B Mosher

LIVES RULED BY PASSION, POWER AND VENGEANCE

KELLY ANDERSON—a fatherless child who refused to be branded by her mother's sin, she grew up to become a titled heiress and a vibrant, exciting woman whose search for happiness was jeopardized by treachery.

GREG MERTON—the ruggedly handsome son of a wealthy Australian rancher, he took Kelly as his second wife, but kept a burning obsession for his first love.

LAURA MERTON—Kelly's fragilely beautiful step-daughter, she was afraid to fall in love, and when she did, it was with the wrong man.

SIR CHARLES BRANDON—a brilliant Member of Parliament and a widower with two grown daughters, would he bring Kelly the fulfillment she craved? Or drag her into a scandal that would shock all of England?

ROSEMARY PAGE—a mysterious and exotic woman, her dark beauty held the key to a secret that could destroy them all.

Spanning five decades of this century and three generations of fascinating women, *FAMILY AFFAIRS* combines the sweep of *THE THORN BIRDS* with the emotional intensity of a Helen Van Slyke novel to create an unforgettable masterwork—TRULY CATHERINE GASKIN'S MOST FULFILLING NOVEL YET.

Bantam Books by Catherine Gaskin
Ask your bookseller for the books you have missed

EDGE OF GLASS
A FALCON FOR A QUEEN
FAMILY AFFAIRS
THE TILSIT INHERITANCE

Family Affairs

Catherine Gaskin

BANTAM BOOKS
TORONTO • NEW YORK • LONDON • SYDNEY

For all the friends of Moira (Pip)

This low-priced Bantam Book has been completely reset in a type face designed for easy reading, and was printed from new plates. It contains the complete text of the original hard-cover edition.
NOT ONE WORD HAS BEEN OMITTED.

FAMILY AFFAIRS
A Bantam Book / published by arrangement with Doubleday & Co., Inc.

PRINTING HISTORY
Doubleday edition published August 1980
5 printings through October 1980
Bantam edition / September 1981

ISBN 0-553-14718-8

Bantam Books are published by Bantam Books, Inc. Its trademark, consisting of the words "Bantam Books" and the portrayal of a bantam, is Registered in U.S. Patent and Trademark Office and in other countries. Marca Registrada. Bantam Books, Inc., 666 Fifth Avenue, New York, New York 10103.

PRINTED IN THE UNITED STATES OF AMERICA

0 9 8 7 6 5 4 3 2 1

Prologue

The General was buried, after a simple service, at Wychwood, with only the members of his family about him, and the villagers who could not be kept away. But his memorial service was held amid the medieval splendor of St. George's Chapel, at Windsor Castle. It was attended by the Knight Companions of the Most Noble Order of the Garter, the most ancient order of chivalry of the Kingdom, designated as the special companions of the Sovereign, and by the many others who had come to commemorate him. His jeweled chain and his star were returned to the Order; his banner had been removed from the place where it had hung over the sumptuously carved stalls of the Garter Knights, to be replaced, in time, by a small plaque bearing his arms. He had been, some thought, too controversial a man to have been given such a signal honor by the Sovereign, a mark of esteem which was only hers to bestow—but he had been so honored, and his friends, and some enemies, gathered there to remember him.

Although it was spring, the day was bleak and wintry, but by a freak of fortune which cameramen pray for, at the moment when the procession of the Knights emerged from the Chapel, the wind whipping their long dark blue cloaks and the white plumes of their broad-brimmed hats, a brief shaft of sunlight touched the ancient gray stones of the building. The cameras focused closely on the General's widow, and those about her. She was flanked on each side by his twin daughters, though they were not her own daughters. They were close in age, these three women, all in their thirties, and each striking in different fashions. Behind them, on a higher step, the fourth was a younger woman, barely more than a girl, whose long blond hair the wind blew across her face, and who turned her head sideways to the popping flashbulbs; she was also a stepdaughter, though not the sister of the twins. The four fell perfectly into the camera frame. The next day the picture was on the front page of all the newspapers, with dignified captions for the serious ones, and anything the copywriters could dream up for the tabloids. One labeled it: FAREWELL TO A HERO.

PART I

Chapter One

I

Kelly was four years old when she and her mother had stood on the platform at Barrendarragh. It was possible that her mother had lied a little about her age so that she shouldn't appear to be so young, and therefore a burden. What Kelly could remember distinctly was that her mother had very firmly disengaged her clinging hand when the woman, having waited for all other passengers to leave the station, finally approached them with a puzzled, ominous frown.

"Mrs. Anderson?"

"Yes. Are you Mrs. Merton?"

"I am. But who is this?"—pointing at Kelly.

"My daughter."

"Your reference said nothing about a child."

"Well—the advertisement didn't say anything about no children. In any case, she's no trouble—no trouble at all. Quiet as a mouse. She won't disturb anyone, I assure you. I keep her well in control."

Kelly, numbed by the long train ride, which had lasted overnight, had been hungry, thirsty and covered with a fine, sandlike grit; she couldn't remember the rest of the talk, the remonstrances, the assurances, the final, very reluctant assent. They were driven in a car whose luxury awed Kelly, over many boneshaking miles by Mrs. Merton, hunger and thirst not assuaged. But she had not complained. It was true what her mother had said; she was kept very well in control.

Afterward, years afterward, she had known how desperate her mother must have been to have the job. It had been necessary to conceal until that confrontation on the station platform that she was bringing a young child with her to her job as cook for the household at a station called Pentland in the northwest of New South Wales, a country of vast holdings, flat plains, boundary lines which stretched to infinity—sheep country. These were the depression years, and even a job that demanded long hours and the flexibility to cope with unknown numbers to feed, working at temperatures often over a hundred degrees, was something eagerly sought. It would not have been offered to someone who brought the inconvenience of a young child. It was probably only the fact that Pentland was now without a cook—the last one having taken a fancy to a stockman who had been there only a few weeks and decamped with him—which decided Delia Merton to take the chance. That, and the fact that she had paid Mary Anderson's train fare all the way from Sydney; Kelly had traveled free, sitting on her mother's lap most of the way. Delia Merton was careful about the money she spent on other people.

They had arrived, after Mary Anderson had scrambled out of the car and opened and closed many gates, at the Home Paddock of Pentland. There, with the late afternoon shadow of tall gums cast across it, was the house—the biggest house Kelly could remember having seen. Its two-storied veranda ran around three sides, supported by thick columns, giving it, to her young eyes, an air of grandeur. At the back were more humble quarters, connected to the main house by a screened passage. Here were the kitchen and the help's quarters; here were the vital water tanks. Beyond were the stables and the stockmen's quarters. The car had swept past the small formal gardens at the front, with their token attempt at a green lawn, to the buildings at the back, there to unload the two bags Mary Anderson had brought, and the tired, dusty child.

Once again Delia Merton had looked doubtfully at Kelly, and this time with some distaste. Kelly did not know why she had earned such a look; she had sat quietly in the car, asked no questions, and not touched the beautiful dove-gray upholstery with her sticky hands. Nor had she dared to say anything about wanting to go to the toilet, so now she wriggled uncomfortably. Mary Anderson intercepted the look. "She *won't* be any trouble, Mrs. Merton. She knows better."

Kelly didn't think, even then or later, that her mother was naturally harsh, but she grew to understand that her life had been hard, her upbringing stern, and that now Mary Anderson was afraid—had been afraid. She was afraid to lose this precious job. That same evening, pausing only to wash and pull a clean white overall from her bag, she had turned to and produced a fine dinner for the family and the two other women servants, Rose and Fran. When Kelly had fallen asleep over her dinner at the kitchen table, Fran had put a rough hand on her arm.

"Ah, sure, poor wee thing. She's worn out. Look, I'll just take her along to bed, Mrs. Anderson. You sit and finish your dinner. Rose and me'll see to the dishes. That's part of our job. We can't turn to no fancy cooking, see. Not good enough for Her Highness out there. That's why neither of us was offered the job."

Mary Anderson had thrust away her plate at once. "No—no, the child is my responsibility. I told Mrs. Merton she'd be no trouble. I can't have you taken away from your job. If Mrs. Merton were to come in . . ."

"Mrs. Fancy Merton hasn't had a meal like that for a long time. So she'd better say nothing. You're a fine cook, Mrs. Anderson, and they don't grow on trees. And not out in the back of beyond like this. Well, sit and finish your tea. I'll slip along and start a bath for the kid. She looks as if she could use it. The poor baby . . ."

"She's not to be babied," Mary Anderson had said quickly. "I don't want her spoiled."

Fran's plain, broad face had creased in a grin. "You'd have trouble spoiling an angel, Mrs. Anderson." And with one swift movement she had scooped Kelly up in her strong arms, and in a little while Kelly felt the blessed sense of being washed in warm, though slightly brown-colored water. "Have to be careful with water out here, kid," Fran told her. "There's only what's in those tanks, and that's the lot till the next rain. But a little scrap like you won't use much, will you? Mr. Merton put in a W.C. for us out here—a blessing it is. We don't have to go out to the dunnyhouse no more, thank the Lord. But you can't flush every time, you understand. This isn't the city, kid . . ." Kelly had fallen asleep as she was being rubbed dry in the big, white towel, harsh from drying in the yard and the fine layer of dust that touched this whole world out here. She had had to be wakened the next morning by her mother.

"Get up, Victoria. Get dressed quickly. Now you can manage it if you try . . ."

Trying, Kelly remembered, was the essential part of life. Trying, and being quiet. No one must know she was there. She could play very quietly on the veranda outside the kitchen, within her mother's sight. She had a worn rag doll; she had a set of building blocks with the letters of the alphabet on them. When her mother took her infrequent breaks to have a cup of tea, she came to sit on one of the straight-backed chairs on the veranda, and she always asked Kelly about the blocks. "Now come on, Victoria . . . A . . . B . . . what comes next?"

"Ah, for the love of heaven, Mrs. Anderson, can't you leave the wee thing alone? She's too young to be bothering about such things." Fran's voice would come from the kitchen.

"It's never too early," her mother answered. "She'll have to go to school by correspondence, and it's I who'll have to teach her."

"But they don't have to start till they're five . . ."

A running battle started between her mother and Fran, big, good-natured, easy Fran, who spent her wages on frivolous things, and a few bottles of gin when she could get into Barrendarragh. She never actually appeared drunk, so there was nothing Mrs. Merton could object to. But Fran liked to sip her gin at night at the kitchen table when the dishes were finally done. By the light of the oil lamp, she sipped her gin slowly, and reminisced about Ireland—a low monologue which Mary Anderson never commented on. "Sure, won't I be homesick forever, Mrs. Anderson. Sure, aren't I longing for the sight of a cow in a green field."

"Never a cow in a green field you saw in your life, Fran," Rose put in. "The back streets of Dublin—that's what you saw."

"I mind the time I was taken to me Granda's place. Green, it was. He died. A fine wake it was. . . . Now where would you be from yourself, Mrs. Anderson? Northern Ireland, I'd be saying."

"Northern Ireland," was the short confirmation. "Belfast." Mary Anderson's harsh Northern accent spoke for itself.

"And you've no family here, Mrs. Anderson?—and you a widow. All alone."

"My parents are dead. Back in Northern Ireland. I've no one here."

"Ah, poor soul. And were they in a way of business, Mrs. Anderson?"

Grudgingly, as if she could spare nothing, not even information, Mary Anderson had answered, "My father was a clergyman."

"Then it's Protestant you are, Mrs. Anderson—for sure, priests don't have children—or shouldn't!" Fran had shouted with laughter, and even the usually silent Rose had joined in. Mary Anderson had remained silent, and the laughter had died away. "How is it then that the kid's called Kelly? Sounds odd to me."

"She only *told* you her name is Kelly. I've no idea where she picked up the notion. Her name is Victoria Jane. We don't know any Kellys."

"Well," Fran said laconically, "Kelly is generally held to be a Catholic name."

Seated at the kitchen table, drinking her glass of milk before she went to bed, while Fran sipped her gin, Kelly herself wondered why she had bestowed the name on herself. She had only the vaguest memory of a time—it now seemed a long time ago—when they had lived with some people in Sydney, some old people, who looked after her while her mother worked. In the way adults have, they had talked across her head as if she had not been present. "Well, wasn't it the disgrace that killed poor Mr. Anderson." The accent had been harsh, like her mother's. "Pity the child bears the name of that good, decent, God-fearing man. When her real name is Kelly . . . or should be . . ." And thereafter, to her mother's great annoyance, and sometimes pain, whenever anyone had asked her name, she had always answered "Kelly."

The time came, a few days after their arrival at Pentland, when Kelly grew bored with the prospect from the veranda at the back of the kitchen; she had stared long enough at the line of gums that screened what Fran called "the men's place," the stables, and a mysterious place called the shearing shed. Her mother had just finished a cup of tea, during which time Kelly had once more been put through the alphabet blocks. She looked at them now with distaste, and very quietly, so her mother wouldn't hear, went down the two steps to the baked earth of the yard, holding the rag doll. The sun smote her; her mother never let her be in the sun without a hat; her dark hair then had a reddish cast, and her fair skin tended to freckle.

She walked along the back of the house, where there was no veranda. She could see nothing within the rooms—the windows were big, but the sills were well above the level of her eyes. Everything was still inside the house; no sound at all. After the men went off on the horses in the morning the place was quiet all day with the quiet of empty spaces. There was so much space around Pentland; far spaces beyond Kelly's imagination, level, dry spaces they called paddocks, and dirty-looking round animals called sheep. Fran had told her these things, but Fran had not told her anything about what went on in the part of the house where Fran did her cleaning—the part where The Family lived. It was this, Kelly thought, she would see when she climbed the steps to the side veranda, which ran along the front of the house. Its whole life and hold on the pillars. Once she was up on it she moved cautiously until she rounded the corner and started down the veranda, which ran along the front of the house. Its whole length was furnished with wicker tables and chairs with brightly colored cushions on them; nothing like the veranda of the kitchen. For a moment she paused, remembering her mother's admonitions, remembering Mrs. Merton's disapproving face; then curiosity banished fear.

She peered in at the windows, one after the other. Blinds were half-drawn so that everything inside was dim, giving the impression of coolness. The corner room was full of books—more books than Kelly had known were in the world. A desk was piled with papers, and books were stacked on the floor around it. There was another room for books, but these were very beautiful books, almost all bound in blue, placed with perfect neatness on their shelves. The room had a blue carpet and blue-covered chairs, and a beautiful little table with a silver inkwell. Kelly moved on; there was a big room where everything was pale gold. She flattened her nose against the glass and saw shining polished floors, golden carpets, the gleam of crystal, gold-framed pictures. She passed the front door—it stood open to the air but a screen door barred her entrance. Blue-carpeted stairs with polished banister, flowers on a table with a mirror behind them—she surveyed it all. Its quiet splendor impressed her. She put her thumb in her mouth, and in an almost forgotten babyish habit, began to hum. She moved on. The next room, she decided, must be where The Family ate. It had a long polished table, a sideboard with silver things on it; Fran complained about always polishing silver. Kelly contemplated the silver things, wondering what they were for. There was a lot of gleaming glass, and there were beautiful blue-and-white plates, but they were hung, oddly, she thought, on the wall, instead of being on the table. Then, having finished her survey of that room, she turned away from the window and saw it.

It too was something new. This world was full of new things. It was at the end of the veranda, and it was a sort of dusty brown and looked rather as if her stuffed rag doll had got itself all knitted into one and had managed to coil itself up in a circle. Coil itself up so beautifully, so neatly, just the way her mother liked things placed. Kelly tiptoed nearer. Then the thing moved—or at least eyes opened where there had been none. Shc advanced a little nearer, and a flat head raised itself out of the neat coil—effortlessly raised itself. It could move then. Kelly wondered what it felt like to touch. Would it feel like the rag doll? She went nearer and put out her hand. The thing uncoiled even more, and she saw it had a mouth, and that there were some long teeth inside.

It was then a hand fell on her arm and she was jerked violently away. The jerk propelled her along the veranda and she stumbled against one of the posts and fell. Then she felt arms gathering her up roughly around her waist; she was almost thrown against the screen door. It opened, and she fell on the polished floor of the hall. Frightened now, and hurt, she began to cry, not softly as she had always cried before, but with loud roars, more like screams. She screwed up her eyes tightly, and screamed.

Then, within a minute, a much louder sound stopped the screams dead. There was a series of deafening bangs very close by. She was frightened now into total silence.

After that the whole household came running—that is, her mother, Mrs. Merton, Fran and Rose. They came and stood staring at her for a moment. Her mother dragged her to her feet, and then they all turned around as a shadow darkened the hall at the open front door.

A boy stood there, a boy with golden hair and blue eyes, a boy who, if he had been a girl, would have been called very pretty. As it was, he seemed beautiful to Kelly.

He held a shotgun in his hand. "Brown snake," he said casually. "The kid was almost touching it. Can you beat that? It was ready to strike. Didn't anyone *tell* her about snakes? Who is she, in any case? Honest, if I hadn't come out just then . . ."

"Your father won't like you having used the gun, Gregory," Mrs. Merton said.

"But he *taught* me how to, Mother. You don't expect me to let a brown snake get away, do you? There's probably another one around somewhere."

They all went out onto the veranda, and from a distance inspected the bloody pulp which had been the neat coil. Part of its body was still intact, and it thrashed horribly. Kelly felt like screaming again, but the pressure of her mother's hand on her was savage, painful.

"What was the child doing here, Mrs. Anderson? I thought I made it quite clear—"

"I'm sorry, Mrs. Merton. She slipped away when I was busy. I'll see that it never happens again. Never." A jerk at Kelly's hand emphasized that.

"Please see that you do."

"But who is she? I didn't even know she was around. Never heard a sound before. I was coming to get some lemonade and I heard this sort of humming on the veranda. . . . Just fancy a kid *singing* to a snake. Dad'll laugh—"

"He won't laugh, Gregory. It's too serious. I'm not sure we can have the responsibility . . ."

The boy looked past Mrs. Merton. "What's your name, kid?"

"Kelly," she whispered.

He smiled, totally ignoring his mother. "I'm Greg. I'll have to teach you about snakes, Kelly." After the harsh voices around her his was gentle, almost soft. It seemed to unnerve her almost more than any other thing of these last dreadful minutes. Silently the tears started to slide down her cheeks. He watched them, his face clouding with dismay. Then he produced a handkerchief, and actually forced her mother to relinquish her hand as he dabbed at them. "Here, Kelly, there's nothing to bawl over *now*. We'll go and get some lemonade." He led her through the shining hall and along the passage that connected with the kitchen. The women, including Mrs. Merton, trooped behind him. He seemed used to it. He went to the pantry and poured lemonade for them both and brought it to Kelly. She choked back her tears as she gazed at him. "Look, come on back with me, Kelly. I've got some lollies. We'll sit out on the veranda . . ." Against the stifled protests of Kelly's mother and Delia Merton, he led her away.

He was ten years old, and Kelly already worshiped him.

Of course he was spoiled; how could he not be? He was the only child of John and Delia Merton, a late child and one longed for. But he had the sort of disposition which shrugged off the overprotective attitude of his mother, and his father tried valiantly, if vainly, not to give him too much of his own way. But the boy was beautiful, and skillful and clever, and it was hard to fault him. His father had taught him to ride when he was three years old; to shoot—and sent off for a handmade gun to fit his size. When there was enough water in it, they swam together in the creek. Sometimes he was allowed to stay out all night with the men when there was a muster in a far part of the station. He was learning to be a man among men; he sometimes displayed an arrogance that came from being a center of attention, but the station hands liked him, called him "The Kid" with rough affection. For all his blond good looks there was never a suggestion that he would be that worst of all things to the Australian male, a sissy. These were his last weeks at home before he went off to a boarding school in Sydney. Some of the men actually said they'd miss having The Kid about.

To Kelly the thought of his going loomed as the first tragedy of her life. She followed him around whenever he would let her. It was useless now for her mother or Mrs. Merton to put strictures on her movements if Greg came and commanded her presence. His first pony, an old, quiet thing who had believed herself forever turned out to grass, if anyone could say the paddocks had grass, was brought back into use. The first small saddle Greg had used was taken down again; even his jodhpurs were brought out of mothballs. Mrs. Merton had kept everything her son had ever used. To see them worn and used by the cook's child was evidently an agony for her.

Kelly listened to them discussing her one day as she waited for Greg. She wondered why adults so often thought she didn't understand what they said.

"Let him do it, Delia," Mr. Merton said. "Have you ever thought the boy's lonely out here? There isn't another kid for sixty miles. . . . Besides, it does him good to teach something to someone else. He'd better get used to the idea that he's not the only person in the world. School's going to be a bit of a shock to him, I'd reckon."

"Yes, but the *cook's* child—"

"Delia, this isn't the Old Country. What choice does he have? Besides, she's a nice little thing. Behaves nicely. Speaks nicely. You can see her mother's had a bit of a come-down in life. You can't hold that against her. She's brought the little thing up nicely. They're clean and decent. Greg watches his manners around Mrs. Anderson, I've noticed. And even Fran's cleaned up her language a bit."

"These things start early, John. It wouldn't do."

He laughed. "For God's sake, Delia! You women . . . I'll never understand you."

II

Kelly was desolate when Greg went off to his school in Sydney. She didn't venture anymore into the big house where The Family lived. She stayed obediently on the kitchen veranda, not caring about anything except the fact that Greg was gone—she stayed, in fact, until John Merton came to fetch her.

"Well, young lady, do you think Greg put in all that time trying to teach you how to ride just to let it all go down the drain? We'll have to be able to show him some improvement when he comes home."

So she got up now as early as her mother, and for a time before breakfast John Merton had her on a leading rein, and the old pony suffered her ineptitude. Merton was patient, endlessly patient, and kind. Fran expressed what was evident. "Ah, sure you can see he's breaking his heart over The Kid being gone, and this wee one is filling in, like. . . . And as for Her Highness . . . well, poor soul, can you blame her for being all wrapped up in Greg? Sure they tell me she had about four miscarriages, and then a baby stillborn. Greg was the last—and the last hope, I'd reckon. Doesn't the sun rise and set on him as far as she's concerned, and it's jealous she'd be of any that came between, even that wee mite . . ."

Because John Merton was so kind, and because Greg expected so much of her, Kelly tried to do and be what was expected. She tried in a different way than she had ever tried for her mother; now it was because she wanted to. Somewhere in the time when Greg was away for his first term, Kelly's fifth birthday arrived, and John Merton demanded a cake from her mother, with candles, and a festive afternoon tea table laid on the front veranda. He paid no attention at all to his wife's frigid silence. He and the servants sang "Happy birthday." Kelly was bewildered and speechless when presents appeared from him and Fran and Rose—a china doll, a miniature tea set, a coloring book, a game of Snakes and Ladders. Kelly shuddered at the snakes, but learned very quickly from John Merton how to play it. From her mother there was a pencil box, a ruler, a slate and chalk. School would begin in earnest now.

Her mother had the correspondence course all ready. Every day while Mary Anderson kneaded dough, stirred cakes, roasted and boiled and stewed and otherwise treated lamb and mutton in every imaginable way, one eye seemed always to be on Kelly, who was now seated at the big kitchen table. She learned by rote, repeating endlessly what her mother said. Multiplication tables were a singsong of memory, and her mother expected ready answers. She could already spell simple words, and she did addition and subtraction. The papers sent off to be marked were models of neatness, though Kelly had to sweat over them. When the first lot came back marked "Excellent" Mary Anderson permitted herself a wintry smile.

"You see what you can do when you try, Victoria? You must always try."

Kelly's only thought was what she would have to show Greg when he returned. How many words would she have learned by the time he came? How well would she ride the pony? Would he approve? It seemed that she and John and Delia Merton waited with equal eagerness for the day.

When it came, Greg unabashedly produced a teddy bear for her. "Dad wrote me you had a birthday party, kid, and I wasn't here to help eat the cake." She took the teddy into her arms as if it were an idol. It didn't occur to her that it was a strange gesture for a boy of ten years to have made. She looked at him adoringly, and was dismayed to feel tears come to her eyes.

"Oh, hell, kid, you're not going to bawl, are you? It was just for your birthday."

As they left together to saddle up the pony, with the sensitivity she had developed to the pitch of Delia Merton's voice, Kelly heard her say, "He brought a present for *her*. . . !"

And the answer. "I'm glad to see he noticed how little she had."

It was worse when he went back to school again. Along with learning to tell the time by the kitchen clock, Kelly learned to read the calendar because the weeks were to be marked off until Greg's next holidays. She worked hard and demanded, and got, holidays when his were due. It was a crushing disappointment on the days when Greg decided to go out with the men into the far paddocks and left her behind. Then she would return quietly to her books at the kitchen table. "You don't own Master Greg, Victoria," her mother said. "Never forget your place in this house. But never accept that it always has to be the same. One day I'll have saved enough money and you'll go to school too. You work hard, and you'll get there. You'll go away from here, and you'll never . . ." Her mother didn't say anymore, but Kelly didn't like the thought of going away. It might mean that she would miss something of Greg, whatever scrap of time he had to spend with her. But the promise of school was something that was evidently sacred to her mother; her face altered subtly as she spoke. "You won't be a servant like me, I mean. I swear you'll get out of this."

Kelly put her head down in her book. Something was wrong with her mother; she had always taught her it was wicked to swear.

III

She was now old enough, had been made old enough by circumstances, to perceive other things about life at Pentland. For one thing, she now knew that John Merton was a rich man—there was wealth in his land and his sheep, and there seemed to be other things that occupied his time, other things he referred to as "business." It was business which took him frequently to Sydney and Melbourne, though he returned always impatiently to Pentland. "It's the best place, Kelly," he would always say. "My father built it up, made it what it is. I hope to leave it an even better place for Greg." His love of the wide silences of his home place was evident; he was at peace there. Kelly had begun to feel sorry for him that Delia Merton did not seem able to share his enthusiasm for all the things that life brought. She was a shy, withdrawn woman, who only occasionally, seemingly as a duty, accompanied her husband on his business trips. "Doesn't she go to buy her clothes," Fran said scornfully, "and with all that money she comes back with just about the same old things she went away in. A real frump. Well"—she sighed—"money's wasted on some people." But Delia Merton spent her money in other ways. Kelly had learned that the rather astonishing splendor of Pentland was Delia Merton's doing. In the main, the houses of the big stations tended to be rather simpler, more homelike places. "Buckingham Palace is what *she* wants," Fran had snorted as she polished silver soup tureens and wine coolers. "She never got over that wedding trip she and Mr. Merton took to England." Delia Merton had a quiet passion for fine things, and her husband's money allowed her to indulge this. She seemed unable to make friends of the other wives on the stations; friendship was not itself an easy thing when most of the women lived so far apart. But when Delia Merton was called to the telephone, she answered with a brevity that verged on rudeness. She seemed incapable of ordinary gossip on which the other women, out of the loneliness of their situation, thrived. She had no small talk. Only reluctantly did she attend the ritual gatherings of the countryside, the weddings, the funerals, often at stations so far away it necessitated an overnight stay. "Sure what did a handsome man like Mr. Merton ever see in a bottle of vinegar like that?" Fran once demanded, sipping her gin in the kitchen while Kelly sat and read.

"Ah, you're very hard," Rose said. "Now you have to admit that in the wedding photos she's real pretty. Comes of a good family, too. South Australia. They're something in the wine trade. I think it's being alone here all the time. If she'd had all the kids they wanted, she'd be a different woman. Now all she has, poor soul, is that blessed needlework of hers, and the books."

It was true that a great deal of Delia Merton's time was spent with the exquisite petit point and gros point which was her obsession. Chair seats, wing chairs, even a whole sofa on which no visitor dared sit, were covered with her work. She had made large tapestries to hang on the walls. "A regular Versailles," John Merton joked. Kelly was too shy to ask him what a Versailles was. And there were the books. Delia Merton did not read the latest books advertised in the *Sydney Morning Herald*. Hers was exclusively a world of the last century. Jane Austen was bound in light blue leather, Dickens in red; Walter Scott was green. There was even a rich purple for Thomas Hardy. The books were ordered and hand-bound in London. They were all in the room where Kelly had first seen the blue carpet and the blue-covered chairs, and what she now knew to be a fine, inlaid table holding the silver desk set. The antiques Delia Merton collected found their way to Pentland from advertisements she read in *Country Life* and other English magazines. She carried on a correspondence with antique dealers in London, with booksellers, and with the shop which supplied the canvases and wools and silks from which she fashioned her needlework. Every six months a volume containing six issues of *Country Life* bound in blue morocco arrived. It sat, each page studied like a Bible, on the writing table, until the next volume came, then it took its place with the others on the shelf. "Sure what does she see in those old things?" Fran asked. "Just old castles and gardens and such. Wouldn't you think she'd get out and about a bit instead of hiding herself in here. . . . Not much of a companion to Mr. Merton, I'd say . . ."

Once, Kelly had ventured into that sitting room which was Delia Merton's kingdom. She had taken a book from the shelf—one with pale-blue binding. *Mansfield Park* the title said. She had started to read. She was not beyond the first page when the book was pulled from her hands, and she felt a stinging slap on the face. "Never—*never* touch my books again. You hear me, you little upstart! And never let me catch you in this room again. This is *my* room."

She had rushed from the room, weeping. The blow had not been hard, but the hurt was great. She refused her lunch, and waited all day on the kitchen veranda until she saw John Merton returning with some of the hands from riding out in the paddocks. When she knew he was in his library, sipping the whiskey he had each night before he dined with his wife in that splendid dining room, she crept along and knocked on the door. She told him what had happened. "I'm sorry, Mr. Merton. I know I shouldn't have been there. I didn't mean to touch Mrs. Merton's books—but they're beautiful, and I wanted to see . . ."

He pointed to the chair opposite, and she sat down. "Kelly, you're too young to understand Mrs. Merton. Her health is delicate. She's what one calls sensitive. She doesn't like noises or intrusions. She likes her own things, her private things. I think she's entitled to them, so I don't interfere. But, Kelly, if it's books you want"—he waved his hand toward the crowded shelves of the room—"Well, you'll find most of the books Mrs. Merton has are here also. Mine are very ordinary editions compared to hers. But the words are the same, and that's all that matters. Most of them belonged to my father. Take your pick. A lot of them are a bit beyond you yet, though. Read what you like—what you can. But don't touch Mrs. Merton's things again, Kelly. Not anything. You can come into this room, but nowhere else."

She had already exhausted Greg's boy's adventure library, so John Merton wrote to Sydney for *Anne of Green Gables* "and anything else of the sort." Kelly began to realize in so many ways how John Merton was striving to make up to her for Greg's absences. He knew he came second in her love, but he seemed satisfied. He was the gentle and kindly mentor who taught her not only to ride and to play tennis, but also to shoot, using the small gun originally made for Greg. The killing of snakes had now become a routine thing. He wound up the Gramophone in his library and she listened to the scratchy records—he liked opera arias best—with wonder and excitement. He gave her all the things he was no longer able to give to Greg.

After the first lot of books had arrived, Kelly was seated, reading, on the side veranda, when her mother had come to speak to John Merton. She listened, unashamedly. There was nervousness in her mother's voice, and Kelly guessed the reason. She, Kelly, was crossing the divide between the servants and The Family. She knew she was what Fran called his "pet." "Sure he can't hide the fact that he loves her, even from his wife."

"I'm afraid you're spoiling Victoria, Mr. Merton," her mother began.

"Have books ever spoiled anyone, Mrs. Anderson?"

"Well, I'd rather she didn't get dreamy notions. I was brought up . . . strictly. Not pampered. There's always the Bible," she added defensively.

"The Bible has its place, Mrs. Anderson, but so do a child's dreams. Besides, when she goes to school, all the other girls will have read those books. You don't want her to be left out, do you?"

Kelly slipped off her chair and raised her eyes gingerly to the level of the window. Her mother was kneading her rough hands as if there had been dough between them. Suddenly Kelly realized that she looked old. They talked, in the kitchen, about what the isolation of these outback stations did to women. The summers were intensely hot, the winters cold. There hadn't been a single holiday for Mary Anderson since she had come to Pentland. She was unwilling to spend the money to take herself and Kelly to Sydney or any other place; apart from the few necessary clothes she bought for them both in Barrendarragh, she hadn't spent a penny of her wages. She allowed Kelly to accept all the gifts of John Merton, including, unasked, his love, but somewhat fearfully. "The poor can't be proud," she remarked to Kelly. And the rich could afford to give, she implied.

"School . . ." She repeated the word reflectively. "Victoria will be ten next birthday. I'm not certain the right school can be afforded. I'd rather she stayed here than went to the *wrong* school. Besides—will the right school take her? They don't take just anyone who applies." Implicit in the bleak words was the knowledge that being the daughter of the cook at Pentland was different from being the son of its owner.

"Yes, Kelly's nearly ten, Mrs. Anderson, and she's hardly spoken to any other children besides Greg. And he's not a child anymore, and he has his own interests, like any boy. Kelly needs to get to know girls, Mrs. Anderson, before she turns into a little old woman. Shall I write to some schools? The right schools. What you can't manage of the fees, I can advance you. A sort of loan for Kelly's education, you could call it. Use me as the bank . . ."

For only seconds Mary Anderson's pride struggled with her reluctance to be further in John Merton's debt. "Very well." She didn't seem to know how to say she was grateful. "But no convent schools, Mr. Merton. I don't want her mixing with Catholics . . ."

It was arranged. After the next Christmas holidays Kelly traveled down by train to Sydney with Greg, and it was Mr. Merton who accompanied them. He had said nothing about it, but Kelly knew from Fran's gossip of the bitter battle which had been waged between him and his wife over this step. Delia Merton had threatened to dismiss Mrs. Anderson if her husband persisted in his folly of bringing the girl up to expectations which were beyond her. "If you do that Delia," Fran reported him as saying, "I will *still* carry out my plans for Kelly. Nothing in life, besides Greg, has given me so much happiness as that child. Not you"—those words were cruel, but necessary—"not money, not Pentland. She has been an unexpected joy come to me late in life. And if you are so foolish as to send Mrs. Anderson away, I shall tell Greg exactly why. Greg, I think, would despise the meanness and jealousy of such an action. You see, Greg loves Kelly, too."

Silently, helplessly, Delia Merton may have raged, but her husband had taken Kelly to Sydney, had put his son on the train for Melbourne, and then gone to the designated department store and bought every single item on the list of required and optional needs for the expensive and exclusive girls' school up the coast to which he was sending her. Every last item of sport's equipment was checked. "You must try to make up for what you haven't had at Pentland, Kelly. Sports are part of it. A proper swimming pool. Basketball. Gym. You're more than good enough at lessons. But Australians love a sport—a real sport. Try for me, Kelly, will you? You're my girl, Kelly.

"Oh, just one other thing, Kelly. When they ask you—they're certain to ask you—just say your mother is housekeeper at Pentland. She really is, you know. It isn't a lie."

It was a lie. She knew it, and accepted its necessity. So she entered the privileged world of the private school equipped with everything John Merton and her mother could, between them, give her. It was a gracious, lovely place to which he had sent her, in the green foothills of the mountains. There, voices were not raised; standards were expected. She was shy; she was not used to girls. They talked of things she didn't know about, things John Merton had not been able to prepare her for, nor her mother. She watched, and copied, and kept quiet, and worked—worked at the sports John Merton had said would make her respected, and worked at her lessons. It was all one long struggle of concentration, and no one must ever see her weep the tears of homesickness. She had no home but Pentland, no love but Greg and John Merton.

Her holidays and Greg's coincided, and she was his devoted follower in everything. John Merton let her go whenever Greg demanded her presence. All three put in shooting practice together, spelled each other at singles in tennis, swam in the creek. "I wish I dared put in a swimming pool," John Merton said, "but that would be tempting the gods. We'd have the longest drought in history." The crown on Kelly's cap of achievement to that date came after her twelfth birthday when she was allowed to accompany the men overnight on a muster in a distant paddock of the station, under John Merton's watchful eyes. He would have no harm befall his beloved Kelly.

The reports from her school were excellent. The headmistress sighed over making the final comment on a report. "Victoria is a model pupil—a tryer in every way, scholastically as well as in games. But she is still a little hesitant with people. However, she is young and she may still develop the one quality she appears to lack—leadership." It happened to be the quality Greg possessed above all others, John Merton remarked to Mary Anderson as he read it.

Greg's passage through school had seemed one of almost effortless success. He was a superb athlete—cricket, rugby, tennis, swimming. He wasn't as good a scholar, but his place in class was always very respectable. There was no doubt that he would go on to University. His beauty as a young boy had developed into a true handsomeness. John Merton found it hard to contain his pride in his son. One winter holiday Greg found a new love, a new excitement. A group from his school went to New Zealand to learn the rudiments of mountain climbing. An exuberant postcard came to Pentland. "It's the greatest thing I've ever tried." Kelly read it with dismay. It seemed one area where she could never follow him.

It was the last winter when such a thing was possible because by September, Australia, a day after Britain, was at war with Germany. Greg chafed that he was not yet old enough to join up, and wrote begging his father's permission. *A little wait won't hurt, Greg. It doesn't seem to me that the war will be over before you get there.* He tried to write lightly, but he wrote the words with dread. His only child, his son, how could he see him go to war? And yet he could not hold him back. He talked of it gravely to Kelly, as if she were already an adult. Kelly knew it was impossible to discuss it with Delia Merton. She grew almost hysterical at the thought of Greg joining up. Kelly heard her cry one night with anguish, "There must be *some* way to stop him joining up. Pentland needs him, and the country needs its farmers." And she heard John Merton's reply, "Do you want him to hate us forever, Delia?"

Greg sat his matriculation certificate before Christmas, and joined the Royal Australian Air Force three days later. By Christmas he was in training camp, and when he next came to Pentland, it was for embarkation leave. John Merton arranged for Kelly to have ten days away from school so that she could be there. Kelly knew that Delia Merton was furious at her husband's action. "It may be a long time before any of us sees him again," John Merton had said. They never ever dared express the fear that this could be the last time they would see him.

He looked splendidly handsome in his uniform, and he was impatient to be on his way to England to complete his training. "I hope I'll get into a fighter squadron. I've always wanted to fly. I wonder if it will seem as good as it does up in the mountains . . ." Kelly heard the words and knew it was yet another place she could not follow him. She didn't know how close her feelings were to Delia Merton's. She wanted to hold on to Greg; never lose sight of him. And yet to try to hold on to him would be fatal. He laughed at her gloomy face. "Don't look so down in the dumps, kid. I'll write to you . . . I'll tell you everything that's happening . . ." She was not then thirteen; he was eighteen. She was a child to him. She had begun knitting the long navy-blue muffler he would take with him. It was a race between her and Delia Merton, though neither knew it. At the end, when Greg looked at both of them, he smiled. "There's sure to be a bloke who needs one. I'll take both." So neither Kelly nor his mother ever knew which muffler he wore.

The next five years of war rolled over Kelly as she lived them through Greg's experiences. They were all thankful that he was still not fully trained when the Battle of Britain raged, though John Merton murmured that if it lasted much longer they must throw even their raw, inexperienced pilots into it. They settled down to wait for letters from him. Kelly felt a particular fury because she was often at school when letters came to Pentland, and although John Merton wrote her their contents, it was not the same as actually seeing them. Her consolation was the occasional letter directed to her personally, a treasure beyond her expectation. He was stationed near London; he loved England, he said. During his leaves he traveled wherever he could, as wartime restrictions and difficulties would allow—Wales, Scotland, the Lake District. He did something mysterious he called "fell-walking." He climbed in Glencoe and the Cairngorms. *One day I'll climb the Alps,* he wrote. He sailed on the Solent in a boat borrowed from people he spent time with during his briefer leaves. *Different from Sydney harbor, and of course we can't go many places because of the mines. They won't let us near the naval vessels, either.* It turned out the "us" was mostly a girl called Dorothy. He sent her picture wearing a WAF uniform. Kelly saw that she was more than just pretty. She wanted to cry with anguish at the sight of it; Greg had grown up and gone away without knowing that she was also growing up. "Wait for me," she wanted to beg him. "Please wait!"

Then he wrote that he and Dorothy were engaged. She was the Honorable Dorothy Harding, the daughter of Lord Renisdale, a press baron and industrialist whose factories had switched from their peacetime occupations to turn out munitions, whose large acreage near Southampton was geared to producing food for rationed Britains. *Of course it's tiny by Pentland's standards, but it's large for here. It's hard to believe how many head of sheep and cattle an acre they can carry here. Dorothy is looking forward to seeing Pentland—living there. But naturally she'll want to come back here every so often. I was terribly afraid she'd turn down Australia—not me!* Kelly wept when she came back from school and John Merton told her the news—but not where anyone could see her. He was not deceived. He recognized the bleakness in her eyes, and hoped that time would take it away. He looked at the picture of his future daughter-in-law, the daughter of a baron, rich and beautiful. And still he wished Greg had waited for Kelly to grow up.

The cold, stunned feeling in Kelly's heart did not leave her; it just became part of her. She continued to work hard at lessons and games, because there was John Merton to please, if not Greg. But she never broke out of the tight little shell which had encased her since she had arrived at school. She did not develop the qualities of leadership the headmistress thought so desirable; she was a remote, rather withdrawn creature, though not unpopular because she was attractive to look at, and she was generous in helping other girls with the things she did well. But she remained a loner, totally at ease only with John Merton. Perhaps the lie of pretending that her mother was housekeeper at Pentland had made anything else impossible; the loss of Greg had hardened that attitude.

Because losses were heavy among fighter pilots, and because he possessed, as John Merton well knew, outstanding qualities of leadership, Greg became in time, Squadron Leader. Then came the Distinguished Flying Cross—and later the bar was added to that. He went with crowds of others to Buckingham Palace to be decorated by the King. He sent back pictures of himself and Dorothy in the Palace forecourt. Kelly was wildly jealous that even in the thick WAF uniform Dorothy looked shapely, the skirt revealed good legs and neat feet. "A Beauty," Delia Merton pronounced. It was evident to them all that she was torn with pride in the sort of bride Greg had found, and the fear that the same girl, used to English society, would find Pentland too dull, and take Greg away.

Mary Anderson guessed Kelly's despair. "You've looked too high, Victoria," she said, unable to soften her tone, though she tried. "People like Greg are not for the likes of you. How would it have looked—the son of this place married to the cook's daughter? Foolish dreams, Victoria. Get them out of your head."

"People do it all the time," Kelly had protested.

"They may sometimes do it in Australia," her mother said, "but not there—not in the Old Country. And the Mertons are more English than Australian, whatever they say."

Then came the news that they had married. Kelly stopped hoping. It was done, over with. She might go on loving Greg, but he never would belong to her. In time came the news that Dorothy was pregnant, and had left the WAF. "It will surely be a son," Delia Merton pronounced. They needed a son, many sons, for Pentland's vastness. But it was a daughter, called Laura. The pictures of her at even a few weeks old showed her as a pretty baby, and Dorothy was a radiant mother. The pride shone from Greg's face as he posed with them. He was more mature, more handsome, Kelly thought. She looked long at the pictures, trying to ignore Dorothy and the baby.

The Allied invasion of Europe was well advanced when the cable came to Pentland. Kelly was at home on holidays. She heard Delia Merton cry out as she answered the telephone and heard the message; Kelly had to go and take the instrument from the woman's frozen hand. "Daisy?" she called to the operator in Barrendarragh. "It's Kelly here. Mrs. Merton's . . . what's the message, Daisy?"

"I'm sorry for the family, Kelly. Tell them, will you? The message reads: DOROTHY KILLED IN V2 RAID ON LONDON. BABY SURVIVED BUT HURT. WRITING. It's signed, GREG. Tell them I'm real sorry, will you, Kelly?"

Dully, Kelly gave the message. A sense of mourning fell on Pentland, for a woman they had never known. They waited long weeks for Greg's letter to reach them. Kelly was back at school, so John Merton wrote her. *It seems Dorothy came up to the family London house overnight to meet Greg. Those bloody* V2 *things come out of nowhere—there's no time to take shelter. The house was demolished, and most of the block with it. They found the baby alive in the ruins. She had a broken leg. Greg had arrived and helped bring her out.* Here John Merton's pen seemed to waver. *Greg doesn't go into much detail, but it seems there was worse than the broken leg. The baby was burned on the side of the face. Her jaw was broken, and one ear damaged. Greg said she will live. She's quite well now. But he says she will need plastic surgery. A great deal of it . . . sometime in the future, when she's older. At the moment she's with Dorothy's parents in the country.*

Kelly felt a sense of pity wring her for the baby, that small beautiful child of beautiful parents, so disfigured. She also knew guilt, because she could not feel the same sorrow for Dorothy's death. She concentrated her sorrow on Greg's anguish, and thought that she would surely be punished by the stern God her mother believed in so single-mindedly. Every day she looked at the picture of Greg she kept hidden away from the prying, desecrating eyes of the other girls. It was now her last year at school; at the end would be the matriculation examination, the time to prove herself. She buried herself in her studies, and tried not to mind that there were no more letters for her from Greg.

She was back at Pentland in the long Christmas holidays when the results of her examinations came. She had achieved one of the outstanding results in the state. John Merton gazed at her with love. "You've made us very proud, Kelly. You were such a little bit of a thing when you came—and now here you are, on the edge of . . . on the edge of what, Kelly?"

She didn't know. It was now early 1946, and the war with Japan had ended last September; the war in Europe had been over since May. There was a sense of the world beginning to stir and look to its future. Young people looked to theirs. "I don't know," she answered.

She sensed that he badly wanted to keep her at Pentland with him, and rejected the thought as a selfish desire. What she didn't know, as they talked of the future together, was that, in his eyes she had grown quite lovely, his young Kelly. She had grown tall and still possessed a faintly coltish awkwardness which would pass; her hair was dark with a faint hint of red in it when the light struck it. Her neck and jawline he thought quite beautiful. She had grayish-blue eyes and pale skin which burned easily in the relentless Australian sun. He urged her to wear a hat always. "I hate the way women let themselves turn into dried-up prunes in this climate," he once said. His own face was seamed with advancing age and the thousands of hours in the saddle, the lifetime of squinting against the far bright horizons of his great territory. She did not know these thoughts; when she looked in the mirror she saw, as girls do at that age, only what was wrong. Vanity was not something Mary Anderson encouraged.

John Merton wanted to send her immediately to Sydney University, but her mother had the last word in the argument to which Kelly listened, but was allowed little participation in by Mary Anderson. "Victoria must learn to earn a living. That's first."

"She could be a teacher, Mrs. Anderson. There's always a living in that for a girl . . ."

Kelly understood what he did not directly say—that there was very little girls could do except marry. They filled in time until then. It was a man's world. "She knows how to cook and sew," Mrs. Anderson continued relentlessly. "What she needs is a good grounding in typing and shorthand—bookkeeping, too. I've saved the money. She must go to Miss Hale's Secretarial College. That's the best. She always gets her girls the best jobs . . ."

He agreed, with the faint hint that when Kelly had finished her course, he could offer her a job as secretary-bookkeeper at Pentland. "Perhaps that's selfish," he admitted, "but I could use one. I've grown tired of trying to keep up with it all." An accountant came from Barrendarragh once a month, and a more specialized one came from Sydney four times a year. "But I really mustn't ask you, Kelly, to bury yourself here at Pentland. It's time you saw something of life." Mary Anderson's body and hands had become tense at that suggestion, so he said no more. Kelly was enrolled at Miss Hale's. The course would start in late February, and she would be there for the rest of the year. She was expected to work hard.

"You have to prove that everything that's been done for you was worth it, Victoria," her mother said. To Kelly's dismay it was arranged, by her mother, that she should stay in the home of the Presbyterian minister and his wife, the McAlpines. "We stayed with them when we first came out from the Old Country. You'll be all right there. A young girl can't be too careful . . . there are bad types around who try to take advantage . . ." There were many more strictures about behavior, the hours she was to keep, the need to study hard to "prove" herself. "You'll get a good job. You'll meet decent young men. I hope you'll marry, and then you'll be safe."

It sounded an appallingly closed future to Kelly. She repeated some of her mother's thoughts to John Merton. "No one who's young is safe, Kelly. That's part of youth. I know you'll make us very proud, no matter what you do . . ." He was sipping his whiskey slowly on the veranda at Pentland in the last of the evening light. He added, almost under his breath, "I wish Greg would come home. But I can't make him."

On compassionate grounds, because of his baby daughter, Greg had been demobilized in England, instead of returning to Australia with the rest of his squadron. He lingered there, and did not write of coming home. He had an allowance from his father which enabled him to do this, and he had by now come into an inheritance from his father's mother, which yielded a further annuity. He could keep himself in England without working, and he could pay the expenses of the care of his baby daughter—for a nanny, for anything that was needed. There was also the fact that the child, Laura, was already receiving the income from a trust set up by her grandfather, Lord Renisdale, in which her mother had shared. Laura still lived with her grandparents. Greg had a flat in

London, and he spent his weeks with a tutor preparing for Oxford or Cambridge; weekends were spent in Hampshire with the Renisdales and Laura. *She's too young to disturb yet,* he wrote. *They're all she's got. It's home to her. She's had one operation to straighten the jaw, but others will be necessary—in the future. They're going to wait for a while before the skin grafts start. She's so young . . . poor kid.* He didn't send any photos.

Kelly knew John Merton couldn't call Greg home, though he yearned for the sight of his son. He could not, would not, command him; nor could he plead that Pentland needed his presence. The station manager was very competent. But John Merton needed his son, and his son needed other things. Unhappily Kelly recognized all this; the closeness between her and John Merton had grown to the point where he needed to express very little for her to guess the rest of his thoughts. They had a letter telling them that Greg had managed to get a visa to travel to Switzerland. He spent the whole of the summer of 1946 there, living in the house of a guide in the high Alps above Sierre. He wrote of a sparse, bare existence, few comforts, and his love of the mountains. *I climb with the guide every day. He says I show promise.* He stayed beyond the time when he should have returned to England and his studies. Kelly knew John Merton felt he was losing his son to nameless, unknown mountain peaks, a white mistress, austere, cruel, unforgiving of mistakes. He sent for books on mountaineering; together he and Kelly learned of the heady wine of the altitude, the goal that was irresistible to some men, those unconquered summits. His son had seen them from the air, and now he wanted to place his foot upon them, and say he had done it. It seemed to John Merton that his little granddaughter, Laura, learning to walk and talk in a gracious house in Hampshire, had little to do with Greg's staying on in Europe.

Kelly went to Miss Hale's, liked it well enough, worked hard, as was expected of her, and hated living with the Reverend McAlpine and his wife. Their family had grown up, married, gone off, and they had only Kelly to care for. They watched her movements as if she were some skittish kitten who would surely find herself hopelessly lodged in a tree, with the hounds of young men's desires baying at her. She returned by tram to Randwick each evening after classes were finished. She was expected at a certain time, and there was no lingering over a milk shake with the other girls. Saturdays were organized. Tennis in the mornings with suitable girls;

the afternoons she spent as a volunteer aid to the nurses at the Prince of Wales Hospital. Sundays were a long ordeal, with services morning and evening. No entertainments—nothing except her books, and they should not be fiction. The Reverend McAlpine was also from Northern Ireland. He observed his Sundays as they did there, with the same stern Presbyterianism as her mother. "I knew your mother's father in Belfast," he said when Kelly first came. "He was a godly man. I hope I know how to do my duty by his granddaughter and keep her from harm."

What harm? Kelly wondered. It was useless to ask such questions. It seemed that in her mother's thinking, and that of the McAlpines, all of life was to be feared as a trap and a snare. "You cannot be too careful," was the almost daily admonition of Mrs. McAlpine.

Her youth was screaming for freedom, expression. Instead she doggedly learned the cryptics of Mr. Pitman's shorthand, practiced her touch-typing, tried to make rules of bookkeeping an excitement to be mastered. She thought of Greg. At the end of the year he still had not returned from Europe; he had moved on to the higher, lonelier valleys of the Valais; he had fallen in love with the treacheries and intricacies of the glaciers. He was an expert skier. There was nothing then but a man's legs to take him to the top of those virgin slopes, to be rewarded by the thrill of the downward plunge. Every few months he returned to England to see his daughter, and then he hastened back to the humble house where he stayed with the family of a guide. He wrote, though not to Kelly, that he shared their life totally. He helped take care of the cows, he sawed wood, he had added the Italian patois of the high valley to his French. John Merton struggled against the temptation to summon him home to take care of what would be his inheritance.

Kelly finished her time at Miss Hale's, and decided to postpone the university for a while. Through John Merton's influence she was offered a job as secretary to the assistant to the managing director of the biggest wool exporting firm in Sydney. "A marvelous chance," her mother pronounced. Then, when Kelly learned that she was expected to go on living with the McAlpines, that life would be exactly as it had been before, as supervised, as hedged in, she sought an interview with the matron of the hospital at which she had been a volunteer aid. She was immediately accepted as a nursing student.

You're throwing it all away, her mother wrote in anger.

You must do as you think best, John Merton wrote. *It's an honorable, noble profession. It will be hard, but if it's what you want, then you are right to do it.*

It was as he had said, a hard life. The young nurses trembled before the gaze of the sister in charge of the ward. They dampdusted, waxed floors, scrubbed bedpans in the sluice room, carried soiled dressings, made beds, but in the beginning were never allowed to touch the patients. They did the most menial work, for little pay; they were not allowed to wear makeup or show hair from under their caps. Kelly thought, as she often dozed over the medical books she had to study in the off-duty hours, that they might as well have been nuns. The parade of the matron and the consultants through the wards was something to be dreaded, in case a bedcover was out of line, in case a mote of dust might be seen. Even the patients seemed rigid with fear. Kelly thought she was probably not really suited to be a nurse, but at least she had made a bid for independence. There were free hours; she had a boyfriend, a newly qualified doctor beginning his struggle up through the ranks. He intended to be a surgeon. It meant years more of study—and of poverty. On Sunday afternoons when they both were free, they rode the Manly ferry across Sydney Harbor. It was all they could afford. She never stopped thinking of Greg. Her brief holidays were spent at Pentland. There she slept most of the time, feeling exhausted. John Merton said she was too thin, and urged her to eat. He insisted on giving her a small allowance and made her promise she would buy extra food. Her mother hated the fact that she had entered nursing. "The scum of Ireland go into the English hospitals," she said. "And you were offered one of the best jobs a girl could wish for . . ." The words were said in bitterness and anger. Kelly didn't care; the world of the hospital was hard, but it was not a smothering cocoon.

She began her second year in nursing, and was allowed, at last, actually to help nurse patients. She began to think that, after all, she would like nursing. One day she would be qualified. Occasionally she pictured herself in the matron's uniform. Her doctor friend laughed and said that one day they would marry; in the beginning she would be his nurse, and his secretary. Later they would have children when he started to make money. He intended, he said, to make money. Kelly said nothing.

Then the telegram came from John Merton. He and his wife were coming to Sydney. Greg was coming home. And Laura was coming with him.

He came by plane, which was still a novelty. They waited at Mascot Aerodrome, three anxious, nervous people. Delia Merton clearly resented Kelly's presence, but John Merton had demanded it, even arranging it with the matron for Kelly to have leave to come back to Pentland with them. John Merton had many contacts, and the matron knew that.

John Merton had tried to keep Greg's arrival secret. Greg had been away from Australia so long, and they did not know what time and the mountains had done to their son, nor did they know what his wife's death had done to him. But somehow the press caught the news, and there were photographers present. The war was still a recent memory, and Greg Merton was an authentic hero, and one with a tragedy in his background, a widower with a little daughter. It made good copy.

As he came down the steps of the plane the flashbulbs began to explode. The little girl he held by the hand looked down, fear in her expression. Long, golden hair hid her damaged ear, and fell across one side of her face, but it could not cover the livid burn mark, nor the irregularity of the jaw line. Kelly felt the wrench of pity. The child would have been not just pretty, but beautiful, if she could be judged by the untouched side of her face. Suddenly, as if in a reaction of terror against the flashes, the clamor of voices, the child began to scream. Greg glanced about. His face was hard and lean, tanned by the sun of the high valleys; there were lines under his eyes. He still moved with that compelling grace he had always had, but to that grace, which had been boyish, was added the maturity of a man. He was a beautiful boy no longer, but a strikingly handsome man. A man who did not ask, but gave commands. He sized up the situation in a second, and the first words he spoke were to Kelly.

"Here, Kelly, take her. Take her and get out of here."

Kelly scooped the child up in her arms, pressed the small face against her shoulder, and ran across the tarmac toward the terminal buildings and, she hoped, a taxi. In the taxi she gave the name of the hotel where the Mertons were staying, and she held the child closely, letting her weep until the weeping was exhausted. She stroked the silken blond hair. She found herself saying things she whispered to the restless, feverish patients at nights, the words that calmed and soothed. She carried the child into the hotel, her face still pressed against her shoulder, and demanded of the manager that they be admitted to the Mertons' suite. It was done. No one dared to cross this suddenly fierce young woman.

She ordered milk and sandwiches for the child; she bathed her and wrapped her in a bath sheet. There were no more tears; Laura was distracted by the toys her new grandparents had waiting for her. Her features, so tortured when the flash-bulbs had begun to erupt, relaxed. She smiled at Kelly.

The door opened and Greg and his parents came in. Laura slipped off Kelly's lap and ran to her father. The bath sheet fell off her as she ran, and he caught her naked, beautiful little body up in his arms. "There, baby, there . . . it's all right. Dad's here . . . Dad's here . . ."

And then, across the child's head, and in his parents' presence, he spoke to Kelly.

"I reckon it's time you and I got married . . . eh, Kelly?"

Chapter Two

I

The opposition that came from Delia Merton was to be expected. Almost without exception, her son was good enough for any girl in Australia, her attitude proclaimed. He was handsome, he would one day be rich as the owner of Pentland, he belonged to Australia's own brand of aristocracy. He had suffered a tragedy, but he had overcome it, in his own individual fashion. Look at him, she seemed to say. Just look at him. Who is good enough for *him?*

The opposition that came from Mary Anderson was fixed and seemed unalterable. She would not discuss it. Greg was impatient and rude about it. John Merton had summoned Mrs. Anderson to Sydney, and all she would say was, "I do not think it suitable, and I think you all know why." Delia Merton was the only one who nodded her agreement.

"In a few months Kelly will be twenty-one," Greg pointed out. "She won't need your permission then."

"When Victoria is twenty-one, she will do as she must. Until then, the law says she must have my permission." And the thin, grim-faced woman, in her plain straw hat and cheap clothes, left the Mertons' suite and went to the small, inexpensive hotel where she had elected to stay.

Later Kelly and Greg rode the Manly ferry; he feasted his

eyes on the harbor as a sight long denied, and vented his fury on her mother. "Silly old bitch," he said, with no apology. "What in God's name is in her mind? She can't hold us up forever . . ." Then his attention was distracted. "Look at that yacht, Kelly! Wouldn't you love to be on it? Look out, you bloody fool . . . God, did you see that? Damn nearly capsized . . ." Then, without change of tone, he went back to the subject. "Well, if we have to wait, we'll wait. That's all. But it's inconvenient."

Kelly was achingly aware that not once had anyone asked what *she* wanted. Most important, Greg had not asked. He had taken her consent for granted. She realized that in her whole life, Greg had taken everything she had ever offered for granted. He had not asked if she loved anyone else; he had not asked if she loved him. She reflected that he knew she loved him. He had always known it.

John Merton tried to soothe over the obvious deficiency. "I know you have the right to ask more of him, Kelly. But remember you didn't ever know each other as romantic lovers. People who grow up together seldom are that. But now he has come home, he has come home to *you*. He had only one girl in mind. And you're the right girl for him. I'm happy Kelly . . . so very happy. If I could have chosen for him, I would have wanted only you . . ." He embraced her gently, a gesture he seldom permitted himself.

Her mother remained rigid and adamant. "You'll always be looked down on in that family," she said bitterly. "You're the daughter of their servant. It doesn't matter that I'm educated . . . I'm a clergyman's daughter. I shall have to leave Pentland . . . that is, if you insist on going through with this madness."

"Why shouldn't I go through with this . . . this madness? If you don't give your consent, I'll do it when I turn twenty-one. Why don't you see that it's inevitable?"

"He is using you," her mother said, with rare frankness. "Can't you see that?"

"I'll be used, then!" Kelly cried. "I love him. I always have!"

"Then more fool you," her mother answered. For one of the few times in her life, Kelly saw her mother's somber eyes blaze with a kind of passion. "Love! What is that but a delusion? A trap. Young girls are caught. Innocent young girls . . ."

"Greg wants to marry me, not seduce me," Kelly said harshly.

A dull, unbecoming flush mounted in her mother's face.

"He will seduce you into doing whatever he wants. You have stars in your eyes now. Wait until you find out what he wants is a childminder, a servant . . . a . . . a . . ."

"A mistress," Kelly finished for her. Then her head snapped back as her mother slapped her sharply across her mouth.

"Slut! Foul-mouthed slut!"

"What are you afraid of, Mother?" Kelly said, when she had recovered. She would not allow her hand to creep up to the burning pain of her face. "What is it that you . . . you and the McAlpines are so afraid of?"

"Afraid of? I'll tell you . . . I'll tell you then. I don't want to produce your birth certificate for your marriage license. You were born in Belfast. And the man who is . . . was—I don't know if he's still alive—your father, was one of your fine young men who talked of love. I believed him. I was younger than you. I'd been sheltered. I used to see him when I knew I shouldn't. I met him without my parents' knowledge. I knew they would never permit it. He was a . . . a Catholic. When I knew I was in the family way and told him, he disappeared. I had to tell my parents. I will say now, and I know it's the truth, that the shock and disgrace killed my father. A Catholic . . . and I his only child!"

"Then his name must have been Kelly."

Her mother nodded, the remembered misery making her face anguished. "I never understood where you got that name from. You were only a bit more than a year old when we came out to Australia. But somewhere you must have heard the name. Yes—his name was Kelly. But there is no father's name on your birth certificate."

It seemed to Kelly that she had always known. "The McAlpines knew?"

"They knew—and were forgiving, for my father's sake. They gave me a home, as good Christians. I only knew how to cook and sew. I worked at whatever I could find, and I helped Mrs. McAlpine. When I was accepted at Pentland I was grateful. It was quiet . . . safe. I wanted you to be safe."

"I'm safe, Mother. Mr. Merton and Greg have seen to that."

"I don't want you to marry him. I sense . . ."

"You *sense!*" Kelly rounded on her in fury. "Where have your senses led you but to misery and fear? I'll go where *my* senses take me. And if not as quickly as Greg wants, then the minute I turn twenty-one. Mother, don't you realize that if you give your consent, there is no question of the birth certificate? No one need ever know. The birth certificate is lost. We'd have to send back to Belfast. . . . All that's needed is your consent. You can't hold out forever against an honorable proposal of marriage. What more can you want? How much *safer* can I be?" The implied lie of all the years was being perpetuated.

"I see that you are caught. Make your own bed. Lie on it." Mary Anderson folded her hands in bitter resignation.

John Merton summoned every friend and acquaintance he had to the wedding reception, but the ceremony itself was quiet and private. It would have been too obvious that there were no friends to gather on the bride's side of the church. Kelly wore the most sumptuous white gown John Merton could find for her. Laura wore a long pale yellow dress which matched her hair, and which delighted her. She carried flowers as she watched her father being married to her new friend by a stern-faced man called McAlpine. She didn't seem aware of the sternness of her new grandmother, or the grim expression of the other lady Kelly had told her was her own mother. Laura accepted Kelly's place in her life without question; she accepted it gladly. She had felt Kelly's comforting hand; she had listened to a gentle voice. Kelly and her new grandfather were twin pillars of security in this strange world. Her father was still her father—kind, when he remembered she was there. But his eyes always seemed to be fixed on some other place.

"Do you really want to bother with her?" Greg had asked when the place for the honeymoon, and whether Laura should go, were discussed.

"She's no bother—and she's too young and too bewildered yet to be left without a sight of you. It's a whole new world for her, Greg. Your parents love her—but they're past the age of taking care of young children. Let's take her with us . . ." He was a shade too ready, she thought, to agree.

They went to an unknown, unfashionable place up along the Queensland coast where the empty, unbroken beach stretched beyond the limit of their eyes, and the surf broke after the mighty swell of the thousands of miles of the Pacific. It was a primitive little place, with no electricity. It was a sort of boarding-house on the beach, the food barely passable. The man and woman who ran it were friendly. They had no idea of the history of the young couple who came to stay with them. They naturally assumed that the bright, though disfigured young child was theirs. She looked, with her blond hair, and especially when her face was turned in profile, so that one did not see that damage, so like her handsome father. They didn't ask what happened to the child. They were nice people. They were glad to see the young wife so in love with her husband.

Greg surfed as naturally as he did everything else. Kelly was used to surfing, but less than expert. It was a new experience for Laura. Kelly held her in her arms and turned her back to the waves. The spray broke across them; occasionally she misjudged the size of a breaker, and they were caught, and dumped on the sand, choking and spitting out the salt water. Afterward Kelly would carefully dry Laura off, and they would wrap themselves in towels, wearing hats against the sun. Kelly never said so, but she was afraid of what too much sun might do to that livid burn mark on Laura's face. They would sit and watch as Greg swam, tirelessly, it seemed, out beyond the line of the breakers, waiting, treading water until he judged a breaker just right. Then with a powerful swing of his arms he was riding it, shooting it all the way into the beach, abandoning it at the precise moment when it began to curl over and threatened to dump him. Then he would swim out again, going through the waves he didn't want, surfacing on the other side, out, out, until his blond head was lost in the dazzle of the sunlit sea. Laura would sometimes grow fearful that he might not reappear. She was fearful of many things, Kelly found. But Greg would at last be finished, would walk up the slope of the beach toward them, and Laura would slip out of the protective cover of the towel and run to him. He would play with her in the waves for a few minutes, able to hold her high above his head when the water crashed around them, able to give her the joy of it without any of the discomfort. Kelly never told her that the coast was notorious for the sharks that could cruise out where Greg swam, could come in quite close to shore. She saw no reason to add to Laura's fears.

Laura was too young to be left alone in a strange room at night, so she slept on a cot on a screened-in porch outside their room. Greg seemed quite undisturbed by the thought of making love to Kelly with his child only feet away. At first Kelly was miserably conscious of Laura's nearness, but the feel of Greg's body against hers, of the powerful thrust of his masculinity was like a narcotic; it both soothed and aroused her. She could forget Laura in Greg—and it was true, the child slept.

Kelly had wondered beforehand how she would overcome

the strictures of her childhood, the sense of something vaguely ugly and distasteful in the act of love that her mother tried to instill in her. She then discovered on their first night together that such feelings didn't exist for her. She had Greg; it seemed a natural and easy thing to please him. All she had to do was let herself slip into the pleasure she had always sensed would be hers with him. He was a skillful lover, but the moments of tenderness were the times she cherished most, the things she daydreamed over as she and Laura sat on the beach. "I'm so damn glad you waited for me, Kelly," he had said.

"But you knew I would. You always knew that."

He laughed. "But I couldn't let myself act on it. It would have been cradle-snatching to have assumed you'd always go on wanting me. I had to wait myself. I had to let you see a bit of life . . ." He almost sounded as if his marriage to Dorothy had never been.

Kelly thought of her time at Miss Hale's, the time of nursing; physically there was nothing about a man that she had not already seen, but to be loved was something that was unknown, and unguessable until it had actually happened. In fact, she had seen almost nothing of life. She suspected that Greg knew that very well. She suspected that some of what her mother had said about him might be the truth. She suspected, and she didn't care. She had Greg. They were lovers, and they were married. If this was the trap her mother talked of, then she was happy within it. Let him use her, if that was what he wanted. It was all, she thought, that she had ever wanted herself.

"Let's not have kids for a while, Kelly," Greg said to her. "Of course we'll have them later on, but there's plenty of time. We've so much to do. And I don't think Laura could stand the competition yet. You're damn good to Laura, Kelly."

"I'm not good to Laura. I love her."

He stroked her hair. "Yes, I know that. I think I sort of counted on that. You never were mean as a kid, Kelly. You always wanted to share. From what Dad wrote in his letters I sort of guessed you'd stayed that way. Laura's a damn lucky kid. I'm lucky . . . listen, Kelly. We'll have kids in time. Lots of kids. You're very young yet. Pentland is the sort of place that was meant for lots of kids. There's so much space to be filled. You'll do it beautifully. But we've got a few things to do yet . . . before we settle down."

It turned out that Greg's idea of what was to be done before they settled down was to go back to England so that he could take a degree at Oxford. Kelly watched the dismay spread on John Merton's face as he heard the news. "Well, Greg, I expected you might want to go on with your education. But what's wrong with Sydney University? You're not starting to turn up your nose at us, are you?" He tried to make the remark sound light-hearted.

Greg laughed. "The only trouble with Sydney is that it's too damn far away."

"Far away from *what?*"

Greg shrugged. "Well, from Europe. I sort of hoped to be able to go climbing a bit. And I'd like the chance to meet all the different types there are at Oxford. Dad . . . look, there's no other future for me but that I'll come back to Pentland. I'll be here the rest of my life. Will a few years away now hurt? It would be something to take a degree at Oxford, wouldn't it? . . . assuming, first, that I make the entrance examinations, and secondly that I make the degree. I don't fool myself I'm a genius. You've always said a man should stretch himself. You've always said that living in the outback was something that tried the soul, and you'd better bring plenty of mental baggage with you. You'd better let me have my experiences while I can. When I come back to Pentland it'll be for good."

"And Kelly? . . . and Laura? What will they do?"

"Well, of course they'll be with me. The war's changed everything, Dad. There'll be plenty of others my age studying for degrees. Men with families, like me. We'll find a place to live. Maybe . . . maybe Kelly would want to study something. Maybe she'd like to go back to nursing for a few years. Except that Laura will be a bit of a handful."

"I hope Kelly's own children—Kelly's and yours, Greg—will be a bit of a handful. I hope to see more than one grandchild before I die."

"For God's sake, Dad, who said anything about you dying? And of course there are going to be more grandchildren. So many we'll fill the rooms at Pentland."

"I devoutly hope that is the case, Greg," John Merton said, and bowed his head in a kind of submission.

II

They found a flat in Oxford, and Kelly settled to grapple with the post-war austerity of England and was thankful for the stream of food parcels John Merton sent; Greg settled to the grind of studies before the entrance examination. "I'm not kidding myself, Kelly. It'll be a tough course for me. But I just want to prove that I can do it."

Kelly thought of all the things she herself had had to "prove" because, according to her mother, she had been so favored. She had now to prove that she would be a mother to Laura. It didn't seem difficult. She loved Laura because she loved Greg, she thought. And then she corrected herself. She loved Laura; she would have done so whomever she had been.

They paid the required visit to Charleton, the big, though somehow cosy Tudor house of the Renisdales, Laura's grandparents, in Hampshire. She had thought she might be resented, as the person who had taken Dorothy's place. Instead she was welcomed with a sense of relief. Lady Renisdale invited her to have a sherry with her in her private sitting room on the first night before dinner. It was a room such as Kelly had read about, with a polished hand-pegged oak floor, hand-hewn beams, and the modern comfort of central heating. Lady Renisdale was a handsome woman with a brisk manner. "I'll tell you frankly, Kelly—" she had slipped into the name everyone called her—"I'm terribly happy about this marriage. Of course we miss our Dorothy. She was a really fine girl. It would have made, I think, a splendid marriage. It wasn't just one of those wartime things. But she went, poor darling. And really, darling Laura was a problem. Greg is very good with her, but he's a man . . . I began to wonder, all that time he stayed in Switzerland, if he was really prepared to take up the responsibility of Laura. We were prepared to go on looking after her, but if possible a child should not be brought up by grandparents. We'll be too old at the time when it matters most to her. You'll have your own children, and Laura will have brothers and sisters. As it should be. We have four children. They have all needed each other. If Greg hadn't married again, I would have sent Laura to live with my other daughter—she has three children of her own. And I'm so glad it's someone who knows Greg so well. I was afraid it might be a sort of . . . well, a marriage to someone he hardly knew. But you're evidently so *right* for him. You're part of his home in Australia. Part of his childhood. And Laura loves you. It's plain to see that. Yes, I'm very happy, my dear . . ."

Kelly looked at her directly. "Did Greg explain just *how* we grew up together? Did he tell you that my mother is . . . is the housekeeper at Pentland?"

Lady Renisdale waved her hand. "We've had a war, my

dear. You could say we've had a revoultion. Those things don't matter anymore. You are a lovely, accomplished young woman. Greg is lucky to have you. Laura is lucky."

"But your own daughter . . . Dorothy. . . ?" Kelly couldn't quite believe this wholehearted acceptance.

Lady Renisdale turned her head to look at the framed photo of Dorothy in her WAF uniform. "We had a lovely daughter. We miss her very much. But nothing *you* did ever caused her or us unhappiness. We are glad to have you in our family, Kelly. You are always welcome here."

They entered the short, dark days of the English winter. It was a quiet life at Oxford. Greg studied, and for exercise he played rugby and squash. He hoped to read History. "I suppose I should be taking a course in agriculture, or something like that, so that it'd help back home. But I reckon if I don't know the ins and outs of a sheep now, I never will. You've got to be a big man, mentally, like Dad, to stay alive in those outback places, Kelly. Store it all up while you're still here. You'll realize how far Pentland is from the rest of the world. Take back things to tell our kids . . ."

In the spring he passed his entrance examinations. It was time for Laura to see the plastic surgeon again. "They told me they have to do it gradually. She's got to keep growing new skin for grafting. There's a lot of work to be done on the ear, and some more on the jaw bone. Poor little kid. She was so damn brave with it all, Kelly, and I felt so helpless . . . I found, for once in my life, that I couldn't do anything. I was helpless."

The operations were scheduled to begin in May. Greg would be there for the first. After that, he planned to join a climbing team which was going out to Nepal. Kelly was dismayed when she heard it, almost without words. "Why . . . ?"

"The beginning of getting together a team for taking a crack at Everest. Oh, we won't try it this time. This is just reconnaissance. We need to know the Sherpas, need to know just what sort of equipment . . . all that sort of thing. They're very high, those mountains, Kelly. There's a different feel, they say, than climbing in the Alps. I'm lucky to have been asked. This is a pretty closeknit bunch of fellows. I'm still a bit of an outsider."

"But Laura . . ."

"Laura has you, Kelly. Already she's much closer to you than she is to me. Well, hell . . . what do you expect? And you even have that bit of medical training. You'll understand much better than I what's going on. I'll be back in time for the new term at Oxford. I've worked too hard to let that go."

She took his hand, forcing his attention. "Greg, what's in the future . . . *your* future?"

"My future? One day, Kelly, I'll climb Everest. I know it."

III

Laura had the first of the operations on her ear, and another skin graft on her face. Greg stayed until she was pronounced satisfactory by the surgeon, then he took a plane to India. "The others have gone ahead. I'll have to catch up."

Against some mild protests from Kelly they had rented a flat in London. "Laura will be going through more than a few operations, Kelly, and she needs a place to recuperate in between. We need a base here. Hotels don't make a home. I'll come down from Oxford every weekend. It'll be much more settled that way. . . . Listen, Kelly, why don't you start taking some courses in something? Why don't you take a teacher-training course?"

"But I'll never have a chance to be a teacher, Greg! I mean . . ."

"Kelly, love, you're going to be stuck on a station in the outback. All the mothers there become teachers whether they like it or not. Wouldn't it be better if you had the proper qualifications? Besides, with what Laura's headed for in the next few years, she's not going to get much regular schooling. It would be great if you were able to teach her. She could be your first pupil, Kelly. Wouldn't that be a wonderful thing for you both?"

He went off to India and left the decision to her. She remembered her mother's words about her becoming a child-minder, and she grew angry—irrationally, not with Greg, but with her mother. So she took a cram course to get a place in a teacher's college in London. She sat by Laura's bed at night in the hospital and studied. When the nurses knew she had had some training they were content to leave her with the little girl, and her presence seemed to calm the patient. "Poor little kid," one of them said to Kelly in the corridor one day. "Rotten luck for you two to get caught in London while the buzz bombs were coming over."

"Yes," Kelly agreed. She realized that the nurse was one of the many who thought that Laura was her daughter. They didn't count ages; they just took it for granted. No mother could have been closer than she to Laura.

When Laura could be released from hospital, they went to

Charleton for two weeks. Lady Renisdale took Kelly's hand in hers when they were alone. "How can I thank you, my dear? You are doing a wonderful job with her. She has more confidence . . . she doesn't try to hide herself as much as she did."

They went back to London. Kelly continued to study at night while Laura slept, and the times when she was taken out by the nanny who came daily. Even in post-war England there remained a few who called themselves nannies, but Laura's was one of the new type who didn't live in. "I like to have a bit of independence, Mrs. Merton," the woman said. She was about thirty-five, Kelly guessed. She had been in the WAF during the war. "There's no way back from that, Mrs. Merton. We took orders then because we had to, but now we want a bit of life for ourselves. So I'll be here nine to five, and you can go to your college—or whatever it is. After that, Laura's yours."

Kelly reflected, as she wrote to John Merton, that it was just as well there was money for all the things that Greg's and Laura's lives seemed to demand. A steady flow of money came from Australia, and there was the income from the trust fund set up for the Renisdale children, and from which Laura now benefited. With memories of the days when her mother had scraped to send her to school, Kelly was almost bewildered by the money that she now could command and spend. She didn't find it easy to spend money, not on frivolous things. She kept the books very carefully, as she had learned at Miss Hale's. It was a skill she had acquired at John Merton's wish, and it would one day be used at Pentland, as he had hoped.

Greg came back from Nepal with a look in his eyes that made Kelly afraid; he seemed to burn with a fire that made him appear like a visionary and a zealot. "I've seen it, Kelly!" he exulted. "We went far enough up the foothills so that one morning I was able to see the summit! My God . . . !" He hugged her and Laura simultaneously, and he talked like a man who has been in quest of the Holy Grail. "How are my two beauties?" He didn't wait for an answer. With infinite gentleness he stroked the hair back from Laura's ear. "Coming along beautifully, aren't you, Baby? You're going to be just gorgeous." Without hesitation he tenderly kissed the place on her face where the new skin had been grafted. It was now a less livid mark than before, but still apparent. In time there would be other operations.

That night in bed Kelly held Greg fiercely. "I've missed you so much Greg. So much . . ."

He kissed her. "I know. I miss you. But I can't tell you how good it is to know you're here to come back to, Kelly. And Laura is so well looked after. My God, how lucky we both are. But Kelly, let me tell you about . . ." He lay in the darkness, holding her, and telling her of the other mistress he had acquired, the one that could only be glimpsed after infinite toil and trial, the one that might never be conquered. "It's hard to imagine what it could be like to stand there one day. I'll do it! I have to!" Kelly listened, and told herself that she would have to be content with the part of him that was left to her. After all, what was there to fear in a mountain—except that it might take his life.

He went back to Oxford and came to London on weekends, as he had promised. He was up at dawn each day, running in Hyde Park; he played rugby for Oxford, and John Merton's letters overflowed with pride; he was on the second Oxford rowing team; he played squash and had trouble staying awake over his books. "But I've got to keep up, Kelly. They'll throw me out if I don't."

During the winter holidays he went climbing—Snowdonia, Glencoe, the Cairngorms—and he always insisted that Kelly and Laura come with him, though they did not join the climbing teams. They grew used to the disciplined comradeship of the climbers—strong, tough men, not all of whom had an Oxford background, or money. The one who came closest to being a friend was Mike Kettrick, an Australian who had drifted to England after the war, and had taken a job as a car salesman. In Glasgow he had married a local girl; when they climbed in Scotland Jeannie sometimes came with him, and shared with Kelly and Laura the rather spartan conditions of the small guest houses which were the climbers' bases. "They're all a bit daft, you know," she once remarked to Kelly as the men set out at first light on a morning of bitter cold. "I don't know why I let Mike go . . . he could so easily get killed. But try to stop him . . ." She shrugged. "What's the use?"

What was the use, Kelly silently agreed. Her own life was almost as disciplined as Greg's. She went on at teacher's college, and she looked after Laura. Outside of the times spent with the climbing team they had little social life. Greg didn't seem to want to spend the time it would have taken to cultivate those who might be considered his social equals. It was hardly a situation anyone would have expected of the son of Pentland, and the granddaughter of the Renisdales. A few times a year, a little reluctantly on Greg's part, Kelly thought, they went to Charleton. Greg filled what he considered idle hours by sailing on the Solent. Kelly and Laura were expected to act as crew, and they quickly learned who was the skipper.

And each year, when the Long Vacation started, Greg was off to Nepal again. "Of course, it's too late for serious climbing. By June the weather starts to turn against you. But I have to get used to the whole operation. When I'm through at Oxford, it's just possible they'll ask me to join a real expedition . . ."

He finished at Oxford with a respectable second-class degree, and Kelly got her own degree and wondered how to use it, except for Laura's benefit. On Coronation Day, in 1953, Greg wept in Kelly's arms when the news was flashed that Edmund Hillary had stood on the summit of Everest. They had had splendid seats for the procession as the young Queen rode in the golden coach through London, and Laura had been almost sick with excitement. Her grandparents had been inside Westminster Abbey for the coronation, wearing coronets and ermine-trimmed robes. Afterward, the Renisdales had given a party in their huge flat in St. James's Square—they never had rebuilt the house in which their daughter had died. There was champagne and delicious food—fatigue after the long day which had begun for most of them near dawn, talk of the ceremony in the Abbey, of the glittering pageantry and, naturally, talk of Everest. Kelly was slightly bewildered by the array of people, many of them still wearing robes, uniforms and decorations. One man detached himself from a group and made purposefully toward Laura; as usual, Laura stuck close by Kelly's side. "You don't remember me, Laura. But I've seen enough photos to know *you*. You were screaming at the front when we last met. I'm your godfather." He looked at Kelly. "And you have to be Mrs. Merton—the Renisdales' beloved Kelly, whom I've heard so much about. My name's Brandon." He was wearing the dress uniform of a Guard's regiment, and a dazzling array of medals, as well as the insignia of a General. Among the medals, Kelly was aware that he wore the greatest of them all, the Victoria Cross. Laura backed away shyly, and Kelly tugged at her urgently to stay. She liked this tall, fair, blue-eyed man whose handsomeness seemed so much to complement the splendid uniform. It was a friendly face—he was smiling as if he were genuinely pleased to see Laura, and to meet her. She realized she was talking to one of Lord Renisdale's closest friends, someone whose name often cropped up in talk at Charleton. Although there was a gap in their ages, Kelly remembered that there had been some sort of wartime association which Arthur Renisdale valued highly. Charles Brandon. That was his name. General Sir Charles Brandon, war hero, confidant of the high and the mighty in wartime councils, as well as friend to press barons, and the powerful of the land, knighted for his military services. But here he was, smiling at them, with a kind of charming humility, as if he really strove to please them both. "Here, let me bring you some champagne—and I'd like to introduce my two girls. Mrs. Merton—Kelly—this is Julia and Kate. And my little goddaughter, Laura. Would you imagine they were twins?" he asked. They were about twenty, Kelly guessed, and very different in appearance and manner, one blond, with her father's blue eyes, classically beautiful features, and a long, beautiful sweep of neck. She smiled gently at Kelly and Laura, but rather absently, as if it were her habit to smile at all the world. The other was shorter, dark-eyed and vivid, without her twin's beauty, but she had an arresting, eager, enquiring expression. Her dark hair was short, and looked as if she had cut it herself. She was carelessly dressed, on a day when most people wore their best. But her smile was open and frank, like her father's; her gaze didn't drift over them vaguely, as her sister's had done. "Hello," she said, and Kelly noticed that she didn't try to avoid looking directly at Laura; her glance didn't slide away from the scarred cheek. "Father's always been keen to meet you again. He always seems just to miss you at Charleton. You're his only goddaughter, did you know?"

Laura shook her head, but her gaze was on the one called Julia. "You dance with the National Ballet, don't you?" The young beauty smiled and nodded. "I try." Laura wriggled with excitement. Somehow, on this great day, this seemed for her to be the high point. Kelly hadn't had any idea that their few visits to the ballet had so impressed the child. She wondered immediately if Laura's shyness could be overcome to the point where she might take dancing lessons. Then Greg was at her side; there were a few more minutes of conversation with General Brandon, whom he had met only at Laura's christening, and then Greg was urging Kelly to leave.

"We haven't met Lady Brandon," Kelly objected, as he led

her away. "It seems rude . . . after all, the General is Laura's godfather."

"She isn't here," Greg said. "She's an invalid. Come on, Kelly. Let's get home."

They watched a replay of the scenes of the day on television that night, and Greg hardly seemed to see them. Laura was asleep, exhausted by the unforgettable day. "I should have been there, Kelly!" Greg said, and she knew he wasn't referring to what they were watching. "And to think it was a New Zealander! Almost out of our own backyard. Trained in New Zealand. I should have joined him. I should have forgotten about Oxford. To hell with the degree. It was only an excuse to stay in Europe. But *he* did it from New Zealand. Oh, damn, I'm ashamed to think I'm so jealous of any man, but I am . . ." He made love to her that night, and she felt as if it were the mountain itself he assaulted.

IV

That summer, after a two-week visit to the Renisdales', they returned to Pentland. They were met at Sydney by John Merton, and Kelly realized that they had been too long away. He had aged; painfully he tried to suppress his joy at the sight of them, and failed. For the first time she saw tears in his eyes. "Welcome home," was all he said. There were no reproaches for the long absence.

So Laura took up the life at Pentland which had once been Kelly's, except the difference lay in the fact that she had a qualified teacher all to herself. And she, in her turn, was caught in the silent struggle which continued between Delia Merton and her housekeeper-cook, Mary Anderson. Kelly's mother had assumed a position at Pentland which had no real definition. There was another cook employed, but Mary Anderson—though she had taken the role of housekeeper, supervising the staff—could still do anything that pleased her in the kitchen. John Merton had built a small cottage near the big house which was hers alone. "I had to look after her, Kelly," he explained. "She was all for leaving Pentland when you were married, and we had a devil of a time persuading her that it was not right. I couldn't have your mother going out and working for other people, could I?" Kelly discovered that her mother had the lifetime use of the cottage, and a small annunity. She saw that John Merton had done these things to protect her from any action Delia Merton might take in the event of his death. Pentland was Mary Anderson's home for the rest of her life.

"I don't know how to thank you . . ."

"You have given more to Greg, to Laura and to me than we had a right to ask. You'll be asked to go on giving, Kelly. I can see it. Greg is an obsessed man, and he settles only for perfection."

"I can't give him perfection."

"You come damn close to it."

But it was a restless man who tried to settle at Pentland. As his father said, he appeared to require little short of perfection, and after the intense discipline of his student and mountaineering years, he found it hard to relax and accept less than the optimum effort. He went to work to help his father on the station, and succeeded only in quarreling with the station manager, whose job he tried to take over. "Look, Dad, I know it all backwards. It could be more efficient . . . we waste a lot of time and effort. When those blokes go into Barrendarragh on a Saturday night to get drunk, you can't get a move out of them on Monday."

"Greg . . . Greg, you know what life is like here. What else do they have? They're a drifting lot, no wives, families . . . or none here. You'll never make an Australian work because you tell him it's his duty, or it's more efficient not to drink. You've got to remember, Greg, that none of them have tasted that high altitude purity you have."

But the station manager left, and another, more compliant man replaced him, and Greg was virtually in charge. Kelly realized that Greg was not popular with the men or quite as popular with the neighbors as one would have expected from the charming boy whom most of them remembered. "Old Greg . . . well, he's just a bit too Oxford for me," Kelly heard one say to another over their beers on the corner of the veranda during one of the Saturday-night supper parties. "Used to be a good sport. Now if I hear about one of those bloody mountains again . . ."

Kelly drifted into the life at Pentland which John Merton had always hoped would be hers. When she offered to help with the books, he accepted gratefully, pretending that he needed more help than he did. As she sorted and sifted the papers, wrote letters at his dictation, she began to realize the extent of John Merton's assets and influence. He held directorships, often nominal, in companies that were far beyond Pentland's scope. She realized why Pentland had survived droughts and bush fires which had bankrupted other men; he had resources far beyond its acres to call on. At last she commented upon it. "It was my father's making, Kelly. He was an exceptionally shrewd and far-sighted man. Pentland was his first love, and he kept expanding here, and improving until the day he died. But he knew it wasn't the only thing on earth. You see the shares in Broken Hill Proprietary. I didn't buy them—he did, when it was an infant company. He got into coal in Newcastle and into shipping to carry his wool. He was a Borderer Scot who came out here with tuppence in his pocket and the will to work. I can't say he didn't have luck—but he had guts, too. A gambler in small companies which grew to big ones. Oh, he had a few setbacks, but his instincts were right. When he handed it all on to me, he also left me a finger in quite a few pies. I know where the bodies lie, Kelly. There's more than one man who owes me—or my father—a favor. I know when to call the score. I do it as little as possible, but I know when to do it. I wanted a lot of children to spread it all out among, Kelly. I got only one. It's a load for Greg's shoulders, and I wish I didn't have to share him with a passion which seems to pull him halfway around the world. But we'll work it out—time will. One day Greg's legs and lungs will be too old to carry him up a mountain. I think it would be safe then to reckon that he'll stay at home."

V

But while Greg was physically present at Pentland, his mind remained elsewhere. Endlessly he wrote, or dictated to Kelly, letters to the men whose friendship or acquaintance he had made on the journeys to Nepal. "I can't let them forget me, Kelly . . ." And he drove his body to the limits, like a fighter in training to stay fit, as if he waited for a call. At last Pentland got its swimming pool. "It's no use putting in an oversize bathtub," Greg said when it was first talked about. "It has to be big enough to give a bloke a chance to really exercise." So it was put in, almost Olympic-sized, and Pentland's water tanks, already enormous, were added to so that the precious rain, when it came, could be stored. There was talk in the district of John Merton's folly; every day so much water evaporated in the relentless sun; every day it had to be topped up. And every day, morning and evening, with near fanatical dedication, Greg lapped back and forth, back and forth. For him there was no frivolous diving, no gentle lolling; he had his set number of laps to cover, and he did it. Because it was Australia, and no other system would have worked, the station hands, and anyone else, were invited to use the pool. In the beginning they did, horsing about, splashing like children, playing with Laura as she rode her rubber raft. But they knew soon enough that Greg thought they interfered with his regimen; he had to break his stroke to avoid them. They came less and less, and finally not at all. Kelly and Laura and John Merton sat about the pool, watching the monotonous lapping of the lean, tanned figure. There was no one to watch him on the early mornings of the winter when a thin sheet of ice slowed him a little as he swam. He went from the pool to an enormous breakfast, to a day in the saddle. Their own generators now gave Pentland electricity, and John Merton rigged up lights on the tennis court, so that Greg could play at night, but none of them, not at Pentland nor any of the neighbors who drove over, were up to his standard, or played with his fierce competitiveness. "It isn't any fun," Kelly heard one of them complain. "He plays as if he thinks he's got to make Wimbledon." When they went to the local cricket fixtures in Barrendarragh, the friendly, easy-going matches became tense as Greg used a particularly aggressive bowling technique. "I thought they taught those sporting gentlemen in England that that's not cricket," someone behind Kelly drawled.

But still, Greg was infinitely patient as he coached Laura at tennis, gentle in a way he was with no one else. He watched the line of her serve, imparted a beauty to the rhythm of her strokes. On Pentland's own cricket pitch he bowled easy balls so that she could have the pleasure of hitting cleanly and well. "You're going to be good, Baby," he would say. "Bloody good!" And he always kissed her on the burn mark on her face. He was equally patient as he taught her the various swimming strokes. "It's how to dance in water, Baby. Men are faster, but there's hardly anything more beautiful than watching a woman do a good backstroke." Laura expanded and warmed in her father's praise. She practiced too diligently.

"He's turning her into the image of himself," John Merton lamented. "Should we send her to school, Kelly? She needs other children—the way you did."

"Not yet. She hasn't learned to be an Australian yet. She's not ready. They know who *you* are. They'll learn that her other grandfather is a baron—and a lot of other things. It takes some getting over—some living up to."

The first winter Greg went off to climb in New Zealand. He had written to Edmund Hillary, and met him. He returned and spoke as if he had talked with a god. "Bloody marvelous man. And he's writing to some of his pals, and he thinks there's a fair chance I could get on the next Everest expedition." Kelly and John Merton heard the news with token smiles.

"Let's hope he doesn't make it," John Merton said that night to Kelly as they paced the veranda together. It was while Greg was away that they had learned for certain that Kelly was pregnant.

Greg greeted the news with enthusiasm. "Marvelous! Bloody marvelous. Dad wants it. Laura's ready for it now. Couldn't be better timing!" Kelly wanted to hear that he wanted the baby himself.

She continued to work with Laura on her schoolwork, to work with John Merton on the books during her pregnancy. She continued to swim, gently. She didn't play tennis, or ride, but she encouraged Laura in both. "I'm dying for it to be born," Laura said. It was her first real instruction in sex; she thought of it simply and plainly in terms of lambs being born. "I do hope it's a boy. Daddy would love a boy. But Grandfather would love a boy even more." How soon, Kelly thought, she had become wise to the needs of men.

It was Laura herself, unwittingly, who caused it. Kelly, in her seventh month of pregnancy, was sitting by the pool, watching as Laura practiced the various strokes her father had taught her. She tried so hard, Kelly thought, but she never displayed the instinctive feel for physical activities which was Greg's by nature. She worked at things conscientiously, bravely, but when she knew that she was doing badly, she seemed to go to pieces. Doing badly, in Laura's terms, seemed to mean performing at less than her father's standard of perfection. At those times she tended to collapse, all her training would desert her, as the superficial thing it was. In the worst instances, as in dealing with a too-fresh or bad-tempered horse, she could panic. Kelly watched for this endlessly. It was a reminder of the day Laura had screamed at the photographers' flash cameras. Kelly guessed that in Laura's mind was a deeply hidden memory of the day the bomb had fallen, and Laura's mother had died with her baby in her arms.

Kelly dozed as she lay in the shade of an umbrella. It was nearly Christmas, and they were in a period of intense heat; even the air seemed baked like the ground. There had been no rain for almost a year; at night the sky was streaked with lightning, dry lightning. Kelly seemed to suck for air; her body was heavy and uncomfortable, hugely swollen. She had reached the stage where she longed for the birth as a release; she dreamed of moving freely again. She watched Laura through half-closed eyes, eyes which did not register the long dark thing that slid over the hot concrete surround of the pool toward the deep end, perhaps drawn there by the scent of water. At that moment Laura finished her practice laps, and started to heave herself out of the water. Startled, the thing suddenly reared itself up, and revealed itself, and struck at the arm that had appeared to come out of nowhere. Kelly was fully awakened by Laura's scream.

The only thing close was the heavy iron pole of the shade umbrella. She pulled it out of its stand and ran to the end of the pool. Laura's screams were interrupted as she sank down beneath the water. The snake waited, rearing itself again as Kelly ran toward it. She managed to strike it before it struck her. Then she hit it again and again, until the thing writhed uselessly. Laura screamed again. Kelly turned and realized that she had gone into one of her states of panic. She appeared, literally, to have forgotten that she could swim. She was drowning here in the deep end of the pool, a victim of her own shock.

Kelly let herself drop in heavily. She had no hope of getting Laura out of that end of the pool, the weight of the child, as well as the sight of the writhing snake was too much. She could feel the awful embrace of the panic-stricken child, and she did what she had been taught. She managed to break one arm free and she hit Laura sharply across the face. Laura stopped screaming, let go of Kelly, and sank again. Kelly lunged for that limp body, swung it around, and grasped the child under the chin; she began the life-saving stroke toward the shallow end of the pool, and the steps. It was the longest swim of her life; she felt the knifelike pains go through her while she desperately struggled to hold Laura in that position, face out of the water. By the time her shoulders hit the first of the steps she was spent. She just lay there, helpless. She propped Laura's unconscious head against one of the wide steps, and started to call for help. When it came it was her mother, and Delia Merton, and then, as the cries grew louder from them, the other women servants. She felt herself half-lifted, half-pulled up the steps and laid on the burning concrete. From there she whispered instructions on what they should do to pump the water from Laura's lungs. Her mother knelt and worked doggedly, ceaselessly; Laura's face was blue. Delia Merton's own face was ashen as she felt for a pulse. It seemed a very long time before Laura gave a faint gasp, and her eyes flicked open for a second. Then Kelly rolled over on her back; the concrete burned beneath her; the last glimpse she had of the sky before slipping into unconsciousness was of a hard, pitiless blue.

Pentland was well used to dealing with snake bites—the techniques were known, the serums on hand. A telephone call was made, and in a few minutes a flying doctor was on his way from Barrendarragh. Gun shots were fired to bring the men from the Home Paddocks. But Pentland was not accustomed to the problem of a woman in premature labor. They heard the sound of the small plane making its approach to the rough, emergency landing strip with relief. The doctor observed the tourniquet on Laura's arm, released it, and administered further anti-venom serum; then he turned his attention to Kelly. As he listened with a stethescope he indicated that his struggle would be to save Kelly; he said nothing about the baby. Looking at John Merton's face, he dared say nothing. When a child was delivered by Cesarean section it was a perfectly formed, seven-month male child, but it was dead. It had not survived the titanic battle Kelly had fought to save Laura.

Kelly was only dimly aware, through drugs, of John Merton's weeping. Greg's hand held hers. "Laura?" she whispered.

"Laura will be all right," came the answer. "She's been flown to Barrendarragh. You'll have to stay here, Kelly. You can't be moved yet."

"Dad . . . ?" John Merton raised his anguished face. "I'm sorry I lost the baby." Then she turned her head into the pillow, and let the drugs engulf her.

VI

Before she was completely well, the invitation for Greg to join an Everest expedition came. There was never any question that he would refuse. "I'd like to take you as far as Katmandu, Kelly—you and Laura. But the others won't have their wives there. Most of them couldn't afford it. But you could come to London. You'd be there waiting when we got back."

You must come and stay at Charleton, Lady Renisdale wrote. *Greg will be gone a long time, and you are not yet completely well. I insist, my dear.* Her insistence was formidable, and the deciding factor was that Greg wanted her to do it. "It'll be good for both of you. Stuck here at Pentland you forget how other people talk—that there *are* other kinds of people. Laura's becoming shy again. At least at the Renisdales' you won't lack company."

There was plenty of company. John Merton insisted that Kelly spend money on new clothes for herself and Laura. "You'll have to learn to be a bit extravagant, my dear." Kelly was glad of his advice as weekend after weekend there was a constant parade of friends at the Renisdales' table. There was a lot of interest in the new expedition being mounted for the assault of Everest, much written about it in the newspapers, particularly the Renisdale newspapers. The attempt had to come before the weather turned in June. There were news reports, and then long silences as communications between Katmandu and the outside world became erratic. There was the terrible morning in May when the news came of the first two deaths; for a time the names weren't known, and Kelly walked the woods of Charleton in agony. But Greg had not died. The expedition moved on to establish Camp 4, preparing for the final assault on the summit. Then two more men died, their bodies lost in a glacier. The expedition was abandoned. Kelly and Laura met a stony-faced Greg on his return to London. "Come on," he said, as if they must start that minute. "Let's go home. That's all that's left."

They went back to Pentland. Greg seemed wrapped in his own private torment. He seldom mentioned the expedition; he had refused to talk to newsmen on his return to Sydney, which made him unpopular. "I wonder what happened to that charming boy who used to get along so well with everyone?" John Merton commented to Kelly. "He can't give you the time of day now."

"You said it long ago, Dad. He's obsessed. When you fall in love with an idea, it's harder to lose it than to lose a woman."

"He hasn't lost it. That's the trouble. Just watch. He'll be off to New Zealand again. You know, Kelly, sometimes I wish there hadn't been money to let him do all these things."

And Greg did go, almost immediately, to New Zealand, taking advantage of the winter conditions. He climbed with, and learned from the famous guide, Harry Ayres, talked again to Hillary. He came home and chafed at the daily routine of Pentland. "There are all kinds of men who can look after sheep. There are damn few who ever climb Everest. Kelly—I'm getting old. Soon it'll be too late." It seemed absurd to hear a man apparently at the prime of his strength and abilities say such a thing, but Kelly knew it was true. And secretly she hoped that the time would pass quickly, that time would defeat him.

The obsession would not be stilled. Finally Greg faced his

father with it. "Get together the money," he said. "It could be an Australian-led expedition. There are plenty of good men I've climbed with in New Zealand—some of them Australians. There were mistakes made last time, Dad. Mistakes I don't think I would have made if I'd been leader."

"You mean *you*, Greg, want to lead it?"

"Why not? Why not me!" He rounded on his father. "If you don't feel like putting up all the money yourself, then put the squeeze on all your pals. Plenty of them owe you favors. Make it a patriotic bit, if you want. Any way—any way you can swing it. Yes, I *will* be the leader. And I'm going to succeed. I've got to do it now, or it'll be too late."

His father went about the task, saying little. What was there to say in the face of such a fever as burned in his son? All he could do, like Kelly, was to pray that this would be the last time, and Greg would return to Pentland, either successful or failed, but here, and safe. The money was forthcoming. John Merton tapped all the sources he well knew were at his disposal, called for the return of all the favors he had ever done. He could have, he knew, mounted the expedition himself, but that would have smacked too much of buying the leadership of it for his son. And he discovered a surprising number of men who were prepared to put up money to see an Australian stand at the summit of Everest. Knowing that the funds were available, Greg began to make his plans. He had to apply to Nepal for permission to mount the expedition, which was difficult to obtain, and, in the end, needed John Merton's influence with his highly placed friends in Canberra to achieve. Kelly was pressed into service as never before. She became a secretary, a quartermaster, a handler of logistics. She was involved as never before. Without ever having seen Everest she began to know it almost too well in terms of numbers and weights; so many tons of equipment to Katmandu, then so many by Sherpa pack to Base Camp, so many to Camp No. 2, less beyond that, less and less as the altitude grew higher, the summit nearer, the oxygen to be carried less. Her dreams were wracked with numbers. It took almost a full year to raise the money and complete the plans. They set off, with Laura, for England in September. An office had been set up in London for the coordination of the expedition, with a manager, a climbing friend of Greg's from the old days in charge. It was still the practice to mount Everest expeditions from London—the British, led by Sir John Hunt, had been the first to do it successfully, though it was a New Zealander, Edmund Hillary, who had stood on the summit. London was still the repository of the greatest experience, and they went there naturally as a base. It seemed odd to Kelly that she was actually closer to Everest on their flight to England as they touched the fringe of the sub-continent of India than she would be in all the time it would take to make the preparations in London. Greg had selected his team, mostly Australian, but augumented by some of the Englishmen he knew and trusted best. Some of them were ones Kelly remembered from the days when she and Laura used to accompany Greg to the lonely Welsh and Scottish farmhouses where the climbing teams gathered. Because of the backing, an Australian would be deputy leader, and Mike Kettrick, the Australian friend who still sold cars in Glasgow to pay for his trips to Nepal, would be in the back-up assault team. It was the realization of a dream for both Greg and himself. They had never lost touch; they had been twice in Nepal together, corresponded regularly, and dreamed the same dream. They would both be given a chance to attain it.

"Take care of him, Kelly," John Merton said to her the night before they left Sydney.

"How can I? What can I do?"

He shook his head. "I really don't know. I just have a feeling . . . My God, I hope I haven't put the instrument of his own death into Greg's hands."

The thought stayed with her all through the long, long flight while Greg remorselessly perused lists, made more lists, dictated memos. "Organization is everything, Kelly. It'll be the best organized expedition ever—and we'll make it!"

They rented a flat in London for convenience, but for Laura's sake they spent many weekends at Charleton. Money was not short, so Greg could afford to take most of his team to Switzerland for the winter months to train together, though it could not offer them the high-altitude tests of the distant, mighty Himalayas, nor the problems of isolation and supply. "The Alps are not to be despised, especially in bad weather—but you always know you're *near* something—help or whatever those efficient Swiss can offer. It's a piece of cake compared to the conditions out there. Once you're there, you know it's the real thing," Greg said. "That's why you can't be satisfied with anything less."

So Kelly and Laura were often alone, Kelly wrestling, along with the small staff at the expedition office, with the typing and correspondence, the purchasing of supplies, arranging the air freight of the materiel needed. In the busy, hurried weeks of that autumn it was easy to thrust into the background the fact that in the summer Egypt had seized the Suez Canal, and that trouble seemed inevitable. Greg didn't worry about it, although the expedition would be journeying out to India and on to Nepal through the Middle East. "It'll sort itself out. And in any case, we're flying everything out. There are always other ways around by air." He thought only in terms of the expedition.

Kelly and Laura were alone, and were staying at Charleton during the desperate days in 1956 when Israel, France and Britain decided to take control, by force, of the Canal from Egypt, and dropped their troops from the skies to carry out that decision. They were at Charleton in the days leading up to the American election early in November, when Eisenhower stood for his second term of office, and whose approval of the combined Suez operation was essential. They had not, Eisenhower said, consulted him, and he did not approve. "What's it about, Kelly?" Laura wanted to know. Kelly wished she had followed it all more closely, and understood it better herself. "Well, Egypt took over the Canal from the people who used to own it—British and French—and now everyone's fighting to get it back. It's because of oil, mainly, I think." Charleton in those days was full of talk about Suez. Lord Renisdale was heavily involved; his newspapers totally backed the bid to retake the Canal. They screamed exhortations at the government and the people. Renisdale's political affiliations drew him in inexorably. He had been a longtime friend of the Prime Minister, Anthony Eden. While he spent most of his time in London, he came to Charleton at weekends, and the sense of crisis followed him. The telephone rang constantly; there was a stream of semi-official visitors. Renisdale made many telephone calls to the United States, to cabinet members, senators and congressmen he knew. "Heaven knows what he can do," Lady Renisdale said, "but he has to try. But after all, if Eisenhower is against it, it's hard to see what anyone can do. But it will be unthinkable for us to have to pull out . . ." Her tone indicated that indeed the end of Britain was in sight if that happened.

A name often spoken during those days was that of General Sir Charles Brandon. "Laura's godfather," Lady Renisdale reminded Kelly, who needed no reminding. He appeared, so far as Kelly could make out, to be in charge of the co-ordination of the three-power attack. "With the French and Israeli generals, of course," Lady Renisdale said. "But he's *our* man." Clearly she regarded him as being naturally superior to his allies. "We just have to hold onto the Canal." It was as simple as that.

And it was as great a shock when the three powers bowed before the will of the United States and began the withdrawal. "It will kill Charles," Lady Renisdale said. "There never was a braver soldier or a greater patriot." It was still possible, in those days, to speak of patriotism without embarrassment, Kelly recalled later.

They did not accept immediately at Charleton the fact that it was the great turning point for Britain. Few could foresee that. Lord Renisdale came down from London and withdrew into a deep fog of cigar smoke and brandy. "We haven't been beaten by those wogs," he thundered over dinner. There were about twelve people assembled around the table, including Kelly and Laura. "The Americans have just made us lick their boots, that's what!"

"Dear—one doesn't say 'wogs' these days," his wife ventured.

"I'll say what I damn well please." Then he turned to receive a message from his butler. "Excuse me—telephone."

When he returned to the table his face was flushed. He was both angry and defiant. "Well, they made it happen!" he announced to the whole table. "Charles Brandon has just resigned. While he stayed in the Army he couldn't open his mouth about politics. Now he means to call it all out—this dirty sellout that's happened. His resignation takes effect immediately. He intends to make a major announcement to the press, and wants time to prepare it. I've invited him here. Of course his London place is impossible because of upsetting his wife. So, my dear, you'd better make preparations for an invasion by the press. And now, I think, we'd better hurry, or we'll miss Eden on the television."

The next days at Charleton were chaotic, with the kind of frenzy which only the press seem to bring with them. Charles Brandon made his resignation from the Army and his position on the Suez pull-out public, and the storm broke. Accusations and counter-accusations were hurled; he was called both a hero and an imperialist reactionary. In turn, he labeled others near-traitors and accused them of bowing before American imperialism. "I have resigned in order to be able to speak out about what I believe to be the truth," he said in a television statement. "I can no longer accept such orders as I have been obliged to carry out."

Laura turned away, panic stricken, from the morning walk she and Kelly usually took when she discovered a television van and cameras in the driveway. Later they went through the kitchen garden and down to the far fields that overlooked the sea. "I wish he hadn't come here, don't you?" she said to Kelly. "It makes everything so uncomfortable. He must have a home of his own. Why isn't he there . . . ?"

"He has a home, naturally," Lady Renisdale told them afterward when Laura asked, "and a family whom I think you've met. You've seen Julia Brandon dance, Laura. Kate's just finished university, and is doing economics and social science at the London School of Economics. She's a bit of a Red, in my opinion. But it's darling Elizabeth, Charles' wife, we care about. She's why he's here at the moment and not at his own London house. It's too sad. Such a tragedy. She has . . . oh, it's called multiple sclerosis. It started when she was quite young—in her twenties—not too long after the twins were born. You know . . . it's something to do with the nervous system. She was using a cane for a while, and then in a wheelchair. And now she's permanently bedridden and becoming more and more helpless. It would have been impossible for her to cope with all this fuss, so Arthur insisted on Charles coming here. It must be such an anxious time for poor Elizabeth. The Army has been Charles' whole life. I don't know what he'll do now he's resigned . . . he doesn't really have any money." She sighed. "Sometimes it seems to me a pity that people have to stick to their principles at all costs . . . if he only could have kept quiet about what he felt—at least in public. Oh, dear . . . I must make a point of seeing Elizabeth when I'm in London next week. She's so brave and cheerful in really rather terrible circumstances. But I'm sure Charles will find other things to do. He's not without friends. And certainly there are a lot of people who admire the stand he's taken over this whole business. Well, Arthur, I'm sure, will have some ideas."

Kelly listened to one of the dinner guests at Charleton who, like half the country, did not agree with the General's views on Suez, remark acidly, "Well, he'd have had to retire pretty soon, wouldn't he? They only keep Field Marshals on forever. This must be as good a time as any. Next week you'll hear he's writing his bloody memoirs . . ."

The General appeared only at meals. For a few days he continued to be the focus of press attention in the continuing Suez row. Lady Renisdale professed to be put out by the commotion, but Kelly thought she actually relished it. "I think he's a very brave man," she said. "He's not letting England go down the drain without a protest."

Kelly sat at the table with the man, who, beside Anthony Eden, seemed the most beleaguered of the hour. He appeared surprisingly calm in the middle of the storm, and always greeted her with that same friendly, open smile she remembered. But they did no more than exchange a few words until the morning she and Laura, on their usual walk, found him already in their favorite place, the edge of a copse which gave a view over the Solent. It was a dark November morning, with clouds scudding low. He was wrapped in a strange combination of clothes, half civilian, half military, from which the insignia of rank had already been removed.

"Hello," he said. "We haven't really talked since Coronation Day, have we? How much you've grown, Laura. How well you look." He smiled at her, and did not avoid her eyes. People who were embarrassed by the mark on her face shifted their gaze, and Laura always knew. He then looked at Kelly. "This is a busy time for you, Mrs. Merton. I hear you're just about dispatching the Everest expedition single-handed."

"Hardly that, General. You couldn't get an Army off to some place by yourself, could you?"

He shrugged, and gave a half-laugh. "I haven't got even a piece of an Army to send anywhere anymore."

"What will you do?" Laura asked with disconcerting frankness. Kelly was about to protest, and then decided not to. She tried never to interfere whenever Laura came out of her shell of shyness.

"Don't know at the moment, Laura. They usually have a few jobs for old codgers like me tucked away somewhere. But I think I'd like something a bit more in the firing line. Funny thing, now that at last I've had my chance to say my piece, I've rather got to like it. I'd like to go on and say a few more things about what I think is wrong with the way we're going on these days. I hate to see Britain end in a whimper . . ."

They walked back to Charleton to breakfast, and the General was once more engulfed in the controversy which had propelled him out of his way of life into something unknown. There were no more conversations with him, and later in the winter Kelly read that he was standing for a seat in Parliament which had become vacant because of the death of a member. She noted that it wasn't a safe seat; it was one he would have to fight against strong left-wing opposition. And he would have to fight on his record of Suez. It was a small satisfaction, in the middle of the preparations for the expedition, to see that he had won it with a tiny majority. She pointed it out to Greg. He nodded absentmindedly. "Good for him," he said. "Tough to have to give up everything the way he did. Must have lots of guts." And then he turned his attention back to what was more important to him.

There were many weeks after the expedition departed before the actual climb began, many weeks when equipment had to be carried to Base Camp, and farther. Kelly had decided that she would be more useful in London than Nepal; in London she could fill any needs of the expedition which had been underestimated, be ready to answer any demand Greg made. She was not in charge in London, but she knew she was useful, so she stayed. And she planned, without talking to Greg about it, and after consultation with a different plastic surgeon, for Laura to have another skin graft.

"Do you think it will ever be finished, Kelly?" Laura asked her. "Will they go on doing this all my life?"

"Every time it gets better, Laura. You're growing all the time, and the skin is changing. Remember how the doctor explained it. And all the time they're learning new things. . . . It depends on how much courage you have to go on. No one will ever make you do anything you don't want to."

"My father would do it," Laura answered. It seemed answer enough for her. "And we don't have to tell him. It'll be a surprise when he comes back."

So she and Laura waited together in what had now become a familiar bond. There was the period in hospital, followed by the period of waiting to see how the new skin graft took, the weeks when Laura's cheek flared an angry red, and then gradually grew paler, the new skin, taken from her inner thighs, growing to meld with the old. At the same time the surgeon had also tried the latest technique at resculpturing her ear. Laura bore it all without fuss, and never complained of pain, although Kelly knew she felt it. There seemed to have been something of heroic endurance impressed into that infant of long ago, when she had lain in her dead mother's arms in the wreck of a building in London.

"She has such courage," Lady Renisdale said to Kelly. "I see some of Dorothy in her, of course—or I like to think I do—but much of it must come from Greg. She tries so hard to live up to him." Abruptly Lady Renisdale dropped her characteristic briskness; her eyes softened. "Laura's been so lucky to have you, Kelly. Sometimes I think you've done more for her than a natural mother would have—perhaps because you've thought you had to, because she wasn't your own. But, my dear . . ." She hesitated. People like Phoebe Renisdale didn't normally probe the private emotions or decisions of other people. "My dear, I do hope you'll have your own family. It's more than time you tried again. You musn't give everything to Greg's ambition, you know. He's having his chance now. After this, it must be your turn. That big place out there—Pentland—you'll need boys for that. It shouldn't all be left to Laura."

"Greg knows it's his last chance," Kelly answered. "If it's successful, perhaps he'll be content."

"He'll have to be," Lady Renisdale said, returning to her usual manner. "He can't go on ignoring his responsibilities forever. And *you* haven't that much more time."

They waited together, she and Laura, through the weeks of that spring, and hardly seemed to notice that the daffodils gave way to the tulips in the parks and window boxes of London. They lived for the short cables that filtered through from Katmandu. Base Camp, Camp No. 1. Camp No. 2. "Nearer . . ." Laura would murmur. Laura could, if necessary, have drawn a profile of the mountain itself and its surrounding peaks. Kelly had studied the terrain on maps, had read every piece of published literature about the mountain, and reluctantly acknowledged the powerful force it exerted on the men who dreamed of climbing it. Over twenty-nine thousand feet, the highest place on earth, it had been named after the first surveyor of the Himalayas, Sir George Everest, but the Tibetans called it Chomo-Lungma, Mother Goddess of the World. That was how Kelly thought of it, an oriental deity, fierce, beautiful, cruel, demanding its sacrifices—glittering, icy, untouchable. How did men dare? Except that men like Greg felt compelled to dare and to challenge it. She and Laura went each day to the office and studied the flags and pins on the big relief maps. "Daddy, do it!" Laura whispered. "Do it!"

There came the morning when Laura almost pounded her awake. "Kelly!—they've done it! They've done it!" She held up the newspaper with its banner headline. AUSSIES CONQUER EVEREST. It had only been a stop-press that had pushed every other item out of place. Just the bare news was flashed from Katmandu, and picked up by the wire services. At the same moment, at a little after six-thirty, the telephone started ringing; it was the press, demanding details. The Renisdale newspapers seemed to assume that they must have natural rights to every aspect of the story. "I don't know anything," Kelly had to admit. After a while, Laura left the receiver off the hook. "Guess what we're having for breakfast? I got it myself, out of my allowance. The man didn't want to sell it to me. It's against the law, he said. So I went to Fortnum and Mason and saw the head man in the groceries there. I told him what I wanted it for. He said he knew Grandmother . . . he'd known my mother, too." She was waving a bottle of champagne around so much that when they finally got it open, it spurted to the ceiling, and rained down on them. Kelly and Laura wrapped arms around each other and laughed with hysterical relief. The private, unlisted telephone started to ring.

"Congratulations, my dear," Phoebe Renisdale said. "Now you will have your husband to yourself again. Now here's a friend of yours who's staying with us and would like a word with you. We're all very proud . . ."

"Charles Brandon here," the voice said. For a moment Kelly couldn't remember who he was, except that she knew the name. Then the voice went on, and she recalled the man, solitary, staring over the Solent, his career behind him, a new one to find. "I would like you to pass my congratulations on to your husband when he comes back. He's done a splendid thing. But I'd like to say that I know he needed you all through it. Lady Renisdale's told me. If there aren't many Greg Mertons in the world, there aren't many Kellys, either."

Somehow, in the long day that they waited in the office for further news, as the telegrams poured in, as the excitement mounted, it was the message that Kelly remembered best. She had sensed a tinge of envy in the older man of the younger one, and yet it was an envy that had given place to generosity. And she remembered the personal part of the message that had been for her.

Confirming reports from other news agencies came in during the day, and yet nothing directly from the expedition itself. It was nine o'clock that night before the brief cable came. OBJECTIVE ACCOMPLISHED, MIKE KETTRICK DEAD. PLEASE INFORM WIDOW. Signed MERTON.

The papers of the next morning carried blurred photos of Greg and Mike together on the summit of Everest, the flags stretched stiff in the wind, their faces indistinguishable because of the heavy masks they wore, their figures bundled. "That's Daddy," Laura said. "He's taller than Mike." Her voice broke. "Kelly, what can have happened to Mike?"

"We'll have to wait, Laura." She waited, alone and wakeful

for many nights, waiting for the telephone to ring, waiting for the personal cable from Greg. It never came. His silence was like a stone dropped in a deep pool.

Quietly the staff at the office began to file and pack. Kelly journeyed to Glasgow to visit Mike Kettrick's widow. Jeannie, whose eyes blazed with grief, shook her head at the words Kelly attempted to say.

"We're bloody fools, you and I, Kelly. All of the women who back up these men. We stand to lose everything because a man believes he had to do something. Men like that should never marry. Women like us should never marry them. That's all, Kelly. I can't say anymore."

Kelly went back to London to await the return of the expedition. There still was no personal message from Greg, although the news agencies had interviewed the whole team at Katmandu. Kelly noticed that Laura began to avoid her eyes; they did not talk of Greg's coming back. They simply waited.

At the appointed time, with the television cameras turning, they saw Greg and the rest of the team file down the steps of the aircraft. Greg put his arms around Kelly and Laura in what both recognized as a mechanical embrace. He kissed Kelly. His eyes held no desire, no triumph, no love. He could have been a man near death in a strange land.

"Let's go home," he said.

Kelly, wonderingly, saw the hard, sun-seamed face of a man from whom the last of youth has gone.

That night, when Kelly went to say good night to Laura, the girl wound her arms tightly about Kelly's neck, as if she were hurt. "What's wrong with Daddy?" she asked. "He hasn't even noticed my face."

"It's because it's so much better that there's nothing to notice. You look just like everyone else."

But it seemed a hollow comfort to offer.

VII

They could not go as soon as Greg wished. There were press conferences to attend, the business of the expedition to wind up. It seemed to Kelly that the team dispersed with a strange haste, once the demands of the press had been satisfied. There was very little talk of Mike Kettrick. "He fell," Greg had said at the first press conference, "on the descent from the summit to Camp 5. We had reached the summit in fair weather, but a blizzard came on suddenly during the descent. It was so fierce I couldn't even see Kettrick when he fell. I got the pitons hammered in, and started down to find him. The wind was blowing so hard it was causing him to sway on the rope. He probably was unconscious. There's only so much stress even a nylon rope can take. It parted. I never saw him again. We waited until the blizzard blew itself out, but we never found him. That was when we decided not to have the second team try for the summit." Yes, he agreed, there had been a change in plans. Mike Kettrick was to have gone on the second try, but finally Greg had decided to take him with him for the first attempt.

When Kelly asked Greg to go to Glasgow to see Jeannie Kettrick, he refused. "What am I going to say—I'm sorry? She must know that. We've done something more practical for her. From the money left in the expedition funds, and from a bit I've put in, we've arranged a trust for her. She should have almost as much as Mike was earning as a car salesman, which wasn't much. But it's something. It's all arranged. I've seen the lawyers. Now, Kelly, let's not hang around here in London. Let's get out. Let's go home."

There wasn't even a farewell visit to Charleton. For most of the long plane journey Greg sat and stared at the clouds beneath him. Kelly had never seen him so utterly unoccupied. He did not open a book for the whole wearying length of the flight. Once, waking from sleep, when the cabin lights were dimmed, Kelly saw him stretched in the seat, staring upward, his eyes wide open. It was as if he could not allow his body to relax. She longed to stretch out her hand and touch him, and for the first time, did not dare.

They arrived to the full paraphernalia of the press. For a moment Kelly thought that Laura would refuse to leave the aircraft, but in the end it was she who went first, and it was Greg who hung back. He descended the steps with seeming reluctance. He kissed his mother, shook his father's hand. He nodded, and even smiled as the congratulations came. There was a combined reception for the press and the most prominent backers of the expedition. They were determined to have their hour. Patiently, but unsmilingly, Greg answered questions, demonstrated on diagrams which were ready, the various stages of the ascent and descent. The other Australian members of the team who had arrived home before him were there, and Kelly sensed the lack of camaraderie which had been so strong among them all through the winter of preparation before they left London. Finally it was over, and they drifted away. The next time they would meet would be at the civic reception to be given in the Town Hall by the Lord Mayor.

During the reception Kelly wondered if Greg might be either about to faint, which would be unthinkable in him, or walk out, which would have been equally unthinkable a short time ago. He endured the speeches, the self-satisfaction of the backers of the expedition; he made a brief speech in reply, in which he gave the total credit to the effort of teamwork. "Lastly, I would like to remember a man whom none of you met, Mike Kettrick." Kelly could see that most of them wished he had not mentioned that name. It put a damper on the spirit of celebration.

Afterward, John Merton spoke to Kelly. "For God's sake, Kelly, get him away—away from all these people. I've never known Greg like this. I don't know whether it's his friend's death, or just the strain of the whole expedition. I feel something's going to snap in him. It would be better if there weren't too many people around if it happens."

"We'll go back to Pentland."

"No—not Pentland yet. Everyone from a hundred miles around will want to come over to see him. It will be one long party. I don't think Greg can take it. What about that place up the Queensland coast where you went on your honeymoon? We'll take Laura back with us."

So they returned. The place seemed hardly different. No doubt in the years in between a few coats of paint had been slapped on the weatherboard frame house, but the sun had blistered each of them. The sagging veranda had been propped up in places. A few miles down the coast the small fishing village had sprouted a few more houses and shops. There was a new hotel there which attracted more business than did the little place they stayed in. The beach was golden and untouched; the long, slow swell of the Pacific came at last to rest within their sight and hearing. In the vast silence, which the sound of the waves and the sea birds seemed hardly to break, a kind of peace sank in upon Greg. At first he hardly spoke at all, but Kelly noticed that the rigid line of his jaw loosened a little. He ventured to have a few whiskeys at night from the bottles she had bought, and a few beers, seated in utter silence, with the man who ran the place.

It was the same couple who had owned it years ago when they had first come, with Laura. There was little hope now that Greg would not be recognized, but the man and woman were discreet. "Bet you need to put your feet up, mate," the man said. "Quite a walk you took up there." It was the only reference to Everest, and Kelly was grateful. Word spread to the fishing place down the coast, and when they appeared to do a little shopping, and sip a beer in the lounge of the pub—women weren't allowed in the bar—a few men came forward and offered their hands. "Good on yer, mate!" and sauntered off.

During the days Greg surfed until his body must have ached from the exertion of it. But he also could now sleep deeply and heavily most nights, which he had not done until now. At last, also, he turned to Kelly and made love to her with a passion that had seemed missing, she now realized, for a long time. One night he said, as he lay close to her, "Maybe it'll be better now. It's over, Kelly. I'm finished with it all. Maybe we can go home now." She held the thought to her, like a cherished gift, through the long days when his head bobbed in the surf, and sometimes disappeared in the brilliant dazzle of the sea; the long days when they walked along the edge of the tide, saying little, mostly saying nothing.

Letters reached them there, letters carefully screened by John Merton from the many hundreds which arrived at, or were forwarded to, Pentland. Only letters which had come from people they knew were forwarded, and mostly only Kelly read them. *I hope all is well with you,* Phoebe Renisdale wrote. *It is high time you had Greg to yourself, and that he applied himself to the business of Pentland. It's high time Laura had family competition, though she's really going to be a very elder sister now. I'm thankful it's over safely, except for the death of that unfortunate man.* The letter rambled on over several domestic matters, into which were mixed some of the affairs which absorbed her husband. It was exactly the mix of Phoebe Renisdale's life, making certain that the dinner was excellent whether for a cabinet minister or the local vicar. *Did you hear that Charles Brandon has been made a Knight of the Garter? Really a tremendous honor, since only the Queen can give it. The vacancy occurred after dear old Hamilton died. I think the Queen insisted on Charles—it's rather a controversial choice because of his position over the Suez. But I think H.M. was rather impressed that he should sacrifice his Army career for his principles. And I suspect she did very much agree with Eden's policy, even though she's not allowed to say so, publicly. She's still so young and impressionable, and I think the Empire—what's left of it—means a great deal to her. We are replanting the old herbaceous border. Rather worn out—as we are becoming . . .* The letter rambled back to domestic matters, and Kelly thought of the time at Charleton when the telephone had never stopped ringing, and the press had clamored round the door; whose dark days of that November seemed very far away now as she gazed out into the blinding light of the Pacific. For a time she had been close to the center of power; since then she had touched the heights of celebrity with Greg. Now she longed only for peace; she longed for the flat brown paddocks of Pentland. She longed for Greg's children.

One morning she woke just as the dawn had flushed the horizon with the violent colors of green and purple it sometimes wore here. Greg lay beside her in bed, smoking—something she had not seen him do for many years. It was a sign that training had been broken, perhaps forever.

"Greg . . . ?"

"M-m-m . . . yes, Kelly, I know you're there. I've always known it, even though I've often neglected to tell you. You've stuck it out all these years. You ought to get a medal, or something."

"I don't think medals are worth that much, Greg."

"You bet they're not. They practically gave me a medal for climbing Everest, and if I don't watch out, they'll pin a knighthood on me, the way they did Edmund Hillary. Well, he deserved it."

"You deserve anything they want to give you, Greg."

He stubbed out the cigarette, and rolled over to look at her. "I deserve nothing but the scorn and contempt they hand out to a coward, Kelly."

"What on earth are you talking about?"

"I let him die. That time when he fell, I hung on with everything I had. Yes, it's true, I hammered in the pitons. I did all the right things. I thought the wind was going to pull me off the face, the way it had him. I tried to haul him up. I couldn't tell whether he was still conscious—you couldn't hear a thing above the wind. And then I began to realize that the pitons were going. One let go, and the strain on the others was going to be more than they could take. I started to hammer in others, but my hands were frozen, and I realized my feet were beginning to slip. I could feel his weight, Kelly—a dead weight pulling me down. There might have been time for a few more pitons, but I'll never know, because I cut the rope."

She lay for a few moments, feeling cold in the dawn, knowing the anguish that had wracked him since that moment. "But you were going . . . you said so. It made sense—"

"Nothing makes sense when you're not sure whether you

let your friend die. I *tell* myself that was what happened. I *tell* myself it would have been senseless for me to die as well. But I'll never know for sure. I'll never know what I did in panic. The fact remains that I cut the rope. It didn't fray, as I told everyone else."

"The others at Camp 5 . . . ?"

"Of course they knew. You can't fake a frayed rope. I told them that I was going too. The pitons were coming out. I had lost my ice axe. I didn't tell them I thought I had had just a few minutes in which it might have been possible to save Mike. But they guessed it. They didn't condemn me, Kelly. It's hard to condemn a man for what he does in those heights in the teeth of a blizzard. But they knew I cut the rope, and there was a sort of agreement, which no one ever spoke about, to stick to the story that the rope frayed. There were only the four of us at Camp 5, and no Sherpas. Let's say it was a gentleman's agreement to cover up. We let the rope get buried in the snow, and every one of us hopes it will never be uncovered. None of us want to talk about it. None of us did. But somehow the feeling conveyed itself to the rest. They knew something had gone wrong—something much more wrong than the accidental death of a climber. Each of us accepted the possibility of death—and the possibility that the death might be his own. But we all counted on one another for our lives. And I, who was the leader, let a man go to a certain death in a moment of fear. I was supposed to be the one who didn't know what fear was. I was supposed to be the one who could be counted on to the very last breath. That's what happened, Kelly."

"But you were going yourself!" she cried. She sat up in bed and stared down at him. "There's nothing in anyone's code that says you have to throw away your own life deliberately because someone else is going to die. It wouldn't have helped Mike—"

"Don't you think I've been all around that?—so many times I get dizzy thinking of it. The others said they would have done the same thing. But would they? One of the others might have saved Mike. I'll never know if just that extra effort wouldn't have saved Mike. How can I? I cut the rope."

It remained the unspoken knowledge between them for the next few days. She did not think he regretted having told her. Something of ease now grew between them that had not been there since the moment she had greeted him in London. It was as if he had laid down, though perhaps it was only momentarily, a burden. He was not hiding from her any longer.

She shared his anguish, and she did not any longer try to argue him away from his guilt. She prayed that time would dim it. They walked the beach together, and for the first time he reached for, and held, her hand.

"We'll go back to Pentland. There's work to be done there. Perhaps I can manage to make something of myself. Perhaps I can finally be my father's son. But will I be able to live with myself? Will I . . . ?"

But there followed a bad night. She had felt Greg tossing through the long slow hours. It was one of the times when the peace, which now came to him fitfully in the quiet of the place, deserted him. Out of a restless doze, she had wakened to find the bed beside her empty. "Greg?" she called.

His cigarette glowed on the screened-in porch. "It's O.K., Kelly. I'm here. Just go to sleep." But she had lain wakeful, watching one cigarette being lighted from the last, listening to the clink of the whiskey bottle against the glass. Both things would have been unthinkable in the Greg of a few months ago. Finally, exhausted, she had slept until the first band of light streaked the horizon directly to the east. It was the sense of being alone which roused her from the bed. She stood at the door to the porch, and was just able to discern Greg's figure as he walked down the beach to where the surf had been subdued to gentle, lapping waves. He always swam as soon as he woke, but never before as early as this. He was naked, and he did not run joyously toward the surf, as he usually did. Instead of the first plunge through a breaker, he just walked steadily on. "Greg!" she called. "Greg. Wait for me." But he did not hear her; he did not turn his head. She lost sight of him in the still-dark sea. She experienced then an agonized sense of rejection, of helplessness. If she could not help him now, what would all the years ahead be like? She lay on the bed and wept, secure in the knowledge that, for the time being, he would not come and see her tears. At last, the tears spent, she slept.

She woke, knowing it was late. She threw on clothes and hurried to breakfast, expecting to find Greg there, but he had not come in. "Stayed out a bit long this time, Missus," the man said. "He's a fair glutton for punishment, is your husband. My missus thought she'd be able to put a bit of meat on his bones while he was here, but blowed if he doesn't go and surf it all off!"

To make up for Greg's absence, she tried to eat the breakfast they put before her, and failed. When she was finished she went out onto the veranda and found that the man had his binoculars trained on the sea, and was searching it, methodically.

"Don't like it, Missus. This is carrying things a bit far," he said laconically. "I'll just give it a few more minutes, and then I think I'd better phone for the blokes in Barrindi to get the boats out. What time did you say he went out this morning?"

"I don't know," she lied, the first terrible fear clutching at her. "I was asleep."

They searched for three days. After the first half day there was no real hope that Greg could be alive, but they made the gesture. They hoped, with faint hope, to find a body washed up on a beach along the coast. Those who knew the currents plotted the search. The news was flashed across Australia, and from there through the world which knew Greg Merton as the conqueror of Everest. The hours of daylight were noisy with the sounds of the boats and planes which came from everywhere. The Australian Air Force sent search planes. Greg had been one of their own. And while those who knew the coast might talk of the currents washing up a body, they all knew of the sharks that were the true deciders of what would happen. That brilliant sea hid many horrors.

John Merton arrived and with him, Laura. "I couldn't keep her away," he said to Kelly. "It seemed cruel to leave her behind at Pentland. I think she knows there's no hope, and she needs you, Kelly."

As she gathered Laura into her arms, Kelly thought of the two women who had been left behind at Pentland. Delia Merton would bear her anguish as she had borne the loss of her other children, the hoped and longed for children, in silence. She would probably retreat further into her world of books and needlework, the perfection of her sitting room. And what of her own mother, Mary Anderson? Would she see this as some judgment of a vengeful God because she, Kelly, had dared to go beyond what Mary Anderson thought of as her station in life? Would she think that it was the hand of the Almighty which struck at one of His creatures who had challenged the summit of His creation, the glittering peak, Everest? The Greeks had called it *hubris*—Mary Anderson would have a more Biblical term for Greg's ambition. Kelly looked at John Merton's wretched, drained face and knew that all hope had been extinguished there. Laura was now all that remained of Greg Merton. Kelly held her more closely, and knew herself the comfort of John Merton's hand on her own shoulder, the gentle stroking of her hair, the same ways he had had of touching her when she had been a small child and had taken a tumble from Greg's pony. She looked at him with love and unspeaking gratitude over Laura's head, and vowed that he would never know, no matter what he might guess or speculate, what Greg had said to her. He would never hear of that last, long walk down to the burning sea, from which Greg would not return.

After three days the search was called off, though unofficially some of the men from Barrindi continued to patrol the places where their long knowledge told them a body would come ashore, if a body remained. John Merton and Kelly and Laura sat on the veranda of the shabby guesthouse, and said hardly anything. The man and his wife told the local telephone exchange not to put through any more calls, and each day they went into Barrindi to collect messages for the Mertons. Sometimes, as Kelly stared at the sea, her confused mind began to see the whiteness that could be snow. She saw Greg climbing, falling. Many times she half rose from her chair because her mind conjured up the image of him emerging, strong, and lean, from the line where the breakers curled over. Once she cried out because she thought she saw a body being whirled over and over in one of these formidable dumpers which had hurled Laura and herself onto the sand long years ago. The man brought the local doctor, who gently suggested that she take some tablets, which would help her sleep. She flushed them down the toilet. It would be a false sleep which overcame the echo of Greg's words: "But will I be able to live with myself? Will I?"

Finally, John Merton gathered himself up from the trance which had seemed to fall on him. He asked the man for one of the boats from Barrindi to come around. He and Laura went walking into the scrubland behind the beach and gathered up grasses and whatever of the wild flowers the land offered. When the other side of the world was going into autumn, Australia was emerging into its spring, the only time it gives freely of its blossoms. They found mimosa, which John Merton preferred to call wattle; there was a small, sweet-smelling boronia which the woman had nutured, and now offered; they found a waratah. They gathered them all into a bunch, and with Kelly they set off in the boat.

When they were far out from the shore, when the line of the shore was no more distinct than the line of the horizon, when the whole world seemed blurred and melted into the fine radiance of the searing sea, when no mark of land or shore or further horizon could be distinguished, John Merton asked the man to cut the engine. They drifted for some minutes in utter silence. They were too far out for the birds to have followed them. It seemed that no land lay before them for thousands of miles. The swell lapped the side of the boat; it rose and fell in quiet rhythm.

John Merton took Kelly's and Laura's hands. He quoted softly, so that perhaps even the man did not hear him. "May the deep sea, where he now sleeps, rock him gently, rock him tenderly, till the end of the time."

Then Laura bent and slipped the rough bouquet they had gathered into the water. They watched it for a minute, perhaps. Then John Merton gave the signal to the man to start the engine again.

They turned their faces toward the land.

Back at Pentland, Kelly was weak enough to confess to John Merton, when they had met so early one morning on the veranda that each knew the other had not slept, her hope.

"You're not well," he had said. "You look so tired. You're too thin. I'll take you in to see Dr. Lacy . . ."

"No, don't. Not yet. It's too soon."

His mind leaped at once to her hope. "Kelly . . . ?"

"It could be due to anything. They say air travel upsets the rhythm. Any number of things. The shock . . ." For a moment she clung to his arm. "Dad, I'm three weeks overdue."

But that night a sharp pain through her belly signaled the end of that last, cruel hope. Greg Merton had not left another child for John Merton and Pentland.

Chapter Three

I

Time, which had been racing in the years when Kelly had striven to keep up with Greg's pace, his ambitions, his demands on her, seemed abruptly to come to a halt. She experienced a leaden weight of time to kill, time in which there was nothing to expect, nothing to anticipate. Day followed day; inexorably they advanced into the Australian summer. She had never noticed before how slow the days were as they lay in the grip of the heat. Sometimes she rode in the Home Paddocks with John Merton, more often she just sat on the veranda, a book unheeded on her lap. She gave the ritual lessons to Laura, and turned her loose in John Merton's library, as she in her day had been. John Merton had to remind her that it was Christmas, and all other children were in the long summer holidays. It was Laura who shook her head. "I've never had holidays—not when everyone else was having them. We always fitted in with what Daddy was doing, and I made up time whenever he was busy. And there were the times in the hospital. Kelly never made me study when I was in the hospital . . ."

John Merton in turn shook his head. "We'll have to do something, Kelly. The child's grown up unnaturally. She's thirteen, and she doesn't really know any other children."

"There are her cousins," Kelly said defensively. Anything that seemed to suggest a criticism of Greg and his life caused her now to tighten and turn away.

"Her cousins are in England, Kelly," he reminded her gently. "Do you want to send her to her grandmother?"

"No! Greg left her in my care. What would he think of my abandoning her? Lady Renisdale is kind, but she's too old to take care of Laura—to make a life for her."

"Then you must, Kelly. As he wanted you to."

It was true. Greg's intention had seemed very clear; his will, made quite soon after they were married, had, along with giving her half his estate, also appointed her Laura's guardian. The remainder of the money, apart from that which in a codicil provided an income for Mike Kettrick's widow, was left to Laura. The idea of having money that was actually her own, not someone else's which she must handle with care and prudence, was new to Kelly. So long as she stayed at Pentland she spent nothing; John Merton had smiled sadly when she had suggested, finally realizing how many weeks and months had passed, that she should pay for herself and Laura. "How can you? What do you cost me? I'd love it if you ran up huge bills for clothes, or some such frippery. I'd love to get a bill from a shop that wasn't for more books for Laura. Shall I begin to calculate the lamb you and Laura eat? How do I estimate the cost of the rooms you live in? My God, Kelly, this house is empty without you—and yet I'm going to send you away."

"Send me *away? Away?* . . . Where? . . . Why?"

"You and Laura both. She has to have companionship her own age. As you must. You're living here with two old women and me. I need you more than ever, Kelly, but I must send you away. You're thirty-one. Have you realized? Time is running out if you're to find someone to marry, with whom you can have children—"

She rounded on him. "How *can* you! Greg's only dead a few months!"

"I am not blinded by my grief, Kelly. I realize I love you quite as much as I loved Greg. Don't you think I haven't worried it through countless nights, wondering how I could manage to keep you here, and yet ensure that you had a chance of a normal, happy life? I've been selfish enough to try to marry you off, in my mind, to every bachelor within a hundred miles of here—and of the few there are, none is half good enough for you. I want to keep you near me, and yet I have to send you away. Laura should go to school."

"Laura's never been to school. She's shy—"

"Kelly, you've been sheltering her too much, and Greg was too preoccupied—or perhaps too selfish—to notice. She must be dragged out of her shyness. The mark on her face must be lived with. She's a very beautiful child, as you know, once you blot out that mark. In time, I suppose, she'll learn to do it with cosmetics, now that it's so much better. Until then, she must start to learn what ordinary, everyday life is all about. She's been both cosseted and had too many demands made of her. Greg was never an easy man to live up to. At the same time she's always had you to support her at every turn. Kelly, tell me—how often has she spent a night away from you since Greg literally threw her into your arms?"

She answered slowly, reluctantly. "Only the nights she was in hospital. And the time Greg and I were . . . were in Queensland. But, Dad, I can't—I can't just shove her into a boarding school. It's too much!"

A compromise was reached. Laura would go to a day school for girls in Sydney, and Kelly would take a flat there. "I wish I could push you farther, Kelly. I wish I could make you go to London, and Laura to school there. But perhaps Sydney is far enough. And I'm selfish enough to want to see you during the holidays. That's something Laura has to learn. That children have holidays."

She took a flat in Vaucluse, which was half of a large house the owner had divided. It was the sort of place she would once have looked on with awe, and hopeless longing. But since then she had been married to Greg Merton. Now she was automatically accepted as a desirable tenant, and there was money to pay for it. As Laura was automatically accepted as a pupil at the right school. Kelly drove her to school every morning, and then wondered what to do with the rest of the day until it was time to pick her up again. It was true what John Merton had implied. She had had no life beyond Greg's and Laura's needs. The vacuum was achingly there.

In time she learned the ritual of the lady of means and leisure who can contribute her time. Her secretarial skills were useful; there was plenty to do for whatever charity she chose to offer her services to. She learned to organize the lunches that brought in money, she learned to persuade and cajole on the telephone. But in the evenings she was short-tempered with the vanities and pettiness of what she had manipulated during the day.

"You know, Kelly—I think you're having a bit rougher

time than I am. It was better when we were planning for Everest."

Over their dinner, Kelly stared at Laura in amazement. She was now fourteen. Kelly knew she had suffered terribly in the first terms at school, and had learned to accept the suffering as she had accepted everything that had been done to her in hospital. She had accepted it and taken it as part of life. And she knew Kelly was experiencing the same thing.

Kelly nodded. Why argue with a girl who knew what Laura knew? "Yes. When you've been to Everest, it's hard to take a stroll through the meadows."

Greg's obsession, his mania, his achievement, his loss, had forever set them apart. In every sense except the physical one, they had both stood on the summit of Everest.

In the holidays they went back to Pentland; it was possible now to fly there, so John Merton met them at the small airfield at Barrendarragh instead of the railway station. Each time Kelly, with a sense of relief, threw herself into the work which had accumulated dustily on John Merton's desk. There was an unspoken agreement between them that he should leave it; to tackle and reduce it to order gave Kelly a sense of achievement, of serving Pentland in some way. Laura seemed to welcome the return to the solitude of the place. She rode with her grandfather, swam, played tennis, read through the long, quiet nights. She was relaxed at Pentland as she never was in Sydney. With the coming of electricity, through their own generators, it was now possible to listen to music. Laura took a delight in bringing records to her grandfather. They sat on the veranda, listening to the music coming from the new equipment in the library . . . Mozart, Beethoven, Schubert . . . it was a learning process for them all. Other changes had come over the years. Fran had moved on, Rose was still there, but working only part time. There was a different manager. The stockhands came and went, as they had always done. Laura experienced the curious situation of being under the eyes of what was virtually two grandmothers in the one place. Mrs. Anderson was Kelly's mother, and still officially the housekeeper of Pentland; Delia Merton kept a jealous grip on the girl, questioning her about the social outings in Sydney, whom she met, where she was invited. It seemed to disappoint Delia Merton that she was unable to question Kelly's care of Laura; the most zealous mother could hardly have done more. The girl was pulled between these two older women, and yet with a sense of amusement she knew what the situation really was.

"I do think they'd die if they didn't have each other to fight with, Kelly," she once said, coming back after her fifteenth birthday. "They pretend to hate each other, but outmaneuvering the other just makes their day. They'd be dead lonely without each other."

Laura, having answered all her grandmother's questions and satisfied her as to her social behavior, and Kelly's, in Sydney, was free to go to Mrs. Anderson, who still had the run of the kitchen, for cooking lessons. "Kelly's made me realize how important it is to be able to cook. I can't tell you the number of times Dad would come home, unannounced—just jump on a train from Oxford without telling us—and Kelly would be able to produce some super thing in an hour." To please Mary Anderson she even tried to learn to sew a little, but it was not a success.

"Well, child," Mary Anderson said, "I suppose if you can sew on a button that will be enough—in your station in life. It's not likely you'll be called on to put patches in your children's clothes." No reference was made to the fact that Delia Merton had failed in her attempt to interest Laura in her great tapestries, her pieces of fine needlework.

"Why is your mother so bothered about money?" Laura asked Kelly. "She makes it sound as if there's something wrong about having anything you didn't actually work for . . . and yet she sometimes talks as if God actually handed money to some people, but not to others."

So Kelly sketched in the little she knew of her mother's life, leaving out the thing that most haunted Mary Anderson—the fact that she had loved and not married a man called Kelly. She explained as best she could the Northern Ireland brand of Protestantism, the hard and often narrow interpretations of the Scriptures, the insistence on work as a virtue in itself. She told Laura how her mother had worked at anything that came her way when she had first come to Sydney; she reminded Laura of the man called McAlpine who had married her and Greg. But Laura did not remember him, only the fact that she had had a long yellow dress. "She reads the Bible so much, Kelly. She brought you up—why aren't you more like her? She's always quoting the Bible to me. Sometimes it's beautiful, but I don't think she means it that way."

"Your grandfather really brought me up, Laura. He knows the Bible as well as my mother, but when he quotes it, it really is beautiful."

They tried, several times, the time-honored customs of

asking one of Laura's classmates to Pentland for the holidays, but it was not a success. "What am I supposed to do with her?" Laura asked. "I feel as if I have to be looking after her all the time, and really I'd rather just be getting on with whatever you or Grandfather is doing. You and Grandfather swim and play tennis and ride better than any of them. Why do I need them?"

"Let's face it, Kelly," John Merton said. "She's been old since the day they dragged her out of that house with her mother. We'll just have to wait until her body catches up with her mind."

To help her overcome her shyness, Kelly enrolled Laura in a ballet class which was held on Saturday mornings in Sydney. To her surprise, once the first agonies of appearing there were over, Laura took to it passionately. She asked for the spare bedroom to be cleared and a *barre* and mirror to be put up. Each morning, very early, Kelly heard the Gramophone records with their insistent beat as Laura went through her exercises. The girl developed a quite fluent grace of movement; she learned to hold her back straight, and her head high, more interested now in how her body looked than her face. Her teacher, a tiny, ancient Russian who had fled the Revolution and kept herself alive teaching ballet, clucked her tongue as she watched the class. "A pity," she hissed at Kelly. "Your Laura could be quite good, but she's going to be too tall. And look—already she has *breasts*. But it pleases her to dance. She forgets herself in it. She cares more than these other lazy lumps I have to try to drill something into."

It was heartbreaking to Kelly to see how eagerly Laura prepared for the small recitals the little Russian gave so that parents could see what they had paid for. She seemed to long for the moment when she was allowed to put on the heavy makeup some of the parts required; she went to much more extreme lengths in this than any other girl, and Kelly knew that Laura welcomed the moment that makeup transformed her face, hated the time when it must be removed. On Sundays, she would often dress in full costume and stage makeup to dance alone before the mirrored wall. Once, Kelly slipped quietly in and watched her without Laura being aware of her presence. The girl seemed to move in a dream world, her movements more graceful, more sure, than when she knew she was observed, her eyes half shut as if to mist the image of herself in the costume, moving to the music of *Swan Lake*. She was dressed, as if for a performance, in the costume of the Black Swan, Odile. Then, as she turned, she saw Kelly, and the dance stopped.

"Laura!—you look so beautiful! Can't I just watch?"

The girl went and turned off the record. "It's no use, Kelly. I dream for a while, but it's no use."

"Why not? We could—we could go to London. You could go to a real ballet school . . ."

Laura's bare shoulders hunched. "It's no use. I'm going to be far too tall. I'd never do for the *corps*—I'd have to be a *great* dancer before anyone would have me. I started too late. And *look* at me! I stick out in every place a dancer shouldn't. A man would have to be built like a muscleman to lift me! I'd look like a carthorse among them all, and I already look bad enough." The body that promised such feminine ripeness was fully displayed in the costume—beautiful but, by Laura, despised breasts, long, beautiful legs, feet folded over in the classic stance, beautiful arms and hands draped across the *tutu*. Tears which finally broke through the mascara, made furrows in the heavy makeup, and turned her from that misted image of grace, into a broken doll. For an instant, Kelly saw again Greg's anguished face in his daughter's—the two, father and daughter, compelled by furies they could not withstand.

For two precious weeks in that time, Laura was within touching distance of the world she longed for. The National Ballet arrived for a tour of Australia, beginning in Sydney. Kelly had booked seats for every night for herself and Laura, and did not discourage the girl when she spent all of her term's allowance of pocket money on lavish flowers each night for Julia Brandon. Julia Brandon had advanced to the stage where her name was being mentioned in the press as a future *premìere ballerina*. Kelly insisted that Laura sign the card on the flowers herself. After the second night Julia Brandon telephoned. "Father said he didn't think you'd mind if I contacted you. We're sort of family, aren't we?" The light voice went on. "The flowers were gorgeous! Our star is quite jealous."

Laura hung on the telephone, hardly able to speak. "I know you must all be terribly busy. And tired. Do you"—Kelly watched as the scar grew vivid on Laura's face—"do you think we could meet? I mean . . ." She looked across appealingly at Kelly. Kelly took the phone.

"From what I hear, dancers really only live after the performance. You work so hard during the day. Would . . . would you and your friends like to come out here for a supper after the performance? Please . . . I'll understand if you feel you can't."

"What! *All* of us! After the performance! Oh, yes. We're all ravenous by then. We just can't manage on these little cocktail bits, and we daren't have a drink before the performance."

Laura had her few hours with them, the idols, but they were really interested only in themselves. They were their own little world. They fell hungrily on the food Kelly had prepared, were polite, momentarily, to the few friends she felt she could invite at that late hour, and still they existed only for themselves. They ate, and they drank the best wine she could find, were happy, kissed her and Laura as they left, but Kelly knew they would hardly remember where they had been. Julia Brandon lingered. "It was wonderful. You were so . . . so good. You didn't expect us to perform after the performance. Oh, and Father asked especially, if we should meet, to send his regards . . ." She looked at Laura. "And his love to you, of course. I think he'd like to know his god-daughter better."

In remote ways, through Lady Renisdale, they had heard of the career of Charles Brandon since that much-publicized and sometimes much-criticized resignation after Suez. As Phoebe Renisdale had predicted, friends had come forward with help; he had been appointed to the boards of a number of companies. The signal honor the Queen had accorded him in making him a Knight of the Garter had set a kind of seal of approval on him in certain places, though there were some who said that the Queen, in making it, had edged much too close to politics for her necessarily neutral role. But the taste of freedom which his forthright statements at the time of Suez had given Charles Brandon had seemed to breed in him the need for more. He had hung on to the seat in Parliament he had so narrowly won in the winter after Suez. He continued to speak out on whatever subject he thought needed airing. He was known as a thorough-going Conservative, but an independently minded one. *He's making quite a stir in Parliament,* Phoebe Renisdale wrote. *Arthur's expecting great things of him. Wonderful—when one remembers how bleak his future looked after he resigned.*

"Father's hoping to get out to Australia some time," Julia continued, "and naturally he'll want to see you both. But it's hard for him to get away. Parliament keeps him busy, and he's got his fingers in a few other pies. He works harder, I think, than he did when he was in the Army. He had a staff then . . ." She sipped the last of her wine, and smiled as she spoke of her father. She was quite strangely beautiful—almost perfection, Kelly thought. Oval face, with wonderfully defined features; her pale blond hair was swept back to reveal her beautiful, long neck. She had an attitude, as if she drifted rather than moved through her life, as if reality did not truly touch it. But she was aware of Laura's longing gaze, and she rewarded her with the only gift she had to give. "If I can arrange it, would you like to watch morning class?" Laura was both ecstatic and dejected when she returned.

"They're all so *good*—and they work so hard. It isn't at all glamorous." She continued her daily practice, but never again was Kelly aware of her dressing, and making-up for a solo, unwitnessed performance.

Against John Merton's own inclination, he had instituted the custom of sending both Laura and Kelly to Charleton each Christmas. Kelly guessed what it cost him to forego their presence at Pentland. He always made the trip to Sydney to see them off on the plane journey, and to give Laura her Christmas presents. "What is Christmas for a girl with three old people in the middle of nowhere?" he said. "At least at Charleton she's thrown together with her cousins. She's forced to dress up. She's forced to talk to some boys, and try out whatever it is they teach her at that dancing school. If we don't watch out, she'll turn into a little nun, and that," he added laughingly, "would be the death of your mother, Kelly. And while you're thinking about it, just watch that you don't turn into a nun yourself."

"Can you find me someone to follow Greg?" she demanded of him. "Just find him, and I'll fall into his arms."

"I'm sorry, Kelly. I'm truly sorry."

"So am I. I always loved him, Dad. And he was always so . . . so different. Beside him, any man who's available, just seems dull."

"You're the wrong age, Kelly. The decent men have married off, haven't yet got divorced, deserted, or killed off their wives." They laughed over it, but it wasn't really a joke. She accepted the growing knowledge that she preferred being alone with Laura to accepting some compromise marriage, even if one were offered, which none were. Sometimes she was taken out by a bachelor, or asked to dinner when someone supposedly eligible was present. But something in her reacted against the situation. And then one night a man, on seeing her home and giving her the ritual kiss, sighed. "Damn it, Kelly. It's no good. I was at school with Greg. He's a damned hard act to follow."

She found the times at Charleton strangely soothing; it was like being dropped back into the times past, except that each year all the Renisdale grandchildren were that much older, their progress was compared, they eyed one another either with interest or disdain. Phoebe Renisdale seemed as concerned over Kelly's future as John Merton was. "I do wish you'd come over here to live, my dear. Oh, I don't mean at Charleton—that'd be almost as bad as burying yourself at Pentland. You should have a flat in London. Laura could go to school here. You'd meet different people. London's such a melting pot. I've never been to Australia, but it seems to me that the society's too small to allow you much privacy. I'm sure you understand, my dear . . ." Kelly was quietly amused that this rather sedate lady was suggesting that it would be more possible for her to conduct an affair in London than in Sydney. Laughingly she told it to John Merton.

"The fact is, she's right," he answered, without a smile. "You've never had the chance to fall wildly in love with anyone—except with Greg, and you did that when you were four. Have you thought what you'll do when Laura is truly grown up, and you'll have to throw her out of the nest?"

She had, and there were, as yet, no answers. So she continued with the routine of keeping house for Laura in Sydney, visiting Pentland in the holidays, visiting Charleton at Christmas, and watching as Laura grew taller and came inevitably nearer to the time when she would be finished with school. One of her women acquaintances in Sydney, who had known her at the school where John Merton had sent her, observed over lunch one day, "Honestly, Kelly, you're a real bore. I know a dozen husbands—and I wouldn't count out my own—who are dying to have an affair with you. And you parade around that hero husband of yours like a ghost on your arm. Why don't you loosen up a bit? You've got a long time to live yet. It isn't fair to burden the kid with it all."

"Burden? You mean Laura?"

"Who else? The way you're going, you two might just as well start up a little convent of your own." The woman never knew how the spirit of Mary Anderson must have shaken at that moment. And yet Kelly knew that the strictures laid on her from the time she could first remember her mother speaking were still there. She often woke at night, and the thought—after the remembrance and longing for Greg which was always the first—which sprang next to her mind was that she might be doing to Laura what had been done to her. She tried never to say, "Be careful."

It was put even more bluntly to her during the Christmas of 1962 at Charleton. Charles Brandon had come down on Boxing Day, bringing Julia with him. It was the day the hunt met at Charleton; they had come to watch it, and to spend the night. Laura, as always, hunted with the local pack. Dressed immaculately in the pale breeches and black jacket, her hair in a neat, netted bun under the hard black cap, she seemed to Kelly strikingly good looking. But Laura regarded the formal riding attire with some dread because the hair style demanded that she fully expose her face, without being allowed the comforting disguise of heavy makeup which the ballet permitted. She arranged her hair so that it came down to cover her ear, and crammed on her cap to keep it in place. She was pacing nervously in the wide sweep of drive in front of the house, watching the horse boxes arrive, watching those who came already mounted walk their horses, watching the stirrup cup being handed around with rather too much liberality. Charles Brandon saw them at once, and approached.

"How good to see you again. How are you, Laura? I really shouldn't ask. Beautifully grown up, I see. Here's Julia—she told me how marvelous you'd been to her when she was in Sydney. My other girl, Kate, is somewhere around too. But she's out there at the gates demonstrating with the anti-blood-sports mob. Kate was never one to compromise where her conscience is concerned. It doesn't matter two hoots to her that the Renisdales are my best friends. In fact, I think it adds just that little bit of spice to the occasion. She can show just how concerned she is if she takes a bit of a bash at Father too." He laughed as he said it.

"You don't seem bothered by it."

He shrugged. "What can I do? Kate is a born radical. She's all for turning upside down the society I've lived with all my life. It's a source of acute embarrassment to her that she belongs to the Brandon family."

"Do you quarrel about it?" Laura demanded with unexpected directness.

He shook his head. "Never. It's a matter of intellectual conviction with Kate. Her heart is something else again. Oddly enough, she likes her family, I think. She likes her sister, wouldn't you say, Julia?"

The fair, beautiful face was turned to her father. "Yes, I'd say Kate does care very much for her family. She'd have to, to stay around. She's become a social worker, did you know? I suppose it's just a natural progression."

Then it was Laura's turn to be mounted, and join the group that the stirrup cup was being passed among. "By God, she's come on," Charles Brandon said softly. "You can see she knows just what to do with that horse—and she's learned a lot of other things as well. You've done a marvelous job, Kelly." That familiar use of her name again, as if they were longtime friends. "What will she do when she's finished school?"

"It's not decided," Kelly said hurriedly. "There's time yet . . ."

All three Brandons stayed the night at Charleton. There was much laughter over the dinner table at Kate's appearance there. "Aren't you the one who tried to bang me on the head with the placard?" the master demanded. "I don't know how Renisdale here puts up with you. I hear there's going to be jugged fox on the menu."

Kate laughed along with the rest of them. The years which had passed since Kelly had last seen her on Coronation Day had produced only a more striking contrast to her twin. The small, pointed face, under a mass of untidy dark hair, had a kind of urchin poignancy to it; she had large dark eyes, and the same pale complexion which made her twin appear so ethereal. "You mark her," the man seated next to Kelly murmured. "There's going to be a remarkable father-daughter confrontation in the House of Commons one day. Kate's a certainty for a Labour seat before she's much older. Brilliant woman, they say. Hear she got an honors degree in economics at the London School of Economics—and studied social science on the side. Strange that neither of them's married, isn't it?"

"Perhaps there just aren't enough of the right kind of men around," Kelly answered with a touch of acid. She was beginning to be tired of men suggesting that the only possible fulfillment for women could come in marriage. Then she watched his expression change, and knew that he was remembering that he was talking to the widow of the Australian chap who'd climbed Everest, and that she probably had impossible standards of behavior in men. Realizing this, she went out of her way to be charming to him for the rest of the meal, which left him totally bewildered.

Her boots crunched on the frosty ground the next morning as she set off on her usual walk. She had left Laura sleeping; yesterday's hunt had been an exhausting one, had continued until dusk, and Laura had stayed with the leaders all the way. Last night's dinner party had demanded the most that a shy girl had to give, and she had made a great effort. Kelly was aware that the sort of nervous energy that had resided in Greg was present also in his daughter, but when it was drawn on too much, it was drained and depleted. One day, if that energy was channeled, Laura might be capable of the sort of effort her father had made; in the meantime it had to be husbanded and guarded.

She was so immersed in her thoughts of Laura that she was at the copse overlooking the Solent before she saw Charles Brandon. He had been standing still, within the dark, leafless trees; he had seemed a part of them, and of the silence. It occurred to her then that for a man who had lived so much of his life in an exposed position, he had a remarkable talent for stillness, for quiet. Once or twice she had observed him in just such a way in the middle of a crowded room. "I hoped you'd come," he said in greeting.

"Oh . . ." Why did she flush, as if she were as young as Laura?

"Do you enjoy it here?" he asked. "Or do you come just for Laura's sake?"

"Both. Lady Renisdale is so kind . . ."

He laughed. "I'd hardly call her that. Phoebe Renisdale is a very good sort, and I'm very fond of her. But she isn't kind in a disinterested way. You've taken a big problem off her hands, and done a wonderful job. She knows it."

"And you? What does she feel about you?"

He shrugged. "Ah, well, now you've touched the unknown. I think I'm the exception that proves the rule. She has no particular reason to be as kind to me as she is, except that Renisdale and I have been friends for a long time. She has indeed been kind at various times in my life, and I *am* grateful. And yet, I almost think she enjoyed the fuss and bother of it all."

He must, she thought, have been referring principally to the time of Suez, when Charles Brandon had caused a great deal of fuss all through Britain, with people who had labeled him both reactionary and the last savior of the nation. Both had been exaggerated claims, but then it had been a time of heightened feelings, and the country had never been the same since. They had crossed into the sixties dragging the remnants of the Suez debacle with them, and Charles Brandon's name was mentioned almost as often as Eden's when Suez was talked of. Eden had been forced into retirement, mostly through ill-health, but for Brandon it had meant a whole new career. He had nursed his tiny majority in his constituency until it had grown to more healthy proportions, but it still was slim, capable of being overturned. There was something in him that appealed to the gut reaction of patriotism in his largely working-class voters. He reminded them of a time that was past; he reminded them that it had been *they* who won the war, carefully leaving out any mention of America. How long could he keep it, Kelly wondered—this loyalty? The young who were growing up knew little of and cared less for the war. As America went deeper into Vietnam, military men were less and less popular. But for a Conservative he had taken a surprising line there. From the beginning he had been violently against America's involvement. Kelly could remember him being quoted from a speech in the House denouncing it, though he didn't go as far as his daughter, Kate, in leading protest demonstrations against it. She was remembering the scraps she had gathered over the years from Lady Renisdale. He was a leading member of the Oxfam organization; he had been on several Royal Commissions. He was a favorite with the press because he could be counted on for a forthright opinion, and wouldn't back down from it. Lately he had had to be more circumspect because he had been made Junior Minister of Defence. "But I doubt he'll stay there, my dear," Lady Renisdale said. "He can't keep his mouth shut when he thinks there's something wrong. And that just isn't politics."

But he had emerged, from being what people had thought of as a purely military man, with a list of decorations, to a man of growing stature in the nation's life. "He had a wonderful war, my dear," Lady Renisdale said, as if war was some sort of social engagement. "All through the Dunkirk business, where he first met up with Alexander. Then he went with Alexander's staff to Burma. That must have been a pretty depressing experience. Then he was under Monty in the Western Desert—he won his Military Cross there. The Victoria Cross was at Salerno, I think—he was wounded there. They brought him back to England, and he was some sort of liaison with Eisenhower's staff preparing for D-Day. Eisenhower must have been very angry about the things Charles said at the time of Suez. The Americans haven't forgiven him for that, and it's amazing that the Prime Minister put him into the Ministry of Defence. Can't have been a very popular appointment with our big ally. Well, heroes aren't always popular, are they?"

No, they weren't, Kelly thought, remembering Greg who

had driven as well as led. And who, in the end, had believed himself to be no hero. Some of the bitter taste of that came back to her that morning as she stood at the edge of the winter-dark copse, watching the gray waters of the Solent.

"What are you waiting for, Kelly?" he asked suddenly.

"What?" She jerked around to him in surprise. "Well, I'm waiting for it to be breakfast time . . ."

"You know that isn't what I meant. When are you going to make some sort of life for yourself? Laura is growing up out of sight. You've done just about all you can do for her. What will you do for yourself?"

She shrugged, suddenly angry that yet another person was interfering. "Why do I have to answer that question? Why don't I just tell you to mind your own business?"

He accept the rebuke without offense. "I suppose I deserved that. It's the sort of stupid, ill-mannered question that always comes to people's minds when they see a beautiful woman who doesn't seem to be going in any particular direction."

"I have my directions. And there's always Pentland."

"Yes . . . Pentland. Pentland. I understand, is a career in itself. I'm going to be in Australia when the House rises next summer. Can I come to Pentland? I've always wanted to see Laura's other home."

She looked at him in surprise. "Do you want to? It isn't a very . . . very brilliant society out there, you know. Sheep farmers. They don't talk about much besides sheep. Except my father-in-law. He'll talk about almost anything you want." She added, as if anxious that there should be no misunderstanding. "Did you know . . . did you know my mother was once housekeeper at Pentland?"

He raised his eyebrows. "Is that supposed to mean something special? Am I supposed to be impressed?"

"No." Again she flushed. "She still is housekeeper, in a sort of a way. She pushed Delia Merton out of the job. She was made a sort of honorary housekeeper when John Merton first sent me to school. He knew it would sound better. In fact, she was the cook."

"You must think I'm some sort of prize idiot—or snob—if you think you can throw me by saying your mother was once cook at Pentland. My dear Kelly, this is the sixties. You're right at the top of the tree. Haven't you realized? You could make a whole career of it if you wanted to. Interviews . . . on all the chat shows on television. I'm sorry . . . I'm teasing." Then he took her arm. "Come on, now. It's damn cold standing still. Let's go back to breakfast."

They walked briskly across the fields white with frost, and were first at breakfast. Kelly hadn't imagined she could be hungry after last night's huge dinner, but she piled her plate. "That's good," Charles Brandon said. "I love to see a woman eat decently. You should see Julia tuck in. Of course, she uses it all up with her dancing. And Kate just burns it up out of natural zeal." He sat down opposite her at the long, empty table. "Are you a good cook?"

"Yes," she replied briskly, and with a certain flipness. "I'm also an excellent shorthand-typist, and reasonable book-keeper. I'm tidy. I know how to file properly. I've had some nursing experience. I have a teaching degree. I don't smoke. I drink moderately. I can sew on buttons. I can organize—" Suddenly she choked on her bacon.

"What's the matter?" He was not smiling.

"Forgive me. I almost said, 'I can organize expeditions to Everest.' Now there's a skill there's not much demand for—"

"Kelly . . ." He reached out his hand across the table and placed it on hers. Then the door opened and Laura came in; her expression, still heavy with sleep, was vaguely accusing.

"You didn't wake me. You went without me."

Charles Brandon answered for her. "Sometimes Kelly has to go on her own, Laura. You understand that. Now get your breakfast and sit down and tell me about Pentland. I've been invited there. I'll see you sometime about August."

Laura's eyes widened. "Will you come? That would be wonderful. Grandfather would love that."

II

At Pentland the news was greeted with skepticism by Delia Merton. "He won't come. Why should a busy man like that bother with us? We're so dull here. Of course we'll give a party. But what will it be? Just a lot of sheep farmers . . ."

"You sell us short, my dear," John Merton said. "He'll come to listen to the opinions of precisely the sort of people he can talk to here. He's not coming out in an official capacity. He's coming to find out about the possibilities of mining uranium as a director of Amalgamated Mining Company. There will be a hell of a lot of controversy about it. A lot of people violently oppose mining uranium because of its use in nuclear weapons. There are opinions to be sounded, things to hear. Things he can hear as well from us backwoods blokes as the bigwigs in Canberra."

Kelly nodded, and kept her smile to herself. She knew that John Merton could pull quite as many, if not more strings in Canberra as General Sir Charles Brandon. The huge contributions to the Liberal Party, and his friendship with the Prime Minister, Sir Robert Menzies. guaranteed that. The press would interpret the visit to Pentland as a sort of public-relations exercise, the salute paid by the visiting V.I.P. to a local sage. John Merton's roots spread very wide in Australia.

But still, Delia Merton read his entry in Who's Who, his career, his decorations, his Order of the Garter, and she fretted that he would find them dull at Pentland. She had an agency in Sydney look out the old press clippings about his role in the Suez crisis. She read what she could find about him. Had there really been a secret meeting with Dag Hammarskjold over the African situation? Had he been used an an intermediary between his Government and the United Nations? After Suez he was not acceptable to the Americans, but who controlled the U.N.? All this she read aloud to her husband and Kelly.

"Believe nothing that's not proven, my dear. The gossip mills grind exceedingly fast."

But before he arrived the gossip mills ground even faster. There was his sudden and unexplained resignation as Junior Minister of Defence and, more startingly, from his seat in the House of Commons. It was a shock announcement, and hinted at very grave trouble between Charles Brandon and the Prime Minister, and his own Minister of Defence. What no one could understand was his resignation from Parliament, except that his majority had been small, and his power base in his constituency not secure. Had the row between him and the Cabinet been so bitter as to require both resignations? And what had the row been about? For once Charles Brandon did not speak his mind. The press noted sympathetically the recent death of his wife, Elizabeth. Charles Brandon would go to Australia purely as a private individual. Kelly, and all of them at Pentland wondered, but Charles' letter, confirming the date of his arrival, hinted at nothing. "You must not ask, Laura," her grandfather felt it necessary to say.

Laura, in her last year at school, was allowed time off to be at Pentland for the period of her godfather's visit. "I should think so," John Merton said. "Who else has a teacher to come along with her? In any case, Laura's going to pass the Leaving Certificate the way she takes a ride in the morning. Kelly's seen to that." Kelly had felt obliged, over the years, to keep just a little ahead of Laura's curriculum, in case there should be an unexpected break in her schooling; in the sciences, though, she had admitted defeat, and left Laura to find her own way.

Charles Brandon came, and the press, which had beseiged him on his arrival in Sydney with questions about uranium mining and his resignation, was left behind. They were left behind because the sheer number of miles defeated them. They could not easily trespass on private property when it stretched for seemingly limitless miles, and stockmen with shotguns sat easily on their horses and asked, in quiet tones, "Got some trouble, mate? Need some help?" In the face of it, even the most persistent turned back.

John Merton, with apologies to Charles Brandon, gave the ritual party for their friends from neighboring stations, and the guests were screened as they opened the first of the many gates that led across Pentland's paddocks. After that, Brandon was left to the quiet of Pentland, days riding in the brilliant sunshine of the early Australian spring. Rain in the autumn had thrown a rare mantle of green over the paddocks; the sheep were fat in their heavy coats, birds of exotic plumage blazed across the hard bright sky, causing Charles Brandon often to rein in and follow them with binoculars. John Merton, Charles Brandon, Kelly and Laura had long days riding, taking their guest to the best places on the creeks that wound through the flat country for the picnic lunch; often the stars blazed in the clear air before they dismounted at Pentland's stables. Kelly knew Charles had won a grudging admiration from the stockhands because, although a "pommy" he sat a horse well, even though he protested he had not ridden for years. He admitted to being stiff at first, but no one offered him the quiet and tired old hacks which were the standbys for visitors.

John Merton asked a few of his special friends over for small dinners which Kelly's mother anxiously supervised from the kitchen. "A few old cronies I like to have a yarn with now and again." There was talk late into the night for the men around the fire in the library. The women stayed in the drawing room with Delia Merton in the time-honored tradition of Australian society. But Kelly and Laura managed to creep into the library under the pretext of bringing more glasses for John Merton's fine old brandy, more cigars, clean ashtrays. And they stayed long after the women went up to their bedrooms, led by a strangely vivacious Delia Merton, to whom the whole occasion was a time of reveling in her position as Charles Brandon's hostess, a time to show off the treasures of her home. Kelly had not seen her so animated since the time Greg had come back from the Everest expedition to meet his hero's welcome. A stir of excitement could be felt all through the house. Mary Anderson outdid herself to give the most varied menus with delicacies which mostly came from tins sent from Sydney; sometimes she even permitted Kelly to help. The silver and crystal shone on heavy damask; the best South Australian wines from private vineyards were produced, and drunk with respect, and tasted by Charles Brandon with amazement. He didn't know that some of the vineyards belonged to Delia Merton's family. At the table one night sat two heads of Australia's most important companies, flown there in a private plane without the press being aware of it; they had spent the afternoon in closed conference with Charles Brandon. John Merton had withdrawn. "It's all top security stuff, Kelly, and I'd rather not know. They'll be reporting to Canberra." But over the dinner table the conversation was of other things, wide-ranging, free; it lasted almost until dawn in the library. Kelly kept building up the fire, and the conversation, along with the brandy, seemed to renew itself. The stars had faded in the growing light before Kelly cleared off the glasses and emptied the ashtrays for the last time.

"I've been too long in England," Charles Brandon said as he drew aside the curtains to watch the light creep upon the land. "I've been listening to civil servants and politicians too long. One gains a little wisdom from just sitting still and hearing what the other side of the world has to say. Pentland's given me more than I expected or hoped for."

She was silent, pondering his words, registering the sounds of the awakening country. John Merton had gone to bed; Laura had gone many hours earlier. Soon the cook would start moving in the kitchen and the mandatory enormous breakfast of the Australian bush would be served. Charles Brandon looked tired, but relaxed. He was, she recalled, fifty-four years old, remembering Delia Merton's reading of Who's Who. It was not just the tiredness of this long night, but of many years of striving, achieving, and being frustrated, many years of carrying a burden.

At last she managed to speak. "I'm sorry about your wife." It had not been possible to say so before; she had not known Elizabeth Brandon. "I hope that doesn't sound trite, or intrusive. It must have been a release for her. I know she had been ill for so long . . ."

"She was glad, I think, finally to go, Kelly. She must have

been so weary of it all. I can't be sure of that. For almost the last year she wasn't even able to speak. But while she could speak we used to talk about what we could do when it got too bad. She tried to get the doctors to promise help then, so that she could go more quickly, but of course none of them would agree to that. She wasn't in pain, but progressively helpless. Her complete dependence on others was what hurt. But I never heard her complain. Her eyes were extraordinary. Right to the last the spirit was there. She never begrudged the girls or me our lives. She was always eager to hear about everything. We all seemed to draw strength just from being with her. She would have lived very fully if she could have. That sort of courage—not to whine—makes medals seem rather cheap currency."

But Kelly was remembering what Lady Renisdale had said of the way Charles Brandon had handled the difficulties of his wife's illness. "My dear, you could only say that so far as Elizabeth's illness is concerned, the man is a saint. He tries to give her everything that will help. You know, he hasn't any money, and everything he could scrape up has gone to give Elizabeth the best. For so many years they've had to have nurses for her constantly. He always refused to allow her to go into a nursing home. Of course, he's always been entitled to Army quarters, but he insisted on making a permanent home for Elizabeth and the girls, so that she shouldn't be disturbed. He once owned a whole row of houses behind Cavanagh's—a Brandon grandfather, or someone like that, owned quite big pieces of that part of London until he lost most of it gambling. Well, Charles sold off the leases of all but two houses in Brandon Place. When Elizabeth had to be confined to a wheelchair after the war, he had the two houses thrown together so that she could have enough space on the ground floor. He had the upstairs of one of the houses converted into flats for the girls so that they could have their own lives, but still see their mother as often as possible. He used to insist that they continue to entertain a little, even though she couldn't use her hands very well for eating. Anything to give her a sense that she was sharing his life. No matter how busy he was when he was away, he was always on the telephone to her, until she couldn't really carry on a conversation anymore. That's why I've had him to Charleton whenever he could spare the time. It was a relaxation for him. I remember the time I went to see her, and she asked me specifically if I would do that. It worried her that he was tied to an invalid. At the time of Suez, she herself telephoned and asked Arthur and me to have him at Charleton. She knew they just couldn't cope with the fuss at their own house, and he had to have somewhere that could. Such a wonderful woman, Elizabeth. Still quite beautiful—and she's so proud of Charles . . ."

All this had been said, at one time or another, but Phoebe Renisdale had recapped it last Christmas, after the three Brandons had gone. "An extraordinary family, aren't they, really? Julia so talented, though so impractical, poor thing. . . . I do hope dear Kate isn't going to give too much trouble. The social work she does is just a preparation. She *means* to be in politics, and that could cause trouble with her father. And he's had quite enough trouble, one way and another. It would be nice if he had just the tiniest gift for making money, but he doesn't seem to share that with the other branch of the family."

"There is another branch?"

"Not close. I think Charles was first cousin to the father—though there was a difference in ages. That was Michael Brandon. They have a place in the Cotswolds. He died just a short time ago. So his son, Peter, inherits, and Charles was telling me that he thinks there's going to be a pile of death duties to meet. Perhaps Nicholas, Peter's younger brother, will come up with it, just to keep the place, you know. It's very historic—quite famous. Nicholas could afford to pay it all out of his own pocket these days if what the papers say is true." Then, impatient at Kelly's non-understanding, she added, "You know, my dear—he's Nicholas Brandon of Brandon, Hoyle, who's become a sort of financial *enfant terrible* of the City. A fortune overnight, sort of thing. Arthur knows him. I think they're in some things together. A pity poor Charles never had the spare cash to put into anything Nicholas was cooking up. He's just got the small income from the ground rent of the houses, and what he earns from Parliament—and whatever he picks up from those directorships, though that's pretty nominal, I think. There's a cottage on the Brandon estate that belonged to his father. Elizabeth and the girls spent the war there. It wasn't used much after that—rather run down, I think. It's a pity neither of the girls looks like making a good marriage. Julia's so beautiful, but, of course, being a dancer she doesn't want to get married and have a family. Someone said she's having an affair with that Russian dancer who defected. No future in *that,* I'd say. I imagine Kate considers herself too busy to get married. It might interfere." Phoebe Renisdale had sighed. "I really don't understand it all now. Modern life is getting a bit beyond me. It makes me feel old. Perhaps it's not such a bad thing that dear Laura's so attached to Pentland. I mean . . . she might just settle down and get married and live there. I suppose there must be some boys in the places around. Or someone she's got to know in Sydney . . ." Kelly realized that Lady Renisdale, having despaired of her making another marriage, had now turned her attention to Laura. At the end of the year Laura would have finished school. That made Kelly herself feel old, as if her task was almost completed. She was thirty-five.

All this she thought and remembered as she watched Charles Brandon gaze out as the light crept across the paddocks of Pentland, the tall, stringy gums standing out against the brightened sky. It was a tired man who stood there, holding onto the last of the night, looking at the dawn. She knew it was a tiredness that sleep did not remove. A burden and a deep worry may have been removed with the death of his wife, but their marks were there. And he still said that medals were cheap currency in the accounting of courage. Greg would have understood that.

At the back of the house a rooster started to crow. Kelly stirred. "It's time to go to bed—or get up. I'll see that Laura doesn't demand that you come for a ride this morning."

"Kelly . . ."

"Yes?"

"Oh—it doesn't matter. It's so late—or so early. It will keep, I suppose." He stretched his arms, not bothering to stifle a yawn. "I suddenly feel old. Funny, I wouldn't say I've ever felt old before. Definitely middle-aged, but not old."

"I was just thinking that about myself."

He smiled at her. She could see the smile, even though his face was in shadow as he stood with his back to the windows. "Why, you're a child yet. Scarcely older than the twins."

"The twins aren't really so young anymore."

"No," he answered slowly. "I suppose they're not. Now that *really* makes me feel old. Come on, Kelly. We'd better go to bed." Then he suddenly burst out laughing. "That doesn't sound so old, does it?"

She decided she felt comfortable with him, as if she had known him a long time. Just before she fell asleep she thought of how many years she had known him, and yet the times when they had met had been very few. She thought of his laughter when he had made that remark about going to bed. It had been comfortable, friendly laughter.

When his time at Pentland was over, and he faced the work that had brought him to Australia, Kelly and Laura flew with him down to Sydney, Laura pulling a long face because she had to go back to school. "Well, it'll be all over by December. I take the Leaving Cert. then. We'll be at Charleton for Christmas." She spoke with the certainty of someone who has not realized that the end of her schooldays could mean a change in her customs and patterns. "You'll be there, won't you, Sir Charles? Granny wrote that she'd invited you all—Julia and Kate as well—to Charleton, and you'd probably be able to stay a while now that . . ." She stopped, aware that she had trespassed on private ground. Had she meant to say, Kelly wondered, that his wife was dead, or that he had no ties to Parliamentary duties or a constituency? "I must talk to Julia," she hurried on. "I have to get a job, you know. She might be able to make some suggestions . . . maybe I could be a dresser in the theater . . . or something."

"Better talk to Kate. She'd have a dozen jobs lined up for you in no time—especially if you'd volunteer to do them for nothing."

"No!" Laura almost shouted at him. "I must be paid! I mean to be paid! Look at Kelly. She's been working like a dog for years at all her old charity things, and she's never been paid. She worked for my father and never got paid. People just take her for granted. Just use her! It isn't right!"

In the instant Kelly felt not only old, but frightened, because Laura could so readily see the hollowness at the center of her being. Soon, not even Laura would need her.

The afternoon of their arrival in Sydney Charles Brandon was on the telephone to her. "Kelly, I know it will seem a terrible imposition, and you must say 'no' at once if you want to. But could you help me out? The secretary they'd arranged for me for this trip is ill. No hope of her being able to do it. It's for about six weeks. Some rather hard work—most of it pretty dull stuff. We'd be going to the Northern Territory, and some mining places in Western Australia. Not very good hotels, I'd imagine. Of course there'd be times in Perth and Melbourne when I have to meet with the directors of the companies. It needs to be handled carefully, Kelly. What I report back to London is in total confidence. I can't risk having an inexperienced person, someone who might let slip a few things to the press. Could you, Kelly? Would you?" He added, "It's for pay. Like Laura, I believe you should be paid."

"Yes," she said at once, like someone clutching at the last chance.

Laura went to stay with a school-friend's family, delighted that Kelly had taken the job. It was true; they worked hard. There was a maze of detail to accumulate and sift through. "You really need someone with a degree in mining engineering," she said as she struggled to decipher her own shorthand. "And I'm a bit rusty, even at this." She found she was often working even when Charles went on to the social side of his work, the necessary gatherings where no business was heard talked, but many contacts were made. John Merton again reached out to all his sources, and doors were opened to them. "You and Sir Charles are related in some way, aren't you?" was a frequent question. Laura Merton's godfather had become a member of the family.

Their journeyings stretched beyond the proposed six weeks, mainly because John Merton had suggested many extra tasks that Charles might undertake; the work assumed a much broader scope when one of the companies of which John Merton was a director and large stockholder asked Charles to represent them directly in London. Laura seemed happy enough staying with her friend's family. *It's good for her,* John Merton wrote. *She'll soon have to be on her own. Might as well get a taste of it. Take your time. After all, there's no great urgency now for Brandon to get back to London.*

They traveled as far north as Darwin, and Charles parried questions about the mining company's intentions concerning uranium, and the uses to which it would be put. "Just exploratory," was all he said. To questions about his resignation from Parliament, and whether he had, in fact, quarreled with the Prime Minister, he would answer nothing. "Personal reasons," he said. "It was time for a change."

Have the changes in General Sir Charles Brandon's life anything to do with the young widow with whom he has loose family connections? one gossip columnist wondered. Mary Anderson sent the Sydney paper, with the sentence marked to Darwin. *It is indecent, the way you are behaving,* she wrote. *If they write this sort of thing, what are they saying?* Kelly tossed the clipping into the wastebasket. "Damn what they say! Let them say what they like!" she muttered. But she hoped no one sent the same cutting to Charles.

Although it was only the Australian spring, it was already getting hot so far north. The air-conditioning system which the hotel had boasted of didn't work. "We're used to it," Kelly said, "but at Pentland it's a dry heat." Then she shook her head. "I forgot you were in Burma, and without ice in the drinks either, I'd bet."

"There wasn't much to drink that I can remember." They sat in the sitting room of Charles' suite, their shoes kicked off, feet propped on the rickety table in front of the sofa. The tropic night had come down swiftly; the cicadas and the frogs made it noisy. The last long-stayer at the working drinks session had departed, and Charles had refused every invitation to dinner. "They'll think I'm a stiff pommy bastard for that, Kelly, but I don't care. We've done enough for one day. We'll just be ourselves. Just as we were in Pentland."

"You liked Pentland—really?"

"I loved Pentland. Partly for the place itself, which is, I suppose, uniquely John Merton's creation—and his father's. But it was also one of the few times in my life when I can remember being quiet for a few hours at a time. Not having to talk. The military's a pretty garrulous place—that is, if you're the sort of officer who sees his advancement through getting on with the rest of them. Only the very brilliant soldier can make it by himself—and I wasn't that brilliant. Parliament's a talking shop. You don't get sent there to keep quiet. It's no place for the loner . . ." For a moment Kelly thought he was going to talk about whatever it was that had caused his resignation; she could not remember in all the weeks they had been together that he had ever himself raised the matter of Parliament. But he passed on. "Pentland was a holiday in more ways that one. I can't really remember having what you'd call a holiday since the war began. Life in the Army in India was pretty well one long holiday for an officer before the war. That ended, of course. Since then . . ." He shrugged. "There's been a lot of travel, but no holidays. Do you have holidays, Kelly?" His eyebrows were raised as he waited for her answer.

"Not the sort you mean. There've always been jobs of one sort or another—proving something. I really don't know what. Proving that I was worth my mother scrimping and saving was part of it. Proving that I was worth the time and money spent on me—worth John Merton's interest in me. I've even had to prove that I was worth Greg's marrying me. I've never really proved that. He left Laura to me . . . and now she'll soon be gone. What will I have to prove then?"

His hand touched hers on the sofa, the lightest touch, tentative, unsure. "Nothing—absolutely nothing. You've proved all there is to prove. Would you do this old man the honor of coming to bed with him? And you have to prove nothing. Absolutely nothing."

Why did she weep so much in his arms? They were tender, gentle arms. He made love to her as if he understood how long she had been unused to it. She felt raw and young again. Greg's love-making had had urgency to it, as if there was little time. Charles had learned the uses of time. She wept in his arms as the vision of the years, those behind and before her passed through her mind.

"I'm sorry. I shouldn't cry. You're a very nice man, Charles."

"Nice!—I'm not nice! I've wanted you for so long, Kelly, and I didn't dare touch you. I was afraid you'd run away—retreat behind Laura or John Merton. Fly off to Charleton—anything. I keep seeing myself as you must. I'm an old bore. I do a boring, tiring job. Many jobs. I have to make ends meet. Did that ever occur to you about General Sir Charles Brandon? He has to make ends meet. Somehow. Physically. Emotionally. Oh, Kelly, dear love. You're too young for me. I'm an old man. Tired. Often beaten. I have no right to you, not even for this little time. But the sweetness of you—the feel of you. God, I wish I could hold this moment forever. No—that wouldn't be possible. I'd wish for something much more prosaic. I'd wish for you to be with me every evening to sit with our feet up, letting the day wind down. I wish I could just think you'd be there—where I was. I wish I could ask you to marry me."

"Why can't you?"

"Because of everything I've said. So many reasons. What have I to offer you? I'm an old man with a doubtful future. And you might agree for the wrong reason—because you're sorry for me."

"Ask me!" she demanded.

His tone was incredulous. "You mean it? You really mean it? Then I do. I'm asking you as quickly as possible. With my whole heart. With all my love. Because I do love you, most lovely woman."

"Accepted!"

He sat up abruptly, and looked down at her face. "My God, I believe you mean it."

"I mean it. I've wasted too much time." She pulled him down to her again.

He insisted that she return alone to Pentland to talk to John Merton. "If he says it's all right, then I'll know it is. He's not a romantic fool like you, Kelly. He'll see everything that's wrong about the situation. I'll wait—and hope. I'll do more praying than I've done for a long time."

"Just wait. That will be enough."

John Merton faced her in the library at Pentland with a wry smile. "You didn't need to come to ask me, Kelly. After all, I've done my best to see that it happened."

"You . . . ?"

"Oh, Kelly, do you really think I want to send you away from here? You and Laura are the most precious things I have in the world. Far too precious to want to see you waste your days and your years alone here. I've hoped—almost fighting the hope—that you'd find a man you wanted to marry. I've sent you to places I thought you might find such a man. Someone you could have children with. I thought there might be other children to come to Pentland. But you've found nobody—not until I saw how you felt about Charles Brandon. He has a power to move you in a way I've never seen with anyone except Greg. He isn't another Greg. Greg was a romantic passion with you. That won't come again. It never does. But this man compels you in a way you've not been compelled since Greg. I've watched you with him, and I've seen what's happened with you both. I wish he were younger, but I can't help that. I think you love him. I think he loves you. It won't be an easy marriage, and it won't be a dull one, either. But you're challenged by him as you were with Greg. They're not ordinary men, the two you've chosen in your life. You don't take easy options. So don't wait any longer for the perfect man. He doesn't exist. Seize the day, I say!"

He clasped her in his arms. "I shall miss you so much. You'll come whenever you can, won't you?" His voice was choked.

It was her mother, Mary Anderson, who was rigidly opposed. "How can you? Twice now! Twice you will have married far beyond what anyone like you has a right to expect. Would you tell him about your birth? Would you tell him *that!*"

"I've told him," she lied. "It doesn't matter. Do you think such a thing could possibly matter at this point in my life? Or his? We're long past that."

"I see." Mary Anderson folded her hand in that familiar gesture of bitter resignation. "So be it. It seems you must marry someone else. You aren't content with the memory of Gregory Merton."

"I live with his memory. I can't grow old on it. I'll marry Charles Brandon."

Laura, when she was told, was almost ecstatic. "Oh, it's wonderful! I think he's wonderful." Then her face clouded. "But Kelly . . . he's so *old* . . ."

"I'm not young myself."

"No," she said gravely. "I suppose not. I've never thought about it."

Laura, vaguely remembering the yellow dress of long ago, had another for this wedding, and was Kelly's only attendant. The church in Sydney was crowded with people when John Merton led her to the altar, where Charles Brandon stood, in full dress uniform, wearing the Garter sash and star. It had been reported in the newspapers that he had had all that flown out from England. "You do me such honor, Kelly," he said that night. "I had to try to bring up every small trapping I have of it to offer you. Kelly . . . such a difficult road you're going on. I wish this second marriage could have been an easy one."

"How do you know it won't?"

"Because my life has never been an easy one. All mixed up. I'm pulled in many directions. No, it won't be an easy one."

"Then it'll be an interesting one."

"That sounds like a Chinese curse." They laughed together. It pleased Kelly to find how many things there were to laugh about together. Charles seemed young and zestful, and the future would not be as he described.

III

The telephone call came from Sydney early one morning to the lodge where they stayed at Koscuisko—Laura's voice, dull and shocked, calling from the friend's house where she stayed. "Kelly, can you come? Grandfather died last night. He just didn't wake up this morning."

A chill gripped Kelly's heart; her life with Charles was only a few days old, and it had not begun easily. They flew to Sydney, and Laura was at the airport, waiting to take the plane to Barrendarragh. They went back to Pentland together, and stood beside Delia Merton at the graveside. Mary Anderson was there, and every hand who worked at Pentland. The people from the stations for a hundred miles around were there, and they mingled with the important and the influential who had flown up from Sydney and Melbourne. Industry and shipping were there, Australia's financial elite, as was Pentland's nearest neighbor, a bent and wizened Irishman who just about managed to survive from one season to another, and who, Kelly knew, had had more than one loan from John Merton to tide him over a drought. They all mixed with the traditional ease of Australians at these times, the sheepmen appearing just the faintest bit superior because they trod their own land. Mary Anderson supervised the food. Barrendarragh had been emptied of every bottle of spirits and beer it possessed, and more had been flown from Sydney. Every bed at Pentland was occupied, and many would stay at stations overnight which were as far as sixty miles away. Delia Merton received them all with severe dignity, wearing a black dress, and demanding that Laura stand at her side. Kelly did not stand with them; her name was no longer Merton, and she knew that Delia Merton was exacting the last ounce of deference owed to the widow of a man whose life had embraced so many diverse fields. She had never fully comprehended its breadth.

But at last it was over. The solicitors stayed on when the last guest had departed. A quiet fell on Pentland. Only then did John Merton's absence strike Kelly with deep pain. Numbly she obeyed the solicitor's summons to the library to hear the reading of John Merton's will. As she sat between Charles and Laura the sun, which with the approaching summer had begun to gather heat, fell on the new band of gold on her finger. Greg's ring had been put away.

The will was a precise document, as she would have expected from John Merton, and his intentions were unmistakable. The usual charities were named, and sums apportioned. Those who had stayed long years at Pentland had legacies. Some income from his blocks of shares and a portion of Pentland's income was to be Delia Merton's for the rest of her life, and she was to remain at Pentland for as long as she wished. Mary Anderson's small house, and her income were also confirmed. On Delia Merton's death her income would revert to the trust long ago established by her husband. The joint beneficiaries of this were to be Laura and Kelly, and they were to have the present income from everything else John Merton owned. Kelly was named along with the solicitors as one of the executors of the will, and was to have discretionary powers along with them, in the trust. Eventually, the whole of John Merton's estate would belong to Laura and Kelly.

Delia Merton turned her head and stared at Kelly, unbelievingly. "It can't be true! *You!* You have control of everything! He can't have been in his right mind. You have exerted undue influence over him. I shall contest it. I shall take it to the courts . . . I shall . . ." Her words were choked by the surge of her fury.

Frank McArthur, head of the firm of solicitors, shook his head. "I beg you not to upset yourself, Mrs. Merton. This document"—he indicated the will—"was executed a number of years ago. It was evident to anyone who knew him that John was of completely sound mind. After all, he has not left you unprovided for. It is quite usual to leave the widow money in trust. Your daughter-in-law had, in John's opinion, exceptional abilities of decision and discretion. I would be obliged to say so in a court of law. I would have to point out the way she has discharged the trust your son placed in her in the bringing up of his child. It would be difficult—in my opinion impossible, Mrs. Merton—to break this will. By all means take other legal advice. I think it will bear out what I have said. It would be a pity, wouldn't it, to drag this through the courts. John was a highly respected man. It would be a sad spectacle to see his widow splashing his name in all the tabloids. It would have grave repercussions in the settlement of the estate. It could be held up for years . . . please think carefully, Mrs. Merton, before you take such a drastic action. Lady Brandon's position will be confirmed, I'm certain of it."

"*Lady* Brandon!" The words were spat out. "And to think she came here a squalling brat, the daughter of a cook. A jumped-up nobody from a dubious background. Well, is this the justice of the world . . . ?"

She left the room. Charles' hand closed on Kelly's. Quietly, Laura began to cry, the first time Kelly had seen her cry openly since John Merton's death. "Can we go soon, Kelly? I mean—will you take me back to England with you and Charles. I can't stay with Grandmother just now . . . I *can't!*"

In her own odd fashion, Mary Anderson was as displeased with the news as Delia Merton. "The high and the mighty! The Bible says: 'Blessed are the meek, for they shall inherit the earth.' But you have not been meek. You have put yourself forward, not content with what God has sent. Your troubles are not over, Victoria. This man you have married . . ."

Kelly didn't stay to listen to the rest of it. Her mother's diatribe had come early in the morning before even the cook was in the kitchen, but Mary Anderson was there, ever anxious that no item of the established routine at Pentland would be overlooked, no matter how exceptional the circumstances. Kelly roused Charles and Laura, and sent word to the stables to saddle horses. They would spend the day visiting the favorite places along the creek that wound through the Home Paddocks where John Merton had taken them. They boiled a billy and ate lunch under a group of massive ghost gums. "You're sure you want to come to England now, Laura?" Kelly asked. "You're going to miss the Leaving. Do you want to do that? You could stay with—"

Laura cut her short. "Grandmother will try to get around me in some way. People will be talking when the will is published, and I don't want to be where I can hear any of it. They gossip . . . everyone talks. I want to come with you and Charles, if you'll have me. I can stay with Granny Renisdale, if that suits you better. There are always ways to take some silly exam. Daddy went back to take an exam to get into Oxford, didn't he? I can do it any time."

Charles reached over and pulled her close to him so that the long blond hair fell across his chest. "Of course you can come with us. And stay with us. Where else?"

Laura raised her face to gaze at him. "I love you, Charles." The words were uttered with what was, to Kelly, a frightening intensity.

They rode back in the gathering dusk, helped unsaddle and water the horses, and walked together to the house. The place was silent and empty after the activity that had attended John Merton's burial. Lights showed at the windows, but there were no sounds. Kelly saw her mother signaling them from the kitchen porch. "The telephone hasn't stopped ringing all day. From England. Lord Renisdale."

"Grandfather!" Laura exclaimed, fear in her voice. "I hope—"

"The call is for Sir Charles. I told him you'd be back by this evening. He's very impatient," she added. "Couldn't understand why I didn't send out for you. As if I would know where to send." Her tone was scornful of those who did not understand the ways of a large station.

It was after eleven o'clock when Arthur Renisdale telephoned again. Charles took the call in the library. When he returned to their bedroom he faced Kelly with an expression that was both exultant and rueful. "Spencer Hunt has died suddenly," he said. "He was M.P. for the Tewford division."

As Kelly still looked at him in puzzlement he explained. "That's the constituency where Wychwood is—the Brandon place. Tewford has sent Brandons to Parliament on and off for a couple of hundred years. Whenever one of them wanted the job. Right back to the days of the rotten boroughs, when you could buy the votes for a song. They've survived the democratic process, and a Brandon can still get elected, because it's a cast-iron Conservative seat."

"What are you saying?"

"I'm saying that Spencer Hunt has died quite suddenly—long before anyone expected him to. Arthur Renisdale telephoned to tell me—unofficially, of course—that I'll be the next Conservative candidate. That is, if I want the job. All I have to do is present myself to the selection committee. The seat will go to whomever they approve. And they want me. All I have to do is ask."

"*Do* you want it?"

He seemed to turn away from her, as if unwilling for her to see his face. He even looked down at some papers which were spilling from his attaché case. It was a long time before he answered. "I think I have no choice. There is no other way back." Then he turned and faced her. "Sorry, Kelly—there'll be no honeymoon at all, it seems. They expect the by-election early in the new year. The Conservative Central Office may not like Tewford's choice, but Tewford will make its own decision. Arthur says they've decided on me."

"You want to go back to Parliament? After you've resigned?"

"I resigned from a very marginal seat because the Prime Minister said he would withdraw Conservative support at the next election. I couldn't have survived. It was better to resign than to be booted out. Now Tewford has been offered to me. The Party can't get me out of there, no matter what they do. It's the way back. I have to take it."

She slept fitfully, and was aware, as the light touched the windows, that Charles also was awake. She asked the question that should have been asked long ago, but which, until now, had seemed irrelevant to their lives. "Charles . . ."

"Umm . . ."

"Why did you resign? What was the trouble?"

His voice was muffled against the pillow. "Kelly, there are things I can't tell you yet. Security. But I *did* tell you it would not be an easy life. There are some things you must take on trust." His arms went around her in a gesture that was one of infinite trust and hope. Their love-making was almost a desperate act, an attempt to hold back the coming day, to stem the tide of things that would take over, take them away from each other.

They left Pentland that day, Laura going with them. To stay on would do nothing to ease the tension between Kelly and Delia Merton. Time might wash over it, soothe it. Delia Merton would spend weeks brooding over what possible action she might take, and probably, in the end, would take none. Kelly's position at Pentland, at this moment, had not changed. What had changed was what took place in Frank McArthur's office in Sydney; what had changed was whose signature was placed on documents. Kelly signed, after carefully reading them, many documents before she left Sydney. "I'll be back in a few months," she said. "I'll be coming to Pentland regularly. I'll have to see to it all as he expected me to. That's what worries me most. I should be there all the time."

"I don't think, Kelly"—Frank McArthur had known her for so long that there was no pretense that the formality of "Lady Brandon" would be maintained—"that that was John's intention. He could have changed his will once he knew you were to be remarried and would live in England. But he knew you well enough to know that Pentland would always be your concern. Perhaps one day it will be Laura's. It's better in your hands than a stranger's, however well meaning. We've instructed the accountant to come out from Barrendarragh once a month to look at the station manager's books, and we've told him that either you—or our representative—is likely to make a visit at any time. And I think he's more respectful of your eye on the books than any nosy-parker from Sydney. I only wish Mrs. Merton were happier with what John had decided. But she'll come around in time, I'm sure of it."

Kelly knew that she left the two women, her mother and Delia Merton, locked in their old alliance of disapproval of her. They had opposed each of her marriages, they disapproved of her inheritance of Pentland. Silently they condemned her and John Merton for what he had fostered in her. Both, in a curious fashion, seemed to close ranks against her, though she doubted they ever spoke together about it. Both had stood watching as they had driven away from Pentland—Delia Merton at the front door of the big house, Mary Anderson from the veranda of her small house surrounded by its stubbornly, insistently cultivated garden. Kelly's throat had frozen at the words of good-bye she had tried to say; she held Laura's hand tightly. It was the first time John Merton had not either driven them to the small landing strip or to the Barrendarragh airport, or had been the last to stand out in the sun, his hat off, waving until they reached the first gate of the Home Paddocks. Pentland had changed forever.

Chapter Four

I

They were greeted at London airport by the press, and by Julia and Kate. Julia carried an enormous sheaf of flowers, the collar of her fur framing her lovely face as if she unconsciously posed for the photographers; Kate wore a cheap little knitted cap pulled down around her ears, her lips were parted in her urchin's grin. It was good newspaper copy on an otherwise dull day, though both Charles and Kelly had to fend off questions about whether he would stand at the Tewford by-election, questions about the inheritance of Pentland and John Merton's estate; Laura clung to Kelly's arm, her old panic in the presence of photographers reasserting itself; her hair was draped across her face. Lord Renisdale had sent a car to meet them, and another to carry the luggage, and Laura plunged into the depths of the first as if trying to find a place to hide.

They drove at once to Charleton. Phoebe Renisdale greeted them as if nothing much had changed, or rather as if everything was exactly as she had expected it would be. It was two weeks before Christmas, and for Kelly and Laura the pattern of many other visits was repeated. But the man at the center of their lives was different. They had been there with Greg, they had been there as John Merton's family; now they belonged to Charles Brandon's family. At times Kelly, with a jolting sense of shock, would feel as if she had been involved in a long slow gavotte, and had turned in the dance to find herself facing a different partner. She loved Charles; she was grateful for the sense of warmth and security he imparted. They were friends and lovers; Charles seemed tenderly appreciative of her. Yet there was still so much to learn about him. For a few days the familiarity of Charleton cushioned the knowledge that now she must fully take up this new life. She could not be half-hearted about Charles Brandon.

But she wished Laura could be a little detached. It was disturbing to see how she had transferred her love of John Merton to Charles. Her grandfather's death had made her deeply vulnerable; she clung to Charles, hardly letting him out of her sight. Even the presence of her idol, Julia, could not distract her from her watchful attention to Charles' every move.

"Poor kid," Kate said to Kelly. "She's had the rug pulled out from under her again, hasn't she? She seems a bit desperate. Strange—she's been into more situations than most women will in a whole lifetime, and yet she's oddly young for her age. You and Charles keep propping her up, and she expects you to do it. It's time she started living for herself a little. Look—I'll tell you—I've got a group in the East End where she could work. Lots of old people who need help, a bit of company. There are other kids her age working there, and that would draw her out a bit. She's such a poor little rich kid. It's time she found out how the rest of the world lives . . ."

"Leave her a little time to find her feet, will you, Kate," her father said. "Trust Kelly. She's taken care of her for so long."

"Too long, if you ask me," Kate answered. Then she shrugged and smiled. "Don't take too much notice of me, Kelly. I'm such an interfering do-gooder."

"Perhaps she'd like to come and watch some of the classes at the ballet," Julia offered. "It would distract her a bit. Maybe there's something useful she can do there. She's such a nice-mannered girl. Wouldn't get in anyone's way . . ." It was all Julia could suggest. She floated through the warm, serene world of Charleton, smiling, talking pleasantly with everyone, and everyone knew she heard hardly a word of what was said around her. She had her own world, and seemed to bring it with her. Telephone calls came late at night for her. "It's after the performance," she would explain. She had been given three days' break from her exacting world, and everyone knew she longed to be back there.

"She really is wildly in love," Kate said to Kelly. "I've never seen her quite so caught up. This Russian, Sergei Bashilov . . . they're dancing together a lot, and providing London with a front-cover love story. Poor Julia . . . what will she do when it's over?"

"Over?"

"The love story and the ballet. Dancers don't go on forever, do they?"

Kelly was grateful for the few days of respite that being at Charleton provided, grateful for Kate and Julia's acceptance of her. Tentatively she tried to say this to Kate. "What nonsense," was the response. "Why shouldn't we? Father's got every right to a piece of good luck like you. It hasn't been easy for him, but he's always put such a good face on it. I'll tell you, Kelly—he was wonderful with Mummy. But then, I think *she* was a wonderful person. They were both generous and giving with each other. None of us expected him to go into mourning when she died. It was a relief—I would think most of all for her. When we heard that he was going to marry you, well, Julia and I could hardly believe his luck. We'd be selfish bitches if we begrudged him his chance of happiness now. Oh, I know—I disagree publicly with him about his politics, but that doesn't stop me from loving him. He's as wrong-headed as he can be about some things, but I still like him. He's managed to be a father as well as a soldier and a politician. I'm beginning to know how rare that is."

Phoebe Renisdale summoned Kelly for the ritual sherry in her sitting room. "My dear," she pronounced, "we couldn't be more happy. How perfectly it's all worked out." Something in the finality of the statement struck Kelly. It was only the beginning, surely?—not the end.

"It's early days to talk about it working out," she ventured. From where she sat she watched Charles and Laura walking across the clipped lawn of Charleton, both wearing riding clothes. Something Charles had said amused Laura; she turned her face to him fully and laughed.

"Well, of course, my dear, there will be adjustments . . . you're too mature to expect a fairy story," Phoebe Renisdale went on. "But I'm so relieved to see you and dear Laura shaken out of that rut you were in. So . . . so *introspective,* my dear. You'll both get a good slice of life served up to you now. Politics is no joke. Wives and families are important. They can so help a man, as I know you will. You'll have a

lot of rearranging to do—Charles will be elected—oh, I [illegible]
I'm not supposed to talk about it, but it's a foregone t[illegible]g, Arthur says. You'll have to fix up that house, and do some entertaining. Trying to reorganize the house will be a major job in itself. Of course, it was all arranged for dear Elizabeth's benefit, but it leaves you with a problem. You can hardly ask Julia and Kate to leave their flats. And I don't think you can turn Laura adrift on her own just yet. And then there's that odd woman, the Russian . . ."

"The *Russian?* What Russian? I know Julia's—"

"Oh, not *that* one, my dear. It's Charles and Elizabeth's Russian. She's been a sort of housekeeper and nurse to Elizabeth since the war. She just about brought up the twins. Didn't you know they both speak quite a bit of Russian? If that dancer fellow didn't fall in love with Julia because she's so beautiful, I suspect he'd love her because she's able to talk to him. Oh, my dear—didn't anyone *tell* you about the Russian woman? Well, you can't know everything about a man before you marry him. It was all so strange. If I remember it—and, mind you, it was so long ago—she stowed away on the plane that Charles was on when he was leaving the Yalta Conference where he'd been as one of Churchill's aides. What made it extraordinary was that she was supposed to be some sort of a heroine in Russia—a nurse who'd been all through that frightful Stalingrad siege. Been decorated by Stalin. Being at Yalta with the medical staff, who always are on standby at these meetings, was some sort of reward for her. The Russians were outraged when they found she'd . . . well, we didn't call it defecting in those days, but that's what it was. They wanted her sent back. They blamed Charles, because he was the senior military man on that plane. And when she landed here, no one wanted her. They didn't know what she was up to. She spoke very good English, even then, and everyone was suspicious of her. The Foreign Office didn't want her, and the Home Office wanted to deport her. There was some talk of shipping her off to America because she claimed she was a political refugee, and the Russians would kill her if she was sent back. America decided not to have her . . ." Phoebe Renisdale poured herself more sherry.

"Oh, dear—it's a long time ago, and I can't quite remember the sequence of events. But I do know that the upshot of it was that Charles sent her down to the cottage they have on the Brandon estate, and Elizabeth took her in. Of course she would. Elizabeth was like that. Then they moved back to London, and the Russian came with them. She was a nurse, remember. So good with Elizabeth. The girls adored her. I seem to remember there were even questions raised in the House of Commons about her—but after all, if Elizabeth insisted on keeping her, and no one else would take her . . . well, I mean, who knows what *might* have happened if she'd been sent back to Russia. *That* was one other thing Charles spoke out about. He said publicly that he refused to have anything to do with sending this woman back to her death, or to a labor camp. He was a war hero, remember, my dear. People liked him for speaking out. It might have cost him his job. But it all quieted down, and people forgot about her. I suppose the Home Office at some point must have said she could stay. At the time of the cold war, the whole thing made much more sense—why she'd wanted out of Russia.

"By then she was indispensable to Elizabeth. She was her nurse long before they needed nurses all round the clock. She ran the house, looked after the girls—she was a sort of nanny to them. A very strange nanny, but there . . . a fixture in their lives. That's probably why no one's bothered to talk about her. She's been there so long, everyone takes her presence for granted. Naturally, I expect Charles might suggest that she move now that you're here, but she's on the same sort of footing as the girls. When Charles converted the second house, and made a flat each for the twins, the Russian had one for herself. Some tiny little thing up in the attic, I think. But she was still supervising the whole thing, organizing the house, the nurses, the housekeeping, everything, when Elizabeth died. That's not so long ago, and Charles has been away for so long in Australia. I expect he hasn't made any arrangement with her yet. She isn't dependent on him for money. I think she got herself a job translating years ago, and never took any payment for what she did for Elizabeth. You can understand how it all might come about, my dear. *Reliable* people are so hard to find. I'm sure Charles couldn't have accomplished half as much as he has if he hadn't had her to rely on all these years. Oh, yes . . . she was married for a while. Some other Russian, I think. It didn't last. Ask Kate and Julia about her. They will tell you far more than I can. She's been a real treasure, as we used to say about old-time servants. But, my dear, the old-time servants always expect to be taken care of. It's one of the problems you'll have to tackle. . . . Life at Brandon Place was always rather chaotic, *I* thought."

"Her name?" Kelly asked. Why was she suddenly so

frightened of this other person, the new addition to the family she had come to share?

"Name? Oh—well, we—Arthur and I—always called her the Russian. Marya something, her name is. You know what these Russian names are. No one can remember them. . . . Have a little more sherry, my dear."

"Marya?" Kate smiled broadly when Kelly asked about her. "You'll love her if you can stand her Russianness. We couldn't have managed without her, I don't think. Fancy Father not saying anything about her. He's got so much on his mind. Perhaps he assumed you knew all about her because everyone else does. We keep forgetting you've never even been to Brandon Place. Of course, we don't see so much of Marya now that . . . that Mummy's gone. The place has been so terribly quiet since she died, and Father's been away so long in Australia. I never have quite got used to seeing that whole house dark and empty." For an instant her mouth twisted in an uncharacteristic downward turn. Then, quite deliberately she smiled. "Well, you'll brighten it up again!"

II

Charles Brandon owned Numbers 15 and 16 Brandon Place. They were, as Phoebe Renisdale had said, one of the few remaining pieces of once important blocks of real estate the Brandon family had developed after a lucky marriage in the late eighteenth century to the daughter of a country squire whose acres had happened to lie west of the City of London. Some of it had been sold as the city advanced. Some had been kept and represented a solid fortune until an Edwardian Brandon had begun to gamble and to attempt to rival the style of that greatest of all London landlords, the Duke of Westminster. The gambling table had won. To pay the debts, most of the streets and terraces and squares which bore the family name had been sold.

As the two Renisdale cars pulled off the main thoroughfare and into Brandon Place, Kelly gave a little gasp. "*This* is Brandon Place! Why didn't someone tell me it was behind Cavanagh's? Oh, yes, Lady Renisdale said something about it, but I just thought it was in the general area." She jerked her head to indicate the solemn Victorian back windows and entrances of one of the world's most famous department stores.

"Didn't I tell you?" Charles said vaguely, sounding like Julia. "I suppose it's because we've all had to learn to forget about it because we couldn't very often afford to shop there. We just try to ignore it."

"*They* don't ignore us," Kate said. "Ever since you left for Australia they've never stopped ringing up and asking if you're interested in selling. I quite like being rude to them. They already own each side of us," she added, for Kelly and Laura's benefit. "They've got the whole of Brandon Place except these two houses. They use theirs for offices, and they'd just love to get their hands on these two so that they could tear the lot down and build a nice efficient block instead of coping with the rabbit warren they've got now. I suppose they thought with Mummy dead you might have changed your mind. They've been after him for years to sell," she said to Kelly.

Laura was standing on the pavement, staring across the narrow street toward the lighted, Christmas-decorated windows of the store. "It's awfully convenient, isn't it? I don't know how you withstand the temptation to shop there." Cavanagh's had been part of Laura's growing up in London. She knew her way about its vast spaces, its food halls, its music shop, its zoo. She had once pointed out to Kelly a door marked FUNERALS, and had giggled. "Fancy having Cavanagh's bury you." It had never occurred to her that people who lived across the road might not shop there.

"Sometimes I don't resist," Julia volunteered. Unconsciously her hand stroked her fur coat. "But I always switched the things into someone else's shopping bag, or took out the labels. Kate's very anti-Cavanagh's."

Charles was helping the Renisdale chauffeurs unload the suitcases, and Kelly turned to look carefully at the houses where she would live. The two, 15 and 16, were uncomfortably distinguishable from all the other tall, narrow houses in the row. Their appearance was oddly at contrast with the new paintwork of their neighbors. Their paint was peeling, the railings around their basement areas bore no discreet little brass plates as the others did, nor did they have small bay trees in tubs lined up at the tops of the shallow steps that led to each front door. Their doors were flat black; all the others were the smart olive-green that was the distinguishing mark of the famous store across the road. Immediately Kelly was taken by a strange affection for these two Cinderellas uninvited to the ball.

Lights showed in the fanlight above each door. Strange that she yet didn't know which house she would live in. So many questions she had never thought to ask. As she stood there looking, the door of Number 16 was flung open. A woman's figure was momentarily silhouetted against the light before she ran down the steps.

"Welcome—welcome!" The woman was wringing Charles' hand, looking as if she wanted to embrace him. "Colonel, we have all missed you. And this is Lady Brandon. Welcome." A great sheaf of flowers was thrust into Kelly's arms. "And this is Laura. Pretty. But come, you must be cold. Kate—Julia, help with the luggage. Go ahead, Lady Brandon. Colonel, go ahead. There is a fire in the drawing room. I shall come directly." Kelly found herself propelled up the steps and into the hall.

"I should be carrying you over the threshold, but if Marya saw that, she'd want to do it for me," Charles murmured. He took hers and Laura's coats. Kelly noted the fresh flowers on a table. They went up the stairs to a shabbily comfortable room that extended the full depth of the house. A fire burned in each of the two fireplaces, there were more flowers, drinks were set out on a tray, and champagne stood in a bucket of melting ice. Charles spread his hands in a gesture of helplessness. "That's Marya," he said. "What can I do? She sees to everything, orders us about, and at times we might have sunk without her. We generally do whatever she tells us." He looked at Kelly. "It won't always be like this, my love. When she's less excited, she's very quiet. She has a little flat at the top of the other house, and one hardly knows she's there. But she *did* manage everything for Elizabeth. I knew I never had to worry."

"Why does she call you Colonel?" Laura asked.

"Because that's the rank I held when she stowed away on the plane from Yalta. I don't think I've ever been promoted in her eyes."

Now the woman herself appeared, and Kelly got her first good look at her. She carried a silver tray with a bowl of caviar surrounded by ice, lemon, crisp toast. She smiled broadly, revealing good but unevenly spaced teeth. Her age might have been about fifty. Her hair was thick and straight, dark but going gray, and cut squarely around an already square face. Her eyes were very dark, and yet seemed full of light, high cheekbones, a rather snub nose—not even good-looking features, but she had an air of great vitality which was, Kelly thought, immensely attractive. Her clothes seemed to be made up of bits and pieces, none of which matched; bracelets rattled on her arms, she wore rings and chains about her neck, big gold earrings which swung as she moved.

"You had a good journey? You got my cable to Sydney?

Yes, Lady Renisdale has telephoned me and told me when to expect you. It is well you went there first. The telephone has not stopped ringing." Kelly realized that the cable referred to must have been one of the many that had come to Charles from England at the time of their marriage. She couldn't, of all the names of people unknown to her, remember seeing one signed Marya. Marya was, as she talked, expertly removing the top from the champagne bottle; it popped gently, and she began to pour into the waiting glasses. When they were filled, she went to the top of the stairs and called down to the hall. "Julia!—Kate! Why are you not here? Why do you make us wait for the toast?"

They came quickly and took up the glasses. Marya raised hers. "Well, Colonel—Lady Brandon. Happiness . . ."

"Marya Nicholievna," Charles responded, "Kelly and I thank you from our hearts. I see my absence, and time, have done nothing to curb your extravagance"—he smiled and gestured to the champagne, the caviar, the many flowers—"nor has it toned down your bossiness. Nor," he added fondly, "your spirit. You're irrepressible—and incorrigible."

"Ah"—she wrinkled her nose as if the bubbles from the champagne had reached her—"What would you expect, Colonel? That I should fall apart, or something? You must never forget that I am a heroine of the Union of Soviet Socialist Republics. One does not become *that* by sitting around and doing nothing. Now"—she tilted her head and drained the glass—"for all you genteel people there is more champagne downstairs. But for this peasant here"—she grinned—"a little vodka." She went and poured a measure, and having toasted them again, tossed it back. "I assure you, Colonel, I shall *not* get drunk. You know I have a head like a horse."

"Horses don't drink vodka, Marya Nicholievna."

"This one does. I tell you I have raided the Soviet Embassy for the vodka and caviar—only export quality, you see. They will shoot their commissar when they find out!" Then she inclined her head. "No—I confess. I went to Cavanagh's. It was easier."

Kate exploded. "Marya, you've betrayed me! You *know* we have a pact about Cavanagh's." She began to chant. *"We never shop at Cavanagh's . . . we never shop at Cavanagh's."*

Marya winked. "Only when no one is looking, eh, Julia?" She was moving among them, refilling the glasses. "Julia, please go and bring another bottle. And telephone your friend. He expects to hear from you before the performance tonight. Otherwise he may dance badly. He may fall and break a leg. Such things I've heard from him over the phone. I'm glad you're back to take him off my hands—and out of my ears." She had come finally to Laura. "Ah, little one, it is both sad and happy, isn't it? You have lost your grandpapa, and the Colonel wrote me that you loved each other very dearly. But you have come to a new family, and we have much love among us to share . . ." One broad, capable hand stroked Laura's bright hair, and Laura, usually so withdrawn with strangers, did nothing to resist. "Welcome home, little one."

And Kelly understood why Marya would stay in the flat at the top of the other house. At the same time, she herself was filled with a sense of belonging to this strange, shabby household. She gulped her champagne, and let Marya refill her glass. A wondering sense of hope clutched at her. What if she should add yet another child to this family? What if she should have Charles' son? The atmosphere seemed charged with promise; the habits of old lives had been shed, new ones assumed. She thought of the child she might have by Charles, and smiled at Marya.

III

The days to Christmas sped by, and Kelly slowly groped her way toward a new identity as Charles Brandon's wife. As Charles resumed his London existence, they often seemed a vast divide away from the pair who had sat with their feet up in a Darwin hotel. She had thought she knew, or guessed, what life would be like with him, but it was both more complex and more demanding. It was true, as Marya said, that in the beginning the telephone seemed not to stop ringing. Many people were anxious to welcome Charles back, to meet her. So often the voice which invited them to dinner would add, "I met you once at the Renisdales'—years ago." Or someone would say, "We knew Greg before Dorothy died." The days began early, often ended late. They fell into bed tired, and into each other's arms, and the hotel in Darwin was there again. Sometimes they just lay together quietly, listening to what each had to say, and listening to the more revealing silences, listening to the late-night noises of London, listening, as quietness grew, to the beating of each other's heart. "Kelly, I love you," Charles would say, over and over. "In all this rushed life we live, never forget it. Never forget how grateful I am. Sometimes I can hardly believe it when I wake in the morning, and you're here. I feel like that man in 'September

Song.' I'm counting the days and the hours, and I want all of them with you."

The household was not as chaotic as Phoebe Renisdale had pictured it. The house they lived in, Number 16, was by any standards an ordinary London house, tall, narrow, many stairs. The only difference lay in the wide glass doors that led, on the ground floor only, to Number 15. Charles explained them to Kelly and Laura.

"You see, when Elizabeth finally had to give in and accept a wheelchair, I was determined she wouldn't be kept upstairs and out of touch with what was going on. So I broke a door through here, and made the front room of Number 15 her bedroom." He showed them the big bathroom with its special invalid's fittings. "This way, she could be involved in all the comings and goings, and she could be wheeled through to the dining room, and the kitchen, and my study in Number 16. I slept in the back room, and if I was away, Marya came down and slept here. Afterward, when she couldn't leave bed any longer, the back room became a sort of day room for the nurses. I fixed up other accommodations for them downstairs, too. But Elizabeth was never left alone with just the nurses when I had to be away. There was always Marya, or one of the girls. Elizabeth had the bed placed where she could see the people coming and going in and out of Cavanagh's. It used to amuse her a little. Not much of a life, but it was all I could do for her. . . ."

He paused, and then plunged on, as if wishing to make up for what had not been told until now. "We had to make a decision at the end of the war. No one could tell us how slowly or swiftly the disease might progress. There can be long stages of remission. But she was already severely handicapped. So we decided to make a permanent home here in London, where the girls could develop independent lives, but Elizabeth would still be close to them. I had no idea where I might be posted, but we decided that if I were sent overseas, it was better for Elizabeth to be here. As it was, there were postings to Germany and the Arab states. As always in the Army, men retired, and I finally made General. It was easier then because I was most often attached to Aldershot. I think the decision not to uproot Elizabeth and take her away from what comforts she could have here was the right one. It happened that neither Kate nor Julia married, so they stayed here. There was always Marya. Elizabeth took the separations very well. Kate or one of the others would write letters for her when it became impossible for her to do it. Strange how these things work . . . she managed a fairly active social life, even from her chair or her bed. She loved people coming, and always made them welcome. She was very interested in the Army. Almost every officer who ever met her would call to see her when he came to London. Some of them—good friends—when they couldn't get a bed at one of the clubs, would stay here. It made a sort of life for her . . . gave her a sense that she was helping me. It was wonderful to see what she managed. When I left the Army it was easier because I was almost always in London then. But none of it would have been possible without Marya. . . . She held it all together . . ."

They looked at the room with its hospital bed where Elizabeth Brandon had spent the last years of her life, and at the room the nurses had used. Julia had her two-room flat on the floor above, Kate above her, and Marya on the top floor. "I'll get it all cleared out," Charles said. "You could have your own sitting room here, Kelly—or whatever you want. Or maybe Laura would like it for a flat. Nothing like keeping the family together, eh?" He smiled at Laura, but he wasn't joking.

But for those first weeks the rooms remained empty, and Laura slept on the floor above Charles and Kelly's. The glass doors to Number 15 were often open; Kate and Julia came and went. Less frequently they saw Marya; she worked quietly, and alone, in her top floor flat. Visitors to Number 15 would often glance curiously into the hall of Number 16. "Perhaps we should put up curtains or something," Charles suggested. Kelly decided to leave it as it was for the time being. She enjoyed the sensation of life that flowed about her. The kitchen of Number 16 was the room facing the street; the dining room behind it. A narrow passage, mostly of glass, led from the hall of Number 16 to Charles' study, a room by itself out in the little garden formed by the spaces at the back of two houses. It had been built after the war, and had the makeshift look of buildings of that time. There was a basement, which Kelly only briefly looked at; it held the furnace for the two houses, bits of discarded furniture and boxes gathered over the years, and Charles' small stock of wine. The basement of Number 15 had been adapted to accommodate the needs of Elizabeth Brandon's nurses. There they had had their own small kitchen and bathroom, and another bed-sitting room, occupied, Kelly supposed, by them whenever Marya or the twins came to sleep in the room near Elizabeth on the ground floor. A small back room in the basement was empty except for the same sort of rejects that had accumulated in the basement next door. It was all empty and dusty now, as silent as the rooms above it where the invalid had lived. The whole of the two houses had a tired, shabby air, which went with their outside appearance. While there were many pieces of beautiful furniture, there also were worn carpets and curtains faded in the folds, chair and bedcovers thin with age and split in places. The kitchen and bathrooms of Number 16 were as they had been in the thirties; the money Charles had had available to spend had gone on remodeling Number 15 into the self-contained flats where the twins and Marya lived. Because of this, Number 15 was in better physical condition than its neighbor. Ruefully, Charles had surveyed the kitchen with its old-fashioned stove and refrigerator, the chipped enamel sink and wooden drainboard, the old glass-fronted cupboards holding the ill-matched assortment of dishes and glasses which were the remnants of the years.

"It's not much of a place to bring you to, Kelly. I really haven't looked at it clearly for years. It all seems much worse than I remember." He shrugged. "It'll cost a fortune to fix it all. Perhaps we shouldn't even try. I could sell both places. Cavanagh's would jump at them. That'd give us the money for one really nice house. Or I could sell Number 15 and use the money here."

"And put out Kate and Julia and Marya? I don't think so, Charles. In their own way, they all have need of it. Where else will they live rent free? Julia never thinks about money, and never saves any. What Kate earns wouldn't pay for a bed-sitter. Marya—? It wouldn't be much of a way to repay her service to Elizabeth, would it? I'm happy with things as they are. We'll do it bit by bit. There's such lovely furniture here, and you'd be amazed at what a bit of paint will do . . ."

She didn't think it was time, yet, to talk of what the money from John Merton's estate would do. She had been forming her own plans for the house, but they could wait. It was a time for groping toward a knowledge of each other. In her happiness with Charles their physical surroundings seemed remarkably unimportant. She was wanted and needed; she felt a flowering within herself that had been missing since Greg's death—perhaps had never been truly present before. She was a mature woman whose needs Charles answered. She looked forward to a full and complete life, and it would be the richer for being shared with the people who had been the center of Charles' existence. She could almost regard the shabbiness of her new home with amused affection. It would all change in time . . . in time. And in time it might be crowded to the roof because she might, at last, have the child she wanted.

Charles made one quick visit down to Gloucestershire to meet the selection committee of the Conservative Party for Tewford. "Don't bother to come, Kelly," he said. "Of course they'd like to look you over, but Charles Brandon's wife, even if she were a Hottentot, would have to be acceptable to that lot down there, or they don't get Charles Brandon to stand for them. I don't believe in pandering too much to them. And I don't want them to get the idea that they're doing me a favor. Oh, yes—when the date is set for the by-election, we'll have to campaign together pretty hard. But until then, your time's your own. And we'll have our Christmas together in peace." So he drove to Tewford alone, and returned late the same night. "It's all set," he said. "They expect the election to be late January. We'll have three weeks of campaigning, and all you've got to do is look as you do now, and they'll be a bloody lucky bunch to get you. I called in at Wychwood," he added. "Peter was there alone. I don't think Louise spends much time there. It seemed odd without old Michael. We were good friends in a funny sort of way, though he was older. He was damned good to Elizabeth and the girls during the war. I always felt, no matter where I was, that at least they were being looked after. You'll like Wychwood, Kelly. It's a lovely old place. We'll be staying there during the campaign. The cottage I own there hasn't been used since Elizabeth left it after the war. I didn't even bother to look at it."

"I'd really rather stay at a hotel if we can't use the cottage. A bit of an imposition, isn't it, living at Wychwood? After all, they're all strangers to me."

"A hotel would be expensive," he pointed out. "And Peter would be hurt if we didn't stay at Wychwood. It might cause raised eyebrows in the Party. The Brandons *are* that constituency, in a funny sort of a way. They've sent members to Parliament since Charles the Second's time. It's *expected* that we'll stay at Wychwood. It's all part of choosing another Brandon to represent them. Peter could have had the seat, but being pretty fuddy-duddy, they really wanted someone older—" He pulled a wry face at her. "And let's face it . . . a small degree of fame—or notoriety—doesn't hurt. They want to feel they've sent to Parliament someone who'll kick up a fuss when it's necessary. They like to see the member for Tewford mentioned in the press now and again."

"It's as certain as that?"

"Not a question about it. The Conservative candidate for Tewford goes to the House. And let the Prime Minister make what he likes of it." It was one of Charles' rare references to the buried quarrel with the Prime Minister and his resignation. "So just let's relax, and enjoy our first Christmas together."

A Christmas tree was placed in the hall near the glass doors so that everyone who came in and out of either house could see it. Kelly and Laura had bought it late one afternoon and barely had it in place when Kate came home. She looked cold, and her woolen cap was misted with light rain, but her face suddenly became radiant. "Oh, how wonderful! That's where we always put it so Mummy could see it. Did you know?" Kelly shook her head. Kate plunged on. "Marya has some wonderful Russian sort of ornaments she used to bring down every year—she's picked them up in junk shops, mostly. Ask her, Kelly. I know she'd love to use them, but I think she'd hold back about suggesting it. And Julia used to bring some of the company back here after the Christmas Eve performance. Some of them, of course, come from the provinces, and they don't get home for Christmas. Oh, I'm so glad it's going to be a *real* Christmas."

Laura went to Cavanagh's and bought colored lights which she hung in the fanlights over the doors of the two houses. "That's just to show them that we're different from the rest of the street." She had caught the habit of referring to the store across the road as if it were inhabited by the enemy, but Kelly noticed that she had not broken the habit of shopping there. "I try to be like Kate," she sighed to Kelly. "But it's a long way to Oxford Street, and Cavanagh's is so . . . well, it's just *convenient*."

Kelly found that she did as Julia had confessed to doing. She also shopped at Cavanagh's, and hid the wrapping away guiltily. She bought extravagant presents for everyone, and then exchanged them for less showy ones; the Merton money must not be too conspicuous yet. With only one present was she reckless, and she guessed that no one would ever know what it had cost. Walking in Beauchamp Place one day she had seen an icon in the window of an antique shop. She blinked a little at the price, but paid. Marya's untidy flat was strewn with objects that were obviously Russian in origin, but she possessed nothing as fine as this. Kelly sensed a deep homesickness which was evidenced only in such slight ways in this woman who could have left Russia with only the clothes she wore. Kelly realized that for the first time in her life she was actively preparing for Christmas with a true enjoyment. She had a family gathered about her which was her own. She tried to say this to Charles one morning as they drank coffee in his study. She had carried the tray there, but there was no room for it on the desk, nor the top of the filing cabinets, nor on the long refectory table which served as a second desk. She sighed, and finally placed the tray on the floor, and poured the coffee kneeling there. "Someday I'll get it cleaned up in here."

He laughed at her. "You will not, woman. You'll leave it exactly as it is. None of that fancy paint you were talking about. And don't let Mrs. Cass move anything, you hear? She can dust a bit, but she's not to touch anything."

"How can she move anything when there isn't room to move herself. And as for dusting—all she can do is stir up the dust." Mrs. Cass was the woman, widowed during the war, who came daily to clean—the last holdover of the staff Charles had provided to care for Elizabeth. She had been with the family, she said proudly, since Elizabeth Brandon had returned to Brandon Place after the war. Kelly liked her; she was comfortable, not too efficient, but endlessly tolerant. She belonged like the shabby carpets, and in her own way had welcomed Kelly and Laura's arrival as wholeheartedly as the twins had done. Kelly had seen her once flapping a duster over Charles' desk. "He'll never change, m'lady. Can't make him get rid of any of this stuff. All these old papers. . . . But then, Sir Charles has had a great career. I daresay he's got a lot of things he wants to keep. He should write a book about it all . . ."

Kelly surveyed the bank of strong filing cabinets, the papers piled upon them, the bookshelves crammed haphazardly, the stacks of books on the floor itself, the magazines, clippings and letters covering the desk. On what little wall space was left photos provided a sort of resumé of his life—the First Eleven at Eton, the wedding photo group with a beautiful, young Elizabeth, pictures with Alexander, Mountbatten, Churchill, Eisenhower, Montgomery. "I was going to suggest that you get a secretary," she said, "but I doubt that you'd find anyone willing to take on all this . . ." She waved her coffee cup to indicate the dusty chaos.

"Can't afford a secretary," he said. "When I get back into Parliament I'll share one there. But I like things as they are here, Kelly. It fits like a comfortable old shoe. Can you bear it?"

"I hardly know how . . ." She put down her coffee and tried to find a handkerchief to put to her eyes which had unaccountably brimmed with tears. Charles saw them, and was quickly seated at her side on the floor. "Oh, Kelly, love! What is it? You're crying. What have I done?" His arms went around her. "Look, if it'll make you happy, I'll try to clean up here. God knows, it could stand some changes. I should try to change myself." He tried to force back her head so that he could look into her face, but she thrust it against his chest, quite helpless now to stop the tears.

"It's so stupid, Charles. I never believed people could cry because they were happy. I don't want you to change . . . to change yourself. Or anything. We'll forget about changing anything. We won't even paint the house."

"What are you talking about, foolish woman? You can do anything you want. You know that."

"Everything I want is here. I'm having a Christmas, Charles. The first Christmas that's really been my own. Family. Presents. Sentimental things. I've had Christmas at Pentland, and Christmas at Charleton, but never a Christmas of my own. All the clutter of this place—the family—even Marya. It's warm and comforting. I've never been happier in my life."

He kissed her tenderly. "Thank you for those words, Kelly. There has never been a Christmas present like that for me. Nothing half so beautiful."

She raised her head. "There is one thing I want from you, Charles."

"Anything, dear woman. Anything—to my last shilling."

"Money won't buy it, Charles. I want to have your child."

Now his hands clutched at her shoulders fiercely. "Oh, my God, Kelly! You're sure? A child—yours and mine. Would you, my love? *Would* you?"

"You don't think I'm too old?" she said fearfully. "It's so late to be having a first baby. Could you stand it? It'd upset everything. Babies aren't easy . . ."

"Dear woman . . . if I can give you that . . . if that's what you truly want. Oh, Kelly, I'd burst with pride to be the father of your child." His grip relaxed a little, and he began to smile. "Shall we go and do something about it right now?"

"With Mrs. Cass cleaning the bedroom?"

"Give her something to think about. She imagines I'm just a doddery old bloke . . ."

"It can wait a few hours longer, I think . . ." She accepted the sheet of Kleenex he had taken from a battered box which stood on the windowsill; it was plentifully sprinkled with London soot. She looked at it, and suddenly laughed as she blew her nose. "This must have been the first box they ever made. I wonder how many years it's been sitting there. Oh! . . . look what I've done!" She had knocked over the coffeepot, and they watched the old brown carpet soak up the liquid which they tried ineffectively to dab up with the Kleenex. They used most of what remained in the box, and she noticed that apparently it never occurred to Charles to offer anything from the stacks of old newspapers. Some things were more precious than others.

That night Charles unashamedly held her hand at Covent Garden as they watched Julia dance Odette/Odile in the full-length version of *Swan Lake*, with her lover, Sergei Bashilov, as Siegfried. Kelly remembered it forever as the night she truly saw Julia Brandon dance. All the air of vagueness, of inattention which characterized her in her everyday life suddenly found its expression in the Swan Queen who only became mortal between the hours of midnight and dawn. The helpless fluttering of the birdlike arms, the utter trust and innocence with which she danced with her prince who would release her from an evil bondage, was the part of Julia she knew and recognized. Most extraordinary was the transformation to the Black Swan, Odile. She gave a glittering, icy performance of technical perfection, enjoying her triumph over the deceived Siegfried; she executed the famous thirty-two *fouettés* with a masterly, scornful confidence. The vision of her beautiful face, encircled by the soft white feathers as she resumed the role of Odette was poignant. Her physical marriage with Sergei Bashilov was evident in every line of their bodies. And yet, for all their closeness, no trace of sentimentality came across in the disciplined movements; the creative tension which existed between them carried beyond the roles they played to impart itself to the audience. Kelly was not the only one in the theater who edged forward in her seat. Afterward there were many curtain calls, many bouquets, the ritual plucking of a flower by Julia to offer to Sergei; but the way he kissed it was not ritual, and the applause went slightly wild. A love story was being twice-told.

They all went backstage, and Julia, surrounded by flowers, looked at them, her face, lovely as the flowers, was nevertheless wrung with exhaustion. She had removed her costume, and wore an old terry-cloth robe, her makeup was streaked with sweat. "Darlings!—oh, God, how my feet hurt! Wait, I must go and get Sergei." She fled along the corridor, pushing past people who had also come to see her. Then she was back, leading Sergei by the hand. Kelly noticed he limped slightly. Without his wig, his face stained with makeup, he still was more handsome than he appeared on stage. "Kelly—Daddy, this is Sergei. And this is my little sister, Laura."

He bowed, and kissed her hand, and Russian flowed from him, which Julia translated. "He says you're beautiful—all of you. He thinks you're a great soldier, and you, Laura, are a beautiful young lady. And both of you are lucky to have Kelly."

Kelly looked at Julia and at Sergei. They were tired and strained. They had danced the greatest romantic-classic role in ballet, and had given a great performance. The glamour was gone; the door was firmly closed against the crowd outside; they wore old gowns and their makeup had crusted into lines of fatigue. Kelly looked into the startling blue eyes of this young Russian—younger than Julia, she now realized. They were as different from Marya's dark eyes as was possible to imagine, but they held the same hungry, slightly hurt look. She turned to Julia.

"Julia, does Sergei have an engagement for Christmas Day? We would be very happy if he were with us."

He had understood everything. He reached and took her hand again, and kissed it with all the grace he would have used before a vast audience. "Madame, you are as kind as you are beautiful. I accept with greatest pleasure."

Quite a number of the company appeared at Brandon Place after the performance on Christmas Eve. There was a sense of leave-taking as well as festivity; in the new year they would start an extended tour of the United States. For some it would be their first overseas tour. They were young and shy in the presence of the stars of the ballet, and Kelly exerted herself to make them feel at home. She was pleased to see how Laura opened up with the younger ones. Several times she had been allowed to watch them at morning class, and at rehearsal, and they remembered her, and talked ballet as only the dedicated can. Kelly had laid in a great stock of food and drink; dancers were always hungry, and they liked to relax when it was safe to do so. Many of them would spend the whole day in bed tomorrow, and for those away from home, this was actually their Christmas Day. Charles beamed on them all, and kept the drinks flowing. Marya was wearing her brightest clothes, and a great deal of fake jewelry. "It's not really our Christmas, but who cares . . ." She conversed rapidly in Russian with Sergei, and they shared vodka, glass after glass of it, tossing it back in the traditional manner. The lights on the Christmas tree glowed, the little Russian ornaments hung there, along with the more usual ones. The party had spread itself over the drawing room and the dining room; couples sat on the stairs. Kate arrived after midnight, having come from a party in the East End. Her face glowed with cold, and she hugged Kelly. "Happy Christmas! It looks as if it's begun well. It's a long time since we've been able to have a party like this. The house has come alive. It was all quite strange when I walked along Brandon Place. The store's lights are out now, and of course there aren't any in the other houses. It almost felt as if we were the only people left in the world. There were lights and laughter and music. I felt as if I were a little girl again and believed in Santa Claus." They sang carols, and then were silent when Marya and Sergei sang a Russian carol. The tears rolled down Marya's cheeks, but she smiled. "It's the vodka, of course, but they're happy tears."

In small groups the guests left, calling their good-byes and their Christmas greetings in the quiet of Brandon Place. Finally Sergei went upstairs with Julia. Wearily, Kelly washed the last glass, and turned to find Charles opening his arms to her.

"They're not the only ones in love. Happy Christmas, my darling. Come to bed."

Christmas Day seemed only a quieter version of the party the night before. Kelly and Charles had slipped out alone to an early church service; Charles bellowed the hymns with more gusto than tune. The others each breakfasted in Kelly's kitchen whenever they chose to appear, eating toast and marmalade and opening presents, drinking strong coffee. Christmas wrapping paper spread out into the hall and no one bothered to clear it up. There were scarves and gloves and sweaters, books and records, the presents exchanged between people who yet didn't quite know the tastes and needs of the others. Marya stared at Kelly's gift of the icon in astonishment. "But I have never had anything so beautiful! I shall cherish it forever. How did you—? Ah, but I must not question a gift. I can see that you meant it to be unquestioned." She touched the icon reverently. "We're such fools, we Russians. We are as tough as people can be, and yet so sentimental." She straightened briskly. "I will put it out of harm's way, and then I will squeeze a great deal of orange juice, because when Julia appears with her Sergei he will be demanding vodka to get over what he drank last night—and he will have it with orange juice. It is a drink I think the Americans invented. So clever, the Americans, but it seems a waste of good vodka." Kelly noticed that she wrapped the icon in a clean dish towel, as if afraid something might soil it. Then she turned to the cooking of the Christmas dinner. Together she and Kelly and Laura had made the stuffing for the turkey the day before, the pudding, ordered from Cavanagh's, was ready for heating. Laura whipped brandy butter, and sipped Marya's orange juice and vodka. "I could get to like this."

"Not too much, little one," Marya glanced at her sharply as she peeled potatoes. "You don't want to end up like me."

"If I don't start to do something seriously, I'll end up like nobody," Laura said. "Kelly wants me to start with a tutor for entrance examinations for Oxford. I want to take typing and shorthand as well, because I want a job. Kate wants me to do volunteer work. Julia . . . well, Julia understands. She knows I can't be anything in her world, so she leaves me alone. It was such fun being with them all last night—but it was only for a night. I have to find something serious to do. And I have to move out of here. I can't live with Kelly and Charles forever."

"Don't be so hasty, my Laura," Marya counseled. "You've only been here a few weeks. No one, I think, wants to push you out."

"I shouldn't need to be pushed out," Laura replied. "There should be a reason for my going."

"Ah, that is another thing. But in the meantime, you cannot settle your life between now and New Year. And there is the Colonel to get elected to Parliament. He'll need your help for a few weeks. You can have, I think, a little more vodka and a great deal more orange juice. It is, after all, Christmas Day, and no big decisions to make."

Dinner was so late that they all listened to the Queen's broadcast from Sandringham before they sat down to the table. As she listened, Kelly fingered the brooch Charles had given her, privately, that morning. It was his regimental insignia, outlined in small diamonds. She hated to think what it had cost him, and knew, whatever it was, he couldn't afford it. As she listened, Kelly's thoughts drifted away from the rather predictable words that the Queen was saying; her gaze went around the circle that had gathered for this ritual of the

English Christmas. First to Charles, who must have his private memories of the Queen—the time when he had received his knighthood, the much more private and splendid ceremonial which would have attended his investiture as a Knight of the Order of the Garter. She had never asked about the reason for that controversial honor, as she had not had time to ask so many things about Charles' life. Julia sat on a sofa with Sergei, her face washed with fatigue, but she looked happy. Marya and Sergei attended to each word the Queen spoke with the seriousness of exiles for the customs of a foreign country. After so many years, Kelly guessed that for Marya it was still a foreign country. For Sergei it was new, and free, but also lonely. He gripped Julia's hand tightly. Kate had invited a young man she had known at the London School of Economics. "He isn't very forthcoming, Kelly," she had said. "But he's alone . . . and I felt sorry for him." Kelly wondered why Kate had to be so defensive about her men friends. This one was about thirty, clean, neat, handsome behind his beard, eyes of an indefinable gray. He wore heavy glasses and spoke with a Scottish accent, and Kelly never heard him called anything but "Mac," which didn't suit him. He wasn't in the least awed by the company, and he spoke a quite fluent Russian to Sergei, a fact that made Sergei spring up to grip his hand. "I have never had so many friends in my life—except in Russia." Mac hardly bothered to listen to the words the Queen spoke; he looked as if he could have written them for her, and didn't take them seriously. But still a hush lay on them all. It was tradition that one heard out what the Queen had to say, whether one listened and remembered, or not. On this her first Christmas with Charles, Kelly thought she might be forgiven for not paying attention.

They ate until a sense of satiation seemed to fall on them. The pudding flamed satisfactorily in the darkened room, the brandy butter, they told Laura, was perfect; Marya continued to fill champagne glasses. They toasted the coming year, they toasted Kelly and Charles, they toasted the coming tour of America. Marya and Sergei exchanged private toasts between them, and tossed back champagne as if it were vodka. They pulled the useless, expensive snappers with which Laura had dressed the table, read out the unfunny jokes that fell from them, put on the silly paper caps, cracked nuts and ate chocolates no one needed, and solemnly passed the decanter of port around the table. It was a merry, noisy meal; they drifted up to the drawing room afterward, leaving the debris behind. "Tomorrow . . ." Marya said, waving her hand toward it.

In the drawing room Charles produced cognac when Kate brought up the coffee. Mac, looking at the drinks cabinet, found a bottle of rare malt whiskey, and whooped with delight. "Man," he said to Charles, respect lighting his eyes, "you have fine taste, or else a very good friend."

"Both," Charles answered promptly.

"What is it?" Sergei demanded. "Something I do not know?"

"Sergei . . ." Julia pleaded. "Tomorrow—"

"Tomorrow is tomorrow. Today it is Christmas. I shall have this . . ."

"Malt whiskey," Mac prompted him. "Scotland's finest treasure. To warm a man's heart and succor his soul."

"For me," Sergei said. "To warm the heart." He seized the bottle and poured a too-generous helping. He insisted on pouring for Julia also. Mac looked at him with something like alarm. "With respect, man. This is not your old champagne."

"Today all is different. I am at home." He twined his free arm around Julia's waist and pulled her with him as he went round the group and insisted on filling glasses too full. He raised his own glass then. "I have one last toast. One. To my new home. To family."

Kelly wondered if he fully understood what he was saying, and she was for just a moment fearful as she saw the hope that momentarily flickered on Julia's face. "To home—to family," Charles said, taking away any sense of strain the Russian's words might have imparted.

Sergei started to drain his glass, and stopped as the Scot tugged at his arm. "To be sipped, man. To be savored." In obedience Sergei rolled the liquid on his tongue. His lips puckered somewhat. "Different . . . not like other Scotch. Not like vodka." Then his handsome features, almost childlike in these moments of abandonment, split with a grin. "What the hell!" he pronounced. "I do not know this word . . . sip." And he drained the glass.

In an effort to distract him Julia had gone to the old, big phonograph cabinet in the other part of the room. After a moment's scratchy hesitation, the familiar notes of *Sleeping Beauty* came. Sergei groaned. "Not today, Julia. Today it is holiday. My feet hurt, my knees hurt. Tomorrow my head will hurt. Today no dance."

"Silly—just not to *have* to dance makes it a holiday," she

answered. But still she hunted through the records until she found a Mozart flute quartet. The light, genial brilliance of the sound washed across them. Sergei, sprawled in a chair, gave a sigh of satisfaction, drawing Julia's untouched glass of malt whiskey toward him. "A shame to waste," he said. And in an instant, it was half gone. No one said anything; tomorrow he would discover what malt whiskey meant, but today it was Christmas. Charles put another log on the fire, and then below, they heard the doorbell ring.

"Who could that be?" Charles frowned. The doorbells often rang in both houses, but in the quiet of Christmas Day it had a faintly ominous sound. "No, Laura—I'll go."

They listened to the sounds in the hall as he opened the front door. There was an instant's hesitation, then his voice boomed out, as if to gloss over that hesitation. "Why, Nick! Nick! What are you doing here? Come in—come in. Not too late to say Happy Christmas, is it? I hope that's what you've come to say. Nothing . . . nothing wrong is there?"

The voice which answered him was lower in tone; they could not hear the words, but they heard Charles' response. "Well—that's fine. Just fine. Glad to see you. The whole family's here. Wanted to make a day of it because Julia's going off to the States on tour . . ." They were coming up the stairs.

"It has to be Nicholas Brandon," Kate said. Her tone was almost like a stage hiss. "Our millionaire second cousin, or whatever relation he is. Whiz-Kid Brandon!" She pulled an expression of mock rage. "You know—grinds down the faces of the poor."

Julia protested. "Kate, he'll hear you!"

"Who cares? He knows what I feel about capitalists making pile upon pile of paper money. He knows he's for the chop when *our* lot runs the country." Then she fixed her face in an angelic smile as Charles and another man appeared in the doorway. "Why Nick Brandon! Happy Christmas. What are you?—the ghost of Christmases Past or Future? Where is Tiny Tim?"

Kelly watched as a thin, tall man, a man with rather dark skin, dark brows knitted, a man with a face too long for handsomeness, but nevertheless arresting looks, swooped toward Kate. "Dear Kate—sweet as ever." He kissed her on the forehead. "Now, if you'd only let *me* run the country my way, why we'd all be rich, and there'd be no more Tiny Tims. Happy Christmas everyone." He bent to kiss Julia lightly, but lingeringly on the cheek. "Julia—more beautiful than ever. You don't know, do you, that I remain one of your most devoted admirers? Always watching you across the footlights, though, my darling cousin. Never near you." Then he turned and was at Kelly's side before Charles could make the gesture of introduction. "You are Kelly, of course. You don't mind my calling you that? And this is Laura. Old Peter and I had a drink together to wish you well on your wedding day, Charles. I hope you got our cable. Lucky man, Charles. Just imagine getting a wife . . . *and* a daughter as beautiful as this. If only I'd got there first."

Marya gave a sort of cackle of a laugh, and raised a wagging finger at Nick Brandon. "You Nicholas Mikhailovich—you make damn sure you don't get anywhere first. You might get caught by a woman. And then where is the life of the happy bachelor?—eh, tell me that?"

"Marya." He embraced her with what Kelly thought was a gesture of real ease and affection. He laughed. "You know me too well. All my secrets."

"Secrets?" Marya laughed again. "Then share just one with me—just for a Christmas present. Tell me how to get rich. I feel like being a capitalist. Sergei—don't you feel like being a capitalist? Such a nice change."

But the rapid English had gone far beyond Sergei's comprehension. He looked baffled, and for a moment, slightly sullen. Kelly had caught his expression as Nicholas Brandon had kissed Julia. It had seemed to be more than a cousinly kiss.

"Well—Happy Christmas, everyone!" Nicholas said again, and raised the glass Charles had put in his hand. "I hope, dear Kelly, you don't mind family dropping in on you this way. I had dinner with friends in Cadogan Square. I'm on my way to other friends. I knew I'd be passing your door, and I wanted to walk off the food. It is all right?" He never for a moment doubted that it would be all right, Kelly thought. He was supremely assured, used to dominating a conversation and an assembly, large or small. She smiled a conventional smile at him, reserving her judgment. "You're very welcome," she said. "Charles—"

She stopped because Nicholas had pulled the glass away from his lips. "Dear heavens, Charles! Is *this* what you serve after dinner on Christmas Day? Marvelous stuff, but highly irregular."

Charles shrugged. "Kate's Scottish friend here, Angus, found it in the cabinet. I didn't tell him I'd been saving it. And I didn't tell him there was no better day than this to save it for."

Nicholas had gripped Mac's hand. "I'm glad to know a man of such excellent taste." He moved on to Sergei. "And may I wish you a happy Christmas in your new home. We're always delighted when someone of your brilliance finds a way out of the Socialist net. It is Russia's loss and our gain."

Sergei struggled to his feet, but responded with a baffled shrug. It had all gone beyond him. "Home . . ." he repeated. "Julia . . . tell me what this man says. Tell me who is this man?" He dropped into Russian. Julia spoke to him quickly, and then turned to Marya when the explanation was beyond her competence in the language. Marya spoke to Sergei, but her words didn't seem to make him happy. Kelly thought that Sergei had reached a point in drink and homesickness when he could not see the light side of anything. One more mention of Russia, and he would be weeping.

It could have been Nicholas' own perception of this which caused him to produce the distraction. He had left packages on a chair on the landing, and he went for them. Beautifully wrapped, there were identical and extravagantly sized bottles of perfume for Julia, Kate, Marya and Laura. How clever he was to have remembered Laura might be there, Kelly thought, and to make no distinction among the four. But it was a gift he might have sent a secretary to purchase; it represented not his time and thought, but only money. He laughed as Kate protested, "Never use the stuff!"

"Never mind. Keep it till next Christmas and trade it off. Perfume's always good for trading."

Then he put a package into Kelly's hands. "Peter and I had quite a time thinking about what we might give you for a wedding present. Finally, he decided to let me choose. I hope you approve."

They all watched silently as Kelly unwrapped the gift. She had a sense of wonder, almost dismay, as she found it wrapped, under the paper, in a heavy blanket of cotton wool; she placed it on a table before gently removing this. She knew it was something precious and special. There were little gasps from the women as the small carriage clock emerged. It was not that the gift of a carriage clock was so different, but that none of them had ever seen anything like this. Gold was intertwined with enamel, blue and crimson, on its case; as Kelly put her finger through the ring and turned it slowly there was the gleam of tiny jewels. Its face appeared to be ivory, its hands of gold, weighted with small rubies and sapphires. "It's . . . it's beautiful!" Kelly breathed.

"My God, Nick," Charles protested. "You and Peter shouldn't have done this."

"You don't get married every day, Charles." Nicholas laughed; he appeared pleased with the sensation the gift had caused.

Marya was kneeling before it; she didn't touch it, but her eyes examined its every detail. "Fabergé," she pronounced. "It could be no one else, eh, Nicholas Mikhailovich? But I never remember that he ever decorated a clock."

Sergei caught at the familiar name. "Fabergé? Never have I seen except in museum." He bent and scrutinized the clock. "Only for Czars—Imperial Family. How does a man buy such a thing in England?"

Nicholas shrugged. "Oh, a few trinkets left Russia when they did. Sometimes one is lucky when one comes on the market."

"You are very rich man," Sergei said. His face was flushed. He seemed to resent the little jeweled clock, to resent Nicholas, almost to resent the people who had been his friends that day. He backed away, reaching for his empty glass and going to the drinks cabinet to refill it. He swirled the liquid moodily and took what was, for him, a modest sip. "Very beautiful," he said, looking at the clock as if it obsessed him. "You think it beautiful, Julia?"

"But of course! Sergei—"

"I do not give you present like this."

"This is special, Sergei. It's for Kelly—"

"Yes, special," he interrupted. "Julia. Record is finished. Put on more music." She hurried to the Gramophone, changing from the silvery Mozart to the familiar music of *Nutcracker*. "Just because it's Christmas," she said, with a glance of appeal at Sergei. His face relaxed into a faint smile.

"Yes, it is Christmas. Good!"

"Cigar, Nick?" Charles said hurriedly. "Oh, damn, this box is empty. Don't use them much myself, and I haven't refilled the box since we got back. Oh, wait—there's some in my desk downstairs. Someone gave me a box before I went out to Australia . . ."

"I'll go," Laura said quickly. She seemed eager to escape the atmosphere of the room. "Which drawer?"

"Top middle," Charles answered.

She was soon back, carrying a cigar box, and something else in a box which Kelly couldn't identify. "I'm afraid, Charles, that it was a *very* long time before you went to Australia," Laura said. She was pinching the cigars and put one under her nose; long experience with John Merton's cigars, kept in a humidor, had made her something of an expert. "These seem terribly dry."

Charles shrugged. "Well, perhaps it was a long time ago. Just remembered coming across them the other day . . . sorry, Nick. Here, let me fill your glass."

"Hold it a minute, Charles. I don't rush this stuff." From Mac he got his first sign of approval.

Laura was holding out the other box. "Charles, you've never shown us this. Have you seen it, Kelly? I'm sorry—I really didn't rummage through the desk. It was right beside the cigars and I couldn't help seeing the inscription. It looked so lovely . . ."

She held out a simple, beautifully tooled and polished mahogany box, with an elaborately scrolled silver plate inserted in its lid. The silver was dark and tarnished; it looked as if it had lain in its drawer for a long time.

"Laura . . . I'd forgotten that thing was there." He reached for it. "It was something the regiment gave me when I was finished in India. I've kept it because it was the N.C.O.s who chipped in to give it to me . . ." He reached for it, and Kelly at once realized why Laura had brought it. Something had been needed to distract everyone's attention from the magnificence of the Fabergé clock, something much humbler but not bought by money only.

They gathered around as Charles brought out a service revolver from its nest in the velvet-lined box. "I never used it. It would have been rather silly to carry such a thing around, but the chaps meant it well." The same silversmith who had fashioned the enscribed nameplate on the box had inserted a kind of silvery marquetry into the dull steel of the handle. "It kind of cocked it out of balance, too," Charles said. "It was meant for a glass case rather than a holster. But still . . . nice thought. A few of us had been on a border mission together, and this was meant to be a sort of souvenir." For a moment or two he held it, balancing it in his hand, smiling a little as if the memories it evoked were good. "Yes . . . I haven't had it out of its box for years. Haven't thought about it . . ."

Laura took it from him. She regarded it in rather the way she had the dried-out cigars. "Charles—I'll bet it hasn't been cleaned or oiled since you got it. Rusting away . . . it would look beautiful if the silver were cleaned up. I'll do it after Christmas. Grandfather was always very particular about the way our guns were kept."

Charles sighed. "Your grandfather, Laura, was a rather hard man to live up to. He—"

He stopped as Sergei reached over and almost forcibly jerked the gun from Laura. "Is handsome." He had tossed back the remainder of his third glass of whiskey in an abrupt gesture before he took the gun. "Julia says you have very great record as soldier. You are General, and have top medal. I—I have never been soldier. In Russia, if boy looks as if he will make a dancer for Kirov, they do not put him to be a soldier. We only play soldiers on the stage."

Suddenly he started, in time to the music, to mimic the theatrical postures of a stage soldier. He twirled an imaginary mustache, raised his hand in the air holding the gun, bent his knees to dance the famous kicking steps that everyone associated with the Cossack. He gave a shout. "Hey!" and his body miraculously was elevated feet off the ground. Even drunk he had an awesome precision, landing lightly on one foot, holding a second, and taking off again to execute a barrel turn which took him to the farther end of the long double room. At no moment did he seem in danger of a collision with any of the furniture. It was as if the impromptu dance had been carefully choreographed to accommodate such obstructions. There were gasps from all of them as he paused; Charles gave a warning shout, and there was a wailing cry from Julia. "Sergei, *please*—" As if her words goaded him, he took off again, with another exultant whoop. "See—Russian soldier! Now Bolshoi—hey!" This time he turned twice in the air, leaping over the sofa. Once again he landed firmly, lightly, on one foot, his balance controlled and perfect. Laura gave a little shout of admiration. "Bravo!"

Then the gun went off. Julia screamed.

The report of the shot and the crash were almost simultaneous, the one nearly drowning out the other. But it was the sound of the pieces falling to the ground that lingered after the sound of the shot had died. They turned, and the little Fabergé clock was in ruins. The glass was shattered; it had been hurled against the wall, and fallen, the face hopelessly blasted, the hands a twisted jumble, the fragile case bent inward as if by the squeeze of a malicious giant.

"You goddamn *fool!*" Charles shouted. "You could have killed someone! Give it to me. Didn't you see it was loaded?"

Sergei looked down at the gun in his hand; the acrid smell of the powder was in the air. A silence held them. Charles moved slowly toward the young man. "Give it to me, Sergei," he said in a much quieter tone, as if he were aware of the danger of the gun and the dancer who had drunk too much.

For a few seconds Sergei resisted the command. "Sorry," he said, finally. "Very sorry. I do not know about guns. Never have been soldier. Very sorry."

"My own bloody fault for leaving it loaded," Charles muttered. He took the gun and turned away. At that moment a harsh barking command in Russian came from Marya to Sergei. Julia, the tears already on her cheeks, her face grayish-white, rushed to Sergei's side. "It was an accident, we know, Sergei. We don't blame you—"

He thrust off her restraining hands. But the instant of his exit from the room, Kelly thought, looked as beautifully timed and paced as his wild dance had been; he played to an audience, and he knew it. She looked at the ruin of the clock, and for a moment wondered if that also had been part of the role Sergei had just danced. She did not believe he had never handled a gun.

The company, with Julia and Sergei, left for New York before the end of the year. After it had gone, a package came for Kelly and Charles. It was a plain gold carriage clock, delicate, beautifully fashioned. The card accompanying it was in a careful script. "So sorry. When I am rich it will be Fabergé."

"I suppose he means well enough," Charles said as he looked at it. And then he added, "Poor Julia . . ."

IV

By comparison to Christmas, the New Year came quietly. Kelly and Charles had deliberately kept it so, refusing invitations. Marya, sensing their mood, took Laura with her to a party. Kate had made her own arrangements. They saw twelve o'clock come up on the hands of Sergei's carriage clock, and they raised glasses of champagne to toast it quietly. They sat on the sofa in front of a banked fire, shoes off, and the feeling of the Darwin hotel was there again. Distantly a church clock tolled the hour. Kelly glanced about the big, quiet shabby room with gratitude, and leaned to take Charles' kiss.

"I'm so glad I'm here. How long it's been since I've welcomed a new year."

They took the glasses and champagne to the bedroom, and they giggled a little, like young children, as they undressed. In the midst of Kelly's happiness there was the discovery of how little she had laughed in her time with Greg. They had been serious, determined years, and it was taking this man, so much older, who had also achieved so much, to teach her that some moments were for laughter and for love. Serious purposes still remained, but they did not dominate. In Charles' arms she felt younger, and, in the first hour of the new year, full of hope.

It was a buoyancy that lasted as they planned the next weeks and months. In the first days of the new year the Prime Minister had announced the date of the by-election at Tewford. It would be early in February. The official campaigning would be in the three weeks leading up to that date.

"The Prime Minister's in a hurry," Charles muttered. "He may not want *me* back in Parliament, but he wants that seat filled with as little fuss as possible. Wants it all out of the way before he goes off to that meeting in Martinique. Doesn't intend to have any of *his* press coverage usurped."

"Is it as bad as that between you?" Kelly asked.

"We certainly didn't part on friendly terms, but who was it said a week is a long time in politics. We'll rub along, he and I, Kelly. One always does if it's expedient."

Kelly realized she was foolish to have hoped for more idealism in a man of Charles' age and background. She found herself wishing, secretly, for some of the fierceness and youthful idealism Kate possessed. But that, in Charles, she knew would have been his ruin. He had experienced far too much not to be toughened and phlegmatic; she was grateful for the moments when he could cast it aside and look at her with tenderness. Too well she remembered the chill, disillusioned eyes of Greg Merton after he had stood on the summit of Everest and seen the world at his feet.

They prepared to go down to Wychwood for the first weekend of January. Laura had asked to come also. "It isn't that I'm hanging on to you," she said, "or that I'm putting off making a start on something. It's only three weeks, but I can be useful—driving you about, stuffing envelopes, answering telephones. The usual dull things, but someone has to do them. You do realize, don't you, that Kate will be down there campaigning for whomever Labour decides to put up? *That's* going to make news."

"Hadn't thought of it," Charles confessed. "Do you think she means to?"

"I know it. She told me. She also knows there isn't a hope

of Labour winning. So they're sending her there to campaign to take as much of the news away from you as possible."

"So cynical?—my Kate?"

"Politics *are* cynical, aren't they?" Laura said matter-of-factly. "Kate's just warming up for the day when they give her her own seat to fight. And she rather enjoys warming up on *you,* Charles. So watch out!" Her tone relaxed into a slight laugh. "It'll be fun the day she does make it to Parliament, won't it? Just imagine father and daughter having a go at each other across the aisle of the House." Kelly listened to this piece of political acuity from Laura with a sense of wonder, and a little dismay. Shy she might be personally, but there was a great deal of both her grandfathers in her makeup. She had grown up in houses where political decisions were made, reputations made, reputations undone. And she was also Greg Merton's daughter, something never to be forgotten.

"Thank you, Laura," Charles said, pulling a face of mock humility. "I most gratefully accept your offer of help. Maybe you'll like to manage the campaign?"

"That isn't so funny, Charles," Laura said, with a touch of acid. "You have a great asset in Kelly, and a damned hard worker in me. You *should* be grateful."

"Believe me—I am." And this time there was no jocularity in his voice.

So Laura drove with them toward the Cotswolds on the cold Friday afternoon in January when rain turned to sleet at times, and pelted against the windscreen. Charles' car was rather battered and far from new. It was garaged in a mews at the back of Brandon Place. "I kept that when I had to sell all the others," he had told them when they had first come to Number 16. "The flat above the garage is rented, but the one thing you have to have in London is a place for the car. Can't spend your life looking for parking places. The old heap's seen better days, but they're so expensive to replace . . ."

Laura regarded the car now with a cool eye as they had set off. "It won't hurt you to be seen campaigning in this. You'll look less like the high and mighty General, and more like an ordinary man. Replace it when the election's over . . ."

There were gaps, Kelly thought, in Laura's perception. She took both the winning of the election and the replacing of the car equally for granted. She had lived perhaps too much in a world where these things were possible; and once more, she, like Kelly, had been caught up in the swift tide of a man's ambition.

They were leaving Oxfordshire and the rise of the Cotswolds was before them when the sleet turned to a damp, sticky snow. "Hardly a good beginning for the weather we need for a campaign," Charles muttered. To Kelly and Laura the country was familiar. They had driven this way many times with Greg and had passed on to the wild mountains of Wales. Remembering those times Kelly was glad that now they would be among these gentler hills, with the villages of warm stone, many gabled, their square-towered churches, the fields of corn, the sleek cattle, the sheep of the upland farms. A kinder country this, even when the wind howled across it as it did now, and the snow mantled the hedge-rows.

Wychwood was ten miles east of Tewford, the market town which was the center of the constituency which Charles would fight. "The cottage is four miles beyond Wychwood," Charles said, "but really is a part of Wychwood's land. Michael did my father a favor by selling him a few acres along with the cottage. Farmers don't like to sell even that much. Though, God knows, Peter will have to sell something if he's going to keep the place. There are some good pictures, but they mightn't bring enough to pay the death duties. He could, I suppose, sell the Eaton Square house, but Louise wouldn't like that." He shrugged. "I'm glad it's his problem, not mine. Funny how things turn out. You can own a house like Wychwood, hundreds of acres of the best farming land in the Cotswolds, and still be scratching around for money. Louise is no help. She fancies herself as a London hostess, I think. Extravagant. Likes to appear in the gossip columns. A rather unlikely person for Peter to have married . . . you'll see what I mean. By the way, she's Lady Louise Brandon . . . an earl's daughter. While you, my love, are just plain Lady Brandon."

Kelly laughed. "And even if you get elevated to Lord High Executioner, I'll never be more than plain Lady Brandon. Oh . . ." They had been driving through an avenue of bare beech trees, the snow lying white on the dark boughs, and then the drive took a sharp swing and Wychwood lay before them. "Charles! But it's beautiful. You never said it was like this."

"And big," Laura commented. "They'd have trouble just keeping the roof mended, never mind paying death duties." She added more softly. "I'd sell *anything* to keep this."

It was a long building of pale cream Cotswold limestone, touched softly here and there with vine, and showing the passage of centuries in its architecture. At the far end was the ruin of a tower which must have been its origin; a deep depression in the earth suggested it had had a moat. More peaceful times had allowed the building of an unfortified house, extended and shaped as the owner of the time had wished it. Tall stacks of chimneys rose against the darkening sky, crenelations topped the facade. Lights from tall windows fell across deepening snow. There was the outline of a terrace and clipped hedges suddenly blurred as the wind drove the snow before it. Charles eased the car to a halt before a deeply recessed door, but before he could get out it had opened, and a man's figure was outlined against the light from the hall. He walked quickly to the car.

"Hello, Charles." On Kelly's side the car door was opened, and Kelly felt her hand grasped firmly. "I'm Peter Brandon. Welcome to Wychwood. And this is Laura . . . come in, come in. Are you cold? Not a good beginning to the campaign, Charles."

They entered the hall, and an elderly manservant came hurrying to help with the bags. Peter Brandon's talk flowed over Kelly and Laura and they scarcely heard it. They stood and looked. At last Kelly turned to Peter Brandon.

"Forgive me—you must think I'm rude. But Charles didn't prepare us. I didn't know it was a treasure."

Peter Brandon resembled his brother Nicholas in certain respects—the dark eyes, the brows. But his features were softer, rounder; the mouth fuller. He had an air of engaging shyness which his brother totally lacked. He shrugged, making a gesture of deprecation with his hand. "A treasure . . . well, I don't know about that. It may well end up in the hands of the Treasury if we're not able to come to terms. And our ancestors never thought about how to heat it."

The Hall had the intimacy of a Tudor building and seemed smaller than the outside of the building suggested. The dark paneling gleamed in the light from the sconces and two fires that burned in opposite fireplaces. The staircase seemed to vanish into the dimness of the high, hammer-beamed roof. There was a screened minstrel's gallery above the big double doors through which they had entered. The impression of dark and shadowy corners was lightened by the masses of what could only have been hot-house flowers. A many-colored tapestry hung above the staircase and seemed to reflect the colors of the flowers.

They had given their coats to the manservant and drawn instinctively toward one of the fires. Charles looked around him with an air of affectionate familiarity. "Well, Peter, it looks as good as it ever did. I miss seeing your father here . . . but you make an honorable replacement."

"Thank you, Charles." It was said in a low, almost humble tone. Peter Brandon looked at Kelly and Laura. "My father would have been delighted to welcome you to Wychwood. The generations got a bit mixed up at some point, so Charles, who was my father's first cousin, is closer to Nick's and my ages than my father's."

Charles smiled. "I wish I *felt* closer to your age, Peter."

Peter was looking at Laura; Kelly noticed that his eyes didn't dart away from the scarred cheek, which, as nearly always when she met a stranger, seemed more obvious than usual. But she didn't try to draw her hair over it, and she returned Peter's gaze firmly. "We're very proud of our hero-soldier in this family, Laura. I wasn't actually here when the news of the Victoria Cross came, but they do tell me just about everyone who could get here turned up that night quite spontaneously—the village people, people on foot and on horse—no petrol in those days, of course—and it was the best party Wychwood ever had, my father used to say. Elizabeth and Kate and Julia were at Mead Cottage, and my father broke the rules to have Elizabeth driven over for the celebration. If it hadn't been for the blackout, they would have lighted bonfires. Of course, we lighted bonfires on V-E night, but it was part of a delayed celebration for Charles. They're still rather old-fashioned down here. An awful lot of them remember that night. They'll turn out, every last one of them, to vote for Charles. Everyone was delighted when they heard he'd agreed to become the candidate . . ."

As he talked he was shepherding them toward a room which opened off the Hall. It was large enough to be termed the Saloon of a great house. Here again was the severe linenfold paneling, but the carved ceiling had been gilded and decorated. It was saved from grandeur by the comfortably used look it wore—somewhat faded chintz covers on the sofas and chairs, newspapers and magazines scattered around. As Peter had opened the door, two golden labradors greeted them ecstatically, tails waving. "I shut them in here when I heard the car. They make such a fuss . . ."

Laura's hand had gone automatically to pat them. "They're beautiful," she murmured. "I've always wanted labradors. We've never been in one place long enough to have a dog—

except for the working dogs at Pentland. And they were Grandfather's . . ."

She and Peter were launched into a discussion of dogs. Charles smiled at Kelly as she looked around the room. The pictures, large canvases, could have been Constables and Turners, the vases on the long table between the windows could have been Ming. There was a crest on the fireback, repeated on the firedogs. There was age here and tradition and a sense of a home much lived-in over the generations. Kelly smiled back at Charles. She liked Peter Brandon; she liked Wychwood. "Yes, please," she said enthusiastically when Peter offered drinks. "It was a long drive, and we didn't stop for tea, because it looked so much like snow coming."

He mixed the drinks, and handed them around. Laura had opted for gin and tonic. It was a wonder, Kelly thought, she hadn't asked for vodka. That thought reminded her of Christmas night when Sergei had destroyed the Fabergé clock, and she wondered if Peter had been told. It had been his present as well as Nick's.

As if he caught her thought, Peter said, "Nick's coming down for the weekend. I heard he dropped in on Christmas Day. Pity about the clock, but it doesn't matter—just so long as no one was hurt. Mad Russians really are mad, aren't they? But then, there's never been anyone better than Marya—and at times *she's* a bit mad, too."

That drew him and Laura into talk of Julia and the ballet. He seemed to have caught all of Laura's enthusiasms, and responded. It was a strange and almost immediate intimacy which sometimes shy people can achieve. Happily Kelly relaxed in her chair and let them talk.

It was ended by the entrance of Lady Louise Brandon. Kelly could describe it no other way. It was as if an invisible stagehand had opened the door. She paused there, as if expecting a small round of applause. Then she came forward, arms outstretched to Charles.

"Charles! How good to see you. It's been far too long . . . and this is Kelly. You don't mind if I call you that? And Laura . . . Peter, darling, I'll have my usual. Laura, I met you once when I visited Charleton when you were a baby. Such a long time ago. I was at school then nearby. Lady Renisdale knew my mother . . ." She might have been at school at that time, Kelly thought, but she would say it, anyway. She was one of those women who never precisely state their age. Kelly noticed that Laura had shrunk back in her chair, and nervously tugged her hair across her face. Louise's

manner was perfectly friendly and was intended to be charming, but something in her tone conveyed that she remembered too well the badly injured infant that Laura had been. "Charles, you're looking so well. Isn't it exciting that you'll be member for Tewford. It's high time a Brandon was back in Parliament again representing this constituency. I'm delighted." It sounded as if it had all been arranged for her personal satisfaction.

Kelly sat back and studied Louise with as much detachment as she could manage while the talk went on. She was quite beautiful, the sort of beauty which comes into its full flavor at her age, which would have been about thirty-five. But there was something that didn't mesh about her. She was tall and slender, with a beautifully oval-shaped face gracefully set on a long neck. She had thick honey-blond hair which appeared to be its natural color; her most arresting feature were her dark brown eyes, improbable with that fair coloring, and delicate, light brows. Cleverly, she wore little lipstick, because when Kelly looked closely, her mouth was narrow and hungry. She had a straight and perfectly modeled nose. Taken separately, her features were good and pleasing, but the personality which came through them was tense and forced. As she listened, the voice was a trifle shrill. As Louise smoked, Kelly was aware of the beauty of her hands. She had beautiful legs. It was, Kelly concluded, just one woman's perhaps envious survey of another. A man would see a different creature.

Kelly forced herself to concentrate on what Louise was saying. She was talking about tonight's meeting. Kelly reminded herself that until Michael Brandon's death, Louise had only been mistress apparent of this house. Now she controlled it fully. And she meant, Kelly saw, to control many aspects of Charles' campaign. She had a list of the members of the selection committee, and a number of key Party workers, and she rattled them off. They appeared to mean nothing to her personally, as if she had met few of them; but she would know them now for these three weeks of the campaign; she would be the ardent political supporter, and, in a small fashion, the political hostess. Being mistress of Wychwood gave her that position. "Poor Spencer Hunt," she said. "A decent man, I suppose, but so dreary. I don't think he ever opened his mouth in Parliament. We're all looking forward to a better showing from you, Charles. The sort of fireworks we've come to expect. The Prime Minister has sort of rushed this election, hasn't he? Perhaps he's planning a Cabinet reshuffle and you'll be back at Defence."

"I'll be firmly on the back benches, Louise," Charles answered. "And the Prime Minister won't be in any hurry to offer me any special sort of job. If I'm to represent Tewford, I'll represent it properly. And when I feel I should open my mouth about any special interest, then I'll do it. One doesn't go looking for fights. They just occur."

"Oh—" Louise pulled a face as if she had been read a lecture. "You'll fight them, Charles, and end up Prime Minister yourself, I'm sure." She had tired suddenly of the political game, and she rattled her ice cubes in her empty glass. "Well, Kelly . . . Laura . . . would you like to go up to your rooms? Dinner's impossibly early because of the meeting, but then half of those earnest people who'll turn up have some sort of high tea, and eight o'clock's the absolute limit they'll wait. But I've laid on a few specials for after the meeting to jazz up the usual tea and dry sandwiches. Have to do our bit . . ."

Kelly and Laura followed her up the staircase, where Kelly would have liked to stop to stroke some of the heraldic beasts surmounting the newel posts. They had surprisingly animate faces, as if the craftsmen who had carved them had enjoyed their work. But there was no pausing with Louise; her talk flowed on. Of course she loved Wychwood, but she found the society deadly dull. "Full of county types in tweeds. I'd go mad if I had to stay here all the time."

"I think it's beautiful," Laura said with that intensity which told Kelly immediately that the girl had found another love in Peter Brandon and his house, something to defend.

Louise actually stopped and turned and looked at her with some surprise. "For a weekend, darling—for a weekend. Never try to spend a winter here."

"Charles told me Kate spent a lot of time alone at the cottage when she was studying for her degree."

"Oh, *Kate*—well, you know how Kate is. She's just as drearily earnest in her own way as these well-meaning types you'll meet this evening. And Kate never noticed how she lives. Sardines and tinned soup. And does she have to dress so badly even if she *is* a Socialist?"

"Kate has ideals," Kelly heard herself say, rather too fiercely.

"I thought people grew out of ideals with their teens. Kate's not a girl anymore, Kelly. She must be—well she must be almost thirty now, mustn't she? And of course, so is Julia. Now there's a lot that's going to waste."

"*Waste!*" The word almost exploded from Laura. "Why, Julia's a great dancer. She's *famous*—she's going to be even more famous when this tour's over."

Louise smiled brilliantly at her, and turned to lead them on again, down a long paneled passage where age-darkened portraits of what Kelly thought must be Brandon ancestors hung. "My dear Laura, I was talking about Julia's future. How many more years can she have to dance? Is she going to subsist on press clippings and giving classes? Julia should get married—and I don't mean to that Russian. He's in the same boat as she is. No future. I mean—well, I know of at least one extremely rich man who was quite interested in Julia. She didn't even know he was there. What I meant was that she shouldn't waste her looks. *They* won't last forever, either . . ." She stopped and opened a door. "This will be yours and Charles' room, Kelly. I hope you'll be comfortable. You must ask for anything you want. I'm sorry there isn't anyone to unpack for you. But nobody has *that* sort of help nowadays."

Kelly murmured her appreciation of the large room, with its canopied, carved four-posted bed, the fire that burned cheerfully, the scent of flowers. Louise shrugged it all aside, implying, somehow, Kelly thought, that she had expected someone from the out-back of Australia, someone called such a name as Kelly, to be impressed. She also implied in her own background a different world, a world in which such houses as Wychwood were usual. Had she somehow caught some thread of gossip that Kelly's mother had been the cook at Pentland—was that why she had so firmly taken over the management of the social part of Charles' campaign? For a second Louise's smile seemed full of well-bred patronage. The mistress of Wychwood, she appeared to indicate, would have no trouble in keeping Charles Brandon's wife in her place. "Dinner's at seven. We won't be changing tonight, of course."

The door closed softly, and Kelly heard her voice fading as she and Laura walked on. She was almost afraid to leave Laura in this woman's charge. She might say something which would upset Laura's precarious self-esteem. But as she began to unpack she reflected that Laura had already taken a step in defense of a house, Wychwood, and a person, Julia, whom she loved. When Laura gave her love, she was as fierce as any female could be in its defense. The scar might blaze on her face, but she would never allow Louise to tear down her idols.

Kelly sighed, and suddenly slumped on the bed. Greg's child was at last growing up.

By the time they sat down to dinner, Nicholas Brandon had arrived. He had dumped his bag in the hall, poured himself a drink, and was seated at the table all in a very few minutes, bringing with him the sense of a world that moved at a faster pace than most others, a world of excitement and even a tinge of glamour. He knew very well the reputation he carried with him—the young genius of the City, the man who had made millions for himself and a few others by daring and imaginative speculation. There was a restlessness in his movements, like a cat who cannot decide where to settle. It was more evident when seen in contrast to the calm quiet of his brother. Where Peter's eyes held a steady gaze, Nick's flickered around, as if afraid he might miss something, something might slip past him. He wore tweed that was appropriate to the country, but it was a citified tweed, the thing to be seen in board rooms on a Friday. There was, Kelly knew, two years difference in the ages of the brothers, but Nick seemed the older, his dark hair thinning, his mouth a sharp crease in that wary, knowing face.

Nick asked briefly about Peter and Louise's two sons, who were twelve and fourteen; Tommy was at Eton, his brother, Andrew, still at a prep school. He listened carefully to Peter's reply. "Tommy seems to be doing all right. I suppose they'll want to go up to Oxford or Cambridge if they can make it," he said. "But if either of them shows any flair for business, it'd be a better education for them to come into Brandon, Hoyle early. Let them get blooded."

"Why not try Tommy in the summer holidays?" Louise asked eagerly. "He'd love it."

Nick regarded her dispassionately. "My dear Louise, I'm quite fond of my nephews, but I'm not in the habit of employing child labor. In any case, I think Peter's right. A boy's summers ought to be his own until a certain age. I had to kick my heels down here during holidays, and it made me restless as hell. It turned out to be very good for me in the long run."

She shrugged. "As you wish, Nick. But you run the risk of turning them into farmers."

"We'll take the risk," Peter said quickly.

"Right!" Nick closed the conversation by raising his wine

to taste it. It was hard to know whether he approved or not. He turned his attention to Laura. "I see you got rid of the Russian. Saw a picture of him and Julia taking off for the States the other day."

"Kate's still here, though." A flash of mischief lighted Laura's face. "And she's coming down to campaign for the Labour candidate."

The dark brows were raised. "Is she, indeed? Rather disloyal of her, isn't it, Charles?"

Charles gestured to indicate his helplessness. "Kate's deadly serious about what she believes in, and she's after the blood of people like you, Nick. After mine, I suppose, in a sense."

"Doesn't believe in private enterprise at all, does she?" Nick shrugged. "Well, it's been around for a long time, and it'll stay. It's in the human system. We all want to do things our own way. This state is stifling the individual, and people like Kate can't see it. If even a Conservative Government is going down those paths, and it is to a degree, I shudder to think of what a Labour Government would do. Kate's so intelligent she knows *she'll* never be a cog in a wheel, but she doesn't make allowances for the less gifted who still might want to do things their own way, instead of having everything spoon fed to them by some governmental nanny. As for buccaneers like myself—well, there have to be some people who find ways to cut through the red tape. Otherwise, the whole damn country will sink and drown in it, and that's what I've come down to hear you say from the platform tonight, Charles."

"Nick," his brother said, "I don't think you have to tell Charles what to say. He's been his own man for a long time, and paid for it. No one ever put words into Charles' mouth."

"Really, darling," Louise interrupted, "don't get so intense. You know very well tonight and every other meeting is a formality. Whatever Charles says will be greeted with cheers. They want a candidate like him, and it's just so much nicer for them that he's a Brandon."

Peter almost snapped back at her. "I think it's so much *harder* for Charles that he's a Brandon. It smacks too much of political patronage, and I don't think Charles ever wanted anything on a plate."

"You're dead right, Peter."

Louise rang the bell for the service of the next course with unnecessary loudness. "Oh, politics—we'll talk about something else, shall we? While we can. We'll have nothing else but politics for the next three weeks." The coldness between herself and Peter became too evident. There was the feeling, suddenly confirmed, that had they sat alone at the table, the silence would have been one of indifference, even hostility. Louise needed company, if only to break that silence.

"Nice wine, Peter," Nick said, finally giving his verdict.

The meeting went off exactly as Louise had predicted, and Kelly knew why Charles would rather have stood for almost any other seat than this one. The Brandons had lived here for hundreds of years. The voters were so sternly conservative in their thoughts as well as the brand of their politics that they would vote in a candidate of the Brandon's choice almost exactly as if this were one of the old "rotten boroughs" of the past, when a seat in the House of Commons had been the gift of the squire, and votes openly bought. So long as the Brandons endorsed the sort of candidate that was expected of them, no further questions were asked. This time, it seemed to the pleasure of every person packed into the village hall, the candidate was himself a Brandon, a man whom many regarded as an authentic hero. Not only was there his war record to point to, but there had been his public stand at the time of Suez. Kelly listened to Charles: "I won't sit quiet and see this country shoved into the back row. We've had a past—a great past. We have a present, and it's a better present than many of those in the places of power would have you believe at this moment. If we do what we should, if we make ourselves felt, if we so steer this country that the individual—the man or the woman who cares and wants to work is guaranteed a fair return for fair labor—instead of letting everything slide into a pappy mess of spoon-fed Socialism, we will have a great future. I say Britain isn't finished—and I pledge my life and my strength to proving that belief."

The applause was just too hearty, Kelly thought, for what had been a rather ordinary speech. But Charles could deliver the platitudes the audience seemed to want with more effect than the words themselves contained. He had talked of no specific plans, no aims. He had not said what he would try to do if he were elected. He had barely mentioned the constituency itself, as if there were no problems in this safe and sheltered place that needed airing and solving. Perhaps that was exactly as the people wanted it. They didn't have big-city problems; they didn't want to hear about them. The local council would look after the laying of a new water line where it was needed, and the defense of the country against every enemy could be safely left in the hands of a man like General Sir Charles Brandon, V.C. They were here to endorse the candidate, and to have a pleasant social evening. No more than that, Kelly thought.

The speeches over with, they mingled with the crowd around the tea urn; there were discreetly placed bottles of whiskey and ale for those who cared for them, as Louise had promised. Kelly felt her hand being shaken in a way that reminded her of the far-off days when Greg had been the new conqueror of Everest. It surprised her to find how many there that evening also remembered Greg Merton and his achievement. They were eager to shake the hand of his daughter as well. So anxious was Laura to help with Charles' campaign that she broke out of her shyness to talk with unusual animation to these strangers. For a moment, left alone, Kelly just stood and watched her stepdaughter, and was a little frightened that even Charles might not be able to live up to the expectations of such devotion.

"Well, it went exactly as it should, didn't it?" Kelly turned to find Nick at her side. His thin mouth was twisted in amusement. "He said what they wanted him to say. He'll have no trouble from *this* lot, not like the last constituency. It was always touch and go there. Once he's in, he's got this seat for life. I wonder how you like the prospect?"

"I wonder more how Charles likes it. He had hoped for something a bit—a bit tougher."

Nick shrugged that aside. "He's a fool to think like that. A safe seat is a marvelous power base. He can work all kinds of things at Westminster without worrying how it will look to the people down here."

"That's hardly what a parliamentary democracy is about, is it?"

"The business of Government is power, my dear Kelly. I suspect you're still a bit of a romantic about such things. You'd have had to have been a bit of a romantic to stand being married to a masochist who'd want to climb Everest for the fun of it, and put you and his daughter through the hoops in the process."

Kelly stiffened. "What do you know about Greg? I don't believe you ever met him."

Nick drew on his cigarette. "You're right. I never did. I knew about him, of course. Who didn't, for a time? It's a small world. I know Renisdale—one hears things. Anyone who goes out and risks his life on a mountain has to be a bit mad, and you and Laura must have been a bit mad to have stood for it."

Suddenly Kelly said what she never expected to hear herself say. "Did we have any choice?"

A strange expression crossed Nick's face; he reached for an ashtray to stub out his cigarette. "Look, I—"

Kelly plunged on. "And what about you? What do you risk? They say great fortunes aren't made by timid men. Aren't you climbing your own mountains? Are you quite sure you're safe?"

He shook his head. "I'm never safe. But you see—I'm not married, either. I'm not dragging a woman and a child up a mountain with me."

"And when—if—you marry, will you start playing safe?"

He shook his head, and his smile now had a little warmth in it. "I may never marry. But one thing I do know—I'll never play it safe."

"Then you have more in common with Greg than you know."

He nodded. "Perhaps . . . perhaps." Then he looked beyond her. "Ah, there you are, Chris. Come and meet Lady Brandon. Kelly, this is Christopher Page. His mother, a wonderful lady, takes care of Wychwood, and Chris grew up here. Chris also happens to work with me at Brandon, Hoyle. A very bright young man is Chris. We only hire the best."

Kelly turned and offered her hand to Chris Page. "I'm very glad to meet you, Lady Brandon." The voice was silken smooth. "The General had always been a hero of mine, and it's good to know that we'll be seeing so much more of him down here now that he's going to represent Tewford."

"I . . . I didn't know people had heroes anymore." Kelly found that her words came haltingly, and that she simply stared at the young man. She registered that he was possibly one of the most handsome men she had ever seen, and would be more so in full maturity. The word beautiful might almost have been used of him. He was intensely dark—hair, eyes, the brows that arched perfectly as if they had been drawn. The lines of the face were very firm and strong, but the jaw had been softened by a cleft; the cheekbones were high, and the shadows under them fell just where a photographer would have wished them. He was tall and slim, dressed in tweeds like Nick. It almost looked as if he went to the same tailor as Nick, except that that might have appeared to be an impertinence in an employee, and this Chris Page looked as if he would be very careful about such things. It was the only fault she could find in him. He had just the slightest suggestion of hesitancy about him. Kelly wondered about that. Men who looked like Chris Page should have been spoiled long ago.

"Oh, Chris is a bit old-fashioned, you'll find, Kelly. And he has a brand of loyalty to the family that is going out of fashion, too. I value him highly at the office. He doesn't mind hard work. I'm expecting him to announce any day that he's leaving us and setting out to make his own fortune."

Then Chris Page laughed, and the laugh revealed perfect, very white teeth. Suddenly Kelly was aware that his skin was somewhat darker than most Englishmen's, dark in the shadows, dark and smooth, like his voice.

"I haven't quite got the courage for that yet—and not enough money for a stake. I think I'll stick around for a while and watch the maestro and see how it's done. It's wonderfully fascinating, like learning to play chess from a Grand Master. But like playing chess with a Grand Master, most of the time I can't keep up with—with Nick." He was a little unsure of using the name, Kelly knew, as if it was something to be used only at Wychwood, and not at the office. "I couldn't even begin to guess what he'll do next. But half the City is trying to do that, so I've plenty of company. And I've got a lot to learn yet." Why was he so polite, so deferential? Kelly wondered. Perhaps she had grown unused to the facade well-brought-up Englishmen wore. In Australia . . . but she wasn't in Australia, she reminded herself.

Having half-turned, he was speaking again, touching the arm of a woman who stood close by. "Lady Brandon, may I present my mother? Mother, this is Lady Brandon, as you already know. Sir Charles is very lucky, don't you think?"

The woman turned fully, and there was no mistaking the relationship between mother and son. His almost too-perfect good looks had their feminine counterpart and origin here. A stately woman, tall, full-figured, with that rare beauty that comes sometimes with the mingling of races, gravely accepted Kelly's extended hand.

"How do you do, Lady Brandon. Welcome to Wychwood. We're all so glad that Sir Charles will be representing us in Parliament. It's been some generations since a Brandon was there, and Sir Charles has much good work to do."

She was Anglo-Indian, Kelly guessed. Her voice still possessed the faintest sing-song rhythm. Perhaps in her late forties, she stood in that village hall, in this microcosm of England, and she was exotically foreign, even in her well-cut country tweed. Kelly noted that she did not attempt to play down her foreignness by imitating the conventional hair styles of the women around her; her lustrous black hair, only faintly touched with silver, was drawn back into that traditional knot. She would have been perfectly at home in a sari except for her height, and the fact that her skin was much paler than most Eurasians', paler than her son's. How beautiful they were, this mother and son, Kelly thought, and almost blurted it out. She wanted to ask, "How did you come here?—why are you here, in this place?" but she managed to make some more ordinary reply about everyone having to work hard to see that Charles was indeed elected.

"There is no doubt of it," Mrs. Page replied in her calm voice. "But of course we shall work. We want it to be a resounding majority. We must show Parliament that Sir Charles has our total support."

How exact her English was, careful, correct. How correct her manner. What had Nick meant by saying she took care of Wychwood?—and that Chris had grown up here? What was her position with the Brandons? Unable to help herself, Kelly said, "You've known my husband—some time?"

The erect head was inclined in assent. "My husband and Sir Charles were friends from school days. They were at Eton and Sandhurst together, and served together in India. I met Sir Charles when they were both posted to Rawalpindi. My husband had to—to return to England just after we were married. Christopher was born here . . . after my husband's death. In the thirties."

She placed a touch of emphasis on those last words, as if she expected someone to refute what she had said. "In the thirties . . ." That was to indicate that she was no part of the new wave of immigrants from India that had appeared so recently in Britain. She had come in the days of the Raj; one part of her was British, she had married a British Army officer, her son had been born in Britain. Her expression was calm, and totally closed. India and her mixed blood were not subjects for discussion.

"Now, if you'll excuse me, Lady Brandon, I must go and help. I see that Lady Louise is being rather swamped. Christopher, you'll pass around the sandwiches, please." It was an order, not a request. "We'll look forward to seeing you during the campaign, Lady Brandon, and, of course, to celebrating the victory afterward." She moved gracefully through the crowd, half a head taller than most other women, followed by her son. Suddenly, although they were unalike physically, this Mrs. Page, so beautiful and stately, reminded Kelly in some fashion of her own mother—her mother whose defenses and guard went up if anyone even mentioned Northern Ireland, her mother who demanded from Kelly total effort and total control. She too had ordered, never requested. They had in common the attitude of a woman who has brought up a child alone, a child in a foreign country. They had also in common, Kelly sensed, that ever-present anxiety that the child might not turn out well. They had the ambition, the will to push—if necessary to goad—the child on. Whatever Mrs. Page's position at Wychwood, Kelly sensed that the young man, Chris Page, had had a childhood rather like her own.

Beside her, Nick's voice was low, hardly heard over the din of the general talk. "Well now you've met her—our beautiful black swan who makes all the other women look just a little like a gaggle of geese."

His sharp, clever eyes seemed to laugh at her, though his mouth did not.

And it was Nicholas Brandon whom she met next morning when she walked early through the parkland of Wychwood, as once she had met Charles at Charleton. It was very early, and Charles had lay sleeping deeply when she woke; knowing the day of activity that lay ahead, she had not wanted to disturb him. In the faint light she had seen shadows of weariness on his face, lines that in the daytime were erased by the energy of his personality; his hair on the pillow lay tousled, and he seemed older than she had ever remembered. His breathing was heavy, as if he could not get enough of sleep. She thought of all the years he had labored, the years of service to military, to politics, to a sick wife. And he had so much more to do, so much farther to travel. She lay watching his face for some time, thinking of the years ahead, the busy, sometimes anxious years, and she felt strangely protective of him, as one would of a child. She thought again about the child she wanted to have with him, a child of her own at last, not more beloved than Laura, or more of a family than Julia and Kate, but a different child. Momentarily she was tempted to lightly tug Charles into wakefulness, to whisper beside his ear, "Hey—what about that baby we're going to have?" But she did not; the next weeks would be grueling, and he needed what sleep he could get. Besides, she thought, as she eased herself from the bed, how did she know she wasn't already pregnant? The sense of oneness they had achieved in that rather ramshackle Darwin hotel had never faded; Charles, the tender lover was still the same, the sense of humor she had so surprisingly discovered in his loving made each time with him something unpredictable, something enjoyed as well as needed, something to be happily pondered afterward. She looked down at her flat belly and thought of the time it would grow rounded and taut. Charles did not feel the light kiss she placed on his cheek before she rose, and went very quietly through the routine of bathing and dressing. She didn't bother with makeup, put on a heavy coat and boots, wrapped her head in a scarf, and went downstairs.

The morning was gray and chill, but the wet snow of last night was already thawing; patches of mist clung about the copses, and along the hedgerows; sheep were vague gray objects on the sparsely cropped fields. The cattle, she thought, would probably be kept under cover through this winter weather. In sheltered pockets where she walked the remaining snow had crusted with frost overnight, crunching under her boots. She approached one copse which stood outlined in its bareness on the crest of a hill, and there a figure moved, as once Charles' figure had moved when she and Laura had approached at Charleton so many years ago. A strange premonition filled her—a premonition of the future, and still a shock of the past, relived.

She had expected it to be Peter Brandon, but it was Nick. It surprised her to find him there. She imagined him the complete figure of the tycoon as he was painted; if he woke this early it would be to telephone Tokyo, or to rouse someone from bed in Los Angeles. She imagined him smoking in silk pajamas by the telephone, waiting for the calls to come through. But he stood beneath the trees, bundled in an old Wellington cape she guessed he had borrowed from the house, his shoes muddy, his head bare.

He voiced her thoughts as she approached. "Surprised, aren't you? Well, I'm used to getting to the office early. Can't stay in bed. This used to be one of my favorite places when I was a kid. Not that I loved it all that much. It just gave me a view of a wider world. I wanted that world. I wanted everything that was out there . . ." Cautiously a feeble sun prodded the mist as he spoke, revealing the folding ridges of the Cotswolds, the hint of stone villages, the occasional wreath of smoke from an unseen chimney. Then his face closed again, as if he had already revealed too much. "You must be an early bird, too."

"One has to be, in Australia. It gets hot so early in the summer. And then—well, I used to have to work rather hard to keep up at school—or rather to try to get ahead. The early morning was the only extra time to study."

"Yes . . . yes." He nodded. "I know. You and me . . . and Laura. All compulsive types. Charles, too, but he's learned to channel his energy rather better, or conserve it. Looking a bit tired, I thought. But this election is already won, so he needn't work too hard. Pity we can't be like Peter."

"And how is Peter?"

"Peter . . . oh, he's really not the compulsive type. Not that I imagine he's not already up. Probably had early breakfast in the kitchen and is off looking at some project or other. You know how farmers are."

"Yes, I know," she answered, thinking of John Merton, and remembering with sadness.

"He'll have the dogs with him in the Land-Rover. He'll stop at a cottage or two and catch some of the men before they go off to work, and have a word with them about something that needs doing, have another cup of strong tea, chat with their wives. I swear he knows every kid on the estate, and remembers their birthdays as well as their names. Peter's soft—oh, not physically. But he's a soft touch. You could almost say he's got a soft mouth, like his labradors. And Louise—she'll not stir before ten o'clock, and have her breakfast in bed, and yawn with boredom at the thought of a day in the country. Can't hear any traffic. No one will ring her up except to ask about flowers for the church, or the vicar's wife will want to know what date will be convenient for the village fete, because of course they go through the motions of pretending that she's interested in such things. She'll be charming to them all, and she'll turn everything over to Mrs. Page. Mrs. Page will decide everything. Louise doesn't have to bother—" He broke off suddenly. "Come on, you're getting cold standing here. I've seen my world. I've got quite a chunk of it. It will keep for a while now. We should have some breakfast. By the way, you look nice without makeup. Your early-morning face is very nice. Few women's are." He spoke with the authority of a man who has seen many women's faces in the early morning, had left them sleeping as she had left Charles, had observed their faces even as his thoughts turned to what waited at the office. Kelly found herself blushing, and was glad that he was not then looking directly at her.

"Mrs. Page . . ." she said, grasping for another subject, but not taking his invitation to return to breakfast. "What does she do here?"

"Well, of course she's the housekeeper. Rather unusual as a housekeeper, you think? And I think we've been very lucky to have her—and Louise is even luckier. Everything runs like silk. She's rather like silk herself, isn't she?"

"How long—?"

He anticipated the question. "I can't remember exactly when it was. My mother died when I was eleven, and we'd had a succession of housekeepers. Mrs. Page must have come just after war broke out. Elizabeth, Charles' wife, asked my father to take her on. They had been good friends in India. Mrs. Page had been widowed very early in her marriage. I do remember that Chris was only a baby when she came. It was rather an odd thing in those days to take on someone like her, and she was very young to be anyone's housekeeper. My father was a bit dubious about the Indian background—thought she'd be unhappy here, and he wondered if she could manage the job at all. Not fit in, perhaps, or not understand how life was here. But he did it as a favor for Elizabeth, and because Anthony Page had been Charles' greatest friend. That counted a lot with my father. And then we did need a houskeeper, and help was hard to come by at that time. Of course, once we had her, we never needed anyone else. She was so anxious to prove that she was more English than the English that it was like having a housekeeper, nanny, guardian angel and social secretary all in one. She must have worked twenty-two hours a day to keep up with it all—perhaps she still does. I can remember being rather thrilled when she first came because she seemed so exotic—so different from anyone I'd ever encountered before. You know how kids are . . . I thought she was some sort of oriental princess, or something. I was just finishing at school and longing to get into the Air Force. Peter was already in the Army." He laughed at the recollection. "Funny what one remembers . . . in fact, I think Mrs. Page's background was pretty ordinary. Her father was English—some sort of civil servant in India. With the railways, I seem to remember my father saying. Mrs. Page once said her mother was of the Brahmin caste, but from the little I know of them they wouldn't give a daughter to a minor civil servant. The surprising thing was that Anthony Page married her at all. Rather an odd—almost an unthinkable thing for an Army officer to do in those days. But he died so soon after their marriage that we suspected he knew he was going to die, and perhaps it was some sort of rescue operation for the girl. I suppose he was in love with her—who wouldn't have been? To give her an English husband was to bring her up in the world in those days. She was, after all, half-caste. Just as despised by the Hindus as she must have been by the memsahibs. Seems madness now, doesn't it? But that was the good old British Raj. If Page knew he was going to die—I have an idea from Charles that that was why he was sent back from India—a marriage would have given her some sort of status, and a small pension. Perhaps he expected her to return to India, and trade on that new position. Well . . . perhaps it was because the war broke out, and she couldn't go. Or maybe she never wanted to return. Luckily for us she didn't. She ran Wychwood as if she were the Quarter-Master General. I think my father might have sunk beneath his problems during the war if it hadn't been for Mrs. Page. You know—trying to run the place, mostly with Land Army girls, the horde of refugee kids we got from London, the rationing. She handled the lot. I can remember when I came back from my bit of the war after being stationed in Germany, I took one look at her and wondered why my father hadn't married her long ago. But they were perfectly formal with each other, always. I don't think the idea ever occurred to either of them. It just wouldn't have been right in Mrs. Page's eyes. She's such a stickler for the correct thing. Old-fashioned. Like Chris. She never talks of India unless you ask her directly, and hardly anyone ever dares to now. I don't think Chris has ever heard a word of Hindi from her. He grew up as an English schoolboy here at Wychwood. Went to Grammar School in Tewford. He's never known any other sort of life . . ."

"Yes," Kelly said thoughtfully, "but he knows he's different. I think Chris Page would give a lot to be exactly that English schoolboy you describe. We odd ones out always feel that way . . . just odd."

His voice was sharp. "You've got strange notions, Kelly. The only odd thing about you is that you seem to make a habit of marrying heroes—"

She turned on him. "And *that*, Nick, is a rotten thing to say. I loved Greg. I love Charles."

"Perhaps you can only love heroes. A woman like you should have remarried long ago, but you had to wait until you could find a Charles Brandon. You're just begging to be used again, as Greg Merton used you. I've heard Arthur Rensdale voice some opinions on *that* . . . Charles will use you in the kindest, nicest possible way, without really thinking about it. You're a woman without a child, but one with three stepdaughters. Shake out of it, Kelly! Women like you aren't doormats. Shake loose from those three. Make a life of your own—make a life for Charles. But make it on your own. Get rid of that God-awful house. Do you have to live with all those memories of a dead woman? Do you have to live with her daughters? Do you have to live with Greg Merton's daughter tied to your apron strings? Ah—" The tirade halted abruptly as her swinging hand caught him across the cheek. The sound was crackling in the cold air.

"How dare you! Is any of this your business? I could ask where *your* wife is?—where are your children? Or are you too frightened to commit to such things? You can push masses of money around, Nick Brandon, but you're afraid of the responsibility of being loved. I doubt you could love anyone. That's what *you* ought to think about."

She began to turn from him, but he caught her arm and pulled her back. He waited for a moment before he spoke; now all the wary caution was gone from his face. "You know, you might be right. And you know something else? If I'd met you before Charles Brandon did, I just might have had the courage to let go—to fall in love. You're warm, Kelly—and I've had very little warmth." Suddenly she was pulled into his arms and he kissed her, ignoring her struggle. His mouth pressed against hers, as did his body. He held her for just as long as he wanted, and then released her so abruptly that she staggered backward.

When she recovered her balance she stood and stared at him. "Don't ever do that again! *Ever!* I'm not available, Nick Brandon. Do you hear? Do you hear!"

She was furious that the twisted smile came back on his mouth. "I fancy you mean the whole world to hear it the way you're shouting. Including your stepdaughter. Here's your little Laura, tied to Kelly's apron strings . . ."

Kelly turned and saw, across the pasture, Laura's figure. The girl was standing still, watching.

"Laura!" Kelly called.

The girl turned and started running—back toward the parkland of beeches and oaks that surrounded the house. Kelly knew intimately the look of hurt and bewilderment her face would wear. Instantly she began to think of what she would tell her, how to explain what had happened, and behind her Nick's voice was saying it.

"You're going to apologize to her, aren't you, Kelly? Tell her she was mistaken. You didn't mean to be kissed. You didn't invite it . . ."

"You bastard!" she said. With difficulty she managed not to break into a run as she started to follow Laura.

Laura was seated alone at the long breakfast table when Kelly returned to the house. She buttered her toast calmly as Kelly helped herself to bacon and eggs from the hot trays on the sideboard, and then sat down opposite the girl.

"I think he's awful, don't you?" Laura said. "I wish you'd hit him much harder. I really wish you'd socked him one, and given him a black eye. He'd have had trouble laughing that off!" The tone was matter-of-fact, but the shiny patch of scar tissue on her face burned lividly.

The election committee came that morning to Wychwood to discuss detailed plans for the campaign with Charles. Kelly, with the rest of the family, attended the meeting, and they often turned to her, not for advice, but to tell her just what her function would be. "Do you speak, Lady Brandon?"

"Speak?" She stared at them.

The chairman of the committee, a man called Marshall, sighed at such political naïveté and inexperience. "I mean—have you ever addressed gatherings?"

"Very seldom. Nothing important. Just some charity committees in Sydney."

"That will do well enough. It won't be very arduous. And the audience won't be critical. Things like the Women's Institute, and such. Promise them you'll come back after Sir Charles is elected and talk to them again. Things like the Everest expedition. I understand you had a lot to do with organizing that. And you can talk about life in the outback in Australia. Make them feel you're a countrywoman at heart. I understand you have some nursing experience, and you're a qualified teacher. They love that sort of thing. Perhaps your stepdaughter . . . the ladies at the meeting last night loved her."

"No," Kelly said quickly. "I'll do anything you want, but you mustn't ask Laura."

"Pity—well, I suppose she *is* a bit young to be talking to political gatherings, even just afternoon tea parties . . ." Thank God, Kelly thought, that Laura had joined the Saturday meet of the Tewford hounds, and as she thought of it she was aware of Nick's gaze on her, the knowing, amused gaze that mocked her and her protection of Laura.

They moved on to other business, and left Kelly wondering why none of them seemed to understand Laura's painful shyness, why none of them imagined what an agony it would have been for her to stand up before any gathering and speak. It could be that she and Laura, having lived with the knowledge of that self-consciousness, were the only ones so keenly aware of what marred her face. Perhaps, Kelly thought, other people simply didn't notice it very much, or dismissed it if they did. Perhaps the long spells of hopeful waiting for the bandages to come off had made them too aware of failure, when they should have rejoiced in success. Perhaps it was time they tried again . . .

"And Lady Brandon will be staying here also, I presume?" Harry Potter, the constituency agent, was speaking. Kelly was jerked back into the discussion she had lost track of.

"Of course." It was Peter Brandon who spoke. Kelly had hardly noticed that he was present. He had taken a back seat in his own house, listening and saying nothing until then. It struck Kelly again that he seemed to have within him that still pool of quiet which Charles possessed so abundantly. "There's plenty of room for everyone."

"Oh—yes!" Louise too brightly echoed his words, as if her thoughts also had been absent from the gathering. Then she added, "I expect there'll be other people from the Conservative Party coming down to speak for Charles? A Cabinet Minister?" Kelly saw the small spark of ambition light in her eyes. It was just possible that this dreary election campaign might yet yield some nuggets of social success for Louise Brandon.

"We've made approaches to the Central Office. Certainly there'll be other MPs. Perhaps a Cabinet member. They didn't promise. This is such a safe seat, and they like to reserve the big guns for the fringe ones . . ."

"It will be a sorry mistake," Charles said acidly, "to treat this as a safe seat. That's an attitude the electorate has a habit of discovering and delights in overturning. Strange things happen in by-elections. The voters sometimes like to give the Government a jolt. If this is going to be treated as a safe seat, and the campaign run that way, then I must withdraw my candidature."

Marshall's mouth dropped open slightly as he considered the words. There was a moment's silence in the room. Then Marshall answered, crisply and sharply. "Yes, sir." Kelly recognized that at some time Marshall had been in the Army, and he was once again talking to a General.

That afternoon she and Charles went to visit Mead Cottage, his house on the edge of the Wychwood estate. "It was built in the fifteenth century," Charles told her as they drove. "It's always been a Brandon house—though not a dower house.

Too humble for that. I fancy some maiden aunt or other has always been tucked away here, or some deserving cousin. Perhaps the idiot relation. . . . That'd about describe me, I suppose," he said, and laughed. "But no . . . my father bought it freehold from Peter's father, Michael. Couldn't stand to be living in a rented house. He paid almost nothing for it, I suspect. It isn't at all grand, you know. And only about five acres with it."

It was, Kelly thought, a house of great charm, long, low, sunk into the earth, of mellow cream stone, with a garden run wild, and an apple orchard behind, which had been left to its own devices. Its small leaded windows looked toward a sequence of folds of the hills, hedgerow trees bare against the sky, sheep grazing in their thick winter coats. They untangled the gate from the briars that had enmeshed it, and walked up the mossy path. Winter-flowering jasmine hung about the doorway. The door gave reluctantly to the key Charles used. The smell of age and damp came to them at once.

It had all the eccentricities of a house of its age, and the beauty. Beautiful floors, such as at Wychwood, dusty and neglected; twisting stairs with a carved banister led to twisting passages from which opened unexpected rooms with unexpected views out over the wolds. The Brandon arms were carved over the huge inglenook fireplace in the big main room which was also the hall, and from which the staircase rose. The kitchen contained a sink with a wooden drainboard, and a great iron stove, which was coated in rust. The only heat would come from the fireplaces which were in every room.

"I'd like to stay here, Charles, while the campaign's on."

He laughed aloud. "Kelly, you really are mad. How could we?" His gesture took in the cold, cobwebbed room, the uncleaned windows.

"It could be changed very quickly. As soon as we got fires going it would be comfortable—and cheerful. There's enough furniture. We'd manage. It would be nice to sit by our own fire at nights."

He sighed. "My poor Kelly. You've really had no honeymoon at all, have you? I don't think you've begun to realize what the next three weeks will be like. There won't be a single night when we'll be sitting at anyone's fire. It will be on from one meeting to another, hoping the weather won't be too bad to keep people away. You'll be sitting on hard chairs in village halls, my love, and drinking lots of strong tea. The wine will have to wait till later. Sorry, Kelly. It just can't be helped."

She looked around her. Of course it had been a foolish notion, a romantic notion without any chance of success. But how little time she had had alone with Charles, and she didn't care for the thought that for the weeks of the campaign she would be eating at Louise Brandon's table. Why did she hear again the hateful words of Nick Brandon that morning. "Charles will use you in the kindest, nicest possible way . . ."

She cut off the thought; why remember what Nick Brandon said. He wasn't important to her. Instead she asked about the times Charles had spent in the cottage.

"Not very much time," he said. "We used it as a holiday house when I came back from India on leave. When the bombing started in London I moved Elizabeth and the girls here. Elizabeth was beginning to be pretty restricted in her movements by then. Couldn't get about much at all. This place wasn't ideal, but it was wartime, and one couldn't pick and choose. At least she didn't have to crawl down into a shelter at nights. By the time the war ended she was completely chairbound." He touched one of the old copper pans, green with mold, which hung over the range. "It wasn't the happiest place. Cut off from everything. She was glad to get back to London. She had friends there . . . some sort of life . . ."

"There weren't any friends around here?"

He sighed. "People were always kind, but they just didn't have the petrol to get around, and this place is isolated. If it had been a house in the village, it would have been very different for her. Peter's father was so busy. Short of help on the farms. Short of everything. Mrs. Page was doing the work of three women, but she always found time for Elizabeth. I can remember her riding up the lane on a bicycle, basket on the handlebars. Mrs. Page was an unlikely sight for an English country parish then. She's part of the establishment now, of course." His lips twisted in a faint smile, and Kelly had a wild vision of that beautiful young woman, as she would have been then, on a bicycle with the sheen of a sari floating behind her, which of course wouldn't have been the case. "Although it was against her ideas of British 'fairness,' still she stole eggs and butter and bacon and such, which should by rights have gone to the Ministry of Food, so that Elizabeth could have them. Elizabeth had been . . ." He turned and bent to peer out of the low leaded window which gave a view of the untended orchard. "Elizabeth had been her friend in India. It was she who suggested Mrs. Page to Michael for the job of housekeeper at Wychwood." He turned back and straightened. "Look, it's freezing in here. Let's go. It's almost teatime at Wychwood. I rather fancy tea by the fire there. It'll be about the last afternoon for three weeks we'll have such a luxury."

They locked up, and pulled closed the garden gate. One hinge was rusted off, and they had to prop it with a stone. Kelly paused for a moment before she got into the car. The house now wore a strangely sad and desolate air, alone, closed, unwanted, it seemed. She would have liked to have flung open the windows, lighted fires, had the floors waxed again. Sometime, she thought. Sometime, after Charles is in Parliament, and he would need to come down here to visit the constituency. She would clear out the smell of old sadness, of a woman, ill and lonely during the war. She would make it bright and filled with flowers. She and Charles would sit by their own fireplace. For an instant she seemed to see the firelight flicker through the dirty windows. She would like her child to be born here.

V

The next three weeks merged into one endless stream of meetings—the constituency was spread too wide and the weather did not encourage anything big enough to be called a rally. Kelly shook hands, asked for people's support for Charles, wore the blue Conservative ribbon. She drank tea and ate too many sandwiches in cold village halls. The winds howled across the winter wolds, and sometimes there were flurries of snow, but no real snowfall. "Just pray," Charles said, "it doesn't rain or sleet or hail or snow on polling day." Sometimes Kelly found herself addressing small groups of women whose eyes seemed to tear open every part of her—clothes, gestures, hair. She wondered how her voice sounded to them, the last, ineradicable remnants of the Australian accent there. They didn't want particularly to know about her politics; they wanted to know about her. She found herself seeking desperately for Laura's face somewhere, always at the back of the crowd, looking to her for reassurance. They seemed to have returned to the close-knit unity of the weeks when they waited for the outcome of Greg's attempt on Everest, only now it was Charles' victory they waited for; he seemed very nearly as absent and distant as Greg had been in

Nepal. He was with them physically, but he belonged to the Party, to the voters.

The Minister for Social Services came down to speak for Charles, and the Party, in the last week before polling. It seemed to be the Prime Minister's peace offering, an acceptance of the inevitable. For that occasion they had booked the largest hall in the constituency. Louise Brandon's inspired gift of hot mulled wine before the speeches had put the crowd into great high good humor. They roared approval of everything that was said. Kelly had heard it all so many times now that she felt it had grown into some weird incantation. It had no reality. She reproached herself for disloyalty, and told herself that when Charles was in Parliament it would be different. The issues would be real; he would no longer talk this mumbo jumbo of catch phrases. She wouldn't be so tired then, and she would listen. She would go to the House of Commons and listen to the debates. She would know what the issues truly were. She would be like Kate, only on the other side. And in the meantime, in the middle of the Minister's speech, her weariness and the mulled wine got to her, and she almost fell asleep. A little squeeze on the arm from Laura saved her from that ultimate shame.

They had encountered Kate several times during the campaign. The Labour Party had encouraged her to go and talk in the constituency, bearing the Brandon name, and bearing the message of the Labour Party. It made interesting headlines in the small local newspapers, and ensured a larger turnout at the Labour meetings than they could have hoped for. The Renisdale national papers played it up to give Charles' campaign publicity. Kelly and Laura met Kate one day in a tiny village high on the wolds, knocking at front doors. Interested eyes watched the strange sight of Tory blue and Labour red ribbons embracing in the middle of the High Street.

One night Kelly and Laura bundled themselves in headscarves and turned-up coat collars and went to hear Kate speak. Kelly didn't agree with all that she said, but the performance was dynamic. Kate's pale, intense face seemed to burn with conviction. She never mentioned her father's name, but attacked Conservative policies. Her words had a passion and a warmth that was lacking in Charles'; Kelly listened, dumbfounded. This was no raw young woman, but a seasoned campaigner. Why, Kelly thought, had she never noticed what magic Kate had in her voice? She could wheedle, cajole and finally demand. She could meet the challenge of hecklers unshaken, and answer with bright flashes of humor which turned their words back on them. When she sat down, the Labour supporters clapped and stamped their feet, and the sprinkling of Conservatives who had turned out to see what Charles Brandon's daughter was like, looked at each other in bewilderment. Kelly read in their faces the secret wish that the father and daughter might have been exchanged. If only Kate Brandon had been a Conservative . . .

"Well," a voice said behind them as they edged toward the door of the hall, "that was a performance that her sister Julia might have envied. They've both got tremendous stage presence."

Kelly turned. "Nick! What are you doing here? Laura and I just thought—"

"You're not the only curious ones. I've been knocking on doors all day, saying the same old dreary stuff, and I just had the thought that I'd like to hear what our dear Kate had to say. Well, she had plenty to say, and some of it was rubbish, to my mind. But the *way* she said it . . . !" He slipped an arm into hers and Laura's. "Come on. It's half an hour to closing time. We've got time for a few quick ones to chase the cold. Goddamn it, but these halls are ice chambers." Kelly and Laura were propelled out of the door and down the narrow village street to the swinging inn sign of the Boar's Head. Their breaths were frosty on the air.

"We can't," Kelly protested. "Charles expects—"

"Damn Charles. *He's* probably got a frozen backside in some other bloody hall, and he'd better understand. Laura, what'll you have?"

"Whiskey, please," she said. She watched Nick's figure as he thrust through the crowd and somehow managed to get instant attention at the bar. "He's . . . he's surprising, isn't he? Who would have thought he'd be here tonight? He's been awfully good about canvassing. I've listened to him sometimes. He doesn't just push a paper into people's hands, he really wants to talk to them. And he's given every weekend. I didn't think he'd care enough—about Charles, I mean."

"I'm not certain it *is* for Charles. I think Nick does most things for himself."

Laura said, "I don't understand."

"I don't quite understand myself either. But I'll get to it some day." Kelly looked up as the drink was placed in front of her. "Thanks, Nick. I think we all need it. Cheers . . ." There was an unspoken agreement between them that what had happened and what had been said that early morning in the copse above Wychwood was done with, finished. Nick might remember it with some amusement, she with regret; they would never talk of it. Kelly put her glass down. "Kate had me really rather shaken. Suppose . . . just suppose the Labour Party had decided to make *her* the candidate against her father. My God!—it would have got headlines all over the country, and I think, if they'd ever got into a personal debate, she'd have wiped the floor with him."

"She'd have done that, all right," Nick agreed. "But the Labour Party wouldn't waste someone like Kate on a fight she can't possibly win. This really *is* a safe seat. They're just grooming her for some really marginal place where a victory from the Conservatives would be a real triumph. She'll get it . . . one day she'll get it. And I say bloody good luck to her."

"Yes," Laura echoed. "Good luck to her. She and Julia are pretty wonderful, aren't they? Both special."

"Listen . . ." Nick laid his hand on her gloved one. His sleeve wiped the damp rings left by the glasses of previous drinkers. "It's about time you began to realize you have some special things about you too, Laura. You may be Greg Merton's kid, but you're Kelly's kid, too. She brought you up. You've got some of her in you, and that's something fairly special. You should use it, Laura. Use it!"

"How?" she demanded, her tone suspended between dismay and hope.

"Something will come. You'll see. Something will come. If you want it badly enough, you'll go out and find it. The trouble with you rich kids is that you have too many doors opened for you. You don't know which one to choose."

"Weren't *you* rich?" Laura snapped back.

He shook his head. "No. I'm rich *now*. I made myself rich. I always knew that what there was at Wychwood had to go to Peter, and so I went out and made something for myself. And I wouldn't be in Peter's shoes even if I had had the choice. Stuck with the estate to run, and the death duties to be found. Stuck with—" His smile was twisted. "Well, I shouldn't say it, but I will. It's all in the family. Peter's stuck with Louise."

"You shouldn't—"

"Oh, come off it, Kelly. We can all see how it is between them. Nothing! We all can see what sort of person Louise is. How he came to marry her, I can't fathom. Well, yes—I suppose I can. She's one of five sisters—there only seems to be about a year's difference in all their ages. Daughters of a Scottish laird who didn't have a penny, and all of them as beautiful as young vixens. They were all cooped up in Scotland during the war. They seemed to burst on London when it was over—all five of them. The Beautiful Buchanans, people called them. Peter was dazzled. I swear the day they were married he could have walked up the aisle with one of the other sisters, and not known the difference. Well, people did crazy things after the war—and she *is* beautiful. That's all. Apart from that, she's a right bitch. Did you see her purring as she watched the dispatch case being carried upstairs to the Minister's room? That's what Charles' election victory will mean to her. She wishes Charles wasn't married, or was still tied to an invalid wife. She rather fancies herself as a political hostess. You're in the way, Kelly."

They followed his Rolls through the dark country lanes back to Wychwood. Beside Kelly, Laura shivered a little, although the heat was turned up full. "He's strange, isn't he? He frightens me a little . . . and yet I think he's generally quite honest. Do you think—what he said about me—something will come? I've got to do something, Kelly. *Something*. I can't hang around with you and Charles forever. I know I'm in the way. I'll find something to do . . ." Her voice sounded a little desperate.

Kelly's hand closed over hers. "We'll think about it all when Charles is elected. There's plenty of time. Plenty . . ."

"But Kelly—I'm almost old. Old just to be starting."

Kelly didn't smile. Laura's brief history had given her too much experience, and yet not enough. Had Nick been right in saying too many doors had been opened? "Perhaps . . . perhaps," she said tentatively, "you'll find someone to marry." At the moment of saying it, it seemed a weak alternative to what Laura wanted to find.

"I'm never in one place long enough to find someone to love. I'm like you, Kelly. I won't marry just anyone. I won't marry just to get married. Nick said there's a lot of you in me. He's right."

They followed the Rolls past the high stone pillars which marked the entrance to Wychwood. It troubled Kelly vaguely to notice how much they both kept referring to Nick, remembering his words. Well, it would soon be over. Next Thursday Charles would be elected, and Nick Brandon would drop back to his former place in their lives.

Nick Brandon had worked hard campaigning for Charles, but Chris Page worked harder. "He stole a march on me," Nick confessed on the last Saturday night as they gathered late for a brandy at the fire in the library at Wychwood. "Took a week of his holiday time to come down here and knock on doors. I told him he was a fool—he'd be better off picking up a nice bit of stuff on a beach somewhere in the Caribbean. No one in his right mind wants to be in the Cotswolds in the winter."

"Chris is very nice. And he works hard. We've been out knocking on doors together." Laura said it rather sullenly; she worked as hard as Chris, but Nick had not praised her.

"Of course he's nice. His mother brought him up," Nick retorted. "How could Mrs. Page do anything other than well? God help Chris if he hadn't turned out 'nice.' She'd kill him."

"I don't think that's fair—to either of them," Peter objected mildly. "And I notice you don't mind taking advantage of how Chris Page has turned out."

"You're damned right I don't. Chris's intelligent. He's got a good instinct for business. He's got the right manners—Mrs. Page would disown him if he didn't! But there's just the right amount of the instincts of the shark in him to take him quite a long way. He's still feeling his way—but don't be entirely fooled by those 'nice' manners."

"I think you're very unkind," Laura said. "Charles—don't you think—" She stopped. She had turned in Charles' direction and her face softened as she looked at his slumped body in a chair, his features blurred by sleep. His brandy sat on the table beside him untouched. "Kelly—?"

"Yes—I'll get him off to bed. Early service over at Stroud tomorrow. And evensong at . . . at"—she consulted a typed sheet from her handbag—"at Duntisbourne Leer. No campaigning on a Sunday, they say. But there's nothing to stop the candidate showing himself at church."

"Mrs. Page has arranged early breakfast for you," Louise volunteered. "Peter's going with you. Too early for me. I'll see you at lunch. We're all invited to Rodmarton."

"Chris too?" Peter said.

Her brow wrinkled. "Darling, don't be tiresome. Chris doesn't go everywhere we do. After all, he's not *family*."

"But he works harder than any of us. Oh well—" Peter stood up, and at once the dogs were on their feet, anticipating their walk. "I'm for bed. Night . . ."

When the door closed behind him and the labradors,

Louise turned to them all. "Well, what am I to do? I just inherited a situation. Chris has been brought up with Peter and Nick as sort of big brothers, but after all . . ." She shrugged. "He is the housekeeper's son."

If being the housekeeper's son rankled with Chris, Kelly never saw him betray it. Mrs. Page lived in what was virtually her own wing of the house, an end portion of that long rambling structure, with its own entrance. Occasionally Chris would appear in the drawing room for drinks, when invited, and discreetly disappear just before the gong announced dinner. Early in the morning they would hear his car in the drive as he set off for the campaign headquarters, or for the villages he had been given to canvass. Quite often Laura was with him. He was present every night of the week he had taken off from Brandon, Hoyle to lend support at whatever meeting Charles was addressing, offering to drive to save Charles' energy. On these evenings he was present with them at the buffet supper Mrs. Page served so that they could be on time for the meeting. He was quiet, efficient, quick to see where a situation needed his presence, adroit at extricating Charles from the clutches of a supporter who had taken too much of his time. He was never ruffled, smiling always at the plainest Party worker, finding seats for the older ones, carrying cups of tea. His manner and voice were just as Kelly had observed on the first evening she had met him, smooth—like silk. Once when she had mentioned his hard work and tact to Louise, a tart answer had come back. "I think he's a slimy little creep. Just too good to be true."

Afterward Laura had indignantly protested to Kelly. "Louise just can't help it, I suppose. She feels guilty and resentful that Mrs. Page runs Wychwood so well, and that she's not needed. She's jealous that Nick thinks so much of Chris and that he's shooting ahead in Brandon, Hoyle. I think she's been hoping that the boys"—she was referring to Tommy and Andrew, Peter and Louise's sons—"would just sort of step into the firm when the time came. But Chris is so far ahead of them, and Nick won't let them being his nephews make a difference."

"The firm's so big—will it matter?" Kelly murmured. She was tired, and she didn't want to think about things that lay so far in the future. She longed for the campaign to be over, for the last speeches to be made, for the victory celebrations to be done with. When would it be quiet again, she wondered?

The first moment came on polling day itself. Charles had always retained his voting registration in the constituency by virtue of being the owner of Mead Cottage; so he turned out early, with Kelly by his side, to cast his vote. It had to be early so that the pictures could make the evening papers. Arthur Renisdale instructed all his editors that that was what he wanted, though the by-election at Tewford was not of national importance. The voting over, a strange lull settled on them all. They had lunched alone. The canvassing was over, there were no more drafts of speeches to work over; Charles' speech of thanks and acceptance had been ready for days. After lunch, all of them had drifted off on their own. Charles, to Kelly's surprise, had said he was taking a walk, and did not ask her to come with him. Thankfully she had gone to their room, drawn the curtains, and slid between the sheets. She woke two hours later, bathed and waited, trying to write a letter to her mother, until it would be time for tea. It was a task she found difficult, almost impossible. There was so little communication between herself and Mary Anderson, no closeness. She wrote the facts of the campaign, the hopes for Charles' career in Parliament, and it might have been a schoolgirl's letter, so self-conscious was it. Laura, she knew, did the same with Delia Merton. The two women at Pentland had to receive the same news, but in separate letters. Each, she knew, would jealously watch the post of the other. Each would somehow contrive to hint, in their few contacts, that she had more news of the doings of Kelly and Laura than the other. She and Laura had entered into another of their almost unspoken conspiracies to see that the balance was kept. Peace at Pentland depended on it.

As she was writing, there was a gentle tap on the door and it opened immediately afterward. Mrs. Page stood there, a pot with a forced hothouse azalea in her hand. She halted on the threshold. "Oh—I do beg your pardon, Lady Brandon. I had no idea you were still here. I thought you'd be downstairs with the others, since it's almost tea time."

"Do come in, Mrs. Page. What a lovely plant . . ."

For a moment that almost forbiddingly untouchable facade of the woman broke. She looked down at the crimson blooms, and a smile touched her lips. "Yes—it is lovely. Haines—that's the head gardener—told me he had a beautiful one just at its peak. I thought it would be a nice little celebration touch for you and Sir Charles. This jasmine, I'm afraid, is past it." She placed the pot on the table where

Kelly sat, and started to pick up two blossoms which had fallen from the vase cloaked by the long trailing sprays of gold.

"You're fond of flowers, Mrs. Page?" Always in her thoughts the woman was 'Mrs. Page,' though Kelly had learned that her name was Rosemary, that most English of names. She was desperate to find something to say to this woman who floated through their lives with such serene dignity, never hurried, never ruffled. Kelly was aware that a huge, late party was planned for that evening at Wychwood to celebrate Charles' certain victory—all the notable names of the county would be there, as well as the most devoted of the campaign workers, but Mrs. Page still had time for replacing flowers which had scarcely shown signs of wilting.

Mrs. Page smiled, her resemblance to her son all the more marked, though the gesture was less exuberant. "Yes—I do indeed, Lady Brandon. I do all the flower arrangements for the house. We had a beautiful garden when I was a girl. I was brought up in my grandfather's house. So many flowers. The house filled with them. Gardeners, though, were so cheap to hire. Always raking and clipping and sweeping. I don't know how we shall manage here at Wychwood with wages gone as high as they have. Haines struggles along, but he really needs more help, and Mr. Peter just can't afford it." She sighed. "Before the war, Mr. Brandon—Michael Brandon, that is—had eight gardeners." She looked down at the crimson and golden blossoms, and the smile left her face. "One wonders what will happen here, now that death duties have to be paid. Will it be like my family, I wonder? My grandfather lost all his money speculating. I can remember all the gardeners were dismissed, and everything went wild."

Kelly realized that she was hearing something that came but rarely from Mrs. Page's lips—a reference to her homeland, but she wondered if it was the truth or some fantasy spun of a wishful imagination. Hadn't Nick said that Mrs. Page's English father had been some sort of minor official with the railways in India? Would he have been permitted to marry the daughter of a rich man?—unless the man was no longer rich, and marriage to an official of the Raj was looked on as some sort of salvation of pride when poverty had struck. How would one know? It was all swept away, lost in the new nation India had become.

"Well, perhaps Nick—" Kelly didn't want to say more. She knew so little of the finances of this Brandon family. Nick was said to be rich, but perhaps it was only paper rich, nothing that could be realized to pay the tax man without sacrificing assets which had not yet matured.

"Yes, there's Mr. Nicholas. Very clever with money. Perhaps he'll be able to pay. But it's a lot to ask of a man when it will all, in the end, go to his brother's son. But still . . . blood's stronger than water. Failing that, Mr. Peter will have to sell the pictures. We would all hate that."

"Yes . . . yes, that would be a great pity." Kelly was reminded again that the problem of John Merton's estate had yet to be dealt with, and that as soon as Charles was settled in Parliament, she would have to make a quick trip to Australia. There would be decisions to be made, but in the case of John Merton's estate, it was merely a matter of deciding which of his holdings might most judiciously be sold.

"The family," Mrs. Page went on, "have been at Wychwood for almost five hundred years. I can't bear the thought that the estate might be broken up. That's why it's so important to have men like Charles—I beg your pardon, Sir Charles—back in Parliament. The other lot—those Socialists—they want to see it all destroyed. Torn apart. Smashed into little pieces. As if everyone could have a share. How can things like Wychwood be shared among the whole common herd? And shame on Kate Brandon that she can stand up on a platform and say so!"

Kelly stared in wonderment at the transformed face of the woman. Who could have imagined her capable of such passion? She had broken her shell of containment. The dark eyes which had seemed so reserved and betrayed no emotion other than what was socially permissible, actually seemed to flash. "A man like Sir Charles would not betray a trust and not expect the betrayal not to come back on him."

"I'm . . . I'm sure he never would," Kelly murmured, uncertain exactly what trust Mrs. Page was referring to. It appeared to go far beyond the election pledges made by a candidate, and, as everyone knew, there was a limit to what one single member of Parliament could either promise or achieve. "Not if he . . ."

But the fierce expression on the other woman altered subtly, became quieter. She began to retreat, the flash of spirit fading as she began to turn away. Something, a sense of pity or compassion, prompted Kelly to try to engage her for a while longer, to soften what might have been interpreted as a dismissal. Although they were so unalike physically, once again she was reminded of her mother; both women wore a sense of solitariness like a mantle against the world.

"Mrs. Page . . .?"

The woman turned. The barrier of impenetrable reserve was once again in place. "Yes, Lady Brandon?"

"You knew . . . well, Sir Charles told me you were very good to his wife when she was here during the war. It can't have been easy to do so much when you had this whole place to see to."

The lips once more parted in a smile, impassive, almost vacant. "It was never a trouble to do anything for Elizabeth Brandon. We were . . . friends. . . . Yes, a long time ago, in India. When my husband died here in England she came to see me. I had his pension, but nothing else—and a boy to bring up. It was her suggestion that I might come here to Wychwood as housekeeper. I . . . I didn't know how to be a housekeeper. But I learned. And Christopher had a good home. He went to a good school—oh, not to Eton, like his father. I couldn't have afforded that, even if he had been accepted. But a good school, all the same. As . . . as his father would have wanted. He was a clever boy, and he knew he had to work harder than the rest. After that, he went to London University. I wished it could have been Oxford or Cambridge, but still. . . . He read English literature there, and took a course in accounting on the side. He even learned shorthand and typing. He believed in being prepared for anything that came his way."

"You must be very proud of him."

"Yes. Proud. And he's earned it all by himself. Scholarships and so on . . . Mr. Nicholas didn't take him into Brandon, Hoyle as a favor. Christopher had to prove himself. He did." She looked down at the vase with the jasmine in her hand. "Well, I must go, Lady Brandon. There are still a number of things to attend to for tonight. I'm sure it will be a wonderful evening. Certainly I'll do all I can to make it so."

"You're very good, Mrs. Page. I don't know how we'd have got through the campaign if you hadn't made us so comfortable here. We've been quite spoiled. I won't know what to do when we get back to London . . ." Kelly was aware that she was saying too much, praising too much, talking for talk's sake. She expected to be dismissed with Mrs. Page's usual faint and distant smile. Instead, at the door, the woman turned back once again.

"There *is* something, Lady Brandon. I wondered . . ."

Rather too eagerly, Kelly responded. "Yes, Mrs. Page—anything . . ."

"It's for Christopher. I must ask it because he'd never ask himself. He'll be angry with me when he finds out I've done it. That is, if I tell him. It depends on what your answer is."

"What can we do, Mrs. Page?"

"Well . . ." For an instant the vase seemed to shake in her hand, and a blossom fell to the carpet. She bent to pick it up. "It's the flat in Brandon Place that's empty now."

"Empty?" Kelly frowned. "There isn't an empty flat in Brandon Place. We're crowded to the roof. There's Julia and Kate . . . and Marya . . ."

"Yes, Lady Brandon. You are indeed crowded to the roof. But you've forgotten the basement flat. That used to be occupied by the nurses when Elizabeth was alive. It's been empty since she died."

"But in the basement . . ." Kelly was thinking of the layout of the house she scarcely knew. "In the basement there's the furnace room, and a box room. You'd hardly call it a flat."

"The other side, Lady Brandon. Number 15. There's a flat there. Living room, small bedroom, kitchen, bathroom. Nothing grand, of course. But Christopher could make it very attractive. He's clever that way. Quite good with his hands. And it's amazing what a bit of paint and fresh curtains will do."

Kelly was remembering a couple of rather dark rooms and a tiny kitchen and bathroom down the area steps, the rather make-shift alterations Charles had had done to give the nurses somewhere to cook light meals. "Chris wants *that!*"

A slight color suffused Mrs. Page's face. "To rent, of course. He wouldn't expect it for less than the going rate."

Kelly felt a fluttering sense of panic. She didn't dare refuse, and yet she didn't dare commit Charles to something he might not want. "Well . . ."

"Perhaps you don't understand, Lady Brandon. Christopher is doing well at Brandon, Hoyle, but he's still young, and young men don't get paid all that much in that sort of business. They're almost expected to pay their own way just to gain the experience. Everyone expects them to have a private income. In Christopher's case, of course . . ." She shrugged. "He has a flat in Croydon now. A nice flat. Big, bright, airy. He even has a bit of a garden. But it's not his sort of place. Suburban. A long journey back if he stays in town for dinner. Not a young man's flat. He'd trade the Croydon place any time for the basement flat. There's a lot of snobbery in an address, as you know. He could be helpful, Lady Brandon. He's used to doing things here at Wychwood. He could tend the boiler and look after the garden. Things have been neglected there. No fault of Sir Charles', of course . . ." Suddenly she held up her hand as if to check what Kelly might say. Another shower of blossoms fell to the floor. "Oh, one hears that *you* have no money problems, but if I know Sir Charles, he will regard the responsibility of the house as his. And it would be good for Christopher to make himself useful. Young people like to know they're needed. Just as much as the old ones do."

"I'll speak to Charles," Kelly said faintly. "It must be his decision."

The vague smile returned to Mrs. Page's face. "Yes, of course. I knew you would be helpful. Christopher will be delighted. He'll transform the place, I promise you."

She bent to pick up the blossoms with her beautifully graceful movements. Kelly stared at the coil of lush dark, silver-streaked hair presented to her gaze. For a moment her vision seemed to waver, and the coil became one of the dreaded snakes of Pentland. When Mrs. Page straightened, she was still smiling. Kelly felt trapped, and somehow frightened. It seemed as if the life of yet another of the Brandon family was being thrust upon her. She hoped Charles would refuse, and that would be the end of the matter. And she despised herself for not having the courage to make the refusal herself.

"Mr. John Haloran, Labour. One thousand and thirteen. Mr. James Semple, Liberal. One thousand, nine hundred and fifteen. Sir Charles Brandon, Conservative. Twenty-one thousand, six—" The rest was drowned in the storm of cheers that echoed through the hall as the returning officer strove to make himself heard. After many appeals the crowd quieted enough for him to make the necessary, but now irrelevant declaration. "I declare Sir Charles Brandon elected. The Labour and Liberal candidates lose their deposits."

It was already late when the count was completed, and the result declared, but the urge to celebrate was strong. The cups of tea which had cheered the waiting gave way to sherry and other wines—and very discreetly spirits for those who preferred them. Kelly wondered if once again it was all provided by Louise—or rather, paid for by Peter. Or perhaps Nick. Or had the Party purse been squeezed just that bit more? Many people wrung her hand. Charles kissed her for the newspaper photographers, and then again when they had finished. The act brought cheers from the supporters. "How will you like being in Parliament, Lady Brandon?" a woman reporter asked.

"But it's my husband who's going to be in Parliament." The woman looked at her with the air of one who has to instruct the innocent, and doesn't quite believe their innocence. "You'll learn fast, Lady Brandon."

It was a relief to find Kate among the throng. "Sorry about your man, Kate. He put up a good fight, and you worked so hard."

The pointed, gamin face wrinkled in a smile. "We knew it was hopeless. The thing was to make as good a show as possible. These are rock-ribbed Tories. We were just here to give them a few bashes in the ribs. But isn't it wonderful that Father's back in the House again? He's been kicking his heels too long. You know, if he just keeps his powder dry, or whatever it is that soldiers do, he could make the Cabinet again. That'll be hard on you, though, Kelly. Member's wives have rotten enough lives, but I should think Cabinet wives have hell. That's why I never intend to get married."

"Why—because you don't want to be a Cabinet wife?"

Kate grinned. "Kelly, you *are* an innocent. Because I intend to be Prime Minister, silly!" They laughed, and hugged, and somehow a photographer, one who had been dissatisfied with the conventional photos of the winning candidate, caught them at that instant. It was the picture which made the front page of the late editions of many of the national dailies, without any prompting from Arthur Renisdale. Most editors captioned it, predictably, IT'S ALL IN THE FAMILY!

At Wychwood they found the celebrations already in full swing. There were people from all over the county, many well outside Charles' constituency. But in the minds of the squires and farmers and the old tenants of the county, it was a Brandon who had been elected, and they turned out to celebrate the name. Class lines dissolved in those moments when they tasted victory. Men who would never sit at each other's tables greeted each other over a drink, offered each other food from the splendidly arrayed buffet. Kelly was amazed at the enthusiasm generated. "You'd think," she said, "they had been expecting some different result . . ."

But Charles wasn't at her side; it was Peter Brandon who answered. "It's always like this. I'm not a political animal myself. It always staggers me to see how wild they go around here when the Tory candidate gets elected—or re-elected. Look at them now. If we'd provided whistles, they'd be blowing them, as if Charles had snatched victory from defeat. Well, Kelly, I hope you're prepared to be a political wife. He's in for life, you know. Once elected to this seat, he's there forever—unless there's a revolution."

"Up the revolution!" Kate had joined them. She had come over from the hall where the returning officer had made his declaration quite naturally with the rest of the family. She was beaming toward the distant figure of her father. "It's marvelous to see him so happy, isn't it? He has his old job back, and now he's got Kelly too. But he'd better watch out, because I'm going to give him a good run for his money."

Peter smiled at her. "I swear when you run for Parliament, Kate, I'll go and register falsely as a voter—wherever it is, so I can vote for you. Count me as a founder member of the 'Kate for Parliament' movement."

"Stand in line," Nick said. "We'll all vote for Kate. But I don't think we'll let her be Prime Minister, so she can't do too much damage." He was holding a glass of champagne, his usually unsmiling face relaxed and affable. "It gets to you, doesn't it," he said to them, nodding to indicate the crowded room, the people who spilled over into the Hall and dining room, some who sat on the stairs. "Even when you know it's a shoo-in, you still get a kick out of it. It'll do the stock market some good tomorrow, even though it's no surprise."

"That's what's wrong with this country," Kate said. "You and people like you make money on elections. It shouldn't—" She cut herself off, shrugging. "Well, I won't spoil the fun. And I'd better get back to my digs. They're not used to people who stay up this late."

"Where are you staying?"

"I'm staying with an agricultural laborer who lives in a tied cottage on the Wychwood estate." She looked directly at Peter. "I told him he'd be risking his job and his home by taking me in, and he laughed at me. He said Mr. Peter would never hold a man's politics against him. And he'd be too soft to turn anybody out of their house. And I told him it was a bloody disgrace that anyone had the power to do just that. And that when I was elected I'd work to see that it became law that no one could. It's Jeffrey Parsons, by the way, Peter, if you're thinking of sacking him."

Peter just smiled at her. "What! Lose my best man because of your politicking, Kate? No chance! Besides, he's perfectly right. My father never turned anyone out of their cottage because they became too old to work—or for any other reason. It's just a bit of a problem to find the money to keep building new ones when we hire a new man."

"It's still a scandal that the cottage goes with the job. Everyone should be free to buy the roof over his head—"

Nick made a face of mock despair. "Oh, for God's sake, Kate, just cut it out for once, will you? This is your father's night—unregenerate reactionary as he may be. Relax and enjoy yourself." He looked past Kate. "Hello, Laura. Happy? Great night, isn't it?"

She looked so pretty, Kelly thought. The long blond hair was carefully draped so that the scar did not show; she was wearing a dress of dark blue velvet which outlined her beautiful, slender body. Kelly had noticed how many of the young men had gravitated to her side. She seemed animated and happy, drawn out of herself. "There's a phone call for you, Nick," she said, "from New York."

"Good—then all of you come into the library with me. I'll take it there. It'll be Julia. I placed a call to her an hour ago. She's not dancing tonight, and I suppose they've had trouble tracking her down. Let's all go and give her the good news. Kelly, could you get hold of Charles. She'll want to speak to him first."

She extricated Charles from a group of well-wishers. "It's Julia," she said urgently, tugging at his sleeve. His face suddenly radiated delight. "It's my *other* famous daughter . . . excuse me." They made their way to the library which Nick had managed to clear of other people. But when Charles picked up the phone, and all of them, Kelly, Laura, Kate, Nick and Peter clustered around, the operator's voice came across clearly.

"Sir Charles Brandon? Well, sir, I think I'd better hold your call from New York. It's Ten Downing Street on the line now, sir. The Prime Minister wishes to speak to you."

They all heard the words he spoke, they heard the forced, muted words of reconciliation. And in the same way, Charles responded. "Yes—Prime Minister. Many thanks. It will be good to be back again . . ." Kelly turned and looked toward the door. Mrs. Page and Christopher stood there. They stood silently, like dark sentinels. How had they known, she wondered? It was not the call from Julia which was important, but the fact of the Prime Minister being on the line. Both faces, the woman's and her son's, were grave, and beautiful. They made no move to withdraw, nor to come nearer. But they had the unshakable air of having earned their right to be there.

Chapter Five

I

They returned to London the next day. It was evident that Marya had been in; the hall and drawing room had bowls of flowers, champagne sat in a container of ice. "It was kind of her," Charles said. And then he sighed. "But I've had rather enough of champagne. I suppose we should drink it with dinner, or she may be offended. Such a good soul . . ." There was an almost illegible note of congratulations in the kitchen from Mrs. Cass. *I'm glad yewll be back there to put them all strait, Sir. I put shepherds pie in the oven, my lady.*

Charles gestured helplessly. "If she only knew how little one can accomplish."

Laura had come in from a shopping foray across to Cavanagh's. She had bought fruit and cheese, and her own two bottles of champagne. "I asked Kate to have dinner. You don't mind, do you? She doesn't want to butt in, but I know she'll have a biscuit and a cup of tea up there by herself unless we drag her in."

Charles spread his hands. "Kelly, is it all right? You haven't had a moment's peace for weeks now." But his expression appealed to her for understanding. Suddenly Kelly felt a sense of happiness which had been missing since they had gone down to Wychwood to start campaigning. She was plunged back into this unlikely household, and she knew she had missed it. When Marya came back from work, Kelly knew she also would join them. They would eat the shepherd's pie, and the things Laura had bought, and they would sit for a long time over coffee. They would start to make plans . . . plans for Laura's future, Kate would talk about her work, and Marya about hers. They would wonder aloud about Julia and Sergei. They would start to be a family again. Kelly wanted it all desperately. She went herself to urge Kate to come down to be with them.

Charles took his seat in the House of Commons almost at once. There was no ceremony to mark the occasion, except a word of welcome before the Prime Minister's question time for the Honorable Member for Tewford. Charles had slipped into his place on the back benches, some old colleagues coming to shake his hand. Kelly watched it all from the Stranger's Gallery. "Don't bother to come," Charles had said. "It'll be a pretty boring session, and nothing special to see or hear."

"If you think I've worked as I have these past weeks just to let you go off to the House on your own . . ."

He kissed her. "Bless you. I would have been terribly hurt if you hadn't been there—just the first time back."

It was, as he had said, uneventful. After Question Time all the sparkle seemed to go out of the procedure. There had been a flash of repartee across the aisle which divided the parties, but when the Prime Minister left, and a debate began on a bill on the Orkney and Shetland Islands fisheries' policy, the benches thinned. Kelly met Charles for a drink in one of the Members' bars. She felt his pride as he introduced her. She saw how quickly he was taking up again the pieces of his old life, how easily he slipped back into the camaraderie of the House, where one could trade insults in the Chamber, and meet as friends in the Lobby. They received many invitations, but all of them provisional on what the business of the House allowed.

"Of course it's all nonsense the way things are run," Charles said on the way back to Brandon Place. "Any sensible body would begin business in the morning, and end at a reasonable hour in the evening. As it is, we could have some all-night sittings. You never know when you'll be free, if it's an important bill that's being debated. Except weekends. And weekends you have to go to the constituency. I intend to keep my promise to get down to Tewford as often as possible.

Even a 'safe' seat has to be taken care of. People begin to resent you taking them for granted. They expect you to be there to listen to their grievances, to write to the appropriate Minister for them. So often it does no good . . . but you have to try."

"We'll get Mead Cottage in order," Kelly said. "Quickly. I don't think I want much more of Louise's hospitality. And the house here . . . we'll have to do some entertaining, won't we?" She added hesitantly, fearful of offending him. "It does look a bit shabby . . ."

At the house Charles brought up the subject again. "Kelly, are you sure you want to go on with this arrangement? Look—you hardly have a moment's privacy. I could sell this house, and let the girls—and Marya—stay put in Number 15. You've a right to a fresh start, without all the clutter and accumulation of the years on your shoulders."

"The clutter can be straightened out, Charles. We could stand new curtains and a paint job. A bit of modernizing here and there. But to go away from Kate and Julia—yes, and from Marya . . . no, I don't think so. It works. I could have a lot of happiness from them." Then she remembered the conversation with Mrs. Page. She told him of the request for Chris to rent the basement flat. She had expected agreement, but Charles seemed almost to explode. "Cheek! No I *don't* want him here! Mrs. Page had no right . . . God, Kelly do what you like about the basement. It's self-contained, and can be shut off. Rent it, if you like, or use it for live-in help—if you can find someone. But I don't want Chris Page here. You've got enough of us camping around you. There's a limit to what she can expect . . ."

She put the case as Mrs. Page had. "He *is* awfully useful, Charles. I think he's quite keen to be near you, and Nick values him highly."

"Then let Nick take care of him! Oh—damn it, Kelly! Do what you want. You're as soft as Peter. But don't complain to me when you begin to find it all a bit too much. You don't have to take on all the Brandons, you know."

"Well, as Louise said, he isn't family . . ."

"No," he said, "he certainly isn't!" He began to move toward his study. "Well, I've got some papers to get through. Can we have an early dinner and an early night? I feel as if I haven't had a decent sleep for weeks."

"Yes, of course. Charles—what am I to tell Mrs. Page?"

"Damn Mrs. Page! Tell her what you like." The passage door slammed.

Kelly sighed. She knew she would never be able to refuse Mrs. Page. And Charles hadn't, after all, done it for her.

II

Life assumed, with a swiftness that surprised Kelly, a kind of routine. Charles went to the House about eleven each morning; the business in the Chamber usually did not occupy him until the afternoon but there were committees to attend and mail to answer. She learned to her surprise that he didn't, nor did anyone except Ministers, have an office to himself, and he even shared a secretary. The salary was small, and the expense allowance meager. He looked at her ruefully. "I told you it was no jug of cream. And it'd be far harder if I didn't have this house in London, and the cottage at Wychwood. Some MPs exist in bed-sitters here in London, and are hard put to pay the mortgage on their semi-detacheds in their constituency. At least I can be grateful to the Brandon family for some things. But you see why it's essential for me to keep on some of the directorships. An MP's salary doesn't stretch far."

"Supposing you become a Minister? You'll have to resign the directorships then."

"We'll face that when we come to it. The Prime Minister might have accepted that it was inevitable I'd be back in Parliament, but he's not about to thrust a Cabinet job at me. I'll be years, if not forever, on the back benches." He kissed her swiftly. "Got to go, my love. I'll be back early. Nothing important to me being debated tonight."

"You'd *better* be back early. We're having six people to dinner. Two of them are on boards of companies with you. Remember?"

His mouth dropped open. "Well—I *would* have remembered. I'll be home in time, I promise." He turned back. "How are you going to manage? I mean, Mrs. Cass's all right, but she can't do anything fancy. It's been so long since we entertained . . . you know, with Elizabeth the way she was, no one expected it."

Kelly pursed her lips, and then smiled. "Well so long as you don't tell Kate, I'll confess. I ordered the whole works from Cavanagh's—cook, butler, the lot. Mrs. Cass will do the washing-up. I've got such beautiful wine I don't think anyone will notice that we could stand some new curtains. Charles—when you have time—can you look at some samples with me? I really don't want to put a green carpet in the dining room and find you hate that shade of green. And will the drawing room be blue or red—or shall I go all out, and let it be a most exquisite pale gold? Shall I be economical and have it painted, or go for French wallpaper?"

He shook his head. "Dear Kelly, you married a poor man, but I'm well aware that *you're* not poor. But I'm also old-fashioned. It troubles me that I can't pay for all these things."

She touched his hand. "Charles, you marired me before John Merton died. I don't forget it. And I can't help knowing what you did for Elizabeth. Try to forget the money—please. And try to tell me what colors you like."

"Didn't you know? I'm color-blind!" He came across the room and kissed her again. "You're a real fool to have married me, Kelly Brandon, but it's done. I'm not color-blind, of course, but I might just as well be for all I'd notice the carpet. And won't we have a good time finding out all the things about each other we don't know?"

So she gave two dinner parties, and attended two others, in those first weeks, learning all the time the art, and in a sense the guile, of being a political wife. She learned that the night did not always end with the dinner party. Often Charles had to go back to the House of Commons while she returned home alone. The separation at first seemed strange and hurtful, but she learned to accept it. She began to grow accustomed to the warm feeling of Charles' pride in her; it was a new feeling, one she had never experienced with Greg. She came to accept his tenderness, to know his moments of passion, to share them joyfully. But she had also to learn the unpredictability of his life. He found her asleep at three o'clock one morning on the sofa in the drawing room, and was wakened by his kiss. "Why didn't you go to bed? Do you know what time it is?"

"I like to wait up for you."

"That may be sweet and loyal of you, my darling, but it's going to mean too much waiting up. I couldn't leave the House tonight. I told you this morning they had put a three-line whip on. They wanted every vote."

She had only vaguely understood before the term "three-line whip," which meant that every Member, unless actually in the hospital, had to appear and vote, no matter how late. "You'll have to promise me you'll be in bed by midnight, Kelly? It matters a lot that you understand. It's a very odd sort of life you've settled for, but I can't help how they run things. When I'm Prime Minister I'll try to change the system, but perhaps it'll have to wait until Kate gets the job. Things move slowly . . . come now, Kelly. To bed." She struggled sleepily to her feet, and let him lead her up the stairs. After that she went to bed at midnight, and waited for his kiss to wake her. Sometimes she woke before him in the early morning, and was always surprised at how the lines of fatigue showed on his sleeping, unguarded face.

She learned not to bother him with the details of housekeeping, or the plans she made. He listened with half an ear, and accepted them all. He was gentle, he smiled at her, and was absent-minded about domestic details, except when it concerned the people he cared about. They spent a whole evening, when Charles did not go to the Commons, in discussion with Laura about her future.

"I know if I took a secretarial course, I could get a job at Brandon, Hoyle."

He shook his head. "That's not trying nearly hard enough, Laura. You'd be someone's secretary. Nice enough, but I think you've got more in you than that."

She went on the defensive. "Well, what am I supposed to do to prove I've got something in me? They don't make it easy for women."

"Go and get the qualifications. Get into Oxford or Cambridge, if you can. Follow Kate, if that's what you want. Get into the London School of Economics."

Her mouth dropped open. "But I haven't even got my Matriculation Certificate from Australia. They wouldn't take me here."

"They'll take you if you qualify. Are you just going to sit down and accept what you are now? Remember when you said you were coming to London with us—you had every intention of going on with your education. Get yourself to a crammer. Dig into your books. Do all the things your grandfather would have expected of you."

"I . . . I was thinking of getting my own flat." Her face flushed. "You and Kelly are marvelous, Charles, but I *am* underfoot. I'll get a flat, and then I'll think about what to do."

He leaned toward her. "Laura, do me a favor, will you? Reverse the order. Get yourself into the university first, and *then* leave here. Maybe you won't want to—specially if you are going to be away from London during the term. I'd like to see you have a foothold here. It's home, Laura. Kelly and I aren't kids. We can love each other without having to hold hands all the time. We're older than that. Romance is great, but love is better, and I think we have that. Don't rush out, Laura. You're very precious to us both. I want to see you make an independent life, and you will in time. But don't rush. It's nice when you're working hard to be able to come home to a hot meal, and someone to ask how the day went. And we'll try, equally, not to get under *your* feet. You don't have to come home, but I want you to know it's here."

Suddenly tears were flooding down Laura's cheeks; the scar flamed. "Charles—I don't know what to say . . ."

"Say 'yes,' my lovely girl, and please this old man. For a while, until you go, it will be like having Kate and Julia young again. You'll make *me* feel young."

She flung herself into Charles' arms, weeping as she hadn't since John Merton's death. Over the flow of golden hair which engulfed Charles' shoulders, Kelly silently thanked him.

Laura talked no more of getting herself a flat. She enrolled with a tutor, and she kept strictly to the study timetable laid out. "I've got to do it now," she said to Kelly. "I can't let Charles and Grandfather down."

"I hope you'll have time for a little fun as well, Laura. You don't seem to accept many invitations." There were phone calls from young men—some she had met campaigning, and some with introductions from her grandmother, Lady Renisdale, but Laura often said she was "too busy" to go out. When she did go she was nervous, her manner strained before she left. At breakfast with Kelly and Charles she had little to say. The theater had been "all right." The young man had been "all right." Sometimes even not that. "A bit of a fool."

Kelly sighed to Charles. "She has a sort of double handicap. She's shy, and she still thinks the scar is the most important thing about her. And she thinks they only take her out because they know she has some money. Without the money, she would know it was because they found her attractive."

"She *is* attractive. At times I think she's beautiful."

"But when will *she* know it?"

During those weeks Kelly gave the final orders for new carpets and curtains, new china and glass. The men from Cavanagh's came to measure for the new kitchen, the fittings for the bathrooms. Everything in Number 16 was pre-war—old and dilapidated. The house possessed many beautiful pieces of furniture. "Some of it was Elizabeth's." Charles said. "Some of it came from my family." There was silver with the Brandon crest. But the china and glass represented what was left of many different sets. Kelly began the task of creating order in what had, of necessity, been a difficult and disordered household. Only when she tried to introduce some order into Charles' study did she encounter serious opposition. "Damn it, Kelly, I told Mrs. Cass not to touch my papers."

"She didn't, Charles. *I* did. They're really . . ."

His face tightened. "Just leave them alone. You understand. This is my room, Kelly. I want it left alone." It was the first time in their marriage he had spoken to her less than lovingly. For an instant she might have been a foot-soldier who was out of uniform, a subordinate who had blundered. She drew back and closed the door of his study, half-expecting him to come after her to apologize. But he did not. She had her revenge by going over to Cavanagh's and having lunch by herself, and ordering extravagantly of garden furniture which Charles would have to stare at from his study window, and which she sensed he would not approve of. She ordered chairs and settees, and a table with a bright umbrella, as if England had summers which needed it. She ordered many tubs which were to be planted with small trees and shrubs. She told Cavanagh's to come and measure the garden for more paving. The sooty grass was almost lost in slippery moss. The garden would be gay, but artificial, as city gardens always are. When she got home Charles had left for the House of Commons, and she went to bed early. When she woke the next morning, later than usual, he had already gone. A note was on the pillow. *A director's meeting at ten. Sorry. I love you. See you for dinner.* He had forgotten that this was the day she had arranged to go down to Mead Cottage to keep an appointment with the men from the local branch of Cavanagh's in Cheltenham. Mead Cottage, she knew, would have to be done from top to bottom, not just new kitchen and bathrooms, but heating as well. It was a task she would have to leave in their hands to be done as quickly as possible so that she and Charles could use it at weekends and be in his constituency. The fewer times they had to stay at Wychwood as Louise Brandon's guests, the happier she would be.

In a strange way Charles' new situation, his return to the House of Commons, and his marriage to someone, Cavanagh's now knew, who had inherited money, was working for and against them. Cavanagh's board had renewed their offer to Charles to buy the two houses which their own property surrounded, and had received his refusal. The orders for the complete refurbishing of the house in Brandon Place gave Cavanagh's no hope that Charles would change his mind. In fact, Kelly, by her actions independently of Charles, had made that plain. But General Sir Charles Brandon was once more in politics, talked of as being once again a possible Minister of Defence. He was the sort of person Cavanagh's still liked to serve, and to speak of as a customer, a client. So the order had gone out that Mead Cottage should be done as quickly as possible—as quickly as Lady Brandon would make her choices of what she required. They had made the appointment at Mead Cottage a week ago; Kelly could not break it now. It would, they all knew, take more than a day to decide all that must be done, and she had reluctantly telephoned Louise Brandon to ask if she might stay the night at Wychwood. To have stayed at a hotel, she knew, would have given deep offense, and caused talk in the neighborhood. "Of course, darling," Louise had replied. "Any time. Don't be in too much of a hurry with the cottage. You can always stay with us." Kelly did not intend that. She showered and dressed in a rush, conscious that she was going to be late for her appointment, drank coffee and ate a piece of toast standing up at the kitchen table while she gave Mrs. Cass instructions about preparing food that Laura could put in the oven for Charles that night. She took time to find a good bottle of wine from the basement. "I'll be back tomorrow night. Tell Laura, will you please, Mrs. Cass, to book us some nice restaurant for dinner. I think Sir Charles needs a change from home cooking. Let's hope he hasn't got something important on at the House that will spoil it all."

III

She drove too fast down to Gloucestershire, and arrived, tense and sweating slightly, to find three men from Cavanagh's waiting in a car outside Mead Cottage. From their expressions one might have thought she was no more than two minutes late. It was nearer two hours.

"I'm so terribly sorry . . . I . . ."

"Please don't worry, Lady Brandon. The traffic can be bad at times." Mr. Aubrey, the head of the decorating department at Cavanagh's London store had come to introduce his colleague, Mr. Pike, who worked through the Cheltenham store, and the architect they had hired, Mr. Randall.

"We've poked around the outside a bit. It needs some attention—gutters, downspouts . . . that sort of thing. I think the roof's all right, but I'll have to climb up there to see. But the fabric seems sound. As they say, they don't build them like this anymore. . . . It'll need a damp course . . ." Amiable, cheerful, she thought. And she knew, as they knew, it would cost a packet.

But she needed them if she and Charles were to live comfortably at Mead Cottage, so they started briskly. They went in through the back door. The kitchen was dismissed with a contemptuous wave. "It'll all have to be redone, of course. Modern appliances, new cabinets—"

"I don't want the character of the other parts of the house altered . . ." Everything she said was gravely noted down. They went upstairs. There was only one bathroom in the house; she wondered if they could have another one without an alteration to the outside structure of the house. That would require planning permission, and could hold up the work for months. "There's space—at the end of the hall here—over the kitchen. It's got the window . . . will you leave it in my hands . . .?"

Thankfully she did. "As long as it doesn't take too long."

"I've already talked to the best local builder. He's lucky to have a couple of real craftsmen. He'll submit an estimate, of course . . . you'll want to see that before giving the go-ahead."

From that Kelly knew that this particular builder was expensive. But she would agree, no matter what the price. John Merton had meant her to have the money from Pentland; he had meant it to be spent at the right time. She nodded. "Let me have it as soon as possible . . ." Damn the expense, she thought. She was moving from room to room with the three men, going back downstairs, answering queries, agreeing or not agreeing to their suggestions, and her thoughts were her own. Damn the expense she said over and over to herself. The time for her and Charles was now, not in ten years. And she would never let him know what it had cost. Strangely, away from Charles and with these strangers, she thought of the child she had imagined being born at Mead Cottage, and she felt the emptiness within herself. But there surely was still time for it, she thought . . . still time. As soon as possible she would see a doctor. The premature birth of her only child couldn't have damaged her as much as that. "Lady Brandon . . . are you coming through . . . ?" It was the architect, Randall. They had gone ahead of her, deep in conversation while she had lingered in the old kitchen with the leaking tap and the rusty Aga cooker. Charles' wartime home; Elizabeth's home. Kate and Julia had been young girls here. So neglected and sad now. Yes, she would bring it back to life, and perhaps even give it new life. Charles Brandon might have a son

. . . why did one always think men wanted sons? She jerked out of the reverie.

"What was that?"

"I was saying that some kind fairy has been ahead of us and left lunch and a fire laid in the hall. I was thinking of suggesting the local pub, but this is much nicer. I must say I hadn't expected a room quite as beautiful as that. It's really old—older than the other parts of the house, I'd guess."

Because it was almost a wing to itself and rose the full height of the house, they had not until now been in the main room, which was also the entrance hall—suggesting that this had once been a small manor house. Mr. Pike was standing still, staring about him. "I *say*—this is rather splendid. Much bigger than it looks from the outside. One doesn't know what to expect from these old places, does one?"

Kelly's eyes had gone to the fire neatly laid, with a basket of dry wood beside it. There was a picnic hamper on the old refectory table, a bottle of wine, a thermos. There was even a box of matches. There was no note with all this, but Kelly immediately read Mrs. Page's signature across it. She wished then that they had gone to the pub.

"I'll go and wash my hands," she said. In the bathroom the basin and toilet had been cleaned, and fresh soap and small towels lay ready. She hadn't noticed them before. It was kind of Mrs. Page, thoughtful, but Kelly wished she hadn't done it. It was as if, silently, Mrs. Page had reached into Mead Cottage and reminded Kelly that Elizabeth Brandon had been her friend.

The afternoon passed in discussions of what needed doing structurally, the rewiring of the house, how the heating system might be installed, and in looking at samples of materials with the decorator. The winter dusk came early, and the house was cold. They agreed to meet again the next morning; Mr. Aubrey, however, with his prime task done, was returning to London that evening. "Nine o'clock tomorrow," Kelly said. "I won't be late. I'm staying at Wychwood, and I must be finished here and back in London by early evening. If you like, we'll have a sandwich at the pub tomorrow. I won't trouble Mrs.—I won't trouble my friend to do this again." They helped her pack the hamper and carried it to the car. It was fully dark as she drove toward Wychwood. It was only February; the gaunt outlines of the trees along the drive stood out against a cold and clear sky. There would be frost, she thought, and she wondered if she and Charles could be in Mead Cottage by the time the trees came to full leaf in May.

And then she remembered that she hadn't asked that amiable architect if there was a chance to get the garden and orchard cleaned up a bit. . . . Between Mead Cottage and Brandon Place, there were so many things to remember. She was happy that, suddenly there were so many. As she stopped the car in front of the main door of Wychwood it was opened; she started, caught in a dream of remembrance. With a sense of relief and pleasure she saw that it was not Louise, or Mrs. Page, but Peter Brandon who stood there.

"Louise is in London," was all he had said after he had welcomed her. He had carried her bag, and automatically she had gone up the stairs and headed toward the room she and Charles had shared. Then she turned, questioning, "Yes—just the same," he said. "Mrs. Page wouldn't like it any other way."

She thought, as she bathed and changed, that Mrs. Page was more conspicuous by her absence than if she had been in the room. The flowers more than anything else represented her. Their winter scent did not cloy or cling; faintly acerbic, like the smell of herbs. A presence.

Peter was waiting when she came down. She had never known Wychwood in its moments of quiet, never before without a small crowd of people, never without voices, questions, answers, sometimes arguments. They sat before the fire in the library, drinks in hand. Peter had put a rather scratchy record on the player—Schubert, she thought. "Sorry," he said, "it sounds awful. But it's one of my favorites. I've never been able to replace it."

She looked closely at him. He seemed no different, and yet he was different. The same tweed suit, the same two golden labradors at his feet. Why had she always thought of him as a second to his brother, Nick—why a sort of shadow to his wife? Now he seemed as perfectly relaxed and confident as she had ever seen a man; no need to talk to her about her day, ask questions, fill the air with anything but the sound of the music. How surprising that was, too. Schubert?—it did not go with the image of the country squire in his Land-Rover, his obedient dogs always at his heel. But why an image? He had never claimed one. She realized that in her time at Wychwood he had rarely spoken. But it was not that he could not speak. Now the music spoke, and it was clearer than anything he might say. " 'The Wanderer,' isn't it?"

He nodded, and for an instant a smile of contentment hovered. They listened until the record ended, and he went to turn it off. He said, unexpectedly, as he sat down, "What of Laura? Will things begin to settle down for her now? You care about her very much, don't you?"

Perhaps it was because she was tired, perhaps the activity since she had been married had pressed on her too much, and she had had little time to reflect. She found herself talking—talking mostly about Laura, but through her, talking about Greg also. Talking about Pentland. In this ancient house, with the smell of old wood about her, the smell of winter flowers, she talked of the dry, bare paddocks of Pentland, talked of John Merton, told what he had done for her, what he had given her. She gestured toward the record player. "He even gave me what little I know about music." Then she went on, with a sense of finality and trust. "I don't know what anyone may have told you about me—except about my being married to Greg—the nursing, taking a certificate in teaching—all those things they put out in the campaign publicity. But no one, I think, mentioned my mother. John Merton told me when he sent me to school to say she was the housekeeper at Pentland. It sounded better. But it wasn't the truth. My mother was the cook at Pentland. She came there on probation, and I came with her, uninvited."

His expression did not change—grave, but the trace of a smile still there, as if the Schubert lingered. "You are a very welcome guest in my house, Kelly."

For the first time she felt totally at ease at Wychwood. The warmth of the fire and the drink spread through her; her body relaxed from the ceaseless thrumming of the questions of the day. There was silence, except for the crackle of the fire, silence and the watching face of the man she realized she had never truly noticed before. There was a center of compassion in that silence, and a mutual respect.

"Will you play the Schubert again?" she asked.

During dinner they talked of the plans for Mead Cottage, mostly for the benefit of the elderly manservant, Tennant, who would spread the news eagerly. Peter asked questions, but offered no suggestions. He merely said, "It'll be nice to have you both coming down regularly. Louise wanted you to make your headquarters here, but I didn't think you'd want that. Always being guests." Then he shrugged. "And I had to point out to her that the future of Wychwood itself is doubtful. The taxmen and I are nowhere near agreement on the death duties. I still don't know what I'll have to pay, or what I'll have to sell to settle them."

They returned to the library. Coffee was left on a tray, and Peter poured for them both. "Brandy? I wish you would have it. You look as if you could do with a good sleep."

She nodded. He placed it beside her. "What about giving up the London house?" she ventured. "It would sell very well—it's such a big house, and in that location. It could sell as an embassy. You wouldn't have the expense of its upkeep, either."

He shrugged. "You don't know Louise. I'll have to sell the pictures before the Eaton Square house. I'd have to sell Wychwood itself—all of it, before she'd agree to letting the house go. She doesn't like the country. You must have noticed that."

It seemed as unthinkable as selling Pentland. "She'd never want that. Your two boys . . ."

He shrugged. "The way taxes are, there may be nothing left in a few years for the boys to inherit. The farmers are squeezed, and we're taxed to the limit. We literally can't afford this . . ." He spread his hands. "The Inland Revenue knows it, and I'm being forced to admit it. Oh, we might hold on for a few years, selling this and that. But you can't support a house like this without its land. If I had any loose change, I'd give it to Nick and hope he'd turn a penny or two on it. But I haven't any loose change. Nick's lending me money to carry on. He doesn't want to see Wychwood go, but, after all, it isn't his concern. Not in the end."

In the end, she reflected. . . . He had put on the turntable one of the Beethoven late quartets, and they listened in silence; but the thought of Wychwood troubled her, though the grave serenity of the music seemed once again to be reflected in Peter's face. It was as if he had accepted an inevitable ending, and was resigned to it. It was almost as if he could not be hurt, though he still could be reached. She wondered about Louise and this man. They were far apart, much further even than Kelly had realized when she had stayed here during the stir and excitement of the campaign. In the silence the picture merged of their estrangement, their indifference to each other. A quiet man who lived with music and his dogs and the bitter promise that he might have to sell his inheritance, and a woman who . . . what was Louise? What did she want? Kelly had no idea. The music ended; the dogs, as if well used to it, stirred expectantly. "I'll take them for a walk. And you must go to bed." He extended his hand to help her up from the sofa. "Thank you, Kelly. I've enjoyed this evening more than I can say . . ."

To her immense surprise and pleasure he bent and kissed her quietly on the cheek. "Good night, my dear."

Mrs. Page arrived when Kelly was ready for bed. Kelly had been expecting her. The discreet tap sounded. "Come in, Mrs. Page."

For just an instant the habitual calm of the woman's face was disturbed. Then she smiled. "You're comfortable, I hope, Lady Brandon." She carried a hot-water bottle in a plush jacket, something as English, conventional and old-fashioned as the house itself.

"More than comfortable, Mrs. Page. It was a wonderful dinner, and I hoped I'd see you to thank you for everything you arranged at the cottage today."

Mrs. Page dismissed it. "Very little, Lady Brandon. You must be very busy these days. So much to do, and get used to. Adjusting to a new life . . ." She was slipping the hot-water bottle into the bed, and removing the one already there. "They get cold, you know."

"Well—it's not that I am so unused to English life . . ."

"Oh, but not used to being married to a man like Sir Charles. And being a Parliamentary wife. And all the alterations and redecorations here and at Brandon Place. The entertaining . . ."

Kelly said coolly, "I wonder how you know about what's planned for Brandon Place?"

Mrs. Page smiled at her innocence. "Lady Brandon, don't you think people talk? That's all there is of interest in the country, you know. They go into Cavanagh's in Cheltenham, and they hear you're going to do all kinds of things at Mead Cottage. And of course the word filters through that the decorators have been called into Brandon Place. After all, you're very much news here still, though it might not seem so to you in London. We hear all kinds of things."

"I expect," Kelly said, "about half of them are true."

"You're wise to take that attitude. People will talk about anything when they've not much of interest in their own lives. Can I bring you anything, Lady Brandon? Perhaps a hot drink—some cocoa?"

"Thank you, Mrs. Page. Nothing."

"Then I'll say good night. I hear you want to be out early in the morning, so breakfast will be ready from eight o'clock on." Kelly wondered how she had heard that. Mrs. Page paused at the door. "Oh, Lady Brandon . . . ?"

"Yes?"

"The matter I spoke to you about?"

"What was that, Mrs. Page?" What had they spoken about? Everything—nothing. Kelly felt bewildered and pressed.

"The flat. The flat in the basement of Brandon Place. I asked—"

"Yes—I'm sorry, Mrs. Page. I meant to speak to you about that."

The straight figure was drawn even straighter, as if expecting a blow. "You mean Sir Charles doesn't agree?"

Kelly now knew she had the decision in her own power. Whatever she said now would be final. She thought of Charles' annoyance at the suggestion of Chris Page living in the basement flat. She thought of the excuse that Charles had offered to her of needing the flat for live-in help. Then she thought of the quiet man, Peter, who was now walking his dogs, and the peace that this woman brought to the outside edges of his life. She wondered if a refusal would not be interpreted as a snub to the Indian origin of this mother and her son. And once again she was reminded strongly of her own mother, alone, fighting and willing her only child to have the things denied herself. Suddenly, in her mind, she was back on that station at Barrendarragh all those years ago, seeing the woman with the small child trying to cling to her hand; she seemed to hear again the persuasion, the near-entreaty her mother had used to Delia Merton. Delia Merton had reluctantly consented, and a new life had opened for Mary Anderson and her daughter. She had become cook, and then the housekeeper of Pentland. That night, Kelly had told Peter Brandon what John Merton had done for her. None of it would have happened if Delia Merton had turned them away.

"Yes . . . it's all right," she heard herself say to Rosemary Page. "Sir Charles hadn't thought of letting it to anyone. It hadn't occurred to him."

"But of course Christopher will pay rent, Lady Brandon. He doesn't expect favors."

Kelly spread her hands. "It can be discussed, Mrs. Page. We'll come to some agreement."

That same, strange impenetrable smile was back on her face. Not pleasure, but satisfaction, Kelly thought. "Well, I shall be very happy to tell Christopher, Lady Brandon. May he come and talk to you about it? He'll telephone. Good night, Lady Brandon."

After the door had closed, Kelly shrugged at her own reflection in the mirror. Mrs. Page had got what she wanted.

The next day was one long jumble of samples and color matches and contrasts, chintzes pretty and exotic, shapes of bath and hand basins. She grew weary of it long before it was all decided. But it had to be decided. In the end she was choosing almost at random, trying to resist the decorator, and finding her resistance slipping as she strove to sort out the multiplicity of choices. "We can't do anything adventurous, I'm afraid," the decorator sighed. "This house just won't stand it. Now if I were doing Brandon Place . . . but Andrew got *that* job," he added, sounding peeved.

"Who's Andrew?"

"Why, my colleague at Cavanagh's in London. Mr. Aubrey's assistant. We work together sometimes."

"You mean you've come down from London just for this job?"

"Well, naturally. It's a whole house, and needs to be done in a hurry. I *had* to see it. It's part of Cavanagh's service. You don't think they keep a decorator at Cheltenham all the time, surely, Lady Brandon?"

She hadn't thought of it at all. The store across the road in Brandon Place seemed to be assuming a large part in her life in these last weeks, and she would be dependent on them for many more to come. "What would *you* have done at Brandon Place? Have you been there?"

"No, but I've seen the plans. It could be opened up more . . ." He gestured expansively. "Sir Charles' study could be a delightful garden room—enlarge those windows. A piece of Victoriana, perhaps . . . the study could be moved upstairs . . ." He sighed wistfully.

Kelly smiled. "You wouldn't get far with Sir Charles, I'm afraid. He won't have anything touched. I doubt I'll even be allowed to have it painted. New curtains and a bit of new upholstery are the most I can hope for."

"Men *do* get so set in their ways, don't they?" he sympathized. "Well, shall we do the big room now? Perhaps we could try something a bit grander here . . . a touch of velvet, perhaps . . ."

The architect, Mr. Randall and a young assistant were measuring up, murmuring quietly in the background. The place overflowed with samples. Kelly couldn't remember what she had chosen. "Well, I think we've got it all, Lady Brandon. You'll slip across to Cavanagh's some time soon, won't you, please, and choose the beds and headboards. And the sofas and chairs, so that we can get on with covering them.

We'll have to do some scouting about in antique places to get a few pieces for this room. It won't be cheap, I'm afraid."

Nothing was cheap, Kelly had decided. They had had morning coffee, and lunch, as the day before, from the hamper Mrs. Page had insisted on providing. Mr. Randall built another fire; the lunch was cheerful, but rushed. Kelly was conscious of time slipping by. From the brilliant morning she had driven out in, the sky had now clouded, and the grayness of the short winter afternoon was nearly upon them. Kelly looked at her watch, and thought of the long drive ahead. "I'll have to go, I'm afraid. Is there anything else?"

"Nothing you need bother about, Lady Brandon," Mr. Randall replied. "Maurice and I have just a few more measurements to take. Look—if it'll save time, I'll leave the hamper back at Wychwood for you. If it's all right with you I'll keep the key. Or, if you like, I could leave it with Mrs. Page . . ."

"No," Kelly said hastily. "Keep it." Mrs. Page already had too much to do with their lives, she thought. And then it occurred to her that Mrs. Page already had a key; there could have been no picnic hamper yesterday without it. "Yes—I'd be grateful if you'd leave the hamper back at Wychwood." She regretted that she wouldn't see Peter again; he had already breakfasted and was gone by the time she had come down that morning. But even if she went back to Wychwood he probably wouldn't be there. And she was conscious of needing to get back to Charles. They had come perilously close to a quarrel the last time they had spoken; the slight breach needed to be healed. She needed to be home to bathe and change, and she hoped Laura had chosen a good restaurant. She hoped no last-minute business would keep Charles at the House. Mr. Randall promised her plans of the alterations within a week. "I'll lay out the kitchen, and you can see what you think. No need to come down just to look at the cabinets. They've got everything on display at Cavanagh's . . ." They saw her to the car like solicitous uncles, she thought with slight amusement. Leave it all to them—and Cavanagh's. She was in good hands, they seemed to say. Trust them. All she had to do was pay the bills. As she drove she thought of John Merton who had made it all possible, and wondered if he would have approved this wholesale handing over of her authority to men she had never seen until yesterday. That had not been how things had been done at Pentland. But times were gentler then, the pressures fewer. She reminded herself that she had wanted these crowded days after the empty years. She had welcomed the turmoil, the rush. She was finished with the deadening quiet of those years after Greg had died. She joined the flow of traffic on the main road to London, and turned on the car radio. As if by arrangement she caught the opening bars of the Beethoven quartet Peter had played last night, that work of infinite beauty and finality, and its hint of impending mortality. An indefinable sense of urgency made her increase her speed.

It was raining as she put the car away in the mews garage. Cavanagh's was closing, and a little trickle of people hurried away from its doors. On the Brompton Road side of the store she knew people would be queuing for taxis, but in Brandon Place it was quiet. She hurried along, head tucked into her coat collar against the rain, fumbling in her handbag for keys. The light in the hall of Number 15 was on, but the fanlight of Number 16 was dark. Charles must still be at the House, and Mrs. Cass would long ago have left. She hurried inside, switching on lights, throwing her coat and bag on a chair in the hall; she fluffed up her hair in front of the mirror and powdered her face, a little amused by the vanity which prompted her to do this in case Charles would return suddenly. She got ice from the kitchen, and brought it up to the drawing room, switching on all the lights there, and drawing the curtains on the Brandon Place side. She went through to the other end of the room, and saw, as she looked down across the garden to Charles' study, that the light was on there. He was home, then, and hadn't heard her come in. Perhaps he also had been in a hurry to get home, because of those few angry words spoken. She smiled a little, and went and poured a drink for them both. They would have it in his study, and she would say nothing about the untidiness, say nothing about the new curtains, and the hope of, at least, having the room painted.

She pushed open the swing door to the passage with her foot, but at the door to Charles' study she halted. "Charles—it's me. I've got my hands full. Open the door, will you, love?" He hadn't heard. "Charles! Charles—open up." Now the silence held disappointment. He wasn't home at all. He must have left the light on this morning—or even last night. She put one glass down on the floor, and opened the door.

He was slumped back in his chair, his arms hung limply over its sides; a newspaper had slipped to the floor, its pages scattered. His mouth was slightly open, but his eyes were closed, and his brow wrinkled as if he had braced himself, and willed himself not to feel something. And she knew it had been pain.

"Charles!" She put the glass down on the desk, the ice rattling violently against its sides. "Charles!" She bent over him and touched his forehead, her other hand going automatically to feel for a pulse. She tried to still the trembling of her hand because she couldn't feel a pulse if her own hand shook. She put her ear beside his mouth, striving to hear the faintest breath, and against his chest, hoping for the sound of his heartbeat. His hand and his forehead were cold. "Charles . . ." she repeated, but now without hope.

She reached for the telephone and dialed 999, asking for the Ambulance Service, but she knew it was uselss. She guessed he had been dead for some time.

Then, with no feeling of urgency at all, she telephoned the doctor who lived in the next square, someone who had attended Elizabeth in the last years. Kelly had never met him. He was at home, and he was at the Brandon Place house in less than five minutes. She opened the door to him.

"Lady Brandon, I'm . . ."

"He's in the study," she said dully. He went with confident familiarity, to the back of the house.She watched as he made the examination, and knew that he would shake his head as he looked up at her. "I'm very sorry. . . . It's terrible for you. There was no indication at his last checkup of heart trouble. Everything appeared normal . . ."

She had begun gathering up the newspaper which lay on the floor. There were bold headlines about something, but she didn't see them. "I was only trying to get him to tidy up a bit," she said, and was aware that she didn't make sense to the doctor.

Then the doorbell rang again. "I'll answer it," she said. "It will be the ambulance."

She opened the door. The uniformed men stood there, and suddenly the reality of what had happened came to her. She found herself unable to say anything. They looked at her, perplexed. "We had a call for this address . . .?"

She licked her dry lips, and no words would come. At that moment Marya came at a run along Brandon Place. She dashed up the steps, thrusting aside the two men. "I saw the ambulance . . . what is it?"

Kelly looked at the questioning eyes, saw the anxiety. "It's . . ." She faltered, and then said, "He's dead."

"My God!" Marya's arms enfolded her as she began to shiver violently.

Julia flew from Chicago, where the National Ballet was then performing, for the funeral. Kelly, Kate and Laura were already at Wychwood. When Julia arrived, looking tired, her face pale and too gaunt, they embraced, but there were no tears. None of them seemed able to talk about Charles, to say the usual things—that it had happened so suddenly, so unexpectedly; that he was too young, that he had so much still to do. There was a kind of dumb disbelief among them. To utter Charles' name as if he were dead would be to admit it, to admit the pain, and none of them seemed willing to do that yet.

The notice in the newspapers had said that the funeral was private, but the little fourteenth-century church at Wychwood, which held effigies of long-dead Brandons, was packed with mourners. The local people had considered that the notice did not apply to them, since this was the Brandon home, and Charles Brandon had come back to be buried among them. All of them, though, resented the photographers who had appeared, and there was a general closing of ranks around the family to protect them. Little murmurs of sympathy reached Kelly as she walked between Peter and Nick to the open grave. Julia, Kate and Laura faced her across it. Mrs. Page and Christopher were behind them, both faces set like molded plaster masks. Louise was theatrically beautiful in black; Kelly caught a glimpse of Marya, red-eyed, wisps of hair escaping her old fur cap. Mrs. Cass looked truly stricken. Phoebe Renisdale squeezed her arm silently. The words were said at the graveside, the symbolic clod of earth fell on the coffin with a terrible sound. Charles Brandon lay beside his first wife, Elizabeth, and in a plot next to his parents. All around, some nearly indecipherable with age, tombstones were inscribed with the Brandon name. The flowers the local people had brought, against the wish expressed in the funeral notices, spread all about them, overflowing onto graves of forgotten Brandons. As she walked down the path to the lych gate, a camera flashed above Kelly; someone had positioned himself on its roof. She was aware of anger, rather than grief.

The big funeral car drove them straight back to London, against Louise's wish that they stay on at Wychwood. They did not return directly to Brandon Place, but went to Heathrow airport. Julia had to be in New York the next day for the opening of the ballet there. Tomorrow night she would dance *Firebird* with Sergei.

"How will you do it?" Kelly said. "You look exhausted."

Julia shrugged. "I never ask myself that question. The company will be around me. They are like another family. Sergei will be there. I will go to class tomorrow morning, and somehow the muscles will warm up and begin to relax. I will be tired, and that probably means I will give it everything I've got. Sometimes I dance very well when it's like that." But her face seemed now not just pale, but gray; her eyes dark blue smudges.

"Be careful, Julia," Marya's cracked voice said. "You wear yourself too thin."

Julia protested that they should not wait at Heathrow until the time of her flight. "You'll only be stared at. I'm going economy class. You have to wait with the mob."

Marya thrust the cigarette into the corner of her mouth as she rummaged in her handbag. "I almost forgot. Nicholas would have killed me. Here is the first-class ticket. He hoped you would be able to get some sleep. Make them give you plenty of vodka." She handed over an already dog-eared ticket to Julia.

They were taken to the First Class lounge, and given the vodka Marya demanded, and finally saw Julia walk up the steps to the aircraft. For once she did not walk erectly; her head was bowed. At the doorway to the plane she paused and looked back at the long line of the airport buildings, as if seeking them. They waved, but the lights blazed on her, and she could not see them. After a moment, she turned and disappeared. "So—there is courage, that little one," Marya said. "Come, we must go back. Mrs. Cass and I prepared a lot of food. We probably won't eat it, but we should try."

It was Marya's arm which propelled Kelly up the steps at Brandon Place, her hand which opened the door. Without it, Kelly thought she might have turned and just gone away. With the opening of that door into the empty hall, she knew that she must finally face the fact of Charles's death.

IV

There was a terrible interval of more than a month when they had to wait for the preparations for the memorial service. This was when Charles ceased to be the private man and became the public one. Officials of the Order of the Garter came to Brandon Place to explain to Kelly what would happen. They guided her through the ritual of the service; the form was set and seemed unalterable. Even the appropriate hymns were suggested to her. She wanted it over immediately, but she must wait.

In the first week the senior partner of Charles' firm of solicitors came to Brandon Place to read Charles' will. Kelly was stunned. She had not thought of Charles' will; it was such a little time since she had listened to John Merton's will being read. The solicitor asked that the family, and Marya, be present, along with Mrs. Cass and Laura. Of his family, there was only Kate to attend. It was a simple will, made in the first week after Charles' return to London with Kelly. It made a bequest of one thousand pounds to Mrs. Cass, and the rest of his estate, real and personal, was left to Kelly "with the certain knowledge that she will deal with my beloved daughters, Julia and Katherine, and with my friend of many years, Marya Nicholievna, with justice and kindness, and will allow them to enjoy the tenancy of Number 15 Brandon Place for as long as they so wish. I also desire that my wife, Victoria Jane"—how strange that sounded—"shall allow my daughters, Julia and Katherine, my friend Marya Nicholievna, my beloved goddaughter, Laura Merton, and Mrs. Hilda Cass to make a choice among my personal effects of any keepsake they may wish to have, always provided that my wife shall have first choice among said personal effects."

Kelly sat, white and stricken, after the solicitor had left. "How could he?" she demanded. "It isn't fair to leave it all to me. What about you—and Julia—and Marya? He should have at least left Number 15 to you."

"He didn't expect to die till we'd all departed, one way or the other, Kelly," Kate said. "Look at it like that. Nothing changes. I presume you don't mean to throw us out? All we'll do is pay rent to you now, instead of him."

In spite of herself, Kelly smiled. "You're a bad liar, Kate. You never paid a penny rent, and you won't start now. Marya, you mean to stay, of course? It won't make any difference?"

Marya's face twisted as she lighted a cigarette. "You are sure you wouldn't like another tenant?" She held up her hand as Kelly started heatedly to protest. "All right—all right. No need to chew me up. I'll stay! I'll stay! It's a big payment though for a trifling service to a woman and a man who were so good to me. Eh . . . how that flight from Yalta hangs on. We'll have some vodka, yes? And have a good cry, if we feel like it. Though the Colonel would have preferred us to laugh, I think."

It was while they sat drinking Marya's vodka, Mrs. Cass perched on the edge of a chair, sniffing at the scentless stuff suspiciously, that the telephone rang. Laura went to answer it, as she had done each time since the funeral. They heard her voice clearly. "Yes . . . yes . . . who? Oh, yes. I see. No, I'm sorry, she's not available to come to the phone. I'll ask her." She returned to the room. "Kelly, I'm sorry. But it's Cavanagh's . . . the decorating department. They're also calling for a . . . a Mr. Randall, an architect in Cheltenham . . ."

"Bastards!" Kate interjected. "Haven't they the decency to wait . . ."

"They want to know," Laura continued, "if, in the circumstances, as they nicely put it, you wish to proceed with the plans for Brandon Place and Mead Cottage. They'll quite understand if you want to postpone everything, but if you want the work to go ahead as you asked, they must know at once."

"Postpone?" Kelly took a large gulp of the vodka; the shock effect of it caused her tongue to pucker and her face to tingle. "No—tell them to cancel it. Cancel. Tell them to send the bills for their time." The two days at Mead Cottage seemed a lifetime away, the plans were dim shreds of memory. She looked at the shabby curtains, the worn carpet, they now appeared familiar and loved, a part of Charles' legacy to her.

As Laura relayed the message, Kelly extended her glass toward Marya. "A little more, please."

"Ah, so you think you want to keep it all as he left it?" the woman said as she poured. "Not so healthy. But perhaps now is not a good time to be disturbed by them hammering and banging. Later . . . perhaps . . . and yet . . ." She also looked around the room. "I also am fond of it. I've known it this way for a long time . . ."

Laura stopped going to her tutor. "Why?" Kelly demanded. "Charles wanted you to do it."

"I don't feel like it," Laura said simply. "Something has happened—almost as much to me as to you. I simply don't feel like going."

They had to fill in time. Life went on, but for them it did not. In the remnants of the London winter, they set off on a round of the sights that brought the tourists. One day, without reason, Laura said, "Would you like to go to the Tower? It's so long since we've been." The roles were reversed. Laura was no longer the young child whom Kelly had sought to amuse and entertain and inform. Now it was she who announced where they were going, she who paid the admission, bought the booklets, guided Kelly through the places. They walked the great rooms of Hampton Court, stood on the steps of the Victoria Memorial in the rain to watch the changing of the Guard. Laura led her into the hushed and empty beauty of the Chapter House of Westminster Abbey; their footsteps echoed with a lonely sound in the cloisters. They went to Greenwich and looked at the misty river from Inigo Jones's great colonnade. They went to Eton and stood in the Chapel where Charles had attended service for so many years. And then, finally, Kelly realized that Laura was walking her across the bridge, and Windsor Castle stood on its height wtih St. George's Chapel seeming to guard it. "No, Laura . . . I don't think I want to go there."

"I think we should. Then it will be easier when the day comes. It's a sort of preparation."

So they entered St. George's Chapel, the home of the Knights of the Garter. It was almost deserted. Few tourists came in March. They stood looking at the intricately carved choir stalls, roped off with red velvet, which also housed the stalls of the Knights of the Garter, their splendid heraldic banners suspended overhead, the arms of all those who had been members of the Order through the centuries wrought in enamel on gilded brass, fixed to the wood above the stalls. They did not ask the attendant if they might go and look at Charles' stall. With his death it was his no more, and at the Memorial Service his banner and Garter star would be offered at the altar.

Kelly gripped Laura's arm tightly. "Yes, we were right to come." They went back to Brandon Place, and Kelly understood the reason why Laura had taken her through the sights of that month. She was showing once again to Kelly the England which had been Charles'; the things that had shaped the man. Kelly understood that, and knew that she had had to be stiffened in this understanding. But, she thought, the days were long, and, dear God, she whispered to herself, the bed was wide and empty.

The crocus which she had hopefully thrust into the sooty ground in the little garden in November appeared and bloomed; then the daffodils carpeted the London parks; the time for the Memorial Service had come.

Kelly was ready an hour before the cars were due to arrive. She paced the hall, dressed in the black she had bought especially for the occasion, hoping that she did not look, as Louise had done, theatrical. One by one the others appeared. Kate, surprisingly, also wore black, a neat new coat, and a small round velvet hat that made her little pointed face look elflike. Laura had chosen a pill-box hat in the style that Jacqueline Kennedy had made famous, which allowed her blond hair to flow freely; the scar was barely visible under her makeup; she seemed more nervous than any of them. Marya sat and smoked; she wore her usual coat, and the old fur hat. Mrs. Cass had new clothes. Julia arrived last. Her beauty could not help but look theatrical; black became her as any other color did. In the two weeks she had been back in England she had not cast off the look of exhaustion which they had seen at Charles' funeral. The tour had ended, a brilliant success, and a personal triumph for her. But she had shown the notices halfheartedly to them, as if, for once, she did not care. There was talk that the great, but aging ballerina who was the star of the company, would finally retire, and Julia would be premiere ballerina. Kelly had read that in a newspaper; Julia did not talk of it.

Kelly paced; there was little talk among the others. Suddenly she turned to them. "If the cars come, tell them I won't be a minute. There's a phone call I have to make." She ran along the passage to Charles' study to the telephone, ignoring the one in the hall, because she needed to make this call unheard by the others. She hadn't entered the room since the day Charles had died there, and she had told Mrs. Cass not to go there either. It was not locked, but it was as if an invisible tape were stretched across its door. In her sudden need, she broke it. She found the number in the directory and lifted the telephone which she had last used to call the doctors to Charles. This call was quickly completed. How easy it was to command things when there was money to pay for them. She went back to the hall.

"Laura, can you get your passport? Do you know where it is?"

"Passport? Why?"

"Because—because if you want to come, I have seats for us both on a Qantas flight to Sydney this afternoon. We should be able to make it after the service."

From all of them, in differing tones, came the exclamations. "Kelly! . . . Lady Brandon!"

"Why?" Laura said again.

"Because I've decided to go home. To Pentland."

The doorbell rang. Laura raced for the stairs. "Tell them to wait. I know where it is."

"Bring mine," Kelly called after her. "Top right-hand drawer of the dressing table."

Mrs. Cass had opened the door. "The cars are here, m'lady."

Kelly witnessed, as if she were far-removed, the procession of the blue-cloaked Knights, saw the cushion which held Charles' banner and star borne to the altar. By June, the Queen would have appointed someone else to fill the vacant stall, and Charles' arms in enamel and gilt would be enshrined there, to remain as long as the Chapel did, perhaps for another five hundred years. She followed the order of the service, did as she was directed, and finally walked down the steps to meet the flashes of the cameras.

"Well," Marya said, after she had managed to gain readmittance to the First Class lounge at Heathrow, "only the rich and the very poor can travel without baggage, but *nobody* can go to Australia without a toothbrush." She handed a package she had bought at the stall downstairs to Laura. "Now have they got some vodka in this place? My God, that church was cold. The kings who lie there must be very cold in their graves."

Somehow she managed to bridge the strangeness of the occasion. It had seemed unthinkable to drive straight from St. George's to Heathrow airport, but now it was done they all knew it had lessened the hurt of the occasion, though Kelly, looking at Kate's face, listening to Marya's flow of talk, watching Mrs. Cass sipping her glass of dark, sweet sherry, knew that the real hurt would come for them when she and Laura boarded the aircraft. She could admit nothing less than that she was running away, finally taking the step she had wanted to after Charles' funeral. And, selfishly, perhaps, taking Laura with her. Their roles were indeed reversed. She was too much reminded of the day Greg had walked down the aircraft steps in Sydney to the flashing of camera bulbs, and had almost thrown Laura into her arms.

The flight had already been announced when Peter Brandon arrived. "Kelly—Kelly!" He called from a doorway where an airline official was trying to keep him out.

"Peter . . .?"

Shrugging, the official opened the door. Peter half ran to

them. "I didn't know when you'd be taking off. I just guessed where you were going. I've had a hell of a time trying to find you."

"How did you know?"

"Saw your cars turning off into the airport. I left Nick to drive Louise back into London. He was furious. I hitched a ride into the airport, and just followed my nose. Couldn't get anyone down at the desk to admit that you were on this flight, but I saw there was one scheduled for Sydney."

"Why?" She had to say it. "Why did you come?"

He shook his head, as if the question had not until now occurred to him. "I don't know. I just . . . well, I just . . . I suppose . . ."

"Qantas announces the departure of Flight No. 260 to Rome, Beirut"—the other stops were jumbled into a blur—"and Sydney."

"But Peter, you shouldn't . . . I didn't want to inconvenience anyone. I didn't want . . ."

"Oh, rubbish," Kate cut in. "Peter's only saying what we all feel. We're sorry you're going, but we know why." The lounge had emptied now. The airline official approached them. "Would you and Miss Merton mind going to the aircraft now, Lady Brandon? The captain informs us that the flight is scheduled to take off on time."

She kissed Julia, Kate, Marya, Peter and, finally, Mrs. Cass. She saw tears begin to streak Julia's eye makeup. To her astonishment, Mrs. Cass bobbed in an old-fashioned curtsy. "Good luck, m'lady. I hope you come back soon."

It was Laura who took her arm as they walked to the aircraft, and Laura who handed the boarding passes to the cabin steward. They were almost alone in the first-class section, absurd with their paper bag of cheap airport toiletries which Marya had bought. "I expect she's got some dreadful lipstick," Laura said. "She always wears such hideous colors herself. But it was lovely of her to think of it, wasn't it?"

"Yes . . . lovely."

Laura leaned over and fastened her seat belt. "You're too seasoned a traveler, Kelly, to forget that."

"Today, Laura, I seem to have forgotten the whole book of rules."

"About time."

V

At Pentland the land lay brown and seared by the summer heat, but the coolness of autumn had come, and at night the stars blazed in the clear, dry air. Kelly drew back the curtains of her room so that she could watch them, because she often lay wakeful, listening to the night sounds of the vast, throbbing land about her. Occasionally a night bird called; there would sometimes be a shrill cry as prey was taken by predator; in the stables a horse would whinny. There were the sounds that had always been at Pentland, unchanging. The human sounds were few. She would sleep from weariness, and be wakened at sunrise by the harsh laugh of the kookaburras, the crow of the rooster.

The days had a sameness. There seemed too much time. She and Laura rode, played tennis, swam in the pool which had been newly filled with water when they arrived. They spoke little; there was little to say. They played John Merton's records, read his books as they had always done. Kelly turned her mind to the affairs of Pentland, and found that she was not much needed. A year before John Merton's death a new manager had been engaged; his name was Bill Blake, and he had a wife, Nelly, and three children. He did his job well. She went over the accounts with him, and found them in order. The accountant, Ian Russell, came out from Barrendarragh, stayed overnight, and checked the books with her. Then a man from Frank McArthur's firm came up from Sydney and reviewed with her and Laura the investment portfolio which John Merton had left to them. "Must I?" Laura asked. "Can't I leave it to you—and the solicitors?"

"The world," Kelly said, "is full of fools who leave others to look after money and wake up to find it out of their hands. Money is a responsibility. It needs decisions. One of the most important is how you will distribute it. These are the charities your grandfather regularly supported. You have to decide if they are the ones *you* want to support. Find out how they are run. Is the money well spent? Most important, do you really want to give it."

"I'd carry on just as he did."

"That's lazy. It might be the right answer, but you should know. And then, Laura, we have, between us, to decide what shall be sold to pay the estate duties. Your grandmother's income must be left intact, and Pentland must not be touched. Some things will have to be sold. You have to listen to advice, and then make the decisions. Eventually we will have to go to Sydney and look for other advice—second opinions. If that offends Frank McArthur, then so be it. But look, Laura, how long ago the Mertons began. Look how long ago these shares in Broken Hill Proprietary were bought—by your great-grandfather. Those are the ones you try *not* to sell . . ."

Delia Merton greeted their arrival almost with indifference. She had never made a fuss of Laura, having long ago accepted that by Greg's wish, she was Kelly's charge. She hardly attempted even to talk to them. The meals were silent affairs, unless Laura and Kelly talked to each other. Occasionally Mrs. Merton would sit with them in the library when they listened to music, working on her tapestry, but mostly she kept to her own sitting room with the shelves of hand-bound books. She sat for long hours on the veranda, staring out at the paddocks, her eyes seeming to be fixed on the first gate, as if she were forever expecting someone to arrive. Few did, and then always having telephoned ahead. She only once referred to Charles' death, and that was several nights after their arrival. "It didn't last long, did it?" she said. "You didn't have much time with him—not enough time to tell how it was going to work out."

"It worked out, though," Laura said sharply. "It was a good time." Kelly said nothing.

They made several overnight visits to the stations about, exchanging news, gossiping. But there was a kind of constraint between them and their hosts, a faint unease. Greg Merton had been almost an exotic stranger among them, but Charles Brandon had belonged to a wholly wider world. That both had chosen to marry the daughter of a woman who had come to Pentland as a cook was still something of a wonder to them all. She might be regarded only as the girl Greg Merton had chosen to be the nurse of his child, and then her teacher-companion; she might be thought of as someone an aging man, newly released from an invalid wife, had happened upon and married in haste, but nevertheless, she had been Greg Merton's wife, and she was now Lady Brandon. She and this young blond stepdaughter who stayed so closely by her side were now the owners of Pentland. In only a few months all this had happened, and in the long days of sipping tea and beer, Kelly knew that over and over again this must have been the topic of conversation whenever people met. She had hoped, by taking Laura to visit some of the other stations, she could somehow break the barriers of strangeness, but it did not happen. She had thought, with hope, that perhaps Laura would show some interest in one or other of the sons of the neighboring families, but that hope died at the moment when she watched Laura among them. They had little to talk about. Laura was the daughter of an Englishwoman, as well as Greg Merton's daughter, and the English side seemed uppermost on these occasions. She displayed flashes of John Merton's acuity at times, and the sophistication of Lady Renisdale's dinner parties. She seemed aloof among these young people who should have been her friends, and how were they to know it was shyness? When the talk turned to horses, hers quite naturally turned to hunting in England; she actually preferred an English saddle. The visits only seemed to throw them both more into isolation, and their own company. They would return to Pentland with a sense of relief.

Kelly's mother was no more unbending than before. Whenever Kelly came to the little house with its garden proudly sporting asters and chrysanthemums in defiance of the bareness all about them, she was received with almost the same indifference that Delia Merton had shown. Mary Anderson commented, without enthusiasm, on the election campaign. "He won—but the papers said it was a safe seat. There was a bit about it in the *Sydney Morning Herald.* And the *Barrendarragh Chronicle* played it up, because of Pentland. But they said the Brandons practically had it in their pocket in any case, so it was no great victory."

"You didn't like him, did you?"

"Like him?" Her mother shrugged. "I didn't know him. What was there to like? He was a big name, and not much to go with it. *You* brought him a lot. He would have had an eye for that."

Kelly rounded on her. "That's not fair. When we married I had only what Greg left me."

"That is as may be, but John Merton wanted the marriage. He might have said something . . ."

Kelly put down her cup of tea. "You trust no one, do you? Nothing is good or decent. There's always some other motive . . ."

Her mother regarded her steadily. "Why should I trust anyone? I did that once, and see what I got. You are the result of that trust. Whenever I look at you, I see *him*—your father. You were tainted from before your birth. No wonder you carry such ill luck with you. Two husbands, and both dead. You shouldn't have married either one of them. I was against it. I told you so then. I still think it. You've no humility, Victoria. You fly in the face of God. The sins of the fathers . . ."

Kelly rose. "I've heard enough of this rubbish. At times I think you must be more than a little mad. Tainted—ill luck. You'll have me believing it if I listen much longer."

"Believe it, woman! You've overreached yourself. And the mighty shall be cast down . . ."

Kelly left, and she did not go to her mother's house again. A few times she encountered her in the kitchen of the big house, but they exchanged few words. She noticed that in the late afternoons Delia Merton and Mary Anderson each sat in cane chairs on their own verandas, within clear sight of each other. She sensed once again that both women had joined in an unspoken alliance against her, their shared disapproval of her binding them closer. Without the cleansing presence of John Merton, the atmosphere at Pentland seemed polluted with malice and ill will. Had it always been as bad as this? Kelly wondered. Had John Merton shielded her and Laura from so much? Or had the simple fact of his death, and the revelation of his will made it so much worse? She couldn't be sure of that, but she began to feel that she was choking in those days of clear, bright autumn sunshine.

She said to Laura, "I think I'd better go to Sydney."

Laura nodded. "Let's go and pack."

The flat at Vaucluse had been given up, and they stayed at the hotel. They spent a lot of time with Frank MacArthur listening to advice about John Merton's estate, advice on how to manage his legacy. She had written briefly to Charles' solicitors in London giving the name of this firm as a forwarding address. They in turn had sent mail to Pentland. There were bills to pay in London. Letters had come from Kate and Julia and Mrs. Cass. She and Laura were missed, they all said, each in her different way. *It's sad to see the dark half of the house*, Marya wrote. *How is it with you out there?—and who was it said you can't go home again?*

She and Laura filled the days, letting time pass over them. They saw acquaintances from the years when Kelly had worked on so many committees; Laura contacted some of her old classmates. Neither of them fitted in with any of them. There was curiosity about Kelly. What would she do now, everyone asked. Go back and run Pentland? Take another flat in Sydney? No one said, "Will you marry again?" but everyone thought it. Knowing that, Kelly was tempted to say aloud, "Whom should I marry? Who have you got for me now that you didn't have before? It's not so long, is it? And is there anyone for Laura?" Instead she said, "I think I'd like to travel a bit. Laura and I have been talking about going to America." They hadn't been, but it sounded as likely a place as any other.

It really didn't need talking about. They found themselves on a plane for Honolulu. "How odd," Kelly said, "that we've never headed East out of Australia before. Do you think we're a bit mad, Laura—all this dashing about? Can't settle. What did I expect of Pentland without your grandfather there? I wasn't really going home. I was running away."

"We'll run a little longer," Laura said. "It doesn't hurt. No, Pentland didn't seem like home, did it? How different it is without Grandfather. Your mother and my grandmother—they never say a word to each other, but the atmosphere crackles between them. What a waste!"

"A waste of what?"

"A house. They really should get together. They're so busy disapproving of everyone and everything that they'd be better teamed up." She began to laugh. "Next time we go back we should suggest that your mother move into the big house, and you and I will have the cottage. It would make better sense."

In the days of the early American summer they drove from San Francisco down the Pacific Coast to Los Angeles. It grew hotter as they turned inland. The roads were better, the driving easier, than anything they had known in Australia. The desert fascinated them—different from their own in a spectacular fashion. They descended into the Grand Canyon on mules. "God . . .!" Laura breathed, "everything's so big!" It was said as if she uttered a prayer. They turned north then, toward Colorado, where the snow still lay on the peaks, and the rivers tumbled in white water. They went where they pleased, stayed wherever the place took their interest. They stayed in big hotels, and small, remote lodges. Some stays were overnight, some were for days. They rode, enjoying the big western saddles, enjoying the splendor of the country, the sense that they were either holding time back, or outrunning it. There had never been a time quite like it in their lives. No one knew where they were; no mail reached them, no telephone rang for them. There were no dates. They wrote a stream of postcards to Brandon Place, and Laura, more out of a sense of mischief than anything else, sent many cards to both Delia Merton and Mary Anderson. "They'll each be trying to read the other's," she said.

They edged East slowly lingering in the beauties and noting the evidence of stark poverty in the Appalachians. They visited the horse country of Kentucky, and rode on English saddles again. They reached Washington, D.C., and Laura demanded that they go each night to stand at the lighted Lincoln Memorial. "It's the most beautiful thing I've ever seen," she said passionately, the idealism of her youth caught by the Lincoln story. They skirted New York, and went on to Boston, and then up to Maine. "I always wanted to see what the real Yankees were like," Kelly said. "Sometimes they're almost too much like Norman Rockwell characters. They can't be real."

It was the end of August before they turned once again toward New York, and joined the summer visitors in its humid heat. Galleries, museums, more postcards, shopping for clothes that seemed different from anything either of them had ever had before. Like most who visited there, they went up the Empire State Building. There had been a thunderstorm the night before, and the air had cleared. At that height the wind whipped them. "Do you know what date it is?" Kelly said. "It's September first. Almost autumn." They could see back and forth along the whole island of Manhattan, across to the New Jersey shore, over to Long Island. They stood for a long time looking at where the Hudson and East rivers flowed together and swept on out to the Narrows, and beyond that to the Atlantic. "Funny, in all these years we've never seen it from this side. Never crossed it." Kelly looked at Laura. "Well—shall we turn and go back, or will we cross it?"

The decision was made for them that night. Laura had bought some magazines from a stall in Times Square. She lay on her bed, half-watching television, and flicking through them. Abruptly she sat up. "Kelly—look here!"

She offered a magazine called *Dance*. Among a number of small items in a column, the name of Julia Brandon leaped out. Julia Brandon will not dance the lead role with Sergei Bashilov in the new Malenkenov ballet planned for the autumn season of the National. Doctors say the broken ankle, the result of a fall in rehearsal, may keep her off the stage for as long as six months.

"Shall we telephone her?" Laura asked. To this point they had never talked of telephoning anyone. In both of them there was a sense that they did not want to lay on anyone the burden of their own loneliness, their rootlessness. They had so briefly shared the lives of those at Brandon Place that neither of them could believe the attachment had been permanent.

"No," Kelly answered. "I think we'll just go and see her." It was an acknowledgment that the time of running was over.

PART II

Chapter Six

I

Kelly and Laura arrived unannounced, and it was one of the few times there had been no one at Heathrow to meet them. But they had grown used to the anonymity of the past months, and it did not seem odd. They took a taxi to Brandon Place, and it was only when they stood on the pavement, Kelly searching in her bag for the now-unfamiliar keys, that a sense of something being different overtook them. It was not just the lack of welcome, but that the place itself wore a strange aspect. Keys at last ready, Kelly froze at the bottom of the steps.

"What's happened?" she half-whispered to Laura.

"Someone's been—*at* it," was the reply.

The old shabby doors had been painted a shade of yellow which seemed subtly to compliment the olive-green of the Cavanagh doors all along the street, the basement area railings gleamed with fresh black paint, the walls of the two basements had been repainted in white. Black-and-white tubs filled with multi-colored annuals—a few late petunias, geraniums, some early dwarf dahlias—stood by each door, their rather gaudy abandon mocking the chic sentinels of the Cavanagh potted bay trees. It stopped there. The facades of the two buildings were as cracked as, and even more in need of paint than the day they had left to attend Charles' memorial service, and had not returned.

"Who did it?" Laura wondered aloud as they moved the bags into the hall of Number 16. "Not Kate—it isn't her thing. Not Marya. She wouldn't—and she's too busy. Certainly not Julia . . ." The September dusk was falling; they turned on lights in the hall of Number 16. The kitchen was tidy and bare; Mrs. Cass's tea cup was upturned on the drainboard, a solitary tin of biscuits on a counter was testimony to the little use the room now received. Laura opened the refrigerator—empty except for a half-used bottle of milk. "Perhaps we should have let someone know . . ." She walked back into the hall, and from long habit unlocked and opened the double glass doors between the two houses. She looked up the stairwell, and saw only the faint glow that came from the skylight at the top. "I don't think anyone's at home." She looked at Kelly. "I've never known it so quiet. It feels . . . empty." She advanced as far as the first landing. "Kate . . . ? Julia . . . ? Marya . . . ? Anyone at home . . . ?" Her voice seemed to echo desolately up the stairs of the tall, narrow and silent house.

They listened and at first they heard nothing. Then there was a muffled crash from the level above Laura, as if something had overturned. There were a few more noises, and then abruptly the door of Julia's flat was flung open, slamming back against the wall. "Laura . . . ? Is that you, Laura?" It was almost dark. Kelly, rushing to join Laura on the landing could make out only vaguely the figure in the doorway. It was outlined against the last of the light which came from the window of the room that overlooked Brandon Place, but it was that slender, unmistakable figure.

"Julia . . . *Julia.* It's us! We're home . . ."

A sound like a sob broke from the figure which now clutched the doorframe. "Kelly! . . . Laura! You're home. Oh . . . you're home!" Then faintly they heard the words as they rushed to meet her embrace. "Thank God . . . oh, thank God."

A walking stick fell from her hand as she stretched out her arms to them.

After the first greeting, lights were switched on. There was a babble of questions and answers not listened to. "All the postcards," Julia managed to say. "We kept getting the postcards, and no one knew where you were. It was awful . . ." Suddenly Kelly was deeply aware of the selfishness of that flight away from Pentland and every sort of world they had ever known; their freedom might have been a novelty, but it had given pain. She saw it now on Julia's face, and with amazement she saw that the beautiful, fragile face was marked with tears. "Oh, damn—I didn't mean to cry. If only you'd let us know . . . I would have been all prepared and smiling."

"We didn't want to bother anyone."

"*Bother!*—oh, Kelly, how could you possibly bother anyone here? If you only knew how we've missed you. It's been so . . . so . . ." Julia never had been very good with words; they failed her utterly now. Her lips twisted in a smile, and a kind of radiance glowed from behind the tears. She gulped, and gave an oddly hysterical laugh. "You know . . . we thought you were lost . . . or kidnapped . . . or something. If it hadn't been for those damn postcards we would have gone crackers worrying. Of course, Marya thought it was all some big plot of the K.G.B. . . . the postcards were faked. At times, after a few vodkas, she had you in the Lubyanka prison. Well, it's over. You're back. You'll all right? Of course you'll all right. You both look marvelous. What were we worrying for?" She bent then and picked up the stick. For the first time they had a chance to examine the cast on her ankle. "I'll tell you—it was pure selfishness. We thought you'd left Brandon Place behind you forever. We were afraid we'd lost you."

Kelly took a deep breath, and carefully wiped the tears from Julia's face with a crumpled tissue she took from her coat pocket. "Of course you knew we'd come back." But they almost hadn't come back. She had lived so few weeks, weeks of happiness and almost breathless chaos, in this house, and she had begun to think of it as yet another way station in her life. But people had waited for her here, waited and hoped. Brandon Place had enveloped her once again. Charles' ultimate legacy had been his family.

They returned to the kitchen of Number 16; Julia, encumbered by the cast, made her way with painful slowness down the stairs. Kelly and Laura said nothing about the injury except, "we read about it in New York." Julia would talk about it when she was ready. She hesitated a moment as they went through the glass doors. "It's so lovely to see them open again—the lights on. Oh, but you *should* have told us. We would have had everything as it should be—flowers, champagne—just the way Marya did it when Father brought you here the first time. Oh, remember that . . . ?" Her voice faltered; she lowered her head and concentrated on moving stiffly toward the kitchen. "There's probably nothing to eat. We could go out, I suppose . . . but I wish just this first night we could all have been together here. I don't know when Kate and Marya are coming in . . ."

"Chinese food," Laura said firmly. "We'll send for it. There's that place on Brompton Road that delivers. What's it called? The Golden Something. We'll have a Chinese feast." She was flinging open the cupboards. "There's booze here from the time we went away, and there's Charles' wine . . . Julia, you should have been with us when we had a Chinese meal in San Francisco! It was like nothing you've ever tasted."

"But I have! The company was in San Francisco . . ." She went off into a string of recollections. She and Kelly began to exchange views on the places they had seen in America. "I *loved* it," Julia said. "I've never felt so alive. There's a vitality there . . . I can't explain it. Sergei felt the same. Being there was the most exciting thing that's ever happened to him. He keeps on talking about it . . ." So Sergei was still there, Kelly thought, still uppermost in Julia's mind; there was still the note of almost adolescent longing in her voice when she spoke of him, as if she had never had another love. Even under the harsh light of the overhead lamp in the kitchen she still seemed to Kelly ethereally lovely, though the delicate modeling of her face appeared perhaps just a shade too pronounced, the bones too fine, almost sharp. She had lost some weight; her hands clasped before her on the table were transparent and blue-veined.

Laura had gone back to Charles' study to bring the telephone books and hunt for the name of the restaurant; now she was on the hall telephone, having a mild argument with the restaurant manager. "Then send the boy in a taxi. We'll pay. Yes—everything!"

"What have you ordered?" Kelly asked when she came back into the kitchen.

"Everything! He kept saying it was too much. But I thought Marya and Kate might come in . . . and I'm ravenous myself." Laura leaned over and touched one of those transparent hands. "Tell me you're hungry, Julia. You *look* hungry. I'll bet you haven't been taking care of yourself properly."

Julia shook her head. "I might have forgotten about food, but Chris never let me. He's been so good. He comes and gets my breakfast every morning, and brings the shopping in the evening. Takes things to the cleaners, posts letters . . ." The words trailed off as she regarded their uncomprehending faces. "What is it?"

"Chris? Who's Chris?" Laura asked.

"Well, you know him, for heaven's sake. Chris Page! From Wychwood. He's . . . he's living in the basement flat." She looked from one to the other. "Kelly, you *said* he could. Have you forgotten? He didn't just make it up, did he? Mrs. Page would die if she thought he was here without your permission. He told us he's been sending the rent to your bank every month. I'm sure one of us must have mentioned him being here when we wrote to Australia . . . well, perhaps you didn't get those letters. The postcards started to come very soon after that. You did say 'yes,' didn't you? We just assumed something informal had been worked out. No one wanted to bother you. Oh, God—did we do something wrong?" Her tone faltered once again on that note which was near tears. For a moment she once again looked from one to the other, her blue eyes wide and defenseless, and slightly panicked.

Kelly managed to smile as she shook her head. "My fault, Julia. I *did* say he could come here. How can one refuse Mrs. Page anything? And as you say, it's only Chris, and he *is* very good. He worked so hard for Charles. But I'd completely forgotten it. He didn't get in touch with me after—after Charles died. It just went out of my mind. I suppose he was waiting until after the memorial service. He couldn't have counted on my doing a bolt right after it. He may well have written to Australia. There were so many letters. If the envelope wasn't typewritten, I didn't even bother to open them. You know . . . those sympathy letters. Yes, Julia—it's all right. I mean, *really* . . ." She took the bottle of Scotch Laura had put on the table and poured lavishly for them all. "Perfectly all right . . ."

"You saw what he's done outside," Julia said eagerly as she added water. "It looks nice, doesn't it? He paid for the paint and tubs and flowers himself—and did all the work. He's painted the whole flat, and put up new curtains. He's got a few pieces of nice furniture—and some of the modern stuff with lots of bright cushions. He's put up shelves. You'd never imagine that gorgeous thing could actually be handy, would you? I suppose, though, if you're Mrs. Page's son, you're naturally efficient. I was amazed when I saw what he'd done with the place. It made me realize we'd been a pretty slovenly, careless lot. Things could have *looked* nicer for very little extra money. None of us thought about it . . ."

"I don't know . . ." Laura said slowly. "Well . . . it isn't my business, I suppose. But I think it was a bit of cheek him actually moving in here when Kelly was away. He might have waited . . ."

"For what?" Julia asked, her voice now sharp with anxiety. "For all we knew, you were never coming back. Your letters didn't say *anything*. We realized it was shock. After all, what did we have the right to expect? We weren't your family. You'd only been here such a short time. We were afraid to ask you to come back because it seemed to be placing such a burden on you."

"So you see," Julia rushed on, "when Chris came and talked to us, it seemed so like you to have said he could have the flat. It was his risk. He had no lease, and he spent his own money decorating it. You could have him out tomorrow . . . if that's what you want," she finished lamely.

"Chris can stay. I *did* tell Mrs. Page he could. If he's been a help—"

"Oh, he has! It's been like having a younger brother. But he's nicer—kinder than I imagine most brothers are."

Kelly shrugged. "There, Laura. That's it. We're rather short of men in this household. And helpful men are hard to find. I think we'd better keep him." She looked at Julia, and the smile grew to warm laughter. "Don't look so guilt-stricken. It's all *right*!"

Julia sighed, and her tense shoulders relaxed. "It's selfish, perhaps, but I was *glad* he was here. It didn't make it so lonely after Father—and you both—had gone. He helped Mrs. Cass clear out all the things from Mother's old rooms—" She nodded toward all the glass doors and the room in which Elizabeth Brandon had spent the last years of her life. "We put an old sofa and a couple of chairs in there. It made a sort of sitting room for us all to use. We didn't think it was right to use Number 16. I suppose we were still trying to be some sort of family, and yet not to get in each other's way too much." Her voice wavered a little, and then she brightened. "The two Brandons have been here quite a lot—Nick and Peter. I think that was when we thought about putting in the sofa and chairs, and a drinks table. Funny, I can hardly remember Nick or Peter coming here before. Oh, just occasionally, to see Mother—but that was more of a duty visit. Now they come because they want to. You made the difference, Kelly, you and Laura. Most of the time we were together we talked about you, wondered where you were."

Kelly poured more whiskey into Julia's glass. "Well, the worry's over. It was thoughtless—but perhaps Laura and I just needed that time away from everything. We were a bit like irresponsible kids. We're back now." She nodded toward the kitchen window where the curtains had not yet been drawn, and the lighted windows of Cavanagh's shone out in the dark. "Perhaps I'll get them to dust off their plans for this house—you never saw them, did you, Julia? Perhaps I'll even think about Mead Cottage again. Not as elaborate as we talked about, because it won't be needed as Charles' constituency office . . ." She found she could now bear to think about Mead Cottage, actually bear the thought of it without Charles. She remembered the dream she had had of a child being born there; the memory still carried pain, but she was no longer unable to confront the pain.

"Yes," she said briskly, "there's lots to do." She realized that she had once again begun to set up a framework of a life, a life without a man in it, but a framework of a life. She looked at Julia, whose gaze was hungrily fastened on her, and she had a sense of gratitude that there was, once again, something to do. "I can't wait for Kate and Marya to come in. I wonder when . . ."

The doorbell of Number 16 rang. "That'll be the food," Laura said. "I'll get it." They could hear the familiar ticking sound of the London taxi motor. Laura opened the door, and ushered in a young Chinese, his arms piled with sealed plastic boxes. He placed them all on the kitchen table between Kelly and Julia. "Everything!" he said, as if he was hugely enjoying the thought. "Shrimp. Pork. Chicken. Beef. Fried rice. Snow peas. Water Chestnuts. Bean sprouts. Spare ribs." Then a grin suddenly split his flat features. "Some party you're having, ladies!" They all laughed, and Laura paid him, paid for the taxi, and added a large tip. He looked at it. "Ma'am, you *must* be hungry! Have a good meal." The front door slammed, and the taxi started up.

Laura turned on the oven, and started looking for dishes to put the food on. "Darling Mrs. Cass. Everything's been kept so clean. Almost as if she'd been expecting us to walk in here just the way we did."

Under the clatter of the dishes, Julia's hand unexpectedly closed on Kelly's. "Thank God you did . . ." Kelly had nearly missed it.

Laura set about transferring the food from the plastic

boxes to the oven dishes. "You haven't said how it happened, Julia." She was squatting down, trying to juggle the dishes in the small oven. "You know—your ankle."

"Well . . ." This time Julia poured her own drink. "Look at me, drinking all this. I won't be able to get back upstairs again. Just as well I'm not dancing tomorrow—" The jug banged against the rim of the glass as she added water. She took a swallow, and another. "Well—it was just unfortunate. You see it happen. It happens to other people, and you hope it doesn't happen to you. Malenkenov had choreographed a new ballet. A Stravinsky suite. Rather harsh, brutal music. At least, that's the way it sounds to me. But he had done it for Sergei because Sergei is mad to try every sort of modern music—to try his technique on it. You know how hamstrung they are in Russian ballet because they never get anything new to dance, nothing to experiment with. Well—this is to be Sergei's ballet. His *real* introduction to the West. *Attitudes* it's called. It's really a display piece of his technique, not his lyrical quality. I thought that was rather a pity because he is such a beautifully lyrical dancer. But he is mad about it. There's no scenery—no plot. The costumes very stark. The lighting—"

Laura banged closed the oven door. "Julia, for God's sake! What happened?"

She took another swallow of her drink, as if bracing herself. "I was coming to that. You see—I was to be his partner. There are only two parts. A wonderful honor. The first ballet created around Sergei and me. We dreamed of dancing it together all over the world. The choreography is very difficult—demanding. But Sergei seemed literally to sail through it—or to fly. I had to put every nerve into it, and I knew I wasn't quite making it. We rehearsed, and rehearsed. I know I was very tired when it happened. I was to make a *grand jeté*, and Sergei was to be there to hold me at the end. But I . . . I missed, somehow. I ended up where I shouldn't have been. Sergei tried to catch me, but I crashed down. My own fault. I don't know why it happened. I was a full two feet from where I should have been. Tired, I suppose. I'd given four performances that week. Of course, class and ordinary rehearsal every day, and then extra rehearsals of the new ballet. Tired . . . so stupid of me. It was just bad luck that it should have been a break, instead of a bad sprain. Sergei blames himself. But it was my fault. Just tired. That's what's so terrifying. To be a dancer and to realize suddenly that you can't go on forever. To know you're wearing out—running down. I thought I was too young for that. You watch it happening to the other ones, but you never believe it will come to you. But it happened to me that day. I just wasn't up to it. So tired . . ." Her eyes seemed to mist with tears, and then she raised her glass again, and drank. When she lowered it she was smiling again. "Well, no one ever pushed me into ballet. I did it myself. You accept the aches, the hurting feet, the bad knees, the bunions. You accept it because you want it. It's harder to accept that it will end."

"But it's going to be all right," Laura protested. "Your ankle will be all right. You'll dance again."

Julia's head snapped back. "*Of course* I'll dance again. I have to wait until the cast comes off. That's the hard part. The weeks are slipping by. Every day I'm away from class means it will take that much longer to get back to form again. Well, naturally I can't expect Sergei to wait for me. The ballet will go on as they planned it. It wouldn't be fair to hold him back. Maria Kalchevna will dance my role. It's a great opportunity for her. They say . . . they say she's very good in it. And she's only twenty-two." Kelly heard more despair in the last words than in all that Julia had said before.

"Sergei?" she asked gently. "Do you see him often?"

"Every day," she said. "Even the nights he's performing he dashes over here in a taxi and we have an hour or so together before the performance. He says he's only warming up on the *barre* up there, but actually he's helping me to exercise—just a little." Her expression took on a defensiveness as she realized that Kelly and Laura were disapproving of that. "Well, I have to do *something*. I can't just sit here. I think the doctors are wrong. I have to move or I'll freeze in place. I must move my hips—take a little weight on that ankle." She gestured irritably. "They just don't understand, those people. If we don't keep on using our bodies they begin to rust. That's what I feel is happening to me. I'm rusting—I'm being rusted into place."

"You won't rust, Julia," Laura said crisply. "I've never seen anyone less ready for the scrap heap. You just need patience—and a little company. Just as well Kelly and I came back. We seem to be needed."

Julia didn't protest anymore. "You don't know yet how much you've been needed," she said softly, and the tears slid down her cheeks once again. She wiped them with her hand impatiently. "Oh, it's the drink. I'm not used to it."

"It's better that I go upstairs and get some vodka." The

voice seemed saturated by too many years of cigarette smoke, but the tone was strangely subdued. Kelly raised her head quickly, and Laura spun around.

"Marya!—oh, Marya!" The strong chunky body of the Russian seemed to envelope Laura in its embrace. "Little one—little one, how we have missed you both!" She rocked the girl for a moment, shorter than she but seemingly possessed of far greater strength. Kelly went to her, and found that somehow Marya's arms were able to encompass them both. "Oh, how we have missed you! This dark, empty house. I used to come and switch on a light sometimes, as if I was lighting a candle to guide you home. I *knew* you'd come back. What a sentimental old woman I have become!"

They found vodka among the half-used bottles. Marya settled herself happily at the kitchen table with them. "Ah, now it gets like home," she said as she drew on her cigarette, and took the first gulp of vodka. "And I hope that is food I smell. Something good. Tonight should be a feast."

"It is a feast, Marya," Kelly promised her. She found herself oddly affected by the sight of the Russian; the great vitality of the woman came across to her strongly, she with the familiar dark and crookedly applied lipstick, the beads, the jangle of bracelets, the trailing scarf, the strong features and dark, thick hair. Was there noticeably more gray in the hair? Did the features look tired, masked somewhat by the snapping life in the dark eyes? Had so much changed since the day Kelly had literally fled this house and this family? She looked from Julia to Marya and knew it had.

They talked, asked questions, hardly waited for answers. "I'm still translating," Marya said. "A few days a week for the Royal Institute—scientific stuff and very dull. But I am also on all the publishers' lists, and occasionally there is a novel to do. I've even tried the Foreign Office again. They have relaxed the old ban to the extent that they let me translate documents of the utmost dullness, and unimportant trade things. They seem to have dropped the idea that I might be a spy." She laughed. "There are enough things being sold to Russia and being bought from her these days that there are always business letters to write. I feel I could write half the contracts myself now, and probably do a better job. Dull . . ." Her eyes shifted from Kelly to Laura. "Tell me about America," she demanded. "Now *that* is a place I'd like to see, if only because its existence annoys and intrigues the Russians so much!"

They talked of their journeying—how restless and aimless

it now seemed. Gradually they began to talk about Pentland, and the two women who inhabited it. They sat around the bare table and ate spare ribs, dabbing with paper napkins at the sauce that dribbled down their chins. It grew late. They stuffed themselves on the Chinese food, and the restaurant manager had been right; there was too much of it. Laura kept portions of all the dishes heated in the oven. "Kate's not away, is she? She'll be in?"

"Oh, yes," Marya said vaguely. "You know Kate. She keeps her own timetable. She's as . . ." She hesitated. "She's as independent as always. No one ever told Kate what to do—or not to do since she was about twelve." She looked at Julia. "Well, you are both your father's daughters. You do not make life easy for yourselves." She switched her attention to Kelly. "Julia has told you about your new tenant?" Her shrug indicated that she was doubtful about his presence. "I held out the longest, though I had no right to say anything. But it was Mrs. Page who really convinced Julia and Kate that it was all right. She came one day and talked to them both. The formidable Mrs. Page. Who could doubt her when she said that you had agreed that Christopher could have the basement flat? For a time I feared that she might take to spending nights in London, with him, but that has not happened. We have never seen her again. I suppose it was Nick Brandon who finally persuaded the girls that it was all right. He seems fond of Christopher. He was anxious that he should have the flat. Indeed, I think he imagined he was going to be some sort of protector for us all here." She gave an inelegant snort. "As if we needed it . . ."

Julia shrugged. "Perhaps we did—until Kelly and Laura got back. God knows, we don't seem to be doing very well with our lives . . ." Once again there was the undercurrent of despair in her voice, a kind of gloom that Julia had never before exhibited. Kelly put it down to the natural depression she was suffering from her inactivity, the loss of the chance to partner Sergei in the new ballet, the loss of dreams. But why had she said, "we"? Marya appeared to be all right, displaying the same feisty toughness that must have characterized her whole life. Julia would recover, would dance again, though she worried that the great roles might now be beyond her. Kate . . .? No one had really talked about Kate.

Kelly brought it into the open. "You don't say much about Kate. She's well, isn't she?"

"In excellent health," Marya assured her. "Robust. Kate is as she always has been. Just as Julia is. You have to be strong to dance. They both are strong." Marya might have been talking as if Julia was not present. Suddenly Kelly felt chilled. It was that time of year, September, when it seemed too early to turn on the central heating because the days were still warm, but at night the chill crept around one. She remembered the fire of New Year's Eve that she and Charles had sat before, toasting themselves and their future in champagne. She could not hold back the memory. All around them the house was dark and empty. She had to bring it back to life, alone, without Charles to do it for and with.

She said, "It's cold, isn't it?" She looked at the littered table before her, remembered how she had stuffed herself with food, how much she had drunk. "I suppose I'm tired from the journey. You forget how many hours you've been on the go. The flight was delayed. When Laura and I started flying regularly from Sydney to London it used to be quite a glamorous thing to do. Now it's like a bus." She realized that she was too tired now; she had sounded maudlin and stupid, complaining when there was little to complain about. She looked at the litter of the table, and hoped that Mrs. Cass was coming in tomorrow. She thought of having to carry up suitcases, and make up beds, and her senses shrieked to revolt.

Marya had been observing her closely. Marya would help, she knew, if asked, but she was being very careful not to overstep the bounds of her own side of the house. Kelly thought of the makeshift sitting room they had set up in the room that had been Elizabeth Brandon's, and she thought of the empty drawing room above them, which no one had dared or wanted to use. They were going to ask her to draw these strands of family together. She welcomed the task, but tonight she was tired.

"Kate!" Marya said, as if she had read Kelly's thought. "She's back . . ."

Laura sprang up and rushed through the glass doors. "Kate!" they heard her call. "Kate, we're home!" The light had been snapped on in the other hallway. There were sounds, exclamations, as the two women clung together. Laura's voice again, high-pitched with excitement and fatigue. "Oh, it's good to be home." They couldn't hear the rest of it, or Kate's reply.

Then she stood clearly in the light from the kitchen, her arm around Laura. Kelly rose, rather unsteadily, to go to her. She felt Kate's arm, as strong as Julia's, as strong as Marya's, around her. "Welcome home, Kelly. We've missed you." It was as close as Kate would ever come to a sentimental statement.

Kelly drew back a little to look at her, and she saw the difference. Kate had gained some weight; the urchin face had lost its famished hollows, the chin was not quite so pointed. Her black hair was still worn short, and it gleamed in the light. Her skin had a kind of glow to it, a radiance Kelly had never seen before. She stepped back a little further. Kate wore a dark red dress, loosely cut, smarter than her usual style. Kate's eyes, though, went to the litter on the table.

"I hope you greedy pigs have kept some for me. Like most mothers-to-be, I'm ravenous. They tell me it's quite usual."

Kelly clutched the edge of the table. "You're going to have a baby, Kate? No one said—"

"Good of them, I'm sure," Kate said crisply, picking up the last spare rib and beginning to gnaw on it. "They wanted me to be able to give you the good news myself. Well, you see"—she paused to chew and swallow—"for me it *is* good news. I've always thought I'd like a kid. That thought never automatically included marrying its father."

Kate drew out a chair and seated herself at the table. Laura had begun swiftly to bring hot food from the oven, clearing a space among the dishes for Kate's plate. She kept her head down, not looking even at Kelly. Kate regarded the food for a moment, and then said, "Got an extra glass there, Laura? It's been a long day, and I'd rather like a drink." Kelly got the glass and poured lavishly. She struggled for words, and found none. Kate herself added a small amount of water to her whiskey. She raised her glass. "Laura, stop fussing and come and sit down." She looked carefully around the table. "Aren't you going to join me? I don't like to drink alone." Kelly found herself with another glass of whiskey in front of her, not wanting it, but knowing she would drink it.

Kate raised her glass, and drank. Then she said, "You're more than welcome home, Kelly—and you, Laura. We've missed you, all of us. I hope my news hasn't shocked you. I'll never marry the baby's father, though I'm quite fond of him in an odd way. I never considered an abortion, though, really, getting pregnant was an accident, of sorts. I wasn't being very careful, so perhaps I wanted it to happen." She dug her fork into the fried rice and bean sprouts, and ate. "He asked me to marry him—but I think he really didn't want it, so I said no. Why go through the motions when it would only end in a divorce? It seemed such hypocrisy. At least, when my kid grows up it will know that *I* really wanted it. I intend to keep it, of course. You wonder how I'll manage for money? I'll manage. Others do on far less, and without the education I've had. All these years working with welfare cases hasn't quite washed over my head. I've learned a few tricks about survival. I intend to survive, and so will my kid."

"Your career . . . ?" Kelly said softly. She despised herself for the waver in her voice, the tightening in her throat, the unreasoning fear that surely was more fatigue than anything else. Tomorrow, she told herself, she would be as calm and confident as Kate herself.

"Career?" Kate put a large butterfly shrimp in her mouth. "My career will go on. It'll test everything that the Labour Party has ever said about women's rights when I present them with a fatherless baby. But I intend to push on, and keep asking them when they'll let me stand for my own seat. If I'm good material for the Party, I'll be as good with a baby as without. Can't you just see all the mums voting for me because I have a gorgeous-looking kid? And as for the ones who don't approve, well I don't want their votes anyway. They'll probably all be Tories. Oh, yes, I'll go on. I intend to take anything the hecklers can give. It's my right to have a child if I want one." She dug into the pile of steaming chicken. "Interesting. The baby's name will be Brandon. If it's a boy, that means Father's name will go on. I wonder what he would have felt about his first grandchild . . ."

She put her fork down and looked at Kelly. "Oh, Kelly, don't go and cry on me. I didn't want to hurt you, or worry you." She rose and went around the table to sit beside Kelly, taking Kelly's hand in her own rather rough one. It's going to be all right." Then her own voice seemed to tighten. "Dear God, Kelly, it's good to see you here. I didn't realize how much I'd been counting on you coming back. Perhaps I'm not quite as strong as I think. A lot up front, and just a little bit frightened at the back. Oh, damn—now I'm bawling too."

Laura said carefully, "I'll help look after the baby, Kate. If you're going to go on working, you'll need baby-sitters. My rates are very low."

Kate had finished her meal and was slowly finishing her drink, when Christopher Page arrived. He halted in the door as they all had done. Kelly looked at him, blinking in surprise. She had not, nor had any of them, heard him come in. Then she realized that he must have gone down the outside basement steps to his flat, and then back up the interior staircase and onto this floor.

"Welcome home, Lady Brandon. Laura." He strode across the room and grasped her hand. She couldn't remember having extended it. "I saw the lights and guessed you'd come. It's good to see you both back." She was aware once again of his almost impossible good looks; his smile and his welcome seemed so genuine. He *was* pleased to see them.

"Forgive me—you look rather tired. I see the bags are still in the hall. I'll carry them up, shall I? The beds aren't made up, but I know where the sheets are. Shall I get on with that while you finish your drink? No, Laura, don't bother. I'll do it. You look tired, too." He turned at the doorway. "I must say I'm relieved to see you safely back here." With a final smile, he was gone. They could hear his whistle as he started up the stairs with the first two suitcases.

Julia spread out her hand eloquently. "You see what I mean. He's done so many things for us—and we've let him do them."

II

Kelly breakfasted on tea and a biscuit, and made out a food shopping list at the kitchen table. Laura seemed still to be asleep, and Kelly envied her the ability to sleep away the fatigue of the journey. She went then to Charles' study and telephoned the grocery order to Cavanagh's; she might as well give up the pretense that they did not shop at Cavanagh's; there was no longer Charles' pride to think of.

When she put down the telephone she looked at the great pile of post that had accumulated, laid on Charles' desk by Mrs. Cass in the order in which it had arrived—a great jumble of letters, bank statements, bills, advertisements, invitation cards, the various journals Charles had subscribed to. She untied the strings Mrs. Cass had put around them to contain them, and they flowed over the desk, a sort of avalanche which slid onto the floor. She sighed, and opened none of it. Then she sat for a time looking around the room. It was untidy, as it had always been. Mrs. Cass had strictly followed instructions and touched nothing, moved nothing. She had obviously tried to dust, but there was little space which was not already covered with papers and clippings. She looked at the bank of filing cabinets against the wall, all of them locked. Charles had always done his own filing, he had said. There had been no money for a secretary once he left the Army, except the one he had shared at the House of Commons. So whatever was here were his own private papers. Kelly wondered where the keys were, but she knew, apart from stacking the papers already here, and putting them under a dust cover, she probably wouldn't do anything in this room, touch nothing. She thought wryly that someone, someday, might want to do a biography of Charles, and theirs would be the task of sorting through those massive files. For the time being they would stay as they were.

She turned and looked for a time at the little garden shared between the two houses. She would go on with the plans to fix it up. Julia could get some exercise by walking here. And then, with a stab of shock, she realized that by next summer they would need the garden for Kate's baby. She got up from the desk and stood by the window, thinking of the baby's pram standing there in the sun—the spring sun. Kate was four months pregnant; the baby would be born in February. Charles' first grandchild. As she stood there she was aware of something unfamiliar, something that had not been there when she had last looked at this scene. For a moment it evaded her, and then she realized what it was. The top of the back windows of the basement of Number 15 were visible from here. She remembered them dark and dirty, rain-washed soot clinging to them, nothing to be seen beyond their grime. Now they reflected the garden in their light. The frames and sashes had been painted white, curtains of bold modern pattern hung at the window—unlined curtains, inexpensive, but striking. She could see white walls, and had the impression that there were shelves filled with books. A plant in a pot hung from a hook in the ceiling, getting what light it could. Chris Page . . . as Julia had said, how could he be other than efficient with such a mother, but who could have guessed at his taste. He was kind, Julia had said. Kelly remembered the bed made up when she had gone upstairs last night, even—she had hardly believed it when her feet had touched it—a hot-water bottle. The suitcases, hers and Laura's, had been sorted out by their labels and were in the right rooms. She had expected him to be clever because Nick Brandon had said he was; he was also skillful with his hands; he had grace and manners. But who would have expected a hot-water bottle? The thought made her laugh. She turned away from the window, left the study, its memories and its pile of post and papers to be dealt with, and prepared to go and meet Mrs. Cass in the kitchen.

The remains of last night's meal had been cleared to the drainboard; the two women sat for a long time over tea, Mrs. Cass occasionally dabbing at tears. "Oh, m'lady, it's so good to have you back home. Poor Miss Julia. I know she's so worried . . . about her dancing. And there's Miss Kate, got herself in the family way. Says right out she won't marry the man, whoever he is. What's the world coming to, m'lady? And Madame Marya . . . well, she used to be able to handle those two very well. But she's a bit down in the mouth herself. I suppose it's one thing on top of another. I can't tell you what it's been like, waiting for you to come back . . ." Mrs. Cass, Kelly thought, had never doubted that she would come back. But then Mrs. Cass had no conception of Pentland, of the life there, of the responsibilities that now rested with Kelly. Mrs. Cass had been born in London; she couldn't imagine that, given a choice, anyone would choose to live elsewhere. "But Mr. Chris, he's been such a help. You saw what he'd done to the outside? Really raised my spirits, it did. It was good to have a man around again, I'll tell you, m'lady. And then Mr. Nicholas, he's been visiting quite often, and Mr. Peter's been a few times. I think they knew everyone was rather lonely. Have you seen the sitting room they fixed up? Quite pretty, the room is. The carpet's still in good condition, and the curtains are all right. Sir Charles insisted a few years ago that there should be new curtains and carpet for that room. He wanted it as nice as possible for Lady Brandon and the visitors who came. What a *good* man he was . . . well, m'lady, you'll be missing him more than any of us, I dare say." She poured herself another cup of strong tea, and added three spoonfuls of sugar. "Well, where would you like me to turn to first, m'lady? I've just kept up the old routine for dusting and hoovering . . ." She ceased talking as the doorbell rang. "I'll answer, m'lady." She sprang up, delighted to have a real task to do.

A moment later she called from the hall. "Did you order from Cavanagh's, m'lady? There are boxes and boxes of things here . . ."

Kelly joined her in the hall. "That's right, Mrs. Cass. I gave an order. We seem to need everything . . ."

Mrs. Cass started to weep again as she surveyed the kitchen table covered with boxes of groceries, meat, fruit and vegetables when the delivery man had gone. "Oh, m'lady . . . it's really as if life's starting up again. I'll just take Miss Laura a cup of tea and a bite of toast, and then I'll unpack this lot." For just a moment, though, she hesitated, and her hand wandered over the apples, oranges, bananas, the packets of biscuits, the pieces of cheese, the fresh bread. She looked like a woman surveying a treasure trove.

III

Kelly and Laura had lunch in Julia's flat, eating cheese, biscuits and apples as they talked. Julia brought out a bottle of white wine. "It's lovely to have someone to eat with at lunch time. I *do* miss the company. There was always something interesting going on—not always nice, but interesting. It's such a bitchy, jealous little world—but I'm at home there."

Kelly had only been in Julia's flat once before—a hurried visit with Charles for a cup of coffee soon after she had come to Brandon Place, and everything had been new and bewildering. Now Julia took them through it as if it were for the first time. Kelly hadn't remembered how spare it was. The sitting room contained only a sofa, two chairs and a low table. The floor was bare polished wood. The wall behind the sofa was entirely covered with framed photos of dancers—some of the great names of the past, dead, perhaps, before Julia was born; some belonged to the generation immediately before her, some were autographed pictures of her own contemporaries. Central to all these was a photo of Sergei in a spectacular leap from *Le Corsaire*, and beside it, another photo of him in practice clothes, drying his face with a towel, standing at the *barre*.

There was space for so little furniture because one wall of the room was completely mirrored, and the wall opposite supported a *barre*. A tape recorder and two speakers were on the floor under the window. It was all as spare and lean as a dancer's body. Only the bedroom gave a hint that Julia, the woman, lived here. The bed was wide and covered with a luxurious down quilt; there was a padded headboard and big soft pillows. The dressing table had another close-up portrait of Sergei. There were cupboards full of clothes, rows of shoes neatly placed. The bathroom seemed one big array of cosmetics and makeup, with a mirror surrounded by theatrical lights. It smelled of bath salts and perfume. Expensive underwear hung on a line stretched across the bath. The kitchen was small and tidy and bare; food did not absorb a great deal of Julia's attention. She managed to walk without a cane as she led them through the flat, but her walk was slow and hesitant. "I suppose you don't remember much of this, do you, Kelly? Kate's and Marya's flats could nearly belong to the same person. Books and books and books . . . I feel such an ignoramus when I go up there. I only read, well . . ." She gestured to the stack of magazines, mostly of ballet and modern dance, on the table. "Chris has been bringing me novels to read—popular stuff. He doesn't expect me to be an intellectual like Kate, and he knows how bored I get . . ."

They sat on the sofa and finished the wine. "Well," Kelly said, "since you've got time on your hands, perhaps you'd like to help me with the house. I've decided I'm going to go ahead with everything at once. We might as well have chaos for a while, and get it all over with. I'll give it all back to Cavanagh's to do. The outside and all. It all needs repointing and painting. I hesitated to do too much before because Charles . . . well . . . I went right up to the top this morning and from the stains on the ceiling, I think the roof needs attention, I must ask Marya to let us look at her flat carefully, because she's right under the roof, and it would show there too. We'll have the builders check everything. I wonder about the central heating. The radiators are awfully old and bulky. It would be a pity to hang expensive wallpaper, and *then* decide to change the radiators . . ." She went on over the list of things which had come to her mind as she had wandered through the house that morning. Julia's eyes had widened as she talked.

"It's going to cost a fortune," she said. "You must be awfully rich." It was uttered with almost a childish naïveté. She had never earned much money, and she had spent it all. All her life she had moved among people who had power or money, and some had both. But the knowledge of how to use these things was alien to her.

Kelly gestured toward Laura. "Laura's grandfather was extraordinarily generous to me. I loved him dearly, and he loved me, I believe. But he didn't have to leave to me as much as he did. I know he expected me to use it responsibly, but to *use* it. It's not sinful to enjoy what money will buy, as Kate sometimes seems to suggest. To redo these houses is an investment in my own life. I think John Merton would have approved. After all, Charles did leave them to me for a reason."

"Grandfather *would* have approved," Laura said firmly. "Why, he'd say it was foolish to leave such valuable pieces of property to run down. Of course they should be done up—from top to bottom. No use putting in new carpet if the roof leaks." She extended her hands, as if trying to explain to Julia. "Why, I'd bet if Kelly took the deeds of these two houses and the mews house to the bank, they'd lend her the money right on the spot. But why pay those big interest rates if you don't have to? Oh, I know Grandfather always said that cleverly used money was never idle—fortunes were made by always being in debt. That would be how Nick would think. I'll bet he's in debt for millions, and the banks go on lending to protect their own investments with his companies. But I noticed that when Grandfather's affairs were all sorted out—Kelly and I went into all that when we were out there—there had never been a mortgage on Pentland. Grandfather always stopped short there. And I think Kelly shouldn't borrow money to redo these houses."

Julia was gazing at Laura with a faint awe. "You're awfully young to know these things. I suppose your checkbook always balances, even though it wouldn't really matter if it didn't."

"Laura's grandfather taught her that there was a difference between having money, spending it, and throwing it away," Kelly said. "A lot of people never learn it. Laura's money is in a trust until she's twenty-one. After that, she's free to use it as she pleases. That's how much faith her grandfather had in her."

Julia took a deep breath. "Well . . . well, it all makes me a bit nervous. But so long as you both think it's all right to spend so much money—then it must be." She began gathering the plates and napkins and glasses onto the tray. "I'd love to help. I'm not very practical, but I *do* love beautiful things. You'll make it charming and beautiful, I know, Kelly." Her pale skin grew flushed with pleasure. She reminded Kelly of Mrs. Cass looking at the boxes of groceries.

They spent the afternoon at Cavanagh's. Kelly had said she could call the decorators over with their samples, but Julia had insisted on their all going to the store. Kelly telephoned the decorating department before they came over. The same Mr. Aubrey and Mr. Pike were waiting. "So terribly sorry about Sir Charles, Lady Brandon," Mr. Aubrey said. "I'd wanted to offer my condolences, but didn't like to intrude. But it's wonderful that you've decided to go ahead with the redecorating. We've still got the plans on file. All the things you'd chosen, colors, samples . . . everything. But I expect you'd rather like to look at it all again. A few months can make a difference in how you think about things." He looked nervously around at the three women, and knew he was outnumbered and probably outweighed. "Would you . . . would you have the same sort of budget? Or shall we cut back a bit here and there?"

Laura looked at him coldly; Kelly saw Greg in that look.

"Lady Brandon likes quality. It should be done right from the first. That's the best way to get value for money."

"Quite so, Miss . . . er . . ." He couldn't remember her name.

"Laura Merton. I'm Lady Brandon's stepdaughter."

The younger man, Mr. Pike, shot a look at his colleague. They had just been introduced to Julia Brandon, whom they had recognized at once, as Lady Brandon's stepdaughter. Julia Brandon, they knew, would be hopeless about money and budgets. She just wanted to purr admiringly over samples of cloth and carpet. This young one, they indicated to each other, was both bold and prickly, and she wanted value for money. Little bitch, the younger man's look said. With a sigh, Mr. Aubrey drew his papers toward him. "You'll want the builder's estimates as soon as possible, Lady Brandon. I think I could get our people over there first thing in the morning to go over the whole house. Very sensible to do the essential things first . . ."

His younger colleague put in a bid for something he had mentioned when he had met Kelly at Mead Cottage. "Lady Brandon—the study that Sir Charles used . . . I drew up some little sketches of a garden room after I talked with you, just in case you'd be interested. Would you consider now—"

"No," Kelly said at once. "Beyond some new curtains, a coat of paint where it shows, and some new chair covers, Sir Charles' study will stay exactly as it is."

The young man's shoulders sagged. The rich could be awfully stingy in small ways.

"Lady Brandon," Mr. Aubrey said, as they were preparing to leave, "about Mead Cottage . . .?"

Kelly hesitated only an instant. She wasn't quite ready for Mead Cottage. "We'll leave it, Mr. Aubrey. We'll leave it . . ."

Nick Brandon appeared unannounced that evening a little after six at Brandon Place. Laura answered the insistently ringing doorbell of Number 15. "I'll have to answer it," she called to Kelly. "Julia's too slow on the stairs." Then Kelly heard her exclamation. She walked through the glass doors, which had stood open all day, and was surprised to see that Laura had been caught up in Nick's arms—or else had offered herself to his embrace, which was another barrier of shyness broken.

Nick also embraced Kelly. "I still haven't forgiven you for giving us the slip after the service, that day. But probably it was the best thing you could have done. Old Peter was on to it like a flash. I must say I wouldn't have thought of you going to Heathrow . . ." He looked toward the stairs where Julia had begun her slow descent. "Hello, Julia. She telephoned me, you know. Told me you were back. I was bloody glad to hear it. They've been carrying on as if you both were lost forever. I had to point out to them the logic of the postcards. You kept getting nearer and nearer." He added, "Kate in?"

"Not yet," Julia said. "You can never tell when Kate's coming and going." She had automatically made for the room that had been her mother's. Then she stopped with the door half open. "Oh, I'm sorry, Kelly. You'd probably rather we all went up to the drawing room." She gestured toward Number 16.

"No—I haven't even seen this. And we'll catch Kate and Marya on their way in—if they come early enough." The room was scantily furnished, but pleasant enough. The curtains and carpet, as Mrs. Cass had told her, were relatively new. There was just a sofa, three chairs, and a drinks table stocked with bottles. Mrs. Cass had left the window open a little and the sound of the rush hour traffic in Brompton Road came to them distantly. Laura brought ice and a jug of water. Nick poured himself a Scotch and sat down in a chair as if it was his accustomed one.

"Welcome home." He sipped his drink. "I've been sponging shamelessly on the girls and Marya. Thought I'd keep an eye on them."

"Don't listen to him," Julia protested. "He's been keeping us all stocked in drink."

He lighted a cigarette and grinned. "Well, I had to have some excuse for getting in. And then I did have to see that young Chris Page wasn't making a nuisance of himself. As I should have expected, he wasn't making a nuisance of himself at all. He was being quite helpful, in fact. I'm glad he's been able to make the move into central London. He's closer to his job. He tends to be a bit of a loner, and he might make more friends if he weren't always dashing for the train—he's too young for the suburban schedule yet."

"Then why," Laura asked coolly, "don't you pay him enough so that he could have had a flat closer in before. Living in a basement isn't much fun."

"Young Laura, with greatest respect, I must point out to you that it isn't our policy to pay our young staff big salaries. We argue that they're gaining experience they couldn't get in a more conservative company. We keep moving them around—exposing them to every sort of situation. And trusting them long before they'd be allowed to do more than shuffle papers in other places. We like having young people in the company. And we expect them to earn their keep. We expect them to get a taste of the market, and put every spare penny of their own into ventures which wouldn't normally be open to them. Chris could have afforded a better flat long ago, if that was what he wanted. He chose to invest in some of our concerns—not big money, but he'll make a tidy profit when he comes to sell. He won't be so foolish as to sell just yet though. Chris would do well to keep his money just where it is. There's such potential overseas—Africa and the Far East. And we're into property development quite heavily now. It really amuses me to think that some day we might be back where that damned Brandon who lost such a big chunk of London was before he—before he washed it all down the drain." He drew on his cigarette and watched the smoke spiral upwards. "You know—I'll confess that I hated that man as I was growing up. I'd listened so long to the stories of how quickly it went. He wasn't tactful enough to have his heart attack and die until there were only a few things left." He jerked his head toward the street. "Brandon Place and the Eaton Square house being some of the few remnants. All of us, as a family, suffered because of him. I used to dream about getting it all back again. Of course, I never will. Not the same properties. But maybe some things a lot bigger. We've got some sites on the South Bank that we're going to pour a lot of money into. Exciting . . . there's an office and residential development we're just starting on a bit farther down the river than anyone's developed before. We'll have a bit of a job persuading firms and the right people to come across the river—but we'll make it so good they just won't be able to say no. Big plans . . ." Momentarily he had lost his usual air of detachment. Kelly had never imagined him being excited, but that was the only word for it. Suddenly she understood that the actual fact of money had very little to do with Nick Brandon's philosophy. It was the power of money, big money, that he enjoyed.

Laura leaned forward. "If you and I are to be friends, Nick, you'll have to stop calling me 'Young Laura.' And secondly, could I say that you seem to be as much a gambler as your unfortunate ancestor?"

Kelly actually saw the gleam of pleasure grow in his eyes. He liked his role of buccaneer, wanted it recognized. "I shall never again make the mistake of calling you 'Young Laura.' You are old and wise—though still young and beautiful. And yes, I *am*, of course, a gambler. From the outside, the company must, at times, look like a house of cards. A strong enough wind, and we might go down, they say. But we won't. When you start from nothing, you either have to do it in a big way, or you might as well go and work as a bank teller. I was never cut out to be a bank teller."

"And Chris?" Laura prompted. "He's not a bank teller, either."

Nick looked down at his drink. "I'm not exactly sure yet just what Chris is—or will be. But I'm certain he's not a bank teller."

Laura's hair swung over her face as she stood up. "Let me give you another drink."

IV

The scaffolding went up on the outside of Numbers 15 and 16 Brandon Place. Viewing it as she walked along the street, Kelly decided that it was as positive a statement as she could make—a statement of intent, a determination to stay, to make a life. Once she had made up her mind, a sense of urgency consumed her. She would not let the repairs and refurbishing consume many months; when she had signed the contracts with Cavanagh's there had been penalty clauses for delays, and for that, she knew, she was paying premium rates. Let it be. She stopped, looking at the shadows cast by the scaffolding on the facade of the houses by the mellow September sunlight. A feeling of excitement and satisfaction gripped her. Not since Charles' death had she felt this surge of optimism and hope—though what precisely she hoped for she could not say.

There had been a brief struggle in Laura's mind about continuing to live at Brandon Place. She had come back one day to announce that she was once again back with her tutor, and wanted to try for a place at London University. "Why London?" Kelly asked. "Your father would have liked you to go to Lady Margaret Hall—or Girton."

"It was easier in his time to get into those places. Besides, I want to stay in London. I've got family here, after all."

"Oxford and Cambridge aren't exactly a thousand miles away."

"I'd like to stay in London," she repeated firmly, and would say no more about her reasons. "Look, Kelly, I'll get out from under your feet. I know I should have my own flat.

I'll do what I planned to do when you and Charles were here. I'd . . . I'd just like to be able to drop in now and then."

Kelly thought of herself occupying the whole of Number 16, thought of how she would miss Laura, and decided that she must never tell Laura that. They were having a late-afternoon cup of tea in the kitchen, and outside the banging and hammering went on, as the scaffolding climbed to reach the roof of the two buildings. An examination of the sloping ceiling of Marya's flat had revealed the same telltale stains as Kelly had found in Number 16. Whether she wished it or not, it was evident that major repairs would have to be undertaken.

She poured a second cup. She had taken to drinking it black, and without sugar. "Let's think about a flat. Of course you should have a place that's your own. You can't—you wouldn't want to stay with me forever. But unless you want a lot of space, there's room for you here. Would you settle for what Julia and Kate and Marya have?"

"How? How could it be managed?"

"The rooms Elizabeth Brandon and the nurses used. There's already that bathroom there. Quite a big one. I'm sure it must be possible to squeeze in a small kitchen. It could be made a self-contained flat as the others are . . ." She hardly dared look up from her cup. Why not confess, she told herself, that she wanted Laura to stay. How to keep her, and still let her go . . .

Laura stood up abruptly, jolting the table. "Could we go and look? It hadn't occurred to me."

They examined the sitting room Julia and Kate and Marya had arranged. Large, pleasant, with the big window looking out on Brandon Place. An interior door opened into a short passage where two doors face each other—the bathroom and a big, walk-in cupboard, with rods where clothes had hung, and shelves, now empty. Another door led into the room the night nurse had used when Elizabeth had been alive. The windows of this room faced the little garden, and Charles' study, and it also had a door opening into the main hall of Number 15.

"Even spruced up, it's going to be barely adequate, Laura. A kitchen could be squeezed into the cupboard, I think. It'd have to be ventilated by joining into the duct from the bathroom. But they can do great things with ceiling fans these days."

"Oh, Kelly, stop it! Adequate! It'll be a palace compared to what most students have. What would I have at Lady Margaret Hall or Girton? One room and sharing a bathroom with a dozen other girls. Well—I don't want that sort of life. I don't want to eat dinner in college every night. I want a life of my own. But not entirely alone. I'd like to stay here, Kelly, if you'll have me."

Kelly hesitated only briefly. "I'm being selfish. I'd like to have you near. I wonder, though, if the Renisdales wouldn't like to see you in something more . . . well, more up to what you can afford. You can afford more than this."

"Who wants it! I wouldn't have a single friend at University if I brought them to anything grander than this. Money attracts the worst sort of person, and frightens off the worthwhile ones. I can say it belongs to you, and everyone will think it comes rent free. Which I'm determined it won't. And as for Grandfather Renisdale—well, he started from something a lot humbler than this, and I think he'd say someone my age shouldn't have more. And Grandfather Merton . . . well, wouldn't he wonder if it wasn't all a bit too fancy?" Laura gripped her arm. "Kelly, what are you afraid of? You know Grandfather trusted your judgment. You're not actually turning me out on the street, but you're letting me off the apron strings."

"I hope I can do just that, Laura."

So Mr. Aubrey from Cavanagh's called the architect once again, and a tiny kitchen was added to the plans for Brandon Place. Until the work was completed Laura would keep her bedroom on the floor above Kelly, and the impromptu sitting room would stay as it was. Laura chose some extra chairs which would be part of her own furniture, found some small tables, bought some vases and kept them filled with fresh flowers, as if the room were already hers; she started looking around the inexpensive galleries for pictures. One day Kelly returned home and found a rather scarred but still handsome mahogany desk being carried through the door of Number 15. "It has to be study and sitting room and dining room," Laura said. She had found the desk in an antique shop on the King's Road. She refused to order new curtains or carpet. "They're perfectly good," she said.

Nick Brandon took in the changes each time he called to visit. "Good for you, Laura. I do think you'll make it despite all the disadvantages of having money." He said it, and laughed. "What are you going to read at London?"

She shrugged. "Haven't made up my mind yet. History or English. I'd like to try economics, but I don't think I'm brainy enough for it. I was hoping"—her tone matched his teasing—"that if I got a degree in economics you'd employ me at Brandon, Hoyle."

"The very last person we'd employ would be someone with a degree in economics. They're all theory and no action. You'd be better selling those skills to the Government, making surveys to show how the capitalist system is breaking down. Just keep reading the *Financial Times* while you've got your head into modern history, and you might actually get a job with us. That is," he added, "if you can also type and take shorthand."

"I'll bet you wouldn't ask for that qualification if I were a man."

"Wouldn't I? Chris Page made sure he had it before he came looking for a job. And it hasn't done him one bit of harm. He's never stuck for a secretary to type a letter or a report if it happens to be the day she decides not to show up. He just gets on and does it himself. A good man, young Chris. He wasn't really expecting any favors when he came looking for a job. His mother didn't ask, either. And I have to say he's worked damned hard. He could make quite a career for himself just as soon as he sheds that last bit of caution."

"Perhaps he's not a gambler like you," Laura offered. "He might want to hold on to what he's got—" She broke off. "Look, he's just gone down the basement steps to his flat. Shall I ask him up for a drink? He never comes unless he's invited, and with you here, Nick . . . well, what do you think, Kelly?"

"It's your flat. Do what you want. That was the whole idea of having it, wasn't it?"

"I will then." She went out into the hall, and they could hear her calling down the steep inside stairs to Chris's flat. His muffled answer reached them distantly. Laura came back at once. "He'd like to, very much." She was already pouring the gin and tonic Chris always asked for. He came, however, carrying a bottle of gin to give to her.

"Hello . . . Kelly." She had asked him to stop calling her Lady Brandon after the first few days, but he still didn't seem comfortable using her name. A hangover, she thought, from all the years at Wychwood when he had hovered in the uneasy position of being almost one of the family, and yet not quite of it. The lingering traces of shyness he still displayed could come from that fact. Perhaps that was why Laura had warmed to him; perhaps she sensed a loneliness in him that matched her own. He didn't appear to have many friends, or if he did, they were invisible and unheard at Brandon Place. Once he had invited them all down to a carefully prepared, beautifully cooked supper, but there had been only one other guest, a young man who also worked for Nick. The evening had not been quite a success, despite the good food and an excellent wine, and despite all that Marya's crackling humor could contribute once she had had enough vodka. Laura, however, had been happy about it. "He's awfully good, isn't he?—I mean, the food and everything? I must ask him for that recipe. All made in one pot. I could use it when I have people in . . ." And she had continued to insist on inviting Chris almost every time any of them gathered in the evening for a drink in the front sitting room. Kelly didn't suggest that she should stop. To see Laura break out of her mold of reserve and shyness to reach to anyone, was something she, Kelly, must not discourage. But at times she wished Chris was a little less helpful and a little less omnipresent. And yet . . . she was too hard on him. Julia had come to rely on his company and help, his willingness to do whatever was needed. Kate treated him in an offhandedly affectionate fashion. Marya, once she knew that his presence at Brandon Place was sanctioned by Kelly, had lavished on him the same open warmth she gave to the rest of the family.

It occurred to Kelly that it was perhaps Marya more than anyone else who missed Elizabeth Brandon. Once Marya had been at the center of this household, depended upon by an invalid and by Charles Brandon for making it run with smoothness. She had been in a mother role to Julia and Kate, a friend and companion to Elizabeth, a housekeeper; she had dealt with the ordinary problems of the nurses who came and went, and with the more intricate demands of Charles' military and political life. She had done all this, and somehow managed to keep up her work translating as well. And it had all ended—all but the translating, and Kelly knew that for Marya that was not enough. It was amazing that she hadn't resented Kelly's coming. But she hadn't appeared to do so then, nor did she now. She would join them when invited to, but never came looking for any of them. It was as if, Kelly thought, the glass doors became a solid wall again. Marya was very careful about the times she came through the glass doors. If friends climbed to the top-floor flat, Kelly was never aware of them. She remembered that Lady Renisdale had told her—how long ago—that Marya had been briefly married and was now divorced. No trace of that married life seemed to linger. She never spoke of it. She never spoke of family left behind in Russia. If one had not known the extraordinary past that this woman must have had, the extraordinary motives that must have pushed her toward the risk of that flight from Yalta, always facing the possibility that she would be returned and handed over to Soviet justice, if one had not known the quiet courage of her endurance, she might have seemed an ordinary woman, earning a precarious living. But the evidence of a past of which she did not speak was in her face, the deep lines under the eyes, the lines running downward at the corners of her mouth, lines that were transformed utterly when she gave her wide smile. Kelly realized that Marya talked constantly, but never of herself, and betrayed only in little ways her eagerness to join the group in the front sitting room whenever she was caught on her way in from the street.

Laura had taken to leaving the door from the hall open so that she could greet and command Kate and Marya on their return. She also listened for Chris opening the gate in the area railings, and descending the steps into the basement, as she had tonight. "Madame Laura's salon," Marya had dubbed it. Kelly knew Laura had been delighted. It was almost as if the possession of this room, the gathering of this little group, was the first time she had truly been able to claim something as her own. She had begun to put her stamp on it. She could invite, order, arrange. Kelly had begun to feel more confident that the arrangement truly would work for Laura. She would . . .

"Kelly . . . you're dreaming. I asked you what you thought about Julia." It was Nick's voice, sharp, but slightly amused at her absentmindedness.

"Julia . . . what about Julia?"

"Do you think she's going to be all right? This is the day the cast comes off. That's why I came. I wanted to know how she was."

Incredible that in the midst of all his activities he should have remembered this day. "She and Marya have gone to Charing Cross Hospital," Kelly answered. "That's where they took her after the accident. They set it in the Casualty Department. They took X rays, of course. Said it looked all right. But I think Julia's frightened that something might be wrong."

"Damn fool," Nick said. "She should have insisted on being left where she was until she got the best orthopedic man in London. These Casualty Departments—and especially Charing Cross—they get every sort of case that comes up in the Soho area. It was no place for Julia. No place for something as important as setting a bone for a dancer."

"And where would you have had her go, Nick?—the London Clinic?" It had been said in a very even, low tone by Kate. She must have come into the house very quietly, and she now stood at the partly opened sitting-room door. She was carrying a string bag with packages and books in it which looked as if it weighed her down. Her expression was both tense and wary; Kelly guessed she had seen Nick's chauffeur-driven car parked somewhere along Brandon Place, and she had expected him to be there. Nick was seated with his back almost to the door, and he had not been aware of her presence before she spoke; it seemed to produce in him the same air of tension that she wore.

"Oh, there you are, Kate. I don't see much of you these days. How are you?" He had risen, and might have offered her a light embrace, but she appeared not to see the gesture. She dropped heavily into a chair.

"Laura, love—I'd love a big fat whiskey. It's been one bitch of a day."

Rebuffed, Nick sat down again. "How are you, Kate?" he repeated.

She sipped her drink deliberately before she answered. "Well enough. The doctor says I'm doing fine. After all, I *do* get the right things to eat, not like half the expectant mothers in this country."

Nick lost his patience. "Oh, quit that for once, Kate. I can't even ask a civil question without getting either a lecture on socialism, or an equally tiresome one on how the rich grab the best that's going. So what if I did say Julia should have gone somewhere else than Charing Cross Hospital? She was probably treated by an immigrant doctor who couldn't understand what she was saying, and certainly didn't know how important Julia is in the world of ballet."

"*Everyone* gets the same treatment!" Kate snapped. Kelly realized with dismay that she was not treating this argument with her usual good humor. She frowned and looked into her drink. "Your stupid prejudices show, Nick. If it weren't for the immigrant doctors and nurses we wouldn't have a National Health Service. And what would you have us do? Go back to the bad old days when you only went to hospital to die? Or be like America where you go bankrupt with a single hospital bill? Julia got no more and no less than anyone else. And I certainly intend to have my baby on the National Health."

"God, you do make me angry, Kate. It isn't a joke. You realize you'll be in some mass-production delivery room, and very likely the birth will be induced so you won't interfere with the doctor's regular hours. And you may not even get a doctor unless something goes wrong. Why must you be so pig-headed? Why won't you accept help?" He looked at Kelly. "Can't you make her see?" He gestured irritably. "Well, I don't understand it. You didn't object, surely, when your father took on the care of your mother at home? That he had nurses round the clock for her, and paid for it himself. Would you rather she had been thrust away in some home, in a ward with—"

"That's enough, Nick. Leave Mother and Father out of this. He did what he believed was right. It *was* right—for her! For me, it's different. Pregnancy is a state of health, you know, not illness. And I happen to believe in the systems of this country . . ."

"Oh, for God's sake, don't start again. Where the hell's Julia. They can't still be running their bloody out-patient's clinic . . ."

All the time since Kate had entered, Chris had remained standing. He was over by the window, staring out into Brandon Place as if he were trying to make himself invisible. Now he said quietly, "Marya's just got out of a taxi—and Julia. The cast is off." He turned. "I'll just nip out and help her."

They waited in absolute silence. Laura was not able to stop herself going to the door. They listened to the confused babble of the voices, but could distinguish nothing. Then Marya came into the room, carrying Julia's handbag and her own. Julia followed, leaning heavily on her stick, limping, and refusing Chris's arm.

"Oh, hello, Nick. Good to see you."

"Let's skip the generalities, Julia. What did he say? How does it feel?"

Julia moved slowly across the room. Her walk seemed hardly different than when she had borne the constraint of the cast. She seemed even less certain of her movement. "Give me a moment, Nick." She sat down, and accepted blindly the glass Laura put into her hand. "I could have done with this at one point this afternoon."

"What do you mean? What happened?" It was Nick who spoke before Kelly could. He was in the edge of his chair, hammering the questions at Julia.

Marya was over at the drinks table. She had already lighted a cigarette, and held it in her lips while she poured vodka. "Take it a little more gently, Nicholas Mikhailovich. Give the girl time." She shrugged, and sagged down on the sofa. All her clothes, her beads, her scarf, the cigarette in her mouth drooped. "I had a little scene with the Sister in charge of out-patients. I protested. I made a fuss. I wasn't English and tight-lipped."

"What happened?" This time it was Kelly who asked, quietly.

"The cast was removed by two porters around the corner out of sight of the rest of the patients. Two porters with shears who acted as if they were butcher's apprentices on their first day. Cut . . . cut. Hack . . . hack. Yes, I know it is the usual way casts come off, and I've seen much worse, believe me. But what I couldn't stand was the sight of our Julia fainting."

"Marya, you promised you wouldn't tell them that! I felt such a fool! It was panic, really. They didn't hurt me . . . they really didn't hurt me. And any rate, it's over now. I'm all right."

"*Are* you all right?" Kelly insisted.

Marya held up her hand. "I'm not so certain. I barged in, of course, once Julia finally got in to see the doctor. Not all the Sisters in the Kingdom could have kept me out then. They wouldn't let me see the X ray, even though I told them I was a nurse. Nurses are not supposed to read X rays. I was there when the doctor examined Julia's ankle—watched her walking on it. A nice young man—far more frightened of me, by then, than he was of the Sister. The consultant didn't seem to be available—Julia says she's never seen him. I don't like it. Even in the Soviet Union we did special things for special people. Or let me say, most *particularly* we did things for special people. In Russia, Julia would be regarded as part of the national heritage. What I saw today . . ." Ash spilled down the front of her dress.

"Julia *how* is it?" Kelly asked. She realized that after Marya's outburst, all of them were tense, and she clenched her own hands in her lap to hide their trembling.

"I'm not sure." Julia was very pale, and her eyes enormous, with a dark smudge of weariness beneath them as if she needed a deep, long sleep. "I hoped to be able to move it much better. It's very stiff. The doctor said that's only to be expected. He said to take it gently. A little exercise every day. Not to overdo it." She gulped her drink in a way Kelly had never seen her do before—Julia who was always so careful about what and how much she drank. "Marya, would you give me my handbag? Thanks." She fished among all the things there, and Kelly was dismayed to see that she brought out a Kleenex and blew her nose. "Sorry. I just feel a bit down. You see, they don't understand about dancers. It could take six months to get back to normal. And by that time I'm really a year behind. Even if the ankle is perfectly all right, it will almost be like starting from the beginning again. And I haven't got that much time." She dabbed under her eyes again, and searched for more Kleenex. It was Chris who came forward and offered her a clean, folded handkerchief, took her glass, refilled it and put it on the table beside her.

"Julia . . .?" Nick said. Now his tone was very gentle, very calm. "Julia—do you have any reason to think the doctor might be wrong? Are you afraid the ankle won't come back?"

Julia raised her head, and looked directly at him. "I have to tell you that I've *always* been afraid of that. When they X-rayed and set it—they said it was . . . it was a very *dirty* fracture. But I expected at least to be able to walk out of there without a stick. Yes, Nick—I am frightened." She fumbled with the Kleenex again.

"Julia, in the morning I'm getting you to the best orthopedic surgeon in London. At this moment I don't know who that is, but I will by then. Everything will be arranged. And you will do what I ask, won't you?"

She looked at him and nodded dumbly.

"Don't you think you should give what's been done a chance to work?" Kate sighed.

Nick sighed. "Kate, do me a favor, will you, and kindly shut up. Run your own life any way you want, but please let Julia run hers. Allow me to give us all a little peace of mind. If this man, whoever he is, says things must take their course, then I'll believe it."

Kate got up, gathering her handbag and the bulging string bag. "Thanks for the drink. I've got some work to do, so I'll go up." She was moving now without the agile springiness which had always characterized her; her body was starting to thicken beneath the loose clothes. She stopped by Julia and softly stroked her cheek. "You do as Nick says, you hear, Little Sister? We'll all be happier when we're sure it's going to be all right. And it will be." She bent lower over Julia. "Are you expecting Sergei?"

"Perhaps. It's never possible to know what time he can get away. And he's performing tonight."

"Well, if you need a bit of company, I'm in all evening. I've got some chicken to cook, if you'd like a bite . . ."

"I also must go," Marya said. She stubbed out her cigarette. She touched Julia's shoulder as she passed. "Don't worry, little one. Do as Nick says, and it will be all right. We will leave it to the doctor Nick will find. Good night." She followed Kate from the room, and they heard the tones of their conversation on the stairs.

When it had died away completely Nick spoke. "Well, you'll leave it with me, Julia? I'll telephone you in the morning, as soon as I have an appointment with this man. I'll send a car. All right? You'll stay in and wait for me to telephone?"

"Yes, Nick. And thank you."

"No thanks, Julia. I should have done it as soon as I knew about the accident. What the hell's wrong with you and Kate that you never ask for help—or advice? I'm surprised that Marya . . . oh, well, never mind. It's all going to be taken care of . . ." He got up. "Chris, walk me to the car, will you? There was something I meant to speak to you about today . . ." He leaned over and kissed Julia's cheek, and touched Kelly's arm in a farewell gesture. "You don't mind if I drop in again, Laura? Good—I'll see you all then."

They sat in silence for a moment after the front door had closed. Julia straightened her shoulders, and took up her drink again. "He's very kind. I didn't want to bother him."

"Rubbish," Laura said. "Don't you realize he *likes* to be bothered. He likes organizing things—and people. And he's right. You should have talked to him immediately after it happened. It wouldn't have done any harm to have a second opinion. I can't really understand why one of the directors of the Ballet didn't insist . . ."

"Dame Katherine did suggest someone else. But I didn't like to. It seemed not to be giving the Charing Cross people a chance. And dancers are so used to injuries . . . half the company is hurting somewhere or other at any given time."

"Julia, you're really such a child," Laura said. "Do you suppose that top athletes don't get the best advice, the best treatment?"

"It's just . . . well, ballet is still really such a new thing to this country. We don't think of ourselves as very important. We're so used to working on a tight budget that we think it applies to us personally. I never thought of asking Nick to help. We used to see him so rarely before you and Father were married, Kelly. We hadn't really got used to the idea that he came around just to see us when you were away.

He's—he's much kinder than I expected . . ." She looked at her watch, and then got a comb and cosmetics out of her bag. Studying herself in a little compact mirror, she said, "What a sight I am . . ." Swiftly she used powder and lipstick, and then with such deftness that Kelly was awed, an eye liner and eye shadow. The face she presented to them was restored, and she was smiling, but the powder didn't erase the shadows under her eyes.

"How lovely you are, my Julia." Sergei was standing in the doorway.

Julia's expression changed from the rather forced smile to a look of radiance. She extended her hand. "Oh, Sergei, how marvelous you could get here. You haven't much time. The performance . . ."

Before going to Julia's side, he first kissed Kelly's hand, and then, with a sort of joking gesture, Laura's. He always did it, and there was no woman who could not be moved by the grace of the action, the feeling that he did it for her alone. They had encountered him many times in Number 15 in the weeks they had been home. Either he had joined them in the front sitting room, and had carefully sipped tomato juice, or they had met him in the hall. A few times he had had a meal with them, but mostly they had wanted to leave Julia alone with him. In the long days while she had waited for the cast to come off, they knew that Sergei had kept her spirit alive. They had never mentioned the mornings they had seen him leave for class from Number 15. It was Julia's life, and at that moment, Sergei was her lover and her support. But Kelly knew fully now what a situation she herself was involved in as she realized that many people had the keys to Number 15. She was certain that Marya did not give keys to anyone—she labored down all the stairs to answer any doorbells that rang for her. But Kate—who knew about Kate, and who wanted to ask? Had her lover—her child's father, whoever he was, been given a key? Kelly had not dared to ask. Kate's sense of privacy and independence would have been outraged. Kelly thought of the glass door that always stood open between the two houses. Was she foolish to leave them open?

She rose and gestured to Laura. "I need a bit of help in the kitchen if we're to eat tonight. How good that you could come this evening, Sergei. Perhaps you could have dinner with us on Sunday? If you're free . . ." She smiled, and tried not to notice that Julia's eyes had never left Sergei from the moment he had stood in the doorway, a longing, wanting look, the look of a hungry child. "Laura—from what I smell, our roast may be a disaster. Good night, Sergei. We'll see you—perhaps Sunday?"

He bowed and smiled. "You are very kind." It was the sort of answer he always gave. Never quite an answer, unwilling to give a commitment, to be pinned down. She wanted to answer to that smiling, too-handsome face, that he needn't bother, but Julia lived in hope of his coming. So she smiled also. "Good night . . ." She closed the door firmly behind herself and Laura.

"Leave them alone. Julia wants him to herself now. She has things to tell him. What she'll tell him, I don't know . . ." She turned, startled, as a figure walked through the front door. "Oh, Chris . . . I didn't hear you."

He shook his head. "Couldn't have heard me. That mad Russian left the door unlocked. I saw it was open so I came up to see what was happening. And he's got a taxi waiting outside, meter running . . ." Then he shrugged. "Oh, well—it's his money, and I'm damn glad he came to see Julia tonight. I think she needs him."

"She needs him," Kelly said. "And you, Chris, if you'll be so kind . . ."

He straightened as if he was being given an order. He couldn't have been more attentive if it had been Nick speaking. "Would you be good enough to hang around here in the hall until Sergei leaves? And then go and get Julia and insist that she come over and have dinner with us." She added hastily, "Of course, you'll have dinner with us, too—unless you have an engagement. There's plenty—if I haven't let it all burn up. We'll eat in the kitchen . . ."

It was the way things happened at Brandon Place. They seemed to be meshed ever closer into each other's lives; Kelly, knowing that she had committed herself, did not resist the inevitable turning of the cogs in the wheels.

Almost against her will, Kelly had found herself turning to Chris more often. That was after the time he had, on Laura's invitation, come into the sitting room, and she had been sitting on the sofa checking a thick pile of bills presented by Cavanagh's. "They haven't given me the labor charges per hour, so I don't know if the totals are right."

"May I?" Chris said.

She had hesitated, but only momentarily. Chris knew about money. He would not be fazed, nor did she think he would be envious of the amount she had to spend on these buildings. Those emotions had little to do with someone who hears millions talked of daily. They were figures to him, figures to be checked. And he had been so helpful about other things.

"He's ever so clever, isn't he, m'lady?" Mrs. Cass said. "You'd never think it to look at him. You know—well, he looks like some sort of poet, doesn't he? And yet, there he is, so handy with his hands, and very practical too. Miss Julia had quite come to rely on him, poor dear. And even Miss Kate asks him to do things for her now and again. Which isn't like her. But then, she *needs* help now the way she never did before." Mrs. Cass's fingers fidgeted nervously with her cigarette as she sat at the kitchen table over her cup of tea. "Oh, dear, m'lady . . . sometimes I can hardly believe what's happened. How could Miss Kate carry on like she does? Doesn't give a hoot that the poor baby won't have a father. I wonder if she'd have been the same if her mother was still alive? Or her father, for that matter. Maybe *he* could have made her see sense." She shook her head. "I don't know what the world's coming to. Why, it used to be such a disgrace. And Miss Kate seems quite proud of it. I just don't know . . ."

Kelly also wondered if Kate might have made a different decision if Charles or Elizabeth Brandon had been there. Or even if she, Kelly, had remained at Brandon Place and had earlier become a sort of sheet anchor for the family. Useless to speculate. Kate carried her child proudly, and let others worry.

It was the last day for some time that Mrs. Cass sat at the kitchen table. Cavanagh's arrived to pull the kitchen apart, and install the new fittings and equipment. Once again Chris had subtly changed the original plans. Kelly had openly asked him what he thought of them when they had been presented. He had studied them, suggested a few things that might make better use of space, and then looked at her directly. "It all looks very efficient, I suppose—and the new appliances should be a great help. I suspect you'll have a bit of a job teaching Mrs. Cass to use the dishwasher. A very new-fangled thing for England, after all. But don't you think—don't you think it looks a bit like a laboratory? All this clinical white . . . it really doesn't look very comfortable." He looked around the kitchen where they then sat. "Just think, Kelly, how many important things in the life of this family happen in this room. Do you want to sit here at a white table and eat in a blaze of fluorescent light?"

Why hadn't she thought of it? Perhaps there had been too many other decisions to make, and she had left too much to the Cavanagh's kitchen "specialist." In the matter of things like dishwashers, she was just as old-fashioned as Mrs. Cass. The next day Chris took his lunch period from work to come with her to Cavanagh's. Laura joined them. "I think Chris's absolutely right," she had said, and showed up at the decorating department without invitation. Mr. Aubrey's eyebrows were raised, perhaps in exasperation, as yet another person was introduced into the refurbishing of Brandon Place, but he showed remarkable patience. No doubt, Kelly thought, the patience would also be added to the bill. Scouring the catalogs, Chris found the cabinets he thought would be right, wooden cabinets with old-fashioned hinges—they were fake old-fashioned, but pleasing. Mr. Aubrey looked at what Chris indicated. "Oh, yes—made by a West Country firm. They're not big manufacturers. In fact, we've never used any of their designs before. High quality—and rather expensive, I'm afraid. They're also the sort of firm which doesn't do things in a hurry, and I doubt they could deliver in time to meet your schedule, Lady Brandon."

"Then why don't you try them?" Chris said. "This would be their first time to do something for Cavanagh's. I imagine they'd jump at the chance." He glanced at his watch. "I'll have to go now, Kelly. If you want to talk about it later, I'll be in all evening."

Mr. Aubrey's eyebrows had gone even higher. "Another relative, Lady Brandon?"

"No—just a friend." She almost laughed aloud. How did one explain the relationship of Chris Page to the Brandons?

V

Julia's ankle was X-rayed and reset under anesthetic; she returned to Brandon Place after two nights in a hospital, her ankle once again in a cast, her face a numb mask that sought to hide fear and despair. She was brought home by Sergei, who was not dancing that night. Kelly put a leg of lamb to roast in the oven, set places for everyone in the dining room, sought the best wine from the cellar, and told Laura to watch for Kate and Marya coming in, and to invite them as well. "And call down to Chris if you hear him. The more we have the better. This is one night Julia mustn't think about herself."

It was after eight when they all sat down. Kelly had placed lighted candles on the table. Elizabeth Brandon's beautiful Chippendale furniture showed at its best, and the shabby walls and carpet were lost in the dimness. Julia seemed to have lost even more weight in the few days she had been away, and her skin had the appearance of translucence in the candlelight; but her beauty now had a haunted, almost tragic look, as if she truly were the heroine of one of the ballets she danced. But she smiled and talked, and found funny things to tell them about the hospital, and most of the time her eyes remained on Sergei. He was charming and amusing as he described the nurses clustering around to see the two dancers leave, and he was very careful about what he drank. "I must never disgrace myself with you again," he said to Kelly, and his eyes smiled at her. He had brought a spray of tiny red rosebuds, which stood now in the center of the table. Kate was wearing a new dress, which made her look pretty. Marya had taken trouble with her lipstick and her jewelry, which meant more of each. Chris was handsome and rather somber in his dark business suit; he seemed more than ever reserved in contrast to Sergei's exuberance. Laura helped Kelly with the food, and said little, but Kelly thought the flush on her face was more one of pleasure than from the warmth of the kitchen. Outside, the early October rain seemed wintry, as it splattered the pavement of Brandon Place. As Kelly carved second helpings of the lamb, and Chris carried the plates, the doorbell of Number 16 rang. Laura went to answer, and came back a moment later with Peter Brandon.

They had not seen him since those last few minutes at Heathrow after the memorial service. He looked around the group. "I didn't mean to burst in. I should have telephoned. But Nick said Julia would be back this evening, and I was only in London overnight. Louise sends her love—she couldn't come. She's at some grand gala thing. I got held up at the club, and I thought I'd just drop around to say hello . . ."

"You haven't had any dinner then?" Kelly asked.

"No—but I'll only stay a minute. Just wanted to wish Julia well."

Laura was swiftly setting a place mat and silverware. "You're surely not going to tell us some polite lie about having a dinner engagement at this hour. The lamb's very good, and there's loads of it."

He smiled. "As a matter of fact, I'm damn hungry." He ate his food, and listened to the talk all around him, and looked like a man who has been alone for too long. He sat next to Kelly, and in a low tone he said, "I'd like to bring the boys some time—maybe half-term—when you have the family together like this. They should get to know their cousins better . . ."

"I'd love them to come."

He put down his knife and fork and turned fully to her. "You know—I really didn't think you'd come back. But seeing you here now it seems inevitable that you'd come back."

"Why inevitable?"

"Because we . . . because you were needed." Then he turned back to his food. She remembered the night she had sat with him so serenely at Wychwood and listened to music. He had been in her thoughts as she drove back to London the afternoon she had found Charles dead, he and the music, the Beethoven late quartet; she recalled now the contentment of that night, lost to her until now because the pain had wiped out the memory.

They had coffee in Laura's sitting room because the drawing room was in the process of having its wallpaper stripped off. There was a smell of new paint hanging over the two houses. Kelly had decided that the hall and staircase of Number 15 should be painted and carpeted to match Number 16. "We shall be too grand," Marya complained. "My friends will think I've come into money." All the fireplaces had been swept of their accumulated soot, and Laura was having her first fire of the winter. Kelly sat watching the flames, sipping her coffee. She was aware of a vague feeling of happiness, a feeling that had nothing to do with excitement. She was aware of Peter's eyes upon her, and she was remembering that he had said, "because you were needed."

Sergei took Julia upstairs, carrying her as if she weighed nothing. Kelly and Laura saw Peter to the door. On the doorstep he stood for a moment in the rain. "When are you coming to Mead Cottage?"

In the midst of the decisions about the work to be done at Brandon Place, she had given little thought to Mead Cottage. It was something for the future, something that perhaps she might never get around to. Now she knew that tomorrow she would go to Cavanagh's, and they would agree on plans. She would have it done. She would plant a spring garden at Mead Cottage.

"Soon," she answered. "Soon, Peter."

VI

Once she had spoken to Cavanagh's, the work started at Mead Cottage. "No need for you to go down yet, Lady Brandon," Mr. Aubrey had said. "The structural things like the roof, and that small new bathroom and the central heating are things we can get on with. You might like to look at the kitchen plans, in view of the changes made at Brandon Place." It was clear that he had not wholly approved of the changes made—he did not welcome independence in his clients, but if they paid for it, it was their privilege. At first Kelly was inclined to do as little as possible at Mead Cottage. The expenses at Brandon Place were heavy, and money flowed out at an alarming rate. She had almost canceled the plans for the new bathroom, but the thought of how many people might use the cottage, once it was ready, almost forced her to go ahead. She thought of where Kate might spend her holidays once she had the baby; she thought of Julia and the possibility of her having too much free time on her hands; she thought of Marya who might not be able to afford a holiday. "Why should you think this way about all of us?" Laura had demanded. "Haven't you had enough, Kelly, after all these years of taking care of me? You're free now. And Mead Cottage should be your place to escape to alone . . ." Her words trailed off as she studied Kelly's expression.

Kelly's gesture indicated the whole of Number 16. "Don't you think I've got rather a lot of space to inhabit all by myself?"

Laura sighed. "Well, if you're determined to saddle yourself with the lot of us . . ."

"Isn't that what I came back for?"

Laura rounded on her. "Kelly, don't you ever think about getting married again? Ever?"

"Find me a good man, and I might consider it. I seem to make a habit of losing good men." Laura said nothing.

There were some who made efforts to see that at least she had contact with men again. Phoebe Renisdale had dropped in to Brandon Place on one of her visits to London. She only occasionally occupied the penthouse flat in St. James's Square which Arthur Renisdale used nightly during the week. "I've always been a countrywoman, my dear," she said. "My father farmed fourteen hundred acres in Yorkshire, and I've never really got over it. London is fine for shopping, and occasionally it is necessary to entertain for Arthur here. But I miss my garden and my dogs . . ." They were having tea in the sitting room of what would be Laura's flat. Phoebe Renisdale had seen and approved the plans for the conversion, and, rather to Kelly's surprise, was enthusiastic about the arrangement of Laura living in Brandon Place. "Yes, I know, my dear—it might be better if she were off on her own. But I feel it's . . . well, it's *safer* for her here. There's always someone coming and going, between all of you. Laura hasn't grown up in a normal way. While she's at this very impressionable age, I think it's better that she feels there's somewhere that's a real home for her to come to, while still being independent. Though, heaven knows, I can't say that either Julia or Kate is much of an example. Julia having this mad affair with the Russian that no good will come of, I'm sure. And Kate—in heaven's name what got into her? What poor Elizabeth would have thought . . ." She clucked in much the same way as Mrs. Cass. "I'd hate to see *that* happen to Laura. But she's so devoted to you that that alone might help her to keep her head. I don't know . . . it's hard to be young these days, I think."

Phoebe Renisdale gave three luncheon parties in her flat for Kelly, to introduce her to her many social contacts, and invited her to two formal dinners. At once Kelly found feelers going out to her to join various charitable organizations. Those on committees sensed one of their own. "Phoebe says you're remarkable at organizing things. I wonder if you'd consider giving some time to our London Fund for the Blind?" She was asked to dinner at a house in Cadogan Square, where they had managed to find an eligible bachelor to balance her at the table. But matchmaking had not been in the hostess's mind. She had trapped Kelly on the sofa over coffee, while they waited for the men to join them. "I've always been conscious of what a tragedy it was for poor Charles that Elizabeth had multiple sclerosis. I have a sister-in-law with the same thing. We're doing all we can to raise money for research. Do you think you might be able to help us a little?" Martin Wyatt, the vicar from Kate's area in Tower Hamlets was more blunt. He asked if he might come to see her at Brandon Place. She had thought at first it was because of Kate, but Kate didn't appear to worry him. "She'll make a splendid mother," he said cheerfully. "Pity there isn't going to be a visible father, but Kate will manage. I've got a lot of respect for her, and so have the people she works with. They know she's deeply committed to what she does, and they trust her. So I think Kate will be all right. Any rate, I pray for her, when I have time. But it's you, Lady Brandon—"

Kelly's eyebrows shot up. "Are you praying for me?"

He laughed. "Not yet. Perhaps I'll have to get around to it. What I need is your time. We're desperately short of people who'll come and spend time with the kids at the social center. Kate was talking about you, and it seemed to me you'd be the right type."

"What makes you think that?"

"If Kate says so, then I don't need any other reason. But for one thing, you're Australian. You've been places. You grew up outside England. You won't put these kids on the defensive by talking down to them. And if you'd agree to come and give us a hand, I'd prefer you called yourself Mrs. Brandon. They don't go much for the 'Lady' image down in Tower Hamlets. . . . Will you give it a try?"

Laura exploded when she heard of it. "You're just being *used* again, Kelly. They'll take every minute of your time, and you'll be paid for none of it."

They were standing in the drawing room, stripped of its furnishings, the smell of paint strong, examining the wall on which a sample of the pale silk wallpaper had been hung. Kelly pointed at it. "In view of that, Laura, would I have the cheek to ask for a paying job? It's a hell of a sight better than spending two mornings a week at the hairdresser."

Laura threw up her hands. "You're not going to meet any likely men in these places, you know. Vicars and do-gooders, and ladies in fancy hats pretending they're raising money for some worthy cause."

"I don't expect I will meet any likely men. I'll leave all that to Lady Renisdale. She's much more energetic in that direction than I am."

Laura sighed. "Well, perhaps you can get her off *my* back. All those chinless wonders she's produced for me. Where does she keep them?"

Kelly laughed. "That's very unfair, Laura, and you know it. She's doing her best to see that you have the sort of social life you'd have worked out for yourself if you'd grown up in London and at Charleton. You've been half-and-half for so long between here and Australia . . ."

Phoebe Renisdale gave two buffet supper parties for her granddaughter, and was merciless on her other grandchildren to see that every young man they knew with an acceptable background was produced. Kelly attended both parties and had been impressed with the numbers who had come. "Oh, it's easy," Laura had scoffed. "You just put it around a Guard's Regiment, or a few stock-broking houses in the City that Lady Renisdale is giving a bash for her poor-little-rich-girl granddaughter from Down Under, and they'll turn up in squads. After all, why not? It's a convenient address, the drinks are free, and the food's first class. What more do they want?"

But afterward the telephone rang quite frequently for

Laura. She pleaded work as an excuse to get off sometimes, but Kelly knew that she went to a few parties and a few dinners at which the hosts were also the cooks. "They haven't all got loads of money," she once volunteered. "They live in places like Chris's—but he's made a better hand of doing his place up than any of them. Far more imagination."

Reluctantly, at her grandmother's urging, she went to spend a weekend with Phoebe Renisdale's second cousins, the Gardiners, at an estate in Yorkshire near where Phoebe Renisdale herself had grown up. She came back ecstatic. "I loved it up there. We didn't do much except look over the whole farm and we went to visit Granny's old home. We walked on the dales—it was *cold*! But no wonder Granny loves it. The Gardiners are nice—very much farmers, running the place themselves. Alex and Ben—his name's Bennett, which was Granny's maiden name—the two Gardiner sons were home from agricultural college, and they had a friend with them. Gavin. He's going to work with his father on their place in Scotland. Alex had a couple of years at Oxford, and then switched to agricultural college. Everyone's very cost-conscious now, and they're not playing around at being farmers. They have to make it pay. They're all planning to manage the places themselves so they don't have the expense of an agent or a manager. They're even talking about using computers to work out the cost-effectiveness. It scares me—but it's interesting. I think you'd like the Gardiners, Kelly. The house, Everdale, is lovely. An old stone place that looks as if it grew out of the earth." Laura appeared happy, and Kelly thought that Phoebe Renisdale might have found the right antidote to the haughty, bored young Guardsmen. And there was much, she reflected, on both sides of Laura's inheritance that responded deeply to the land, to the things that grew from it, and those who worked on it. In her enthusiasm she seemed to have brought back some of the bracing, sparkling air of the Yorkshire dales. She talked happily of having been invited back.

Kelly drove down to Mead Cottage several times while the work was being carried out. The first time it was massively scaffolded, as the men swarmed around to mend roof, gutters and downspouts, lay the pipes for the new bathroom and the heating system. The local builder, Conegar, whom Cavanagh's had found, was the rare kind. His vowels were broad Gloucestershire, and he loved his work. "A real beauty, it is, m'lady. Does your heart good to see something put back in right shape and not spoiled. I've got good stonemasons. Master draftsmen, they are—father and son. Father's more 'an seventy now. Mr. Peter, he came along and talked to me before the job started, and I moved my two men from another job, because he asked. I'd do a lot for Mr. Peter. And of course, as it's for Sir Charles' family. . . . Knew the first Lady Brandon, I did. A right lovely, brave lady . . ." He pushed his hat back on his head and stared at the outline of the building against the raw November sky. "Don't you fret now, m'lady. If weather's right, we'll have you snug in here before the spring."

The same firm of Somerset cabinetmakers who were doing the Brandon Place kitchen had been engaged to work here. They clearly reveled in it, and the head of the small firm told Kelly that he thought he knew where she could get hold of the right sort of tables and chairs for the kitchen. "There's a big place going for auction, packed with furniture. The right sort for this house. There'll be dealers from all over the country there, looking for good pickings. But the family solicitor owes me a little favor. I might be able to get you in ahead of the dealers . . ."

Kelly went and was able to buy a stretcher table and carved oak chairs, a sideboard and dresser, a beautiful chest, two cupboards, a settle and two stools, and an assortment of copper, pewter and earthenware jugs and pots for flowers. Mr. Aubrey examined them carefully. "All late Tudor, or thereabouts—and all of it fine craftsmanship. May I ask where you found them, Lady Brandon? What sort of prices did you pay for them? Not too much, I hope."

"Not too much, but enough. And no, I can't tell you where I got them. Let's say someone did me a favor."

A wintry smile played about Mr. Aubrey's lips. "It was a favor, and I wish I knew your source. Well, you've just about done my job for me. With this as a basis, the upholstered chairs and sofas and curtains will be easy." He turned around and looked from the windows of the main room toward the orchard. "It will be beautiful when the garden is cleaned up. So satisfying to see work being well done."

Each time she went down to Mead Cottage she stayed at Wychwood. Only once was Louise there. Peter shrugged away her absence. "Louise gets bored here. Especially when there aren't guests. I suppose with Mrs. Page to run the place, she feels superfluous. There isn't any scope for someone like Louise. She's clever and creative, and she really ought to be doing some sort of real job. She redid the Eaton Square house, and everyone says it's a marvel—though I'm never quite comfortable with it, myself. But then, I'm old-fashioned. I've urged her to try something on her own. Open a dress shop, or something like that. But perhaps that's naïve. And it would need capital, which I haven't got. She gets restless here. I'm sorry for her sometimes. She was brought up in the remote Highlands. There were seven children growing up in a bone-chilling castle, and not a penny to spare. I think she's never got over the hatred of isolation and penny-pinching. There were five daughters, and all of them beauties. The sort of thing that *Country Life* loves to go and photograph, with them all sitting on the stone staircase in their plaids and white blouses. But they always had to stay with cousins or friends when they came to London, and sometimes borrowed their clothes for parties, and the taxi fare as well. They all became dab hands at fighting their way through sales to find the real bargains. It seems when you're nineteen, cheap clothes don't matter . . ."

"When you're tall, and have the bones Louise has, almost no one sees the clothes," Kelly observed.

"That's not what Louise thinks now." He smiled a little ruefully. "The four sisters all married men much richer than I—and of course Louise has to keep up. The four of them all have houses in London too, and there's a pretty active social life just there, without needing to go any further. But they all do. Between them, they're all into everything that's talked and written about. Well . . . why should I begrudge her her fun. Life's dull enough here, if you look at it that way . . ."

Kelly said nothing to that. She saw the name of Lady Louise Brandon often enough in the gossip columns to have an idea of the extent of her social life. It seemed to be an accepted thing that she lived that life in London, and only visited Wychwood when she wished to entertain friends. "She's always saying *I* don't have to stay here, either," Peter volunteered, as if he had read her thoughts. "It's hard for her to understand that I want to be here—that I want to farm my own land. I try to point out to her that it isn't exactly like banishment to the Highlands, but she really seems afraid of being trapped here."

It was as close as he had come to saying that their marriage was virtually over. Kelly thought of the two sons whom she had not yet met, and wondered if it was they who held together the last threads of this relationship. There seemed a streak of stubbornness in Peter which would not yield to the fact of this failure; which refused, for this moment, to admit it. And for that beautiful, rather wild child of a penniless Scottish peer, perhaps she was not yet prepared to venture beyond the conventional safety of her marriage and the background of Wychwood. Then Kelly dismissed the thought; it wasn't her business.

The routine of her visits to Wychwood had become established. The same room she had occupied with Charles was ready each time, the perfume of flowers in it, the hot-water bottle. Mrs. Page was hardly seen, but her presence was felt everywhere. Without her, the absense of Louise would have been much more marked. Kelly even, with a sense of trying to do Louise justice, began to wonder if indeed Mrs. Page was part of the reason for Louise staying away. Only the strongest will could have effected the slightest change in the prescribed ritual at Wychwood.

Mrs. Page spoke of Chris having taken over the basement flat only once. "I consulted with Mr. Nicholas before advising Christopher that I thought it would be correct, Lady Brandon. After all, you had said he could have it—"

"Yes, yes, Mrs. Page," Kelly answered, a trifle impatiently, unwilling to be involved in a discussion of Chris. But the silence following unnerved her. She felt obliged to add, "Chris has been very helpful to—to everyone."

Mrs. Page nodded, unsmiling. It was only, her manner indicated, what she expected to hear of her son. "For his age, Christopher is a thoughtful young man—not selfish, I mean. I had a lovely letter from Miss Julia telling me that she'd come to rely on him. Brought up as he was, without a father, Christopher tends to be rather aloof. Being at Brandon Place is, I think, bringing him out of that." She spoke, Kelly thought, as if they at Brandon Place were lucky to have Chris's presence. And indeed, Kelly conceded, they had been lucky. But at times one longed for a slight mistake, to see the perfection of either mother or son ruffled, just to prove that they were human.

Peter had taken to inviting a few guests to Wychwood whenever Kelly came down. The evenings were completely informal, the guests were often farmers like himself, though some, she thought, farmed many fewer acres. The wives seemed relaxed, as if coming to dinner at Wychwood when the hostess was absent was something they were used to. They tended to talk to Kelly about the campaign Charles had fought. There had since, of course, been another by-election, and the new member, Tim Carpenter, long ago installed in the House. "He's a good man," one woman said to Kelly, but, with bias, added, "but Sir Charles was just what we wanted. A Brandon, who practically grew up here . . . a wonderful man to represent us. What a pity . . ." She hurried on, perhaps worried that she had trespassed too much on personal territory. "We tried to persuade Peter to stand, but he says the farming takes too much time. He can't do both." She rattled her coffee cup, as if remembering the disappointment.

Kelly had fallen into the ritual of listening with Peter to some music after the guests had gone, and before the dogs got their walk. Her mind went always back to Pentland, and the first music she had heard with John Merton. Peter had qualities of silence which reminded her strongly of the older man; there grew between them a feeling of complete ease at these times, with no need for words. At the end of the music she would rise without comment and say good night. The dogs would go eagerly toward the front door. And a fire and the scent of flowers always greeted her in her room.

In November Sergei and Maria Kalchevna danced the premiere of *Attitudes*. It was a gala benefit for charity, with one of the Royal Family present. Kelly found that Louise had organized a box, and they all, Laura, Marya and herself, and of course, Julia, were expected to attend. Even Kate, who hated the idea of dressing up, reluctantly agreed to come. "Julia needs all the support she can get," Marya had insisted, and she brought from her wardrobe a long, flowing gown, with bands of embroidery on the wide sleeves. "It would fit a pumpkin, and we will just tack a piece of velvet on the hem to make it longer. No one will look at your feet."

Nick sent a car for them, and he, Louise and Peter were waiting when they reached Covent Garden. Louise looked dramatic in dark green silk, and she wore an emerald and diamond necklace and earrings. "Borrowed, of course," she said, fingering the necklace. "The jeweler likes the advertisement . . ." But her fingers touched it lingeringly; several times in the darkness of the box, during the two short ballets which preceeded *Attitudes*, Kelly saw her fingers on it again. Between acts, Louise introduced them to many people, but the most important to her obviously was a man called Jack Matthews. He spoke with the accent of the East End, and he wore diamonds in his dress shirt. "And he didn't borrow *them*," Louise laughed. "Jack arranged for me to have the necklace and earrings for tonight."

As they moved through the crowd to return to the box,

Nick leaned close to Kelly and said, "Now *that's* a man to watch. Matthews. He's made a few million on everything that's trendy these days. They say he just missed owning the Beatles. If anyone is in there promoting the image of Swinging London, it's Jack Matthews. He's into boutiques, rock, recording companies, cheap clothes—and anything else that'll sell. And little Louise had better watch herself. That's high-powered company she's playing with."

Attitudes was an extravagantly modern ballet, and it had been created for the male dancer of the pair. The ballerina was given her moments, but the spectacle was created to show off the particular talents of Sergei Bashilov. He danced its formidable choreography with a grace and strength that brought gasps from the audience. Effortless in the great turns and leaps, he still could come out of a head-spinning series and light on one foot and stand in utter stillness, compelling a like stillness from the audience, until the cheers and bravos broke through. At the end, as he and Maria Kalchevna took their bows, he displayed a charming modesty, always deferring to his partner. But the evening was his. As they were taking their final bows, Sergei straightened and turned directly toward the box where Julia was seated beside Louise. He kissed the rose Kalchevna had given him from one of the bouquets, and, standing on his toes, he aimed it toward Julia. Encumbered by the ankle cast, she was slow to get to her feet, and her outstretched hand missed it by inches. It fell among the audience below. Sergei bowed to Julia, bowed again to Kalchevna, and the audience roared its approval. And Kelly watched as the tears slid helplessly down Julia's face.

"Damn!" Kate muttered beside Kelly. "This was to have been *her* night. I don't know how she can stand it."

"She loves him—that's how. For her, it's *his* night. And he threw the rose to her."

VII

Nick's voice was quiet, as always, on the phone. "Kelly, tell the others you're going somewhere else and come around and have dinner with me, will you? Just the two of us. There's something I want to talk to you about. Eight o'clock, right?"

She had twice before been to dinner parties Nick had given in his top floor flat in St. James's Place, overlooking Green Park. She remembered them as glittering occasions, a mixture of people from the theater, journalism and the financial world, as carefully selected as the wines to complement each other, as beautifully presented as the food. But that evening it was quiet; not even all the lights in the drawing room were switched on. The curtains on the wall that faced the park were not drawn, and she could see over the top of the winter-bare trees to the lights of the Mall and Buckingham Palace. The clock in St. James's Palace around the corner chimed the quarter hour. Nick was late, which was unlike him. The butler had served her a drink; there was near-silence about her. The traffic flowing on Piccadilly was only a distant hum. She gazed at the spectacle of the winter London before her, the mist clinging softly about the tops of the trees. There was a faint melancholy about it, which seemed to suit the mood of the time they had just passed through. Two days ago she had watched on television the burial of John Kennedy, and had been moved by the sight of the young and beautiful widow with her two children, and that same woman who walked with the heads of state from a dozen countries to his funeral service. Laura had let her tears flow unchecked as she had watched. They had all shared the same shocked bewilderment. "I hate to see someone like that go," she had cried. "He seemed to be so *right*—he was young and he could still laugh. He gave people a sort of hope." It was the strong streak of idealism in Laura which had been touched, but she was expressing the sentiment of many at that moment.

Kelly cut off the thought and turned to survey the room behind her. Empty and quiet, it was a different place from the one she had known filled with people and talk. She hadn't realized how stark it was—deeply luxurious, but furnished in severe modern taste. She went from picture to picture—all were abstract—brilliant splashes of color in an otherwise almost totally milk-cream room. A silken Chinese rug of deep green was laid on the milk-colored wall-to-wall carpet, which also covered the entrance hall and dining room. There were a few colored silk cushions on the dull cream-covered sofas; there were glass-topped tables and a few pieces of wonderfully delicate Chinese ceramics, as spare and pale as the room itself. She wondered if the pictures and the ceramics had been Nick's choice, or a professional decorator's; but she had seen a de Kooning signature on one picture, a Hans Hoffmann on another, and there was a breathtaking Jackson Pollock. These were not decorator's pieces, and she guessed that a small fortune rested in the pale cream lines of a Chinese bowl.

"Excuse me, m'lady," the butler said. "Mr. Brandon's assistant has just telephoned. He apologizes for Mr. Brandon's lateness. He has just left his office and is on the way. May I bring you another drink, m'lady?"

She surrendered her glass, and when it was returned, surrendered herself to the stillness of the room. There were some freesias in a pale celadon vase, their perfume pervaded everything, reminding her subtly of the way her room at Wychwood smelled. She wondered if Nick had sought to create this pool of deep quite in the middle of London as his own version of the essence of Wychwood, which for Kelly was captured in the moments when she and Peter sat listening to music, the lustrous heads of the labradors reflecting the firelight. She decided that it had been Nick who had made this room, not a decorator. The absence of clutter was a statement of the man.

He stood in the doorway. "How quiet you are," he said. "I've never seen a woman who fidgeted less. Very sorry I'm late. There was someone who was taking a flight tonight from Johannesburg, and we had to settle something before he left."

"I've been enjoying it." Nick took the martini in a chilled glass from the butler. He sipped, and the severe lines of his face relaxed. Then he sat down across from her, sighing a little as he took another sip.

"It's beautiful here," Kelly said. "I've never had a chance really to look at it before. The pictures . . ."

He smiled. "Rather different from the Constables and Turners at Wychwood I grew up with. When it came to buying something for myself, I found I wanted something very different . . ." The talk drifted on in generalities. How they had both reacted to *Attitudes*, and how long it might be before Julia had her chance to partner Sergei in it. They went in to the candlelit dining room. Two places were set close together on the bare polished table. They ate fish in a delicate sauce, a succulent roast beef, and a lemon sorbet. "Do you always have wines like this?" Kelly asked. "Or am I dreaming? I thought the food at your dinner parties was superb, but simplicity like this is achieved only by a great cook."

The tired, rather tense lines in his face softened. "I try to keep everyone up to scratch. I'll help you buy some wines if you like. Or at least introduce you to my wine merchant."

Kelly laughed. "That's one introduction I might not be able to afford."

Over coffee in the drawing room they talked about plans for Christmas. "Louise is planning a big bash at Wychwood. A bit of a mix-up. Friends of Tommy and Andrew from school—little maharajahs, I suppose, who aren't going home for the holidays. That would be the sort Louise would encourage. And then she'll have her own set—the Swinging London lot. Personified by Mr. Jack Matthews, no doubt. There's always a bit of a do for the tenants and the farmers around. I wonder how the two lots will mix?"

"Will you be there?"

He pulled a face. "Not if I can help it. I'll send presents and regrets, and find some urgent business in Australia. I'm waiting to be invited to Pentland, Kelly. When are you going to do it?"

She put down her coffee cup. "And when are you, Nick, going to tell me what was suddenly so urgent to say? You're a marvelous host, but I'm growing impatient."

He rose, and went out into the hall. She heard him speaking to the butler, and then he returned and closed the door. "More coffee? I'm having a brandy. Will you join me?"

She nodded. He seemed maddeningly slow and heavy as he performed those tasks, he who usually was quicksilver light and swift. He sat down opposite her. Suddenly they seemed a vast distance from each other, the cream-whiteness of the room expanded, the mist beyond the windows made it seem to stretch into an indefinite space; the light struck the almost translucent surfaces of the ceramics and reflected back tiny images of the bright squares of paintings. Nick saw at some distance from the nearest lamp, and his face was shadowed. His expression seemed to Kelly to grow grim, almost anguished.

"Kelly, I want your help."

The thought that she could help Nick Brandon seemed ludicrous. "How can I help?"

"With Kate. Kelly—Kate is having my child, and I want to marry her. She refuses."

It was cowardly to turn away from him and reach for the brandy. For a few seconds she closed her eyes, and inhaled the bouquet, and heard her own heart thudding in her chest. She heard the clock in St. James's Palace chiming the hour, and even counted the strokes. Ten. So short a time . . . she opened her eyes.

"Forgive me, Nick. It's a surprise. I confess I've often wondered about the father of the baby. In my wildest imaginings—and some of them have been wild—I never thought of you."

He shook his head. "No you wouldn't. Nor would anyone else. On the surface, it doesn't make sense. She and I are so unalike. Most of the time she annoys me intensely. I don't like the way she talks, the way she lives. God help me—I *hate* the way she dresses! I think most of the things she says are nonsense. I've grown weary of arguing with her about things in which we're so fundamentally different that we shouldn't even be in the same room, much less the same bed. But we have been in the same bed, and I enjoyed it more than I ever had with any woman. All her fierceness is there—and that damnable honesty. It's for the things she doesn't have that I've come . . . well, let's say I've come to have a very high regard for them. She has no guile, no greed, no sham. She has a quite brilliant mind, disastrously set on the wrong course. But you don't have to go to bed with a political viewpoint, and Kate and I have been to bed. Oh, most certainly we've been to bed—gloriously, joyously to bed. In these last years I've never been to bed with a woman whom I was certain wanted nothing of me but myself. Kate? Kate wants nothing. I can give her nothing, not even my name. She already has that. My child will be called Brandon, whether Kate marries me or not. I want my child, Kelly. I never thought it possible to care so much about a child. But I want this child."

"Do you want Kate? Do you love her?"

He shrugged. "I've asked her to marry me, many times. Love? I'm not sure I know what that means. I'm not romantically in love. I never have been. I see all of her flaws, and few of her virtues. But the virtues she has compel me to respect her. She can't be bought, and I find that a very rare quality—in a man or a woman."

Kelly took another sip of brandy. The smoke from Nick's cigarette curled toward the light from the lamp; the mist seemed to press more closely against the windows. Despite the warmth, the food and wine, despite the luxury, the air seemed chill. She thought of the brief, unlikely affair between these two—on the surface so disparate, but somehow each possessing a quickness and fire which Kelly could well imagine igniting into that physical passion that Nick, so unsentimental, had chosen to call joyous, glorious. For a second she reflected on the blood tie between these two—how close was it? Charles had been Michael Brandon's first cousin, so Nick and Kate were what?—second cousins, or second cousins several times removed? The relationship was distant enough not to matter; the child who inherited the genes of these two people seemed unlikely to be anything less than they were themselves—sharp, clever, quick. She thought of Kate's strain of high idealism melded with Nick's streak of ruthlessness; it would be a more than interesting child.

She answered slowly. "She can't be bought—I think there's your answer in your own words, Nick. If you could offer her love, she might be persuaded. But you've your own kind of honesty. You haven't said you love her."

He shook his head. "No—I've never said that. But I've never said it to anyone else, either. Kate knows that. I've offered her a relationship that I think could be made to work. She rejects it. If it weren't for the child, I think I could walk away and forget it. There are other women who would be more comfortable to live with, God knows. Women who would also give me children. But when Kate and I came together, even though the time was so brief, it was with an almost . . . well, an almost explosive force that I've never experienced before. Kate has a strange . . . a sort of compelling power. It's the kind of thing that makes Julia a star the moment she appears on the stage. It is the thing that made us all sit up and listen when Kate spoke in that damnably cold and uncomfortably hall during the election campaign. It's the sort of quality Charles had that made him both loved and hated. If I do love Kate, then love is not at all the sort of emotion I expected it to be."

"How long—how long were you lovers? Are you still lovers?"

He shook his head. "No. I hardly see her now, except those few minutes at Brandon Place. She won't come here anymore. And how long?—well, it started just after you went off to Australia. Your going was a bit of a shock. To all of us. It's hard to explain why. I took to going around to Brandon Place regularly. Julia wasn't there often—you know what a dancer's life is. Marya always seemed to have work to do. I found myself taking Kate out to dinner quite often, furious with her because she refused to go to good restaurants—or if she did consent, she wore the clothes she'd been working in all day. We argued through every meal. I started asking her here. It was all very brief—and at times rather painful. She can be so abrasive. But it ended when she told me she was pregnant, and I asked her to marry me. She laughed at me, Kelly! She *laughed* at me!"

Clearly it had been a long time since anyone had laughed at Nicholas Brandon. Kelly had a sudden vision of Kate's mocking pointed little face under its spiky haircut, the huge dark eyes lighted by wit and intelligence and conviction. She tried to imagine Kate in this room. It was an unlikely picture.

"What do you want me to do?"

"Ask her. Persuade her. Tell her how much easier life will be for her and the child. She can continue just as she wants to. She can even go on with that damned silly social work. She can stand for Parliament when they give her a constituency. But I want her and I want my child . . ."

Nick's chauffeur was waiting to take her home. They turned into St. James's Street as the Palace clock chimed the half hour.

The light was on in the hall of Number 15, and looking up from the street, Kelly saw that the light in Kate's flat was showing through the drawn curtains. She went up and knocked at the door. "Kate?—it's Kelly."

She answered the door immediately, wearing a shapeless dressing gown stretched over her swollen body. "Kelly—come in! It's ages since you've been up here." She held the door wide. "What would you like? Coffee?—tea? I think I've got some brandy . . ."

"Nothing, Kate, thank you. I've had plenty." Kelly found a place on the sofa which was strewn with newspapers, books and magazines. A gas fire added to the warmth of the central heating. A single reading light burned beside a big chair. Kate settled into it, and put her feet up on an old leather pouf. She was wearing lambswool slippers, curling over at the sides. She did not look in the least like anyone the immaculate, fastidious Nick Brandon would want to marry. Bulging, sagging bookshelves were on every wall of the room, almost to the ceiling. The only space left was over the fireplace, and there was displayed only an unframed poster, the Picasso peace dove. The room was as much a statement of Kate as anything could be, as strong a declaration as Nick's cream-white room had been.

"I've just had dinner with Nick."

Kate sighed, and stretched out her hand for a cigarette. "I've been trying to keep off these damn things because the doctor said I should. But if you're going to talk to me about Nick . . ." She struck a match and lighted the cigarette. "Well . . .?"

"He told me that your baby is his."

"He has? Well, I won't deny it. I've no need to make him out a liar. But being the baby's father doesn't give him any rights over me. None at all."

"It gives him natural rights, Kate. And he still wants to marry you."

Kate drew deeply on the cigarette. "I told you the night

you came home that I had no intention of marrying the baby's father. That still goes. Can you see me married to Nick Brandon? The idea's ludicrous. I still am amazed that we ever had a relationship. We spent our time arguing—except when we were in bed. That part of it was good. Quite amazingly good. Nick suddenly stopped being patronizing and condescending and maddening." She added, with the faintest trace of regret, "He was a good lover."

"Don't you think you could build on that? A lot of marriages don't even have that."

Kate stabbed at the air with her cigarette. "*That* is no real basis for a marriage. The fact is that I don't respect Nick. I hate what he stands for . . . the way he makes his money. You only become filthy rich in a few years by doing things that are questionable, and investing in things where people work like slaves for almost nothing. Do you think I could live—or I could let my child live—on the proceeds of black labor in South Africa? Or textile sweatshops in Hong Kong? That money stinks! I would choke on the smell of it. I don't know how I let Nick Brandon take me to bed. But I did. And I wasn't very careful. But when I knew I was going to have a baby, I wasn't sorry. I want my baby. But it will be mine—not Nick Brandon's."

Quietly, slowly, Kelly recited the benefits that a marriage would give to the child, the possible anguish of growing up illegitimate. She talked only of the child. Kate listened to it all, and still shook her head. She took her feet down from the pouf, and leaned toward Kelly.

"Just let me ask you one question, and I think you'll see that any thought of marriage between me and Nick is impossible. Kelly—can you see me in that awful Ice Palace of his? Can you see me presiding over his dinner parties which have no purpose except to advance Nicholas Brandon? Can you see a child growing up there."

"Nick could change."

Kate shook her head. "Nick is forty-two. He'll no more change than I will." She looked around the room, at its cluttered, shabby warmth. "No, my baby will take its chances here, and they're not such bad ones."

Kelly nodded. "Well, I did what I promised Nick I'd do. And I don't think the baby's chances are so bad, either." She got to her feet. "Would you like a hot drink? Shall I make some tea, or coffee?"

Kate smiled. "I'm glad *that's* over. You're a good sort, Kelly. No coffee or tea. The doctor says I drink too much of it. Make it cocoa. All milk." She patted her belly. "I have to think of the baby."

Kelly went into the little kitchen to heat the milk, glad that she no longer had to face Kate's sharp gaze. Did the other woman, she wondered, sense the envy with which she viewed the swelling belly in the shapeless gown? Kate, without a husband, would have a child. She, Kelly, had had two husbands, had three stepchildren; but the child she longed for had not been given to her. And time was running out.

Chapter Seven

I

The two houses in Brandon Place suddenly seemed to flower. The roofs were mended, the exterior painting finished, the scaffolding started to come down. They were painted the same white as the Cavanagh houses on either side, but Kelly decided to keep the yellow on the front doors that Chris had chosen. He permitted himself a rare display of pleasure when she had mentioned it to him. "I'm awfully glad. I thought perhaps you'd think I'd over stepped myself doing what I did."

He had taken out the last perennials in the tubs beside both front doors and replaced them with trailing ivy, and a mixture of miniature conifers. "Too busy!" the young decorator from Cavanagh's had sniffed as he passed them. But Kelly found herself consulting Chris when the decision about a tree to be planted in the small garden had to be made. He took the matter seriously, and spent some time at the public library, and telephoned a nurseryman he knew near Wychwood. "If you're brave you could try a *Prunus Autumnalis*—winter flowering cherry. It's very sheltered there between the buildings, and there's nothing better to look at on a dark winter's day. Otherwise you'll have to settle for a plane tree—and the roots of that'll get too big. Get into the drains. Summer is easy. We can fill it with tubs of this and that—any fool can do a summer garden." The little garden took on a rather more austere look than the decorators at Cavanagh's had envisaged. Teak furniture had been ordered, rather than the white wrought iron they had suggested. "It costs a fortune," Chris had said, "but you'll have it forever. I'll oil it a couple of times a year. It's no more trouble than painting the other stuff." Subtly, the garden took on the look of a Japanese scene. Between the irregularly laid squares of flagstone, Chris planted spreading junipers. "It will look better when the moss starts coming in and blurring those edges." The tree was planted and staked. As the weather grew colder they waited for the first of the tiny pale pink blossoms to appear.

"Perhaps it won't bloom this first season," Laura said.

"It had *better* bloom," Chris answered, with what was for him an unusual flash of humor. "I've spoken to it sternly."

It was Chris who had scoured the antique and second-hand shops to find the table and chairs for the kitchen. None of the chairs matched exactly—all were versions of the spoke-backed Windsor. They were admired by the older of the two craftsmen who had come from the West Country firm to install the cabinets personally. He fingered the patina of the old, big scarred table Chris had found. "Lovely bit of work that, m'lady. Goes right well with the cabinets." He viewed the potted plants that hung in front of the windows, suspended from old iron hooks Chris had produced. "Right clever young chap, that is. Got a feel for things . . ."

"Oh, m'lady," Mrs. Cass had sighed when the kitchen was finished. "It's beautiful." She ran her hand over the unknown, terrifying dishwasher, the refrigerator with its separate freezer that was bigger than any she had ever seen; she stared aghast at the number of dials and knobs on the cooker. "It's beautiful—but it still looks like home." Then she examined the set of French copper saucepans hanging from their iron rack over the table. It had been Nick's gift brought over from France after he had seen the final plans for the kitchen. "I'm sure they're very beautiful, m'lady, and they do say nothing cooks better than copper. But Mr. Nicholas doesn't have to clean them." Nevertheless, they became Mrs. Cass's point of pride, polished unnecessarily and lovingly.

So it was easier to turn to Chris when it came to the final clearing up of Charles' study. It was a damp cold Saturday in December. The rest of the house was almost finished. On Monday Cavanagh's people would start to lay the new carpet right through the house; after that the curtains would be hung, and the newly reupholstered furniture put in place. But no one, so far had done more than measure Charles' study for the curtains and the carpet, and have them made up. The passage that led to it had been painted right to the door. Kelly still had not faced the problem of making the study ready for the painters on Monday morning.

Laura had presented herself in old slacks and sweater to help; she looked at the room despairingly. "*How* did he collect so much paper? And how did he ever know where anything was?" She studied the bank of filing cabinets. "I hope they send along some burly men on Monday morning. It'll take an Atlas to move these while they paint behind and get the carpets laid. Shall we just pile the loose papers and stuff in the passage? At least that will get them out of here, and give them a better chance to work . . ." Kelly was tempted once again just to close the door and forget about it, but Laura's and Chris's waiting presence prevented that.

"Yes—let's put all the loose papers in piles, and we'll cover them with dust sheets. Then when the filing cases go back, we can stack them on top again."

"You're not going to sort through it?" Laura asked.

Kelly shook her head. "Perhaps some day . . ." She started by clearing the desk of the few papers now on it. Over the weeks she had worked steadily away at the pile of mail which had gathered there, the letters of condolence. She had even bought a filing cabinet of her own. All the things she had been taught at Miss Hale's secretarial school came once again into play; all the skills Greg had needed and demanded of her were used. The bank statements were neatly filed, the correspondence dealing with Pentland and the other Australian interests had their own folders, Laura's trust fund statements and her own had been scrutinized. She had bought a typewriter. She had cleared one of the drawers of Charles' desk for the pens and paper clips and rubber bands she needed, and left his own potpourri of such items alone. The keys of the filing cabinets had been in Charles' pocket when he died. With such items as his watch they had been handed to her, and lain undisturbed in the top drawer of the desk. She looked around and felt a sense of desolation as Chris and Laura began to move the papers and clippings and journals stacked on top of the filing cabinets. How bare and empty it looked without them—how unnaturally tidy. She began to take down the pictures, revealing the sooty marks on the wall. She looked at each of them carefully—there was

Charles in all the various phases of his life—with the officers of the regiment in India, with Mountbatten, with Alexander, with Montgomery. He was in the background with three other officers as a smiling Eisenhower greeted King George VI; he stood with a row of officers behind Churchill, Roosevelt and Stalin at Yalta—that would be a fateful picture to Marya. There was one, probably from one of the Renisdale newspapers, of him entering 10 Downing Street at the time of the Suez crisis. Kelly recognized the background of Charleton in one as Charles had faced the television and newspaper cameras after his resignation from the Army following that crisis. There again were the steps of St. George's Chapel, Windsor, with Charles among the company of the Knights of the Garter following the Queen in procession. That was the one Kelly loved most, studied most often. If ever a man seemed born to grace that medieval costume of cape and plumed hat, it was Charles; he wore it effortlessly. She decided that when the decorating was done, she would have one of the photographs of their own wedding framed, and she would hang it here. She would also return to its place the yellowing print of Charles with Elizabeth Brandon in her wedding gown of the style of years ago, as well as the photographs of them both outside Buckingham Palace on the day he had received his V.C., Elizabeth in a wheelchair, her face turned upward with an almost fierce pride toward Charles. She thought she might even put a photo of Greg there—the photo of him when he had stood on the summit of Everest. Laura would like that. . . . She realized that she had gone off into a reverie, and Chris was standing beside her, waiting to take the photo of Charles in his Garter robes from her hand; he must have stood there silently for some time. His face was grave as he also studied the photo, and turned to look at the others still on the wall.

"He had a remarkable life, didn't he?"

Kelly nodded wordlessly, and passed the picture on.

The work was almost finished when Laura brought mugs of coffee and a plate of biscuits from the kitchen. They stood around the desk while they drank it. "I suppose we ought to take the drawers out of the desk and put them in the passage too," Laura said. "It'll lessen the weight for the men to move it." Idly as she talked, she slid open the top drawer. "Good heavens—it's still here. I'd forgotten all about it." She took out the box with its silver plate bearing the inscription from the company Charles had lead to the Afghanistan border. She opened the box, revealing the beautiful revolver, with its fanciful inlay, and took it up in her hand.

"Laura, put it back!" Kelly said sharply.

"Oh, it's all right. It's not loaded. Charles made sure of that after Sergei got so wild with it. Look, here are the bullets . . ." She weighed the gun in her hand, extending her arm to feel the balance. "I promised him I'd clean it—and polish the silver." She laid the gun down gently in its velvet-lined niche. "Well, I will. Before everything is put back here, Kelly." As she closed the box she said to Chris, "Do you think your father was on that patrol into the Khyber Pass? He was in the same regiment, and he was Charles' best friend . . . I wonder if they were together then?"

"It's likely," Chris said. "They did a lot together, right from the beginning. They were at Eton and Sandhurst together. Passed out together. Sir Charles was head of his class, I was told. My father's in the photo of the officers in India."

Laura's eyes widened. "He is? Let me have a look at it."

Chris shrugged. "Too much trouble to dig it out from all the rest now. You'll see it when we're putting them all back." He nodded toward the filing cabinets. "His whole life story must be there . . ."

Laura gave an exclamation. "Kelly!—look at this!" She had brought out a small box, opened it, and revealed a medal on a mauve ribbon. "That's his *Victoria Cross*! Can you imagine just leaving it here in the drawer, with all the rubber bands and paper clips and bits and pieces. Really—it should be mounted—or in a glass case—or something . . ." For a few moments they all stared at the simple, unadorned medal, with its stark words, For Valour.

"Can you imagine him doing anything else?" Kelly answered.

She felt her throat tighten, and didn't want either of them to see the sudden brightness of tears in her eyes. To sit in Charles' room to work was one thing; actually to handle his possessions, to weigh his achievements, to see the landmarks of his life come down from the wall was quite another. She began to pick up the empty mugs. "Another biscuit, Chris?" She tried to smile at him, and knew that the smile was falsely bright. He shook his head.

Laura was farther into the drawer. "Surely this newspaper can go, Kelly? It's just stuffed in here . . . at least it would be one out of the way."

Glad of the distraction, Kelly turned to look at it. It was the *Evening Journal*, one of the papers owned by Lord Renisdale. The big black headlines were intended to catch the eye of the homeward bound commuter at the railway stations and the entrance to the Underground. "PHILBY IN MOSCOW? Is He the Third Man?" She concentrated on it, to keep back the tears. It referred to the disappearance from Beirut of Kim Philby, linking him to the notorious Burgess and Maclean, who had defected to Russia years earlier, taking with them secrets that had caused one of the biggest diplomatic rows in memory between the United States and Britain. Philby had been connected with both Burgess and Maclean; there had been accusations that it had been he who had tipped off the two and allowed them to make their escape. But the Prime Minister and the Foreign Officer had continued to say that the connection was circumstantial. Philby had been, however, forced to leave the Foreign Office, and had worked as a journalist until his disappearance. She and Laura had been in America when the news had broken that most definitely Kim Philby was in Moscow, and the old anger against the British Security network had broken out afresh, with renewed bitterness. But this paper had been published before that fact had been established. It had been an evening headline teaser.

"Yes, Laura. I'd like it kept. I put it there."

"Oh . . ." Laura looked at it again. "I'm so sorry, Kelly. I just didn't think . . ."

Kelly took one more look at the big headline, remembering how she had gathered the scattered pages from the floor. It was the evening paper published on the day Charles had died.

The biscuits spilled from the plate as she put it back on the tray. At once Chris was at her side, putting them back, placing the milk and sugar beside him. "I'll take them, shall I—?"

For once her grief broke through, her resentment toward the invasion of the privacy of her home, her relationship with a man whose life she had scarcely begun to know.

"Oh, for God's sake stop being so bloody helpful!" She picked up the tray and charged along the passage, the milk sloshing over onto the tray, the feeling of remorse already with her. She shouldn't have said that to Chris, but she had.

II

In the second week in December Kelly went down to Mead Cottage with two thousand daffodils in the boot of the car to plant. Peter laughed at her. "Instant garden? You'll need a bit of help. In fact, if you're going to plant on that scale, you'd better be doing something to the whole orchard. It hasn't been touched for years. The trees need heavy pruning, of course, but that can be done during the winter. Haines might be able to spare some time for that, I think. What the soil needs now is rotovating, fertilizing and reseeding with grass. Then the bulbs will plant easily, and next summer you'll have a little crop of hay to sell me . . ."

It wasn't Haines who came to Mead Cottage with the rotovator, but Peter himself. The day was fine with a pale sun, and warm for that time of year. "No rain for a week—you're lucky. The soil can get damn heavy when it's wet." He worked in gum boots, and eventually pulled off his sweater, and rolled up his sleeves. His powerfully muscled arms had the look of often being worked that way. Kelly followed as quickly as she could, dropping the bulbs into the freshly turned earth, scattering them randomly and planting where they fell. The trees were old and lichened, with many dead and hanging limbs. She thought of how it would look in spring, the drifts of yellow and gold and white blossoms turned to the sun, the spring she had once imagined sharing with Charles. She would put some wooden seats in the orchard, and in the summer they would have tea there. Who were they?—Kate's baby in its pram, perhaps?—Julia taking a few days rest with Sergei? Dancers never rested. Would she have to strip the carpet off one of the rooms and install a *barre*? Thoughts as random as the bulbs she planted.

They ate their lunch sitting on the empty plastic bags from the fertilizer Peter had spread. It was the usual beautifully prepared food Mrs. Page always sent. They sat and viewed the cottage clothed in its scaffolding. "It's going to look great," Peter said. "I love seeing it come back to life. It's looked so sad and neglected all these years since Elizabeth and the girls left. What a pity Charles . . ." His hand closed over hers. Despite the gloves she had worn, her hands were caked with dirt, and the earth was heavy under her fingernails; she realized how few times Peter had touched her. She was only now discovering that his hands were nearly as hard as a laborer's. "Well," he continued, "at least you're making a life for yourself. Shaping it around something. I think Charles would have been pleased that you decided to come back here. Places, like people, can be a nuisance and a burden. But belonging to no one and no place can be a pretty sad sort of existence."

But she did belong also to Pentland, she thought—and dared not say it lest he should sense the tug of her loyalties. The isolation of Pentland, shared only with those two women, Delia Merton and Mary Anderson, seemed bleak indeed by comparison with the rich mixture of the life she was making here and at Brandon Place. But what she owed to John Merton, the trust he had placed in her, was something which could never be forgotten. Sometimes, in the sleepless passages of the night she wondered what she would do if Laura should marry and make her life completely in England? Then she, Kelly, would carry the burden of Pentland alone. Instantly, she was closer in understanding with Peter Brandon, who labored for his inheritance, who struggled to save it for his sons. It occurred to her that John Merton would have liked him very much.

"But you?" she said. "Will you always have Wychwood? Will you be able to hold on to it? Pass it on to Tommy? The estate duties . . . are they going to let you keep it?" It had been a thought nagging at the back of her head ever since she had returned to Wychwood and Mead Cottage. Somehow, life here, without Peter's proximity, seemed a cold, less pleasing prospect. How, in the short time, her dependence on him had grown. A dangerous dependence, perhaps.

He let out a deep breath. "Thank God for Nick. He's paying the lot. We can keep the land and the house. At least this time around we can keep it. When it comes to Tommy's turn . . . well, that's anyone's guess. He probably won't have a brother like Nick."

"Nick is paying *everything*?"

"Every last penny. Don't ask me how he's managing it. It's nearly half a million. It's taken him months to arrange, but the Revenue people are prepared to be patient when they scent that they're actually going to see their money. They really don't like the idea of selling up a place and a farm like Wychwood any more than most people do. The thought of the bad publicity when yet another estate is sold up to pay death duties doesn't exactly give them joy. It isn't so easy to find a buyer for a house like Wychwood, so the land would have gone first, and that takes the gut out of the whole thing. At times I was so frantic I thought of taking in guests to keep it running—but I suspect I'd make a rotten hotelkeeper." He laughed.

"Nick must be selling shares in Brandon, Hoyle."

"He is, I think. He won't be specific about it. I don't know in what sort of position it leaves him. He had the majority holding in the company, which gave him control. But he says there are ways to arrange things so that his position is secure. I don't know how he juggles it all. I almost have the feeling that half a million or so doesn't mean very much in Nick's way of thinking. But to me it's the difference between life and death—keeping Wychwood and losing it."

"Does that mean Nick's got a share in Wychwood now?"

He shook his head. "He refused it when I offered. Said he wanted no part of it. Frankly, I don't understand it, and I don't think he means me to. All I know is that early in the New Year the Revenue people will be paid off, and I can breathe again. Ever since my father died and we began to realize the size of the death duties, I've been waiting for the axe to fall. It seems it's not going to, after all—and Nick has chosen to make it that way."

"I didn't think Wychwood meant so much to him."

"Nor did I. He hardly ever comes here. I realize I know my own brother . . . well, what I realize is that I don't know him at all. I wouldn't have believed there was a sentimental bone in his body."

Kelly was silent for a few moments; she became aware that she was still holding Peter's hand, and holding it quite unselfconsciously. "I'm so happy it's going to be all right. But Nick . . . well, I don't understand him, either." She plunged on. "Did you know . . . ? Did he tell you about Kate?" As soon as she had said the words she wanted to withdraw them. She was, possibly, violating a trust, Nick's and Kate's; was possibly laying another burden on Peter. But hadn't he said that burdens were the rock of existence; she had believed him.

His hand gripped hers more tightly. "I'm glad you know. He only told me a few weeks ago. The same time he came down to tell me he'd got things worked out about the death duties. That was when I really tried to push a partnership in Wychwood on him because he's going to have someone to inherit. But he just laughed and said that his kid was going to have a pile of shares in Brandon, Hoyle—not a slice of a crumbling old house and a few acres."

"Kate won't marry him."

"I don't think he believes it. This baby has taken hold of his imagination. He wants it. I was amazed. I just don't see Nick as a father."

"Neither does Kate. She won't marry him. He sent me to ask her again."

He shook his head. "Strange that those two ever came together in that way. But it's not strange that Kate won't marry him. They couldn't last together. Anyone can see that."

"If she married him, he'd have legal rights to the child . . . a say in the way it was brought up . . . how it lived. Kate is determined he won't. She'll bring it up the way she thinks it should be. Do you know what she called Nick's flat?—the Ice Palace. Perhaps there is more than a little truth in that."

Quite slowly, he raised her hand to his lips. And then pressed it against his cheeks. "And if you don't think I feel like a bloody fool doing this . . . and yet, what can I say?" He lowered her hand and looked at it, rubbing the dirt-engrained lines between his fingers. "What burdens we've laid on you, Kelly. All of us. You know what'll happen if you don't get out from under? You'll end up bringing up Nick's kid! That's what families do to you. Welcome to ours."

He let her hand fall into her lap. The workmen in the cottage had finished their lunch break; the sound of hammering came to them. "Well, two thousand daffodils are a hell of a lot of daffodils. And you're a hell of an optimist, Kelly. We'd better get back at it."

III

Cavanagh's had achieved what had seemed impossible; the refurbishing of Number 16 Brandon Place, and the work needed on Number 15 was completed a few days before Christmas. Kelly came downstairs one morning to find Mrs. Cass standing in the hall, her coat and scarf still on, shopping basket over her arm, twisting her gloved hands together, her lips trembling slightly. "Mrs. Cass—what is it? Is something wrong?"

"Oh, no, m'lady. Nothing wrong . . ." Kelly was dismayed to see that she was on the edge of tears. "It's just . . . well, it just struck me as I came in. It's all so beautiful now. Everything." She gestured to the Christmas tree which had gone into its former place the day before, and last night had been decorated. All the old decorations had been brought out. But Mrs. Cass's gesture took in the hallway, the staircase, the newly painted and carpeted hall and stairs of Number 15 visible through the glass doors. Kelly had had a heavy curtain made which could be drawn over the glass doors, but she guessed it would be seldom used. Mrs. Cass moved to the open door of the kitchen; she was still unused to its new splendor. Then she went on to look at the dining room. Elizabeth Brandon's beautiful furniture had come into its own. "It never looked like this, m'lady. I came right after the war, and you were only allowed to spend a hundred pounds or thereabouts on repairs and decorating and such things. We just got a lick of paint here and there and made do. And then, when Sir Charles got permission, he spent so much money making

Number 15 into proper flats for the girls and Madame Marya . . . and the alternations for poor Lady Brandon and the nurses. There was never a penny over for making the place *look* nice . . ." She gazed at the silk wallpaper which the Chippendale furniture demanded, the silver-gilt framed mirrors Kelly had found for each end of the sideboard. She went over and touched the flowers which were reflected in another mirror over the marble mantel. She turned to the curved window that looked into the little garden, the winter-flowering cherry staked in place, the irregularly laid flagstones with their spreading juniper laid to Chris's direction, a pear tree espaliered on the wall of Charles' study, where it would catch the only sun the garden received. A ground cover of vinca mingled with the juniper. Mrs. Cass took off her gloves and touched the pale green damask curtains, looked at the faint imprint her shoes had made on the silken pile of the carpet.

"It always was a nice house, m'lady . . . and now you've made it beautiful. If only Sir Charles could see it . . ." She sniffed, and turned abruptly. "Well, this won't get my work done. Have you had breakfast, m'lady? I'll just put the kettle on. Will you have it in the kitchen, or will I bring it in here?"

"I'll take a tray to the study, Mrs. Cass. I've still got some Christmas cards to write . . ."

She sat at Charles' desk, sipping her coffee, not touching the pile of cards waiting to be written. She thought of the big drawing room, with its windows looking both onto Brandon Place and the garden, the room that had been transformed by the pale golden silk wallpaper, the golden damask curtains, the sprinkling of red upholstered chairs through the golden ones, Elizabeth Brandon's Regency side tables and commodes and mirrors at last having the background they deserved. Kelly remembered what Phoebe Renisdale had said when she had come the other day to see Laura's finished flat, and view the final results of the redecoration. "You've done wonders, my dear Kelly." They had sat in the drawing room drinking tea, served reverently in the Royal Doulton tea set of the old Imari pattern by Mrs. Cass, a tea set found on one of the upper shelves of the old kitchen, dust and grime-covered, and never, Mrs. Cass declared, used in her time. "Yes, wonders . . ." Lady Renisdale repeated. She looked around the room again. "It always cried out for this, but it was never possible for Charles. What a pity . . ." She set down her cup. "I can't help saying it. It's such a pity Charles didn't live to benefit from the help you would have given him. With a wife able to entertain, and a house like this to entertain in . . . you would have been very good for Charles' career, Kelly."

Kelly remembered it, thought about it, and began to wonder why she had done it. In the beginning, in the first flush of her welcome back to Brandon Place, it had seemed the obvious, the right thing to do. And now it was done, what would she do with it? Who would use it? Even Laura had moved over to Number 15. Would she, Kelly, sit alone in the golden drawing room at night? Unlikely. She would sit here, or in the room Charles had used as a dressing room next to the big bedroom, now refurnished as a sitting room with a television set and record player, bookshelves, three deep, comfortable chairs. And the golden splendor below would remain undisturbed. It frightened her to think that perhaps she had allowed to be created something as untouchable as the icy splendor of Nick's room. Where would the life come from that it had been meant to hold? Who would dare put the first spot on that golden carpet? She thought of the promises she had made to give time to various groups to raise money, to give time to the center in Tower Hamlets. She was back, almost, to the way she had lived in the years between Greg's death and Charles' advent, available to everyone because there was no life of her own urgently demanding to be lived.

The fresh brightness of the house about her seemed to take on a brittle sheen.

Julia had had the cast taken off a week before, and the surgeon had pronounced himself satisfied with the results. Julia smiled, and talked about soon dancing again; she walked without a stick, and almost without a limp. "He says it will grow stronger all the time. I'm to exercise regularly, but not too strenuously. Physiotherapy every day. I can't wait for the day I'll be able to take morning class again—but I will have to wait."

Kelly had invited her and Sergei to a drink in the drawing room. Sergei was not dancing that night, and normally he would have been relaxed, would have permitted himself a few swift shots of vodka. But he drank his vodka slowly, carefully, perched in unnatural stiffness on one of the golden chairs, gazing around the room as if he mistrusted his surroundings. His expression had brightened a little at the sight of his carriage clock. "You don't forget I owe you a Fabergé," he said. Then he sat down. "I liked it better before. More like home."

"Oh, Sergei," Julia wailed. "How can you say that when Kelly's taken so much trouble. It's *beautiful*!"

He shrugged. "I'm sorry. Maybe it will look better when it gets a bit dirty. Too clean."

"Is that Russian complaining again?" Marya said. Kelly had left notes on the hall table in Number 15 where the post was always put, asking her and Kate and Laura to join them. Marya poured herself a vodka, and sank down on a red chair, doing it exactly as if nothing in the room had changed. Kelly silently blessed her for the gesture. Julia went to bring the tray of canapés Kelly had prepared; it was a pleasure to see her move unencumbered by the cast or stick, and it was evident she took joy in her freedom of movement.

"Cheers," Marya said, tossing back half the vodka. She bolted down two of the canapés while Julia held the tray. "Good! I had no lunch. I was late for an appointment with a publisher, and then *he* was late, so I sat in the waiting room with my tummy rumbling. However, he liked the translation, so I can expect more things from him. How bored I get with these scientific and medical things. And the contracts! All very important, no doubt, but I never see the result."

Laura arrived. "I see you've taken over my salon," she said.

"Sergei was saying the room was too clean. I thought we ought to start dirtying it up a bit."

Laura surveyed it all, the ladened drinks table, the tray of canapés being passed around, the second one waiting under a damp cloth. "Well, I can see I won't be able to compete with this. But I do hope some of you will drop into my humble abode from time to time. Mr. Harris says I'm doing quite well, and I'm to get my head out of the books during Christmas." Mr. Harris was her tutor. "He says—" She stopped and walked back to the open door of the drawing room. "Kate? We're all up here. Kelly's taken over. I'm not needed anymore."

They heard Kate's voice as she came up the stairs. "I except a little more consideration for an expectant mother. Having to climb these stairs and then my own—and after two drinks. I think I'll patronize your pub, Laura. It's handier."

She also settled in a chair as if the new splendor of the room had quite escaped her. She looked well, Kelly thought—in the expression so often used about pregnant women, she was, in fact, blooming. She appeared to have experienced a serene and uneventful pregnancy, never seeming to be ill, never complaining of anything but her growing size.

After Christmas she would have leave from her job, and would stay out for two months after the baby was born. She seemed, as far as Kelly could tell, to have made little preparation for the birth. She did not talk of baby clothes, or prams, or arrangements about who would look after the child when it came. Kelly decided that after Christmas she would talk to her about it all, pin her down. She would have to point out that a baby was not like a book to be stored on a shelf until next required.

Laura had wandered around the room, and then positioned herself, drink in hand, by the windows overlooking Brandon Place. She seemed unusually tense, and Kelly realized that she was waiting, watching for the return of Chris Page. Finally, after ten minutes during which she had taken no part in the conversation, she turned to Kelly.

"Chris has just gone down the area steps. Did you leave a note for him, Kelly?" Chris had his own letterbox fixed to the basement rails. He did not use the hall table as the others did.

"Awful of me," Kelly lied. "I forgot. He's so quiet I just forget he's there, and since you moved over into your own flat, I hardly see him."

"Well, then, shall I go and ask him?"

"Of course," Kelly heard herself say. The others had not seemed to notice the exchange, except Marya, who stared at her for a moment, fixedly, and then tossed back her vodka.

Chris came up with Laura to join them, as careful, quiet, as clever as a cat picking its way through a field of obstacles. He had come home early, he said; the City was in a pre-Christmas slump. They exchanged information, joked, were serious, ate everything that was on the two trays, and drank to wash it down. At last Kelly said, trying to hide her nervousness, trying to make her voice casual, "Unless anyone's in a desperate hurry . . . well, I've got a big pot of stew on the stove. We could all eat in the kitchen." They mustn't know, any of them, how much she wanted them to stay—yes, even Chris. She was afraid that her eagerness sounded pathetic, the cry of a woman alone. They agreed. None of them wanted then to go and cook alone.

"I like your kitchen," Sergei said when they went downstairs. "It is real home."

"I have Chris to thank for that," Kelly said. She could not begrudge him the acknowledgment. If there were any rooms in the two houses which would keep them all together, it would be the kitchen and Laura's sitting room. And Chris Page had helped to bring both into being.

IV

As they had the year before, many of the ballet company came to Brandon Place after the Christmas Eve performance. Sergei greeted Kelly with a warm kiss. "Everything not so clean after this, eh?" The party spilled over the two houses; they ate ravenously, drank wine, broke into impromptu Christmas carols. From Laura's flat came the sound of the Beatles; in Kelly's drawing room a group tried to listen to a Mozart quintet. In the midst of the gaiety, Kelly missed Charles' presence acutely. Last year he had been the heart of this gathering. But she shared the pleasure when somone pointed out that the winter-flowering cherry had, for the occasion, miraculously burst into bloom; and she shared the laughter when it was discovered that the blooms were made of paper, glued onto the bare branches by Chris. Laura held one in her hand, laughing, and received Chris's kiss. "Happy Christmas, Laura. I meant it as a surprise for tomorrow morning." Both things were an uncharacteristic gesture from him, but he fell back into place by leaving immediately for Wychwood to spend Christmas with his mother. The words "Happy Christmas" echoed down Brandon Place as they had done the year before. The faintest blurring of snow showed in the light of the street lamps.

Kelly had wakened early by the ringing of the telephone at her bedside; the first sharp apprehension was instantly stilled when she heard the voice and the words. "It's covered in snow here, and it's beautiful. Just the way you first saw it. Happy Christmas, Kelly."

He remembered she had come to Wychwood in the snow. "Happy Christmas, Peter."

V

By late February Mead Cottage was ready. Kelly went down alone on a Thursday; for this first visit she would have liked to have Laura with her, but she did not invite her. Hers and Laura's lives would have to diverge, and this was as good a time as any to begin. Laura had planned a month ago to go to the Yorkshire cousins, the Gardiners. The visit seemed to have been arranged to coincide with Alex Gardiner being home from agricultural college. Laura said little about the visit, but Kelly knew she had bought some new clothes recently, and all of them had a distinctly "country" look. She had bought stout boots for walking, and a sheepskin coat.

Kelly had done her own clothes buying after Christmas,

and not from Cavanagh's. She had been accepted at the Tower Hamlets center as "Mrs. Brandon," but on the first visit she knew her clothes set her apart. So she went to Oxford Street and bought some inexpensive sweaters and skirts, cheap shoes, and a coat which looked all right on the rack, but she knew would soon begin to lose its shape. "I don't know," she confessed to Kate, "what I'm supposed to be doing there."

"It just matters that you're there," Kate answered. "You're there to talk to anyone who wanders in. To listen when you can get them to talk. You're there to dish out tea and sandwiches. You're there to play table tennis or chess with any kid who feels like trying. And watch out for the ones who need help with their reading and are too ashamed to admit it. There are a lot of those—the kids who hide the fear behind the cigarettes. The ones with the 'what have you got to show me?' attitude. The 'prove it to me' kids. If you help to keep even one of them out of Borstal or a remedial center, you'll have done a lot. And the Girl Scout attitude won't work. You have to try to imagine what it's like to be their age, and with damn-all ahead of you except some bloody boring job—if they're lucky enough to get a job."

Kelly came back from those afternoons and evenings at Tower Hamlets exhausted and strained. She seemed to be up against a wall of indifference, when it wasn't downright hostility. At times she thought she hated the teenagers who reluctantly showed up at the center—probably because it was too cold on the streets. And she guessed that some of them hated her, were suspicious of her despite the cheap clothes. Her hair was shiny, and she didn't have hands like their mothers'; her eyes weren't tired and defeated. These things she couldn't disguise. But the warm luxury of Brandon Place seemed at times overwhelming when she returned. She began to fear the wrath of the young, the fury that would mount when they came to the age when they knew for certain that the reality of their lives would never match their expectations.

So she went down to Mead Cottage with a slight sense of exhilaration, shaking off the depressing conviction that she could do nothing at Tower Hamlets, that all attempts to help or understand would founder on the rock of the vast divide between her life and theirs. And yet as she looked at them she knew only the hairsbreadth of chance had saved her from becoming one of them. Her mother's determination, Pentland and John Merton had saved her. She struggled to give some of this back. But she knew she could not change their pasts, and she could, by only fractions, influence their futures. She thought of Mead Cottage with a mixed sense of guilt and of pleasure.

There was a moment of painful remembrance as she swung open the gate of the cottage. It moved so easliy now on its new hinges; the path had been swept and weeded, the jasmine cut back from the door. She looked around, half expecting to see the stone with which Charles had propped up the gate the only time she had been there with him. That, like much else, was gone. She had brought groceries from London with her, and she carried them to the front door, fishing in her handbag for the key. Everything moved with well-oiled smoothness; the heating was on, the warmth greeted her. And something else. A fire burned in the big fireplace of the main room. The basket that Mrs. Page had so often sent over was on the long oak table; Kelly didn't need to look at it to know it was filled with the usual excellent food. But the sight of it angered her. She had believed, from now on, that she would be free of Mrs. Page. She neither wanted the fire lighted, nor the basket of food. And then she saw that a silver wine-cooler with a bottle of champagne set in it stood behind the basket. Mrs. Page would not have gone so far. It was Peter who had lighted the fire, brought the basket, set the wine to chill. Peter would come this evening.

She put the groceries away, put the casserole she had cooked in London into the oven, and took her bag upstairs. Mr. Conegar, the builder, and Mr. Aubrey between them had done well by the cottage. It was warm, comfortable, and had an atmosphere of ease about it; but it had retained its sense of age and intimacy. Areas of hand-pegged oak floor were visible; no one had blindly covered it all with carpet. The curtains and bed covers were small-patterned chintz, not fighting with the low, oak-beamed ceilings. She breathed a silent apology to Mr. Aubrey as she bathed in the tiny new bathroom. She had left so much to him, and if she thought that he had made Brandon Place perhaps a bit too splendid, he had treated Mead Cottage as the entity it was, and left it intact. The sleet rattled against the tight-fitting windows, and no drafts stirred the curtains.

She set the table for two in the main room, and waited until nine o'clock before taking the now dried-out casserole out of the oven, and eating a solitary meal. She added wood to the fire and sat reading, and at ten thirty she went upstairs. She lay in the big bed in the room she and Charles were to have shared, and listened to the wind sweep down from the wolds. The old timbers of the house seemed to creak a little—time was something even Mr. Conegar could not overcome. She listened to the soughing of the wind through the old boughs of the apple trees in the orchard; it spoke of times and happenings long past, things she would never know about. And she thought how strange it was that she should spend this first night in what was an ancient home of the Brandons quite alone.

Eventually she fell asleep and heard the wind no more.

The ringing of the telephone was distant and faint. Kelly woke and didn't remember where she was. The room was dark, the ceiling felt close—and the wind still howled.

She put on lights, and groped her way down a still-unfamiliar staircase to the phone in the big room. She expected and hoped to hear Peter's voice. She had no idea of the time.

"Kelly?" Laura's voice was controlled, but at the same time excited. "Kate's had her baby. It's a boy. Everything's fine. It all happened very quickly. We just about got her to the hospital before he was born. He's marvelous, Kelly. Beautiful!"

"Kate?—how is Kate?" It was a week ahead of time, but then Kate hadn't bothered to inform them very accurately.

"Kate is wonderful. I was with her most of the time. I saw the baby born, Kelly!" Laura's tone rose almost to a pitch of exultation. "Kate says I'm to be godmother—if there ever is a christening."

"When did the labor start?"

"Oh . . ." Laura was vague. "Kate just came down the stairs, with her bag packed, and asked me if I'd find a taxi to take her to the hospital. I said we should telephone for an ambulance. She said there was time for a taxi."

Laura talked a great deal more; Kelly listened, making the appropriate responses. "Will you be going up to Yorkshire, then?"

"No—of course not! Kate's got to be visited. We have to get things ready for her coming home. I . . . I don't think she's made many preparations."

"Do you want me to come back?"

"Of course not! We're able to take care of everything."

"Yes—you can take care of everything. No one better . . ." They talked for a while longer. When she put down the phone she went out to the kitchen to make tea. It was a little past six o'clock.

Kelly dressed and drove to Wychwood. Mrs. Page, even at that early hour, was dressed and presiding over breakfast in the servants' quarters. She looked pointedly at Kelly. "Is there something wrong, Lady Brandon?"

"No, nothing wrong. I'd like to talk to Peter."

Mrs. Page's body grew even more erect. "Mr. Peter . . . well, he's been gone all night. He's out with the shepherds. It's lambing season, you know, Lady Brandon."

"Oh, yes . . . lambing season." She remembered the lambing season at Pentland. The paddocks were often miles from the homestead, but John Merton could never stay away from them. His ewes were producing lambs in many separate paddocks, but he could not detach himself from the drama of their birth. Within the pens, he worked as hard as any of his stockmen, knowing that there were many other ewes, out in the distant paddocks, who would give birth alone and would take care of their young without human help. And that some would die.

"Do you know where he'd be likely to be?"

Mrs. Page rattled off a number of places Kelly had not heard of, and did not know how to find. "If I were you, Lady Brandon, I'd just wait here for him. Eventually everyone goes home for breakfast."

But she didn't wait. She went off in the car searching the still-dark folds of the valleys for the sight of a light out in the fields. She stopped the car twice, and walked through light, but still driving snow, to the sheepfolds. Strange men raised their heads to her. "Aye, mistress, he's been here and gone. Gone over yonder, I reckon. Beyond the next farmhouse. Can't stop Mr. Peter moving around at this time o' year."

She came on him finally. He was in the insecure shelter of a hedgerow, and a movable sheep pen, a short piece of canvas stretched to protect him, the ewes and the shepherd from the wind. She watched him for some minutes. By the light of a lantern and a torch he and the shepherd struggled to deliver a lamb; it was a breech birth, Kelly knew, having watched it many times before. Peter, with his shirt stripped off, reached his hands into the ewe's body, and bloodily delivered its lamb. For a second he sat panting, and the shepherd hastily wiped the lamb, and the ewe reached around to find it. Feebly, the lamb reached for its mother's teats. She licked it, and claimed it.

"Peter . . . ?"

He sat back on his heels, wiping his hands in a piece of towel. "Kelly . . . ? What . . . ?"

"Kate has had a son."

They went back to Mead Cottage. They opened the champagne, which Kelly had left sitting in its lukewarm water. It spurted, as she remembered the champagne had spurted on the morning when she and Laura had learned that Greg had climbed Everest. They drank it, eating cold meat and cheese. They toasted each other, the birth of the lambs and the birth of Kate's son.

Then Peter telephoned Nick. "Well, old man, your young man made it. There's another partner in Wychwood!" Kelly heard Nick's voice only as a gravelly burr on the telephone, and she realized it was the first news he had had of the birth of his son.

They carried the last of the champagne upstairs to her bedroom. Peter still smelled faintly of blood and manure and sweat. They made love and slept, spent, in each other's arms.

Kelly stayed two more nights at the cottage, unable so soon to withdraw, and she knew that she loved Peter. He came to eat supper with her each night, did a round of the sheep pens, and returned in the early hours of the morning to her bed. They said many things to each other, asked many questions, with the eagerness of lovers who must quickly try to make up time; they asked about each other's past, seeking to furnish out the bareness of that territory. In gaining knowledge, one of the other, reaching out to attempt to share memories, there was a dauntingly long way to go, but the knowledge of each other's bodies, desires, wishes, pleasures, seemed instinctive. To Kelly, Peter combined the urgency of Greg's love-making with the patient tenderness of Charles'. But she did not say this, because memories of past loves was something they had not yet come to talk about. She woke to Peter's dark head on her shoulder, and was satisfied. For the moment, she wanted nothing else.

They could talk of the past, but not of the future. The future was something that they did not yet dare to explore. "I have to go back," Kelly said. "Kate will think I don't care about the baby. I do care about him—but I care about you more."

He accepted it. "I wish I could make you stay. When will you come back?"

"Soon—very soon."

"Louise will know," he said. "I'm a bad liar, and this is something I don't care to lie about. Mrs. Page will know first—and make her disapproval known, though she'll say nothing, not to me or to anyone else. Soon the people around here will know. You can't hide things like this in a country place—and I don't want to hide it. I want you, Kelly—all the time, and forever."

It was as far into the future as they ventured. The present was such excitement and tenderness and, Kelly believed, love. "I love you," Peter said. "I think I've loved you for years, long before I knew you. Would you believe that? Something in me recognized you the first time you came here. I brushed it away, because you were married to Charles. But every time I saw you, there were more things about you I recognized. The way you moved and spoke. The things you said. More important, the things you didn't say. I remember the time I realized that silence was a large part of the woman I had recognized from somewhere else. Do you believe in dreams foretelling the future? I would have said it was nonsense. But when you came you fleshed out some image I had from the past—a very fuzzy image that suddenly took on a definite form. I tested you in a hundred small ways, to try to knock down the belief that you were the person I had always known. But you were always there before me, anticipating me, as if you knew—all that time ago when you were Charles' wife, you *knew*."

"And how did *you* know that day that I was going to Heathrow—to Pentland? I had only decided an hour before the service."

"How does one know anything? Did I dream that also? Oh, Kelly, I'm such a long way from being a young man blindly in love. I'm not blindly in love. I see you with open eyes. The image isn't fuzzy anymore. I'm not in love. I love you."

PART III

Chapter Eight

I

"You just can't believe the baby," Laura had said. "He looks as if he was born at the London School of Economics, and has got his professorship already." Kelly remembered the words the first time she saw him. The dark gray eyes seemed questioning, he had Kate's pointed chin, and even his hair, full and black, framed his face in spiky points. He struggled to focus his eyes on the ring Kelly wore as she put a hand gently toward him, and he amazed her by the sudden, darting grasp; his tiny fingers latched onto hers and he held her with a show of determination. Having achieved his object, the shining ring, he smiled fully, and seemed to laugh. Then she saw Charles in him.

"He doesn't look like Charles, but he acts like him. He would have liked to see this grandchild, Kate."

"He's a doer, isn't he," Kate said, quite unable to keep the pride out of her voice. "I think he's already in a hurry. We'd better get alphabet blocks and a Meccano set because he'll be ready for them in a few days."

Kelly found that Kate had made more preparations for the arrival of the baby than she had expected. Kate shrugged. "What's so difficult about buying baby clothes, and a cot? I got one of those collapsible prams. I can leave the frame in the hall and not have to pull it upstairs. I've got a baby bath, a rattle, and I've even got his first Teddy bear." She laughed at Kelly's expression. "It's what you call planning ahead. Someone gave me a playpen for when he's older. I wonder when he'll be able to sit up. . . ?"

"From the way he's going, I'd say in a few hours. He really is such a big, healthy-looking baby, Kate. And I thought you weren't taking proper care of yourself. I should have known you'd be as efficient in this as everything else."

Kate grinned. "I did do rather well, didn't I? Cut right down on smoking, drank milk, ate proper meals . . . all the things I didn't usually bother about. But I was determined that this kid was going to be as healthy as I could make him, if I had any say in things." She paused. "But I'll tell you, Kelly . . . while I was pregnant, it was a sort of academic matter. I read all the baby books, and I did what the doctor told me to do. And I assumed that what I produced would be a perfectly healthy child. But when he was actually born I couldn't wait to get a look at him. After he'd had his first feed he just lay back and grinned at me, as if he knew already that I was besotted with him. You'll just have to watch me to see that I don't spoil him rotten."

Kelly said, "Well, I don't have too much experience of motherhood."

"Rubbish! You made a great job of Laura, with that formidable Greg Merton watching your performance, and Phoebe Renisdale keeping an eagle eye on developments."

"Ah . . ." Kelly said softly, "but you didn't know *John* Merton. The best there is in Laura comes from him. And now that your young man has arrived safely, I suppose I'd better think about making a trip back to Pentland. John Merton left it to me to be looked after, and no matter how good the manager is, it matters very much that either Laura or I show ourselves there regularly . . ." She disengaged the still-clinging fingers of the baby. "Well, I suppose this makes me a sort of stepgrandmother."

Kate smiled. "Hello, Granny." Then her eyelids drooped. She shifted the baby in her arms and offered him to Kelly. "Take him back to the nursery, will you, Kelly. He's had a walloping great feed, I've burped him, and he'll sleep like a log. Funny, the one thing I hadn't reckoned on, besides being madly in love with him, was how tired I've been, now it's all over. I just want to sleep my head off."

Kelly left the ward, with its evening visitors, fathers, grandparents—perhaps no other stepparents, like herself. The baby had been born at the Westminster Hospital. As she walked along the corridor, she could see the face of Big Ben almost unnaturally close since this floor of the hospital was at about the same level as the famous clock. The baby had already heard its chimes; Kate had joked that he had been born in the division bell area, and that gave him a birthright to being elected to Parliament. "Just try and stop him. I wonder if it will be the first mother-son succession in the history of the Commons? I must research it."

Kelly was jerked out of recollection of that joke as Nick approached her. He looked paler than she had ever seen him, his face, always thinner and more pointed than Peter's, now looked almost haggard. When he saw that she was carrying the baby, he went to the nearest ashtray and stubbed out his cigarette.

"Kelly, they wouldn't let me in! I've been here every visiting hour. I can't say I'm the father—and being a sort of second-cousin isn't enough. If she were in a private room, it would be different . . ." He stood several feet away from her, as if afraid to approach.

"You can look, Nick. He's beautiful—and perfect. And he does look a little like you, but a lot more like Kate."

"Kate would see to that!" He edged carefully nearer. The baby, who had been lying contentedly with closed eyes, suddenly opened them. Nick was wearing nothing that shone to attract that as yet unfocused gaze, but the dark eyes seemed to sharpen, and fix on his father's face. Nick had reached to turn down the fold of the blanket, and suddenly the energetic, demanding little hand reached up. Nick found himself helplessly grasped by an infant.

"Oh, God, Kelly. This is my son. What am I going to do? I have to have him. I'll fight Kate . . . I don't care who knows."

She drew back from him, but the baby's hand still held, and he moved with her. "Nick, if you try to do anything to take this baby without Kate's consent, I'll personally fight you on every point. I'll prove that she's the best and most caring mother that ever was, and I'll paint you the blackest villain in legal history. I'll stand up in court and say so, if necessary. If you don't care who knows, then I don't either. Be careful, Nick. Don't do anything to hurt this baby. I'd rather he had two parents than only one, but if that's the way Kate wants it, then she has the absolute right to decide. Believe me, Nick. Children without fathers sometimes manage not at all badly."

"Kelly . . . I beg you. Try with Kate again, will you?"

"Yes, I will try. But you know Kate even better than I. You probably know what she'll say. But I'll try."

A nurse came hurrying along the corridor. "Is that Baby Brandon you've got there?" She was young and anxious, and she broke into a kind of nervous giggle. "For a moment we thought we'd got some kind of kidnapping on our hands. He wasn't in the nursery, and he wasn't with his mother." She extended her arms to take the baby from Kelly. "Well, there now. Back we come, little one. Oh, look . . . he's so sleepy after his feed, but he just doesn't want to give up. He's going to be a ball of fire, this one."

Nick took Kelly's arm, and they waited in silence for the lift. It seemed to take a long time to come.

Kate brought the baby home, but she refused to let life at Brandon Place revolve about him. "He's just a baby—an extraordinary baby, of course, but just a baby, and we all have to get on with our lives. But we'll try to let him grow up without too much fuss, shall we?"

She looked at the faces which surrounded her as she sat with the baby in her arms, a position that seemed to Kelly to be already a relaxed and comfortable posture for both Kate and the baby. They had all gathered—she and Laura had gone to bring them home from the hospital, Julia was waiting, and Marya and Mrs. Cass had joined the group. Sergei had arrived, bringing a quite absurd number of toys which the baby wouldn't be able to play with for several years.

Mrs. Cass bent over and touched the baby's cheek. "He does have a look now and then of Sir Charles. What will you call him, Miss Kate?" She appeared to have forgotten her disapproval of the whole situation; the arrival of the baby had transformed everything. She was as helpless before him as any of them.

For once Kate had no quick answer. "I haven't thought of a name for him yet. It just seemed to matter to get him born safely—and for him to be healthy."

"Well, he'll have to be named," Marya said. "And properly. You must have him christened at Wychwood."

"I hadn't thought of having him christened. I don't believe—"

"How do you know he won't be a believer?" Marya said fiercely. "Let him make up his own mind, but you must have him christened in the church where most of the Brandons have been christened. Let him know where he belongs."

"If you don't have him christened," Laura said, "how can I be his godmother? You promised, Kate."

"It was a moment of weakness," Kate answered. "But—all right. He'll be christened at Wychwood, if the vicar can stomach the idea of an unmarried mother. It'll be rather a test of his own Christianity, won't it? And if he won't do it, Martin Wyatt at Tower Hamlets will . . . he's always christening the kids of unmarried mothers."

II

It was mid-April when they all went down to Wychwood for the christening. The vicar had done no more than barely raise his eyebrows at the request to christen Kate's son. "God is always pleased to receive a soul. And I am happy to see this new Brandon join us."

All of them from Brandon Place came, even Mrs. Cass. They filled every room at Mead Cottage, and Laura was to sleep on one of the sofas in the main room. Kelly paused as she prepared the meal on the Saturday night before the christening, listening to the sounds of their voices, the opening and closing of doors, the footsteps in the passage and on the stairs. It was now as she had intended it to be—lights, fires burning, the hungry cry of a baby. She remembered that one occasion she had come here with Charles, and envisioned all this, though then the baby was to have been hers. And here, she had taken another man to the bed she would have shared with Charles. She came here most weekends, and Peter came also. They still did not talk of the future. Kelly knew that for herself she grasped at the present because the future seemed too insecure; she could not afford dreams of a life shared with Peter, and yet she could not imagine a life that did not hold him. So she counted the hours with him, and was happy, asking no more, daring to ask no more.

Marya was at the sink blanching tomatoes for a salad. She turned and brought the bowl over to the big table. "Well, this is the real place of your heart, isn't it? Home." She looked around the kitchen, seemed to listen, as Kelly had, to the sounds of the house, smelled the warm fragrance of the food. "I am glad you have revived it. This was the first haven I knew in England. The Colonel brought me down here when no one knew what to do with me, and Elizabeth Brandon gave me a home, and the girls accepted me as if unknown, penniless Russians were a normal thing to have around. They gave me clothes—took away my soldier's uniform. The house seemed a palace to me . . ." She smiled at Kelly. "Ah, I get too sentimental. Mrs. Cass has scented bath water, and we will all wait on *her* tonight, and make it a time she will remember forever. You draw us together, Kelly—as once our love for Elizabeth kept us together."

"Oh, rubbish—what else have I to do?"

Marya shrugged. "All right. I will say nothing, otherwise you will get a big head. But I wish the Colonel . . . well, he would have thanked you too."

Kelly went to a cupboard and began to load bottles on a tray. "We'll take them out to the fire, shall we?" They went through the passage into the living room.

Laura and Kate and the baby were there. Mrs. Cass came down soon, wearing very obviously new clothes and smelling of the bath salts Marya had noticed. She beamed on them all. "Lovely, it is, m'lady. All just lovely." She accepted a glass of sherry. "Miss Kate, you'd better make up your mind quickly about a name for that baby. You can't stand in front of the vicar tomorrow and not have a name ready."

"I'll think about it."

Kelly sat and let the talk flow about her. It was an altered vision from the one she had dreamed that day with Charles, but it was an authentic one. The baby slept in Kate's arms, contented now that he had been fed. Laura put aside the history book she had been reading; she had stuck firmly to the course she had set herself, and was cautiously hopeful about her exams in June. Gradually she was fashioning a life for herself. She went out, and gave small supper parties in return, and no longer expected Kelly to be part of them. The bond between them was as strong as ever, but each was making a conscious effort a built a life that was independent of it. Kelly wondered if Laura yet knew that she and Peter were lovers. It was something that would be talked of in time, but Laura hovered around the edge of the subject, only hinting obliquely at it.

"Kelly. . . ? Kelly, what do you think?"

She looked at Kate, startled. "Sorry, I was just staring at the fire and feeling rather smug. Think about what?"

"Julia. How do you think she's coming along? I'm worried, myself. I think she sneaks off to see that surgeon Nick found for her from time to time, but she never says anything. Have you noticed, when you catch her without her party face on these days how worried she looks . . . and dreadfully thin. I know ballerinas are meant to be like sticks, but really, she's gone too far. Does she ever talk to you about dancing?"

"Not directly. She goes to class every day."

"That is it," Marya said. "She goes to class, but we hear nothing about what she does there. She does not talk about rehearsal. She does not talk about when she will perform again. She says nothing. She lives for Sergei, and sometimes I am afraid when I see her eyes."

"I think you're all being too pessimistic," Laura said. "You know it takes time for bones to strengthen and get flexible again. She goes to class . . . it's only a matter of time now."

"And time is the one thing a dancer hasn't a lot of," Kate muttered.

Mrs. Cass put her sherry on the small oak stand beside her. "Perhaps I shouldn't tell you this . . . but then we all care about her . . ."

"What is it, Mrs. Cass?"

"Well—last week—Tuesday afternoon it was. I was all alone in the house, and I was cleaning the mirror in the hall. Everything was quiet. The doors were open between the houses . . . I suppose you must have left them open the night before, Lady Brandon. Then, all of a sudden, I hear the music. Gave me quite a turn, it did. I thought she was out—at the ballet, for certain. I hadn't heard her come back. I was feeling ever so glad—you see, I remembered the music. She's been practicing to it for as long as I've known her. Well, I just thought I'd slip up and have a word with her—I hadn't seen her for about two weeks, and I'd got used to her being at home all those months. Thought I'd ask her if she'd like a cup of tea, I thought she'd like a break . . . maybe. . . ."

"Mrs. Cass, what happened?"

She drew in a breath. "Well, I went up quietly, and tapped at the door, and she didn't hear me, what with the music, you know. I opened it. She wasn't practicing—you know those things she does on that rail, all the stretching and such. She was wearing the usual old rags she wears when she's exercising. But she wasn't exercising. She didn't see me. She had her head down on the rail, and she was crying the way I've never heard Miss Julia cry. Fit to break her heart. The music went on and on, and she just had her head down on the rail, crying. I didn't . . . well, I thought it was too personal for me to butt into. It wasn't anything that a cup of tea would fix."

A log slipped in the grate, and ashes fell to the hearth. Laura went to lay on a new log. Kneeling, she turned and faced them. "What do we do?" she said.

"Better ask, little one, what *can* we do," Marya said.

Kelly heard the car stop in the lane in the early hours of the morning, heard the subdued voices. Laura was there to let Julia and Sergei in; Sergei had been performing the night before, and Julia had waited in London to drive down with him. The kitchen table had been left set for them to eat—cold ham and chicken and roast beef, and Laura had said she would scramble eggs for them if they wanted it. A bottle of wine was chilled. The smell of percolating coffee came to Kelly as she lay awake, and she almost went down to join them, and then decided to leave them alone. She guessed that the performance had gone well—Sergei was full of good humor, and his laugh sounded through the house as they forgot to be quiet. She hoped they wouldn't wake the baby until it was time for his feed. It all seemed so normal and ordinary; what was happening was what she had dreamed might happen in this house. But the baby who would be christened the next afternoon had no recognized father, and Julia wept when she was alone at the *barre*. Kelly turned restlessly, trying to escape the thought, and longed for the comfort of Peter's body beside her. The pleasure of the present moment was all any of them had.

When Louise had heard that Julia and Sergei were coming down, she had offered to accommodate them at Wychwood, and had been politely refused. "We don't mind crowding," Julia had said. "It makes a sort of party." The words had seemed to spark the idea in Louise's mind because she decided to give a christening party at Wychwood. She regarded Kate's baby as something that everyone must inevitably think of as unwanted, an inconvenience—but the baby was a fact that couldn't be ignored. "One just has to put the best face possible on it," she had said to Kelly. "Better bring it all out in the open than pretend it didn't happen. Though whatever madness possessed Kate to go through with having this baby . . . it could all have been . . ." She made a gesture of impatience, as if she considered Kate had committed a grave social blunder. "Of course everyone wants to come to meet Sergei and Julia. Amazing how the doings in London reach the ears of this backwoods lot. There can't be many of them who've ever actually *seen* a ballet. But stars are stars, and people love to gape . . ."

Although Louise had not suggested it, Peter had insisted that the baby wear the christening robe worn for almost two hundred years by all Brandon babies christened at Wych-

wood. The lace an[illegible] was yellowed and fragile. Kate regarded it warily. "I think if he gave one good kick the whole
thing would come apart."

"Then it will have a marv[illegible] nish with the latest of the
Brandons," Peter said cheerfu[illegible] me a favor, please,
Kate, and put it on him. I'm a se[illegible] fool about tradi-
tions."

She pulled a face. "Oh, all right. For yo[illegible]"

So the baby lay in Laura's arms, the old [illegible]
spilling down. He made cheerful noises throug[illegible]
ceremony, waving his arms about, staring at a[illegible]
things he saw. When the vicar took him to the f[illegible]
poured the water, the baby gave a yell of surprise, a[illegible]
mighty heave, and suddenly snatched at the vicar's glasses. [illegible]
baptize thee John Michael." He pushed his glasses back up
on his nose.

At the last moment Kate had made up her mind. "I'm going to call him after a man I've never met, but one I would have liked to have known. I'm calling him after Laura's grandfather. And Michael is for Peter's father." Peter was godfather. So the name that was entered in the parish register was John Merton's name and the name of the father of both Peter and Nicholas Brandon.

The christening party at Wychwood was well attended; Peter's friends came in force, and there was a good sprinkling of the tenants of the Wychwood farms. The showers of the morning had given way to sunshine; Wychwood lay bathed in it, as if the old golden stone of the house acknowledged one more winter's storms withstood. Daffodils naturalized under the beeches; in the distant pastures the spring lambs skipped around their mothers. "It is all too much," Sergei declared. "Pretty. Clean. All spring. Where are the serfs? We could make a ballet of it. Woodcutters . . . hunters . . . village maidens. I hope there is no wicked fairy that someone has forgotten to invite to the christening."

"Oh, *don't*, Sergei. It's such a happy time." Julia was almost superstitiously ready to believe the stories of the ballets. They all laughed at the look of anguish she cast toward the baby, and over the assembled guests, as if seeking for the dreaded arrival of the forgotten guest whose christening present would be a spell of disaster.

But it seemed that no disaster threatened for the baby whom Kate was already calling Johnny. The guests spread out through the sun-filled great rooms of Wychwood. Peter,

in a fit of extravagance, had decided to [illegible]rovide champagne.
"Well, heaven knows when there'll b[illegible]nother Brandon baby to christen and wish well. I wa[illegible]ng Johnny to have as good a start as any." He adde[illegible]tly to Kelly, "And I have so much else to celebrate[illegible]eprieve from the tax-gatherers. A new season." [illegible]ed his glass to her. "And a celebration of all t[illegible] and bright and beautiful. And I don't care who [illegible]sentimental fool."

Kate loo[illegible] gifts that people had brought. They ranged f[illegible]er spoon, which no one would admit hav[illegible]the silver mug Peter had insisted on present[illegible]—he'll bash in his front teeth on it, but it's part [illegible]ion, and he *is* my godson"—through the blankets ing[illegible]ing bowls and china mugs, to the hand-knitted [illegible] and bootees that smacked so heavily of the Women's [illegible]titute. For a moment Kelly thought Kate'e eyes misted with tears as she touched the gifts laid out, her hands lingering on the little knitted jackets, the blankets, the bootees. "Honestly, I didn't know people could ever be so kind. Just look at it all—you'd think they really wanted to show Johnny he's welcome. I . . . I don't know what to say, Kelly.

"And what do you think of this?" she added. She handed an envelope to Kelly. It was unmarked, and contained a thousand shares of stock in Brandon, Hoyle.

"He had the good sense not to show up, but he's already turned Johnny into a bloody little capitalist." Her lips twisted in a half-smile. "I'd like to send it back, but it seems such a heartless thing to do. I can't be angry at Nick. After all, I got Johnny from him. But I do hope he stays out of our lives. I've got enough to handle in that young man out there." She went off to try to prize Johnny out of Laura's arms, and lost the battle.

"Lady Brandon?" A thin, gray man was addressing her. He wore a sober, gray suit, and the low sunlight, striking his glasses, masked his eyes. "I'm Harry Potter. Of course you don't remember. It's been so long—and there were so many people around you all the time."

"Mr. Potter . . . of course." Kelly offered her hand and found it taken in a surprisingly strong grip. "You're the agent for the constituency. You worked so hard for my husband. Thank you for your letter. I'm sorry it took me so long to answer it. Things . . . well, I just didn't feel up to it."

"I understand perfectly, Lady Brandon. It was a wonderful experience working with Sir Charles. He worked like a soldier at it. With all a soldier's best qualities. He was always so frank and honest. Qualities I admire, Lady Brandon." He went on, before Kelly could comment. "It's rather wonderful, watching what's happening with . . . with Miss Kate." He didn't know what else to call her. "Miss Kate, she's always been different. I've always got my ear to the ground around here, and believe me, many people admire her for going ahead and having her baby. And they're glad to have another young Brandon among them—especially as it's Sir Charles' grandchild."

Kelly studied him carefully; he had moved a little, and she saw the blue-gray eyes behind the glasses looking at her steadily. "Thank you for saying that, Mr. Potter. I will tell Kate. Yes . . . I'll certainly tell her. I expect Kate will be bringing the baby down quite often . . . to let him get some fresh air." She smiled a little ruefully. "Or I'll be bringing him down by myself. I suddenly find that I'm a sort of grandmother. Between Laura and Julia and Marya he doesn't lack for surrogate mothers. What he needs is a few more men in his life."

"Well, Peter Brandon will see to that. And there's Christopher Page. I understand he has a flat in your house in London, and he's doing very nicely at Brandon, Hoyle. The Brandons have been very good to that young man."

"Oh, I think it might be the other way around. How would the Brandons have got along without Mrs. Page? You must have known her a long time, Mr. Potter. She's something of a legend in the family, it seems to me."

He chose his words carefully. "Well, I wouldn't say I *know* her, Lady Brandon. She's a very good lady—very quick to offer help if anyone's in trouble, you know. But you'd never really think of going and *telling* her your troubles. She finds out whatever is needed, does it, and then just sort of . . . well, withdraws. Christopher is rather the same. He grew up here, but you couldn't say he had any friends left here. Some boys he went to Tewford Grammer School with still live hereabout, but he hasn't kept up with them. Well—I expect he's been too busy in London." He broke off, and stared past her. "Look, now, Lady Brandon. There's Mrs. Page and Christopher, and *that's* I think, their christening present. I rather wonder how Miss Kate will take to that. I do hear she's a freethinker, for all she's had her baby christened in church."

Kelly turned, and saw that the Pages had somehow edged aside the group that surrounded Johnny, still in Laura's arms. Mrs. Page bent over the baby from her stately height and swung something on a silver chain, something that flashed and glittered in the low rays of the sun. Moving nearer, out of curiosity, because such a display of even slight emotion seemed out of place in Mrs. Page, Kelly saw that what swung on the end of the chain was a silver crucifix. The baby stared at it, fascinated by the darting light. "Mrs. Page is a very strict Christian observer," Mr. Potter murmured. "Which always strikes me as odd when you remember where she comes from. I imagine her mother was born a Hindu. Though really what it matters I don't know. Oh! . . . oh, goodness me!"

Johnny, reaching with his astonishing energy had managed to catch the dangling object, a mere fluke, Kelly thought, but one which evidently pleased Mrs. Page, because she bent until her face was almost level with Johnny's and a faint smile came to her lips. Kelly saw a sudden, swift movement of the baby's hand, and a cry came from Mrs. Page. She straightened, holding the palm of her hand above her right eye. She took it away slowly, and looked at it. There was blood on it, and a thin line of blood had already started down her face.

"Oh, my God!" Kelly breathed, Johnny had evidently lunged out with his usual forceful movement, holding the crucifix, and the edge of it had struck Mrs. Page over the eye. Kelly moved forward, as Laura began to back away in dismay. "Mrs. Page . . . here, please let me."

Chris had offered his handkerchief. "It's nothing, Lady Brandon," Mrs. Page said. "Just a trifling cut. The poor child's worn out with all the excitement and fuss. I should have known better than to let a young child have a sharp object as a plaything." She even managed a tight smile. "Young Master John doesn't know his own strength. No, Christopher . . . don't fuss. I'm perfectly all right. But may I suggest, Miss Laura, that perhaps it's time the baby went upstairs? It's well past time for his nap."

Then Johnny, who had laughed all through his christening, who had not cried at the touch of the water nor the taste of salt, suddenly began to wail. As always, he did everything in an emphatic fashion. He didn't merely cry, he bellowed. Kate came quickly from the Hall. She had not seen the incident with Mrs. Page, nor the crucifix. "There, I knew he'd give up eventually. It's time for his feed, and he's determined I won't forget it." Without looking at anyone she took Johnny from Laura, and hurried away. They listened to the cries diminishing as she carried him upstairs.

Behind Kelly, Sergei said to Julia, "Who is the dark lady? Is she the fairy godmother who didn't get invited?"

Chapter Nine

I

For the first time Kelly traveled back to Sydney without Laura seated beside her in the plane. "About time, too," Laura said as she kissed her good-bye. Laura hadn't even gone to Heathrow with her because Peter had come to Brandon Place with his car to take her. "I've got a lot of work to get ready for Mrs. Harris tomorrow," Laura had said. "Peter will look after you—and stay if the flight's delayed." But she stood on the pavement at Brandon Place and waved after them until the car turned into Brompton Road. Mrs. Cass had stood behind her on the steps, waving also. Kelly thought of the good-byes, the supper party Laura had given for her the night before when they had all gathered in Laura's flat, with Johnny sleeping in his carry-cot, and she wondered what the welcome at Pentland would be.

She turned rather desperately back toward Peter when the flight had been called and she had gone to present her boarding pass. "I don't think I'll go—"

He kissed her again. "You'll go and do your job, and come back quickly. Quickly, Kelly. I'll only be half alive until I see you again. When you come back we'll start to work something out. We've got to work it out . . ."

She had held the words with her through the long hours on

the plane, just saying them over and over as a sort of talisman against a fate that might once again take away a man she loved. She stayed a few nights in Sydney, seeing Frank McArthur about Pentland's affairs, and reviewing the portfolio of hers and Laura's stocks, discussing changes, what to sell against the death duties which were now being levied, striving to perform all these tasks with the same concentrating as before, but Peter's words kept appearing on the pages as she read, and sometimes made nonsense of the figures she studied. She heard the words when she woke in the morning, and when she tossed restlessly in bed before sleep came. "You're looking wonderfully well, Kelly," Frank McArthur had remarked when they had lunched together on the first day. "I was a bit worried when you left here—after Charles died. You seemed so strained. But everything you tell me about Brandon Place, Laura, and the two Brandon girls sounds good." He swirled the last of the beer in his glass. "And may I also say, as an old man who has always had a very high regard for you and no designs on you, that you've turned into a beautiful woman. You were pretty and fresh and attractive when you were married to Greg. Now you're beautiful."

"Rubbish, Frank . . . but still, thanks." She smiled gratefully as she thought of Peter.

They discussed Delia Merton. "She's apparently given up all notion of contesting the will. I suppose that was just a momentary thing. I heard from one of my colleagues that she came down to Sydney and discussed the situation with another solicitor. Obviously, he advised her as we had done. She went back to Pentland, and no one's heard a word from her since. It beats me why she stays there. She doesn't spend a fraction of her income, and she isn't any more interested in running the property than she ever was. I don't know what she does with her days. She hasn't got John's interest in what's happening in the outside world. She's still rereading the same books she was reading forty years ago, and of course there's the needlework. There can't be many more chairs left in the world to cover with her tapestries. . . . God help me, I even suggested that she go and pay a visit to her cousins in Adelaide, and she just looked up from the bloody needlework and said, 'And why would I do that?' I gave up then."

"She's very shy," Kelly said, and with the words, realized the fact fully for the first time.

She remembered them again when Delia Merton came to

the veranda as the car started across the Home Paddock, and entered the area of the garden. The thin figure stood at the top of the steps; she wore black as she had from the day John Merton had died. The manager, Bill Blake, who had come to meet her at the airport, covered his embarrassment by making a great fuss with the bags. "I'll put them up in your room, Kelly, eh?—the same one, Mrs. Merton?"

"The same one." Delia Merton waited until the man had gone whistling up the stairs, and then held out her hand formally. "How do you do? So you've come back."

Kelly felt like laughing, and still wanted to weep. She couldn't remember when Delia Merton had last willingly touched her. They shook hands like the strangers they were. "Dad—Mr. Merton—expected me to come back. Pentland is not something that can be looked after by letter. He expected me to come regularly. It's a responsibility—"

"Yes—" Delia Merton turned back toward the house. "Yes, you always made a show of taking your responsibilities seriously. I expect you want some tea now?"

Kelly bit back her angry retort. Things would not change. "Yes—I'd like some tea. But please don't trouble about it. I'll go and have it with my mother."

Delia Merton turned back and looked at her. "You are half mistress of Pentland. You will have your tea where you shall have it, in the drawing room with me. After all, you always wanted to live in the big house, didn't you?" She led the way into the drawing room, where the curtains were drawn fully back to allow the room to get the full strength of the autumn sun, where a fire burned, and the most precious blue-and-white Meissen tea set was laid out. The spirit lamp burned under the silver kettle, the Georgian silver tea service sparkled with fierce light. The tiny scones were warm from the oven; little iced cakes were set out. "Your mother made them. She was always the best cook we ever had." Kelly nearly choked on them.

They talked mostly of Laura during that half hour they spent together. "She's going to do well in her exams. I think her grandfather would have been pleased."

"He would have preferred her to go to Oxford or Cambridge rather than London University. From what I read, London's become a very dangerous place for a young girl. The things that happen there . . ."

"She refused to move away from London—and I suppose she's really better off where she has a family around her."

"They've taken her over, haven't they—the Brandons?

When she writes she can't write about anything else. Got her under their thumbs. And that Kate with her baby. I don't call *that* a good influence."

"It's rather the other way around," Kelly said. "Laura has become rather bossy, in fact—at least where Julia and Kate are concerned." She made an effort to reach Delia Merton. "Laura's . . . well, Laura's trying very hard to come out of her shell. You know how shy she's been. There are times now you'd hardly know her."

"It doesn't sound much of an improvement."

Afterward Kelly went across to the little cottage whose windows sparkled in the sun, whose garden bloomed with chrysanthemums of prodigious size. She had to wait for her mother to answer her knock, though she knew her approach had been seen from behind the starched lace curtains. "Come in," her mother said in greeting. "You've taken your time about coming back, haven't you? All that gallivanting around America. Ridiculous postcards. Was that what Mr. Merton expected of you? And you must have spent a fortune on those houses and on the Brandons. You watch out, my girl. They'll have the lot off you before you know what's happened."

Without being invited, Kelly collapsed into a chair. "Is *that* what you have to say to me? It was hardly worth coming back to hear that."

"What else do you expect a mother to say? I've always watched out for your interests—never wanted you to get into trouble. And you had better watch out for Laura. I don't think it was wise to leave her alone. You never know. The girl has money, and men come creeping after that. Always have. You have to guard against her getting in the family way."

"I think," Kelly said, "that I may safely leave that to Laura. She's too old to keep on reins, and I credit her with a good deal more common sense than you do."

"Common sense, is it?" Her mother's faded eyes seemed to grow darker. "And was it common sense what happened to Kate Brandon? Brought another bastard into the world. What kind of common sense is that? A woman of her education, her position. It's a disgrace."

"Kate has a beautiful son, whom we all love. She called him after John Merton, because Laura loved her grandfather so much. Laura is Johnny's godmother."

The thin, aging woman leaned forward, her eyes flashing. "You don't mean to tell me that *that* child has been baptized in a church? What is the world coming to? Is there no shame anymore?"

Kelly said, "John Michael Brandon was baptized and received into the Church of England with all due ritual. He wore the christening robe the Brandons have worn for two hundred years. And no one will ever call him a bastard."

"More's the pity! The sins of the fathers—"

Kelly pulled herself wearily out of the chair. "I can see that your God is still a God of vengeance."

"And why not? Whatever happened in my life—or yours, my fine lady—to prove otherwise? Things of the world you have. Money—all that goes with it. Are you happy?"

Kelly turned toward the door, impelled by a mixture of fury and pity. "Have *you* ever been happy? Why the God? Why the prayers? What have they brought you?"

"I expect nothing in this life. I sinned. I have to repent—"

"They once told me," Kelly said before she crashed the door closed behind her, "that God is a God of mercy and love. Have you ever thought of it?"

What sounded like a scream of rage—perhaps anguish—followed her across the paddock to the big house. Laura had been right. Two houses were wasted on two women as mad as these appeared to be.

She spent her days at Pentland as John Merton had intended, had wished. She inspected the books, talked at length with Ian Russell, the accountant from Barrendarragh, spent a long time on tours of inspection with Bill Blake, ate with his family, and heard from them all the local gossip she would never hear from Delia Merton or her mother. The Blake family, Bill, Nelly and their three children used the swimming pool, as did any of the station hands who wished to. "It's funny," Bill remarked, "but it strikes you as a bit odd that no one from the house uses it. All that big place with no one in it but an old lady who doesn't see anymore. A shame, really. People used to come for a while after Mr. Merton died—sort of forced themselves on her to keep her company. But they pretty soon found out that she didn't want them. No one comes now."

But the Australian summer was gone, and now no one but Kelly used the pool; it would be emptied soon, before the danger of frost cracking it. As she swam alone when the mid-day sun had warmed it, she thought of Greg's relentless lapping of the pool each day. She wondered if the mastery of his own body, the total self-discipline he had achieved had brought him any joy. In some ways, it had caused others to dislike, even to fear him. The old ghosts were resurrected as she slipped through the water, using the balanced overarm, the regular breathing John Merton had taught her, and Greg had perfected. She remembered the day the snake had struck at Laura, the day she had lost her child. Pulling herself out of the water, she glanced over at the veranda of the big house, and thought of the snake there, and of the day Greg had entered her life. Her life had probably begun that day. It was the day she had started the impossible pursuit of excellence in all things—not because her mother expected and demanded it as a payment for what had been sacrificed, but because excellence was something that Greg Merton had taken for granted.

She found the accounts of Pentland and all its physical aspects in complete order. The house and outbuildings had been recently painted, the roofs were in good repair, the fences sound; the stables, shearing sheds, sheep dips and pens were in the immaculate order John Merton had demanded. A sign of the innovation was that there were fewer horses and more Land-Rovers for the work of the station. She rode out during the day with Bill Blake, inspecting the stock. There had been some heavy rain that autumn, and the paddocks were an unlikely green, the sheep were fat, the wool well grown for winter. She rejoiced in the feeling of the sun on her body, and ignored the stiffness of her muscles, unused to the saddle for so long. Sometimes she drove out in a Land-Rover with Nelly and the children, tempting them away from the lessons that were done by correspondence, as she, in her own time, had done them, to picnic at some of John Merton's favorite places along the creek. "Pity Mrs. Merton doesn't feel like coming," Nelly said. "It'd do her good to get out of that house." Kelly couldn't ever remember Delia Merton joining a picnic in all the years she had been at Pentland. It hadn't seemed strange to her; it was just Delia Merton's way.

More for Laura's sake than her own, she made contact with the neighboring stations, and paid the ritual visits, often staying overnight because the distances were too great to allow her to return. She did it for Laura because she was aware that one day Laura, or Laura's children might live at Pentland. They would need these distant contacts; it would not do to stay aloof. So she exchanged gossip, telling them about the American trip, about doing up the two houses in Brandon Place, opening up Mead Cottage, Laura cramming for her exams, Julia's bad luck with her ankle. She tried to steer the conversation away from Sergei and from Kate's baby, but somehow these also had slipped into local gossip, and the women asked questions. They lived isolated lives, and they fed on news. One of them, about Kelly's age, sipped a gin-and-tonic as she prepared dinner in the kitchen; the cook had moved on the week before, struck by the restlessness that often touched those who had opted for the great wide spaces of the country. The restlessness of those who had to stay was evidenced in their avidity for news. She said, "It sounds O.K., Kelly—but what's *your* life going to be? You're not getting any younger." And then, as Kelly didn't reply, "Oh, why don't you tell me to shut my trap? It wasn't your fault Greg died—and then your General. Tell you the truth, Kelly, there are a few around here who aren't exactly weeping tears for you. You pulled off something, marrying Greg Merton. Got in where more than a few others would have liked to. And then Greg seemed to get a bit too big for us all here. Him and Everest! And then that snooty-nosed Laura, with her English accent. And then your General. *Lady* Brandon. . . ! Well, you can imagine what a few of the girls had to say about that."

"I can imagine it. I can't change it, though."

"No—I reckon you can't." She refilled her glass. "A lot of us wonder what's going to happen to Pentland. A place that size needs to be taken care of. Oh, Bill Blake's a good bloke. But he's just a manager. John Merton was the heart and soul of that place. He stood for something in this country. If you wanted to look at the best around here, you looked at John Merton. And he loved Pentland. But you—you're away in England. What's going to happen to Pentland?"

"There's a lot of John Merton in Laura. You could find her back here someday."

"Yeh, I'll bet. And using an English saddle, too."

Kelly sighed. The visits, which were undertaken for Laura's sake, were not always a success. But she had come to fulfill John Merton's expectations of her, and this ritual was part of it. The only times when she felt truly comfortable were the times riding alone. These were the times when she wrote letters to Peter in her head, letters which were never posted. Why give Mrs. Page a chance to examine the Australian postmark? In her head, she told John Merton about Peter, imagined showing the wide stark country to Peter, imagined him comparing it to his green, gentle land, even its largest fields mere patchwork beside the smallest of these paddocks. She tried to imagine how he would react to Pentland and its neighbors, how they would react to him. They would meet halfway because he was a farmer. But he was a foreigner, alien to them, with the appearance of an English gentleman which seemed to irritate some of them so much. She even wondered, in her wildest imaginings, hardly daring even to admit the thought to herself, if Pentland might provide the answer to their dilemma. Would Peter ever come to Pentland to be with her? No, Peter would never leave Wychwood. If Pentland was ever to have its family once again, the necessary heart which had been lacking since John Merton had died, it would have to come from Laura.

So she spent the weeks at Pentland in the way she thought was required, time enough to give Bill Blake and the whole countryside the assurance that Pentland would never be secondary in her plans. She spoke of the time, next year, when Laura would have her summer vacation from university, and she also would come to Pentland. She strove to impart a sense of continuity from John Merton. "Laura is lost to Pentland," her mother said. "By the time she's finished at university, England will have her completely. Where will she find a husband who will want to come to *this*?" This was Pentland, its ease and splendor, its harshness, the magnificence of its size, the cruelty of its isolation. Kelly attempted no answer.

The day before Kelly left she had tea with Delia Merton in the drawing room. "I shall be coming with you tomorrow," Delia Merton said.

"To Sydney?—I'll be glad of your company," Kelly said politely.

"To London. I wish to see Laura. She is my only grandchild. I wish to see how she lives there."

Kelly managed a weak smile. "That's—that's wonderful. Laura will be delighted. How . . . how long is it since you've been in England?"

"Not since the wedding trip I took with John. A long time ago . . ."

She traveled to Sydney with Kelly, and waited passively at the hotel while the arrangements were made. Her passport had long ago expired; she seemed to find the necessity of a new one an irksome piece of bureaucracy, to have to obtain permission to visit England was a piece of nonsense. Kelly and Frank McArthur between them managed to have it expedited. Before they left, Kelly telephoned Laura, and heard her incredulous gasp on the phone as she received the news.

"Whatever for? She hasn't been further than Sydney . . . well, since I've known her."

"She wants to see you, she says."

"Well, if that's it, I'll be waiting. I'd better alert everyone—Granny Renisdale and so on. Is she going to stay at Brandon Place?"

"She can't stay anywhere else."

The woman in black sat beside Kelly during the interminable hours of the flight. It had never seemed so long. Delia Merton had never flown in anything larger or faster than the small craft which shuttled between Sydney and Barrendarragh, but she made no comment on the plane, the food, the service or anything else. She refused the magazines offered by the hostesses, and worked on a piece of petit point. When they landed at London she prepared to leave the craft as if it had been a half-hour car journey. However, she betrayed some irritation when they had to queue to pass the immigration officers, and to wait for their baggage. "It used not to be like this. And where is Laura?"

"Laura can't come past the customs. She'll be outside."

"In the old days, people came aboard the ship." Porters took their baggage, and Delia Merton walked past the customs men as if they did not exist, an old woman in an expensive but dowdy black coat and hat. Laura was there to meet them.

"Grandmother! How marvelous of you to make the trip! Have you got all your things? Grandpapa sent a car."

Delia Merton submitted to having her cheek kissed. "Why would I not have all my things?"

"Oh—the airlines often mislay baggage. There's so many people traveling." Delia Merton glanced at her stout, heavy suitcases of real leather, and her look said that they would never be mislaid.

She examined Brandon Place and its occupants without enthusiasm. There was a sense of nervousness in Julia and Kate that Kelly had never witnessed before; in the kitchen as she prepared food, Marya smoked and drank vodka. "Give me courage," she said to Kelly. "That is no grandmotherly soul." The dining room was laid for a formal meal. The graden beyond was planted out with tubs of bright flowers. "Chris worked half the night getting it all ready," Laura whispered. It was a summer garden, cheerful and pretty. Delia Merton said not a word about it. The telephone rang, and it was Phoebe Renisdale, with an invitation for them to go to Charleton that weekend. Delia Merton inclined her head in assent. "Very kind." They ate a meal of smoked salmon, veal in wine sauce, and fresh strawberries, none of which could readily be present on the table at Pentland. Delia Merton made no comment. Kate and Julia drank their coffee quickly in the drawing room, and excused themselves. Kelly saw them go with a kind of desperation. She so badly wanted to talk to them. She wanted to see Johnny; she wanted to ask Julia about her ankle; she wanted the kind of home-coming they had given her before at Brandon Place. She longed to telephone Peter. The presence of the woman in black silk and pearls, sitting in the drawing room, forbade all that.

"Dear God," Laura said to her when finally Delia Merton had gone upstairs to the room Laura had once occupied, "*why* did she come?"

"I have no idea."

The next morning Laura carried a breakfast try to her. She returned to the kitchen swiftly. "Do you know what she said to me? 'Are there no servants?' " She giggled. "I wonder what she'll think of Mrs. Cass?"

"I wonder what Mrs. Cass will think of *her*."

"Thank God I've got my exams over," Laura said as they stacked the dishwasher. "I think I'd have a nervous breakdown if I had to take them with her here. What shall we do with her? How long is she going to stay?"

"I haven't had the courage to ask. I just keep reminding myself that she is your grandmother—your grandfather's widow. And this is the only thing she has ever asked of me in my whole life. Whatever she wants, for however long, she must have it. Nothing less. It's what your grandfather would have expected."

That morning, after a minute but silent inspection of Laura's flat, after glancing up the stairs of Number 15, but declining an invitation to have coffee with Kate and Marya, both of whom had stayed at home in order to receive her and to show off Johnny, she asked Laura to call a taxi and go with her to a shop in South Audley Street. "They have been supplying me with canvases and silk and wool for many years. The old proprietor has died. I have a few complaints to take up with the new one. She is the daughter of the lady who had it before. And there is a china shop nearby I would like to visit."

"They have a marvelous needlework department at Cavanagh's," Laura said hopefully. "Wouldn't you like to walk through Cavanagh's, Grandmother? It's the most wonderful place."

"I knew Cavanagh's when service was service," Delia Merton said. "I hardly think it can have escaped the modern trend to sloppiness."

That afternoon they went to Charleton. After tea, when Delia Merton had gone to her room to rest, Phoebe Renisdale detained Kelly and Laura. "It's early, I know, but I'm going to have a good stiff Scotch before I go and change—before Arthur gets here. Poor man, he doesn't know what he's in for this weekend." She turned, decanter in hand. "My dears, how have you *stood* it? It almost makes me glad my Dorothy never got to Pentland. I begin to understand why Greg was so keen on climbing mountains."

Laura laughed. "I suppose it's easier if you've grown up with her, as we both did. You just get used to her saying nothing and approving of nothing."

"All I can say Laura, is thank God you had Kelly out there." She shook her head. "My goodness . . ."

The weekend dragged to its close. "I would like to see Mead Cottage," Delia Merton said. "Can it be arranged?"

"Of course." Kelly telephoned Wychwood. She had hoped to find Peter at home, but Mrs. Page answered. Kelly explained what was happening; she hated to have to ask Mrs. Page, but no one had been in the cottage since the weekend of the christening, except the local woman who cleaned only two days a week. "I understand perfectly, Lady Brandon. It will be a pleasure to do anything for your mother-in-law. You may leave it all to me."

"I'll bet I can," Kelly said to herself as she hung up.

It was, of course, as immaculate and beautiful as Mrs. Page's skillful hands could make it. The best of Wychwood's picking garden had been stripped to fill the vases and copper pots. The bathrooms shone, clean linen was on the beds, the refrigerator was stocked. Mrs. Page herself waited for them. "Mr. Peter has asked for the pleasure of your company at dinner, Lady Brandon. He would very much like to meet you, Mrs. Merton." The head was inclined in its stiff assent.

"I met your son on Friday morning, Mrs. Page—out watering the garden very early. An extremely nice, polite young man."

"Grandmother!" Laura exclaimed. "I didn't know you'd been down so early. I didn't know you'd met Chris."

"I have no need to tell you everything, Laura."

The dinner at Wychwood followed the pattern of the weekend of Charleton. Delia Merton said little, praised nothing.

Peter took her through the house, and she stopped often to examine a painting, a piece of china, her hand occasionally touching the carvings in the old dark wood. From room to room she went, moving from one thing to another with what only Kelly and Laura could recognize as eagerness. At the end she asked to see Mrs. Page. "I have enjoyed myself very much," she said.

When they drove away, she added, "*That* is the sort of person one wants to have around. No doubt in reduced circumstances, but a lady. She could only have come from the *old* India."

Before she went to bed at Mead Cottage she announced that she had some places in England she wished to visit. Kelly and Laura waited eagerly. Delia Merton volunteered that since she had visited England with her husband, all those years ago, certain changes—socialism, in fact, in the form of punitive taxes—had forced some people to open their houses to the public. "I should very much like to see some of them." She had the list ready. As she read it, Kelly's thoughts went to the volumes of *Country Life* at Pentland, bound in their pale blue leather. How many times had Delia Merton studied the articles and pictures of Chatsworth, Hardwick Hall, Haddon Hall, Knole, Windsor Castle, Longleat, Blenheim? How many years had she kept to herself this simple ambition to see them for herself? "Of course—when would you like to start out?"

"In the morning."

Kelly telephoned Mrs. Page and told her. "Well, naturally I understand, Lady Brandon. It *is* Mrs. Merton's pleasure you are concerned for. Please leave everything to me. I shall see to the linen and such things. I'll take away the flowers and clear out the refrigerator. Please don't thank me, Lady Brandon. It is no trouble."

Later Peter telephoned. "When shall I see you? The old black dragon had me completely tongue-tied. How long are you staying here?"

"We're not staying. We're leaving in the morning."

"Oh, God, Kelly! No! You *must* stay. Why can't you stay? Why do you have to be at the beck and call of that terrible old woman?"

"She's Laura's grandmother. She's John Merton's widow."

"And she's Greg Merton's mother," he added. "And you have to show her what a wonderful daughter-in-law she got! How long's she staying in England?"

"Who knows? A month. A year. No one dares ask."

"If you cared about how I feel, Kelly, you would ask her. I want to see you—alone. Must I wait on her?"

"We all must wait, I'm afraid. It is one of the things John Merton wouldn't have just asked me to do. He would have *expected* it."

"Blast John Merton—and his son! And his mother!" He hung up, and then ten minutes later called to apologize. "Of course you have to do it," he said. "I'm a crude boor—but I love you. I'll wait as long as I have to."

They drove through England for ten days at the height of the tourist season. It was high summer, and for England, it was warm. It was dry; the wheat and barley sheaves were beginning to turn gold, their heads heavy. The sheep looked fat and clean, the cattle impossibly sleek in their rich pastures. Delia Merton frequently turned her head to gaze at all this as they drove, but she never commented, never asked questions. Laura and Kelly shared the driving; one of them would go with Mrs. Merton through whichever house it was she wished to see, and the other would go off frantically scouring the countryside to find accommodations Delia Merton would deem acceptable, standing at reception desks begging the manager for the first chance at a cancellation. Several times, in desperation, Laura telephoned her grandmother at Charleton. "Granny—do you know anyone near Chatsworth who'd put us up for the night—and wouldn't mind Grandmother Merton?"

"My dear, I'll ask Arthur to call in all the debts owed. He must know *someone* . . ."

They managed, between hotel guides, reception managers who were impressed by a title, and the acquaintances of Arthur Renisdale who didn't mind being in good standing with a press baron, to find accommodations which Delia Merton didn't actually complain about, though she was never again as gracious as she had been to Mrs. Page. She seemed oblivious of Laura's and Kelly's efforts. She would stride through the crowds of tourists, ignoring the guides who argued with her to remain with the group, would stand minutes before pictures, ceramics, tapestries, pieces of furniture, saying nothing. She would walk through the famous gardens, pausing now and again, as if she suddenly recognized a landmark, a picture held in her head for many years. She would indicate when she wished to leave, return to the car, and be driven to the next place.

"It's weird," Laura said. "I never realized she really was quite so batty."

"These last years without your grandfather to give her a hold on reality must have been hard. When you are alone at Pentland, you are very much alone."

"The aloneness of Pentland is the only kind worth having," Laura responded with a perception that startled Kelly. "If I had my choice of being alone in London or being alone at Pentland, I'd choose Pentland any day."

They worked determinedly through Delia Merton's list of stately homes. Some were the obvious ones, famous and crowded, with lines of touring coaches in the parking lots. Others were highly individualistic, opening only one or two afternoons a week, hard to find in a maze of country lanes, and no doubt present on that list for some reason which had struck Delia Merton years ago when she had read about them or seen pictures of them. They worked their way through the Home Counties, and after seeing Knole, held to be the largest of the stately homes, she indicated that she would like to return to London. "I will go home as soon as possible," she added.

That night, seated in the dining room at Brandon Place, picking at a meal hastily assembled by Marya after Kelly had telephoned from Kent to say they were returning, Kelly thought that Delia Merton looked more than usually worn. It was not surprising. She had seen—Kelly did not venture to use the word experienced, because she had no idea what Delia Merton could experience—more in the past two weeks than she had seen in the last forty years. She was an old woman, and she now looked it. She had asked that Christopher Page, if he were at home that evening, be invited to join them. She acted as if Julia and Kate and Marya did not exist. Chris had come willingly, and Kelly was grateful for his presence, for at least he was someone for her and Laura to relate the sights of the tour to—they had long ago exhausted the mutual conversation they could conduct in Delia Merton's hearing. But although she had asked for him to come, Mrs. Merton did little more than bid him good evening, and say, "I met your mother. A charming lady." She went to bed early. She had a seat on a flight to Sydney at four o'clock the next afternoon. She had brushed aside Laura's offer to accompany her on the journey. "They will attend to my needs. That is what they are there for."

"I suppose there's really nothing that can go wrong once she's aboard," Kelly said to Laura. "I'll ask them to watch her and make her as comfortable as possible, but if I know her, she'll work at the tapestry all the thirty-six or whatever number of hours it takes to get to Sydney. Mrs. Merton is not a person likely to fall asleep in public." She had already telephoned Frank MacArthur to meet Mrs. Merton in Sydney. She knew he would see her safely on to Barrendarragh and, finally, Pentland.

Kelly was startled, coming downstairs early the next morning, to find Delia Merton standing alone in the dining room. Because of the late summer twilight, the curtains had not been drawn the night before, and the garden, with a pale early sun just beginning to creep down the wall of Charles' study, was pretty and fresh and well watered. Chris had also been up early.

"Mrs. Merton. . . ?" Kelly said tentatively from the doorway. "Is there . . . may I do something for you?"

"A cup of tea, if you please. I miss my early tea. They bring it to me at half-past five in the summer at Pentland."

"Of course . . ." Kelly lingered. She was struck by the final anachronism of Delia Merton's life. Because Pentland was so isolated, so far from Barrendarragh or any other settlement, it had always been necessary, vital, to have live-in servants, at whatever cost. Delia Merton had not, therefore, experienced the whole post-war revolution. She did not even appear to be aware that these days, most people did things for themselves; she would never be required to learn. She still lived back in that world of her nineteenth-century novelists, where even the poor had those still poorer to work for them. Kelly's throat tightened as she remembered once again that first day when she had stood on the station at Barrendarragh, when her mother had had to beg to be allowed to serve Delia Merton.

Delia Merton seemed not to be looking at the garden, but at the dining room itself, the furnishings, the silk wallpaper, the mirrors. With careful fingers she touched the back of one of the twelve Chippendale chairs. "This belonged to the General's . . . the General's first wife? Elizabeth Brandon? That was her name, wasn't it? And now all this belongs to you?"

"Yes. Charles—"

"She must have had fine taste, or been fortunate enough to inherit all this."

"Both."

"And one day, I presume it will belong to Laura?"

"Elizabeth had two daughters. Don't you think they should come first in the matter of what had belonged to their mother?"

"One is a dancer who could care nothing for such possessions. The other is a slut who cares less. Laura should have it. She should have everything."

"We'll see. I'll make your tea, Mrs. Merton."

"This wallpaper—do you have any of it left over?"

"There are some scraps in the basement. We kept it in case some places might be damaged and need patching."

"I'd like a piece. It's a pleasing color. Such a light green. I thought—perhaps we might repaint the kitchen at Pentland this color. It's cool looking . . ."

Delia Merton visited the needlework shop in South Audley Street accompanied by Laura once again that morning. By noon Laura had brought down the heavy leather suitcases. They ate a lunch of smoked salmon and fresh raspberries, and then went to the waiting car, which had been sent by Arthur Renisdale. Mrs. Merton had not asked to see Julia, Kate or Marya before she left, and they were thankful not to be asked. Mrs. Cass helped the chauffeur carry the bags to the car, and received a stiff nod by way of thanks. She stood shaking her head as the car moved off toward Brompton Road.

The flight, to Kelly's and Laura's relief, took off on time. Laura had wheedled permission to go with her grandmother to the steps of the aircraft. A hostess was waiting. Laura kissed her grandmother's cheek, and handed over to the hostess the flight bag containing the tapestry and toilet articles. Delia Merton climbed the steps of the aircraft slowly, but scorned the offered hand of the hostess. She did not turn to look at her granddaughter before she vanished inside.

Laura returned to Kelly. They sat for a time, waiting to be sure the flight had departed before leaving the airport. A silence of exhaustion hung on them.

"Why?" Laura asked, as she had before.

Kelly shook her head wearily.

II

The sudden sticky heat for which London is notorious descended on the capital that afternoon. Kelly and Laura returned to Brandon Place in Arthur Renisdale's car, listless and almost wordless; the activity and the strain of the two weeks of Delia Merton's presence with them had seemed to drain away any sense of pleasure Kelly had had in her return. It had been, in a way, a false return; she had been robbed of the home-coming she had anticipated.

It changed when they reached Brandon Place. Marya must

have been waiting at the kitchen window; she came and opened the door and ran down the steps. Her arms were about Kelly in the familiar embrace, her bracelets jangling. "Now you are really home! How we have missed you!"

She led them into the garden. Julia and Kate were there, Johnny seated in Kate's lap. Kelly reached out for him instinctively, and he showed no surprise or fear at being taken into the arms of someone who must now be a stranger to him. "He's grown huge! My God, he's so heavy." Kelly had only glimpsed him sleeping in his cot since she had come back. The demands of Delia Merton had not permitted more than that.

Kate grinned. "He's not too bad, is he? I'm back at work, you know. Mrs. Cass's sister comes every day to take care of him. Mrs. Nelson, her name is. You'll have trouble telling them apart. Of course she spoils him rotten—but he gets plenty of spoiling from us all. I don't know . . . discipline won't stand a chance . . ." She looked relaxed, cheerful, her face not quite as sharp as it had been; she had let her hair grow a little, and the ends curled softly about her face.

"We made a Pimm's cup in honor of London having a summer's day," Marya announced. "Lots of ice from your monster refrigerator. And the fruit's so good for one, don't you agree? We are finishing up that smoked salmon from lunch which you rich people didn't want . . ." It was laid out on pieces of toast, and Marya had indulged in her favorite extravagance of caviar, presented on a silver tray, with lemon and chopped egg.

"I'm glad you're back, Kelly," was all Julia said.

Kelly sat down, still holding Johnny. He seemed to want to sample the caviar. She put a few pieces of the black roe on her finger and transferred them to his tongue; he paused to consider the new, salty taste, and then smiled. In his smile Kelly was once more reminded of Charles. "I'll say this for him," Laura commented, "he's developing expensive tastes early. I hope you can afford to support them, Kate."

"Well, if there isn't bread, he can always eat cake."

The conversation was desultory. Laura's exams—Kate had read the set papers, questioned Laura on how she had tackled them, and seemed to think she had a fair chance of getting through. "For a spoiled, rich brat, Kelly, I have to hand it to her that she knows how to knuckle down and study. She was so disciplined while you were gone . . . baby-sat with His Highness there any evening I wanted off, and really cracked the books."

"Hardly surprising. You've seen Delia Merton now. You know what Greg accomplished. When the Mertons put their minds to something, that's that." Kelly smiled across at Laura. It was oddly moving to see the easy affection which had grown between these loosely related women. They could not know of the incredible self-discipline Laura had imposed on herself during the many operations on her face and jaw and ear; the pain she had accepted without complaint. They couldn't know what her father had expected of her, or of the weekends spent in the cold of the Cairngorms and Snowdonia where toughness was a part of life, and no complaints were listened to. That she should learn to study and complete her education through all these distractions was also part of the Merton tradition. Self-discipline was in Laura's nature, especially the self-discipline to throw off disappointments, to force herself to break through the barrier of her shyness. But she flourished in this atmosphere of camaraderie and affection.

Marya went to make another pitcher of Pimm's cup. Chris came home, and they saw him open the back window that looked up toward the garden. Kelly was too lazily relaxed to mind that he really had to be invited to join them. It was Laura who called out the invitation. "Come and join us. Grandmother's gone, thank heaven, and Kelly and I are feeling we've been let out of prison."

"Poor lady," Chris commented as he sank down next to Laura on one of the teak garden seats. "She really is so sad, isn't she?"

To her own surprise Kelly found herself defending the thin, grim woman who had been a sort of silent black spider among them. "She was extremely pretty when she was a girl. You'd have to see the wedding photos . . . I think she so desperately wanted to give her husband a lot of children. Three miscarriages, a stillbirth, and then Greg's death. I think it took everything out of her. She can't help being possessive . . . she's lost so much." Why, she wondered, did she see it only now, when her own days at Pentland were so few, when the old antagonism between her and Delia Merton had no sting in it, when it no longer mattered to fight an old lady. She felt vaguely ashamed, and then, looking around, realized that much of this new wisdom may have come from the very people who surrounded her, the family Charles had brought her to.

"I have," Marya announced, "raided your cupboards, Kelly, and have produced an enormous Salade

Niçoise—tuna, olives, artichoke hearts, anchovies, beans. There is fresh French bread, slathered with garlic to put in the oven—a dry rosé in the fridge . . ." She cocked her head. "But perhaps you were planning to go to some grand restaurant to celebrate the departure of the black lady?"

Laura fell back in the seat in mock horror. "Marya, we'd just planned to kick off our shoes, eat a crust of bread and cheese, and have a good laugh. I don't know what there's to laugh at, certainly not poor Grandmother. Come on, Chris. We'll set the table. We'll have dinner in the kitchen, won't we, Kelly?" She got to her feet, slowly stretching. In that one natural relaxed action Kelly was aware of the extreme sensuality of Laura's body, quite unconsciously expressed. Chris rose more slowly, his face tightening, even as Laura's had relaxed. "Yes, of course I'll help."

Julia, who had contributed nothing but little sounds of agreement to the conversation, rose also. "Let me help. Marya's done all the work, and I feel so useless." She moved ahead of Laura and Chris, almost in a hurry to be away from them.

Kelly proffered her glass to Marya to refill. On her lap, Johnny was growing sleepy, and was sucking his thumb. She put the glass beside her on the table, and turned directly to Kate and Marya. "Now, tell me what's wrong with Julia."

"Sergei," Marya answered. "What else could be wrong with Julia? Apart from the fact that she cannot yet dance, which tears her apart. Julia is not yet able to dance a full role. She takes class every day. She exercises alone. But the ankle will not stand the strain. After a little dancing, it crumples. She cannot stay *en pointe*. The company directors have been good—but they also know the quality they have in Julia. She is employed. She is coaching. It seems some of these silly young things do not know how to use their hands and arms. Their faces. There is much more than legs and feet to a ballerina. Julia still had the most perfect extension. Something for them to marvel at. To learn from . . ."

"Marya, what about Sergei?"

"Ah, Sergei. During the summer break he is in America. He has been invited to give a few guest performances with the American Ballet Company. It excites him. To him, America is the ultimate freedom."

"And he didn't ask Julia to go with him?"

"I do not know if he asked. All I know is that she has not gone."

After supper was eaten and cleared away, and they had all gone, Laura lingered. "I telephoned the Gardiners—you know, Granny Renisdale's family up in Yorkshire. I asked if they'd like someone to help out with the horses or around the farm for a few weeks. I could make myself useful. I just don't think I can stick around London waiting for the exam results. It's too nerve-racking. I need to get tired enough to be able to sleep at night. They said they'd be glad to have me."

"You could always go to Mead Cottage."

Laura shook her head. "No, Kelly. I'm not going to hang around you forever. I've always said you need your own place . . ." Then, as she was about to close the glass doors, she added, "Oh, and I telephoned Peter. Told him that Grandmother had gone. Perhaps that was a bit of cheek, and I should mind my own business, but I thought he'd want to know as soon as possible. Good night, Kelly."

Kelly was in bed when the telephone rang. "When are you coming?" Peter said.

"As soon as I can load the car with groceries in the morning. I should go down to Tower Hamlets, and should look in on the Blind offices, and the Multiple Sclerosis offices. I should start the paperwork on the desk. But I'm being selfish. I'm doing none of that. I'm coming down to the cottage."

"If you'd said anything else, I would have come and dragged you down here myself. I'm sorry for all the people who need you. I need you more."

They had two days together—a time when Peter hardly left the cottage. They made love and talked and ate and slept. They talked of Pentland and of Wychwood, resuming the dialogue begun in February when they had started to attempt to make up for the years when they had not known of each other's existence. "I saw you there at Pentland, but it wasn't real," Kelly said. "I tried to fix you there, but you wouldn't stay. You belong here."

Those were the two days before Peter let the world of Wychwood intrude. "But I can't stay forever. Tommy and Andrew have been staying with a friend in Scotland. They're due back, and you will have to meet them, Kelly. It's all beginning now. Before you went away I told you we'd have to work out something. We have to make a beginning . . ."

She went to dinner at Wychwood. Tommy and Andrew were there, but not Louise. She was relieved to find them ordinary boys, good looking without being overly handsome, well-scrubbed but untidy, polite enough, given to a bit of boisterous manhandling of each other. They were thirteen and fifteen, and Andrew had that year joined Tommy at Eton.

"Tommy thinks he's no end of a swell now just because he's called Brandon Major," Andrew said to Kelly. "*Major*—why, he wouldn't even make Private in the Army. I say, I remember the General, Lady Brandon. He only came here a few times. Grandfather used to talk about him a lot, though. I expect you miss him—but he was much older than you."

"Andrew!—you don't say things like that."

"Dad, you're always telling me to say what's on my mind. How am I to know when it's the right time or the wrong time?"

"Stupid," his brother said. "You're just stupid." He made a feinting punch at his brother. "Fathead—"

Andrew wasn't to be distracted. "Dad says you've got one of those big sheep stations in Australia. I'd like to go there sometime."

"You wait until you're invited," Peter said.

"Oh, everyone wants to go to one of those outback places. It's all pretty tame here. Scotland's better. This chap's place where we were staying was very wild. We did a bit of climbing. Is it true your first husband climbed Everest? You must have had an odd sort of life."

This time his brother thumped his shoulder. "You bloody silly ass! You're rude, do you know that? You don't *say* things like that. Dad, can I have a sherry? I'm almost sixteen. Andrew can't have one. He'll say even worse things. Lady Brandon, I apologize for my brother. He doesn't mean to be rude. He just can't help it. He's rather stupid, you see."

Kelly's relief showed itself in her laughter. "I'm sorry . . . you don't even know what I'm laughing at, do you? Can I tell you what I was afraid of? I was afraid you'd both be young versions of Chris Page."

They both groaned. And then Tommy said, "Well—Chris isn't so bad. In fact, he's jolly decent to us. It's having Mrs. Page for a mother. She expects him to be perfect. Pretty hard thing to be."

As they went in to dinner Andrew said, "When's Mother coming down? It seems ages since she's been here."

"I don't know," Peter replied. "Soon, I suppose."

Tommy waited until Kelly was seated, and then sat down himself. The cheerful good humor had vanished from his face. He stared glumly down at the table. "It's that stupid boutique she's started. I've never heard of anything so stupid.

London's crammed with shops like that, and she had to start another one. Just because it's trendy to have a boutique. I suppose we should be glad she hasn't started a disco. That'd be even more stupid."

"Tommy, I don't want to hear you talk about your mother that way."

"Sorry, Dad." Then he looked up at his father. "But it does seem pretty stupid. At least, that's the way it seems to me. I can't understand someone wanting to have a silly boutique in London when they could be at Wychwood." He took a spoonful of soup. "Dad, when I'm finished at school, and everything, do you think there'd be something for me to do here? I mean a real job on the farm. I have to earn a living. But could Wychwood afford me? Now that Uncle Nick's fixed up everything, and we're going to be able to keep it, I'd like to know if there's something for me here." He looked apologetically at Kelly. "I'm sorry, Lady Brandon. I didn't mean to start talking about all this, but I've been thinking a lot about it while we've been in Scotland. The chap we were with there is going to farm. There's not much there but sheep, and it doesn't pay very well, but he's going to stay and work it with his father. He's planning to go to agricultural college instead of university. I thought I might—"

"We'll talk about it, Tommy. If you want to work at Wychwood—really work, there's pretty sure to be something for you. We'll talk about it, but you don't have to make any big decisions yet."

Kelly ate her soup in silence, only distantly listening to the talk of Peter and his sons. The tentacles of his family were reaching out to her. Until now, these two boys had been names to her. Now they were identities, with rights and desires and hopes of their own. Her relationship with Peter could no longer close them out. She looked at them half-fearfully; whether she wanted it or not, they were there, and their futures must be weighed along with her own.

Peter drove her back to Mead Cottage. "I've talked with Louise. I've told her I want a divorce."

"You're sure, Peter?"

"Would I have gone that far if I weren't? You know me—I'm the slow, stodgy type. I don't make impulsive gestures which are just gestures. All the time you were away I thought about it. Not hearing from you was hell, but I thought you meant it to be that way forever. I thought perhaps you'd never come back from Pentland, or if you did, you wouldn't come back to me. But you did, and the moment I saw you, even with that poor woman, Mrs. Merton, looking on, I knew it hadn't changed for you. We're together, you and I, Kelly. I am right, aren't I? It's more now than even it was before?"

"Yes."

"So I told Louise. She simply laughed. She said there was no need to be so deadly serious about it. People have affairs all the time, was how she put it. We could have our affair, and no one's life need be disrupted. After all, she'd had her affairs, and hadn't turned my life upside down over them. She implied that eventually we'd probably tire of each other, and why go to all the trouble of a divorce. When I said it wouldn't be like that, she got a bit more serious. She said she wasn't going to give up. She likes her life the way it is and sees no reason to change it. When I told her I'd go ahead in any case, she threatened to name you in any divorce action. So I told her if she did, that I'd name Jack Matthews, and perhaps a few others. So it all became pretty ugly, and I could read the newspaper stories as if I wrote them myself. She has a price for letting go without all this. Money. A lot of money. It would mean the end of Wychwood. This time, finally. I owe Nick for what he's already paid for it, and no matter what he says, I mean to repay it, if it takes the rest of my life. If I were to give Louise what she's asking, Wychwood would have to go. I think Louise may be making these demands with the hope that once again Nick will come up with the money. I'll never let him do it . . ."

Kelly laid her hand on him to silence him. "No more, Peter. You will not sell Wychwood. Do you think I could accept that, live with you having had to pay that price? Even Tommy and Andrew . . . could I take that away from them? We'll wait, my love . . . we'll wait. And if we can never marry, that is how it must be."

With his arms about her, the future seemed neither so bleak nor so bitter as the words she had just had to speak.

She stayed a week at Mead Cottage; it was both too long and too short a time. Too short because the hours with Peter were so few, too long because Tommy and Andrew took too much of a hold on her, and the thought of being the instrument of overturning their lives became the unthinkable thought. She worked in the garden, and unasked, they cycled over each day to help her. She sensed that it was more a need of her company, of her presence, than any great love of the work itself. "Can we call you Kelly?" Andrew asked as they rested in the shade of the orchard. "We're almost family, aren't we?" He drank the lemonade she had made, and ate biscuits, and he seemed younger and more vulnerable than the evening when she had first met him at Wychwood. He was a boy just into his teens, as yet without Tommy's commitment to Wychwood, utterly vague about what he wanted of his life, betraying just the edge of panic because he recognized that a part of what he had taken for granted might be swept away. "I wish Mother liked gardening," he said suddenly. "She doesn't like getting dirty and sweaty. She's always so cool and clean, and she thinks we should be like that too. I wish she'd stay at home more. She wants us to go and be with her in London next week. I hate the London place. It's always full of people who are smart and trendy—and they talk down to me."

Kelly refilled his glass and tried to steel herself against the unspoken plea, and could not. Andrew didn't really know all that he was touching on, did not realize the implications for the future. But he had instinctively reached to her to make her an ally, to make a treaty so that she would not undermine his world. Perhaps his mother's increasing absences had been bearable until Kelly had arrived to pose a threat, to become a potential enemy. He sought to disarm her.

"Oh, Andrew, stop *whining*," Tommy said. "You're such a crybaby." He reached over and tugged on his brother's dark hair, which was worn as long as the school rules permitted. They both wore threadbare jeans and old faded shirts; their skin was young and soft and beautiful. Seeing them as Peter's sons, Kelly's throat tightened. Was she forever to be involved with other people's children? "Don't blame Mother," Tommy went on. "Oh, she just likes a good time. I know I said the boutique was stupid, but if you grew up the way she did, up there in the wilds with no one but your own family, perhaps you'd feel the way she does about it. She's got all her sisters there in London. They all have a great time together. Wychwood must seem as dull sometimes as the place in Scotland where she grew up. I mean, be fair, Andrew. You really can't see Mother handing out tea at the Women's Institute, can you? If you wanted to be away from here, would you want someone stopping you? Well, we're grown-up, aren't we?—you and I. We're not kids anymore. We shouldn't expect her to be here every minute just because . . ." He rolled over and put his face into the long grass.

III

Kelly slipped back into the London rhythm. At the Tower Hamlets center some of them looked at her with a faint hostility. "You've been away a long time."

"I have to go Australia every now and again. I've got family there."

"My dad once wanted us all to go out to Australia. They turned him down. No skills, they said. They pick and choose who they'll have, that lot. My dad wasn't good enough. He's a milkman now."

The boy who had said it wandered off to the snooker table. Kelly knew he had left school a year ago and hadn't yet found a job. No skills.

At the London Fund for the Blind, and the Multiple Sclerosis Society they were more understanding, and grateful enough to have volunteer help so that they didn't complain. People were always joining up, and dropping out, and coming back again. Kelly started addressing envelopes and getting on the telephone to appeal for support, contributions, patronage. She always went away vaguely unsatisfied, since she never saw the end product of her efforts. She thought of asking to be trained to work with the blind, and realized that it was a commitment and a responsibility which would bind her as closely as anything had ever done in her life. The blind were people, not envelopes or telephones. They could not be put down at her convenience. The experience of forming even the slight bond she had done with Peter's sons had made her wary. In committing herself to Peter she had also committed herself to them. She wondered how many more people must she made her life encompass; to how many more must she assume the role of keeper?

Marya came and had dinner with her one evening soon after she returned. "You look tired, Kelly. I think you care too much about those kids at Tower Hamlets. Do what you can for them, but don't take their failures as your own."

"I don't think they've failed. There's so little for them to try to reach, that's the trouble."

Laura telephoned that evening from Everdale, the Gardiners' house in Yorkshire. "I'm in! It's O.K.! I passed my exam! Mr. Harris telephoned. He actually seemed pleased." She overrode Kelly's congratulations. "You know I *had* to make it. For you and Dad and Grandfather."

"You're sure you don't want to apply for Oxford or Cambridge?"

"I'll stick with London. I miss the family . . . I miss that little brute, Johnny. The Gardiners are wonderful to me. But even if I do say it myself, I earn my keep. So everything's fine. I'm getting a bit of riding, too, in my spare time. It's wonderful country up here, Kelly. They want you to visit. Granny Renisdale's been filling them in on you. You can see the dear old thing is trying to marry you off, but I don't see anyone likely up here. Of course, there's Alex and Ben, but I think you'd consider them a trifle young. I hinted that you were spoken for. They're all getting over the notion that I'm a spoiled London brat. I keep telling them that anyone who grew up at Pentland with Dad and Grandfather would have to know how to turn to." Her talk ran on. She sounded happy, pleased, exhilarated. "Look, Kelly, I hate to lay anything else on you, but I think I should return the Gardiners' hospitality. Alex and Ben would like a few weeks in London, but they can't afford a decent hotel. Do you think. . . ?"

"Of course," Kelly said. "Now that your grandmother is out of the room, it's theirs. I'll be glad to have them."

"Oh, that's marvelous, Kelly. I promise I won't let them be a bit of extra work for you or Mrs. Cass. In fact, they're pretty handy, both of them. They don't often get to London, and it would be nice to let them have a bit of a break before they go back to agricultural college . . . before I begin at university. I'm going to lay on some theater tickets, and I'm sure Julia can get us in on the opening of the ballet. I told them Grandmother Merton had given me a present to spend as I wanted. Of course, it never struck them that that would be the last thing Grandmother would ever think of . . ."

With Kelly's return it was possible for Nick to visit Johnny. He came one day to ask her to arrange it. "I can't get through to Kate. I can't ask to have Johnny by myself. But if you were to have him for a few hours once a week—well, I could just come and see you, and I'd be seeing him."

"Is that wise, Nick? While he's a baby, he won't notice. His life is full of people. We all take turns to baby-sit, and sometimes Kate even takes him and leaves him with friends at Tower Hamlets if Mrs. Nelson can't get here. He's a happy baby, and he takes to everyone. But in time he'll begin to wonder why you're coming around. He'll begin to see that you don't fit the pattern. Children catch on very early."

"You can say," Nick answered, "that I am trying to reach Kate through Johnny. It's the only way left. If I continue to come and see Johnny, it may persuade her that I care about him very much. That I'm not giving up. I want my son, Kelly."

"Kate won't give him up just because you want him."

"God, there's so much I could do for him. There's so much I could give him. How can Kate afford to bring him up—educate him properly? Even if, against all odds, she does manage to get into Parliament, she'll still be squeezed for money." He stubbed out his cigarette savagely. "God, she's a stubborn bitch. Is it possible to be as clever as Kate is and still be so stupid?"

"I expect she'd say she has her own wisdom. All right, Nick, I'll try to persuade her to let me have Johnny here, and I'll tell you the time to come. I warn you—spending time with a young child can be exhausting and mostly pretty boring. He's not quite up to discussing the *Financial Times* with you, you know."

But she set up the playpen in the kitchen, and bought a high chair, and about once a week Nick would come around and have a drink, and make an effort to talk to, to play with, his son. At first he made the mistake of bringing expensive toys which were beyond Johnny's comprehension, and then discovered that banging two saucepan lids together provided greater pleasure. "Is he advanced for his age, Kelly?" he demanded.

"About average, I'd say." And then she laughed at the disappointment in Nick's face. "Don't worry. He's on the way to being a genius, but it's better to let nature take its course." Johnny was crawling now. Very soon he would be trying to pull himself upright against the leg of the table. She didn't tell Nick that in certain ways Johnny was advanced; Nick already was too concerned about him, marking his progress every week as if it were something to be put on a graph. There were times when Johnny was fractious because he was teething, and Nick backed off. "You'd be wailing too if your gums hurt," Kelly objected. "It's all part of having a baby around, Nick. They're not always cooing and crowing. And he has his touches of temper tantrums—which is exactly the sort of temperament I'd expect him to have inherited from you and Kate. He's strong-willed, and he wants his own way. Watch out for him when he's five years old. He may be a bit of a devil."

"I swear by the time he's five years old he'll be living with me. I'll have persuaded Kate by then . . ."

"You might marry someone else."

Nick looked at the child in the high chair who was trying

to flip his food off the spoon and onto the wall. Kelly tried to visualize him in any part of Nick's elegant, cool flat, and failed. She guided the spoon toward the baby's mouth; he swallowed half of the food, and the rest went down his chin. She wondered how Nick took to the sight of a baby feeding messily.

"I won't marry so long as there's even half a chance that I might get Kate to marry me. I want my son, Kelly. It's as simple as that, and I won't change."

The Gardiner boys, Alex and Ben, paid their visit. For ten days before Laura was due to start at London University and they to return to agricultural college in Gloucestershire, they acted like young people on a spree. There was four years difference in the ages of the Gardiners, and they were not at all alike. Alex had a polish about him that it seemed Ben would never acquire—was not interested in acquiring. "Alex is the glamour boy," he said one morning to Kelly, as they shared an early breakfast before she set off for Tower Hamlets. "He's the white-haired boy at home. Well—I don't mind that. He's earned it. He was in the First Eleven at Malborough. He had two years at Oxford and did pretty well. Then he decided to switch to farming. That was quite a shock. I was supposed to be the farmer. We all thought he'd go for law, or something like that, because he's got the brains. Well, Dad . . . he couldn't quite manage to hide the fact that he was pleased Alex was going seriously into farming. He wanted the eldest to have the place. Now he says there's room for the two of us. But I wonder . . ." He nodded enthusiastically as Kelly suggested more eggs and bacon. "Here, let me cook them," he said. "I'm not bad at cooking this simple stuff. More coffee?" He poured for her, and then resumed his talk. "I've enjoyed Laura being at Everdale with us this summer. I think she's great." He pulled a wry face. "Of course, when Alex is around, she hardly knows I'm there. But I'm used to that, I expect younger brothers always are, when the elder one is the glamour boy. And I suppose it's natural with Laura, having a father like Greg Merton. And she has another hero to worship in the General. I think she admires him even more than her own father. Probably because she was older when she knew him. Well, competition like that makes it hard on an ordinary chap like me. I'll have a tough enough time just passing my exams. I don't think I'm going to climb Everest or win medals. A pretty dull prospect, I'd say." But he grinned at her as he turned from the stove. "I don't let the prospect depress me, though. I intend to enjoy life. I'll just make what I can of those stupid, dumb sheep up there in Yorkshire, and leave the glamour to chaps like Alex."

He had rather ordinary, blunt features, a square chin, sandy hair and light hazel eyes. A plain sort of a face that was utterly transformed by his smile. Kelly knew that she liked him a great deal more than his handsome, polished brother. And she regretted that Laura seemed more attracted to Alex. But Laura was still uncertain enough of her own attractions so that she still tended to see beauty in others as a special grace. It was true what Ben had said; there was an element of hero-worship in her relationship with Alex. He was older, good looking, and he would make the perfect gentleman farmer. He could ride, dance, talk about politics with Kate, and ballet with Julia. He had once started to quiz Marya about Stalin, but she refused the bait, saying she had viewed him only at a distance. "But you've got some sort of medal from him, haven't you?"

Marya shrugged. "After the siege of Stalingrad there weren't enough generals to go around for all those who had medals pinned on them. Stalin would have been up all night if he'd had to do it all himself."

Only with Mrs. Cass did Ben shine more than his brother. "That's a lovely young man, m'lady. Just lovely." And she didn't explain why she thought so.

In September the National Ballet started its new season; Sergei was back from America, and the trouble started. When he came to Brandon Place he was unusually quiet, almost melancholy. He went to see Johnny put to bed, and then he returned to the kitchen of Number 16. He sat silently through most of the meal, only answering in monosyllables when he was questioned about dancing in the States, the places he had been, what he thought of the company.

Julia, who had sat gazing at him and almost forgotten to eat, answered for him. "The truth is, Sergei thinks there is no other place but America. He's unhappy to have to come back here because of his contract." She said it as if she were reading out the sentence of her own execution.

Sergei shrugged. "They are free. The dance is alive. Is growing. There is no end."

"We've done a lot of creative things here, Sergei. It's not like Russia at all."

"No, not like Russia. Much better. But in America it lives. Different. They"—he struggled for the word—"dare more.

Will make mistakes, but dare more. Even some dancers produce their own ballets. They do not all take . . . take instructions."

The trouble that was to become a storm burst into the newspapers when Sergei had a public row with the management and chief choreographer of the National. He refused the classic interpretation of a classic role. He demanded that *Attitudes* be produced more often so that he could dance his tailor-made role. He attended class punctilously, but gave trouble at rehearsals, and when performing his solos would often ignore the choreography to produce such audacious feats of skill and grace that the audiences were gasping. He never wrecked a performance, but in his deportment toward his partner he declared his boredom with the supportive role. His lifts and holds were mechanical, as if he wanted to indicate to the audience that any schoolboy could have done them. In his solos he took flight. Whenever Sergei danced, the company suffered. The public began to come to witness the war between them, and the press made more than it should of the situation. *Temperament or truth?* one story was headlined. *Does the National need this self-indulgent boy wonder?* another asked.

"He's doing it deliberately, of course," Laura said, "to get the National to release him from his contract."

Julia said nothing. She attended classes, attended rehearsal as an onlooker, and continued to coach in individual roles which did not demand sustained effort from her. There was no mention of a time when she might appear on stage. She made no comment on the sympathetically whispered rumor that she would never perform in public again. She was present at every performance that Sergei gave.

The end came quite suddenly. Sergei, after a stormy rehearsal session, went out and got drunk, and was unable to give a performance that night. A young dancer went on in his place and scored a minor triumph in *Attitudes*. Sergei was waiting at the end of the performance and punched the young man as he came off after taking his last curtain call. No appeal from the directors was able to stop the young dancer from pressing charges of assault and battery. Sergei appeared before a Bow Street Magistrate, and was fined one hundred pounds with costs. The press had a field day, and the National offered to release Sergei from his contract. He accepted.

Two weeks later the American Ballet Company had arranged a visa for him to work and live permanently in the United States. He came to say good-bye to Kelly. "The best times since I came out of Russia I have had in this house. I have come to see little Johnny because I have promised him I would teach him to dance. It must wait a while. And I owe you a Fabergé clock. I don't forget."

"Sergei, what about Julia?" In the two weeks since he had left the National he had spent much time with Julia, but she did not speak of his plans or her own. He shrugged, and lifted his hands in a gesture of exasperation and defeat. "Julia knows I must dance. It is my life, and it is short. In America they will let me do more. They give me a chance to choreograph, to go on with the ballet after I have finished dancing. I have explained all this to Julia. She can come with me if she wants. . . . This I have said. She refuses."

"Refuses?"

"Well, she has decided not. There is no place for her with the American Ballet. Here she has a place, a home. Perhaps, just maybe, a chance to dance again. In America—well Julia Brandon is not one of their own, and there are many younger dancers waiting for their turn. In America . . . no job. No dance . . ."

So he left Brandon Place after he had seen Johnny. No one knew when he last saw Julia. What they saw was Julia's haggard face, with eyes that burned feverishly in it. For a week she stayed away from classes at the National, asking Kelly to telephone Dame Katherine Meredith to say that she was ill. She stayed in her flat, and played records all day and half the night. Almost by force, Kelly got her down to the kitchen of Number 16 to eat some meals. At other times she or Marya would take food to Julia's flat, and stay while she toyed with it, pushing half of it aside. She played listlessly with Johnny, but refused to take him for walks in his pram, or to go out at all. Finally, over dinner at Number 16, Marya tackled her. "So, Julia, the time has come that you have always known would come. When you first knew Sergei he was a young man in flight from a system which stifled him. What he found here was freedom, and he loved you because you seemed the best embodiment of it. You brought him to your home, and you even spoke a little Russian with him. But you knew always that it would never be permanent. You were the first taste of freedom, and now you cannot compete with what he was offered in America. I am brutal—no? But I am right. Younger women and older women he will find in America. He will not be faithful for long. I do not think he is scheming enough to use each one deliberately, but each will be used. He will have all the attributes of a great star in a country that worships its stars. It is heady for a young man, and he wants it. You could not go with him, and very wisely you decided not to try. But what now of your own life?"

"What of it?" Julia countered. "There's not much of it, is there?"

Marya pulled on her cigarette. "So you have nothing to contribute? You break your heart over a young man who was never wholly yours. And I ask myself is this the daughter of the Colonel? Is *this* Elizabeth Brandon's daughter? If she were still lying in that bed now, would you dare face her? You make me ashamed I know you."

"Marya," Kelly objected, "that's cruel."

"It is cruel and it is true."

Julia got up and left the kitchen. The next morning she went early to class. Two nights later she was in the audience, frozen-faced, to watch a gala charity performance of *Firebird.*

IV

Kelly went down to Mead Cottage each weekend, and Peter was always waiting there for her. They accepted the fact that people around them must, by now, know of their relationship. Kelly realized that she was partly isolated from the reality of it because once she reached the cottage, she seldom left it until early Monday morning when she set out for London. But Peter's absence from Wychwood was remarked upon, and people began to discover that if he could not be reached by telephone at Wychwood, they might find him at Mead Cottage. For her sake, Peter insisted on returning to Wychwood each night, however late, and he cursed the hypocrisy of it. "If it were London, it wouldn't matter a damn. But people notice things in a country place, and they talk. It's different talk from London talk. I don't mean that people don't break marriage vows around here—if I can use that quaint expression these days—but it's covered over. There's a sham in it that I hate, but for a while I have to go along with it. In time, people will take it for granted. Give Louise a little more time, and she'll change her mind. Do you ever read the gossip columns? She and Jack Matthews are what they call 'a constant couple.' She'll want all of Jack Matthews' money, not just a part of it. I suppose you could say he's as much the sort of man the sixties threw up as Nick is—rock records, films, discos, boutiques, designers, cosmetics. Matthew lives off the publicity machine, and Louise likes that. At last she's more important to the press than any of her sisters. She has more money to spend. She flies to New York for a weekend. She's jet set, and she likes it."

"Why doesn't she marry him?"

Peter laughed. "Perhaps he hasn't asked her. Who knows? Perhaps she's not certain that she can give up the Wychwood background. She wants to have her cake and eat it. It isn't so long ago that someone like Louise, an earl's daughter, would hardly have thrown a word to a character like Jack Matthews. Now it's trendy, and so long as there's success and money, who cares? The Profumo affair seemed to blow the lid off a lot of things apart from one man's career. People down here read about it. They shake their heads, and no doubt say my 'poor Peter' and aren't surprised that I spend my time here. What I don't like is the idea that anyone would think that we were no different from Louise and Jack Matthews. That part of it hurts, and I don't want you hurt, Kelly."

"You must think I'm very fragile. I'd go a long way farther than this for you. And I can wait a long time. I can out-wait Louise. I think I've been growing toward this all my life. Time—there's all the time in the world, and I can wait, so long as I can wait with you. I'm holding on. This time I don't mean to let go." She couldn't have explained exactly what she meant by 'this time.' She felt as if she had wandered a long way in darkness after Greg's death, and again after Charles' death; had moved mechanically to do things because they were expected of her. With Peter, a part of her long untouched had become awake and aware. There was freedom, movement. But she was also once again committed.

V

It was that September that the first faint clouds of doubt began to gather around the bright pinnacle of the success of Brandon, Hoyle. An article in the business section of the *Sunday Journal* raised the question of the financing of the South African subsidiary, a question of whether or not money might have been raised on collateral which existed largely on paper, and on future prospects not yet realized. On the stock exchange the next day the shares of Brandon, Hoyle fell sharply.

It was one of the evenings Kelly had arranged with Nick to have Johnny with her, one of the evenings Kate would be out. She had prepared Johnny's supper and begun to feed him when Nick arrived. He went automatically to the kitchen after she had answered the doorbell. He stood looking at his son for some time, watching the flaying hand dabbing at the food. "He's grown," he said.

"It's only a week since you saw him, Nick."

"Well, I tell you, he's grown. Look, he knows me. I swear it." He put out his finger tentatively and touched Johnny's cheek. "Hello, young man. How are you? In pretty good form, I'd say. Look at him. He's sitting up straight as a die."

"In fact, Nick, he's pretty firmly anchored in that chair. There's not a lot he can do except sit up straight. But, yes, he's in pretty good form, I'd say. The doctor thinks so, in any case."

"Kate takes him regularly to the—what's he called—the pediatrician?"

Kelly poured him a Scotch. She now kept a supply of drinks in the kitchen because it was more often used there than in the drawing room. At times she wondered what the drawing room was for. "Nick, you ask that question every other time you come here. You know she does, and you know the doctor thinks Johnny might be a touch *too* advanced. He grows and puts on weight just a little ahead of schedule. He's making all the right noises and movements. He's interested in everything. He likes people. He shouts when he's pleased about something, and that's pretty often. He doesn't howl except when he's hungry. He hasn't even had a sniffle since he was born. You know Kate. Once she decided she was going to be a mother, you know she'd put everything she had into it. To have a child without a father is only a further challenge to her to make that child as happy and healthy as she can. Don't ever forget, Nick, she sees a good deal of the other sorts of children—the other kinds of parents—in her job. She knows the signs of a child who's not well. She can't hand Johnny a certificate of happiness, but by God, she'll see that he goes into the fray as healthy as any child can be. So let's hear no more of it."

He nodded, sipped on his drink, and carefully blew the smoke from his cigarette away from the baby. "I know . . . I know. I sound like a fool. Kate's great when she isn't being as irritating as hell. Sorry, Kelly. It's been an edgy day."

She let Johnny get down a few more spoonfuls of food, and then went and poured a Scotch for herself. "I listened to the financial report on the news, Nick. Brandon, Hoyle took quite a tumble." She put another spoonful in Johnny's mouth.

"Oh, *that*. Yes, well that was part of it. Some days just have problems. And the shares—nothing to worry about. One slightly off-putting article in a newspaper, and all the Nervous

Nellies rush to unload. Maybe they call it profit-taking. But they unload. We always pick them up again. There's always someone ready to pick up the stock at a lower price. That's what the market is all about. We all trade in mystique . . ."

"Then there was no truth in that article in the *Journal* yesterday?"

He shrugged. "There's always a grain of truth in almost anything any journalist wants to say about a company. You can always find something if you dig hard enough. A lot of journalists make their living by that sort of digging. It's what they're good at. It's no problem, Kelly. It will go away once something more interesting comes along. Brandon, Hoyle's all right. It'll continue to be all right so long as people don't put out scare rumors. Scare rumors—" He stopped, and Kelly looked around from her task of getting more food into Johnny.

Kate had come through from Number 15 and stood in the doorway of the kitchen. She so seldom allowed herself to encounter Nick that her presence there had to be deliberate. She was unusually flushed, her eyes bright; it was one of the times when she looked decidedly pretty.

"Hello, Nick." She wandered over to the Scotch bottle. "Do you mind, Kelly?" Nick got to his feet, found a glass for her, added water to what she poured. "Talking about rumors, I suppose you've been paying *some* attention to the rumors going around that Alec Douglas-Home was about to dissolve Parliament and call a General Election? Well, the word's out, and it's more than a rumor, that he'll announce it in the Commons tomorrow afternoon. Election Day will be the fifteenth of October."

"You're sure?" Nick said. "Home could hold on a while longer."

"He won't. He'll call an election, and the Conservatives will lose. Labour will be in."

"You're looking pretty pleased about it."

"Naturally. I have a rather personal interest in it. That's what I've come to tell you. The selection committee for Beckenham South East, who've been flirting with a few possible candidates, have finally made up their minds. I've been adopted. I'll be fighting the election there for Labour."

"Kate!" Kelly put down the spoon, and stared at her.

Kate held up a hand deprecatingly. "Oh, don't get excited. They don't give me a snowball's chance in hell of winning. Beckenham South East is a part of London neither of you would know much about. It's not your sort of place. Not mine, either. They're pretty solidly Conservative, with a fringe of Labour in the newer parts of it. But basically it's one of those places where people are scared stiff of even a whiff of Socialism. They live in solid little semi-detacheds, and worry about the mortgage and their pensions. They don't like people stirring up their lives. They're afraid of change—any sort of change. I suspect the selection committee have let me have it because no one else is very keen to fight it. But it's my first chance to fight an election. It means the Labour Party has its eye on me, and with luck I'll be given another try. Maybe a by-election with a better chance of winning. This is where I'm going to be blooded, I suppose."

Nick looked at her steadily, and then raised his glass. "A Labour victory will play hell with the stock market, but I have to wish you luck. Oh—the selection committee *does* know about Johnny?"

"Of course they know. I don't doubt it'll be the first thing some heckler will shout from the back of the hall. Don't you see—Labour has thrown me this seat because it's impossible to win, but they want to see how I'll perform. Whether I can take the pressure." She sat down and took the spoon from Kelly, and began feeding her son. "And Johnny is very much part of the pressure. If I can't take the things that will be said—if the electors are too offended by the situation, then I doubt I'll ever be offered another chance. I'm a woman, I'm too young, and I've got a baby. The whole thing is stacked against me. But I intend to squeeze out every vote I can."

"You can do with campaign contributions," Nick said.

"Much as I need the money, I think you'd better stay out of it, Nick. Kelly, I'd be very grateful if you'd ring doorbells for me, but you can't give more than a nominal donation. I don't want anyone suggesting the Brandon money, or Merton money, or anything else is working for me. It would be a total about-face if the Renisdale press were favorable to me, but the Renisdale press is there in the background, nonetheless. The kindest thing they could do would be to ignore me."

She took up a mug of milk and waited patiently as Johnny tried to get his two hands around it; she guided it to his lips and let him think he had done it himself.

"So from tomorrow on it's going to be a campaign. Thank God a campaign can only run for three weeks, and these may turn out to be three weeks of hell. I have to know for *myself* if I can take it."

In Beckenham South East things did not go as either party had expected or planned. The Conservative member, who had represented the constituency for twenty-eight years, was retiring and not standing again. The Conservatives, sure of their majority, had chosen as a candidate a solid man of fifty-two; he was a solicitor, and this was his first time to stand for Parliament. He toured the district faithfully, wearing his blue rosette, and his speeches, like his face on the posters, excited no one, and neither were remembered. In the midst of a general election through the whole country, there was no interest for the national press in Beckenham South East. It was assumed by both parties that Mr. Henry Saunders would win. If he had continued on his routine, proper course, he would have won, but he made a mistake. Watching the polls in the local paper record a slight dip in those intending to vote Conservative he had panicked, and inexperienced, he had blundered. He attacked Miss Kate Brandon, the Labour candidate, as an immoral woman and unfit to represent Beckenham South East in Parliament.

That personal attack caught the attention of the national popular press. Kate Brandon was both denounced and applauded by columnists, tipsters, erudite pundits and political correspondents. She was interviewed on radio and television. She was asked to defend her position, and she refused. "You accept that fact as it is, or you don't accept it. I have a son, and I am not married. That is all I intend to say. My baby will not be exploited by either Party. I'm fighting to represent Beckenham because I think I have something to offer the constituents. It's possible I have something to offer the country. Something constructive. Yes, I'm Labour, but if I'm elected I won't vote the straight Party line. I will not be in Parliament to keep either Party in power. I would vote every issue as I thought it right to vote."

"Does that, Miss Brandon, mean you wouldn't accept the Party whip?"

"I'll accept nothing that goes against what I think is right—right for Beckenham and right for the country."

The glasses of the television interviewer glinted as he lifted his head from his notes. "Aren't you . . . aren't you, Miss Brandon, a little young to think you know what's right for the country?"

Suddenly Kate had flashed that grin that utterly changed her face. She looked relaxed and confident. "That is what youth is for, Mr. Sargent. Don't you think we've had enough of the mess the old men who've been running this country have made? I hope the voters of Beckenham will give *me* and other young candidates a chance . . ."

Nick sat watching the interview with Kelly. "She just committed political suicide. The Labour Party will dump her after this. She hasn't got the right to talk like that until she's been in Parliament for twenty years. They'll never forgive her. Honestly, although she's with the other Party, it's Charles all over again. Never knew when to keep quiet . . ."

Kelly said coolly, "I think she's got a point—about all the old men. The old and sick men." She was thinking of Eden at the time of Suez, too ill to know what he was doing, too ill to give Charles the backing he had wanted. She was thinking of Macmillan who would not be pushed off his perch until illness had done it for him. She thought of Macmillan's unlikely choice to succeed him. However able, a fourteenth earl, even if he renounces his title, as Alec Douglas-Home had done, is not a natural in politics. The country had not taken to him.

Suddenly the country, in the form of the popular press, took to Kate. "Let youth have a chance!" was on the front pages. The evening papers carried pictures of her campaigning in Beckenham, the wool cap looking impossibly jaunty. The ballerina, Julia Brandon, was photographed ringing doorbells, as was her stepmother, Lady Brandon. Laura swung her hair over her cheek, and smiled for the photographers, and the picture emerged as one of those freaks which is both innocent and sexy. The press had found something other than politics to write about. They wrote about the Brandons and the Mertons. They wrote about the four women of the family. They dug out from the files the pictures of Kelly and her three stepdaughters on the steps of St. George's Chapel. The Renisdale press tried to keep off the subject, but in the end succumbed. Arthur Renisdale had tried to bar pictures of Laura appearing in any of his papers, and his editors had pointed out that since she was campaigning for the Labour candidate, Kate Brandon, it would appear as a petty piece of overprotectionism—indeed he would appear as a spoilsport. He gave in, and telephoned Laura to apologize. "Don't worry, Grandpapa. I'm enjoying it all because Kate's such good fun. She's wiping the floor with that stupid Saunders man . . ."

As hard as Kate fought to talk of the issues of the election, in Beckenham it had become a contest of personalities. She refused to talk about Johnny, refused to allow him to be photographed. But an enterprising cameraman, arriving outside

Number 15 Brandon Place early on a Sunday morning, got a shot of Kate carrying Johnny down the steps, and Laura following with the pram. Johnny, always enchanted by anything new, waved his arms at the flash of the camera, and the man took another photo. No one noticed how nervous it made Laura. The splash picture that appeared on the front page of of the country's largest-selling tabloid on Monday morning was of Johnny with both arms held high, his face close to Kate's. It was captioned: THE VICTORY SALUTE?

That day, Kate sent Johnny, in Marya and Mrs. Nelson's charge, down to Mead Cottage. There were no more photographs of him, but that single one was enough. Beckenham, bemused, found itself at last on the front page. The country at large had never heard of Beckenham; no one could remember the former Member ever saying anything of note in the House. He had toed the Party line, voted dutifully, and left an apathetic electorate for the next Conservative candidate, who was supposed to slip quietly into his shoes. It was not going to be quiet. Beckenham liked having itself written about, mentioned on television. Kate Brandon was asked back again to appear with other candidates on a prime-time evening show; the personality that came off so well on the platform was even better on camera. She made her points quickly, neatly, and managed to get a laugh out of one of her opponents. Interviewed in the High Street in Beckenham the next day, a middle-aged woman with a shopping basket remarked, "The Parties?—they're all much the same. I vote Conservative myself, but I must say it's a nice change to see someone in politics actually smile. Perhaps she's right about these old men. . . . Yes, I like Kate Brandon, and I think she's entitled to her baby and her private life, like anyone else. He looked like a nice, healthy baby to me." A young man in jeans shrugged at the pollster's questions. "I dunno . . . I never voted before. But I read she listens to the Beatles. I might vote for *her.*"

An anonymous Labour supporter bribed someone at the newspaper office to get hold of the negative of the picture of Johnny. It was printed hastily and appeared by the thousand on walls and hoardings in Beckenham. *Who says this baby's mother isn't good enough to represent Beckenham?*

Nick telephoned Kelly in near-anguish. "For God's sake, Kelly, get Kate to stop it."

"How can she? She didn't do it. Hold on to yourself, Nick. On Thursday it'll be all over. Publicity never made a successful candidate."

"Publicity, my dear Kelly, can do anything. And who should know it better than you? You've lived with enough of it. And now *this*!"

"She won't win, Nick. She can't. No publicity could ever overturn that Conservative majority. By Thursday it'll be all over," she repeated.

Kelly had not calculated, as neither the Conservative or Labour Parties had done, what twenty-eight years of being represented by the same, predictable member had done. Beckenham had not changed much, but its fringes had, and the fringes were young. They came from the new, featureless housing estates and high-rise blocks; no one could accurately assess the character or opinions of those who lived there. They turned out in surprising numbers at the polls. Beckenham had the distinction of scoring the highest ratio of registered voters to turn out at the polling stations. When the results were in they had the youngest member of Parliament, and Kate Brandon was one of an overall majority of five which put Labour into power. In Beckenham they had turned out to vote both for and against Kate Brandon. She had a majority of only two hundred and fifty-seven. Henry Saunders demanded a recount, and got it. Labour waited another day to announce that Miss Kate Brandon was among its back-benchers.

Kelly, Laura, Julia and Marya were in the Stranger's Gallery as Kate, along with all the other members of the newly convened Parliament, slipped into their places. There was no business of any note on that first day. They left early, and joined Kate in the Lobby. Mrs. Nelson had waited with Johnny in Kelly's car, parked in Old Palace Yard. The same photographer who had caught them at Brandon Place followed them from the House. He managed one shot of Johnny before Laura put her elbow in his stomach. He gasped, and then took it in good humor. "Fair's fair, Miss Merton. Your grandfather wouldn't approve of that."

The next day there was a front-page picture of them all. THAT BRANDON BABY AGAIN, was the caption.

But one of the Sunday papers, with a more serious readership, and no habit of commenting on the personal lives of members of Parliament, mused over the composition of the new House. The article ended: *Miss Kate Brandon helped give Labour its narrow victory. While not agreeing with his politics, one likes to speculate—had not Sir Charles Brandon died last year—on the fascinating idea that father and daughter would have debated each other across the aisle of the*

House of Commons. There seems little doubt that Kate Brandon will go on to greater prominence, possibly to high office. As the youngest member of this Parliament and the daughter of a former member, the new member for Beckenham South East has already been touched by history.

VI

One of the unexpected, unwanted results of Kate's election was the reaction in Tower Hamlets. Looking out of the kitchen window the morning after Kate had taken her seat, Kelly recognized the face of one of the girls who sometimes drifted into the center at Tower Hamlets, a rather sullen, difficult girl, given to wearing the extreme of fashion in its cheapest available form, who smoked constantly and had never had more than a job at a chocolate factory, which she held for six weeks before quitting. She went to the labour exchange, went for job interviews, and never got another job. "Same old thing," she had said to Kelly, "They want you to work like a slave for a few quid a week." Kelly had tried to interest her in a secretarial course which was being offered as a training scheme. "Can you see me in one of the toffee-nosed West-End offices? They don't take people like me. I talk wrong—I'm not their sort, see?" But she had consented to see a career's officer again, and said she would "think about it." Now she stood on the street outside Number 16, gazing at the two houses, the planted tubs, the still new-looking paint.

Kelly went to the front door. "Marilyn? Are you looking for me? Or for Kate? Is there something wrong? You'd better come in." Kate had once been assigned to the family as a social worker, trying to deal with the problem created by an unemployed father who drank too much.

"Don't mind if I do." The girl came up the steps slowly, staring into the hall, gazing through the glass doors into Number 15, looking up the stairs.

"Come into the kitchen," Kelly said. "Would you like some coffee? It's just made."

"Don't mind if I do." She looked around while Kelly got another mug, poured, pulled out a chair for her. Her eyes lingered on everything, the plants, the shining copper pots, the handsome wooden fittings, the big refrigerator. She put three heaping spoonfuls of sugar into her coffee and stirred lazily.

"What is it, Marilyn?"

"Nothing."

"Nothing?"

"That's what I said. Nothing. I just was curious. Wanted to see it for myself. Saw it in all the newspapers." She sipped the coffee, which was too hot, and took a biscuit and dunked it before eating. "You really think we're a load of rubbish down there, don't you—in the Hamlets? Think we can't read, or something? All that stuff Kate comes on with about the working people getting a better crack at things. Getting jobs—training—all that sort of stuff. All right for *her* to talk. All the time she lives in a place like this. She and her grotty clothes. Told us she lived in a place off Brompton Road. That's O.K. Lots of cheap places off Brompton Road—the other end of it. This ain't cheap, *Lady* Brandon." She laughed aloud. "That was a load of rubbish, too! *Mrs*. Brandon. You should have heard the kids when they saw the pictures in the papers. You and Miss Laura Merton. Her grandfather's a lord or something, and owns newspapers. And that Australian place you go to—the two of you, you own some great bloody big farm out there. And you have the cheek to come down to Tower Hamlets and tell us we have to get jobs! Have you ever had a job, *Lady* Brandon?"

Kelly tried to keep her temper. "I once trained as a nurse, and I have a teaching certificate. Yes, I've had jobs."

"Nurse . . . teacher . . . wouldn't you just know it! Miss Goody-Two-Shoes jobs. Pushing people around. Telling them what to do. Just like Kate. They said on the telly she's got some big degree or other. Well, I don't suppose we'll be seeing *her* anymore. Too busy on the telly, and posing for photographers. Felt sorry for her, we did, bringing up a baby all by herself. Seemed just like one of us. But look where she's bringing up the baby—and she's got a whole bloody great family doing it for her! What a load of rubbish," she repeated. "Thanks for the coffee, Lady Brandon . . ." She rose and looked around the room carefully again. "Funny, you people. You dish out a load of money on places like this, and you can't even buy a new table. My mum wouldn't give this lot here house room."

She gathered her coat with its bedraggled piece of fake fur trimming about her like a grand cloak, and walked out into the hall. Coolly she paused to look about her again; she even took a few steps forward so that she could see into the dining room. She said nothing more until she was standing on the pavement outside, and then she turned and looked back at Kelly. "A bunch of hypocrites, that's what you are. A whole bunch of hypocrites!" She edged between the cars parked at the curb, and for a moment rocked back on her thin high heels. "I think I'll go and have a look over there." She jerked her head toward Cavanagh's. Her gaze ran over the whole, neat, prosperous face of Brandon Place, the two yellow doors set among the sleek olive-green doors, the prim bay trees in their tubs. "Handy for you, isn't it? I bet you buy your groceries there." Then as she stepped jauntily out into the road, a driver stood on the brakes of his Jaguar, and brought it to a screeching halt a foot from her. He rolled down the window and shouted something at her. "And up yours too, buster!" she retorted, and flounced across the road. Kelly watched her vanish behind the brass-and-glass doors of Cavanagh's.

Chapter Ten

I

After the hectic activity of the election campaign, the period that followed seemed oddly quiet. "We haven't had time to think," Kelly said to Peter. "We've barely had time to eat. We all thought it was going to be for nothing—just a chance for Kate to fight her first election. Now she's in Parliament. It's so strange. Almost overnight everything's changed. She seems suddenly to have moved into the limelight, and Julia is backing out."

They sat in the kitchen at Mead Cottage, ate the food Kelly had cooked, and looked at each other with the hunger of two people who have been long parted. It was no more than a month since Kate had made her announcement of her adoption as a candidate, and Peter had been to London several times since then to see Kelly. But it seemed they had spent no time together—a snatched hour or two, a hasty meal, the telephone always ringing. After Kelly had sent Johnny and Marya to Mead Cottage, Peter had stayed at Wychwood. "I can't leave them alone," he said on the telephone to Kelly. "I don't know what the press will get up to, and if I have to act the heavy, and stand with a gun at the gate—which really isn't my style—then I'll do it." He and Mrs. Page had kept Marya supplied with food, newspapers, cigarettes and vodka. "Mrs. Page says nothing. It's evident she approves of nothing in the whole arrangement—not Johnny or Marya or you or I. But Mrs. Page isn't my life—you are." He put out his hand and touched hers across the table. "I want to live with you, Kelly."

She smiled lightly. "I thought we were already living together."

"This isn't nearly enough. I want you all the time. I want you at Wychwood with me. I want to marry you."

"That's a lot of wanting all at one time."

"I know it's a lot of wanting, and I'm impatient. I've only just realized that so much time has gone by me, and I've hardly been living. Now I grudge the days—the hours. It's one more gone, every time I count. I'm getting like that man in that song—what's it called? I haven't got time for the waiting game."

"You must wait a bit longer on Louise, or you could lose Wychwood. You almost lost it once, and now it's been given back to you. Hold it, Peter. You'd only be half yourself without it, and I know that even better than you. I don't want only half of you. I'm impatient and greedy myself, but I'll wait. Patience will win this game. Something will happen . . . I don't know what will happen, but something will happen."

"How can you be sure? I know I said we'd outwait Louise. I said she'd tire of the game first. But can we be sure of that? Perhaps we're just waiting—and losing time—for nothing."

"After Greg—and Charles—don't you think I have a sense of things happening? About to happen? Things will seem to stand still, but they'll move on . . ."

"I don't understand you, Kelly. I don't know what you're talking about."

"I don't completely understand myself. I'm just saying 'Wait awhile.' Love me, and wait." She put her other hand down on his, so that he was gripped. "We've had a spring and a summer and an autumn together. Let's see the winter through. By spring, something will have happened."

He looked down at her hands grasping his. "Yes—by the spring I'll be one year older. One more Christmas will have gone. That's the way I look at it now. I must have been mad ever to have said we could wait."

"By spring Tommy and Andrew will be a year older. They will be that much closer to understanding that what happens will be inevitable. Louise will be one year older. Time runs on for her, too. The clock will have stopped for none of us.

Things have happened so quickly for me since the moment Charles came into my life at Pentland. A whirlwind that seemed to sweep me up, and then quite as suddenly dropped me. I would like to draw breath. I would like a time without tumult. I can easily wait the winter through—forever, if I have to."

"It's not because you're not sure, is it? Not sure that you want to be with me?"

"I want you—and I've learned to wait."

II

Things did happen—small, almost imperceptible things that seemed of no great magnitude at the time of their happening, but each of them marked a change, or the beginning of a change.

Julia began to take night classes in shorthand and typing. She still continued her morning class with the National, still coached individually in the afternoon, but, without telling anyone at Brandon Place, she began evening classes. It was only when Kate heard the clatter of the typewriter in Julia's flat that any of them were made aware of it. Kate brought it up one evening when they had gathered in Kelly's kitchen for supper. Gradually, after her return from Pentland, Kelly had established a pattern by which all of them at Brandon Place knew they were welcome at a meal on Wednesday evenings. Kelly would prepare food that was almost infinitely stretchable, filling it out with fruit and cheese, and whomever was at home that evening and cared to appear was welcome. Almost against her will she had felt compelled to include Chris Page in that invitation. He always exercised usual tact, and appeared infrequently, always bringing wine and often flowers with him. He would make his excuses and depart early, leaving them to talk over coffee.

This Wednesday evening the kitchen had gathered in Julia, Marya and Kate. Johnny lay asleep in his carry-cot, and later would go upstairs with Marya; Kate was due to go back to the House of Commons for a late debate, and to vote. In the erratic rhythm of Kate's days, Kelly relived the few weeks when she had shared that same strange schedule with Charles. It was a time she recalled with vivid clarity, but yet a time which now seemed an age ago. As she had tried to voice it to Peter, time had a way of pausing, and then running on too swiftly. Time was not the same for any of them, but the clock did not stop.

"Have you taken to novel writing, Julia?" Kate joked. "Did I hear you banging away at a typewriter?"

Julia colored. "I didn't think it made much noise."

"That isn't an answer, dear sister. What are you writing?"

"Nothing. I'm trying to learn to type. I find it's almost as hard as learning to dance. I'm so slow and clumsy. I'm too old to be learning new things, I think. And as for the shorthand—I'm hopeless . . ."

Marya put down her cigarette and stared at Julia in astonishment. "*You* are learning to type—to take shorthand? Good God, whatever for? Why do you need to type?"

"It's quite simple. I need a job. I have a job, of sorts, of course, with the company. But it doesn't pay very much. And I've had an offer—"

"What are you talking about?" Kate demanded, no longer joking. "Of course you have a job. You have a job dancing."

"Perhaps you haven't noticed," Julia said slowly. "I'm *not* dancing anymore. I'm taking classes. I'm doing a bit of coaching, but I'm not dancing." She took a deep breath. "Even I have had to admit it at last, I'm not going to be dancing anymore. It's quite definite now. My doctor—the one Nick sent me to—even he has come out and said it. It's a year since the operation. From every aspect the ankle is perfect. Every aspect except a dancer's, that is. It just won't take the punishment. I can do little bits and pieces very well. Then, quite suddenly, it goes. I suppose it might be possible to merge back into the *corps* where I wouldn't have solo pieces to dance, but that wouldn't do. The star system doesn't allow that. From time to time there may be a character role to dance . . ." Her tone wavered dangerously. "I may dance a witch or a Dowager Queen . . . and people may say, 'Remember when she danced *Firebird*?' Well, I don't want to dance the witch. I'd rather be gone."

They sat silently. So long as Julia had continued to attend morning class, they had all assumed that eventually she would dance again. Kelly realized that Kate's election campaign and her entrance into the House had masked a grave crisis with Julia. The smiling, beautiful face of the woman who had rung doorbells in Beckenham had seemed more beautiful because she was facing the full realization of her own loss, and must have been then making her plans. And she had said nothing. The twins who seemed so unalike had in common a strength which could have been an inheritance both from Charles and from Elizabeth. Kelly felt the guilt of her own absorption with Peter, seeing him, loving him, to the exclusion of everything but the most obvious events. She topped up the wine in Julia's almost untouched glass, and the bottle rattled against the rim.

"You said 'an offer.' What sort of an offer? Who with?"

"The National. They can use a bit more secretarial help. They want to keep me with them. And it's useful to have someone who already knows how things are run, who knows the people involved. I know who's dancing what, with whom, all over the world. Who's on tour, who's dancing at home. They don't have to break in an outsider. Dame Katherine said there'd be some public relations involved. And they desperately need help when the company's on tour. I don't know how I'll work out at that part of it. I'm not a very well-organized person myself, so I don't see how I'll manage organizing others. But at least I do know what the company needs. If they complain about something, I'll know what they mean." She looked at the silent people around the table. "Well, it's something, isn't it? Better than nothing. Better than pretending everything's going to be all right again, and that I'm just waiting until I'm ready to perform. I'll never perform again. It's better to come right out and say it."

Kelly felt the tears prick her eyelids, and managed to hold them back. But it was Kate who spoke first.

"Must it be with the company? Couldn't you go somewhere else?—find something else? Wouldn't you be better away from it all? Not to be reminded day after day—"

Julia shook her head. "I don't want *not* to be reminded. It's the only world I've ever lived in. I don't understand any other sort. I'm used to performances and crises and triumphs and disasters. I'm used to the whole crazy world that it is. We're not like other people. It's just that I . . ." She sipped her wine, and then went on. "I simply want to stay with my own kind, and they've made it possible." She added with a trace of wistfulness, "I wish I had your sort of cleverness, Kate. Then I'd be more useful to them. But they're making room for me, and I expect to be able to help them in ways other people can't."

Marya stubbed out the butt of one cigarette and lighted another. "Julia, couldn't you have talked to one of us? Discussed it before you made this decision? Can we be of no help?"

Julia shrugged. "Did you think I was going to bother you all in the middle of the campaign? There really was no decision to be made, Marya. It was made for me. My ankle won't take certain things, and that's that. It was finished. Done. What decision was there to make?"

After Kate had quietly departed, and Marya had taken Johnny upstairs, Julia lingered with Kelly. "Perhaps I should have talked about it more, but honestly I didn't see what anyone could do or say about it."

"Have you let Sergei know?"

The gesture of her hands dismissed the thought. "I've written a few letters to him, and I've had a few notes back. Sergei finds writing in English very difficult, and my Russian isn't that good. But he's not the sort to write letters, anyway. Never could be. And letters . . . letters like that are like sending for luggage you've left behind. That's over with, too, Kelly, and better to realize it. I had Sergei for a time. I always knew it would end. But I just kept on thinking we would dance together—be together—for a few more years. It ended both ways sooner than I expected. You can't *hold* someone like Sergei. And he's not going to marry anyone, not for a long time. That's part of the freedom he wants—needs. He will remember me, I hope, with love. If I'd tried to hold him, the love would have gone sour."

"But you—you still love him?"

Julia drew her coffee cup toward her, and answered slowly, "I know this sounds ridiculously romantic. But I think I will always love him. It was a special thing. I won't pretend I haven't believed I was wildly in love before. Of course I've been in love. But with Sergei it was different. He could be so tender—and at times quite mad, as you know. While he loved me, he was the perfect lover. But he made no promises that it would be forever. And so it came to an end."

She looked up from her coffee to Kelly, looked around the room, seemed to listen for a moment to the autumn rain that touched the window. "I made it all sound better than it is . . . than it will be. But I'm clinging to the company because it's all I have—apart from you, and the rest of the family . . . Marya, Laura. If I hadn't had you all in these past months I think I would have fallen apart. The loneliness . . . I try to fill the days and the nights. I find, suddenly, at this age, that I don't know the world at all. I want to stay within this little group because I don't dare go beyond it. I've lived to dance . . . and to love. I don't quite know how to face the end of it all. Some mornings it's as much as I can do to make myself walk down the stairs and out of this house. I want to hide . . . from everyone, from myself. Some days I don't want to paste the smile back on my face. I want to cry, and feel sorry for myself, just the way I'm doing now. Sorry, Kelly . . ." With infinite slowness Julia's head began to go down until her face was hidden, and all Kelly could see was the bright hair. The sound of her weeping was, with the rain, part of the autumn night.

III

One of the other things which happened that autumn and early winter, little shock waves that no one knew presaged the earthquake, were the persistent rumors and reports in the financial press that Brandon, Hoyle was in trouble. Close to Christmas the reports moved over from the financial pages to the general news.

Nick drank his Scotch with Kelly in the kitchen at Brandon Place as he watched his son being fed. "It isn't anything serious," he insisted. "But while these self-proclaimed experts continue to cry gloom and doom, confidence slips in the shareholders, and confidence is what the game is all about. We're sound enough." He waved his cigarette deprecatingly. "Oh, we're a bit tight in some places—over extended, but it's nothing that most companies don't face from time to time and pull through. But when the public keeps on hearing about stock prices falling, they rush to unload. And new investors are harder to find. The small man doesn't want to risk it, and the big institutions—the pension funds and so on—tend to look askance at anything that isn't at least a hundred years old."

"Why?" Kelly asked. "Why has it happened?"

"That," Nick replied, "is what I'd really like to know. It started with one bloody report. Almost like a deliberate leak to the financial correspondent of the *Journal.* And then the rest of them were on it like a pack of bloodhounds. It had just one grain of truth—about the South African holdings—and the rest was sheer speculation. You know, Brandon, Hoyle has always been suspect by the old guard. It was a bit of a glamour stock with the public—spectacular rise, and all that bit. The whiz-kid stuff. There are certain people in the City who'd just love to see this upstart get his nose bloodied. It would teach the investing public not to put their faith in shooting stars. Well, it won't come to anything. It's a matter of riding it out. You have to be able to play good poker, Kelly, to win in this game. I intend to win."

He switched his attention to Johnny, who was growing impatient with Kelly feeding him, and wanting to do it himself.

"Let him have a go," Nick urged. "Let him try anything he's ready for."

"Most of it," Kelly explained patiently, "will end up on his chin or in his ear. He tends to get hungry if he gets only half his food. As you would."

Nick leaned nearer. "Here—let me." He put his cigarette and whiskey glass aside, and took the spoon from Kelly. "Listen, old man, there's really nothing to it. Look, you hold it like this—and then you just let it find its way to that hole in your face—you know, that place where you stove the stuff when you get hungry. Oh, hell—" The spoon with the strained carrot on it hit one of Johnny's emerging teeth and turned sideways, spilling the food down the baby's chin and onto his bib. Nick gestured helplessly to Kelly, and handed back the spoon. "Well, no need to rush things, I suppose. He'll get the hang of it in time." He leaned back in his chair and took up his cigarette again, drew on it, and studied his son. "He looks fine, doesn't he, Kelly? Does he cry much?—I mean at times when I'm not here."

"Only when he's supposed to. He can bellow his lungs out at times, which is healthy. But he laughs a lot more. He's good at amusing himself. Talks like a streak if only one could understand what he was saying. Mrs. Nelson, who's with him more than anyone else, dotes on him. She'd spoil him—but she's just old-fashioned enough to know when to hold back. She brought up three of her own, and now they're out at jobs, she's just ready to start mothering again. Kate's very lucky to have her. It's like having one of those old-fashioned nannies without all the snob bit that goes with it."

Nick shrugged. "Then he doesn't miss having a father around?"

"I'd like to flatter you, Nick, and say he needs you desperately, but I don't see it. He's really too young to know that there should be a father around. There are so many people coming and going in this house, and he's passed from one to the other so often, that he doesn't realize it isn't a normal family. In fact, he's got a rather old-fashioned family—the sort there used to be with grandmothers and aunts and such. He goes from one to the other with the utmost good humor, and doesn't cry for Kate all the time, though he loves it when she comes back to him. In time, he'll come to want the uncles and the grandfathers, but he doesn't know yet that he hasn't got them."

"He could. He could have them. He could have a father. I haven't let up on Kate. I telephone her. I've even waylaid her in the Lobby of the House. She was furious with me. But I won't stop." He looked at the child in the high chair with the spiky hair that had remained black, the eyes that had retained their first snapping look of humor in their dark depths. "I knew before he was born that I wanted very much to have my child. Now that he's here, and I know him, I want him more than I ever believed possible. I want—"

"Nick. . . !" Kelly stopped him. "Please don't say that in front of Johnny. Not ever again. You'll make a habit of it, and before you know what's happened, *he'll* know. It has to come from Kate, or not at all. It's her decision."

"Kelly, what do I do? I've told her I'll change the way I live. Do it any way she wants. Anything . . ."

"You can't stop being the Nick Brandon who built Brandon, Hoyle. That's what Kate can't get around. Take it slowly, Nick. Give her time to settle down in the House. Give her time. . . . She'll get used to the idea that she can't change the world overnight just because she's in Parliament. She may get used to the idea that she can't change you, or you her. And that could be the beginning."

"She won't even see me. How do I convince her?"

"Well . . ." Kelly smiled and scraped the last of Johnny's bowl. "We're having a party next week—on Christmas Eve. We've done it before—mainly just for Julia's friends in the company. But this year we're expanding a bit because—well, everyone's life is expanding. Why don't you come?"

"I was planning to be in Hong Kong—and then to go on to Australia. The Melbourne office keeps wailing to me that they need me there for a press conference so that they can get the message to the stockholders that everything's all right. But I suppose around that time of year's a rotten time to expect people to pay attention to the financial news. Well . . . I'd like to come. Louise is giving a big bash at Wychwood, and I've begged off that, but perhaps I'll go after all. It might be nice to see my nephews. They're not bad kids. In fact, I like them. I saw them at half-term—took them out. They talked about you. They like you, but they're a little afraid you're going to upset things for them. But I think they already knew that it was their mother who was doing the upsetting right from the beginning. Hell, Kelly, you're in as bad a situation, almost, as I am. How are you going to work that one out?"

"It will work itself out. Things have a way of doing that." She wiped Johnny's face with a damp cloth, lifted him and put him down on the floor; he immediately crawled to Nick and grasped his trouser leg, trying to pull himself up and falling back, and yelling impatiently at his failure. Awkwardly, Nick lifted him and held him on his knee, gingerly beginning to bounce him. Johnny crowed his delight. Across his head, trying to conceal his pleasure, Nick said, "You're going to do that—just let things work themselves out? You should—"

Kelly held up her hand. "Concentrate on being an uncle—or a grandfather. Stop worrying about me. Yes, and do come to our party. Kate's asked along a few of the new Parliamentary pals. You might like to meet them. Leave Hong Kong and Melbourne for a bit. Everyone's at the beach at Christmas time, anyway. They won't be the least interested in Brandon, Hoyle. And go down to Wychwood after the party. Peter and Tommy and Andrew would like that. You may be a whiz-kid in the City, but you're incredibly solid and stuffy beside the Jack Matthews lot. Peter feels he owes Wychwood to you, and he wants to share it. So come here first, and then go down there, and you'll have a nicer Christmas than you expect. Oh—just one thing. Please, Nick, don't arrive laden like Santa Claus with expensive presents. Kate would probably throw hers at you. And for Johnny—remember he isn't a year old yet. Just wait a while before you give him his first Monopoly set, will you?"

He continued to bounce Johnny, and he laughed. "But you do agree that he's really pretty advanced, isn't he?"

IV

The Christmas party was different from the previous ones, itself a small but significant change. Julia had moved from the role of dancer toward those who produced the dance, and the transition had altered her. She seemed less exuberant, a little more withdrawn, more formal. She had stayed at Brandon Place to help with the preparations instead of attending the performance, as she had always done before. Dame Katherine Meredith, the director of the National, and the choreographer, Malenkenov, had accepted an invitation, as well as several members of the board. Two of the Arts Council would be there. "I've hardly ever spoken to them before," Julia confessed of the board members. "They tend to think dancers are all mad—and they could be right." On Christmas Eve the ballet was never well attended. "They'll be glad of an excuse to leave at the interval. They won't stay as late here as the company." There was an unusual flush on her pale face, and she moved around nervously, carrying bottles and glasses and food. Because the party was bigger than before, and already had the sense of being more formal, Kelly had engaged three waiters, through Cavanagh's, to help, and there was confusion in the kitchen as Marya and Laura tried to do their accustomed tasks, and it was politely suggested that they should go and enjoy themselves and leave the work to the professionals. The Christmas tree was placed where it had always been. Johnny had been brought down to see it lighted before he went to sleep. Seeing the dawning look of wonder and delight on his face as he watched the tiny blinking lights, Kelly felt her throat tighten, and was glad that Nick was not present to witness his child's reaction. There were many extra wrapped packages under the Christmas tree and they were there because of Johnny. Kelly remembered the previous parties—the one she had shared with Charles, almost impromptu, totally informal, the next without him with the house newly decorated and Sergei promising it would not be so clean thereafter. Charles was gone, Sergei was gone, and Johnny was here. She looked around the faces as one of the waiters opened the first bottle of champagne—Julia, Laura, Marya, Kate and Johnny. "Before anyone arrives—let's toast ourselves," Kelly said.

Chris Page had arrived after they had drunk their own Christmas toast. How did he manage, Kelly wondered, always to be in the right place, but never before time? Nick came too early. "Damn it—can I pass up the opportunity to talk to Kate before she gets too many around her?" he had whispered as he kissed Kelly. He deposited packages of a modest size under the Christmas tree. "Is that because shares in Brandon, Hoyle are dropping?" Laura laughed.

Nick turned on her. "Listen, you heartless female, that isn't funny. Laura, you look gorgeous. Marya, that dress is fabulous. You must have pinched it from some Russian museum. Julia, darling—how do you manage it? You actually look more beautiful than before. Can it be that you're getting more rest at last, and eating more than a lettuce leaf?" He held out his hand to Chris. "Happy Christmas. Don't look so gloomy, Chris. We'll not bankrupt. We'll sail through it."

"Of course we will." Suddenly Chris flashed the smile that, because it was so rare, seemed to have a special significance. His attitude brightened. He held out his hand to Laura. "Come on. We'd better get some music going." He leaned down from his height and his hair seemed to brush hers.

A moment later *I Want to Hold Your Hand* blared out from Laura's sitting room. Nick took Kate by the elbow.

"Lead me to the food. I'm starving." It was the one plea Kate could never resist. She went with him into the dining room and they had it to themselves.

It had been an odd mixture, Kelly thought, but it had worked. Friends of Laura's had come from London University, Kate had invited Parliamentary friends and their wives—all of them new back-benchers like herself. She had also invited her secretary at the House, and a number of the Party workers who had helped to get her elected in Beckenham. Several had been young, and wore jeans and had been either hostile or shy, but soon relaxed. The members of the board of the National had got mixed up with the dancers, who arrived just before midnight. The Arts Council members had tended to remain aloof but had thawed as Julia worked feverishly to see that they were introduced, had enough to eat and drink, and most particularly that they met some of the young *corps de ballet*. But only Kelly had seen her with a tall, sober-faced man with silver-gray hair, handsome in a hawklike way, talking quietly in the curve of the bowed windows of the drawing room. The activity of the evening had drawn her out of herself. For once, Kelly thought, she is not remembering Sergei. For just those few moments, while Julia strove to entertain someone who was obviously a distinguished guest, but whom Kelly had not met, the ghost of that delightful tempestuous, tender lover had not seemed to stand by her side.

Nick had left early to drive down to Wychwood; Kelly didn't remember when Chris had gone—somchow he had missed his usual punctilious thanks. The Cavanagh waiters had stayed to clean everything up, packed the hired glasses and dishes back in their boxes. All Kelly had to do was open the windows to let out the cigarette smoke. She stood now by the big windows of the drawing room with the curtains drawn back, the smell of the damp night air coming to her. This year no snow had fallen, and the cherry tree had put out its own blossoms. Then she saw that, although the new curtains in Charles' study were heavily lined, they had not been completely closed; a chink of light fell across the little garden.

She went back downstairs. Number 15 was now silent and dark. The passage leading to Charles' study was dark. She was almost certain that she had locked the room before the first guest had arrived. There were letters and papers spread on the desk and she had not wanted anyone to go in there. The door, however, was still locked, and she opened it with the key she had brought. The desk lamp was lighted; had she forgetfully left it that way herself as the early afternoon dusk had gathered? It was the only explanation. But as she stood in the darkness for a moment after she had switched it off, she thought she smelled cigarette smoke. She shrugged it aside; cigarette smoke would have penetrated every room in the house this evening.

She went to sleep, and in a few hours woke to Peter's telephone call.

V

Before Johnny was a year old Kate had made her maiden speech in the House of Commons, and had had a major row with the Minister for Social Services. She had had the good luck to have drawn the right to present a Private Member's Bill—one not sponsored by the Government—and instead of choosing something safe and non-controversial, had decided to attack the failure of the new Government, her own Party, in its outline of bills they intended to introduce in that session of Parliament, to provide any extra benefits for mentally handicapped children cared for at home.

It was an emotive speech. Julia and Kelly and Marya sat in the Gallery to listen to it. Kate looked almost fragile seen at this distance, dark hair and eyes emphasized by the dark red dress she wore. Under the rules she was allowed only ten minutes to speak. She used the first five to draw the picture, garnered from her years as a social worker, of the plight of the mentally handicapped, the burden of the care on their families, and she made the word "love" shine from among the statistics. Members began to drift in from the lobbies to hear what "the Brandon woman" had to say. They were there when the slight body seemed suddenly to grow in stature; the voice, low-keyed until now, was whipped to a pitch of fury. "A crime" she called the neglect of these children and their families. "A social disgrace that makes the position of the Government on this matter stink to high heaven. I have heard the word 'tolerance' used too often in this House. To tolerate this injustice lays bare the hypocrisy of those who mouth one sentiment and legislate another. It is an affront to this House and to this nation."

Unexpectedly Nick's voice whispered next to Kelly's ear. "*That's* not the way to make it to the Front Benches. The Party'll give her hell for this." She turned to look at him in surprise. "Did you think I'd miss it?" he said.

Kate was called to the office of the Minister. She returned

to Brandon Place undismayed. "I got what I expected, and a bit more." She mimicked the Minister's tone. "Don't I know how new I am to Parliament . . . I have to learn the rules . . . there's the matter of Party loyalty and Party discipline. He, of course, knows how slim my margin was at the election. He threatened that if I didn't toe the line in future, official support might be withdrawn at the next election. To which I replied that if they were a halfway decent Government, they'd stay their full five years, and five years in politics is an eternity. And I would continue to do what I thought was right whenever I was lucky enough to get the opportunity."

And then she laughed. "And do you know what he added as I was leaving, presumably, in his thinking, with my tail between my legs? He said, 'Well, you're your father's daughter, all right. And you know what happened to him. He got kicked out.' So I turned back and said, 'And remember, Minister, what happened after that? He got elected for Tewford. And he could have held Tewford forever . . . and continued to say whatever he liked.' "

The press attention was disproportionate to the weight of the act Kate proposed, but the press was short of something to write about that day. It emphasized the row with the Minister which had leaked out. *New member's stand on mentally handicapped,* the heavies reported. *Independent line taken by new member.* The mass circulation dailies put it more pithily, *Kate won't toe the line.*

Kate studied them ruefully. "I might," she said to Kelly, "have just as well been talking about the monkeys in the zoo for all the good it will do. I haven't a hope of getting the bill through. But I'm going to keep on it . . . and on it . . . and on it. They'll get sick and tired of hearing Kate Brandon lobbying on the subject. But they won't shut me up."

Nick talked to Kelly about it the next time he came to Brandon Place. "You know, a year ago, I doubt Kate would have decided that she was going to defy the Party by talking about that—and attacking them. But since then she's had her own baby. I didn't think about it myself—but while she was speaking in the House I suddenly felt so damn grateful that Johnny's quite normal. It never occurred to me before that there was always the chance that he might have been one of the ones Kate was talking about."

The change in Julia was subtle but on-going. She reached the point where she mastered the typewriter, and laughed about her shorthand. "But I scribble something down and it makes sense later—to me if not to anyone else." She was more and more working for Dame Katherine Meredith than with the *corps*, and often there wasn't time to take morning class. So more frequently Brandon Place heard, early in the mornings, the practice tapes because Julia had to work alone at the *barre*. She never talked of Sergei. The pictures of him remained on the wall, but Kelly noticed, one of the times she brought Johnny up to Julia to baby-sit, that the big close-up of him had gone from her dressing table.

Kelly noticed also that her clothes altered. As if in complete rejection of the star image, she took to wearing plain, almost non-descript clothes, shades of gray and brown and beige, tweed skirts and sweaters decorated only by a thin gold chain. She had her long, beautiful hair cut. "Silly girl," Marya commented the first time she saw the new style. "You think you are turning yourself into some kind of nun, but it has only made you look a little more like an angel." It was true, Kelly thought. The hair, relieved of its weight, curled softly around her face, giving her the appearance of one of those almost sexless beings of the old masters. Her blue eyes, so like Charles', were faintly wistful, and now that she no longer followed the punishing routine of the ballet she had gained just the amount of weight that filled out the too-gaunt hollows of her face. The sheen of her skin was less translucent. "She actually starts to look healthy," Marya said. "I don't know if her heart is broken, but her body looks mended. She is no longer quite so . . . so . . ." She groped for the word. "So tragic?—is that what I mean? When she was with Sergei one always felt it was bound to end, and Julia would be hurt. She knew it too."

One Wednesday evening when they had all, except Julia, gathered in the kitchen, Laura mentioned the large, chauffeur-driven car she had seen waiting at the curb as she had come in. "Who's going out?" She looked around them all in their everyday clothes. "None of you, I take it." She made sure the glass doors were open as Julia came down, and invented an excuse for going over to her own flat. "*Well!*" she said, as she saw Julia. "You look *gorgeous!* Must be something very grand."

"A gala of *Bohème* at Covent Garden," Julia said briefly. She tried to slip past, but Laura grasped her hand and led her through to the kitchen. "Look at our Botticelli angel, will you?" Julia wore her gown of off-white silk jersey as only someone used to costume can; pearls, which Kelly thought were the ones she had seen on Elizabeth Brandon in one of her photos, circled her lovely neck, and threw light into her face.

"More like *Venus Rising from the Waves*," Marya said.

Julia flushed. "Oh, stop it! It's just a new dress, that's all." She slipped the fur coat that had been one of the symbols of her stardom around her shoulders. "Now that I'm so broke I'm glad to have a few relics of glory left." She stroked the soft, dark fur.

"The dress," Laura observed, "doesn't look as if it came from Oxford Street."

"Oh—my friends in the rag trade are kind. I can still get big discounts, and in return I get them tickets to the ballet on important nights when *they* want to be seen. And they still like me to wear their clothes."

Laura touched the fabric gently, appreciatively, and then bent a little to kiss Julia softly on the cheek. "Have a good time, Angel. I hope the man who sent that gorgeous car is filthy rich and knows he doesn't deserve you."

The faintest frown appeared between Julia's brows. "Oh, *that*—that's nothing. It's just one of the board members. He's on the boards of half the artistic bodies in the country. I'm just a convenience date. Very formal. I barely know him."

She was gone, leaving the fragrance of her perfume in the air. Kelly stirred the meatballs in their sauce on the stove, and plunged the spaghetti into the big pot. "Well, after that angelic vision I think we'd better get down to the rather more earthy business of eating. I don't know . . . Julia's someone I really wish had lots of money. She just seems born to swansdown, doesn't she?" She raised her head, and her voice brightened rather artificially. "Oh, hello, Chris. Come in. I thought you weren't going to make it." He had telephoned during the day, as usual, to ask if it was all right for him to come, and as always, she had pressed him to do so. "Oh, Lord, you have been extravagant. Nuits St. George. Thank you, we'll enjoy it."

"Julia looked beautiful, didn't she?" he observed. "I just caught a glimpse of her."

"But who's the man?" Laura questioned. "Julia wasn't talking."

"The man?" Chris said. "Oh, it's Clive Wallace. You know, the family that's pharmaceuticals and glass and synthetics. Just about everything, in fact. His brother's chairman of Consolidated National Chemicals, but Wallace is vice-chairman and managing director and does all the work."

"Oh . . ." Marya pulled on her cigarette. "And how did you know who the man was? There wasn't anyone in the car, and Julia didn't say."

Chris shrugged. "Well, the car was standing there at the curb as I was coming in. I just asked the driver who he was, and who he was waiting for. I thought I should . . . it could have been anyone."

"You mean," Marya shrieked, "that a chauffeur from a big car is going to break in here and rape us all! Oh, Chris. . . !"

They all collapsed in laughter, and Chris, after a slight hesitation, also broke down. "I suppose I did sound ridiculous."

Laura said, "But you did know who Mr. Clive Wallace was?"

He stopped laughing, and looked at her as if she had said something stupid. "Naturally. All the Wallace family are big names in the City."

For Kelly, time moved in jerks—the seemingly endless week to be got through in London, busying herself with the tasks she had assumed, and the swift passage of the weekend at Mead Cottage, the hours with Peter that sped like seconds. Lambing time was long over, the daffodils bloomed and the orchard bore its blossom. "What are we waiting for?" Peter said. "I can't wait for you much longer, Kelly. I'll give Louise what she wants, and be done with it."

"You will not give up Wychwood for me," Kelly said. "I could never compensate for that. I don't intend to try. Wait, Peter, just a little longer. In June, when Laura's done her first year examinations, she and I will both go to Pentland. When we come back—then we'll look at things again. Perhaps then we'll make a decision."

"I don't see what will be different."

"Something will be different. It always is."

Kelly continued to go to Tower Hamlets. It was neither better nor worse than before; Marilyn's visit to Brandon Place was the last she ever saw of the girl. She had asked the vicar, Martin Wyatt, about her, describing the morning at Brandon Place. He sighed. "She's left home, and no one knows where she's gone. I've spent quite a lot of time walking the streets of Soho looking for her. I've asked about her." He shook his head. "I've turned up nothing. Her family doesn't seem to care. They regard someone like Marilyn going on the streets as just about inevitable." He looked at her over the rim of the mug of tea he held, and then looked around the now deserted center. "Sometimes, God forgive me, I despair. All this work here, and I never seem able to reach them. The Church has the message, but we don't seem to have the right words for today. I suppose there has to be some success, but I don't see it. All I know is the numbers who go to Borstal, and six months after they're released from that, they're in jail. I think of the girls who go on the streets. I perform shotgun marriages, and then I christen the babies, and I don't see them any more. I try to visit them, and I know they don't want me. Sticking my nose in, that's how they see it. More and more, I'm looking after the old, and losing the young . . ."

Kelly had no words of comfort because she experienced the same feeling of futility herself. But Martin Wyatt's suit was shabby and his house was in need of repair. He had three children, and his wife looked perpetually tired. Sometimes he worked on the petrol pumps at a local garage to earn extra money, to the annoyance of his bishop, and the outrage of some of his parishioners. "He thinks I'm one of those Commie worker-priests," Martin Wyatt said. "But I have to find a few extra quid somewhere when my kids need shoes." Kelly knew that he would never accept outright charity from her, but she ensured a holiday for the family by offering him Mead Cottage during the time she and Laura would be at Pentland.

"I miss having Kate around," he said. "She was good at her job. Quick to spot something going wrong before it actually happened. She had an almost uncanny sense of when a child was in danger of being battered. Those were the times when just by being there and getting the mother to talk, I think she may have saved a child. But you never know what you've prevented happening. You just know the times you've failed. Yes . . . I do miss Kate. I comfort myself by thinking that she may be able to do more for children all over the country by being where she is than down here." He smoked the rest of his cigarette in what seemed to Kelly to be the silence of defeat.

Kate herself, Kelly knew, was restless under the strictures of her Party. "Oh, I know I was full of idealism," she said one Wednesday evening over Kelly's supper in the kitchen. "I knew I couldn't move the world, but I didn't expect to feel quite so helpless. I thought I could count for something. But it's just one more vote they want to be certain of. I read all the Bills, attend the debates, speak when I feel I know enough about the subject to try to get a point across. It's all written down in Hansard, and it just doesn't seem to matter, I have a long way to go in politics before anyone will really start to listen. I don't have any *clout* . . ."

She was once again before the Parliamentary Party for abstaining on a vote. "They gave me a telling off as if they owned me—as if I hadn't been elected to represent people. I thought it was a bad Bill, and I didn't want to vote for it. But I couldn't quite bring myself to vote against it. I suppose it's naïve to think that being elected gives you the right to vote by conscience . . ."

Marya observed dryly, "The consciences of the young are tender . . . thank God."

"You don't seem so young to me," Laura said. "You're Julia's twin, but most of the time you seem a hundred years older."

"Our dear Julia," Kate said, her tone soft with recollection, a touch of compassion, "despite the brutally punishing work and discipline the ballet requires, always seemed to live in fairyland. She grew up a fairy-tale child, beautiful as a fairy-tale princess, and lived to dance the Princess in *Sleeping Beauty*. She regularly fell in love with the handsome prince. But don't let's sell her short. I think she truly loved Sergei, and losing him almost broke her heart. But look how she's carried it off. I often feel I should go and beg her pardon for ever thinking she was made of the stuff of dreams. She has had to come down to earth, and as always, she's landed with grace—and courage."

"I'll drink to that," Marya said. "In Russia they either would have kicked her out right after the injury, or they would have given her a state pension and a dacha. The price of democracy is that they leave it to oneself to work things out."

"I wonder," Laura said, "if Clive Wallace isn't helping her to work things out. He sends his car quite often for her—and it isn't always a gala when he needs a convenient partner in the official box."

"How do you know?"

"You know me—I've got a big nose. And now that the evenings are getting longer, and I leave the curtains onto the street open, I see that big fat black car waiting for her. I just wish, though, that it all was a bit more romantic. It would be nice just for once to see Clive Wallace drive up himself—preferably in a small red sports car. I'd like to see Julia borne off into the night, the way Sergei would have done."

"*That* wouldn't happen in a million years with Clive Wallace," Chris, who was present that evening, observed.

"They're one of the ultra-conservative families of England. Of Quaker origin. Full of good deeds, and great patrons of the arts. The grandfather started as a chemist with a little shop in Birmingham, made a fortune out of his pills and potions, and the family have been trying to give it away ever since. They give a lot away, and they continue to make even more. That chemist shop in Birmingham has got Swiss affiliates and American subsidiaries, and they make soup and soap and stockings as well as pills."

"Has this . . . this Clive Wallace ever been married?" Kelly asked.

"Oh, yes," Chris said. He seemed to be enjoying the role of having information to impart, as if he were a messenger from a distant country. "His wife died last year. Cancer, I think it was. Ironic that all the Swiss drugs couldn't save her. They say he was devoted to her. He has two children. Early teens, I think. I must make a point of looking it up in Who's Who."

Laura cleared her throat. "Can I admit to being just a bit more nosy? I notice that when the big black car comes back, a tall gentleman sees Julia to the front door, and then the big black car drives off again. He never goes upstairs—that is, presuming Julia has ever invited him in for a drink . . ."

"Has anyone ever seen this Clive Wallace?" Marya demanded. "He sounds altogether a good deal too cautious for my liking."

"Of course you've seen him. Didn't you know? He was here at the Christmas party," Chris said. He sounded shocked, as if everyone ought to have known Clive Wallace on sight. "He's a member of the board of the National."

"That silver-hawk man?" Kelly asked.

"Yes—that would be he," Chris answered. "I wanted badly to go and talk to him, but in the end I thought I wouldn't have anything interesting to say. I could hardly discuss the stock-market reports. And I certainly didn't want to discuss Brandon, Hoyle."

"Well, if you didn't discuss Brandon, Hoyle, you'd be about the only person in the City who isn't discussing it these days," Laura said. "It's beginning to look rather bad, isn't it?"

Chris turned to her grimly. "You only make it worse by talking about it. If everyone would stop talking and just let us get on with the job, there'd be no trouble. There's nothing Nick can't pull us out of if people just keep quiet and don't lose their heads."

"You have great confidence in Nick," Kate remarked.

Chris seemed to take it as a challenge. "Yes. I have the utmost confidence in Nick."

But Brandon, Hoyle was increasingly in the news, and not in a favorable light. The journalists who had started digging into the ramifications of the South African company, had unearthed a lead to a Nigerian company which had participated in some dubious deals. The President of Nigeria disclaimed any connection with it, but he was known to be a close friend of the managing director. There were hints that Brandon, Hoyle had been involved in arms shipments, but the law of libel, so tight in Britain, prevented any journalist from coming out and saying so. Then, as the news began to peter out for lack of confirmation, a new source of information on the Australian company opened up. Brandon, Hoyle, through a holding company, was involved in the sale of small amounts of uranium to unknown sources, it was alleged. An immediate connection was made to Sir Charles Brandon's long visit to Australia, as the director of another company, to explore the extent of possible uranium mining, and how swiftly deliveries might bc made.

"But it was nothing to do with Brandon, Hoyle," Kelly had protested when the story broke. "I was with him all the time. I took the minutes of the meetings. I typed the reports. I *know* what was in them. There weren't any secret deals being done." But, uncomfortably, she remembered certain documents given to Charles which he had read and made no comment on, reports which he had kept locked away and which she had never seen. She had taken it all as part of Charles' natural discretion. He was someone—a soldier who had been an aide and sometimes a confidant of great men—who was not given to gossip. She had taken that part for granted. But the contrived link between Charles and Brandon, Hoyle made her uneasy.

"We could have done without this," she said to Laura. "I think the press has had quite enough of us for the time being."

"No they haven't. They'll go on boiling us down for soup as long as there's any meat on the bones. You can bet on it." Laura's tone was defensive, truculent, and edged with bitterness. Kelly examined the face of the girl who had grown into a woman, and realized that it had become tighter, more withdrawn, even suspicious. The publicity given to Kate's election and to Brandon, Hoyle had done that. The circle around Laura, which at times seemed to be opening out, was in danger of closing. More and more she sought her own haunts, the people she had come to trust.

More and more she went to Yorkshire. She had bought a Mini car, and didn't seem to mind the long drive on Friday night in order to have a full weekend there. "Are Alex and Ben able to get away from college so often?" Kelly enquired.

Laura shrugged. "I don't go just for Alex's company. The place is wonderful. The Gardiners are super people. Really involved in farming their own land—you know, the way Peter is about Wychwood. I just like being there. They leave me alone to do as I please. I can ride or walk or study. No one tries to entertain me. No one asks questions. They mind their own business."

But some weekends, Kelly knew, Alex was at home at Everdale, and those times Laura came back with a special radiance. "Oh, I've walked my legs off, and I'm full of fresh air." She was, Kelly decided, full of something more. She seemed filled with a hope, an idea for the future, and it seemed to center on Alex. Remembering that handsome, clever young man, Kelly grew anxious for Laura. If her feeling was not returned, the blow could be hard. The scar of her childhood was rooted deeply in her personality. She had hidden behind the fall of long blond hair and trusted few. When she had given love, it never had been given lightly.

That spring Laura turned twenty-one, and Lady Renisdale had insisted on giving a large party at Charleton. Laura resisted violently, but was forced, in the end, to agree. "My dear, I've given it for all my grandchildren. I don't see why you should be different. You don't have to make any of the arrangements. Just buy a nice dress, and be here."

Laura had appeared to enjoy it more than anyone expected. Kelly wondered if it was because Alex Gardiner had come, and they had danced together many times. Phoebe Renisdale had beamed at them. "She looks charming, don't you think, Kelly?"

Ben Gardiner put it more succinctly as he danced with Kelly. "Laura looks smashing! I wish I could get near enough to her to ask her for a dance."

Kelly couldn't help being aware that many people knew that on reaching twenty-one, Laura had also reached the time when she was given control of the shares placed in trust for her by John Merton, and that she also inherited the part of the Renisdale trust that had been her mother's. Being related to Phoebe Renisdale, Alex Gardiner would be among those who knew. Kelly watched them as they danced, that golden young man smiling at Laura, and Laura smiling back, her body moving in graceful abandon, too much of her feelings showing on her face.

One Saturday afternoon in late spring Ben Gardiner telephoned Kelly at Mead Cottage and asked if he could drive over from the college to visit her. Kelly had greeted him happily, realizing again how much she liked this rather stocky, blunt young man, liked the patent honesty in his light hazel eyes, the openness of his expression. "Hope you don't mind my coming? Hope I'm not in the way? I'm just sick of keeping my nose in books. Exams are in June, but you can't swot all the time . . . I thought I'd like a break and someone to talk to."

"Don't you have a local girl friend?"

He shrugged. "Occasionally I take a girl to the flicks and a couple of beers. Nothing serious. Look—I'm no genius, but she is rather stupid, even though she's pretty. I get bored by the debutante type."

He took another sandwich and ate as if he were hungry. "Alex has a few girls on the string, though. Of course, he's always had his pick."

Kelly decided to plunge in. "Ben, I think Laura's in love with Alex. I've never known her to be this way before. She talks about him a lot. She seems to be building on something. She loves to be with your parents, and she talks about Everdale as if it were home. Do you think Alex . . ."

Ben shrugged, "Alex doesn't confide in me. I'm still very much the younger brother—the plodding young brother. Maybe he's taken by Laura, but I don't know. Alex is a pretty cool guy. He'd think of every angle—the fact that Laura gets on with my people so well, that she likes a farming atmosphere. And no one like Alex can overlook the fact that Laura is pretty well off. It would figure in the way he thought. He'd never do anything rash. I don't think he'd ever be so impetuous as to fall in love."

"That seems sad—never ever to fall in love."

"Yes, well—that's the way Alex is. I hope if Laura really is in love with him, he has the good sense to know it. He'd be a bloody fool to miss having her."

"You like Laura, don't you?"

"I think Laura's a terrific girl. She's bright and pretty and she's got guts. But I don't think she's had much experience in handling this sort of thing. She's so shy . . . in spite of the sort of life she's had, with all you people, I get the impression that she's still groping her way through things that most of us go through just like having mumps. She's a big dazzled by Alex." He smiled ruefully. "I just wish sometimes she'd turn around and see me. I don't think she'd notice me unless I put out my foot and tripped her."

He finished his tea, had a beer with her, and drove away in his battered little car. Watching him drive down the lane Kelly wished that in some fashion he could indeed put out his foot and trip Laura. "It might," she said later to Peter, "shake some of the stardust out of her eyes."

"Don't expect her to be any wiser than anyone else when it comes to falling in love. Most people would say you could have chosen a lot better than me, Kelly."

"Then they'd be mad." She touched his hand. "And they'd better mind their own business."

May passed, and the position of Brandon, Hoyle grew worse. Almost every day the financial pages seemed to carry some fresh news of a slip in its stock price brought on by fresh selling. The story of the uranium deal grew, and now the financial correspondent of the *Journal* claimed to have information of loans made by one subsidiary in Singapore to the Australian holding company on assets which did not exist. The correspondent, Humphrey Watson, stated that he had seen files which traced the transactions through various merchant banks, some of which had deliberately contrived to help cover it up. Nicholas Brandon threatened to sue for libel.

His face was tight when he came to Brandon Place that week. "Damn it," he said to Kelly, "that man's sniffing around like some sort of bloody hound. And he has more information than he should have. If I weren't absolutely certain of everybody who works for us here in London, I'd say there had been a deliberate leak. He has too much information for an outsider. But for anyone in the London office to do it deliberately would be absurd. It only brings the house down around their own heads."

"Then the things he's saying are true?"

Nick looked at her sharply. "Not all of them. Oh, damn it, Kelly. Of course you switch things around from one company to another. Banks help you out because they've already lent you so much money that they have to protect themselves. But don't forget they make a big fat profit when everything goes well—as do the stockholders. You only hear screams like this when someone's got a deliberate set on you—as this Watson fellow has. He's been fed a certain amount of information, and he—and others—are now hell bent on getting more. He's just a lightweight journalist who's trying to make his name by butchering Brandon, Hoyle."

His attention was distracted as Johnny hauled himself to his feet by holding onto one of the legs of the kitchen table. He took two wobbling steps toward Nick, and then abruptly sat down. He howled with frustration, and Nick went to pick him up. "There, old man. You'll do it." He looked at Kelly over Johnny's head. "He's going to be a world-beater, isn't he?"

She took no notice of his question or of Johnny's yells. "Is it serious?"

"Serious enough. It could do a lot of damage. The maddening thing is that it need never have happened. That first leak was like a crack in the dike. If we could have stopped it there, we'd be all right now. It means I've got a lot of shoring up to do, and when confidence gets shaky, that's just so much harder. I'd like to get my hands on whoever started it . . . someone with a grudge, and some inside information. That's all it takes."

"But if it were perfectly straightforward, you'd be able to prove it, and there wouldn't be a question of confidence, would there?"

"You know that very little in any business is perfectly straightforward, Kelly. If you succeed and make money for everyone, you're a hero, and no one asks about how you did it. If you lose, then you're a scoundrel and a crook. And I'd say there's more than a little of a scoundrel and a crook in almost every successful businessman."

Kelly felt the first real fear as he spoke. It was the beginning of an admission. He handed Johnny to her, and went to the counter and poured himself a large Scotch. For a moment he leaned back against the sink, and drew silently on a fresh cigarette. His thin face was more strained than she had ever seen it. "You know, since this business started the only thing I have to be grateful for—apart from our young man here—is that Wychwood is safely out of it. There was a time while I was raising money to pay the death duties when a run on the stock like this could have put the whole thing in jeopardy. For just a few weeks, Brandon, Hoyle *owned* Wychwood—though I never told Peter that. But it's all free and clear now. Even if they succeed in bringing Brandon, Hoyle down, they can't touch Wychwood."

"I didn't think you cared so much about Wychwood."

"There are people like me, Kelly, and there are people like

Peter. I'd go stark raving mad if I had to stay down there and do his job. And he wouldn't last one day at mine. But the feeling about a parcel of earth where you know you belong persists. And I know Peter will take care of Johnny. Johnny will always know he has a place at Wychwood. Peter will see to that. That's the only thing I'm certain of right now."

The fear grew in Kelly. "It can't be as bad as that?"

He smiled, slowly and deliberately, and there was no truth in the smile. "No, of course not. Nothing's as bad as it seems at the fag end of a rough day. Let's not frighten our young Johnny, shall we? Funny—about Peter. I can remember times when I've thought him pretty dim. Well, let's say I've thought him stodgy. Now I'm glad he's the way he is. There's one man who, even if he knew how to be a scoundrel and a crook, wouldn't be one. It's lucky for us. He's clean of it all. And he'll take care of Johnny."

"You talk as if Kate doesn't exist—as if she wouldn't be able to take care of Johnny."

"Kate's going for big things. She could end up a big name in politics. I know she'll always take care of Johnny. But what's Brandon Place, after all? Only a little piece of real estate in the middle of London. Nothing to get attached to. Peter will see that Johnny learns to ride and use a gun responsibly. That he knows a duck from a goose, and an oak from an elm. Those are things neither Kate nor I can give him. Only Wychwood and Peter can make him someone who knows more than politics and money. If everything else went, there'd always be Peter and Wychwood."

Kelly put Johnny in his high chair, fighting against the sense that a tide was flowing strongly against her, threatening to take her off her feet. This couldn't be the strong, confident Nick Brandon who was speaking. He talked of Wychwood as the last resort—for his son, but not for himself. She was afraid to turn and face him. With shaky hands she went and poured herself a Scotch.

VI

Early in June Laura took her first-year exams, and she and Kelly planned to go to Pentland immediately after. The last weekend before the exams, with Laura crouched over her books at Brandon Place, and the weather suddenly turned warmer, Kelly insisted on taking Kate and Johnny down to Mead Cottage.

"Remember?—he's not supposed to grow up a London baby. Now you know Martin Wyatt is going to use the place over the summer while Laura and I are away. Well, you're to come down too as often as you can get away. Martin's expecting you. Peter's expecting you. You are going to let Johnny play in the mud now and again, aren't you? The Wyatt children will be good for him. You'll all squeeze in somehow."

"You make me ashamed," Kate said as they settled in for dinner at Mead Cottage on that Friday night. "It's so lovely here, and Johnny should be here more often. I keep remembering what Laura said when he was born—that he looked as if he were already a professor at the London School of Economics."

"Why don't you turn him over to Peter for a few weeks this summer?"

"If Peter had the sort of wife he should have, I'd happily turn him over. But our Louise will only be at Wychwood to get a bit of beauty sleep, and when she wants to entertain her friends. And as for turning him over to Mrs. Page . . . well, I don't think so. I don't want Johnny turned into a carbon copy of Chris."

During the weekend Kelly remembered the slight, gray man who had spoken to her during the party that followed Johnny's christening. "Do you mind, Kate? I've always meant to ask Harry Potter and his wife over here for tea. You remember Harry Potter, don't you? The constituency agent? He's rather an admirer of yours."

"I'm all for having admirers. Go ahead."

It was a bright sunny afternoon when the Potters came. They had tea on the old tables and benches in the orchard, among the uncut grass. Mrs. Potter delighted in Johnny, asked to be allowed to feed him, and didn't mind when he put honey on her blouse. "I'm used to it, Miss Brandon. I've brought up four . . ."

Harry Potter talked randomly about constituency affairs. "It's not as simple as it used to be here, Miss Brandon. Times are changing so fast. Television's bringing in the outside world. It'd be hard to say we're a completely rural constituency anymore. Those new housing estates on the edge of Tewford, they've brought a new element. The farms aren't big enough to absorb all the young people, and they have to look for other kinds of work. We have a few light industries now. At one time you could just say it was a straightforward farmer's vote, but it isn't that way anymore. We're getting different sorts of problems, and it needs a member who's closely in touch on the constituency level. Mr. Carpenter has been very conscientious about that. Has a clinic every Saturday and encourages people to come and talk to him. He does what he can in the House . . ."

He savored, as only someone to whom politics is the breath of life, Kate's election victory at Beckenham. He smiled at the recollection. "Even though it was a seat to Labour, Miss Brandon, I was really pleased you won. You deserved it—and your father would have been proud of you. I knew no one gave you a chance of pulling it off."

Harry Potter was a man who read widely on all sides of the political debate—he even read the *Tribune*, although its left-wing policies were anathema to him. Soon he and Kate were deep in conversation as to the direction the Labour Government might take the country in the next years; there was argument, but a surprising amount of middle-ground agreement. "You're not as much a Socialist as I thought, Miss Brandon."

"Well, let's say I've had my views a bit modified since I've been in Parliament. I've had to realize that it isn't enough to wish things could be perfect. The practical steps to getting things even slightly improved are hard and slow and often boring. Such a little step at a time. Just working away at it . . ."

Mrs. Potter had started to talk to Kelly about her going to Australia. "It's hard for me to imagine having a life in two countries, Lady Brandon. I was born five miles from where we live now. They tell me it's a very big place you have out there—and you look after it for Miss Laura." She gazed at the bright, leafy greenness, the golden stone of the cottage that appeared to have taken on the color of the afternoon. "I don't see how you can leave this."

Kelly, looking up, saw Peter coming through the gate, the labradors following. Mrs. Potter's words, innocently expressed, had at this moment, a terrible weight. It was Peter, not Mead Cottage, that Kelly did not want to leave.

Peter had tea, and took Johnny from Mrs. Potter and held him so that the baby seemed to be riding on the back of one of those gentle, tolerant dogs. The conversation went on between Kate and Harry Potter. Mrs. Potter smiled at the sight of the child and Peter and the dog. "No, truly—I don't see how you can bear to go."

But they went, Kelly and Laura, the day after the exams were finished. This time, both went with reluctance. Peter had come to drive them to Heathrow, and Laura almost caused them to be late for the flight. She was only half-packed an hour before they were due to go. "Oh, stop fussing, Kelly," she said irritably. "After all these years don't you think I know how to throw a few things into a suitcase?" She was about to go into the car when she heard the telephone ringing in her flat—the door of Number 15 and her flat door were both open. She almost knocked Mrs. Cass down in her rush to get back to answer it. "Don't worry, Miss Laura. I'll take a message . . ." Mrs. Cass called after her.

She came back, a few minutes later, her expression halfway between gloom and hope. "It was Mrs. Gardiner. She . . . she just wanted to wish us a good trip. Alex . . . Alex and Ben are still doing their exams."

She left Peter and Kelly alone in the departure lounge and went off to the bookstall. Seated beside Kelly, she didn't speak for a long time after the flight had taken off.

"Well, I suppose this is the first time both of us have hated the idea of leaving. I wish there was something I thought we absolutely had to do at Pentland. I wish I could believe we were needed there."

"What's needed is our presence," Kelly said. "You just have to show Pentland—everyone there—that it matters. That's what your grandfather intended. It involves great responsibility as well as great privilege."

Laura nodded. "Kelly, as soon as you talk about Grandfather, I melt. I was just being sore-headed because Alex hadn't telephoned. It was only half-right that his mother did it for him. Well, at least *she's* on my side. Let's order some champagne, shall we, and put a good face on everything? We'll just have to think up lots of marvelous sparkling conversation to carry us through those meals with Grandmother Merton. I got her a present I think even she won't sniff at. Went around to that needlework shop in South Audley Street and got their newest canvas. They assured me it was a design she would like. They seem to know her taste just about as surely as if she'd been old Queen Mary . . ."

They ate and dozed and read through the long hours of the flight; Kelly thought of Peter, and was just as aware that all Laura's thoughts focused on Alex. They had grown closer in age and feeling because for the first time they both were women in love.

Chapter Eleven

I

At Sydney they were met by Frank McArthur. "You'd better go straight on to Pentland," he said. "Mrs. Merton wouldn't let me tell you, but you'll know it for yourselves as soon as you arrive. She's dying of cancer. She was down here for several operations. One of her doctors contacted me to say that it was time you both were told, but she wouldn't permit it. She's a game old lady, I'll say that for her. Insisted that Laura's exams weren't to be disturbed. She doesn't even pretend that there's any hope. We don't know how long . . . a few weeks, maybe. They've done everything they could for her here, and now the local man's just keeping her comfortable."

Laura's face was white as she listened. "My God, and to think I didn't want to come. Poor thing . . ."

As they waited for the connecting flight to Barrendarragh, Kelly said to Frank McArthur, "Do you think she knew last year when she made the trip to England? Could it have been as long ago as that?"

"Almost certainly. The doctor told me that she'd had her first operation by then—though she never told me about it. She must have been feeling pretty bad. But she's hung on. The doctor's surprised at how long she's hung on."

Kelly sat silently thinking of Delia Merton's pilgrimage to all the places of her imagination, filling her eyes and mind with the things and sights that had been her preoccupation for so many years. She envisaged the feelings of Delia Merton as she had seen those pictures from *Country Life* become reality. That gaunt figure in her dowdy black dress assumed the stature of courage. When she had got on the plane in London she had never expected to see Laura again. She had expected the isolation of Pentland to engulf her finally in her self-imposed solitude.

It was Mary Anderson who stood on the veranda at Pentland as the car came through the Home Paddock. Her lips were unsmiling as she greeted them.

"You know, then?"

"Yes, Frank McArthur told us. You should—"

"She forbade it." Mary Anderson turned to Laura. "You got your examinations finished, I hope? That is the first thing she will ask. I hope," she added, "you did well."

"Mrs. Anderson, I won't know that for a long time. I did the best I could."

"She *expected* that. Now you should go and see her, but don't stay too long. She has little strength, and as you well know, she never was one for idle chatter."

Bill Blake had met them at Barrendarragh. "Your mother moved into the big house as soon as she knew your grandmother was failing. She was with her the two times she was in Sydney for the operations, and she threatened me with everything under the sun if I even mentioned that to you when you were here last year, Kelly. It beats everything I've ever seen. Those two—you'd say they'd been fighting like two silent cats for years, and finally Mrs. Anderson takes over and becomes Mrs. Merton's nurse. She's the only one Mrs. Merton will let near her. Not even Nelly is allowed to do anything for her. Dr. Lacy's out every day, of course, and gives her her drugs. But Mrs. Anderson does everything else. Washes her, cooks for her and takes it to her. She's been ordering every sort of thing you can imagine from Sydney to try to tempt her to eat a little. Nothing's too much trouble. Of course, your mother always was a very conscientious woman, Kelly—very responsible. But here I've always thought the two of them hated the sight of each other. Well, there's just no telling . . ."

"I think in the end," Laura had said slowly, "Grandmother just realized that there was no one left who knew her so well—knew her life. Kelly's mother has been here more than thirty years. She went all through the war years with Grandmother—the time my mother was killed. And Dad was killed. And Grandfather died. They must have known each other very well, in the end. It's a pity they never got around to talking."

"Perhaps they just didn't need to," Kelly said.

The days flowed into a pattern of waiting. Delia Merton's sere and wasted body seemed so fragile that Kelly thought she couldn't have the strength to draw a further breath. But she endured, her face yellow and sunken, her bones showing skeletally through the blankets. Despite the almost antiseptic cleanliness, there was the pervading smell of sickness which Mary Anderson endeavored to overcome by filling the room with flowers. When the last of the blooms in her little garden had been exhausted, she began to send to Sydney for flowers to be flown up each day. She placed them where Delia Merton could see them without turning her head. Hardly a word was spoken between the two women, but Mary Anderson seemed instinctively to understand and anticipate the other's needs. She slept in an adjoining room with the door open and rose several times during the night to go to Delia Merton's bedside. Dr. Lacy, who made the long journey from Barrendarragh each day, tried to persuade Delia Merton to have a nurse so that Mary Anderson's nights might be undisturbed. Mrs. Merton had questioned the other woman with her eyes, and Mary Anderson shook her head. "No need. I don't believe Mrs. Merton would want an outsider. Don't worry about me. I sleep well enough for an old woman . . ." She had even learned to prepare and give the injections that now were necessary every few hours.

She rejected Kelly's offer of help. "Remember, I did once have a little training in nursing," Kelly said.

"I remember. It isn't needed here." But Laura was permitted to sit with her grandmother while Mary Anderson went to the kitchen she had officially left years ago and cooked the light and delicate things that Delia Merton might be induced to swallow. A fire burned in the grate day and night against the cold of the Australian winter which was settling on them. Laura was reading to her grandmother. Unbidden, she had brought out the blue-bound volumes of Jane Austen; Mrs. Merton listened impassively as once again the familiar names and scenes were evoked, her eyes fixed on the flowers that

Mary Anderson brought daily. She spoke little, her voice a thin whisper when she did. Kelly came several times a day to Mrs. Merton's room, but the sick woman barely recognized her presence, and Kelly would go away, frustrated and helpless.

"It can't be long now," Dr. Lacy said. "It beats me how she manages to hang on. She's got a strong heart, and it just doesn't want to give up. I'm glad Laura got here in time. I wanted to write go you about it, but quite honestly I didn't have the nerve to face Mrs. Merton and tell her that I had. She set great store in Laura sitting those exams. It's as if Laura has to be everything Greg and John Merton were rolled into one—which is a bit hard on Laura."

Thinking of what he had said, Kelly decided, with Laura's connivance, to practice a small deception. She went with Laura one morning to Delia Merton's room. "I've had a telephone call from London—from Kate Brandon. Laura's done extremely well in the exams. Of course, it's only the first year—but the first year always weeds out those who won't be able to stay the course. It's wonderful news, isn't it?" She hated herself as she spoke the words, hated what she might be doing to Laura. There had been no telephone call, and it would still be some weeks before there could be any examination results. But Delia Merton would not last those weeks.

Almost imperceptibly the head nodded. Laura bent to hear the whispered words. They were, however, not congratulations, but instructions. Laura obeyed them, and went to the bottom drawer of a tall rosewood bureau, one of the most beautiful pieces of furniture Pentland contained, and considered a treasure by Delia Merton. From the drawer she brought out a pile of canvases, with an intricate flower pattern worked on them in petit point; the background was the pale green of the wallpaper in the dining room at Brandon Place. "Chair covers," Laura whispered. "They're for me?" Her lips trembled. "For . . . for the chairs in the dining room. For *me* . . . oh, Grandmother, they're not my chairs . . ."

"Yes, they are," Kelly said. "I'm giving them to you now. And the table. They belong together. When you have your own home . . . well, perhaps it will be here at Pentland—I hope it will be here at Pentland—the chairs and table will be yours."

Once again there was the faintest nod of Delia Metron's head, as if to signify the rightness of the gift. With a slight fluttering of her fingers she signaled that they should leave.

Outside the room, Mary Anderson rounded on them both. "It is never right to lie—not even to make a dying woman happy."

"There was no lie. I'm as certain as I can be of anything that when the exam results come, they will be excellent. And I *did* just give the chairs and table to Laura. They are mine to give."

Her mother conceded grudgingly. "Well, I suppose in the circumstances . . ." For a moment she fingered the canvases Laura held, looked at the fine work, the infinitesimal stitches. "She worked at them night and day. When the pain came she didn't sleep very much, but I worried that her sight would give out. Such fine things. But she never did say what they were for . . . I never imagined . . ."

There was so much Delia Merton had never said, and would not now say.

The accountant, Ian Russell, came from Barrendarragh and went through the books with Kelly. She had regularly received copies of the accounts from Frank McArthur, but going through the books was as much a ritual, as much expected of her as the minute inspection of every building on the property. She thanked Bill Blake for the care he gave to Pentland; it had the same appearance of good husbandry as at any time when John Merton had been there to oversee it. He nodded as she spoke. He was in the library with her and Ian Russell, and she could not avoid the question that they both wanted to ask.

"I'm glad you think it's in pretty good shape," Bill Blake said. "We had to do a bit of hand-feeding during that dry spell, but the wool prices rose because of it, so that pretty well offset the cost. The stock's fine, and we should get a good lambing season." He spoke with the ease of someone on whom the question of ready cash did not press too heavily. Pentland could outlast more than one season of drought, thanks to the diversification of John Merton's other interests. Pentland owed no money, and even with the death duties paid, the reserves were solid. Kelly had given instructions that no debt must ever rest on Pentland itself. It had been John Merton's most prized, most loved, possession. She and Laura had been trained in the tradition of thinking that it must be the last ever to go.

Ian Russell finally asked the question. "What will happen when the Old Lady—I'm sorry, Kelly—when Mrs. Merton goes? The big house will be empty. Laura's got a few more years at the university to go. And even then, unless she's married . . . well, you could hardly expect her to live here by herself. If she were only a . . . well, a sort of ordinary girl . . . she might have married a bloke from around here. But Greg, he made sure she'd never be like any other kid. And perhaps Mr. Merton wasn't so wise in sending her off to England so often. The kid really doesn't know where she belongs."

"I think you can leave that to Laura to decide when the time comes. Mr. Merton did what he thought was best. As much as he loved Pentland, I don't think he ever meant it to be some sort of prison for Laura. If she decides to come back here, it'll be because she wants to, not because she feels she must. He didn't want her to feel that all she was was Greg's child."

"Could be," Bill Blake admitted. "But I hope to God she doesn't bring some pommy husband back here who thinks he can run the place like one of those potty little farms in England. We could take an Englishman so long as he didn't try to tell us our jobs."

"Well—we'll see," was all Kelly could say.

Bill Blake had kept the pool filled, though in the early mornings it was shiny with ice. Kelly and Laura swam when the sun had warmed the water a little, the icy plunge seeming to shake off the smell and sense of the sickroom. They rode for a time every day, sometimes taking a picnic to some of John Merton's favorite places along the creek, as they always had. But they never went beyond the Home Paddocks, and each time they returned, they expected to see Mary Anderson waiting on the veranda, her face already giving them the news.

Each day Kelly noticed how Laura watched for Bill Blake's return from the post box at the point where Pentland's land fronted the main road. There the post was delivered and collected. The batches of letters were given first to Kelly. She saw the flush mount in Laura's face when she handed over an envelope with a Yorkshire postmark.

Laura looked at the handwriting, and her mouth drooped. "It's from Ben . . ." She slit the envelope and scanned the pages. "Not much news . . . they haven't had the exam results yet. Alex is in Scotland." She read to the end. "Ben sends his regards to you. He says he's sorry about Grandmother . . ." She crumpled the letter. "Damn Alex! I wrote to him about Grandmother, and he's left it to Ben to reply."

She left the room. Later, Kelly, watching from an upstairs window, saw that Laura was lapping the swimming pool in the same, dogged methodical manner as her father once had, back and forth, back and forth, until the girl's body must have been near exhaustion.

In the time that they waited Kelly scanned the financial section of the daily Sydney newspaper for reports on Brandon, Hoyle. They appeared with ominous frequency; the statements issued from the Melbourne office increasingly had a note of desperation about them. The news was always of a further run on the stock and a fall in its value. The letters that came to Kelly from Peter were no more cheerful. *I wish to heaven I understood these financial tangles. Nick's in real trouble, I think, but he's admitting nothing to me yet. There've been more leaks to the newspapers, starting with that Watson man. Something to do with a dummy company set up in the Bahamas. Nick has finally sued Watson for libel, and he's pressing for the case to get to court as quickly as possible because of the damage the rumors are doing. Nick says the information has to have come from within the company, and Watson is refusing to name his source.*

Kelly read that part of the letter to Laura. "Kelly, I wish we were back there. The awful part of waiting here is that we can't do anything for Grandmother."

"She'd never say so, Laura, but the sight of you must help her. You're something for her to be proud of. Since your grandfather died, you're all she's got."

"I know," Laura said unhappily. "And I feel it's just too much to live up to."

She continued to ride and swim and read in the sick room; she continued to hang around each day when Bill Blake brought the post. There were no more letters with a Yorkshire postmark.

The word came as the cold blue dawn was breaking. Kelly felt her mother's hand on her shoulder as she slept. She struggled to sit up.

"She's gone. Got rest her soul."

Mary Anderson had arranged Delia Merton's body in a position of repose, had combed her hair and straightened the bedclothes before she called Laura.

Laura touched the sunken face briefly. "She was brave. I wish I had understood her better."

They gathered at Pentland for Delia Merton's burial in much the same way they had come to honor John Merton. It was a salute to the things that were long gone rather than to the almost unknown woman who had just died. The cousins came from Adelaide; Frank McArthur came from Sydney; some of the companies in which John Merton had large holdings sent representatives. As always, the people from the stations bordering Pentland came in complete family groups, not caring where or how they slept, bringing cooked food to swell Pentland's larder and ease the burden of feeding so many. Many curious, speculative eyes looked at Laura and Kelly. With Delia Merton gone, the income of which she had been the beneficiary would revert to the trust. Some years had passed since John Merton's death, and as yet Pentland had no natural heir.

With the funeral over and the people gone, Frank McArthur asked the cousins from Adelaide, Kelly and Laura and Mary Anderson to gather in John Merton's library to hear his widow's will read.

"I have asked you all," he said, "because I wish to make clear to you that this truly is the will of Delia Merton. To some of you it may be surprising. I have absolutely no doubt in my mind that she made it with all due consideration. It is dated shortly after the first operation she had in Sydney. I urged her to think carefully about its contents, and as it happens, she had a rather unexpectedly long time to do so. It nullifies, of course, any earlier wills."

Delia Merton had had no disposition of the income from the Pentland trust. But she had owned, outright, a parcel of stock in the vineyards in South Australia of which her father had been a founder, along with the fathers of the cousins who now sat and listened. Some could not repress the short intake of breath when they heard the news, in those dry, unemotional legal phrases, that Delia Merton had left her stock in the now considerably enlarged and prosperous company, to the one-time cook and housekeeper of Pentland, Mary Anderson. "I do so in recognition of her long dedication to my family and to the interests of my late husband."

Mary Anderson's face twisted strangely as she heard the words. Then she rose and walked, with a stiff back and quick steps, from the room. Despite the vigor of those movements, as if she had seen her mother clearly for the first time since she had returned, Kelly recognized deep fatigue. She knew that if she had remained in the room, Mary Anderson's life-long reserve might have broken.

Afterward, before the last meal which the cousins and Frank McArthur would have before leaving for the plane at Barrendarragh, one of the cousins spoke to Kelly. He was a big man, somewhat overweight, looking a trifle uncomfortable in his dark suit, but wearing the assurance of someone who had always moved in the right circles. "Well, I have to hand it to you, Kelly—you and your mother. I've no idea how she managed it, that dried-up old stick. We always thought there was no love lost between her and Delia. In fact, mostly because of you taking John's fancy and then marrying Greg, we got the impression that she hated the sight of your mother and you. Look—we weren't expecting anything ourselves. But we thought it would naturally go to Laura. Her only grandchild, after all. . . . But now I expect the stock will eventually go to you. It's a pretty fair chunk. My kids could have used it and used it well. They've worked in the business all their lives. You don't even know anything about our wines, do you? Some of the best South Australia produces, and right up beside anything France can turn out. We've even got one little vineyard whose wine we don't even offer for sale. It's special reserve for the Governor-General and the Prime Minister, and to give as presents to visiting bigwigs. And now *she* owns a piece of it. I don't think that's right, but I'm not going to challenge it. If I know Delia, this will was just some joke her twisted mind thought up—she always was a bit mad."

Laura was beside him. "Uncle Charlie, I don't think you should say anymore. You don't know Mrs. Anderson. She was—"

He took a huge gulp of whiskey. "What was she, my little English sweetie? Don't tell me now that *you* care about that old hag. By God, you and Kelly, you're really something. Thick as thieves. I hope you realize, dear Laura, that you've been tricked out of something pretty good. And to make it worse, I'm told that the old bag of bones wouldn't even let a drop of wine pass her lips."

He turned and went to the sideboard and poured lavishly from the whiskey decanter. "Some wine lover, *that*," Laura muttered. "He must have a palate as delicate as old shoes.

Come on, Kelly. We've got to get this meal over, and then it will be done. We'll be rid of them."

"You heard what he said, Laura. You don't think there is some justice in it?"

"Whatever Grandmother wanted was done, Kelly. You saw her and your mother together. Grandmother wouldn't have let anyone touch and care for her that way if she hadn't trusted her—felt something about her. In the end, they almost seemed to me to be the same woman. You know the way people sometimes grow to look alike when they've been living together a long time. We've all made the mistake of thinking that just because they didn't talk, they disliked each other. But there must have been something that built up over the years. Especially, I think, since my grandfather died. A mutual respect perhaps—a concern. They both cared about Pentland. As you said, perhaps they didn't talk because they just didn't need to."

That night the lights once again shone from behind the lace curtains in Mary Anderson's house. She had refused the suggestion that she remain in the big house of Pentland. "What for?" was her uncompromising reply. "*I* don't set myself up as mistress of Pentland."

For the next few days Nelly Blake and Kelly and Laura worked in the house, covering everything in dust sheets. Kelly paid off the two women who had cleaned and cooked for Delia Merton, and added the bonuses that Delia Merton's will had neglected. Nelly sighed as she swathed one of the chandeliers in the drawing room. "Well, it's going to seem awfully quiet around here now. Mind you, it's been terribly quiet since Mr. Merton died, but at least we could see a light at night, and the girls were always chattering in the kitchen. My kids were always running in and out—though not to *this* part of the house. Mrs. Merton didn't care for that. But now it's going to be empty, with me just looking in every day to see that everything's O.K. A shame . . ." She looked hopefully at Laura. "How many more years at the university?"

"Two," Laura answered, and would not be drawn further.

"Oh, well," Nelly said. "I suppose you'll be back from time to time, Kelly. But, God," she said again, "it's going to be awfully quiet. This big house . . . and no one in it."

It was Mary Anderson who stood, dressed in black, on the veranda of her own small house when Bill Blake drove Kelly and Laura away. She had walked over to the big house to make her formal, terse farewells when the bags were being loaded into the car, but had not lingered. Kelly had put her lips on her mother's paper-dry cheek, but had received no response. "I hope those exam results are as good as Victoria told Mrs. Merton they were. Then it won't be a lie." To Kelly she said, "Be sure you have those chair covers put on as soon as you get back. And remember, the furniture belongs to Laura. Take care of it." To them both she said, "Mrs. Merton used to place flowers every Sunday on Mr. Merton's grave. Mostly they were the flowers I grew myself, and during the week Mr. Blake used to drive me to the cemetery so that I could keep the grave weeded and tidy. I'll do it for her. You can count on that." Kelly and Laura were silent at the revelation that both women visited John Merton's grave regularly, but never together. Mrs. Anderson continued, "And I'll watch the house. I'll write to you if there's anything needing attention." She fixed her eyes on Bill Blake as she said this, as if daring him to neglect any detail.

She took a few steps away, and then turned back to them. "You know, I never expected it. I didn't know. The will . . . what does an old woman like me need with such things? I have everything. . . ."

She gestured toward the cottage, with its trim garden, fresh paint, shining windows. She stared at it, and then looked back at them. "Your grandfather took care of everything. There was no need . . ." Abruptly, she turned and walked stiffly away. She remained standing on the verandah of the cottage until the car was about to go out of sight. Looking back, Kelly saw, as if it were a gesture most reluctantly made, a stiff arm slowly raised in a single gesture of farewell.

Bill Blake had observed it in the driving mirror. "Well, no matter what she says, she's what's carrying Pentland on for the time being. She's the only one left."

They stayed only two days in Sydney, hurrying through all the routine matters that had to be discussed with Frank McArthur, making decisions, signing papers. Kelly knew the impatience in both herself and Laura, but she was more used to waiting; Laura was only learning. Kelly came into the sitting room of the suite they shared in the hotel to find Laura talking on the telephone. "That call I placed to Yorkshire, operator—would you cancel it, please?"

She looked over at Kelly, and the scar burned on her cheek. "I put in a call to Alex. And then I decided that I just had to have a bit more pride than that."

Frank McArthur came to the airport to see them off. In the last minutes before boarding, he bought a newspaper. For an instant he scanned the headlines, and then pointed to a stop-press item. *London stock exchange suspends trading in Brandon, Hoyle securities.*

Chapter Twelve

I

Peter was waiting at Heathrow. Kelly saw his face among the crowd which waited outside the customs area, and she felt a strange sense of weakness in her, as if she had not quite the strength to go forward and grasp the reality of having returned to him. "I can hardly believe it," she whispered as she clung to him. "I'd begun to think I would never get back, and that you really didn't exist. I feel as if I've been much farther this time, and for much longer."

He shook his head. "Never again. I'm not going to let you go again." He kissed Laura. "You're going to have to do your turn from now on."

Laura smiled at him. "I know . . . I know. Kelly's done enough." But it was a grave smile, as if she was reaching an acceptance of something that had had only vague substance before. The responsibility of Pentland would be more surely hers in the future. The memory of the empty, sheet-shrouded house lay with both of them, and would not be shaken.

They were waiting—Kate, Julia, Marya and Johnny—at Brandon Place. There was champagne and vodka and caviar—tears in Julia's eyes, and tugs at Kelly's skirt from Johnny, who was stumbling around the room on unsteady legs, and trying to decide whether or not these two were strangers.

Strangers or not, he adopted them quickly, since they seemed to be the center of attention. "He seems to have grown a couple of feet," Laura said. "Almost too big to lift now." But she did, nonetheless, waltzing him around the room. Suddenly, with Johnny in her arms she turned to Kate. "I can't tell you how good it is to come back to someone young, whose life is just beginning. It was agonizingly slow for poor Grandmother. And there was the awful feeling that she was leaving life without ever having known it. That's probably pretty presumptuous of me to say, but seeing her go like that I just felt so determined that I was going to *live* my life, not just let it pass."

"Oh . . . oh, watch out," Marya warned. "Are we to see another Everest expedition, or something of that nature?" Then her tone grew more sober as she reached out and for a moment placed one hand on Laura's face and one on Johnny's. "Yes, little one, you are wise to celebrate life and not death. And to live every minute there is."

Laura, with Johnny still in her arms, looked at each of them in turn, seeming to recall what she knew of each of them, as if their varying histories were flashed before her eyes, and now were being woven together, presenting some piece of a pattern whose final shape was not yet determined. "I can't know the end of it all," she said, "but I certainly intend to live it."

Chris had sent flowers to Kelly and an extra bottle of champagne. "That's our Chris," Kate remarked. "Tactful as always. He invented some pressing engagement tonight, so as not to intrude. It would do him a world of good just to break out one day and forget some of those totally English manners his mother drummed into him. But I shouldn't complain. He's awfully good. When all else fails, I know I can always park Johnny on him for a few hours. Chris has even discovered a creative toy place, so now we all have to buy terribly earnest toys so that Johnny's mind will develop in the right way. Nothing nasty or violent like guns or soldiers. Imagine the grandson of a general without toy soldiers." Johnny, sitting in his mother's lap, reached out and tried to take the glass of champagne from her; he managed a sip of the liquid before it spilled down his chin.

"Well, there he is, on the road to ruin," Peter said. "And on Chris's champagne, too."

Kelly and Laura flicked through the post that was waiting. "There's probably some still on its way out to Australia,"

Julia said. "We forwarded on anything that looked of interest, but of course we didn't know you'd be back until Peter telephoned and told us."

There was a small bouquet of flowers for Laura. "From Alex," she said.

"I would rather," Marya murmured quietly to Kelly, "that the young man had come himself. It is too polite for someone in love." She shrugged. "Well, perhaps I am very stupid. I spend my life translating back and forth from and into the English language, but I can never pretend I understand the English themselves."

"We don't understand ourselves, Marya," Peter said. "So many of us are afraid . . . don't realize . . ." He looked at Kelly, and faltered.

"That," Marya countered, "is not the English. That is everyone."

Over supper, which by common agreement was moved from the formality of the dining room to the kitchen—"After all," Kate said, "Johnny can make a mess there, and it doesn't much matter"—the talk had inevitably to come around to Brandon, Hoyle. They had all appeared to be avoiding it, to savor the pleasure of the homecoming, but in the end it had to be talked about. "It's bad," Peter said. "There just seems to be a flood-tide now of accusation and rumor. Everyone's onto it. The Stock Exchange is saying that there *have* been what they call 'irregularities.' Nick is denying it and saying it's normal business practice. But at any rate, the trading in Brandon, Hoyle has been suspended until an enquiry is held. A lot of shareholders bailed out before it was stopped—and took the losses. Nick keeps saying it will all come back, and he's buying up more of his own company. Of course, Allen Hoyle himself got out years ago, when the shares were riding high. Retired and sold out to Nick. Nick kept the name, because it was well known, but now he's been left holding the bag. Allen Hoyle claims to know nothing about the deals that are being investigated. But wherever the chap Watson got his information, he's still leaking it, a bit at a time. He's become a sort of hero on Fleet Street—the small, clever, industrious journalist digging away and uncovering the big shark entrepreneur. But Nick says the fact is that he didn't uncover so much himself—it was fed to him. And there may be more to come. All Nick can do is file a libel suit against him, to try to force him to reveal his source. If Watson doesn't reveal it, and the case goes against him, he may end up with a short jail sentence—and be an even bigger hero. But whatever happens to Watson, Nick's been seriously hurt. It needs millions in cash to shore Brandon, Hoyle up all over the world, and because the stock has crashed, there just aren't the millions available. The banks are starting to ask for their money. Nick says it isn't there."

They let him talk without interruption, the food growing cold on their plates, the champagne growing flat.

They drifted away, Kate first because Johnny had to be put to bed, then Marya, then Laura to unpack; Julia stayed to help stack the dishwasher, to wash and dry the pots. Peter sat at the kitchen table, chewing an apple. Kelly went into the dining room and brought back brandy and glasses. "Stay and have a small one with us, Julia . . ."

Julia smiled softly, and sat down. "I'm sorry you've come back to such bad news about Nick, Kelly. But I have to say it's wonderful to have you back. The house goes . . . well, dead, when you're away. We missed our Wednesday nights. Marya kept them going in a sort of a way . . . but, well, it wasn't the same."

"What have you been doing?" Kelly asked. "You wrote letters that said absolutely nothing. You might just as well have sent the ballet programs, and be done with it. You left it to Kate to tell us about the O.B.E. You had to have known before we left you were going to get it, but you didn't tell us." The award of the Order of the British Empire had been announced as part of the Queen's birthday honors list.

Julia spread her hands. "The O.B.E. was just like giving me an official handshake, because they can't give me a pension—that's all. And one's not supposed to say anything about it beforehand. What else there was to say I found I couldn't put into a letter. There's nothing concrete, and even if there were, I still wouldn't know what to say."

Kelly sighed. "You make it sound very complicated."

"It's not complicated, because there isn't anything *yet*. There may be, and if it comes, I won't know how to answer."

Peter sipped his brandy. "You'd better get your tongue around it, Julia. It's Clive Wallace, isn't it? Marya told me . . . I'm breaking a confidence, and please don't be upset with her. She wanted Kelly to know."

"It is Clive Wallace," Julia admitted. "There's nothing else. No one else. I've just been doing my job with the National, and I've been seeing Clive Wallace. I've been *seeing* him, that's all."

"Then what are you so twisted up about?"

"Because I know I'm being weighed up. And I find the feeling very uncomfortable. He doesn't commit himself, but I feel he's going to ask me to marry him . . . after he's thought about it a bit more. Perhaps I'm wrong, and I'll just be dropped from the list of possible wives for a man like Clive Wallace."

"It doesn't sound like a romance."

"It's not. I think Clive would find it hard to talk about love. He hasn't fallen in love with me, but he might ask me to marry him. I'm not sure I'd know what to answer."

She looked at them both, twisting her long pale hands together. "I've been invited to family dinner parties, and some of his business dinner parties. He seems to regard the fact that I was once a well-known dancer quite intriguing, but the background of ballet is less his style. Of course he knows about Sergei. He's trying, I think, to forgive me that. His whole family are very much into the arts, and he enjoys the fact that I'm well-known in that world. But Clive Wallace's wife—like Caesar's—has to be above reproach. It is one thing to patronize the arts; quite another thing to be involved in them. His family make a thing of the fact that I was Julia Brandon. They try to overlook the rest."

"You *are* Julia Brandon," Peter objected. "You're beautiful, intelligent, charming Julia Brandon. What man could miss that? It all sounds pretty cold-blooded to me."

"It's not quite like that. I haven't been fair to Clive. He's being careful, not rushing. Don't you think there must be a number of women who would like to marry Clive Wallace? But he sees it as a position, a job, that has to be well and gracefully filled. There are the two children. A girl and a boy—Jennifer and Mark. I've been to stay at his place in Kent when they've been home from school—of course, always with other guests. He wants to see, naturally, how we get along. I find myself quite tongue-tied with them. Rather frightened. I wouldn't know how to go about being a stepmother . . ." She looked at Kelly. "I haven't your gifts in that way."

"Julia, there's only one question. Do you love Clive Wallace? Do you want to marry him?"

"No, Kelly, that's *two* questions. I still love Sergei. I think I always will. But I also knew, right from the beginning, that he would never marry me. So now there is Clive, and you ask me if I want to marry him. I think I do. And why . . . ?"

She paused, and her hand slid across the table to the

brandy glass. "Because I'm frightened. I see what's happening to me, and I'm frightened. Not to be able to dance anymore—it's to grow old overnight. I know I wouldn't have been able to go on forever, but I would have had time to get used to the idea. What am I in the National now? Nothing but a general factotum—everybody's dog's-body. I'll get less and less important as time goes on. One day I'll hear one of the new little girls—the little girls who show such promise—ask another, 'Who's that?' 'Oh, she used to be prima ballerina. She's written up in the books.' And there I'll be, trailing around after Katherine Meredith, notebook in hand. The clothes I had as a star will wear out, and there won't be any need for the furs, because I won't be going anywhere to wear them. There'll be fewer and fewer invitations. I'll come home every night, and hang around hoping you, Kelly, will ask me to eat with you, even that Kate will ask me to take care of Johnny. I'm afraid. I'm afraid of being left alone. I'm afraid of growing old . . . I'm afraid of everything. I have to hear myself say it. I'm my father's daughter, and my mother's daughter, but I'm a coward."

"There are other men in the world beside Clive Wallace," Peter said. "You talk as if no one else could ever want you, or love you. That's nonsense."

"There are plenty of other men in the world," Julia answered. "There are plenty who've been married once, and divorced, and want their freedom. They don't at all mind having an affair, living with you for a while. But who wants marriage? This is the Swinging Sixties, Peter. All the old rules seem to have gone. I lived by the new ones myself—but then I thought I had everything still ahead of me. The other side of thirty is colder. I can't dance anymore. And Sergei is gone."

Kelly took a deep breath. "I admit all those things. I wish Clive Wallace were less cautious. A woman as beautiful as you—someone with your nature, is a prize."

"The world is full of beautiful women, and lots of them younger than I am. I'm looking for lines on my face now, where I never thought of them before. I'm afraid of putting on weight. I'm afraid of so much." She turned to Peter. "I'm sorry, but I *hate* it when there are new stories about Brandon, Hoyle because that seems to put the whole family in a bad light—and the Wallaces have been City conservatives for so long. I find myself wishing that Kate was respectably married, and she would keep her mouth shut in Parliament. I wish Louise hadn't taken up with Jack Matthews. Oh, all kinds of things I wish because I'm afraid Clive *won't* ask me to marry him. I'm so ashamed of myself, and I can't help it. I want the security he can give me. I don't know how to cope for myself in this world. You think ballet is tough, but once you've made it to the top, they give their own kind of protection. I've lost it now. I'm exposed. I'm alone. And I find I haven't the courage for it."

Kelly and Peter watched helplessly as the first tears rolled down her face, causing her eye makeup to streak, giving her, prematurely, the look of age she dreaded.

"I'm not *Firebird* anymore. I'm a little brown-gray sparrow." She put out her hands and touched both of them briefly, and then she left.

For the first time Peter came upstairs with Kelly at Brandon Place. She took him into the room she had made into a small sitting room beside her bedroom, and they finished their brandy; after so long a wait, there seemed to her, miraculously, to be no hurry. They were hungry, but within sight of a laden table.

"Out of so much bad news, there's some good," he said when they had settled on the sofa. "Louise has become frightened. She knows now that there's no hope of Nick coming up with the money she asked for. She seems to have decided that being married to Jack Matthews now is better than being left high and dry with no one. You know—she's hung on to Matthews for so long—or he's hung out on her. Because basically Louise is a snob. She's wanted his money, but she's never quite been able to settle for his background. Now he looks to be the safest refuge. She's seen Brandon, Hoyle go down, and she's frightened she may lose out on this lovely swinging world. Whatever happens, she'll always have her title. She'll always be Lady Louise whatever . . . that may be about as much as she has to trade these days."

"What will happen?" Her voice was tight, dry, as if hope was something she did not dare express.

"I've offered her the Eaton Square house, and she's decided to accept. That's to be her settlement—her payment, I suppose. I think she's decided that she'd better take it quickly while it's still on offer, because it might vanish with the rest. She's settled for a quick divorce so that she can marry Jack Matthews. The boys will stay with me. She can see them whenever she wants to, but their home will be Wychwood—for however long we have it."

Kelly sat quietly, her eyes closed, thinking about it. "I said something would happen . . . I didn't think it would have anything to do with Nick's trouble. But I can see—it's pushed her, hasn't it?" She opened her eyes and turned to him. "Why in God's name didn't you tell me sooner? The minute I got off the plane? All the talk this evening—about other things. This is our future. But you didn't tell me!"

He put his hand on hers, his thumb stroking the back of her palm. "I had to talk to you alone. It's not all good news, and we're a long way from the end yet. The divorce is the first step. But Nick—well, there could be so much trouble ahead, and I may end up with almost nothing to offer you. I've called in Christie's to look at the Wychwood pictures and give me an idea what they might bring at auction. Nick's going to need money for legal fees, no matter what he says, and I have to be able to offer it. The pictures would be the first of the assets to go—after all, they're only still at Wychwood because Nick paid off the death duties. In a sense they really belong to him. But if it comes right down to it, and Nick needs the money, and Wychwood itself has to go, then that's how it must be."

"Nick told me it was free and clear of Brandon, Hoyle. They owned no part of Wychwood."

"That's true—but I can't see Nick in this trouble and not offer back the only thing I have. It will be easier to sell the land than the house—who but a madman wants a place like Wychwood these days? I know the sale of any of these things can't prop up Brandon, Hoyle itself—that'd need millions. But it might buy Nick some time to extricate himself. In the end—in the end, Kelly, it might keep him out of jail."

"It's that bad . . . ?"

"Yes, it's that bad. Nick says what's come out so far is only a part of it, and he still insists that what he's done isn't so unusual. It's being found out that's his crime. If he'd been able to go on as he was, it would all have worked out. The shareholders would have taken their profits and been happy. But you know, Kelly—what Nick says and what the lawyers may be able to prove could turn out to be rather different. He does admit that there have been some dealings that won't look so good if they come out. But so many people are now demanding a full enquiry that a lot of it is bound to be dragged up. It's going to be a long, messy, expensive business. It's so complicated that I can't begin to understand it. Nick's had to fire more than half the staff here in London. The other offices—South Africa and Hong Kong and Melbourne—are getting by on a shoestring. You see, the cash flow into Brandon, Hoyle completely dried up. It really didn't need the

Stock Exchange to order the suspension in trading. There were all sellers and no buyers."

She finished her brandy and turned to him. "Whatever happens, you have to keep enough land to be able to get by as a farmer, however small. You might not have Wychwood, but there's Mead Cottage. The sale of the last couple of hundred acres isn't going to help Nick, and I think one of the things he's going to need most is the knowledge that Johnny has somewhere to go. He once said to me that he didn't want Johnny growing up only knowing about money and politics. He knew you would see to that. He counts on you. So all of the land can't be sold. You owe that to Johnny. If Nick saved Wychwood for you, he was also saving something for his son."

She stood up and pulled at his hand. "Come to bed now . . . come and hold me because I feel tired and bewildered and old. I said something would happen in time. I didn't think of all of this. . . . Hold me, Peter. There's a storm howling around us. We haven't any idea what'll be left by the time it's blown out. Except you and I . . . we have this, and always will. Oh, love . . . how I've missed you . . ."

She woke in the morning to feel his sleeping weight against her, and to the thought, the first time that she had known it as a certainty, that they would wake together many mornings. The clock ticked beside her, inexorably moving time on. Upheaval awaited them before the day when they would lie together in peace. She held his body for comfort, and cursed the ticking of the clock.

II

Laura drove to Yorkshire that week at Mrs. Gardiner's invitation. "I don't know what to expect," she told Kelly. "I'm a bit afraid to face Alex, and yet I know I have to. He's finished at agricultural college now, and he's going to be making some decisions . . . I haven't any idea whether I'm part of them or not."

"Surely you have to make your own decisions. It can't all be Alex's doing."

"The way I feel about him, I could do just whatever he says."

Two days later she was back. The doors to Number 16 were open, and she came through. "Kelly . . . ? Are you home?"

Kelly called back back. "Here . . . in the study." She walked through the passage and found Laura standing in the hall, holding onto the newel post of the stairs. She wore an expression Kelly had never seen on her before—hurt and outrage and pain. She wore no makeup. Her hair was dragged back from her face and held by a rubber band. There were dark circles of weariness beneath her eyes.

"Can we make some tea?" Without waiting for an answer, she went into the kitchen and put on the kettle.

"Laura . . . what's happened?"

"In a minute. Some tea first. I've driven down from Yorkshire without stopping except to get petrol. It never seemed such a long drive before. And the rain . . ." The early evening had been darkened by rain; Kelly pulled the curtains, shutting out the sight of the wet street and Cavanagh's lighted windows. It was another autumn.

Laura drank a full cup of tea, and poured another. Kelly had made her a sandwich, but it remained untouched beside her. She waited for Laura to speak.

"Alex asked me to marry him."

"I thought that was what you wanted."

"I thought so too. In fact, I still want it. But I want it because he wants it. Not because it seems a good idea."

"What are you talking about?"

"Alex asked me to marry him because he'd *thought* about it, and obviously, in the end, it seemed like a good idea. Alex doesn't love me, Kelly. He expects to marry and settle down to farming. He's looked around, and weighed everything up. I turn out to be the best value."

Kelly felt a sense of relief sweep her, but Laura's stricken look prevented her from expressing it. "You're sure?"

"I'm sure. I'm in love with him. Foolishly, stupidly in love with him. And I think he's in love with himself. All that time at Pentland I thought about him . . . and thought. I imagined what it would be like the first time I saw him again. I felt it—but he didn't. He saw Laura Merton, the girl with the scarred face and some money. She'd be grateful . . . who would expect Alex Gardiner to look at her. He could do better. Or could he? I was suitable. I like farming and Everdale. I could be expected to settle down happily, have children, bring them up. And always adore Alex." Her fingernails drummed the table. "You know, Kelly, I had the feeling that it was all arranged. The Gardiners wanted me, and Granny Renisdale wanted it to happen. I'd be nicely settled, wouldn't I? Dear, darling Laura, who has a bit of a problem, would be nicely settled with a young man she was devoted to. The trouble is that Alex isn't devoted to me. He's been up in Scotland staying with the family of a girl he's been seeing a lot of. I asked him—why not her? He said quite bluntly he'd decided against it. Then why decide on me? He said he thought it was a good idea. I don't want to get married because it's a good idea. I want it to be the *only* idea."

"There's more, isn't there?"

"Kelly, I hate to say it, but I think the money part of it mattered most to him. He expected to use my money. To use *me*. I had the most terrible dream—vision—whatever you call it. I saw myself ten years from now. I wouldn't be in love with him anymore. I'd have three or four kids, and he'd be unfaithful to me whenever someone else took his fancy. And he'd be surprised that I was hurt. Well, in the end, I decided not to go through those ten years. I can skip them. I can do without them. If I'm going to be hurt, I'll get over with now. I could have kidded myself about Alex for just a while, but not forever."

The bones of Greg's face showed through the taut lines of Laura's. Hurt was there, but also the determination to ignore it, as Greg had ignored so many physical pains. Laura's own experience of pain had brought a kind of terrible wisdom to her. She had learned, from pain, to sift and sort. She had learned that to be in love was not enough; she wanted love in return. While Kelly silently rejoiced that it would not be Alex Laura gave herself to, she also wondered who would meet these standards Laura had set, who could breach the barriers she had erected about herself. The scarred face that seemed such a slight thing to those who loved her, still assumed giant proportions in Laura's own mind. That and the money seemed to make an impossible obstacle.

Unexpectedly, Laura's lips forced themselves into a smile that was more like a grimace. "You know what I'll have to do, Kelly? I'll have to go off somewhere—somewhere that no one knows about me. Take out a begging bowl, or something. Then if someone wants me for myself, face and all—no money, then I'll know it's right. Oh, damn, Kelly! Don't look like that! You couldn't help it. I know you've never been mad about Alex, but you didn't interfere. I know you want the right things for me, but you can't *give* them to me. You're not like Granny and the Gardiners. You don't think it can all be arranged. Look, I wasn't blind about you and Dad. You loved him, and he let you love him. And he used you. Perhaps *that's* what I saw in Alex. Don't be hurt, Kelly, because I saw it. Dad wasn't unfaithful to you, I'd swear that. But he didn't mind what he asked of you. And he wasn't grateful for what he got. He just expected it. He was Greg Merton, and he expected the best. In my opinion he got it. If I learned just enough from that to be able to see some of it in Alex, then it's saved a lot of heartache. Oh, it aches like hell now, but I'll get over it. It's a late case of puppy love. I seem to be more than slightly retarded in a lot of ways . . ."

She broke off the corner of her sandwich and chewed it. "Take it easy with Granny, will you, Kelly. I've a feeling she's going to be awfully disappointed. Mrs. Gardiner was, I know. And I think she wanted me for myself. They just about had the champagne cooling when I arrived. Perhaps that's what made me think a bit. Everything taken for granted, most especially me."

"And Ben . . . did he say anything?"

Laura looked at her with some surprise, as if she hadn't thought of his existence. "Ben wasn't there. He'd left just before I got there, they said. Gone off to an interview for a job on a farm somewhere up in Northumberland, I think it was. Mr. Gardiner said something about there being enough for both Alex and Ben at Everdale, but I wouldn't have a doubt about who'd expect to be boss. The way I'm looking at things now, Ben's well out of it . . ." She looked past Kelly to the kitchen door. "Oh, hello, Chris . . . what's the matter?" Chris, Kelly knew, had seen Laura briefly on the night before she had gone to Yorkshire, so there were no other greetings to be exchanged.

"It's your car, Laura. You left it unlocked, with the key and your luggage in it. I've put your bags in the hall, and here's your key. I knocked at the flat door . . . and then I saw the light in here."

Laura sighed. "Oh, Lord, I'm stupid, I know. Serve me right if the whole lot had been pinched. Thanks, Chris."

Chris hesitated a moment, and then the words came in a rush. "You look all in, Laura. You know, you didn't give yourself any time to get over the plane trip before dashing off to Yorkshire."

Laura pulled a face at him. "Yes, Uncle. I'll remember in the future."

"Do I sound as middle-aged as that?" he asked. "I hoped not even Johnny thought of me as an uncle. I tell you what, Laura. Prove to me I'm not quite middle-aged. Come and have dinner with me. Somewhere there's dancing. You must know all the places. . . . Just for once I feel like throwing off these middle-aged shackles."

"I know some places . . ." Laura's face had brightened,

but she kept the last reserve. "Now hold it, Chris, I know that Nick has put everyone he's kept on at Brandon, Hoyle on half salary. I'll only go if you let me pay my share."

"Then I've just uninvited you. I asked you. You either accept or you don't. We've had a few dinners together before—remember? In the beginning, before you got to know all your trendy friends. You let me pay then. If you don't now, I'll be offended. Besides"—he advanced farther into the room—"I really need some company tonight. I need cheering up. That bloody man Watson has got hold of something new on Brandon, Hoyle—or else he's had it all along, and this is just the latest he's prepared to release. The whole place just about shut down when we read the afternoon papers. Well . . . there aren't so many left there anymore, so you hardly notice the vacant desks. It's almost come to a 'will the last person to leave please turn off the lights.' So, dear Laura, will you please do me the favor of coming out to dinner, and find some place where the music is loud and the lights are low so no one will notice how clumsy I am on the dance floor."

She looked at him, blinking. "Yes—I accept. With pleasure."

To Kelly's astonishment Chris quickly moved to Laura's side, and bent and placed a kiss exactly on the scar. Laura's face flamed, but it came to life. Then Chris's hand was on the elastic band. "You have such beautiful hair. Why do you drag it back like that? Go and take a bath, and put on some perfume and your prettiest dress. Tonight I feel like being like my boss—Nick the Spender. I want to forget everything that's happened. I want to enjoy myself. Will you help me, Laura?"

She put her fingers where his lips had touched her cheek. With her other hand she dragged the elastic band off her hair, but she did not let the thick curtain of it swing across her face, as was her habit. She raised her face to Chris, and the light fell directly upon it. "Yes, Chris, I'd love that. I've got a bit of forgetting to do myself."

III

A week later Ben Gardiner telephoned Kelly and asked if he could come to see her. "I'm just passing through London—on my way to Canada and the States. I thought I'd like to see you, if it isn't inconvenient."

"I'd like very much to see you, Ben. When do you want to come?"

He hesitated. "Well, I'd rather not see Laura, if that can be managed. I think she's had rather enough of the Gardiners for the time being."

"I think she has lectures all this afternoon. It's Wednesday. She often has dinner with me and the others on Wednesday."

"I'll be gone before she gets back, then."

He came, and she carried tea up to the drawing room in case Laura should come home early. "I'm in a hotel on the Cromwell Road," he said cheerfully. "It's a dump, but it's a bed. I'm going to be traveling on very little money, and I'd better get used to it." He munched the sandwiches hungrily.

"Tell me what happened when Laura went up to Everdale."

"She probably told you I wasn't there. In fact, I got out deliberately. I knew even if I'd been offered the job I wouldn't take it, but it was an excuse to get out. I really didn't want to be around when the champagne corks began to pop. As it happens, there wasn't any champagne being drunk. Mother was very disappointed—she's genuinely fond of Laura. Dad's pretty keen on Laura too. He was delighted when he thought she and Alex might get married. I think he's always been afraid of the sort of girl Alex might wind up with. Laura seemed . . . well, I suppose, *safe*. That sounds an awful word to use about a marvelous girl like Laura, but that'd probably be how Dad would see it. Alex is the light of his life, and he'd be pretty concerned about whom he married."

"And Alex?"

Ben permitted a slow grin to spread on his face. "I suppose this sounds a rotten thing to say, especially when you think that Laura must have been pretty badly hurt. I think she really was in love with Alex—probably still is. But when she turned him down, it was the biggest shock Alex ever had in his life. It must have been the last thing he ever imagined happening. All his life, all he's ever had to do was lift his finger and everything came his way. And after a certain point, the girls did too. I thought Laura was going to be a walkover for him. He did too. He still hasn't come out of shock." He accepted more tea from Kelly, and kept on talking and eating. "You know, Kelly, I think it's a good thing she turned him down. He's my brother, but I don't really like him. He's capable of treating whomever he marries rather badly. And I care enough about Laura not to want to see that happen. Especially as he's my brother, and I'd feel . . . in a way . . . that I was partly responsible."

"Do you care about Laura?"

He waved the teacup at her. "Yes, I care about Laura. I haven't been allowed to get to know her very well, because whenever Alex was around, I made myself scarce. I knew I wasn't any competition for him. And even I buck at playing that game. But, Laura . . . yes, I care about her. I might even be in love with her, if I were certain what that meant. But when a girl has hardly looked at you, how can you say you're in love with her? I know I admire her. I said to you before that I think she has guts. Now I think she's shown pretty good judgment too. It must have taken a hell of a lot of determination to say 'no' to Alex. She may be eating her heart out, but I think she's done the right thing."

Kelly relaxed in her chair. "So do I." The smiles they exchanged had a slightly conspiratorial air.

They talked about Ben's trip. "I'm using up everything I've saved, but I thought I had to get out and see a bit of the world before I took a job. Canada first—because the winter's coming, and I thought later I'd work my way down south in the States. If the money holds out, I could last until spring. Then I really do have to find a job back here. I don't feel like working at home. No matter how Dad tries to rationalize it, there really isn't room for both Alex and me. Not unless I decide to take orders from Alex, and I don't feel like doing that. In fact, I suppose I've been hoping I'd find some job in farming in the States—but the immigration laws are pretty tough, and I couldn't expect anyone to favor me over an American when it came to handing out a job. But if I can talk my way into them, at least I might see a few of their farms—the really big places. I'd like to see some of the big wheat farms in the prairies in Canada and the Dakotas—and those big cattle ranches in Texas. I suppose it sounds like a little boy wanting to play cowboy. Perhaps it is. Dad's given me one or two introductions, but I don't know if they'll work. I can hardly expect some Texas rancher to remember the name of the man he bought a prize bull from, can I?"

Thinking of Pentland, and the way news and memories were cherished in the isolation of the vast holdings, Kelly said, "You might be surprised how well they remember. Particularly if the man went to Yorkshire to buy it. I wish I knew some people over there . . ."

"Don't worry. I'll just knock about as long as the money lasts. If I keep my eyes open I'll learn a lot—and that's what the whole trip's about. I don't feel that I know it all because I've got a degree from an agricultural college." He got to his feet. "Kelly, it was awfully nice of you to have me here. I've enjoyed it. I'll send you a postcard or two from the States. Don't say—"

Downstairs a door banged; the sound seemed to have come from Number 15. Kelly looked at the clock—Sergei's clock she always called it in her mind. "It could be Mrs. Cass leaving—I told her not to tell anyone you were here. You know, this is a house where it's very hard to keep secrets . . ."

Laura's voice drifted up the stairs. "Kelly—you there?"

Kelly went to the door. "I'll be down in a minute. Just finishing tea."

"Is that Granny there?" Laura's voice was nearer. "You don't usually have tea in the drawing room . . ." Kelly looked at Ben and shook her head.

"Sorry," she murmured. In a moment Laura stood in the doorway.

"Oh . . ." She stared at Ben in surprise. "I didn't mean to interrupt. Sometimes I suspect I'm more than a bit of a nuisance to Kelly. I don't really seem to know what side of the house I belong on. How are you, Ben? I missed seeing you when I was up there last week."

"I didn't get the job, Laura, so I missed seeing you for nothing. Well, it wasn't much of a job, anyway. I'd already really made up my mind about something else. I'm taking off for a bit. I'm flying to Toronto tomorrow. And then as the bad weather sets in, I'll be moving south through the States. I might pick up a casual job or two along the way. I'm not particular what I do, and it'd all be experience. England seems a bit small at the moment. I was telling Kelly . . ."

Laura advanced cautiously into the room. "They haven't sent you, have they?"

"Who's they? And why would I be sent?"

She shrugged. "Oh, I just thought Alex . . . or your mother . . . or Granny . . ."

"Laura, I may be the young brother, but I haven't turned into an errand boy yet."

"Sorry." Laura turned to Kelly. "Any tea left?" She looked at the delicate china on the tea tray. "I'll go and make a fresh pot, shall I?—and bring a mug for myself. I don't know how Ben came to rate tea in the drawing room."

"Maybe I should be left to decide those things myself, Laura—in my own house."

"Oh, sorry. That was rude. It's been that sort of a day. I don't seem to have understood one word the professors were saying. Really dense. I cut the last lecture. Listen, please stay awhile, Ben. I'd like to hear about where you're going. I didn't think the Gardiners broke out of bounds like that. Alex—" She clamped her lips on the word. "It's going to be pretty silly if I keep saying 'sorry' all the time. Take it as said, will you? I'll just go and get the tea." She paused at the door. "It's Wednesday . . . Kelly, forgive me for sticking myself in again, but have you invited Ben . . . ?"

"Thanks, Laura, but I've already got a date."

"You're an awfully bad liar, Ben. Kelly, may I invite him, please? Has Kelly told you about Wednesday nights? There's an infinitely stretchable supper. I'd really like to offer you some hospitality, Ben. I owe your mother so much. When I write to her I'd like to be able to say you had supper with us all. May I, Kelly?"

Ben spoke first. "In that case, Laura, I'd like to take you out to dinner."

She shook her head. "You don't know what you'll be missing here. It's family." She looked at the clock. "And I just have time to get into Cavanagh's before they close. I'll get some *gateaux*, Kelly—and a few other things. Wine . . ." She had brightened. "Yes—why not? It'll be *my* party tonight. A farewell party for you, Ben. Canada . . . America . . . I think that's marvelous . . ."

"Can I come shopping with you, Laura? I'm pretty good at carrying things."

She laughed. "Yes—you look as if you could heft quite a load. All right—quickly. We've only got about twenty minutes before closing, so don't think you can agonize over vintages and all that rubbish."

It was one of the nights when everyone came. Even Chris Page was there, bringing the usual bottle of wine, and some flowers. "It's been another of thos long-faced days at Brandon, Hoyle. Everyone but Nick left early. All glad to go, I think." He shook hands with Ben, and didn't refer to Laura's last trip to Yorkshire. "Good to see you again." Kelly told Chris about the American trip. "I rather envy you that. I'd like to clear out for a bit myself, but it would seem like deserting Nick right now. Tell me . . ." They sat together for a while, talking, the kitchen grew warm and fragrant from the smell of the ragout. Laura laid out the pastries and fruit and cheese.

"Ben lost his head and insisted on buying the wine. I think they saw him coming and sold him the most expensive thing within reach." She turned laughingly to Ben and Chris. "You know, Chris, you could give him a tip or two. He's too easily parted from his money."

"Since I seldom have any, that's all too easy, Laura."

"I wouldn't underestimate him," Chris said. His tone was slightly reproachful.

"I see I'm back to saying 'sorry' again. This just doesn't seem to be my day." Laura poured a shot of vodka for Marya, who had just come in, and one for herself. She was flushed, and her speech was rapid and staccato. She set the table, poured more drinks when Julia arrived, and greeted Kate and Johnny loudly. "You know, it's party night. Where's Mrs. Nelson? Has she left yet? I wanted her to come and have a drink with us. Mrs. Nelson . . . ? Mrs. Nelson . . . ?"

"She's gone," Kate said. "And calm down, Laura." But Laura had swept Johnny up in her arms. "Look at this big boy, Ben. Just look at him. He's gorgeous, isn't he?"

"Put Johnny down, Laura, and behave yourself," Kate said.

"Yes—yes I will. It's time I shut up and behaved myself. I don't know how Kelly stands me." They, all of them, realized that she was letting go the emotion that had seemed bottled up since the return from Pentland, and from Yorkshire. They let her say whatever she wanted. She drank too much, but there was the knowledge in all of them, that she was safe with them. She kept pouring drinks, and when the food was served, she kept pouring wine.

Finally, she looked across the table at Ben. "There's one thing I'll bet you haven't thought of."

"What's that?"

"Well . . ." She swirled the wine in her glass and smiled at him mischievously. "It's one thing to go somewhere as a tourist—even if you expect to do it the cheapest possible way. It's another thing to go and hold down a job."

"What exactly are you talking about? I'm . . . well, when you're in this mood, I'm not quite with you."

"I'm talking about a real job. No casual work, where you can get out whenever it suits you. No pampering. No luxuries. Just what everyone else gets. I'm talking about Pentland, Ben. Bill Blake would give you a job if we asked him to. A job with no favors attached. You'd bunk in with the rest of them. You'd do whatever came to hand. You'd get used to sheep who can't be mollycoddled. There are just too many of them. You'd ride until your bones ached. That's Pentland, Ben. You'd never see the inside of the big house, as they call it. You'd have to take an awful lot of leg-pulling and perhaps some prejudice because you're what we call a pommy. You're an Englishman, and that's a disadvantage. But there's a job there, and not a tourist ride."

All of them at the table were stricken with silence. Laura held up her wine glass as if in challenge. Ben looked across at Kelly. She nodded.

"If it's a real job, then I accept."

Kelly telephoned Bill Blake. "It's to be a real job, Bill. No favors. He'll do exactly the same as every other man you hire. Same wages, same conditions."

There was a hesitation in the answer. "You're the boss, Kelly."

"In these things, I'm not. You do the hiring and firing. You have to run Pentland. If you don't want him—if you really can't use an extra hand, or you think it won't work out, then say so."

"I can use someone who's willing to work. A bloke left two weeks ago, and I haven't replaced him yet."

"Give him three months probation, Bill. He may want to come back to England at the end of that time. He may want to stay forever. Would you give him a try?" She didn't say that Laura had already made the offer.

"Anything for you, Kelly. How soon can he got here?"

Two days later, Ben, with a temporary visa, was on a plane for Sydney.

That one outburst from Laura seemed to mark a turning point. To Kelly she seemed visibly to retreat from the small outside world she had been building. She attended lectures, and she studied, and appeared to do little else. She refused invitations to Charleton and Kelly's urging to spend some weekends at Mead Cottage. Most nights Kelly heard the record player used for hours on end, and she was unhappily aware that Chris Page had taken to spending a good deal of time in Laura's flat.

IV

Julia took the occasion of a Wednesday night gathering to wear a spectacular solitaire diamond ring and to announce that she was going to marry Clive Wallace. "In three weeks time," she said.

Marya patted her hand. "It's good. It's good for you to be married, Julia."

Kate nodded. "Good luck, lovely fairy princess."

"Why?" Laura asked. "Do you love him?"

Julia chose to respond to Laura's question. "I'm marrying him because at last he's asked me, and there's nothing else I can do. Love him?—that's really not the point. I'm grabbing him because he represents security and a certain position. He'll give me the things I seem to need. I wasn't aware that I needed them, but I do. It sounds a dreary reason for getting married, but I've stopped believing in all the fairy stories. I intend to make him a good wife—as good as I can be. I hope not to disappoint him."

"Perhaps you should wait a little longer—think about it," Kelly said quietly.

"Wait? That's what I've done. I've waited for him to ask me, and each day I pick up the newspapers I'm terrified that one more scandalous thing may be rumored or said about Nick and Brandon, Hoyle, I'm marrying Clive as quickly as possible before things can get any worse—before he decides to back away from me. He's taken a long time to make up his mind. I don't want it to be changed. So the invitations for the reception will go out tomorrow. The wedding itself will be quiet—in a registry office. Just his children, and his brother's and his sister's families. And all of you, of course."

"I wish you looked happy," Laura said.

"Happy? In a sense I'm very happy. No—I'm glad. I'm relieved. I feel as if I've stopped struggling. He's a good man, and I've stopped thinking that the prince has to come out of the wings with a spectacular leap. In fact, I don't want any more princes. I intend to be very, very careful."

Julia invited them all, Chris included, to supper on the evening before she was married. It was a simple meal—cold chicken, salad, potato salad, fruit, cheese—all, Kelly guessed, bought at Cavanagh's. Julia did not claim to be a cook. There was laughter when it turned out that each of them had bought a bottle of champagne to contribute to the supper. "We'd better not drink it all," Laura said, "or we'll disgrace Julia tomorrow by looking sadly hungover." But they did toast Julia, rather solemnly, Kelly thought. It seemed that the fact of marrying Clive Wallace was a rather solemn one, and they all reacted to it.

They had all given Julia gifts, but Laura's was the most imaginative. From the National she had begged photos of Julia in all her most important roles, and had had them hand-bound in calf and morocco. "I know you wouldn't want to hang pictures of yourself all around, but I thought you'd like to look at these sometimes."

Julia put the book away quickly. "It is a lovely thought, Laura. To be quite honest, I don't know how often I'll want to look."

"Well, perhaps not you—but your grandchildren. It will be quite a thrill for them to see how beautiful Granny was—is. You'll be just as beautiful when you're eighty. I know it."

"I'm not sure Clive wants more children. We haven't really discussed it. I think I'm rather too old to be starting . . ."

"Go ahead and have them, no matter," Kate said. "Clive will love them once they come. It'll make him feel like a . . . a dashing young man. Good for the ego." She dropped a light kiss on Johnny's head as she spoke.

Kelly thought there was a rather strained gaiety among them that night. They laughed a lot, and talked of just about everything except tomorrow's ceremony—and the state of Brandon, Hoyle. Julia's bags were packed. The bare living room with its mirrored wall and *barre* was only a little barer. The ballet pictures were gone from the wall. "I'll be keeping up my exercises, and Clive has arranged for me to have a *barre* in both the houses. But I won't need the mirrors." From behind the sofa she took out the two pictures of Sergei that had hung on the wall—Sergei in the great, exuberant leap from *Le Corsaire,* the wonderfully intimate one of him in practice clothes wiping his face on a towel as he stood at the *barre*. "Marya, will you keep them, please? I hadn't the heart to throw them out. And you always understood him better than any of us."

A few cardboard boxes stood around on the polished floor. Julia was taking none of the furniture with her. "What would be the sense?" she said. "You can let the flat furnished, Kelly. It only needs a table and a few chairs."

"Well—I hadn't thought about letting it." The idea of a stranger walking up those stairs was distasteful. She would have to keep the glass doors locked; they would lose some of their sense of family. She joked, "Well, perhaps I'll just keep it until Johnny's grown up, and needs it."

"Perhaps Chris could move out of the basement," Laura said.

Chris held up his hand warningly. "Hold it. If things don't improve at Brandon, Hoyle I might not be able to afford the basement. Kelly could have a handsome rent for this place." He smiled. "After all—one of the most exclusive areas of London."

"And smack in the middle of one of the most notorious families. Brave person, whoever took it on."

Julia seemed to shake, and shrink into herself. She twisted the great gem on her finger.

"Stop it! Oh, stop it—all of you! It isn't a joke. Don't you think I'm afraid that even now Clive will telephone and say it's all off. Yes—we're a great family—the Brandons, the Mertons, the Renisdales . . . on and on it goes. Families. But we're an unlucky family. Even now the telephone could ring. I just pray it won't before tomorrow."

The next day Julia Brandon was married to Clive Wallace in a civil ceremony, and afterward they held a reception at the Savoy. Julia's fragile beauty was enhanced by the gown of blue which almost exactly matched her eyes, and the large-brimmed hat of the same color. Cilve Wallace, the silver-hawk, as Kelly always thought of him, looked proprietarial as he stood with Julia to receive the guests; he looked, Kelly thought, as if Julia was some new acquisition.

All the tabloids carried pictures of the couple as they emerged from the registry office. Only one columnist was unkind enough to resurrect the memory of Sergei.

Kelly had received a package by Special Delivery on the morning Julia was married. It contained a Fabergé Easter egg, and a note in careful handwriting which looked as if it had been laboriously composed. *I could not find a clock. Perhaps I destroyed the only one. This should be for Julia, but I know she would not wish to receive anything from me. Please kiss her for me.* Sergei's signature had more of his characteristic dash.

V

At four A.M. of the day after Julia had been married, the telephone rang at Kelly's bedside. "Kelly?—Bill Blake here. I've been trying to get through for a couple of hours."

"Yes, Bill—is it my mother?"

"That's right, Kelly. I'm sorry. It's all over. Nelly didn't see her about this morning, so she went over to the cottage to check. She was sitting quite peacefully in her chair with the reading light still on. She looked as if she'd just fallen asleep. There seemed no sign of pain—as if she'd struggled, or tried to call for help. We've had Dr. Lacy out and he confirms that her heart just gave up. There hadn't been any sign of previous trouble that we knew about—or Lacy knew either. But then you'd never know with Mrs. Anderson. She wasn't one to complain, or ask for help."

"I know—I know that."

"Kelly, I'm sorry, but we'll have to go ahead with the burial. We can't wait for you to get out here. It'll be done properly, you can be sure. We'll see that flowers are sent from you and Laura. We just wondered if there was anyone else we should notify. Was there any family in Australia? She never spoke about her family—either here or back in Northern Ireland."

"There was no one I know of, Bill. No! Wait! There are the McAlpines, the people we lived with when we first arrived in Australia. I don't know if either of them is still alive—but you could try." From memory of the place that was ineradicable, she dictated the address. "As to the rest—yes, please, do go ahead. And thank you, Bill. Now, let me talk to Nelly, will you?"

"She's right here."

Nelly's voice was fainter; she sounded as if she might have been weeping. "Sorry it's come like this, Kelly. But it's so much better than the way poor Mrs. Merton went, isn't it? She seemed to go right down since Mrs. Merton's death—as if there really wasn't anything to go on for. But she kept busy. Every day she used to go into the big house. She'd take one room at a time, and dust and polish just as if someone was living there. All the books have been taken down and dusted—she'd even put some stuff on the leather bindings to preserve them. It's shining like a palace in there—and she'd never let me help her. She used to bring flowers in there, too. Put them in the hall, or the drawing room, or Mrs. Merton's sitting room. The only thing she'd ever let anyone help with was washing the windows. I know it sounds queer, but we let her alone because that's what she wanted. But she must have been lonely. She never was one to come over and have a cuppa and a chat, as you well know . . ."

They talked for some time, mostly about the funeral arrangements. "It'll be nicely done, Kelly. I promise you that. We'll put the coffin in the drawing room of the big house. People are starting to come from the places around . . . just the way they did for Mrs. Merton. People never got to know your mother, Kelly, but they certainly had to respect her."

Bill Blake came back on the line to say good-bye. "Oh, Kelly—I hope you don't mind my saying so at a time like this, but that Gardiner bloke you sent out . . . He's O.K.

Works well—wants to learn everything. A decent bloke, but I don't think we're going to be able to keep him."

"Why not?"

"Well—you remember the Fergus place? It's got a bit run-down because the old man's really not up to it anymore, and there isn't any close family to take an interest in it. Well, Fergus was speaking to me, and saying he thought he might offer Ben a job as a sort of manager. Of course, Ben's inexperienced, but he's dead honest, and Fergus could do a lot worse. I'd help him out if he were stuck and didn't know what to do about something—and then old man Fergus would be watching him all the time. I wouldn't stand in his way, but I'd be sorry to lose him, just the same. It wouldn't be the cushiest job in the world, but it'd be great experience for him to have under his belt. I'd have to advise him to take it. Just thought you'd like to know."

"Thanks, Bill. Thanks for everything . . . you and Nelly . . ."

"Right, Kelly. I'm sorry you're not here—but everything'll be done properly. Nelly'll write you all about it."

She went down to the kitchen and made some tea, resisting the temptation to go and wake Laura, and share the news. But the tea grew cold in her mug untasted as she thought about her mother, Mary Anderson, who would claim no one as a relative, whom no one but she, Kelly, would claim. In Northern Ireland, Mary Anderson had had parents; she may have had brothers and sisters. All that Kelly knew of her mother, Mary Anderson, if that indeed was her true name, was that she once had had a lover, who had been a Catholic, and who had not married her, and that his name had been Kelly.

Later Frank McArthur telephoned from Sydney. "I'm just on my way to Pentland, Kelly. I wanted to be there—sort of to represent you and Laura. But I'd have gone in any case. She was one of the old breed, and they don't come like that anymore . . . Pentland will miss her."

For the first time tears came to Kelly's eyes as she listened to the words—not tears for her mother's death, because Mary Anderson had lived her life, and had had, in the end, little left to live for. The tears were for the woman she, Kelly, had never known, for a relationship missed, passed by, undeveloped. She might have tried harder to know her mother, if Mary Anderson's unyielding nature had ever permitted it.

"Thanks, Frank. I feel rather badly—I feel I could have made a better effort to know her. I neglected her . . ."

"You didn't neglect the Merton family, Kelly. That's what mattered to your mother. They came first. If she was ever the sort of woman who could allow herself to be proud of a child, you made her proud. But then she'd consider pride a sin . . . so I don't see how . . . well, it's all past now. All past . . ."

He went on. "She came down to Sydney just after you and Laura went back to London. Wanted to redraw her will. She'd only had a simple thing drawn up by the local man in Barrendarragh, and she wanted to be sure that this was all straight and right. There wasn't really much. The little house, of course, belongs to Pentland now that she's gone, and the pension John Merton provided for her will go back into the trust now. She had some savings. I take it she didn't spend much on herself. But it was the shares in the vineyards that Mrs. Merton left her that were bothering her. She never wanted them. What she wanted to make sure of was that everything should go back to Laura. The shares, and whatever money came from them—though in these few months she'd had them there wasn't all that much. But the money's untouched. All her personal possessions go to Nelly Blake. I'm sorry, Kelly . . . she doesn't mention you in the will except to say that you are already well provided for. There wasn't even a little keepsake, or anything. . . . Well, she was a strange woman, all right. I'm sure if there was anything you wanted from her things, Nelly would be only too happy . . ."

"No, Frank, thanks. There's nothing. She didn't owe me anything."

It was surprising how much it hurt, that last denial by her mother.

Then came the letter from Nelly. *It was beautiful, you'd be amazed at the people who came . . . the flowers. I'm enclosing a list. A lot of letters have come for you. I'm forwarding them.* At the end of the letter a paragraph had been added on a fresh sheet, as if it were something Nelly had been doubtful about writing. *Kelly, I hope you don't mind that she left me her things. I suppose she thought that over there you wouldn't have need of any of them. But be sure I'll take good care of everything. When I was clearing out I found that all the drawers of the sideboard were stuffed with papers and some scrapbooks. She kept every single thing that had anything to do with you. All the old school reports, the photos, all the press cuttings about your wedding. All about Greg and what you did to help organize the Everest expedition. All the newspaper pieces when you were married to the General. I have a feeling she probably never said a word about all this to you, but it's pretty clear she was very proud of you. No one ever knew what Mrs. Anderson was thinking.*

No, Kelly thought, no one ever knew.

Chapter Thirteen

I

It was as if Julia's fears about the growing notoriety of the Brandons had been realized. Three days after her picture as she had left the registry office as Clive Wallace's wife had appeared in all the tabloids, Kate was there in her place. She was pictured as she left the House of Commons, having been censured by the Parliamentary Party for voting against her own Party and Government. It had been a bill which no one had expected to attract much attention, so only a one-line whip had been called. Kate's vote against the bill defeated it.

"It just wasn't common sense," she said to Kelly. "It concerned a group of docks—the St. Mary Docks in the constituency adjoining mine. The Member has been ill, and he sort of asked me to read up on it, and find out everything about it. Well, I did. It's a privately owned group, doing well—who've gone in heavily for containerization. That makes them very unpopular with the unions, who don't seem to like that sort of efficiency. This was just a nasty little bill the Government hoped to sneak through to nationalize them and bring them in with all the other ports—without anyone paying much attention. A lot of the union action is sheer bloody-mindedness, and some of it, I haven't a doubt, is Communist inspired. All around them this group has seen docks close down because they're hopelessly uneconomic, and then whole areas become derelict. That was the writing on the wall for this one. But the unions seem willing to see even the jobs that have been saved there go rather than back down. It's straight confrontation."

"Kate, I thought you believed in everything being nationalized. I thought that was real Socialism."

Kate sighed. "Kelly, I'm all for what will be right for the most of the people. When common sense tells me something that the Government decides to do just because it happens to suit the unions is wrong, then I don't just abstain, I vote against it. They don't like it. No, I'm not for Socialism for its own sake. I want this to be a just and equible and free society. *Free,* Kelly. I want to be free to vote my own conscience, no matter what. I think they've decided they can do without me."

"Without you? But you've been elected!"

She nodded. "They can't throw me out until the electorate does—or the selection committee refuses to endorse me. But they can do every sort of thing to frustrate me, and make the rest of my time in this Parliament almost completely wasted. They'll see I won't be allowed to introduce any new bills. They could see that I never make a major speech—or I suppose any speech at all unless it's about stray dogs at three o'clock in the morning when everyone else has gone home. And when it does come to the next election, depending on how strong they are—depending on whether or not they need me—they could just withdraw support, and I'd be finished. They could bring pressure on the selection committee. Remember how small my majority was? I couldn't say I got big support in Beckenham. If Labour decided not to put any effort in to help me, I'd be finished."

"Then what are you going to do?"

"I suppose I can do what Father did—I can resign."

"Kate!—but Parliament's your life! What are you going to do to get back in? After all, it was only a fluke that Charles got Tewford. The member died, and there was the by-election."

"You don't have to remind me, Kelly. I know it all by heart—remember I campaigned against Father in that election. But even if I could forget the smallest part of it, Harry Potter is determined I won't."

"What on earth are you talking about?"

They were alone in the kitchen. It was early evening, and Mrs. Nelson had agreed to stay on an extra hour to see to

Johnny being fed and bathed, and Kate had come looking for Kelly. Kelly, who had been making a salad, put down the big chopping knife, drew out a chair, and motioned Kate to take one also. "Sit down. What about Harry Potter?"

"It seems he's been following my career in the House with more than a small amount of interest. He's been to hear me speak a couple of times when I haven't noticed it—which is more than my own constituency agent has done, even though he's only a few miles away, and Harry Potter has to come from the Cotswolds. Well—he's willing to chance his arm. They're hunting a new candidate. Poor Tim Carpenter has had a heart attack. They've kept it very quiet, because they don't like people to know that their member isn't attending the sittings, and isn't looking after constituency business. He's recovering nicely, but he's been told he'll have to give it up. No more of these all-night sittings, and the rest of it. You know, he's a solicitor, and he's got nice, quiet, steady work that doesn't exert any pressure. But he's been hanging on just waiting until Harry Potter and the selection committee come up with the right person. Harry Potter thinks I'm that person."

"Kate!" Kelly was aware that she did little but repeat that name. She shook her head. "But that would mean leaving the Labour Party. That would mean standing as a *Conservative!* You couldn't do that!"

Kate looked grim. "Who says I couldn't! The compromise would be that I would stand as an Independent Conservative. God help me if someone else in Tewford comes along with a better claim, and the committee decides to adopt him or her. I'll have resigned Beckenham, and I'll have nowhere to go. But Harry Potter says he's almost certain. He's been to talk to nearly every member of the committee. Some are cautious. They don't forget that I campaigned for Labour against my own father. Some are dead against it—unless they can be persuaded by the rest of the committee. The fact is that Harry Potter really is a sort of political genius. He can scent things. The Brandon name goes a long way in the constituency. Strangely enough, there's a lot of sympathy for Nick among the die-hard Conservatives. And there's something else that's bothering a lot of them. It's that fringe element that they don't understand. The young ones in the new housing estates. Nobody they've got in mind to replace Tim Carpenter has ever dealt with that before. In fact, there's something serious that's worrying them all, and it's about to burst in the papers. There's been a case of child abuse—consistent child battering that no one seems to have noticed. Or didn't want to report, or thought was none of their business. The poor kid died. And now the whole thing is going to come out in an official enquiry. That sort of thing isn't supposed to happen in a nice, rural constituency like Tewford. None of them know how to deal with it. None of them can think of a candidate for Tim Carpenter's place who would know how to deal with things like that in the future. Harry Potter thinks I can. He remembers that my maiden speech was about a better deal for mentally handicapped children. He remembers that I won Beckenham in spite—but I really think he means because of—Johnny. Suddenly I've changed from being an immoral woman into one who loves children so much that she'd never sacrifice one of her own—for any reason. Certainly not a political reason. So I'm to wait until he's canvassed the whole of the selection committee, and if he can get a majority, then it's 'go.' Tim Carpenter will announce he's retiring, and I will resign Beckenham and stand for Tewford."

"They'll call you a turncoat."

"They'll call me that, and a lot more. Let them call me what they like. I wouldn't be the first by a long shot to have crossed over the aisle of the House. Including such people as Winston Churchill. Don't forget I'd be standing as an Independent Conservative. I'd be free, Kelly. I'd never have to accept the party whip. The gamble is, can I win Tewford? If I can win it once, I think I can win it as many times as there are elections. It won't be the easy win it was for Father—it isn't a cast-iron seat for someone like me. I have to convince the voters that I can do more for them than anyone else. It'll be winning the first time that will count. Harry Potter thinks I can do it."

After a lengthy interview with Kate, the selection committee voted narrowly in favor of adopting her as candidate for Tewford. Some of the committee resigned in protest and declared they would find another candidate to run as an official Conservative. Others, troubled by the changes that were occurring in the constituency, voted for Kate with misgivings. The Conservative Central Office was thrown into an uproar, not certain if they should endorse Kate Brandon or not. She had, the day before, resigned her seat at Beckenham, and Tim Carpenter had announced his retirement. The Labour Party branded her a traitor; the Prime Minister declined to announce immediately the date for the by-elections in both constituencies. The Conservative press, led by the Renisdale papers, welcomed Kate Brandon into the ranks of the Conservatives, and went back into Parliamentary history to name the many prominent members who had switched parties. They then accused the Prime Minister of being afraid to name the date for the two by-elections—that at Beckenham, the seat which Kate had vacated, and might now be retaken by a Conservative, and the Tewford one, which would certainly be won by a Conservative, whether it was Kate as an Independent, or a possible Official Candidate. Angry, and hoping to throw the unprepared party workers in both constituencies into disarray, the Prime Minister named the day which gave all of them the shortest possible campaigning time—three weeks.

"It's on," Kate declared that Wednesday night in Brandon Place. "I'll either make it, or I'll be finished in politics. The Labour Party will never take me back. If I lose, the Conservatives may never want me."

The three weeks of that campaign were nothing like the weeks of Charles Brandon's campaign to win the same seat. Kelly moved down to Mead Cottage with Kate, Marya, Johnny and Mrs. Nelson. The campaign seemed to be run from the kitchen there, not from the drawing room, as it had been at Wychwood. There was no longer Louise's presence to appear to grace it. Laura could come down only on weekends.

"It's very odd at Brandon Place with you all gone. I'd be absolutely alone if it weren't for Chris. Funny how quiet it is—just the Cavanagh offices and the store across the road, and nothing at all happening at night. Funny, I never realized how isolated we are in that street."

She flung herself into the weekend campaigning with a zest that pleased Kelly, though she always campaigned in company with Chris Page. Mrs. Page was as consistent as ever in her support of anything that concerned the Brandons, though Kelly guessed that she did not wholly approve of Kate, nor the fact that she was splitting the Conservative vote in what had once been such a solid seat. The dissident members of the selection committee had put forward their own candidate. Central Office was torn between the two committees, and as the time was so short, and the voters more interested in the candidates than in whether London approved of them or not, the indecision was hardly noticed. The Liberals, knowing the Conservative vote would split, fielded a candidate in the hope of picking up the disenchanted or the undecided. Labour said loudly that whoever voted for Kate Brandon was really voting for Labour, and washed their hands of the whole affair.

The national press got involved to a degree that Tewford had never known before. The Brandons did not seem the impeccable family they had once been. The stories about Brandon, Hoyle were raked through, the separation and impending divorce of Lady Louise Brandon and Peter Brandon was brought into the open, the fact that the Independent Conservative candidate had had a baby without troubling to get married was once again news.

"It's not even three years since this was about the dullest electoral seat in the country—especially when a Brandon ran for it," Peter said. "And now we seem to be a hot-bed of scandal. But Harry Potter's right. There's a feeling among the people that times and conditions are changing quicker than anyone ever supposed, and we can't afford a stick-in-the-mud Member. The case of that little girl who died has really shaken people up. That sort of thing's not supposed to happen in Tewford. Everyone thought that was strictly big-city stuff. But here it is, right on our doorsteps."

Julia did not come to help in the campaigning, but then no one had expected her to; the candidature of Kate Brandon was too controversial for Clive Wallace's wife to be involved in. The honeymoon, which was also a business trip, was extended. "Our fairy princess is slipping away from us," Kate said.

As it came closer to polling day even Harry Potter's optimism began to show signs of wearing thin. The informal polls Kate's supporters were taking through the constituency showed her trailing behind the official candidate. "Never take any notice of polls," he said. "They're never right." But it was not said with great conviction.

"If I lose, I'll probably never get another chance."

"I'm sorry, Kate," Harry Potter said. "You at least had a seat, and might have won Beckenham again." They were sitting in the kitchen with Kelly and Peter late at night, after returning from a meeting. It had been well-attended, but the crowd had not all been sympathetic. From the back of the hall a heckler shouted. "Do we want the Brandons? Haven't we had enough of them?"

Kate shouted back, "What this world needs is *more* Brandons," and had managed to wring a laugh from the audience.

She stirred her tea thoughtfully. "Harry, that isn't the point. Politics is taking chances in the hope of being able to accomplish something. In Beckenham—with the Labour Party—I was getting nowhere. I took my chance when you made it for me. It was always a gamble, and we knew it—"

She broke off as the telephone began to ring. Kelly had had a temporary extension put in the kitchen for the period of the campaign. It rang at all hours, but this call was later than most.

"Yes?" Kelly said. "Yes, Nick. Oh, everything's going well. It's a bit neck and neck, but we're hopeful." She listened for a while as he spoke. "Oh . . . Nick, I'm sorry. Of course you'll come through it. Yes . . . yes, I'll tell Kate . . . and Peter. I'll be back in London immediately after the election. Come and see me, please. Yes, *please,* Nick . . . good night."

She looked at them all. "I don't know . . . but that may be the end of the fight. You may have lost it, Kate. Nick seems to think so, and he doesn't know how to apologize."

"Oh, for God's sake, Kelly, what is it?"

"He was ringing to tell us, before we heard it on the news or saw it in the papers, that he's being charged tomorrow with corruption and conspiracy to defraud. The enquiry into Brandon, Hoyle has brought out enough for the Crown to say there's evidence to warrant a trial, so he's being charged. He'll get bail, of course. The police have already asked for his passport. He says he's sorry, Kate. He tried to hold them off until after the election, but he thinks it was a piece of deliberate timing prompted by a couple of influential Labourites. It's just the worst possible time . . ."

Around the table no one had the energy to refute the statement.

Harry Potter rose. "I'd best be off. Tomorrow's another campaigning day. When you've watched the game as long as I have, you know that some funny things can happen. You *never* give up until the count is in."

"Brave little man, isn't he?" Kate said when he had gone. "I wish I had half his guts."

There was a strange change in the mood of the constituency in the next two days. The papers headlined Nick Brandon's arrest, and his being granted bail. THE FALL OF THE BRANDON EMPIRE one paper labeled it. The Renisdale press played it down. *Nick Brandon is going to be given what he has always asked for—a chance to establish that there has been nothing criminal in his activities.* The local press made much of the story, reporting it in a neutral fashion. The constituents were not neutral. Some people went out of their way to come and shake Kate's hand. "I liked your father—and Nick Brandon's father. They were both good men. And if we had more people with Nick's enterprise, this country wouldn't be going downhill." One woman strode up to Kate in a shopping center on the outskirts of Tewford. "A crying shame, I call it. Real smear tactics. Your father stood out against the bigwigs up there, and you're doing it too. They're out to get you, but I don't think the people here will let them. If they think we're a lot of country yokels to be led around by the nose, they might have a big surprise."

It was that day that Kate's car, which was parked on the edge of the shopping center, was spattered with eggs. Mrs. Nelson was waiting in the car with Johnny, the window partly rolled down. One of the eggs caught Johnny on the side of the face. Instead of crying, he put up his hand, wiped the gooey mess firmly into his hair, and laughed. Kate, who was near the car, and was being followed by a reporter and a cameraman from the local paper, rushed to him and took him up in her arms. He laughed again at the flash of the camera.

The next morning the national dailies had a print of the picture. *The Brandons can take it!* the Renisdale press proclaimed. The local newspaper, however, was more concerned. *Have we come to this?* it demanded. *Shame!*

It was only a few days before polling when Nick rang Mead Cottage again. It was early evening. "Is Kate there?"

"No," Kelly said. "She won't be back until late. There's a meeting over at Barns—"

"Well, listen, get hold of her somehow. Get her to call a press conference. Every local newspaper in the Cotswolds. Get some handbills printed—I'll pay the expenses. I've got an issue for her, and it might just make up for the damage I've done her."

"What is it?"

"I heard a rumor, and I set someone digging. The Ministry for the Environment was holding up the news until after the election. They're about to sign an agreement with NATO to reactivate Everston Air Force Base. And it won't be just an ordinary Air Force Base. They're giving permission to U.S. jet fighters and bombers—ones capable of carrying nuclear missiles—to refuel in the air from tanker planes based at Everston. All this is going to go on over the heads of the Tewford constituency. Tell Kate she's got to challenge the Ministry to deny it. If she gets elected, she's just the sort who could fight it, and possibly stop it. There are thousands of empty acres up in Scotland where they could do the same thing at a fraction of the risk. Try to get her to telephone me. I'll be here all evening, and I have all the details. No one has to know the information came from me. But it's absolutely true, Kelly. I have it on the best authority. I still have a few friends in high places."

Kate managed to hold her news conference two days before the election, and the national papers as well as the local ones picked up the story. From the Ministry came only waffling and dissembling replies, but no clear denial. "Talks are going on" they were finally forced to admit. The concern and anger in Tewford pushed the Nick Brandon story and any further consideration of Kate switching from the Labour to the Conservative Party out of people's minds.

"I lived here during the war," Kate said in her eve-of-the-poll address. "I remember Everston. I remember the bombers taking off from there, and coming back. We were grateful for them—glad to hear them. But they weren't carrying nuclear weapons, and Everston wasn't a fuel dump. Think about it. In Parliament I intend to fight it."

They waited until after midnight for the results to be declared. Kate was in by a majority of only a little over a thousand. There was not, as there had been for Charles, a champagne party at Wychwood. Kate thanked the tired party workers, a modest amount of drink was circulated, and then they returned to Mead Cottage.

"Well, there's really no telling, is there?" Harry Potter said. "It could have been concern about Everston. Or it could have been a genuine backlash against the way the Brandons have been treated in the press. Whatever happened, they swung your way, Kate. You'll have to look after them very well. They'll be expecting it now. Next time it'll be a much bigger majority. We'll go on building and building. If we do the right thing by this electorate, this seat can be what it was for your father—a seat for life. A real power base for you."

II

Kate, Johnny, Marya and Mrs. Nelson went to London early the next morning. Kelly remained to tidy the cottage a little, get linen ready for the laundry, make lists of what had to be replenished. The cottage now had a more worn look than it had possessed before; it had been thoroughly and well used, and looked it.

At twelve she drove to Wychwood. Peter had pressed her to come there to have lunch. "I know—it's cozier at Mead Cottage, but one day you'll be living at Wychwood—that is, if I still own it. People have to get used to the idea. You too. Besides, the place has been awfully lonely and quiet. Just for once, I need to see you again by my fire."

He wasn't there when she arrived. Mrs. Page came to the door. "I'm very sorry, Lady Brandon. Mr. Peter was called away suddenly. There's been some sort of accident at Traynor's farm. I don't think it's serious. He expects to be back for lunch. You know how he likes to see to these things himself. . . . May I give you a drink?"

Kelly took dry sherry, pouring for herself. Mrs. Page had better get used to that, also, she thought.

"Very gratifying that Miss Kate won, wasn't it? How hard she's worked! She's very determined, of course—always was. At times very headstrong—like her father. But I think she'll serve the people here very well. They're lucky to have her . . ."

"Yes . . . lucky. . . ." Why did she find it so hard to talk to Mrs. Page? The woman was hovering, moving about the room in a proprietarial way, adjusting one of a mass of mixed blooms in a vase, touching the fold of a curtain as if it did not already hang perfectly, running her finger across a piece of intricate carving as if seeking for dust. "Seems strange, doesn't it, Lady Brandon, how things have changed? Look—the pictures have gone. Christie's took them. They've advised Mr. Peter to hold them for their big auction next season—June, or thereabouts. That's when all the important buyers come from overseas. Hard to think of this house without those pictures. Constable and Turner—they've always seemed the essence of England to me—as Wychwood is. What's to become of us all, I wonder? With Mr. Nicholas in such trouble, and Mr. Peter determined that he's to be defended at any cost. . . . And Lady Louise gone—" She stopped, as if the subject was too delicate to proceed with.

She moved about the room with what was, for her, almost a restless movement. "Naturally, I don't believe a word of what the papers say about Mr. Nicholas. But it could cost everything to prove him innocent . . ." She touched a silver-framed photo of Peter and Nick with their mother when they had been young children. "I never knew her. I came long after she died. They did tell you about that, didn't they? How Elizabeth Brandon got me this position after my husband died. She and I were great friends . . . in India. As Sir Charles and my husband were great friends. . . . It was only because of Elizabeth that Mr. Peter's father gave me a trial as housekeeper. I'd had no experience. How could I? And I was very young. But Christopher and I needed the money, you see. We needed money and a home. Just so lately come to England . . . knowing no one but the Brandons . . ."

"They have been very fortunate to have you, Mrs. Page . . ." Kelly was uncomfortable as the woman continued to move about the room, fractionally repositioning a china ornament, plumping up a cushion which didn't require it. Once again Kelly marveled at the grace with which she moved. Beauty was in every movement, the turn of her head, the length of neck. The smooth black hair was liberally streaked with silver, but still gave the impression of infinite darkness and shifting light; her hands were long and graceful as she touched things. Kelly was reminded of what Nick had said of her. "Our beautiful black swan." What a long time ago it seemed, that time when she had first come to Wychwood, a time when she and Charles had been happy together, when Nick had been riding the peak of his success, Julia and Sergei a partnership of love and dance, Laura seemingly poised at the beginning of a flowering, Kate with all before her, and the child, Johnny, unthought of. Before she, Kelly, had done more than touched Peter's hand.

Mrs. Page's smooth, silken voice went on, a monologue. "Yes, I wonder what is to become of us all, Lady Brandon. What will become of my Christopher, I wonder? He's given even more to the Brandons than I have. A young man's life—and loyalty. The Brandons have had everything from us both. All we could give—"

"Everyone is most grateful, Mrs. Page. They never stop saying that they couldn't—"

"Grateful!" Suddenly that floating, gliding figure stopped. "What do *you* know of it? You came from nowhere! A nobody! You earned nothing. It was given to you. Handed to you on a plate. From one husband to another. Why do you think *he* married you—Charles? Because of what you could give him! He didn't see where justice lay, but what best served him. All his life he's done that. Taken what he wanted, when it suited him. I *knew* him. Like all the Brandons, he was one great mass of deceit and lies. And now my Christopher is dragged into the mud with them. My beautiful son . . ."

Kelly had only one more look at the agonized, contorted face before Mrs. Page turned. She heard the rapid movement of her feet over the rugs and polished boards. But the last gesture was characteristic of the woman that they thought they had all known. The door was closed softly.

Kelly wrote a note for Peter. *Sorry, love. Couldn't wait. Telephone me tonight.*

On the car radio she tuned to the Third Programme, hoping for some of the Schubert or Beethoven she and Peter listened to together. There was a break in the midday concert. Someone was giving a talk on the habits of the Black Widow spider.

When she reached Brandon Place Mrs. Nelson was waiting in the kitchen with Johnny. "Miss Kate had to go to the Conservative Central Office, m'lady. Quite a change for her, isn't it, going there instead of the Labour place. I was wondering, m'lady, if I could leave Johnny with you now—that is, if you're free to look after him until Miss Kate gets back? I've been away from home so long now—and there's shopping and all to do on the way. George's pleased as punch about Miss Kate—he's voted Conservative all his life—but he's getting a bit browned off eating boiled eggs. Men are funny, aren't they, m'lady? Twenty-seven years he's watched me in the kitchen, and all he can do is make a cup of tea, boil an egg, and burn the sausages. We got one of those pop-up toasters, and would you believe it, he still burns the toast! He brought me breakfast in bed on my last birthday because it was Sunday. I couldn't eat a mouthful of it."

She looked and sounded absurdly like her sister, Mrs. Cass, as she stood putting on her coat and hat, taking her shopping basket. Kelly watched as she kissed Johnny with a naturally affectionate gesture; there was so much good in these two women that they helped to ease the memory of that sudden revelation of the dark side of Mrs. Page. Kelly had almost begun to wonder if she had imagined those strange, twisted words, that shocking accusation against Charles, the hysteria and hate evidenced as the smooth facade had shattered. There was no knowing what degree of fear for the future of her son had prompted that outburst—whether those thoughts had lain festering all the years she had been at Wychwood and had erupted only because she saw Chris's career threatened. The sheer normality of Mrs. Nelson's chatter was a blessed antidote.

"Oh, m'lady—Mr. Nicholas Brandon telephoned. He said was it all right if he came round about six o'clock. He said to telephone his flat if it wasn't convenient." She looked around the kitchen, which now seemed as much her domain as her sister's. "Well, that's everything, I think. I've left Johnny's supper ready. It just has to be warmed up. I gave him his bath early so Miss Kate wouldn't have to do it when she got back. Be a good boy, Johnny. I'll see you tomorrow." Then she looked at Kelly. "I expect Miss Kate will be wanting to make some different arrangements now, seeing as how she'll have to go down to Tewford pretty regularly. I could work all day Saturdays instead of half day. Or I could sleep here one night a week and let her get away. Always difficult, isn't it, m'lady, when a mother has to work. But that sort of work is life to Miss Kate. You couldn't imagine her not doing it. . . ."

Nick came early. He came by taxi instead of his chauffeured car. "One of the little things that had to go." He looked almost cheerful. "Had a cable from New York this morning. They've sold my Pollock and the Hans Hoffmann. Got a pretty good price. Should keep the lawyers happy for a bit. I can't let Peter go ahead with this crazy scheme of selling off the Wychwood pictures. Or any part of Wychwood. What does he think I've been working for all these years?" He dropped a light kiss on Johnny's forehead. "How are you, old man? I see your mother's been up to her old tricks. Winning elections could become a habit."

To his obvious delight Johnny said, "Nick!" quite distinctly, and banged on the table of his high chair.

"Well don't break it, old boy. No—you can't get down. Can't you see Kelly's got supper for you?"

Kelly seated herself beside Johnny and nodded to the bottles set out on the counter. "Help yourself, Nick. Was there something special you wanted to see me about?"

He looked at his son, choosing his words carefully. "Oh, no. Just a social call. Haven't seen any of you lately." He went and poured himself a Scotch and came back and stood leaning against the counter, watching as Kelly fed Johnny, who ate hungrily. "That's right, old man, eat it up. You need to be tough and strong to survive in this world." Kelly realized that Nick had become cautious of what he said in front of his son. He strictly abided by the agreement that only Kate should have the right to tell Johnny, if she chose to do so, who his father was. He was determined that no chance word of his before the child would break this agreement.

Kelly wondered what pretext he would make to see Johnny as the baby grew older.

"Sorry about the Brandon, Hoyle thing blowing up in the middle of the campaign. I couldn't stop it. But it seemed that the Everston information helped. Hope it did, anyway."

"Kate and Harry Potter are sure of it. What matters is that she's in. The next time won't be so difficult."

"The next time the Brandon, Hoyle thing will be settled—one way or another. I'll either be clear of it all, or I'll be in jail."

"Nick, please—don't joke."

"Wish I were joking, Kelly. But it'll depend on how the jury looks at the whole business. There were some things that were done not strictly by the books. And yes—there were presents—well, let's use the less pretty word—there were bribes. But it's a terribly long and complicated business, and they're going to have to go into half a dozen countries and get extradition orders agreed to before any of us will stand in the dock. I'm going to fight, Kelly . . . I'll do my damndest. You know, I don't fancy jail."

"It doesn't seem your sort of place." Kate had come across from Number 15. "How are you, Nick? Or need I ask?"

"Have a drink," he said by way of an answer. "Scotch? How did it go with the dear old Conservatives?"

"They're still in a state of shock at finding me in their ranks. And not at all sure of me—in that I'm an Independent. They can hardly lecture me about Party loyalty, and all that, because I wasn't elected on their platform. Thanks for your help, Nick. And the contributions. I don't think you should have sent so much, though. Brandon, Hoyle can hardly be flush with money these days."

"You let me worry about that, Kate."

She took her drink from him and pulled out a chair. Quietly she lighted a cigarette, and savored it. "Nick?"

"Yes?"

"Remember that marriage offer you made? You said it was good at any time. Well, I've decided to take you up on it. What do you say?"

Nick deliberately turned and went to the sink and added some more water to his drink. "Thanks, Kate. I appreciate it. All your impulsive, altruistic nature coming out again. Anything to help a lame duck, eh? Sorry, Kate, the offer's withdrawn. You've got your young man there to think of."

Abruptly he tossed the remainder of his drink into the sink. "Thanks, Kelly. I'll be off now. You won't mind if I drop in again sometime?" He paused in the doorway. "Thanks, Kate. You're a sweet, generous fool, you know."

They heard the door bang, and his shouting in Brandon Place for a taxi.

When Peter telephoned that evening Kelly made excuses about her abrupt departure. She seemed unable to find the words to tell him about Mrs. Page's utterances. Even set at the distance of a few hours they seemed bizarre—unthinkable. She tried to dismiss them as the overwrought reaction of a woman who believed that her whole life and her son's future were threatened. "I'll be with you soon . . . soon. Next weekend. I've neglected Tower Hamlets again, and all the other things . . ."

"One day you'll have to give them all up. You'll be with me. I want you full time, Kelly."

She lay and thought about life when she would be married to Peter. And over and over again she heard Mrs. Page's words. "What's to become of us all, I wonder? . . ."

Chapter Fourteen

I

The autumn weather which had held fair all through the campaign seemed to advance with dramatic suddenness into a too-early winter. With the election safely over, and Kate Brandon appearing to have achieved a degree of respectability with it, Clive Wallace seemed to judge it safe to bring Julia back to England. When Julia telephoned, Kelly at once asked them both to dinner at Brandon Place. Tomorrow's Wednesday—remember?" She heard a little intake of breath on the telephone, the hesitation before Julia attempted a reply.

"Eh . . . well, I'll have to ask Clive, Kelly. There's so much been piling up while we've been away . . ."

"Oh, darling Julia, don't worry. We'll all be on our best behavior. We'll eat in the dining room, and it'll all be very correct."

Julia sighed. "Does Clive really seem as stuffy as that? I'm dying for one of your Wednesday nights in the kitchen, but let's ease him into it gradually, shall we?"

"We've missed you, Julia. We really have. It hasn't been like the times when you were on tour. I'm awfully conscious of the flat being empty. You know—I've kept forgetting until now that you and Kate are twins, because you're so unalike.

But I think she's missed you too. In a special sort of way. Despite all the rush of the campaign. Well, try to persuade Clive to come, will you?"

"Unless he's got dinner with the Prime Minister, which I doubt, Clive being a die-hard Tory, we'll be there. By the way, he's really pleased about Kate's switch. He says the Party needs new young blood like her. But who would have thought she could make the switch and get away with it?"

"As always, Kate's deadly honest about whatever she does, and people know it. I don't know that it bodes well for her political future that she doesn't seem able to lie. But it's nice for us."

Julia and Clive came the next night. Drinks were served in the drawing room at seven thirty; dinner was in the dining room at eight o'clock. Everyone was there in their best clothes and most formal manners. Mrs. Cass was staying to help in the kitchen, and Mrs. Nelson was taking care of Johnny. "I really don't think Mr. Clive Wallace is quite ready for Johnny in his high chair yet. I'm sure his own two children were perfect models of behavior," Kate said. She sounded slightly waspish, but she had put on her favorite red dress, and warned them that she had to leave early to go back to the House of Commons. *"That* might impress Mr. Clive Wallace." Marya took only one shot of vodka, and looked vaguely unhappy, until Laura prevailed on her to have another; then she relaxed and began to tell some unprintable stories about the publishing business. She was wearing more beads and bracelets than Kelly ever remembered. Laura had appeared in a new dress of brilliant green velvet; her hair seemed more golden than ever before, and Kelly wondered if she had had it tinted. It swung heavily over her cheek. Chris Page had had to be invited—it was both at Laura's insistence, and because of the need to have another man present. Chris had dressed for the occasion in a dark suit, and Kelly had to admit to herself, once again, that he was more handsome and graceful than most men she had ever seen.

Julia was suntanned and smiling; she had gained a little weight, which only made her more beautiful. She looked rested and her eyes were brilliant. She wore a pendant of a single large emerald set in diamonds; her pale chiffon dress made her seem to float as she moved.

"Oh, darlings!—it's so nice to be home," she said as she embraced them. "It's so nice to be with the family."

Looking around the oddly assorted group, Clive Wallace seemed to reserve his judgment as to the matter of family, but he clearly was eager to be pleasant and to please Julia. Kelly noticed that his gaze rested often on Julia with an undisguised fondness, almost a tenderness, as if she were some lovely child who had given him her trust, someone to be shielded and protected. Kelly began to have hopes that Julia would indeed achieve that safe world she had declared she needed, and in time the ghost of Sergei would be no more than that—a ghost.

The dinner went well, the wines were good, the talk flowed easily. Laura told Clive Wallace the story of the petit-point tapestry seats on the dining chairs, and leading from that, some of the story of Pentland and Kelly and Greg. He must already have known the outlines of that story, but he listened attentively. It was one of the times when Laura, out of her need to help and contribute, broke out of her shyness, and her story-telling took on the quality of fascination—the story of John and Delia Merton, of Everest, the story, so far as she knew it, of Mary Anderson. "Well, Laura—if I may call you that—it's a remarkable family. You have great things to live up to."

Afterward Julia went upstairs with Kelly. She put her arms around her. "Kelly, it was wonderful what you did tonight. Laura was magnificent, wasn't she? Clive liked her—I could see that. He'll relax a bit more in time. He really does have a tremendous admiration for people who fight and endure. I could see he liked the story of your mother best of all."

"Julia—how is it with you? With you both?"

Julia turned away to look in the mirror, and then applied powder to her chin. "He's kind, Kelly. He's so very kind—and patient. I . . . I have a lot to learn."

II

For the first time, as the autumn advanced to the winter, Kelly became seriously worried about Laura. The break with Alex Gardiner appeared to have been more than the loss of someone she believed she loved; it brought a change in her behavior. After the first weeks when she had studied furiously, she seemed to cast aside the discipline of the books. More and more she was out at night, and very often in Chris's company. When Kelly saw her, her conversation was nearly always about the theater or a concert they had attended together. On the nights she was at home, Chris almost always had dinner with her in her flat. She was hardly ever available to baby-sit for Kate, and the task fell on Marya and Kelly.

"I'm pretty sure she's not attending all the lectures she should," Kelly said to Marya. "I often see her leaving as late as midday to get to the University. And she's out so often I wonder when she gets any work done."

Marya drew deeply on her cigarette. "One might have expected it. She has been in love, and now she feels betrayed. All her life she appears to have done the right thing—worked hard, was respectful of the attitudes of those who advised her, been the traditional good little girl. And it has not brought her the one thing she wanted—which appears to have been Alex Gardiner's love. That we all think he was not good enough for her is beside the point. She fell in love with him, and he did not fall in love with her. So now she is, as they say, kicking over the traces."

"I wish it weren't with Chris."

Marya shrugged. "With Chris perhaps she feels safe—not exposed, not vulnerable to being hurt again. She's used to having him around. He's the faithful family friend. And he is, after all, a very handsome and quite charming man. We must not forget, Kelly, that you and I do not look at Chris with the eyes of a young woman who believes that she is unattractive because her face is not perfect. We would not be flattered and reassured by his interest, as she is. She is an intelligent, sensitive, but flawed young woman—who also happens to have money. It is, I think at times, a highly dangerous combination. But give her time. Her good sense will reassert itself. To be wounded in love is part of living. It had to come to her, at one time or another, in one way or another. No more than Julia is she the fairy princess who must, in the end, get her prince."

Kelly listened to Marya, and managed to keep silent with Laura. Marya was right. It would be only a few months of a fling. A sense of balance would be restored; the pendulum would swing back.

Nevertheless she was surprised when Laura took Chris down to Charleton for a weekend. It was the first time Laura had ever done such a thing. It should have pleased her grandmother, but apparently it did not.

"Granny's a terrible old snob," Laura had burst out on the night she returned. "She was barely civil to Chris. I suppose it's because he's the son of the housekeeper at Wychwood. Because his mother is Anglo-Indian. What prejudices come out when people are really put to the test! Of course she hasn't forgiven me for turning down Alex. She doesn't know how kind Chris is . . . how thoughtful. Look how he's stuck by Nick. They've only got a skeleton staff left now, on very little pay, but he hasn't gone looking for work anywhere else. There's so much preparation to be done for the trial. The Queen's Council Nick has engaged doesn't seem to know much about finance—at least not on the scale Nick's been operating. It's people like Chris who have to instruct him. Nick isn't giving it half the time he should—he's letting things slide, and enjoying himself as if he were certain he was going to jail in any case, and was determined to have every last moment of pleasure. He's still running up huge expense accounts, Chris says, even though he's supposed to be broke. And taking a lot of women out. He's even got a car and chauffeur again. It's all mad!"

"And how is Chris managing for money, I wonder? He takes you out a lot."

Laura flushed. "I pay my own way. No, I *don't* pay for him. He's too proud for that. But why shouldn't I pay for my own concert ticket? Pay my share of the dinner? Women are supposed to be getting liberated, aren't they? That's all part of it. After all, I'm not spending someone else's money."

"No one suggested that."

"Well then, don't look at me the way Granny does. I thought you were my friend."

Kelly's mouth fell open. "Laura, you and I can't be quarreling, can we? Not about Chris! Not after all this time!"

Laura sighed. "Sorry. It's just that Granny made me so angry—and ashamed. She doesn't realize how things have changed. Chris could get a marvelous job in the City with another firm. A lot of the others who worked with Brandon, Hoyle have. It's considered quite a plus to have had experience with them. Just because Chris chooses to be loyal . . ."

"Chris is everything you say, Laura. Kind and thoughtful and loyal. And it's wonderful that you have such a friend." What she wanted to say, but did not dare, was, "I hope he isn't also a lover."

"The only hope of helping Laura through this time," Kelly said to Marya, "is not to drive her away."

III

A cold December sleet rattled against the windows as Kelly prepared for bed; the Third Programme, with a recording of the Mahler Fifth, had just closed down as she sank back against the pillows. It had been an exhausting and in many ways, a frustrating day. She had searched the stores in the morning for Christmas gifts and found nothing she thought unusual; that afternoon she had spent four hours at the Tower Hamlets Center, and found Martin Wyatt gloomy about a more than usual shortage of funds, and pessimistic about falling attendance. Nick had come at six, and even the sight of Johnny had failed to cheer him. "They're saying that with or without the extradition requests being granted they're going to fix the trial for March. They seem so sure of a conviction that I think they've come up with something I don't know about. God knows, there's plenty of evidence spread around the world. They seem to be putting the pieces together pretty well. Of course, if there's a conviction, I'll appeal—that is, if I'm allowed to. The trial's going to take a hell of a long time . . ." He had drunk his Scotch and chain-smoked. Kelly felt tired, and for the first time she could remember, she had the distinct feeling of being old. Was this what age was, she wondered?—the sense of energy draining away, of hope diminishing, of horizons narrowing. In the darkness she closed her eyes, the Mahler music still with her, and drifted toward sleep . . . she was coming close to forty.

Below, the doorbell rang with a jarring shrillness—rang and rang again. Almost at once, before she even had the bed-side lamp switched on, she heard running footsteps on the stairs and Laura's voice. "Kelly . . . Kelly . . . come quickly. Quickly!"

She flung on her dressing gown and raced down the stairs. Laura had not waited for an answer to her call. When Kelly reached the hall the doors to Number 15 were open, and the lights on. A wave of cold air greeted her as she went through. The hall door stood wide open. The door to Laura's flat was also open, and she heard the urgent tone as Laura spoke on the phone. "Ambulance, please. An accident at Number 15 Brandon Place, South West One. Yes—behind Cavanagh's. Someone's been run down. Please hurry."

For a moment Kelly paused on the doorstep of Number 15, sleet striking into her face and momentarily blinding her. But there was a terrible familiarity about the two figures out there, one lying in the gutter, the other hunched over it. Laura came running out, her arms piled with blankets.

"Kelly—it's Marya. She's been run down! We heard a car, and then she called out. It didn't stop. It speeded up like mad."

Chris looked at Kelly when she approached. "She's—I think it's bad."

Kelly bent over the fallen figure. Marya was wearing a raincoat and the scarf she had on her head did not disclose the extent of her injuries. Not until Laura opened the door of Number 16 and put on the lights there, and brought a torch from her flat, did they see the blood seeping through the scarf and soaking the collar of the raincoat. They piled the blankets about the still figure, but the melting sleet ran as water in the gutter, and the water was stained with blood. Kelly felt for a pulse and found it feeble. "My God—no, Chris, don't try to move her. It's better to leave her in the water than move her. Don't touch her head . . . oh, my God," she breathed again.

"Shall I bring brandy, or anything . . . ?"

"Nothing. She should have nothing. At any rate, she's not conscious." But as she said it, Marya's eyelids fluttered. Her lips framed something, but although Kelly knelt beside her, her ear almost against Marya's lips, she heard nothing. The pulse fluttered.

Kelly felt something wrapped around her shoulders. "Here's a raincoat. They shouldn't be long. It's five minutes since I telephoned." Kate had joined them. Kelly looked helplessly along the length of the deserted Brandon Place. Across the road, the lighted festive windows of Cavanagh's seemed garishly unreal. There seemed to be no one in the world except themselves and the still figure lying in the gutter. It seemed to be an hour in the cold sleet before they heard the siren, and then saw the flashing blue light of the ambulance. It was, she learned later, only a few minutes.

One of the ambulance men examined Marya briefly. "Hit her head on the curb, looks like. Right—we're going to St. George's. Car knocked her down, did it? Have to notify the police." As he spoke the two men were lifting Marya carefully onto the stretcher. She was now covered with their own red blankets. Laura's, wet with sleet, and one end soaked with blood, lay discarded in the road. "Any of you know her?"

"Yes—all of us. She's . . . she lives here."

"Well, one of you can come. Only one. You others—you wait here for the police."

Laura thrust Kelly forward. She found herself in the ambulance. The vehicle started gently, but then moved quickly, the siren screeching. Kelly leaned across and under the blanket sought Marya's hand. They turned, against the light, into Brompton Road, and then when they reached Wilton Place, they cut across the traffic to avoid having to go around Hyde Park Corner. The Emergency entrance of the hospital was within sight when Marya's lids fluttered open. Her gaze moved about, as if she were puzzled; then she seemed to recognize Kelly. Again the lips moved, and Kelly bent to listen. At first she could make no sense of it. Astonishingly then, the broad smile that Marya used when she joked, seemed to flash across the shockingly gray face. "Don't worry . . ." The words were so faint they were almost not there. "It's hard to kill a heroine of the Socialist Soviet Republics . . . don't worry . . ."

"Don't let her talk," the man commanded.

"I've never been able to stop her," Kelly answered.

The ambulance drew up to the casualty doors, and the two men carried the stretcher in. Kelly followed. A nurse came hurrying. "Bad. Get a doctor." They lifted Marya onto a trolley. There were a number of other people waiting attention. Another nurse approached with a blood pressure cuff. The yellow woolen scarf was almost completely red. The ambulance men, their job done, moved off.

A young doctor came along. He took no notice of Kelly, bent over Marya, felt for a pulse. The nurse was cutting away the scarf and a great deal of Marya's thick hair. The extent of the skull wound became visible, a deep gash which showed shattered bone; but the blood had ceased to flow. Marya had not moved since they had placed her on the trolley. The doctor rolled back the slack eyelids, then set the stethoscope on her chest which the nurse had uncovered. He listened, moved the stethoscope, listened again. Then he took the stethoscope away. For the first time he looked at Kelly.

"You a relative?"

"A friend.

"I'm sorry. She's gone." He began to fill out the D.O.A. form. *Dead On Arrival.*

Kelly waited while they completed more forms, asked questions. Name. She spelled it carefully for the nurse. Address. Age. How old was Marya? How old had she been when she stowed away on the aircraft that had taken her from Yalta? The aircraft whose senior officer had been Charles? Nationality. What nationality was Marya? Had she ever become a British subject? Kelly didn't know, but she gave answers. How little, in the end, she had known Marya.

She herself signed a release for an autopsy, since she was unable to say that Marya had any close relative in England. Later she stood at Hyde Park Corner with the raincoat held around her dressing gown, waiting for a taxi to come. Her body shook with cold and shock. She hadn't thought to telephone Brandon Place, had just walked out of the hospital when she had given the answers to all the questions they had asked. A nurse had tried to call her back, and called out something about a cup of tea, but she had gone. Now she stood in her sodden slippers; the sleet had stopped. She put her hand to her wet face and realized she was weeping.

The police had already left Brandon Place when she got back. Laura paid off the taxi. She led Kelly upstairs and made her get into a hot bath. The blood-stained gown and raincoat were taken away. Later she went downstairs. Laura and Chris and Kate were in the kitchen. Kate poured hot tea and brandy. "I've been in touch with the hospital. And a funeral director. I told the funeral people that she'd be buried at Wychwood."

The police came again about ten o'clock in the morning. Mrs. Cass, her eyes swollen and red, showed them into the dining room, and called Kelly and Laura and Chris. The Inspector went over the notes that had been taken the night before, and took a statement from Kelly; she had heard nothing before Laura had rung the doorbell to summon her. Laura and Chris repeated their statements. They had been together in Laura's front room. It was close to midnight, and they were putting away gramophone records. Both had heard the sound of a car being driven very fast, and accelerating violently after a single cry from a woman. They had pulled back the curtains and, by the light of the street lamps, and from Cavanagh's windows, had seen the woman lying in the gutter. By the time they had reached her, the car had vanished into Brompton Road.

"There was no one else about?"

Chris shook his head. "There seldom is. The whole of this side of the road is Cavanagh's offices. There's never anyone in them late at night. A few cars use the road as a short cut. Not many. You can get caught by the light at the end, and so you don't save any time."

"We'll talk to the night watchmen at Cavanagh's. Someone may have heard something. Was it Madame . . ." He stumbled over Marya's name. "Was it her practice to return about that time at night?"

"Most nights she was at home—working," Kelly said. "But she came and went as she pleased. We didn't ask where. She had some friends in publishing . . . there were a few contacts with the Foreign Office. I don't know who exactly . . ."

There were other questions, and finally the man put away his notebook and left.

They all went into the kitchen and had a cup of coffee with Mrs. Cass. "It was deliberate," Chris said, his face cold and strained. "I tried to suggest that last night, but they weren't buying it. Or didn't seem to be. There were no cars parked outside here, or on the other side of the road, so she couldn't have stepped out right in front of whoever it was. He was driving at a terrific speed—Laura and I looked at each other, because it's so unusual to hear a car going at that rate. And he accelerated like mad. It was deliberate."

"He must have been drunk," Mrs. Cass offered.

"Could have been, but I don't believe it. There wasn't any sound of braking—a drunk would have done that just instinctively, even if he decided then to speed up and get out of it. It was all too—too smooth."

"But you're saying Marya was *murdered!*" Kelly cried incredulously. "Why? Why should anyone want to kill her?"

Chris looked at her directly. "Do you *know* anything about Marya, Kelly? Have you any idea who she really is? I mean—not just her name, but what her background is. What did she do beside translating? Who were her friends? We don't know, do we? We really don't know anything about her."

"Why," Mrs. Cass cried indignantly. "Why, I've known Madame Marya since . . . well, since the first Lady Brandon came back from the country after the war. She's always lived here—except for that little time when she was married to that Russian chap. That didn't last long. He went off to America . . . or somewhere. Of course we know who she was. She was Madame Marya. She took charge of the place—a sort of housekeeper and a nurse for Lady Brandon. She practically brought up the girls. *Of course* we know who she was! Whatever are you suggesting? Murdered? It was a terrible accident, and I hope they give a big jail sentence to whoever did it. But deliberately? Why, that's a terrible thing to say, Mr. Chris. I'm surprised at you. No wonder the police didn't pay any attention to it . . ."

She collected the coffee mugs, and banged them into the sink. Around the table, no one said anything.

When Marya's body was released after the autopsy, which found the cause of death to be a massive injury to the skull, she was taken to be buried among the generations of Brandons who lay in the graveyard of the little church at Wychwood. Flowers were sent; some friends from her publishing life came down from London. Condolences were offered to Kelly and Julia and Kate. They were standing in for a family none of them knew. A few people stood in the graveyard who did not come forward to identify themselves, and who slipped away quietly afterward. It was always that way at funerals. Kelly thought. People who appear momentarily, and then go, not wanting to intrude. She could see nothing to suggest Chris's sinister strangers.

Julia had come down from London in her husband's chauffeured car; she was returning immediately after the burial. She clasped Kate under the lych gate. Kelly watched them, and was amazed again to remember that they were twins. The dark and the fair heads were close together. "I can't believe it, Kate," Julia whispered. "It seems she's been with us forever. What will it be like without Marya? I can't imagine what the house will be like without Marya." She entered the car and drove off. Nick took Kate's arm and started on the short walk to Wychwood. Peter fell in with Kelly. They were trailed by Laura, Chris, Mrs. Page and Mrs. Cass. Everyone who had appeared at the church and graveside was invited back to Wychwood. A straggling little procession formed.

The inquest brought in a verdict of manslaughter. The police could offer no clue as to the identity of the person responsible. It was over very quickly.

Kelly had patiently, in the days before the inquest, been through all of Marya's possessions, after the police had made their own examination. She had no idea whether they put any credence in Chris's idea that Marya's death had been a deliberate act. The police had more information than she had had to offer that night at the hospital. The Home Office contained a file on Marya, started at the time she had stepped off that plane which had carried her from Yalta. Kelly now knew Marya's age—fifty-four. She had become a British subject. And that was all she knew. In all the mass of books and papers in Marya's flat, there was nothing to tell her more than that. There was no single name or address of anyone in Russia. There were no letters beyond the business ones she wrote to publishing houses. The only names listed in her telephone book were from the same sources. A woman who spoke perfect English, had some medical training, and was a heroine of the siege of Stalingrad; if the Home Office file contained anything more, the people there were not revealing it. The books and papers and magazines, the wardrobe of flamboyant clothes, the many necklaces and bracelets, the vodka and the dark, evil-smelling cigarettes—there seemed to be nothing else to discover about Marya, nothing left behind to tell them more. Kelly now knew hardly more than she ever had done, except that she had come to care deeply about this woman who seemed to have no past.

She descended the stairs from the flat. Sometime later she would clear it all out. A simple will, made years ago, had left all Marya's possessions to Julia and Kate. But as she passed the flat Julia had occupied, she realized that there was one more empty space at Number 15 Brandon Place.

They abandoned plans for Christmas at Brandon Place. The sight of Cavanagh's festive windows across the street had become sickening. They went to Mead Cottage, and for Johnny's sake, Peter put up a Christmas tree, and they trimmed it. Instead of lavish presents they had given in other years, they bought inconsequential things locally—soap and cologne, diaries, kitchen scissors, candlesticks from a local potter. The day they left London a huge hamper and a case of champagne had arrived from Julia and Clive. *Darlings,* the note read, *I know you don't feel like doing anything festive. You can pick away at these instead. All my love. Julia.* They unpacked it all at Mead Cottage, the smoked salmon, pâté de foie gras, caviar, potted shrimp, smoked oysters, turtle soup, many different cheeses. In the middle of it Laura suddenly turned to them, her face streaming with tears. "It's no good, is it? Think of the joke Marya would have made of it all. She would have had us all laughing. And where's the vodka? I even miss the smell of those foul cigarettes."

They made a show of unwrapping presents on Christmas morning for the pleasure of watching Johnny unwrapping his. Peter, Tommy and Andrew, and unexpectedly, Nick had appeared. They all brought simple presents, and received them. For his son, Nick brought only a large white rabbit. "There, old man. His name's Harvey. Don't pull his eyes out too soon." He took Johnny for a walk down the lane, leaning down to catch the small trusting hand, before they all went over to Wychwood for Christmas dinner.

Because Laura had insisted on having Chris there with them, Mrs. Page had had to accept the invitation also. "Well, everything has changed, hasn't it?" she said to no one in particular as she cautiously sipped a half glass of champagne. A Christmas tree stood in the Hall, the table was dressed with holly from Wychwood's lanes. Peter directed Mrs. Page to the chair Louise would have occupied. Johnny's high chair had been brought over. No one attempted to interfere as Nick placed himself beside it, cut up Johnny's food, and tried to stop him throwing most of it around the long table. "It isn't that he's not hungry," Nick explained, "he just wants to see how far he can throw." He neglected his own food to see that Johnny got some himself. "That's right, old man. Makes you strong for throwing things in people's eyes. A useful skill, that."

Chapter Fifteen

I

By February the winter began to seem endless. It was impossible to step out into the rain-washed street in Brandon Place without remembering Marya. Her comings and goings had always seemed unobtrusive, but her presence now was missed. They missed the sound of that rather harsh laughter, the jangling bracelets. Her absence from the kitchen table on Wednesday nights was a larger absence than any of them expected. There was no one to make jokes about her own vodka-drinking habit, to offer the occasional extravagance in the form of caviar. The group seemed diminished by more than the sum of just one person.

The winter was made more dreary by the fact that Humphrey Watson of the *Journal* had come up for trial on Nick's charge of libel. Little could be said at the trial, because so much of the evidence involved matters that would be brought up at Nick's own trial, and could not be discussed for fear of prejudicing a future jury. But Humphrey Watson continued to refuse to name the source or sources of the information which had started the whole investigation of Brandon, Hoyle and its slide into insolvency. He was acquitted of the charge of libel, but for refusing to divulge his source when ordered to do so by the judge, he was found guilty of contempt of court, and sentenced to one month in prison. His newspaper, which was paying his costs, immediately appealed, so he was still free.

"It was pretty stupid of me to bring that libel action," Nick admitted. "I felt the threat of it would shut the man up, but of course it didn't. Now this sentence has turned the rest of the press against me. And if Watson does go to jail, it makes him a martyr and me a bigger villain than ever before. I must be losing my touch. I clamped absolute security on everything in the office as soon as Watson started those stories, but whoever leaked information must have already handed over everything that was needed." He shrugged. "And once the hunt was on, all the overseas deals came out. I couldn't be sure of absolute security anywhere. For all I know, Watson may have got his information from one of the overseas offices in the first place. Those people know almost as much of the overall picture as we do, and it just needs some determined digging, and a little bribe money. And there are people who dislike me enough to shell out to see me lose my head . . ."

Nick came more and more often to Brandon Place, and more and more Kelly found herself giving him dinner. At first he had insisted on taking her to restaurants, but they both found the experience uncomfortable; too many heads turned, and too many eyes refused to meet Nick's. "Even my coterie of dolly birds is slipping away," he confessed ruefully. "They don't like the smell of impending doom. It doesn't do their social life any good to be seen with me . . ."

"Nick, will you shut up about doom," Kate said crossly. "You've got yourself convicted before there's even a trial."

He could have been a little drunk. He drank more these days than he used to. He looked at her levelly. "Sweet Kate, you don't know as much as I do."

The trial was only a few weeks off.

Every weekend Kelly went down to Mead Cottage; the time there was the solace of the dark days of that winter. She and Peter listened to his favorite Schubert; they hardly dared talk of the future. Louise had started her divorce action; she was in a hurry. "I think she's afraid Jack Matthews may slip away from her."

"Even for Louise time doesn't stand still," Kelly said. "I think most women get a little afraid when they get close to forty."

Christie's was still advising Peter to wait until the important summer sales to offer his pictures so as to get the best prices. "Nick keeps saying he's got plenty of money to pay the legal fees, but there's simply no knowing how long the trial will go on, or what it will cost in the end. If he's ordered to pay costs . . . well, it won't only be the pictures, but it will have to be Wychwood as well. I'm getting used to the idea." He looked around the sitting room of Mead Cottage. "Somehow I never expected not to have a home to offer you, Kelly. If I kept about three hundred acres, I could make it pay reasonably well. But there wouldn't be luxuries . . . and I would be coming here to live in your house. Tommy and Andrew would be coming here. It doesn't seem fair."

"I'm getting rather used to having a crowd around me," Kelly said dryly. "I'd miss it if the pack suddenly departed. You'll just have to swallow your pride, Peter Brandon, and live in your wife's house. You know, I think I was always meant to be a farmer's wife. A farm—if you could call Pentland that—was where I started." It was as far into the future as they dared to go. The long ordeal of Nick's trial reduced the future itself to the weeks and months that it would have to be endured.

"It's lambing time again," Kelly said. "I always get hopeful when it comes around. Here . . . and at Pentland . . . it was always the toughest and best time of the year."

II

Mead Cottage was full on that last weekend of February. Kate and Johnny had come down; Kate came most weekends to hold a Saturday constituency "clinic" in Tewford. Harry Potter was delighted by the way she attended to constituency business. "The people are coming to her and writing to her, Lady Brandon. It's not possible for her to put everything right, but at least they know she's here and ready to listen. She's fighting hard against reopening Everston, and they all know it. It's that sort of thing that builds a solid majority the next time around." Because Peter was completely occupied by the spring lambing, Kelly had urged Kate to come to Mead Cottage and bring Johnny. "You don't need Mrs. Nelson. I'll baby-sit." Kelly herself had come down on Thursday, tired of the London round, excusing herself from a meeting of the Multiple Sclerosis Society. The first snowdrops had bloomed. "I can't wait for the daffodils—to feel the sun again," she said to Kate. And a wan sun did appear on that Saturday. She took Johnny for a walk down the lane, looked for the unfurling fronds of the new bracken, searching the bare limbs of the trees above her for the first swelling buds. Johnny was two years old.

When they returned, Laura's car was standing outside the cottage beside Kelly's car, and the rather battered old one Kate now drove. "Hope you don't mind my barging in," Laura said. "I got so fed up with Brandon Place. It's so empty without you all. This winter . . . well . . ." She spread her hands and sighed. "I thought of going to Granny's, but she's been so snooty to me since I took Chris there. She keeps going on about Alex—as if I could do anything to change that. Or wanted to. Can I go and make up a bed? Am I being a nuisance, Kelly? I seem to hang around your neck just as much as ever."

Kelly brushed back the long swath of hair. "I'll be poorer when you stop hanging around. You know that."

She nodded. "I think I always know how you feel . . . but I rely on you too much." She picked up her bag.

"Wasn't Chris at Brandon Place this weekend?"

"Chris?" Laura was offhand. "Oh, yes. He's busy on something. Work for Nick, I suppose." She went upstairs.

Peter joined them all for supper that night. Kate bathed and put Johnny to bed, and came down, looking weary. "You have to listen to people's problems, and it's heartbreaking knowing how little, in the end, you can do about them. Sometimes I understand revolutions because it seems you can do things quicker that way . . ."

Laura was falsely gay, and on edge. "If there was a revolution, they'd pitch all of our lot out. This way to the tumbrels, everyone . . ." Unexpectedly, she had produced a bottle of vodka. She poured some on ice for herself. "Here's to the revolution—and to Marya. Kate—can I go and read some nursery rhymes to Johnny?"

"Johnny is—thankfully—asleep," Kate sighed. "And please let sleeping tigers lie."

All evening Laura continued her restless moving—starting a conversation and then abruptly changing the subject, playing Beatles records, and switching to Bach. "I think I'd better go back to London tomorrow morning. I meant to stay until Monday, but I've got a paper I'm due to turn in on Wednesday, and it's not nearly ready."

"Then you should be back there working on the paper," Kate said, rather coldly.

"Thanks," Laura snapped back. "All I need is lectures from you. Oh, God—sorry, Kate. I'm in a bitchy mood, I know. But it's just . . . well, this winter. I don't know. London seems so foul right now. And I can't make myself get terribly worked up about the effects of the Black Death on trade in the French provinces, which is what I'm supposed to be writing about. Oh, well . . . God, it would be good to feel some sun!" She turned to Kelly, "Sometimes, don't you miss Pentland terribly? I mean the sun—the space? Being able to get off by yourself where there isn't even a chance of meeting anyone. Out on a horse—there's only you." She looked at Peter. "I don't know how you're going to work it out with Kelly after you're married. This green, gentle, pretty place you live in . . . it's country, but it's all so *closed.* A part of Kelly has always to be back there."

"I'm grateful for the part of her that's here, Laura. And Kelly will go to Pentland whenever she wants."

Laura nodded. "I thought you'd say something like that. You're such a nice guy, Peter. So damn nice that at times I can't believe it—"

"Laura!" Kelly's tone was angry.

"I'm sorry. I think I'd better go to bed. I'm only upsetting everyone. It's this endless winter . . . if Marya hadn't died . . ." She went upstairs.

"If Marya hadn't died," Kate repeated. "And if she'd been able to make herself believe that Alex Gardiner was in love with her. If Nick hadn't been in such desperate trouble. If Julia hadn't left us. If she could look in a mirror and believe in herself. . . . So many things Laura wishes. I just hope she doesn't believe that Chris can make up for all that went wrong." She poked the fire with a gesture that conveyed both irritation and gloom.

At midday on Sunday Nick telephoned from London. "I've heard Peter's been up all night with his lambs, and Mrs. Page told me sternly he wasn't to be wakened. No one's home at Brandon Place—I've tried. Who am I to take to dinner? Who's going to entertain me?"

"I hadn't intended to come back until tomorrow morning," Kelly answered. "I'm due at Tower Hamlets, but I thought if I left early . . ."

"Come back this evening, Kelly," he pleaded. "Peter can spare you. Make Laura come back, too. I'll take you both out to dinner. When do I get a chance anymore to take out two beautiful women? Please, Kelly . . . ?"

Kelly handed over the receiver to Laura. "Do you want to say 'no'? I find it hard to."

"Nick"—Laura's tone was jaunty—"I want the best dinner in London. And I'll bring Kelly back. I want a great night on the town. If that can be had on a Sunday night. Come to Brandon Place and have a drink first. We'll be ready."

"I'll do my best, Princess. Thank you."

"You're on," Laura promised. She hung up and turned to Kelly. "We've got to go. He's desperate. Have you ever heard Nick sound like that? I think it's beginning to close in on him. All the feelings . . . the trial . . . possibly going to . . ." She stopped. "It's a bit of a nightmare, isn't it? He needs company. *I* know how that feels."

It was Kate who spoke. "Well, why don't you go and keep him company yourself, Laura? You don't need Kelly. You're old enough to charm and distract and flatter any man. Go and try it. Nick's a very sophisticated and intelligent and well-read man. He can talk to you about the Black Death in the fourteenth century, or yesterday's price of wool in Sydney. Go and try him."

The painful, familiar flush started; Laura swished her hair across her face. "I won't go without you, Kelly. You heard him. He invited *you* first. I promised we'd both be there."

Kate threw up her hands. "Go on! You're both helpless and hopeless when a Brandon asks anything of you. And you, Laura. You'd better toughen up. You're not living in a little girl's world anymore!"

III

On that cold, rainy afternoon at the end of February, traffic on the road back to London was light; most of the time Kelly kept Laura's Mini in sight. She listened to a concert on Radio Three, her mind going over and over the events the next months would bring—Nick's trial and its outcome, Peter's divorce, their marriage. Marriage. Once again she would be married. Before the year was out she would be married, and she must also go again to Pentland, to the big empty house, to her mother's small empty house. Laura should go to Pentland by herself during the summer vacation, but would she? If Nick's trial was still in progress, it would be hard to make her go. How did one tell a young woman . . . the jumbled thoughts continued . . . Laura, Louise, Peter, Nick. Brandon Place was deserted, and Laura was just taking her bag out of the Mini when Kelly drew up behind her.

She took out the key to Number 16. "Let's have a cup of tea, shall we? Then a bath. Are you going to wear that green velvet dress? I think you look stunning in it . . ." The door swung open and they walked into the hall. The glass doors to Number 15 stood open. Kelly stiffened. In a low voice she said to Laura, "Did you leave them open? I was pretty certain I locked them." Laura and Kate both had keys to the connecting doors. Laura shook her head. She pointed to the door at the end of the hall that led to the passage to Charles' study. It also was open. At the far end, they could, in the gloom of the February afternoon, see a thin crack of light at the bottom of the study door.

"Someone's there," Laura whispered. "Shall we telephone the police?"

Swiftly Kelly's mind ran through the people who had keys to either Number 15 or 16, who might have keys to the connecting doors. Mrs. Cass . . . Mrs. Nelson . . . what would they be doing here on a Sunday afternoon? Chris Page . . . was it possible Nick had a key?—had arrived early and was waiting for them? He would be furious if they called the police.

"We'll just see . . ." She walked quietly into the passage which gave a clear view of the window of Charles' study. The curtains were drawn, and no light shone into the garden. Nor was there a light in the window of the back room of Chris's flat. There had been none in the front room that looked onto Brandon Place, either. Beside her, Laura whispered, "For God's sake don't, Kelly. If it's an intruder you could get hurt."

"It could be Nick." She raised her voice. "Nick? Is that you, Nick? Is there someone there?"

For perhaps thirty seconds there was silence. Then slowly the door opened. Chris Page's tall figure was outlined against the light.

"Hello, Kelly—Laura. You're a little early, aren't you? I thought it was tomorrow morning you were coming." His tone was calm, casual, offhanded.

"And so what are *you* doing," Laura half-shouted at him. "What do you think you're doing in Kelly's study?"

He shrugged. "Having a look around. I often do."

"You *what!*" Kelly exclaimed.

"Just exactly what I said. I often have a look around. Interesting things here in this room, Kelly. Very interesting."

She walked toward him; as if it were a perfectly usual situation, he stood aside to let her and Laura enter the room. A drawer of one of Charles' filing cabinets stood open; files and papers were spread on the desk.

Laura stared at it in disbelief. "You've been into the files! Why—you bloody little sneak!"

"And how," Kelly said coldly, "did you get the files open? They're always kept locked."

"Oh, Kelly, you're so careless and so trusting. You left the place in perfect disarray when you ran off to Australia that time after Charles died. Any fool could go through everything here and pretty soon find the keys. Getting duplicates was simple. You really haven't guarded Charles' secrets very well, have you?"

"Secrets? Why should I need to guard secrets? They were Charles' papers. I thought some day I'd go through them all. I thought there might be material for a biography."

Now Chris strolled casually into the room after them, and dropped lightly into one of the armchairs. "In fact, that was exactly what I was doing. I've been preparing my own biography of General Sir Charles Brandon, Victoria Cross, Military Cross, Knight of the Most Noble Order of the Garter, the oldest order of chivalry . . . and all the rest of the rubbish. Just the way I prepared a biography, if that's what one may call it, of Nicholas Brandon, financial genius, swindler and crook."

"You . . ." Laura's tone rose to a pitch of fury. *"You!* It was you who gave that material to Humphrey Watson!"

"Yes, I, dear Laura. And it gave me great pleasure to do so. I had the whole picture assembled before the first article from Watson appeared. I gave him all of it, but the agreement was that he would only write a piece at a time. Keep up the suspense, you know. Make everyone thoroughly frightened. Give everyone in this family many months of misery. Give the stock plenty of time to tumble all around the world. Give other journalists who hadn't any particular inside knowledge of Brandon, Hoyle the urge to do some digging on their own. I knew it only needed time and some determined investigation until Mr. Nicholas Brandon's world would come crashing down around his ears. I caught him at a time when Brandon, Hoyle was vulnerable. He hadn't quite time to cover his tracks in every place he'd fiddled and bribed. Some people talked out of fear—some out of sheer ignorance of what they were really involved with. All I had to do was start the ball rolling, and sit back and watch the crash. I've enjoyed it—enormously!"

"You *bastard!"* Laura breathed. She had moved behind the desk, and now she dropped into the chair. It was as if the words were expelled from her. For a second a flicker of emotion crossed Chris's face, and then he smiled. Kelly had by now gone to the open file drawer; she saw spaces there, and the papers spread on the desk. She had no idea what Chris had discovered; the untidy files of Charles' life had always been for her a task for the future. Now she felt a sense of fierce anger, as if a desecration had been committed.

"And I suppose you were prying into Nick's life in just about the way you've been prying into Charles'—and mine. You've lived on trust."

"Exactly. For such a sophisticated man, Nick was oddly trusting. From the day I first went to work for him I established the reputation of being the hard worker—the one who always stayed late. I learned to type and take shorthand because if there was something very confidential that you didn't want the office boy gossiping about, I could be trusted to look after it. You know, even the most confidential documents go by post when it's to the other side of the world. If you're the last one in the office, it takes no time at all to open an envelope, see what's there, and retype another. I gathered a whole set of miniature cameras, and found someone to develop the results—someone I paid enough to keep his mouth shut, even if he could have understood what the documents were about. Nick could sometimes be very careless with his keys—as you were, Kelly. It only needs a few minutes to make a wax impression. And if you've seen a man operate the combination of a safe often enough, you begin to know the numbers of that combination just by where his fingers stop—without ever seeing the numbers. You don't have to be a genius for that—just observant and careful. People like Nick get used to treating people like me as a faithful dog's-body. After a while you're just part of the furniture. They simply don't notice what you do. By the time Nick knew that there had been a leak of confidential transactions, and woke up and started to be careful of what papers were available to whom, I already had all the information I needed. After that, it was the domino effect. As one piece of information was either published or unearthed, another would come to light as a result. I really hadn't anything to do then except sit back and watch things take their course. It was very stupid of Nick to sue Watson for libel. It made virtually every journalist in the world his enemy, which helped along my work very well."

He paused, and surveyed them both, relishing their silence. "Oh, yes," he resumed, "Nick Brandon will go to jail all right. For a very long time. What will come out at the trial is his involvement in an attempted cover-up in South Africa. A cover-up that ended in a murder to silence someone. Not that he did it, of course—but it was done *for* him. That will come out, and Nick knows it. He's desperate. He will be an old man before he leaves jail—if he ever leaves it."

Kelly listened to those chill words and tried not to believe them, tried not to remember Nick's increasing gloom, his desperate search for distraction, for forgetfulness for even a few hours. He knew, and feared, what was coming.

Laura broke the silence at last. "And what did *you* get out of all this?"

"Satisfaction, Laura, dear. Satisfaction. I've taken second best from the Brandons all my life. I've grown up with the feeling that they expected gratitude, service—loyalty. Loyalty was supposed to be my strong suit. It was what made Nick trust me when he shouldn't have."

"But *why?*" Kelly said faintly. She leaned back against the filing cabinets. It wasn't real. But the cool, beautiful face of the young man sitting so calmly in the chair defied her unbelief. "Why ruin Nick? Weren't you losing a lot yourself?"

"I was losing nothing but my position as an underpaid servant. You really don't think I was so stupid as not to protect myself financially? I saved—I bought every penny's worth of stock I could afford. I took my mother's savings and bought stock in Brandon, Hoyle. I borrowed money to buy stock. And I sold when it was at the top, before I handed over the information to Watson. I made quite a lot of money. Nick Brandon is not the only one with a flair for money. Yes, I gambled—but I knew when to get out."

"That," Kelly said, "doesn't answer my question. Why do it at all?"

He looked at her coldly. "I thought I'd made that clear. I loathe all you Brandons. I've grown up in your shadow. But always second best. Sent to the local Grammar School instead of Eton. Went to London University instead of going to Oxford or Cambridge. Studied accountancy in my spare time. Typing and shorthand so I could be a sort of super-secretary. But then, wasn't I doing very well for the housekeeper's son? Wasn't I fortunate to be able to grow up at Wychwood? To have Nick and Peter as sort of big brothers—so long as I was nice and respectful, and knew my place. And kept to it. Kept to my side of the house. I and my mother, perfect servants to the Brandons."

Laura put her elbow on the desk and rested her forehead in her hand. Incredulity was still in her expression. "But it wasn't anyone's *fault* that your mother was housekeeper at Wychwood. It was just unlucky your father died—"

"My father didn't die. Not until a long time later. My father died here in this room."

"What!"

"That noble and honorable soldier, General Sir Charles Brandon, was my father."

"You're mad! You're truly mad!"

"Does my mother seem to be mad? Hardly. It was she who told me. And she didn't tell me until the time when what was her due was taken from her—or at least was denied her—by you, Kelly."

"What are you talking about?"

"You didn't even know my mother existed when Charles and you were married. But *he* knew. He could hardly have forgotten. It was his greatest friend, Anthony Page, who had been persuaded to marry my mother in Rawalpindi. Because she was going to have Charles Brandon's child. Because Anthony Page knew he would die soon, and at least he could help out his friend, Charles Brandon, and give a name to a bastard. They were together at Eton, together at Sandhurst. Honor among friends and gentlemen. Uphold the honor of the regiment. My mother was Anglo-Indian. Socially barely acceptable at the time of the British Raj in India. But she was also extremely beautiful . . . beautiful then, as she is now. Being a gentleman, of course Charles Brandon was conscience-stricken when he knew that she was going to have a child. He told his friend, Anthony Page. And Anthony Page, being a gentleman, stepped in to save his friend, and his friend's mistress and child. Elizabeth Brandon knew, of course. Why do you think she was such a friend to Rosemary Brown?—Rosemary Page as she became. To protect her beloved husband's reputation. To protect her own future. She knew she was ill, and she needed desperately to hold on to Charles Brandon. He was her only future. My mother told me it was actually Elizabeth Brandon who persuaded Anthony Page that it would be a very noble thing for him to do to marry this half-caste, and give Charles' child a name, if not a father. It was she, of course, who got my mother into the position at Wychwood, got Michael Brandon to try an experiment with a half-caste. No matter how well educated my mother was, no matter how high the caste, she still was half-caste. Before the war, that was a very unfortunate situation."

Kelly felt she could stand the smooth silken tones no longer. How strongly now they reminded her of Mrs. Page's own.

She remembered the strange outburst that day she had fled Wychwood, the day she had witnessed Mrs. Page's hatred and rage. She could even remember the words Mrs. Page had used of Charles, "He didn't see where justice lay." She repressed a shiver.

"Oh, for God's sake, stop it! Even if it were true, it's over. It's done with! You can't undo it. But I don't believe it's true."

For a moment anger blazed on Chris's face. "Say what you like. You can no more disprove it than I can prove it. There are no letters, no documents. There's nothing but a marriage certificate to Anthony Page, and a birth certificate to say I'm his son. All I have is what my mother told me—and she didn't tell me until the day she received the news that Charles Brandon had married *you*."

"She . . . ?" Kelly couldn't keep the shadow of doubt hidden.

"She waited, of course. All the long years of Elizabeth Brandon's illness she waited. She was perfectly certain that when she died, as everyone knew she would, that Charles Brandon would marry her. She was Elizabeth Brandon's friend. There was an unspoken agreement. No one wished to hurt Elizabeth Brandon, or upset her world. My mother was content to wait. She said . . . she said she had always loved Charles Brandon. She was confident that he would wait a decent length of time, and then they would be married. To marry someone like my mother in the sixties was a very different thing from doing it in the thirties. Acceptable. Advanced. And Rosemary Page was more English than the English by then. She was quite confident—until the news came that he had married you. *Then* she told me. The hurt and bitterness was too great to keep to herself any longer. She knew what Charles Brandon had done. He'd married someone much younger than himself, someone with the prospect of money—someone with connections. That was Charles Brandon. And so my mother was going to be housekeeper at Wychwood for the rest of her life. That was the time I decided I would look much more closely into Nick Brandon's more dubious business dealings. I didn't care how I achieved it. I was going to bring the whole house of cards crashing down around the Brandons. And enjoy doing it."

Laura was staring at him, her face white, and the scar blazing on it. "You really went the whole way, didn't you? You wormed your way into this house as well as into Nick's confidence. Into the confidence of all of us. You cheap little bastard!"

"You can call me a bastard as long as you like. It happens to fit. Yes, I did the lot. I'm nothing if not thorough. Yes, Laura, I went as far as any of your lot would go. You—the Brandons, the Mertons, the Renisdales—all with money and position protecting one another. All you liars and cheats and hypocrites. I went every bit as far. I wanted to be here so I could see the damage I was doing at firsthand. I got my mother to ask about the flat because I wanted to be under Charles' eyes, where he couldn't escape me. It was too bad he died so soon. I would have enjoyed watching him squirm."

Suddenly Chris raised a finger and pointed it at Kelly. "I'd bet anything I had that he didn't take it very well when you said you'd agreed to my having the basement flat. Can you remember how he reacted, Kelly? I'm sure you do. Oh, you were such a soft touch for my mother. You didn't dare say 'no' to her, did you? Anything to please Mrs. Page. And I'll bet Charles didn't dare say no, either—for fear of what Mrs. Page might say to *you*. How do you think it felt for me to see you come here, where my mother was meant to be? I took the basement flat—the basement seemed to be the position I'd always occupied with the Brandon family. I took the basement flat and prepared to stick around to watch the fall of the house of Brandon. Kate and Julia—so bloody superior, and being kind to their friend, Chris Page. And Miss Laura Merton, the kid with the silver spoon, always anxious to prove how democratic she could be. Invite Chris . . . include Chris . . . Chris will do it . . . leave it to Chris . . . Chris is so nice, and obliging, and above all, Chris is loyal. Trust him with anything. Trust Chris even to the extent of having an affair with him when Alex Gardiner didn't come up to scratch. Chris was all right to have an affair with, but you'd never have married him, would you, Laura? The Renisdales wouldn't have liked it. The Brandons wouldn't have liked it. Good old loyal Chris—"

"Shut up!" Laura screamed. "Shut up, you bastard! Yes, I said it. I'll keep on saying it. You're a thief and a coward and a liar. I don't care *what* your mother told you. She's lying, too. So easy to lie when you've nourished secret daydreams for years of what will happen when a poor, sick woman dies. Of course she was in love with Charles. Plenty of women must have been at one time or another. Women invent fantasies—especially at her age. You said there was no proof. There's no proof because it isn't true."

"No one but my mother will ever know," Chris answered. "Charles Brandon is dead, and so is Elizabeth. Anthony Page is dead. There is no one left in India who matters. They're all dead. The only one who knows for certain is my mother—and she's alive. I choose to believe her."

Kelly felt sick. The vision of that agonized, contorted face of Rosemary Page which had been turned to her that day at Wychwood would not be banished. She was sickened, too, to hear confirmation of what she had feared—that Laura and Chris had become lovers, as Laura had flung herself violently away from Alex Gardiner, and had not known how to regain her balance.

"Choose to believe what you like," Kelly said. She put out her hand and held the back of the other armchair; her knees seemed about to buckle and she strove to hide this from Chris. She lowered herself until she was seated on the arm of the chair. "Choose to believe what you like. As you said, there is no proof. Only what your mother has told you. You've done the damage now. You've managed to ruin Nick. You may also ruin Peter. What is there left? Why are you here?—here in this room? What more is there for you? You've taken everything now." She didn't want to betray to him the extent of her shock and near-despair, to afford him more of the satisfaction he craved, but it wasn't possible to hide it completely. His story was just barely possible, even believable. Laura had called Mrs. Page's story a fantasy. But there was just enough that was strange in the whole history of Mrs. Page to lend the story credibility. Kelly took a deep breath, trying to control the sense of distaste and near-fear which seemed to crawl through her guts.

"You'd better leave," she managed to say at last. "You had no business here in the first place."

He didn't stir in his chair. "Oh, I intend to leave. Leaving will be easy. I would have hung on a little longer if you hadn't found me here today. But what I've got now is sufficient. I came searching in this room, you know, in the first place because I thought there just might be something to give tangible proof of what my mother had told me. He might have kept a letter—a photograph—even something that Elizabeth Brandon had left behind to tell me that my existence mattered to him. Perhaps I came here wanting—hoping—to find myself. After all, I am his only son. It should have mattered to a man—even a man like Charles Brandon."

"But you found nothing, did you?" Laura demanded. "You

found nothing of the sort because nothing you've said is true. There could have been nothing."

A strangely dangerous smile played on Chris's face. "No, I didn't find what I came looking for. But I did find things so damaging that Charles Brandon's reputation will be blown sky-high. Nick Brandon may be ruined, but when I pass on the information I have collected about Charles Brandon, the very name of Brandon will stink in this country. It will knock Kate out of Parliament. It will ruin Julia's marriage. You and Peter will live together tied by that name, Kelly, and be despised by all those good souls to whom the Brandons of Wychwood have been the very essence of all the decent and respectable virtues that the English so admire."

"And what madness have you dreamed up now?" Laura said.

"Not at all mad when one thinks that spies are only successful in so far as they appear to be people who couldn't possibly be spies. It hasn't been cloak and dagger stuff for a long time, has it? It has been a steady drip of information. People in high places who have access to secret information which may or may not be vital to the enemy. Bits and pieces put together. They never know when the bit they supply will fit the jigsaw being put together in Moscow—or Washington—or London."

Kelly shook her head uncomprehendingly. Laura's mouth hung open in disbelief. "You—you really *are* crazy," she breathed. It was the first time her tone had been quiet since they had discovered Chris there.

He smiled again. "But I'm not. There's enough in those files to tell the story. I came searching for one sort of information, and found another. Very amateurish of the General to leave so much of it there—but then he never expected to die when he did. People like Charles Brandon never expect to be suspected. After all, he'd built his whole life on service to his country—but which country that is, is the point that matters. A spy to one lot, is a hero to the other side."

"Charles won the Victoria Cross," Kelly said slowly. "He had the trust of some of the most senior commanders during the war. He was, if anything, too right wing. He chanced his whole career on the stand he took on Suez." Her tone wavered as she pointed to the filing cabinets. "There can be nothing there that contradicts the evidence of his whole life. You could have said he was an old-fashioned patriot."

"People gain convictions for all kinds of reasons," Chris said smoothly. "In the beginning I neither understood nor believed some of the things I turned up. But you surely haven't forgotten the Burgess-Maclean affair, and how they were shielded and tipped off by a man who had given his life to an elaborate structure of appearing to be right wing. Kim Philby. The Third Man. All those years ago Philby began to build his cover by reporting the Spanish Civil War as an anti-Communist. The powers that be obligingly let him into the Foreign Office, as they did Burgess and Maclean. Even when they began to suspect that it was Philby who had tipped off Burgess and Maclean in time to let them escape to the Soviet Union, Philby was still protected. No one directly charged or challenged him. He had to leave the Foreign Office, but the Establishment found jobs for him—nice reporting jobs where he still could have his ear to the ground. Possibly the most highly placed spy in history—except for the ones we don't know about. And that includes Charles Brandon."

"What have Burgess and Maclean and Kim Philby to do with Charles? This really is fantasy."

"Do you happen to remember what day it was that Charles died? Died of a heart attack."

"Of course I remember. It was—"

"The date really isn't important, Kelly. Do you remember the newspaper here in Charles' office—the last one he ever read. Just tossed, like everything else, on the desk. Of no significance until one reads some of the material, the memos, in those files. The headline story that day was of Kim Philby's disappearance from Beirut. What it must have done to Charles—the fear that Philby wouldn't make it to the Soviet Union. That he would be caught, and he would talk. Name names. Was Charles the Fourth Man—or the Fifth? The Twelfth? The fear killed Charles that afternoon."

"You're a monster. A despicable, lying monster."

"I wonder if the Prime Minister who threw him out of his job at the Defence Ministry would agree. It was all smoothed over—covered up. Because they had to. They couldn't afford the sort of scandal it would cause. Charles didn't only resign from his post at the Ministry, but his seat in Parliament. Whatever pressures they brought on him were enough to cause him to do that. They mustn't have had quite enough information, but enough suspicion. There was a complete rift, remember, between him and the Prime Minister—until, by greatest good luck, that very safe seat of Tewford was offered to Charles. He was back—and the Prime Minister had to swallow what was pretty unpalatable. You have to have pretty strong proof to accuse a person like Charles Brandon, and the very accusation—coupled with the fact that that Government had given him a very sensitive post, where he was privy to more defense secrets than ever he'd been while he was in the Army, could easily have brought the Government down. That's how Philby survived for so long. The fear the Government had of admitting that they'd kept him in his job for so long, despite the suspicion. It was just unthinkable that Charles Brandon could have been a traitor. So they didn't let themselves think it . . . or not very often. Charles survived, and was even permitted to make that trip to Australia to investigate the very sensitive subject of uranium. What he sent back to his masters from there must have been most interesting."

"I was on that trip," Kelly said. "There was nothing I didn't know."

"You're quite sure of that, Kelly? No papers so confidential that they were for Charles Brandon's eyes only? No information of quantities, availability . . . all the rest of it. I'm sure if you went back in your memory you'd find you weren't at every single meeting—didn't type every single paper. Bluff and deceit were a large part of Charles' life. He deceived you—as he deceived most people."

"You don't have any proof of this. No more than you have proof that you are Charles' son. It's an invention."

He shook his head. "Not so. I've taken my time over those files. Most of it is of little interest, but there are just a few items which are very damaging. Possibly he overlooked them himself—or became too careless. I have made copies. There isn't a lot, but there's enough. Enough, at any rate, to cause charge and countercharge. The Defence Ministry could be very embarrassed. The man himself isn't alive to answer the charges. The newspapers will have a field day. After all, I had only to set one ball rolling to start the avalanche that brought Nick Brandon's empire down. When you put together the little bits and pieces of Charles' life, and then couple them with the fact of his long association with Marya—well, it begins to look very damning."

"What has Marya to do with it?"

"Marya? Marya was his controller, of course. His spy master. Charles never had to make direct contact with his Russian masters. Marya did it for him. Why do you think she was on that plane from Yalta? She didn't stow away on it. She was *put* on it—the defecting heroine. Someone who supposedly couldn't stand the Stalin regime. Someone whom

Charles so nobly took into his own house when officialdom was doubtful of her. Someone whom, again, Elizabeth Brandon befriended—most probably in order to please Charles. Why would a woman as intelligent, as educated as Marya, ever leave Russia? To come to the sort of life she had here? Only if she was ordered to. Ordered to establish the sort of deep cover Charles already had."

Kelly turned her head away from him, unable to look at him anymore. "This is the purest speculation. You have no proof . . . none at all. Don't you think people more skilled than you have investigated Marya?"

"Then why was she killed? She *was* killed. I've already told you that. She was of no further use to her Russian masters. With Charles' death her contacts were cut off. The one chance she had to be of service to them again might have been through Kate, but Kate abandoned the Socialist cause. They wrote Kate off as a possible recruit. Then Marya may have asked for her ultimate payment—which would have been to return to Russia and her reward. The special position—the dacha, the perks. She'd waited a long time. Perhaps she became too impatient. Perhaps *they* didn't want their traitor, Charles Brandon, uncovered. It strains relations between countries when things like that happen. If Marya had demanded to be returned to Russia, then she had to be eliminated. They don't care about things like that. She'd served her purpose. There are several notes in the files, in Russian, in Marya's handwriting which I've taken copies of. I haven't had them translated yet because I didn't dare. I was holding back. I was going to wait until Nick was convicted, and trying to appeal, and then I was going to let it all go. Keep out of it myself, but let it go to a really top political correspondent who would have understood all the implications, and who could be trusted to take the whole thing much further. Ask the questions. It only needs the first suspicion cast from the right quarter, and then you see Charles Brandon in quite a different light. Enough muck thrown, and some will stick. The Brandon name will stink." He opened his hands, and shrugged, as if the end was inevitable, was already waiting, immutable.

"I was going to wait, but now you force my hand. It will have to come out now. The lot of it."

Kelly felt her body sag. Despairingly she looked at Chris. He seemed so sublimely confident; it may have been the confidence of madness, but it was there, just the same. Mad or not, whether the facts that he claimed he had were even partly true or not, the damage he could do before the truth was established could be enormous. He was right in his statement that just the stirring up of suspicion could be enough. Enough people would be ready to believe. He had already proved what malicious intent had done to Nick—but then Nick had confessed to some guilt. Was Charles guilty? She glanced back at the bank of filing cabinets which held—God knew what they held. She was frightened. She turned back to him.

"Is it any use my appealing to you not to do this? I don't believe that what you say you have can be damaging to Charles, but I must beg you not to reveal it. Why must you hurt the memory of a man whom I think was a very good man?—a man who served his country—"

"Don't tell me what Charles Brandon was. I *know.*" Chris's even tone grew shrill. "I know what he was, and I intend that everyone else shall know. I intend—"

"Please . . ." Kelly said. *"Please,* Chris. . . . Is there anything I can offer you? Any way that—"

"Don't insult me further." He turned directly to her, away from Laura. His voice was now angry. "I'm not one of the ones Nick could bribe so handily. The only thing that could ever have been offered to me was that Charles Brandon should have acknowledged what he had been—was—to my mother. He could have made the single gesture of marrying her after Elizabeth had died. Then none of this would have happened. He had his chance to put right something that went wrong a long time ago. He didn't take it—ignored his obligation. That fine gentleman who belonged to that most exclusive order of chivalry! No—there's nothing you can give me, Kelly. Not money—not anything now. I'll have my satisfaction—"

Laura spoke. She had been quiet for so long, listening, her eyes fixed on Chris. "Kelly, one doesn't bargain, or plead, or make deals with a snake that's slid in where it shouldn't be. One doesn't temporize. One just kills it."

Kelly and Chris turned and looked at her in the one instant. She was still seated behind Charles' desk. The narrow top drawer had been silently opened. She held Charles' presentation revolver with the elaborate silver ornamentation in both her hands, steady in the aiming position. They heard the safety catch slipped off.

"You were so busy with the files you forgot this, didn't you, Chris? Didn't you even notice that I'd cleaned and oiled it as I said I would? Where I come from, we respect guns."

Chris's body tensed. He leaned forward, the mask of smooth complacency slipped from his face. "What—?"

"I'm going to kill you, Chris. I'm going to shut your lying mouth forever."

"No!"

"Laura!"

Kelly's and Chris's voices both were mingled with the sharp sound of the gunshot. As Chris had struggled to rise from the deep armchair, Laura had gently squeezed the trigger. The bullet entered his forehead above the right eye. He fell back.

Kelly was frozen in disbelief. "My God—oh, my God, Laura!"

Laura's eyes had a wild and manic glitter. "I always was a good shot. Grandfather saw to that. But at this range I could hardly miss, could I? This was the only time it really mattered . . ." She remained seated behind the desk, still holding the gun with both hands raised, as if she expected to fire again.

Kelly had gone to Chris and bent over him. Now her voice was a low moan. "My God . . ." she repeated, a desperate prayer, unanswered. The bullet had made a neat entry, but the back of his head which rested on the upholstery was a bloody mess. He was already dead.

"Laura!—you *killed* him!" It was as if she begged Laura to say otherwise, to deny it, to deny the evidence of her own eyes.

"I meant to kill him. I told you that." Her tone was deadly calm. "I meant to kill that lying, thieving son-of-a-bitch. I meant to stop him before he could do any more damage. He's destroyed Nick. He meant to claw at you and Peter—to destroy Kate—and Julia. Pull all of us down. He was going to destroy the memory of a great man. I loved Charles, Kelly. I loved him the way I loved Grandfather. I was proud of him—everything he stood for. And Chris was going to destroy all that."

Kelly moved to her. She had to prize Laura's fingers loose from the gun. Laura kept on talking, as if she were an automaton. "I can't forgive him because we trusted him—all of us. Perhaps I trusted him most of all. I was . . . we were lovers, Kelly. I thought I loved him. He seemed so . . . so kind, so gentle . . . after Alex. I trusted him with the only real thing I had to give . . . not money, but love. I trusted him with that. And I sat here and listened to that madness, that obscenity, that sickening mass of lies. I realized that he'd stolen and schemed and robbed. He'd wormed his way in here like the deadliest snake there is, and I kept remembering that I'd trusted him with everything I had. It was a snake I kept thinking of. Something that strikes, then slides away. We kill snakes, Kelly. We always kill them, don't we?"

Kelly touched the frozen arm of the shocked girl. "Laura . . . you . . . oh, God, what will happen now?" She tugged at her urgently. "Come away now. Please, Laura, come out of here. I have to think . . . I have to think what to do now." She was still pulling at Laura's resisting arm when the doorbell rang.

In the silence of that quiet house, on a Sunday evening, it was like another pistol shot. Kelly's hand dropped away from Laura.

With utter calm, as if she were in a trance, Laura rose. "It's Nick. I'll go and let him in."

"Wait! . . . *wait!* It could be anyone."

"Does it matter? Everyone will soon know. I shot him. I shall simply say it was a lovers' quarrel. What matters is that he's dead, and he can't pass on any of those sickening lies about Charles." She moved with great deliberation past Kelly as the doorbell rang again.

IV

Nick moved swiftly into the hall, looking from one to the other, anxiety growing in his face. "What the hell's the matter with you both?"

"You'd better come." Kelly led the way back into the study. Laura followed slowly, seeming to hang back; her features were stiff, her eyes had assumed the glaze of shock.

Nick stood in the doorway, his glance going from Chris's body in the chair to the gun on the desk. "Tell me," he said.

He edged carefully around the chair in which Chris lay until he was standing with his back against the filing cabinets. Kelly dropped down into the chair behind the desk which Laura had occupied; Laura remained in the doorway as if reluctant to come farther. She leaned against the frame, staring fixedly at Chris.

Kelly told Nick, remembering as well as she could the sequence of the talk, the things Chris had said, the things he had alleged, the bizarre accusations he had made. Nick listened in almost total silence, interrupting only once or twice to clarify a point.

"So it was our loyal friend, Chris," he said at last. "Bloody little bastard—I'd have done him in myself if I'd had the chance. Little sneaking bastard. Yes, I tightened security when it was too late. Too late for everything. But he had enough on me. If it's all there with Watson, it will all come out. He was right on one thing. It's the end of Brandon, Hoyle. And the end of me. Yes, I'll go to prison, as he said, for a long time. And he would have laughed. As for the rest—it's all rubbish, of course. I simply don't believe it about Charles and Mrs. Page. She may have *told* him it was so, and he must have wanted to believe it. If you think of a twisted little mind like that—envy and hate growing over the years. I haven't a doubt Mrs. Page has been dropping hints to him ever since he could understand that he was entitled to much better than he had. She's a woman with a very highly developed sense of importance, is Mrs. Page. She brought up a perfect son with what has turned out to be an exaggerated sense of his own destiny. And a highly developed imagination. It took daring and envy to pull off what he's done to Brandon, Hoyle, but it took a very warped imagination to make the accusations he has about Charles. A whole load of rubbish, of course . . ." And yet, as he spoke, Kelly saw his glance flick nervously to either side of him, to the bank of filing cabinets, to the drawer that was open. "And dragging in poor Marya. . . . My God, he *was* mad." But there was, Kelly thought, in his tone and glance, just the faintest shade of doubt. "I wonder what the little bugger found to make him say all that? Or did he merely want to frighten you? He's obviously been enjoying himself hugely all this time. He would have enjoyed coming to visit me in jail. Bring me cigarettes and so on . . . just to see how I was taking it."

He reached automatically into his pocket and brought out his own cigarette and lighter. Kelly watched as he slowly went through the ritual of lighting and taking the first draw. Time to think.

Suddenly, from the doorway, Laura spoke. Her words were slow, as if she were trying to drag something from her memory. She looked at Chris's body in the chair as she spoke.

"You see I had to do it, don't you, Nick? I never imagined I was capable of killing anyone. But I saw him as some sort of animal. I kept seeing a snake . . . a snake in a dark place. A snake lying there when you step over a log in the bush. A snake on the rafters of an outbuilding. A snake that's slid in to get the warmth in the winter. I didn't see a man. I didn't see the Chris I'd trusted, but something so evil it had to be destroyed. I didn't think then about what would happen to me. It didn't seem to matter. All I thought about was what he'd done to you, and what he intended to do to Charles—and through Charles to the whole family. Destroy us all. I felt myself dying as he talked—as he strung out those filthy lies. If I was dying, then he would, too. It was the only way I could stop him. I did a terrible thing—but I stopped him. He could not live to create more misery. The last thing I could not forgive him or myself was that I had let him become my lover. He was waiting—after Alex he was waiting to catch me as I fell. Gullible, trusting, Laura. The kid who never grew up. I felt degraded because I had been his dupe, as all the family has been. I suppose he saw me as just another of the family he could injure in a very personal way. Because I am of this family, Nick—just as much as Kelly—or any of you who are called Brandon. He was out after all of us. Whoever could be a victim, would be a victim. He would concoct any lies he could about Charles and Marya. Make any hideous slander—anything that would hurt this family. If only I could have stopped him before he hurt you, Nick. But that was done a long time ago. He's been here among us, gloating . . ."

She stared, her gaze horrified, at Chris's dead face. "He was so beautiful . . . I've always worshiped beauty. But when I looked at him this time I saw something ugly and evil. I killed it." Her body sagged in the doorway.

Nick stood silently for perhaps a minute longer. Then he went to the desk and picked up the revolver. Taking a clean handkerchief from his breast pocket, he began to wipe it carefully.

"That's no use, Nick," Laura said. "We can't just invent an unknown murderer. I really didn't know what I was doing when I shot him—except that I knew I had to get rid of this evil thing. But I shall have to tell the police that I did it. We can't just spirit him away and pretend it never happened."

"Shut up, Laura. I want to think a bit. And I don't need any advice from you." He touched Kelly's arm. "Look—the two of you go and pour me a brandy, will you? Out in the kitchen—I'll come and get it. I need to think a bit about all this. There are ways and ways of telling the police. We won't rush this one. Just a bit of time to think . . ." Gently he forced Kelly out of the chair. "Now go on, there's a good girl. We could all do with a brandy, I'd say. But even I don't fancy it in Chris's company . . . slimy little bastard."

Kelly took Laura's arm, and half led her through the passage. A February mist that was almost fog had come down.

The unlighted back windows of the Cavanagh offices looked down on the little garden. The back windows of the houses on the next street had their curtains drawn against the damp and the cold. When they reached the kitchen Kelly placed Laura in a chair; she was now shaking. Kelly drew the curtains to shield them from the street, and then went to the drinks cupboard. She found the brandy, and took out three glasses. She poured for Laura, and guided her cold and shaking fingers until they closed over the stem. "Try to take a little, Laura. It'll help warm you . . ." Gently she forced the glass toward the girl's lips. She could hear the rim striking Laura's teeth, but she did take a small amount. She shuddered, as if the taste was unpleasant.

Kelly had the bottle poised to pour for Nick when they heard the shot.

When they reached the study Nick lay face-forward on the desk, a gun-shot wound in his temple. Frantically, Kelly felt for a pulse, lifted him to try to feel for a heart beat. Laura remained clutching the doorframe, making a low, moaning sound of fear and pain.

Kelly gently laid Nick's head back on the desk. "He's dead . . . he's dead . . ." she murmured unbelievingly. She was about to move away from the desk, to take Laura in her arms, when she saw the paper. It was a piece of her own notepaper taken from one of the drawers, and it contained Nick's bold, sprawling handwriting.

I got the sneaking, thieving little bastard. At least he'll never have the satisfaction of seeing me in jail. I took him with me. Nicholas Brandon.

Kelly took the paper to Laura. The girl's shocked eyes seemed unable to focus. She stared uncomprehendingly. Kelly was forced to read it aloud.

"He was looking after you, Laura. Don't you see? He killed himself—and he saved you."

Laura's mouth opened and closed, but for a time she could force no words out. She was now shaking violently, staring at the paper, then at Kelly, then at Nick's body slumped on the desk. "Then I've killed him too! Nick!—I've killed *Nick!*"

Kelly parried desperately. "No—no you didn't. He would have done it in any case. Nick would never have gone to jail. Never! You understand. You didn't kill him. It just came sooner."

She put the paper back on the desk, and once more led Laura through the passage. All the back windows overlooking the garden still presented their blank curtained facades, undisturbed.

"You have to go back to Mead Cottage," Kelly said.

"Why?" Laura asked, numbly.

"Because you weren't here. You never left Mead Cottage. You're not going to be involved at all. Tell Kate what's happened when you get there. I don't dare risk telephoning her. But you must go at once. At once, Laura! *Now!*"

"The police. I have to tell the police . . ."

"Nick has taken care of that. Why should you be sacrificed too? I'll tell the police. It's quite straightforward. I came back, found Chris in the study—he told me what he'd done to Nick. I don't have to say anything about Charles and all the rest of his lies. Nick came, as he'd arranged to. I told him what Chris had said about leaking information about Brandon, Hoyle. Nick shot him, then shot himself. That's what the note says. He's done it for you, Laura. He couldn't save himself, but he saw this way to save you. You have to go—"

"I can't. I can't leave you to face it all."

"You have to go."

"I can't drive. I'll never be able to drive—not the way I feel."

She was still wearing the coat she had driven up in. Now Kelly took the lapels and shook her. "Pull yourself together. You've *got* to drive. It's dark. No one will see you arrive back at Mead Cottage. No one will see you leave here. Nick did it for you, Laura. You can't let him down." She took Laura's scarf and tied it under her chin so that it half-obscured her face. She went through Laura's handbag until she found her keys. "Here are your keys—money—driving license. Right . . ." She picked up Laura's suitcase. "Now drive carefully. Don't speed. Don't do anything to attract attention. In the morning you'll come back with Kate, and you'll stay out of the whole business." She switched out the light in the hall. "Give me your keys. I'll get the car open and put the suitcase in. When I'm certain there's no one on the street, you can come out. . . . You do exactly as I say. You understand, Laura."

"What will happen to you? You're alone—with them." Laura's head jerked in the direction of the study.

"Nothing will happen to me. So long as I know you're safe, I'll be all right. It's going to be all right . . ."

She waited, with the hall lights off, the door slightly open, while Laura slid into the Mini. She watched until the car, driven cautiously, signaled that it was turning into Brompton Road. She closed the door, and leaned back against the wall in the dark hall, and the trembling that she had managed to suppress while Laura was there, overtook her. She heard her own voice whisper in the silence. "Lord—what am I going to do?" It was, once again, a prayer and a plea.

She thought of all the years that Laura had been her charge and her care; she thought of the love there had been between them—Greg's child, John Merton's beloved grandchild. The thought of John Merton steadied her; the thought of Nick strengthened her. Nick had expected her to carry through with what he had begun. He had not given his life as an empty gesture. The cool courage of the act was his total redemption; whatever he had done that was questionable, dubious, even criminal, seemed washed away in this final gesture of concern for Laura. Nick had finally given his love. In those seconds as she stood in the dark hall, trying to still the racing of her heart, incredibly there flashed into Kelly's memory the words she had used against Nick that morning, so long ago, when they had stood in that cold mist-shrouded copse above Wychwood, and she had accused him of being unable to make a true commitment. He had done it now; he had made the final commitment. Kelly breathed deeply, the calmness of desperation creeping over her. The task was unfinished. Nick had trusted her to see it through.

But her hands still trembled as she washed and dried the glass Laura had used. Then she went back to the study; the sight of the two bodies there almost unnerved her. With gloves on she made herself search Chris's pockets until she found his keys. Then she went to his flat and began a frantic search for the papers he said he had collected on Charles. What, she wondered, if he had kept them some other place—at Wychwood? What if Mrs. Page knew of their existence? It was possible—no, she told herself—it was certain that they did not exist at all. None of what Chris had said about Charles could possibly be true. But there, in the locked bottom drawer of the desk in Chris's flat was a legal-sized folder tied with pink tape. She glanced quickly at its contents. Some of it was on Ministry of Defence stationery. Some of it was marked Secret or Confidential. There was no time to read the papers, no time to discover whether they were not things which Charles was perfectly entitled to have in his possession, things which had never passed beyond his office at the Ministry and the study at Brandon Place. She had no idea whether any of it would have been of the slightest interest to an enemy. There were two documents which related to Australia, documents she did not herself recognize. There were a couple of scattered pages of Russian in Marya's handwriting. It was, in all, a slim collection of papers, and they may have had no significance at all. She had to believe that Chris's warped and overwrought imagination had read into them things which were not true. She had to believe it, but she could not risk leaving them for the police when they came, as inevitably they must, to search Chris's flat.

She returned the heavy bunch of keys to Chris's pocket, loathing having to touch his body, but it had to be done. She noted that duplicates of the keys of the filing cabinets were on the ring—how easy it had been for Chris to enter and steal what he wanted. She thought of the months she had been away at Pentland—of the weekends he had been here alone. She thought of the many nights when Number 16 had been empty, and he had had leisure to pursue his search. Just as he had done with Nick. How innocent and trusting they had all been—how foolish. She put the file she had taken from Chris's flat into her own filing cabinet—the one marked Pentland, Tower Hamlets, Multiple Sclerosis, Fund for the Blind—and locked it. Surely the police would not ask to examine all those files. They could not. There could be no reason. Her thoughts ran on and on, trying to anticipate the questions, conscious of the minutes slipping away.

Finally she took off her coat. Then she dialed the police. They would be here in a few minutes. She had time just to make one call. She prayed it would be Peter and not Mrs. Page who answered. It was Peter. "Come at once. Something terrible has happened. It's Nick. He's dead, Peter—and so is Chris Page."

She went to the kitchen and poured brandy into three glasses. She took the contents of one in gulps, which made her feel sick; she poured again, and this time sat sipping it, waiting for the sound of the cars that would stop outside. They came; they came far too quickly.

The man was Inspector Harris. She couldn't tell whether he believed her or not. Her greatest fear was that they would discover the difference in the time between Chris's death and Nick's—could they do that? Would anyone else have heard the shots? Would the whole elaborate structure come down on this basic point? Nick's note was irrefutable, but the story sounded thin. She had driven up from Mead Cottage to keep a dinner engagement with Nicholas Brandon. She often saw Nicholas Brandon, but this had been a spur-of-the-moment decision. She had not been expected until Monday morning, when Kate Brandon and Laura Merton, her stepdaughters, were also expected. She had found Christopher Page in her study—which had been her husband's study. A file drawer was open, and he had some of its contents on the desk. He had not tried to excuse himself. He had laughed at her, and told her the story of having leaked the information about Brandon, Hoyle to Humphrey Watson.

"Why would he have done that, Lady Brandon?"

"I'm not sure of all of his motives, but he seemed to be highly jealous of Nick's success, and very bitter about the fact that his mother has been housekeeper to the Brandons all these years. 'Servants'—that's what he said they both were. He was very resentful of that."

"But why was he going through *your* files—your husband's files?"

"I got the impression that having done the worst he could to Nick, he was now trying to find something discreditable about my husband. I don't know quite what he was looking for. By this time—by this time I was beginning to be convinced that he was mad."

"Most people would have thought it extremely unlikely that anything seriously discreditable to Sir Charles Brandon could be found." The Inspector did not say whether he himself was among those people.

As much as possible she stayed with the events as they had happened, but trying to blot out the memory of Laura's presence. She told the Inspector of Nick arriving. "I told him what had happened. Chris was sitting in the chair, smiling. He seemed very pleased with himself. Nick—well, I believe Nick's been convinced for some time that eventually he would go to prison, and now he knew Chris was responsible for it. Had brought it about. Nick always maintained that he hadn't done anything others hadn't done and got away with, and that, given time, he could have set everything straight. But . . . but whatever Chris said to him when I was out of the room must have convinced Nick that whatever information had been passed on, he had no hope of extricating himself. Or else, in blind anger, he shot Chris. And then, knowing what would happen—well, he shot himself."

"You were out of the room, Lady Brandon? Why?"

All the time they had talked they had been sitting in the

kitchen. She indicated the glasses and the brandy. "Nick asked me to go and bring some brandy. He said he wanted a long talk with Chris."

"I see you also poured a glass for Christopher Page."

Her mouth twisted bitterly. "Force of habit, Inspector. Chris Page was in and out of here all the time. We included him in everything. That's what made it so . . ."

He waited for a while. "The shot, Lady Brandon . . . you must have heard the first shot? Why didn't you go to see what had happened? There was time for Nicholas Brandon to write that note before he killed himself. Why didn't you investigate?"

She looked at him with blank, deliberately stupefied eyes. "Does one *expect* to hear a shot? Even if I registered the sound I took no notice. My mind was on . . . well, it was the *second* shot I heard distinctly. It was a shock. I'd forgotten about the gun being there."

"Ah, yes—the gun, Lady Brandon. How would Nicholas Brandon have known about the gun, and where it was kept? It would be a help if you could explain that."

"Nick . . . Nick has known for a long time about the gun—and where it was kept. You see . . ." She told him the story of that first Christmas she had spent at Brandon Place, the Christmas when Sergei had become drunk, had danced like a madman, and destroyed the Fabergé clock which Nick had brought as a wedding present. As she spoke, the Inspector nodded, almost imperceptibly. The love affair between Sergei Bashilov and Julia Brandon had been common knowledge. And there would have been a number of witnesses to the destruction of the Fabergé clock.

All the time Kelly and the Inspector had talked in the kitchen, police had been in and out of Number 16, and been down the stairs of Number 15 to Chris's flat. Once, Kelly had gone back to Charles' study, and found police photographers there, and men dusting every inch of the furniture for fingerprints. She knew hers and Nick's were on the note he had written, but not Laura's. There was a calm rhythm to the way these men worked, quickly but painstakingly. They knew the time was on them when the press would be informed, and the photographers and journalists would once again gather outside in Brandon Place.

"You didn't telephone us immediately, Lady Brandon." The Inspector's tone was neutral, neither accusatory nor protective.

"No—I knew they both were dead. It was . . . it was a great shock. I was stunned . . . stupid, I suppose. I came back here and just . . . just sat down. The brandy was here . . . I drank it. I don't know how long it was before I thought of telephoning you. I'm sorry . . . it's all been . . ." She indicated the brandy. "You don't mind if I have another?" Now she could allow her body to shake; she had told her story. Either he believed it or he didn't.

The few hours until Peter got there seemed endless. "I telephoned Nick's brother just after I telephoned the police, Inspector . . ." She made pots of tea and coffee, and even made sandwiches and set them out in the kitchen, and the men working in Charles' study came through, one by one, ate and drank, murmured their thanks, and went back to their work.

Peter arrived at last. He formally identified his brother's body and that of Christopher Page. He identified his brother's handwriting on the note. The bodies were taken away. The first of the press had begun to gather outside in Brandon Place. Peter sat drinking hot tea in the kitchen with Kelly, his arm about her shoulders. "We're going to be married soon, Inspector Harris."

He adjusted his glasses. "Yes, I do recall reading something about that in the press, Mr. Brandon."

And then, for the first time in all the hours since he had arrived at Brandon Place, the Inspector closed his notebook and consented to have a small brandy.

Then, finally, they were all gone. Kelly sat holding both of Peter's hands as if they were a sort of lifeline, and told him what had really happened. Then Peter telephoned Mead Cottage and spoke briefly to Kate. "They're starting back at once—Kate and Laura and Johnny."

It was still very early when they fought their way through the crowd of photographers and reporters outside in Brandon Place. The news had been passed on by the police too late to make the morning papers, but the evening papers were in plenty of time, and the news was on the first bulletins on the radio. Julia arrived, pale and distraught looking. "I had to fight my way through them out there."

They had all moved into the dining room to get away from the noise of the newsmen. Mrs. Cass had come early, after hearing the news on the radio. She kept a supply of tea and coffee going to the dining room, and made sandwiches from the fresh bread she had bought on the way to Brandon Place. She worked with the curtains to the street drawn, and the lights on. In the dining room they had to look out into the little garden, and the drawn curtains of the study, which the police had sealed. "It's just temporary, Lady Brandon," the Inspector had said. "I don't want anything disturbed just yet."

He returned again that morning. "I'm glad to find you all here," he said. "This shouldn't take long."

He went again over the story Kelly had told him about Nick's visit on that Christmas Day. Julia, her voice trembling, gave her version. "I'm afraid Sergei was very drunk. He seemed jealous of Nick because the clock was so valuable, and we'd all had such expensive presents from him. Sergei *said* he couldn't shoot worth anything . . . he was just fooling around." Her professional pride in Sergei took over. "It was a stupendous piece of dancing, though—especially for someone who was drunk. But I was never sure that hitting the clock was accidental."

"Why was the gun brought up to the drawing room at all?"

Now it was Laura's turn to answer. Kelly tried to keep her eyes off the girl. She told of how Charles had sent her for the cigars, and because she had wanted to take Sergei's attention off Nick, she had brought the gun with her. "It was so beautiful—and I was curious about where it had come from. Charles told us about it being a gift from the regiment. I promised that I'd clean it. I did, too. Cleaned and oiled it properly, the way my grandfather taught me. I polished the silver—on the gun and on the box."

"Did you load it?"

Now Kelly couldn't keep her eyes away from Laura's face. Would the telltale flush come? Would the scar burn on her face? It remained as white as it had been in the cold dawn when she arrived back from Mead Cottage. "Yes, I loaded it."

"Wasn't that a rather dangerous thing to do, Miss Merton?"

Kelly felt her stomach tighten. Laura's fingerprints would be on the cartridges, but the girl had already thought of that. "Yes," she answered. "Yes, now I see that it was a dangerous thing to do. Stupid, I suppose. But, after all, I'd found it loaded in the first place. Charles had left it that way. I never felt inclined to change anything of his. Just the way Kelly never threw out any of his papers . . . or anything. And then, at Pentland . . ." She paused.

"Yes, Miss Merton?"

"Well, the place where I grew up in Australia—where

Kelly grew up too—we're used to guns. We're always taught to clean and oil them when they've been used. And there's always at least one of them around the house that's loaded ready for use. There are snakes, you see, Inspector. They come very close to the house—sometimes onto the verandas. The first day my father ever saw Kelly, when she was just a little girl, he killed a snake with a gun on the veranda because she was going to touch it—she didn't know what it was. We shoot snakes, Inspector. We always shoot them. We always keep a gun ready. So when Charles had left this service revolver loaded . . . well, I just naturally put the cartridges back. The spares were lying in the drawer. There seemed to be everything in that drawer. Even his Victoria Cross."

"And did Christopher Page know of the existence of this gun—and where it was kept?"

Laura shook her head. "I haven't any idea. He didn't come to live here until after Charles died. But if he'd been snooping around, as Kelly found him, well, probably he did know. I suppose it never occurred to him that Nick would use it."

Very carefully she reached out and took a sandwich and began to nibble on it. In that gesture, the coolness of it, Kelly suddenly saw Greg Merton, Laura's father, totally in command, looking through those blue eyes. She also saw, with fear, the hauntingly taut face of the man who had, with his friend, climbed to the top of Everest and then cut a rope; she saw the man who had never been able to forgive himself for that act. She saw the blinding glare of the Pacific and the deserted beach, the empty, empty sea. She feared for Laura, and knew that very soon she must get her away from Brandon Place, from London, from everything that had to do with this terrible event. Nick's supreme gesture would be lost if Laura should break. Nick had intended that Laura must live her life in freedom so that his own death should have value.

"Lady Brandon . . . ?" It was Inspector Harris's voice.

She looked at him, startled. "Yes?"

"I was saying . . . did it never occur to you, Lady Brandon, to lock the drawers of that desk?"

"I was never able to find the keys. As Laura said, Charles was very untidy. The files were locked, but not the desk."

"Christopher Page had one of the filing drawers open—there were files spread on the desk."

"Chris seemed to be able to get into anything he wanted

to. He boasted that he got into Nick's files—even learned the combination of the safe at the Brandon, Hoyle offices. After what I learned last night, I wouldn't be surprised at what Chris got into. From what one reads, most locks are pretty worthless once a person gains any expertise . . ."

The Inspector nodded. "Unfortunately, yes." He must have known, Kelly thought, even as he asked that question, that the keys to Charles' filing cabinets were on Chris's key ring.

He questioned Kate routinely and briefly, about the Christmas Day incident, about her knowledge of Chris's habits. "He was omnipresent." Kate said sharply. "After a while we hardly noticed him. I very much blame myself that we didn't check fully with Kelly before letting him have the basement flat. But his mother assured us that Kelly had given her permission, and we couldn't contact Kelly because she and Laura were traveling in America then—it wasn't long after my father died, and Kelly needed to get away from here. So we—Julia and I—took it upon ourselves to let Chris in here." She looked directly at the Inspector. "Nick even urged that on us. Chris was a favorite with him. And Julia and I had, in a sense, grown up with him when we lived at Mead Cottage during the war." She was, Kelly realized, using her most forceful Member of Parliament manner, reminding the Inspector that she had fought, and against all odds won, two difficult elections. She was the one whose obedience no Party could command; she was, she implied, the incorruptible.

Of all of them there, Julia, with her chalk-white face, and hands which trembled so much that her cup rattled against the saucer, was the only one who did not know the true events of the night before. And never would know, Kelly vowed.

As the Inspector prepared to leave, Kelly spoke. She struggled desperately for calm, struggled to find that right note that would almost approach nonchalance, as if what she was asking was hardly of importance. "Inspector . . . I was wondering . . "

"Yes, Lady Brandon?"

"I was wondering if you'd be needing Laura—Miss Merton—for further questioning? One or the other of us has to keep going out to Australia. We jointly own a property there. I was planning a visit quite soon, but Laura could go in my place. I assume you'll be needing my evidence at the inquest. Of course, if it's important that she stay, we'll make arrangements. The manager and one of the accountants could fly here. It's just that on the property they expect one or the other of us to come regularly. Mr. Merton—Laura's grandfather—my father-in-law—set great store in personally managing the property. He didn't look kindly on absentee landlords." Swiftly she invented a future for Laura. "Laura's planning to live there permanently once she's finished university. Of course, she could be back here quite quickly if you felt she should come."

He paused and looked around all of them; that keen gray stare told Kelly nothing. Laura was not yet safe. "We're aware of the Australian property—" He consulted his notes. "Pentland, isn't that right? Well, we haven't a report on the fingerprints on the gun yet, but since Miss Merton cleaned it, one assumes the last thing she would have done was give it a final polish with the cloth. Mrs. Wallace's and Miss Brandon's testimony about the Christmas Day incident should be sufficient. As to Miss Merton's leaving . . . well, I should know . . . let's say I should know if that's all right fairly soon Lady Brandon. Within the next day or so." He thanked them for their time, and left.

They would, Kelly knew, need at least until tomorrow to check on any unusual occurrence in Brandon Place last night. They would question the people whose back windows overlooked the Brandon garden; they would ask about the sounds of gunshots. They would probably enquire at Mead Cottage. They were, most likely, at this moment interviewing Mrs. Page.

There was a lot of time, she thought, to find out a lot of things.

It was two days before Nick's body was released, after the autopsy, for burial. Christopher Page's was released at the same time. Nick was taken to Wychwood for burial. They did not know where Chris was taken. By the time Peter returned to Wychwood, Mrs. Page had packed and left.

Once again they gathered at Wychwood for a burial; the newspapers had splashed the story, but in the two days there had been no further developments, so it had lost much of its interest. A murder, and a following suicide—it was a common enough happening, though the fact that it had happened in the Brandon family added spice. Once again there was a picture which managed to group Kelly and her three stepdaughters as they walked under the lych gate at Wychwood.

It was a further agonizing two days before, on Inspector

Harris's orders, Charles' study was unsealed. He paid a call on Kelly to inform her that she should hold herself available to give evidence at the inquest, the date of which had still to be set. "Oh—and I don't think we'll be needing Miss Merton's evidence. Miss Brandon and Mrs. Wallace can corroborate anything you will say about Nicholas Brandon's knowledge of the gun."

The next day Laura was on a plane for Sydney. She kissed Kelly and Peter good-bye at Heathrow, but the eyes that looked at them were grave, almost cold. Kelly tried to repress a shiver as she once again saw the agonized gaze of Greg Merton. In those days of waiting, when Laura had sat in her sitting room and listened to Bach, when she had stood over Nick's grave, she had seemed to leave behind the last of the girl Kelly had known. Not once, as the flashbulbs had popped, had she swung her hair over her face. Before Kelly's eyes, Laura had appeared to become totally Greg Merton's daughter, accepting discipline and pain, accepting the bitterness of death, and yet she was still reaching for life.

"I may not come back, you know," she said to them. "Not for a long time. Unless they decide they want me, after all, for the inquest . . ." For just a second her lips trembled, and when she spoke again, her tone wavered in the first words. "I have a lot to do. I have a lot to make up for. I have to do something worthwhile with my life because of what Nick did. Grandfather would have understood that. Charles would have understood it. Honor meant a great deal to Charles—and to Grandfather. I have that to try to live up to . . ."

She held her head high as she walked away from them, and Kelly knew that it had never occurred to Laura to doubt that Charles could ever have been anything less than honorable.

Kelly telephoned Bill Blake, telling him about Laura's coming, and asking him to get the house ready. Because of the Merton and the Brandon, Hoyle connections, the Australian papers had run stories of the events at Brandon Place. Bill Blake could only make shocked and sympathetic murmurs. "Thank God Laura was out of it all," Kelly said. By now she knew her tone carried absolute conviction. "Bill—would you give me the number of the Fergus place? I'd like to talk to Ben Gardiner."

She reached Ben almost at once. "Ben, Laura's coming out to Pentland. She'll probably be staying for a while. You've heard what's happened here, haven't you? Well—I want you to be in Sydney to meet her. Not Barrendarragh—Sydney! Don't ask questions. Take her just as she is. You'll find she's a rather different girl. No, she's a different woman."

Epilogue

The May sunshine streamed through the windows of Numbers 15 and 16 Brandon Place as Kelly took a last tour of the empty rooms. The movers had left little bits of debris; odd boxes and pieces of packing paper lay about. On the walls of Number 15 were the marks left by the books that had been stacked there over the years; she passed down from Marya's flat to Kate's—they might have been inhabited by the same person. Then on to Julia's, tidy and bare. The *barre* and the mirrored wall for just an instant seemed to give back the vision of the woman who had been *Firebird*. Laura's books had been sent out to Pentland, as she had asked, the furniture sold. Kelly did not go down into Chris's basement flat. Long ago movers, on Mrs. Page's orders, had come and packed and taken away every single item it had contained.

She lingered a little in her own house, Number 16. The furniture was gone. Elizabeth Brandon's chippendale dining furniture was on its way to Pentland. The two years since the house had been redecorated could be counted—marks on the walls which showed where the bookshelves had been, the outlines on the silk wallpaper of the pictures and mirrors. The kitchen seemed bare and forlorn without its plants and copper pots; the big table and beautiful Windsor chairs had gone. She made a last cup of tea with the few utensils which were left, standing at the sink drinking it, and staring across unseeingly at Cavanagh's windows. Traffic and people passed, as they always had done, but for Kelly, Brandon Place would always wear the same aspect as it had done on the night when she had put Laura into her car and sent her back to Mead Cottage. It would forever be haunted by the specter of uncertainty and fear.

The inquest which she had so much dreaded had been almost a formality. The press had been there, of course, but she had become nearly inured to them. She was the chief witness and had given her evidence in a dry, unemotional voice, keeping her eyes on Peter as if he were some sort of talisman of luck. Kate and Julia and Peter had all testified as to Christopher Page's involvement in both the household at Wychwood and Brandon Place. A former member of Brandon, Hoyle had talked of his position of trust in the company. One of the more sensational newspapers had made a reference to "a nigger in the woodpile," and that in turn had brought accusations of racialism. Mrs. Page was not called. She had sat in court, dressed in black, and had stared at the Brandon family with eyes which appeared not to see them. The prime exhibits had been in court—Nick's note and Charles' gun. They made good copy for the papers. But in the end the verdicts were as everyone had predicted; murder and suicide.

In the weeks that had passed, the business of Brandon, Hoyle had been put into the hands of official receivers and was being wound up. Since Nick had, until now, been the only member of the firm charged with crimes, the proceedings against Brandon, Hoyle had, for the time being, come to a halt. Investigations were being continued of some of the companies which had been associates of Brandon, Hoyle, or had been wholly owned by them, but there would not now be a Brandon to stand in the dock. The family could now only be touched by association, not directly. Peter's pictures had been returned from Christie's to Wychwood. Louise, having made her bargain with Peter, could not now demand more money; the divorce would go through.

The sunshine warmed Kelly as she stood at the sink. The time of the daffodils had passed at Mead Cottage, and the orchard was in bloom. Kelly had made over the deeds of Mead Cottage to Kate; it would be used as a base for her constituency work. "A good thing for her to have a permanent home here," Harry Potter had said. "You know, now she's made it in Tewford, she's in for life. She'll always be in the House of

Commons." Kate had taken a small flat in Marsham Court, within the division bell area of the House of Commons, and she came every weekend to Mead Cottage. During the week Johnny lived at Wychwood with Mrs. Cass as a sort of nanny. "Well—it's right, isn't it?" Peter had said. "Nick could always be sure I'd look out for Johnny." Mrs. Cass declared she was homesick for London, but made no suggestion that they should find someone to take her place. "Not after all these years, m'lady. The Brandons are my family."

Kelly turned from the window, and for a moment once again the kitchen seemed crowded. She saw Marya with her vodka, and the ash from her cigarette always threatening to fall into the food, joking, laughing, the bangles rattling. She saw Julia's lovely ephemeral presence; Julia had been there, but she had rarely spoken. There was Kate—dynamic, dark, inviting argument, glorying in it, Kate, whose destiny, Harry Potter said, should be at least the Cabinet. "Who knows, perhaps one day there'll be a woman Prime Minister. By that time she may have got around to getting married—or perhaps no one will bother with such things." There was Nick, his eyes riveted on every movement of his son, the love that he had never allowed himself to declare to any woman was plainly, openly there on his face as Johnny had banged the table of his high chair. And there—just on the edge of her vision—there was Chris Page, beautiful, haunted, damned Chris Page, moving in and out, graceful and evil, perhaps mad.

And there was Laura. Laura in the moments when she was confident and full of life; Laura when she had suffered some blow, and had come creeping back, apologizing for coming, unable to stay away. Letters came from Pentland. *I'm well—I miss you all, and I'm a little lonely, but I'm well. I've always thought that Pentland would be the best place in the world to be lonely. I read a lot, and I ride out and help Bill Blake and the men when I can be useful. Bill says it's been the best season for lambs since he came to Pentland. There's been an unusual number of twins . . . There's a lot of time to think . . . as if I could ever forget . . .* There were references to the future as well as the past. *I've been accepted for next term at Sydney University. I have to get my degree. I owe that to Grandfather—and to Nick—to finish something. I owe the best I've got to Pentland. Most of all, to Nick. He always expected me to make something of myself. Remember he said it—that first time there at Wychwood?*

The letters seemed calm, thoughtful. *I keep thinking of it all the time. Wondering why—and how. And I haven't any answers. I keep wondering was it the same person who did it, that night? Was I a little mad—and am I sane now? Nothing can excuse what I did, so perhaps I have to spend my life trying to make up for it. Perhaps Kate's ideas are the right ones. The only way to repay is to give. I have to give . . . and so I have to prepare to give responsibility. I think I'm beginning, at last, to understand what money and the power that goes with it really is. Perhaps there are things I can do in Australia I never thought about before. Things that could help other people . . . I may become one of Kate's do-gooders yet. . . .* There came as if an afterthought, the words, *When you start really thinking about other people, it's surprising how little a scarred face matters.*

Threaded through the letters were references to Ben Gardiner. *He drives over from the Fergus place every Sunday to see me. It's good to have him here. He's comfortable to be with. We're comfortable together. Is that enough for marriage, Kelly? No, don't answer that. I'll have to find out for myself, and so will Ben. Is passion gone, I wonder?—all burned up in that one terrible night? Can Ben and I be lovers—and still friends? Or is that an impossible condition? We'll find out. But I do know, if we marry, it'll be because we both want it.*

As she drank her tea, Kelly took the latest letter from her handbag and reread it. *Ben and I talk about England a lot—about England and Everdale. But neither of us wants to go back for more than a visit. Old Mr. Fergus is talking about some sort of partnership for Ben. So, you see, Ben doesn't need any help from me. It's Sunday, and I'm waiting for Ben. Every Sunday I wait for him to come. He always does.* She took the loneliness, the isolation of Pentland as if it were a natural condition. The tone of the letter was almost serene.

Then there was an abrupt break. A new page had been started, the writing urgent, scrawled across the page.

I've told him! I've told him every single thing that happened! We sat up all night talking about it. He seems to understand why I did it—how I could have done it. It doesn't make it any less terrible, Kelly, but he knows, and he understands! I could never have married him without telling him. We talked all night. And then I started to cook breakfast for him before he left. When I was doing the eggs at the stove he suddenly said, "We'll call our first boy John Kelly Charles Nicholas." I cried, Kelly. I cried with relief because it was all said, and he didn't reject me because of it. I cried because

Grandfather would have been so happy at the thought of my being married to someone like Ben, and having children. And Charles. And Nick. I know you'll be happy. You understand, as no one else can, about Pentland. Whatever I'm able to accomplish in life, whatever I try to do to make up, Pentland will always be the base, the first concern, as it was with Grandfather. Pentland, and the children Ben and I will have. . . .

Kelly put the letter back in her handbag.

The only room she had not visited was Charles' study. It had been bare since the day the police had said she might use it again. She had removed her personal possessions, and had never gone there again. Charles had died there, and Nick and Chris. The filing cabinets and all the papers had been taken by removal men down to Wychwood, and she and Peter had burned every single item without reading any of it. They would never know if what Chris Page had said on that dreadful night contained any truth. They did not want to know. She had taken Charles' pictures from the wall, and she would find a place at Wychwood to hang them. Charles' honor was left untouched. His coat of arms was still fixed in the Garter stalls in St. George's Chapel, Windsor.

She tossed the remainder of her tea into the sink, leaving the mug on the drainboard. She put on her coat and took her handbag. Her suitcases were already stowed in the car standing at the curb. It would be a fine day to drive down to Wychwood. She had nothing more to do now but walk across the road and turn over to Cavanagh's, the new owners, the keys to Numbers 15 and 16 Brandon Place.

ABOUT THE AUTHOR

CATHERINE GASKIN was born in Ireland, raised in Australia, and has lived in the United States (where she met her husband) and the West Indies. She uses all of these places, and others, as settings for her romantic family sagas.

Miss Gaskin was still in convent school when she wrote her first novel and had her mother deliver the manuscript. *This Other Eden* became an instant bestseller on two continents—and both her publisher and the reviewers were astonished to discover that the acclaimed new novelist was a seventeen-year-old schoolgirl! She followed this success with seventeen other splendid novels, including *A Falcon for a Queen, Edge of Glass* and *The Tilsit Inheritance*. Her newest bestseller is *Family Affairs*.

Catherine Gaskin and her husband now make their home in a lovely restored farmhouse in County Wicklow, Ireland.

Here is what some reviewers have said about Catherine Gaskin's works:

"An excellent example of the intensely feminine novel of private terror and romance out of *Wuthering Heights*, by way of *Rebecca*. . . . For all devotees of Mary Stewart."

—*Library Journal*

"Catherine Gaskin has mastered true romance."

—Pittsburgh *Press*

"Fascinating . . . escape literature in the finest sense."

—Chicago *Sunday Tribune*